Praise for

THE SECRET COMMONWEALTH

"Coming back to [Lyra] after all these years is such a profound pleasure that I can do nothing else but sit back and watch her charge forward into the night, ready as she always was to remake the world in her own image." —*Vox*

"Pullman's best novel so far . . . a work of extraordinary depth and humanity." —*The Observer*

"Pullman's writing is simple, unpretentious, beautiful, true. The conclusion to the Book of Dust can't come soon enough." —*The Washington Post*

"Not only is it a worthy second installment in the Book of Dust trilogy, it continues to prove this sequence will be every bit as excellent as His Dark Materials." —*Seattle Post-Intelligencer*

"*The Secret Commonwealth* is ablaze with light and life. The writing is exquisite; every sentence sings." —*i*

"The novel gallops forward, full of danger, delight, and surprise." —*New Statesman*

"*The Secret Commonwealth* is a majestic return to Lyra's next chapter with all the magic, folklore, and fantasy only Philip Pullman can provide." —*Hypable*

"Exhilarating." —*Kirkus Reviews*

"For Lyra, the journey really is the destination. Engrossing. *The Secret Commonwealth* is a vivid portrait of the often painful transition to adulthood and autonomy." —*Financial Times*

THE SECRET COMMONWEALTH

THE BOOK OF DUST

VOLUME TWO

THE SECRET COMMONWEALTH

THE BOOK OF DUST
VOLUME TWO

PHILIP PULLMAN

ALFRED A. KNOPF   NEW YORK

THIS IS A BORZOI BOOK PUBLISHED BY ALFRED A. KNOPF

Visit us on the Web! GetUnderlined.com

Educators and librarians, for a variety of teaching tools, visit us at RHTeachersLibrarians.com

Library of Congress Cataloging-in-Publication Data is available upon request.
ISBN 978-0-553-51070-6 (tr. pbk.)

Printed in the United States of America
10 9 8 7 6 5 4 3 2 1
First Knopf Paperback Edition 2020

TO NICK MESSENGER,

fine poet and indomitable friend

AUTHOR'S NOTE

The Secret Commonwealth is the second part of The Book of Dust. The central character, Lyra Silvertongue, once known as Lyra Belacqua, was also the protagonist of a previous trilogy, His Dark Materials: in fact, her name was both the first word and the last in that work. In that story, she was about eleven or twelve years old.

In the first part of The Book of Dust, *La Belle Sauvage*, Lyra was a baby. Although she was central to the story, most of the action of that book concerned a boy called Malcolm Polstead, himself about eleven years old.

In this book, we skip ahead twenty years or so. The events of His Dark Materials are ten years in the past; both Malcolm and Lyra are adults. The events of *La Belle Sauvage* are even further back in time.

But events have consequences, and sometimes the effects of what we once did take a long time to become fully apparent. At the same time, the world moves on; power and influence shift, or increase, or diminish. And the problems and concerns of adult people are not necessarily the same as the ones they had when young. Lyra and Malcolm, as I say, are not children anymore.

Philip Pullman

Every thing possible to be believ'd is an image of truth.

—William Blake

CONTENTS

THE SECRET COMMONWEALTH

THE BOOK OF DUST

VOLUME TWO

ONE

MOONLIGHT AND BLOODSHED

Pantalaimon, the dæmon of Lyra Belacqua, now called Lyra Silver-tongue, lay along the windowsill of Lyra's little study-bedroom in St. Sophia's College in a state as far from thought as he could get. He was aware of the cold draft from the ill-fitting sash window beside him, and of the warm naphtha light on the desk below the window, and of the scratching of Lyra's pen, and of the darkness outside. It was the cold and the dark he most wanted just then. As he lay there, turning over to feel the cold now on his back, now on his front, the desire to go outside became even stronger than his reluctance to speak to Lyra.

"Open the window," he said finally. "I want to go out."

Lyra's pen stopped moving; she pushed her chair back and stood up. Pantalaimon could see her reflection in the glass, suspended over the Oxford night. He could even make out her expression of mutinous unhappiness.

"I know what you're going to say," he said. "Of course I'll be careful. I'm not stupid."

"In some ways you are," she said.

She reached over him and slid the window up, propping it open with the nearest book.

"Don't—" he began.

"Don't shut the window, yes, Pan, just sit there freezing till Pan decides to come home. I'm not stupid at all. Go on, bugger off."

He flowed out and into the ivy covering the wall of the college. Only the faintest rustle came to Lyra's ears, and then only for a moment. Pan didn't like the way they were speaking to each other, or rather not speaking; in fact, these words were the first they'd exchanged all day. But he didn't know what to do about it, and neither did she.

Halfway down the wall he caught a mouse in his needle-sharp teeth and wondered about eating it, but gave it a surprise and let it go. He crouched on the thick ivy branch, relishing all the smells, all the wayward gusts of air, all the wide-open night around him.

But he was going to be careful. He had to be careful about two things. One was the patch of cream-white fur that covered his throat, which stood out with unfortunate clarity against the rest of his red-brown pine marten fur. But it wasn't hard to keep his head down, or to run fast. The other reason for being careful was much more serious. No one who saw him would think for a moment that he was a pine marten; he looked like a pine marten in every respect, but he was a dæmon. It was very hard to say where the difference lay, but any human being in Lyra's world would have known it at once, as surely as they knew the smell of coffee or the color red.

And a person apart from their dæmon, or a dæmon alone with their person nowhere in sight, was something uncanny, eldritch, impossible. No ordinary human beings could separate in that way, though reputedly witches could. The power that Lyra and Pan had was peculiar to them, and had been dearly bought eight years before in the world of the dead. Since coming home to Oxford after that strange adventure, they had told no one about it, and exercised the most scrupulous care to keep it a secret; but sometimes, and more often recently, they simply had to get away from each other.

So now Pan kept to the shadows, and as he moved through the shrubs and the long grass that bordered the great expanse of the neatly mown University Parks, feeling the night with all his senses, he made no sound and kept his head low. It had rained earlier that evening, and the earth was soft and moist under his feet. When he came to a patch of mud, he crouched down and pressed his throat and chest into it, so as to conceal the treacherous patch of cream-white fur.

Leaving the Parks, he darted across the Banbury Road at a moment when there were no pedestrians on the pavement, and only one distant vehicle in sight. Then he slipped into the garden of one of the large houses on the other side, and then through hedges, over walls, under fences, across lawns, making for Jericho and the canal only a few streets away.

Once he reached the muddy towpath, he felt safer. There were bushes and long grass to hide in, and trees up which he could dart as quickly as a fire along a fuse. This semi-wild part of the city was the place he liked best. He had swum in every one of the many stretches of water that laced Oxford through and through—not only the canal but also the wide body of the Thames itself and its tributary the Cherwell, as well as the countless little streams diverted from the main flows to power a mill or feed an ornamental lake, some running underground and out of sight until they emerged beneath this college wall or behind that burial ground or brewery.

At the point where one of these streams ran next to the canal with only the towpath between them, Pan crossed over a little iron bridge and followed the stream down to the great open space of the allotment gardens, with the Oxpens cattle market to the north and the Royal Mail depot beside the railway station on the western side.

The moon was full, and a few stars were visible between the racing wisps of cloud. The light made it more dangerous for him, but Pan loved the cold silver clarity as he prowled through the allotments, slipping between the stalks of Brussels sprouts or cauliflowers, the leaves of onions or spinach, making no more noise than a shadow. He came to a tool shed, and leapt up to lie flat on the hard tar-paper roof and gaze across the wide-open meadow towards the mail depot.

That was the only place in the city that seemed awake. Pan and Lyra had come here more than once before, together, and watched as the trains came in from the north and south to stand steaming at the platform while the workers unloaded sacks of letters and parcels onto large wheeled baskets and rolled them into the great metal-sided shed, where the mail for London and the continent would be sorted in time for the morning zeppelin. The airship was tethered fore and aft nearby, swinging and swaying in the wind as the mooring lines snapped and clanged against the mast. Lights glowed on the platform, on the mooring mast, above the doors of the Royal Mail building; railway trucks clattered in a siding, a metal door somewhere closed with a bang.

Pan saw a movement among the allotments to his right, and very slowly turned his head to look. A cat was creeping along a line of cabbages or broccoli, intent on a mouse; but before the cat could spring, a silent white shape bigger than Pan himself swooped down from the sky and seized the mouse, to fly up again out of reach of the cat's claws. The owl's wings beat in perfect silence as it made its way back to one of the trees behind Paradise Square. The cat sat down, seeming to think about the matter, and then resumed the hunt among the vegetables.

The moon was bright now, higher in the sky and almost clear of the cloud, and Pan could see every detail of the allotments and the cattle market from his vantage point on the shed. Greenhouses, scarecrows, galvanized-iron cattle pens, water butts, fences rotted and sagging or upright and neatly painted, pea sticks tied together like naked tepees: they all lay silent in the moonlight, like a stage set for a play of ghosts.

Pan whispered, "Lyra, what's happened to us?"

There was no answer.

The mail train had been unloaded, and now it blew a brief whistle before starting to move. It didn't come out on the rail line that crossed the river southwards just past the allotments, but moved slowly forward and then slowly back into a siding, with a great clanking of wagons. Clouds of steam rose from the engine, to be whipped away in shreds by the cold wind.

On the other side of the river, beyond the trees, another train was coming in. It wasn't a mail train; it didn't stop at the depot, but went three hundred yards further on and into the railway station itself. This was the slow local train from Reading, Pan guessed. He heard it pull up at the platform with a distant hiss of steam and muted screech of brakes.

Something else was moving.

From Pan's left, where an iron bridge crossed the river, a man was walking—or rather hurrying, with an air of furtive haste— along the riverbank where the reeds grew thickly.

At once Pan flowed down off the shed roof and ran silently towards him through onion beds and lines of cabbages. Dodging through fences and under a rusting steel water tank, he came to the edge of the allotment grounds and stood looking through a broken fence panel at the grassy meadow beyond.

The man was moving in the direction of the Royal Mail depot, going more and more carefully, until he stopped by a willow on the bank a hundred yards or so from the depot gate, almost opposite where Pan was crouching under the allotments fence. Even Pan's keen eyes could hardly make him out in the shadow; if he looked away for a moment, he'd lose the man altogether.

Then nothing. The man might have vanished entirely. A minute went past, then another. In the city behind Pan, distant bells began to strike, twice each: half past midnight.

Pan looked along the trees beside the river. A little way to the left of the willow there stood an old oak, bare and stark in its winter leaflessness. On the right—

On the right, a single figure was climbing over the gate of the Royal Mail depot. The newcomer jumped down, and then hurried along the riverbank towards the willow where the first man was waiting.

A cloud covered the moon for a few moments, and in the shadows Pan slipped under the fence and then bounded across the wet grass as fast as he could go, keeping low, mindful of that owl, mindful of the man in hiding, making for the oak. As soon as he reached it, he sprang up, extending his claws to catch at the bark, and propelled himself up onto a high branch, from which he could see the willow clearly just as the moon came out again.

The man from the mail depot was hurrying towards it. When he was nearly there, moving more slowly, peering into the shadows, the first man stepped out quietly and said a soft word. The second man replied in the same tone, and then they both retreated into the darkness. They were just too far away for Pan to hear what they'd said, but there was a tone of complicity in it. They'd planned to meet here.

Their dæmons were both dogs: a sort of mastiff and a short-legged dog. The dogs wouldn't be able to climb, but they could sniff him out, and Pan pressed himself even closer to the broad bough he was lying on. He could hear a quiet whisper from the men, but again could make out none of the words.

Between the high chain-link fence of the mail depot and the river, a path led from the open meadow next to the allotments towards the railway station. It was the natural way to go to the station from the parish of St. Ebbe's and the narrow streets of houses that crowded along the river near the gasworks. Looking from the branch of the oak tree, Pan could see further along the path than the men down below, and saw someone coming from the direction of the station before they did: a man on his own, the collar of his coat turned up against the cold.

Then came a "Ssh" from the shadows under the willow. The men had seen the new arrival too.

Earlier that day, in an elegant seventeenth-century house near the Cathedral of St. Peter in Geneva, two men were talking. They were in a book-lined room on the second floor, whose windows looked out on a quiet street in the somber light of a winter afternoon. There was a long mahogany table set with blotters, pads of paper, pens and pencils, glasses, and carafes of water, but the men were sitting in armchairs on either side of a log fire.

The host was Marcel Delamare, the Secretary General of an organization known informally by the name of the building they occupied, the one in which this meeting was taking place. It was called *La Maison Juste*. Delamare was in his early forties, bespectacled, well groomed, his perfectly tailored suit matching the color of his dark gray hair. His dæmon was a snowy owl, who perched on the back of his armchair, her yellow eyes fixed on the dæmon in the other man's hands, a scarlet snake winding herself through and through his fingers. The visitor was called Pierre Binaud. He was in his sixties, austere in a clerical collar, and he was the Chief Justice of the Consistorial Court, the main agency of the Magisterium for enforcing discipline and security.

"Well?" said Binaud.

"Another member of the scientific staff at the Lop Nor station has disappeared," said Delamare.

"Why? What does your agent say about it?"

"The official line is that the missing man and his companion were lost among the watercourses, which change their position rapidly and without warning. It is a very difficult place, and anyone leaving the station must take a guide. But our agent tells me that there is a rumor that they entered the desert, which begins beyond the lake. There are local legends about gold—"

"Local legends be damned. These people were experimental theologians, botanists, men of science. They were after the roses, not gold. But what are you saying, that one of them disappeared? What about the other?"

"He did return to the station, but set off at once for Europe. His name is Hassall. I told you about him last week, but perhaps you were too busy to hear me. My agent believes that he's carrying samples of the rose materials, and a number of papers."

"Have we captured him yet?"

Delamare composed himself almost visibly. "If you remember, Pierre," he said after a moment, "I would have had him detained in Venice. That idea was overruled by your people. Let him get to Brytain, and then follow him to discover his destination: that was the order. Well, he has now arrived there, and tonight he will be intercepted."

"Let me know as soon as you have those materials. Now, this other matter: the young woman. What do you know about her?"

"The alethiometer—"

"No, no, no. Old-fashioned, vague, too full of speculation. Give me facts, Marcel."

"We have a new reader, who—"

"Oh yes, I've heard of him. New method. Any better than the old one?"

"Times change, and understandings must change too."

"What's that mean?"

"It means that we've discovered some things about the girl that were not clear before. It seems that she is under certain protections, legal and otherwise. I would like to begin by taking down the network of defense around her, unobtrusively, quietly, one might say invisibly. And when she is vulnerable, that will be the time to take action. Until then—"

"Cautious," said Binaud, standing up. "Too cautious, Marcel. It's a big fault. You need to be decisive. Take action. Find her, acquire her, and bring her here. But have it your own way; I won't overrule you this time."

Delamare rose to shake his visitor's hand and see him out. When they were alone, his dæmon flew to his shoulder and they stood at the window to watch the Chief Justice bustle away, one attendant carrying his briefcase, another holding an umbrella against the snow that had just begun to fall.

"I do dislike being interrupted," said Delamare.

"I don't think he noticed," said his dæmon.

"Oh, he'll be aware of it one day."

The man coming from the railway station was moving quickly: in less than a minute he was almost at the tree, and as soon as he got there, the other men struck. One stepped out and swung a heavy stick to strike him at his knees. He dropped at once, grunting with shock, and then the other man was on him, chopping down with a short club, striking his head, his shoulders, his arms.

No one uttered a word. The victim's dæmon, a small hawk, rose into the air, crying and fluttering violently, and kept falling down as her man weakened under the blows.

But then Pan saw a flash of moonlight reflected on a knife blade, and the man from the mail depot cried out and fell, but the other attacker struck again and again, and the victim fell still. Pan heard every blow.

The man was dead. The second man stood up and looked at his companion.

"What'd he do?" he said quietly.

"Cut my bloody hamstrings. Bastard. Look, I'm bleeding like a pig."

The man's dæmon, the mastiff-cross, was whining and writhing on the ground beside him.

"Can you get up?" The killer's voice was thick and muffled, as if he was speaking through catarrh, and he had a Liverpool accent.

"What do you think?"

Their voices hardly rose above a whisper.

"Can you move at all?"

The first man tried to push himself up. There was another grunt of pain. The second man offered his hand, and the first managed to stand, but it was obvious that he could only use one leg.

"What we gonna do?" he said.

The moon lit them all brilliantly: the killer, and the man who couldn't walk, and the dead man. Pan's heart was thumping so hard that he thought they must be able to hear it.

"You stupid sod. Couldn't you see he was holding a knife?" said the killer.

"He was too quick—"

"You're supposed to be good at this. Get out the way."

The first man hobbled back a pace or two. The killer bent down and picked up the dead man's ankles, and hauled the body backwards and into the rushes.

Then the killer reappeared and impatiently beckoned the other man forward.

"Lean on me," he said. "I got half a mind to leave you here on your own. Just a bloody liability. Now I gotta come back and deal with him meself, and that bleeding moon's getting brighter all the time. Where's his bag? Wasn't he carrying a bag?"

"He never had a bag. He never had nothing."

"He must've done. Sod it."

"Barry'll come back with you and help."

"Too noisy. Too nervous. Give us your arm, come on, hurry up."

"Oh Christ—be careful—aargh, that hurts. . . ."

"Now shut up and move as fast as you can. I don't care if it hurts. Just keep your bloody mouth shut."

The first man put his arm around the killer's shoulders and limped along beside him as they moved slowly beneath the oak tree and back along the riverbank. Pan, looking down, saw a patch of blood on the grass, shining red in the moonlight.

He waited till the men were out of sight, and then prepared to jump down; but before he could move, something stirred in the rushes where the man's body lay, and something pale and bird-sized fluttered up, falling and flying up again, failing, dropping, but with a last burst of life making directly for Pan.

He was too frightened to move. If the man was dead . . . But this dæmon looked dead herself—so what could he do? Pan was ready to fight, to flee, to faint; but then she was right there on the branch beside him, struggling to stay there, almost falling off, and he had to reach out and catch her. She felt icy cold, and alive, but only just. The man wasn't quite dead.

"Help," she whispered raggedly, "help us—"

"Yes," he said, "yes—"

"Quickly!"

She fell off and managed to flutter down to the rushes. In a moment Pan had flowed down the trunk of the oak and bounded across towards where she'd vanished, and found the man lying there in the rushes, still just breathing, with the dæmon pressing herself against his cheek.

Pan heard her say, "Dæmon—separate—"

The man turned his head a little and groaned. Pan heard the grating of bone against broken bone.

"Separate?" the man murmured.

"Yes—we learnt to do it—"

"My lucky day. Inside pocket. Here." He raised a hand with enormous effort and touched the right side of his jacket. "Take it out," he whispered.

Trying not to hurt him, and fighting the great taboo against touching another person's body, Pan nosed the jacket aside and found a leather wallet in the inside pocket.

"That's it. Take it away. Don't let them get it. It's all up to you and . . . your . . ."

Pan tugged, but the wallet wouldn't come, because the jacket was caught under the man's body, and he couldn't move; but after several seconds of difficulty, Pan got it free and pulled it out onto the ground.

"Take it right away . . . before they come back. . . ."

The pale hawk dæmon was hardly there now, just a wisp of white shadow fluttering and pressing herself to his flesh. Pan hated seeing people die, because of what happened to their dæmons: they vanished like a candle flame going out. He wanted to console this poor creature, who knew she was going to disappear, but all she wanted to do was feel a last touch of the warmth she'd found in her man's body all their lives together. The man took a shallow, rasping breath, and then the pretty hawk dæmon drifted out of existence altogether.

And now Pan had to carry this wallet all the way back to St. Sophia's College, and Lyra's bed.

He gripped it between his teeth and pushed his way up to the edge of the rushes. It wasn't heavy, but it was awkward, and what was worse, it was saturated with the smell of another person: sweat, cologne, smokeleaf. It was being too close to someone who wasn't Lyra.

He got it as far as the fence around the allotment gardens, and then stopped for a rest. Well, he would have to take his time. There was plenty of night left.

Lyra was deep in sleep when a shock woke her up, like a sudden fall, something physical, but what? She reached for Pan, and remembered that he wasn't there: so had something happened to him? It was far from the first night she'd had to go to bed alone, and she hated it. Oh, the folly of going out by himself in that way, but he wouldn't listen, he wouldn't stop doing it, and one day they'd both pay the price.

She lay awake for a minute, but sleep was gathering around her again, and soon she surrendered and closed her eyes.

The bells of Oxford were striking two o'clock when Pan climbed in. He laid the wallet on the table, working his mouth this way and that to relieve his aching jaw before pulling out the book with which she'd propped open the window for him. He knew it: it was a novel called *The Hyperchorasmians*, and Pan thought Lyra was paying it far too much attention. He let it fall to the floor and then cleaned himself meticulously before pushing the wallet into the bookcase and out of sight.

Then he leapt up lightly onto her pillow. In the ray of moonlight that came through a gap in the curtains, he crouched and gazed at her sleeping face.

Her cheeks were flushed, her dark-gold hair was damp; those lips that had whispered to him so often, and kissed him, and kissed Will too, were compressed; a little frown hovered on her brow, coming and going like clouds in a windy sky—they all spoke of things that were not right, of a person who was becoming more and more unreachable to him, as he was to her.

And he had no idea what to do about it. All he could do was lie down close against her flesh; that at least was still warm and welcoming. At least they were still alive.

TWO

THEIR CLOTHES SMELLED OF ROSES

Lyra woke up to hear the college clock striking eight. In the first few minutes of drowsy surfacing, before thought began to interfere, her sensations were delicious, and one of them was the warmth of her dæmon's fur around her neck. This sensuous mutual cherishing had been part of her life for as long as she could remember.

She lay there trying not to think, but thought was like a tide coming in. Little trickles of awareness—an essay to finish, her clothes that needed washing, the knowledge that unless she got to the hall by nine o'clock there'd be no breakfast—kept flowing in from this direction or that and undermining the sandcastle of her sleepiness. And then the biggest ripple yet: Pan and their estrangement. Something had come between them, and neither of them knew fully what it was, and the only person each could confide in was the other, and that was the one thing they couldn't do.

She pushed the blankets away and stood up, shivering, because St. Sophia's was parsimonious where heating was concerned. A quick wash in the little basin where the hot water knocked and shook the pipes in protest before condescending to appear, and then she pulled on the tartan skirt and the light gray jersey that were more or less the only clean things she had.

And all the time Pan lay pretending to sleep on the pillow. It was never like that when they were young, never.

"Pan," she said wearily.

He had to come, and she knew he would, and he stood up and stretched and let her lift him to her shoulder. She left the room and started downstairs.

"Lyra, let's pretend we're talking to each other," he whispered.

"I don't know if pretending's a good way to live."

"It's better than not. I want to tell you what I saw last night. It's important."

"Why didn't you tell me when you came in?"

"You were asleep."

"I wasn't, any more than you were just now."

"Then why didn't you know I had something important to tell you?"

"I did. I felt something happen. But I knew I'd have to argue to get you to tell me about it, and frankly . . ."

He said nothing. Lyra stepped out at the foot of her staircase and into the dank chill of the morning. One or two girls were walking towards the hall; more were coming away, having had breakfast, stepping briskly out to the morning's work, to the library or to a lecture or tutorial.

"Oh, I don't know," she finished. "I'm tired of this. Tell me after breakfast."

She climbed the steps into the hall and helped herself to porridge, and took her bowl to a spare place at one of the long tables and sat down. All around her, girls of her own age were finishing their scrambled eggs, or porridge, or toast, some chatting happily, some looking dull or tired or preoccupied, one or two reading letters or just eating stolidly. She knew many of them by name, some just by sight; some were friends cherished for their kindness or their wit; some just acquaintances; a small number not exactly enemies, but young women she knew she would never like, because they were snobbish or arrogant or cold. She felt as much at home in this scholastic community, among these brilliant or hardworking or gossipy contemporaries, as she did anywhere else. She should have been happy.

As she stirred some milk into her porridge, Lyra became aware of the girl opposite. She was called Miriam Jacobs, a pretty, dark-haired girl, sufficiently quick and clever to get by academically without doing more work than the minimum; a little vain, but good-natured enough to let herself be teased about it. Her squirrel dæmon, Syriax, was clinging to her hair, looking stricken, and Miriam was reading a letter, one hand on her mouth. Her face was pale.

No one else had noticed. As Miriam put the letter down, Lyra leant across the table and said, "Miriam? What is it?"

Miriam blinked and sighed as if she were coming awake, and pushed the letter down onto her lap. "Home," she said. "Something silly." Her dæmon crept onto her lap with the letter while Miriam went through an elaborate demonstration of not caring that was wasted on her neighbors, who hadn't been watching anyway.

"Nothing I can help with?" asked Lyra.

Pan had joined Syriax under the table. Both girls could sense that their dæmons were talking, and that whatever Syriax told Pan would be in Lyra's knowledge very soon. Miriam looked at Lyra helplessly. Another moment and she might burst into tears.

Lyra stood up and said, "Come on."

The other girl was in that state in which any decisiveness, from anyone, is seized like a lifebelt in a rough sea. She went with Lyra out of the hall, clutching her dæmon to her breast, not asking where they were going, just following like a lamb.

"I'm sick to death of porridge and cold toast and dry scrambled eggs," said Lyra. "There's only one thing to do in a case like this."

"What's that?" said Miriam.

"George's."

"But I've got a lecture—"

"No. The lecturer's got a lecture, but you haven't and I haven't. And I want fried eggs and bacon. Come along, step out. Were you a Girl Guide?"

"No."

"Neither was I. I don't know why I asked."

"I've got an essay to do—"

"Do you know anyone who hasn't got an essay to do? There are thousands of young ladies and gentlemen *all* behind with their essays. It would be bad form to be anything else. And George's is waiting. The Cadena's not open yet or we could go there. Come on, it's chilly. D'you want to get a coat?"

"Yes—just quickly then . . ."

They ran up to get their coats. Lyra's was a shabby green thing that was a little too small. Miriam's coat was of navy cashmere and fitted her perfectly.

"And if anyone says why weren't you at the lecture or the seminar or whatever, you can say that you were upset and nice Lyra took you for a walk," Lyra said as they went out through the lodge.

"I've never been to George's," said Miriam.

"Oh, go on. You must have."

"I know where it is, but . . . I don't know. I just thought it wasn't for us."

George's was a café in the Covered Market, much used by market traders and workers from round about.

"I've been going there since I was young," said Lyra. "I mean, *really* young. I used to hang around outside till they gave me a bun to go away."

"Did you? Really?"

"A bun or a clout. I even worked there for a bit, washing dishes, making tea and coffee. I was about nine, I think."

"Did your parents let— Oh God. Sorry. Sorry."

The only thing Lyra's friends knew about her background was that her parents were people of great family on both sides who had died when she was young. It was understood that this was a source of great sorrow to Lyra and that she never talked about it, so naturally their speculation flourished. Now Miriam was mortified.

"No, I was in the care of Jordan by then," Lyra said cheerfully. "If they'd known, I mean if the Jordan people had known, they'd have been surprised, I suppose, but then they'd have forgotten about it and I'd have kept on going there anyway. I sort of did what I wanted."

"Didn't anyone know what you were doing?"

"The housekeeper, Mrs. Lonsdale. She was pretty fierce. I was always getting told off, but she knew it wouldn't do any good. I could be quite well behaved when I needed to be."

"How long were you— I mean, how old were you when— Sorry. I don't mean to pry."

"The first thing I remember is when I was taken to Jordan for the first time. I don't know how old I was—probably just a baby. I was being carried by a big man. It was midnight and stormy, with lightning and thunder and pouring rain. He was on a horse, and I was wrapped up inside his cloak. Then he was banging on a door with a pistol, and the door opened and it was all warm and light inside, and then he handed me over to someone else and I think he kissed me and got on his horse and rode away. He was probably my father."

Miriam was very impressed. In truth, Lyra wasn't sure about the horse, but she liked it.

"That's *so* romantic," Miriam said. "And that's the first thing you remember?"

"The very first. After that, I was just . . . living in Jordan. Have been ever since. What's the first thing you remember?"

"The smell of roses," said Miriam at once.

"What, a garden somewhere?"

"No. My father's factory. Where they make soap and things. I was sitting on his shoulders, and we were in the bottling plant. Such an intense sweet smell . . . The men's clothes used to smell of it, and their wives had to wash them to get it out."

Lyra was aware that Miriam's family was rich, and that soaps and perfumes and such things were behind their wealth; Miriam had a vast collection of scents and fragrant ointments and shampoos, and it was a favorite occupation of her friends to try out all the new ones.

Suddenly Lyra realized that the other girl was weeping. She stopped and took Miriam's arm. "Miriam, what is it? Was it that letter?"

"Daddy's bankrupt," Miriam said shakily. "It's all over. That's what it is. So now you know."

"Oh, Miriam, that's awful!"

"And we won't—they can't—they're selling the house, and I'll have to leave college—they can't afford . . ."

She couldn't go on. Lyra held out her arms, and Miriam leant against her, sobbing. Lyra could smell the fragrance of her shampoo, and wondered if there were roses in that too.

"Hush," she said. "You know there are bursaries and special funds and . . . You won't have to leave, you'll see!"

"But everything's going to change! They're having to sell everything and move to . . . I don't know . . . And Danny will have to leave Cambridge and . . . and it's all going to be horrible."

"I bet it sounds worse than it is," said Lyra. Out of the corner of her eye, she could see Pan whispering to Syriax, and she knew he was saying just the same sort of thing. "Course it was a shock, learning about it in a letter over breakfast. But people survive this sort of thing, honest, and sometimes things turn out much better than you think. I bet you won't have to leave college."

"But everyone will know. . . ."

"So what? It's nothing to be ashamed of. Things happen to people's families all the time and it's not their fault. If you cope with it by being brave, people will admire you for it."

"It's not Daddy's fault, after all."

"Course not," said Lyra, who had no idea. "Like they teach us in economic history—the trade cycle. Things that are too big to resist."

"It just happened, and no one saw it coming." Miriam was fumbling in her pocket. She brought out the crumpled letter and read: "'The suppliers have simply been so unreasonable, and although Daddy has been to Latakia again and again, he can't find a good source anywhere—apparently the big medical companies are buying everything up before anyone else can—there's absolutely nothing one can do—it's too awful. . . .'"

"Suppliers of what?" said Lyra. "Roses?"

"Yes. They buy them from the gardens over there and distill them or something. Attar. Attar of roses. Something like that."

"Won't English roses do?"

"I don't think so. It has to be roses from there."

"Or lavender. There's lots of that."

"They—I don't know!"

"I suppose the men will lose their jobs," Lyra said as they turned into Broad Street, opposite Bodley's Library. "The men whose clothes smelled of roses."

"Probably. Oh, it's awful."

"It is. But you can cope with it. Now, when we sit down, we'll make a plan of what you can do, all the options, all the possibilities, and then you'll feel better at once. You'll see."

In the café, Lyra ordered bacon and eggs and a pint of tea. Miriam didn't want anything except coffee, but Lyra told George to bring a currant bun anyway.

"If she doesn't eat it, I will," she said.

"Don't they feed you in that college?" said George, a man whose hands moved faster than anyone's Lyra had ever seen, slicing, buttering, pouring, shaking salt, cracking eggs. When she was young, she'd greatly admired his ability to crack three eggs at once into a frying pan with one hand and not spill a drop of white, or break the yolk, or include a fragment of shell. One day she got through two dozen trying it herself. That had earned her a clout, which she had to admit she deserved. George was more respectful these days. She still couldn't do the egg trick.

Lyra borrowed a pencil and a piece of paper from George and drew three columns, one headed *Things to do*, the next *Things to find out*, and the third *Things to stop worrying about*. Then she and Miriam, and their two dæmons, filled them in with suggestions and ideas as they ate. Miriam finished the currant bun, and by the time they'd covered the paper, she was almost cheerful.

"There," said Lyra. "It's always a good idea to come to George's. St. Sophia's breakfasts are very high-minded. As for Jordan . . ."

"I bet they're not austere like ours."

"Socking great silver chafing dishes full of kedgeree or deviled kidneys or kippers. Must keep the young gentlemen in the style to which they're accustomed. Lovely, but I wouldn't want it every day."

"Thank you, Lyra," said Miriam. "I feel much better. You were quite right."

"So what are you going to do now?"

"Go and see Dr. Bell. Then write home."

Dr. Bell was Miriam's moral tutor, a sort of pastoral guide and mentor. She was a brusque but kindly woman; she'd know what the college could do to help.

"Good," said Lyra. "And tell me what happens."

"I will," Miriam promised.

Lyra sat there for a few minutes after Miriam had gone, chatting to George, regretfully turning down his offer of work in the Christmas vacation, finishing her pint mug of tea. But eventually came the time when she and Pan were alone again.

"What did he tell you?" she said to him, meaning Miriam's dæmon.

"What she's really worried about is her boyfriend. She doesn't know how to tell him because she thinks he won't like her if she isn't rich. He's at Cardinal's. Some kind of aristocrat."

"So we spent all that time and effort and she didn't even tell me the thing she was worried about most? I don't think much of that," Lyra said, gathering up her shabby coat. "And if that's how he feels, he's not worth it anyway. Pan, I'm sorry," she said, surprising herself as much as him. "You were just going to tell me what you saw last night, and I didn't have time to answer before." She waved to George as they left.

"I saw someone being murdered," he said.

THREE

LEFT LUGGAGE

Lyra stood still. They were outside the coffee merchant's, by the entrance to the Covered Market, and the air was full of the smell of roasting coffee.

"What did you say?" she said.

"I saw two men attack another man and kill him. It was down by the allotment gardens near the Royal Mail depot. . . ."

As she walked slowly out into Market Street and headed back towards St. Sophia's, he told her the whole story.

"And they seemed to know about separation," he said. "The man who was killed and his dæmon. They could do it. She must have seen me on the branch, and she flew straight up—well, with an effort, because he was hurt—and she wasn't frightened or anything, I mean, not frightened of me being alone, like most people would be. And he was the same."

"And this wallet? Where is it now?"

"In our bookshelves. Next to the German dictionary."

"And what was it he said?"

"He said, 'Take it away—don't let them get it—it's all up to you and your . . .' And then he died."

"All up to us," she said. "Well, we'd better have a look at it."

They turned on the gas fire in her study-bedroom at St. Sophia's, sat at the table, and switched on the little anbaric lamp, because the sky was gray and the light was gloomy.

Lyra took out the wallet from the bookshelf. It was a simple one-fold wallet without a clasp, the whole thing little bigger than her palm. There had originally been a raised grain in the leather, like that of morocco, but most of that was worn away to a greasy smoothness. It might once have been brown too, but it was nearly black now, and marked in several places by Pan's gripping teeth.

She could smell it: a faint, slightly pungent, slightly spicy smell, like that of a man's cologne mixed with sweat. Pan waved a paw in front of his nose. She examined the outside carefully for any mark or monogram, but there was none.

She opened the wallet and again found it perfectly normal, perfectly ordinary. There were four banknotes, six dollars and a hundred francs in all—not a large sum. In the next pocket she found a train ticket for the return journey from Paris to Marseilles.

"Was he French?" said Pan.

"Don't know yet," said Lyra. "Look, here's a picture."

From the next pocket in the wallet she took out a grubby and much-handled card attesting to the identity of the owner, with a photogram showing the face of a man of forty, possibly, with black curly hair and a thin mustache.

"That's him," Pan said.

The card had been issued by His Majesty's Foreign Office to Anthony John Roderick Hassall, who was a British citizen, and whose birth date showed him to be thirty-eight years old. The dæmon photogram displayed a small hawk-like bird of prey. Pan gazed at the pictures with intense interest and pity.

The next thing she found was a small card she recognized, because she had one identical to it in her own purse: it was a Bodleian Library card. Pan made a small noise of surprise.

"He must have belonged to the university," he said. "Look, what's that?"

It was another card, this one issued by the university Department of Botany. It certified Dr. Roderick Hassall as a member of staff of the Department of Plant Sciences.

"Why would they want to attack him?" Lyra said, not expecting an answer. "Did he look rich, or was he carrying something, or what?"

"They did say . . . ," said Pan, trying to remember. "One of them—the killer—he was surprised that the man wasn't carrying a bag. It sounded as if they'd been expecting him to. But the other man, the one who'd been wounded, wasn't interested in thinking about that."

"*Was* he carrying a bag? Or a briefcase, or a suitcase, or anything?"

"No. Nothing."

The next paper she found was much folded and refolded, and reinforced with tape along the creases. It was headed LAISSEZ-PASSER.

"What's that?" said Pan.

"A kind of passport, I think . . ."

It had been issued by the Ministry of Internal Security of the Sublime Porte of the Ottoman Empire, at Constantinople. It said in French, English, and Anatolian that Anthony John Roderick Hassall, botanist, of Oxford, Brytain, was to be allowed to travel through the realms of the Ottoman Empire, and that the authorities were to give him assistance and protection whenever needed.

"How big is the Ottoman Empire?" said Pan.

"Enormous. Turkey and Syria and Lebanon and Egypt and Libya and thousands of miles east as well. I think. Wait, here's another. . . ."

"And one more behind that."

The other two documents had been issued by the Khanate of Turkestan, including the regions of Bactria and Sogdiana, and the prefecture of Sin Kiang in the Celestial Empire of Cathay. They said much the same thing, in much the same way, as the laissez-passer from the Ottoman Empire.

"They're out of date," said Lyra.

"But the Sin Kiang one is earlier than the Turkestan one. . . . That means he was coming from there, and it took him . . . three months. It's a long way."

"There's something else in here."

Her fingers had found another paper hidden in an inside pocket. She tugged it out and unfolded it to find something quite different from the rest: a leaflet from a steamship company advertising a cruise to the Levant on a vessel called the SS *Zenobia*. It was issued by the Imperial Orient Line, and the English-language text promised A *world of romance and sunshine*.

"A *world of silks and perfumes*," Pan read, "*of carpets and sweetmeats, of damascened swords, of the glint of beautiful eyes beneath the star-filled sky* . . ."

"*Dance to the romantic music of Carlo Pomerini and his Salon Serenade Orchestra*," Lyra read. "*Thrill to the whisper of moonlight on the tranquil waters of the Mediterranean*. . . . How can moonlight whisper? An *Imperial Orient Levantine Cruise is the gateway to a world of loveliness*. . . . Wait, Pan, look."

On the back there was a timetable showing the dates of arrival and departure at various ports. The ship would leave London on Thursday, April 17, and return to Southampton on Saturday,

May 23, calling at fourteen cities en route. And someone had circled the date Monday, May 11, when the *Zenobia* called at Smyrna, and drawn a line from that to the scribbled words *Café Antalya, Süleiman Square, 11 a.m.*

"An appointment!" said Pan.

He sprang from the table to the mantelpiece and stood, paws against the wall, to scrutinize the calendar that hung there.

"It's not this year—wait—it's next year!" he said. "Those are the right days of the week. It hasn't happened yet. What are we going to do?"

"Well . . . ," said Lyra, "we really ought to take it to the police. I mean, there's no doubt about that, is there?"

"No," said Pan, jumping back onto the table. He turned the papers around to read them more closely. "Is that everything in the wallet?"

"I think so." Lyra looked through it again, pushing her fingers down into the pockets. "No—wait—there's something here. . . . A coin?"

She turned the wallet upside down and shook it. It wasn't a coin that fell out, but a key with a round metal tag attached to it, bearing the number 36.

"That looks like . . . ," said Pan.

"Yes. We've seen one of those. . . . We've had one of those. When was it?"

"Last year . . . the railway station . . ."

"Left luggage!" Lyra said. "He put something in a left-luggage locker."

"The bag they thought he ought to be carrying!"

"It must be still there."

They looked at each other with wide eyes.

Then Lyra shook her head. "We should take this to the police," she said. "We've done what anyone would have done, we've looked to see who it belonged to and—and . . ."

"Well, we could take it to the Botanic Garden. The Plant Sciences place. They'd know who he was."

"Yes, but we know that he was killed. So it's really a matter for the police. We've got to, Pan."

"Mm," he said. "S'pose so."

"But there's no reason why we shouldn't copy a few things. The dates of his journey, the appointment in Smyrna . . ."

She wrote them down.

"Is that everything?" he said.

"Yes. I'll try and get them all back in the right places, and then we'll go to the police station."

"Why are we doing this? Really? Copying these things down?"

She looked at him for a moment and then turned back to the wallet. "Just being curious," she said. "It's none of our business, except that we know how it came to be there in the rushes. So it is our business."

"And he did say it was all up to us. Don't forget that."

She turned off the fire, locked the door, and they set off for the main police station in St. Aldate's, with the wallet in her pocket.

Twenty-five minutes later, they were waiting at a counter while the duty sergeant dealt with a man who wanted a fishing license and who wouldn't accept that it was the river authority that issued them, and not the police. He argued at such length that Lyra sat down on the only chair and prepared to wait till lunchtime.

Pan was sitting on her lap, watching everything. When two other policemen came out of a back office and stopped to talk by the counter, he turned to look at them, and a moment later Lyra felt his claws dig into her hand.

She didn't react. He'd tell her what it was about in a moment, and so he did, flowing up to her shoulder and whispering:

"That's the man from last night. That's the killer. I'm certain of it."

He meant the taller and heavier of the two policemen. Lyra heard the man say to the other, "No, it's overtime, completely legitimate. All done by the book. There's no doubt about it."

His voice was unpleasant, harsh and thick-sounding. He had a Liverpool accent. At the same moment, the man who wanted the fishing license said to the duty sergeant as he turned away, "Well, if you're sure, I've got no choice. But I'll want it in writing."

"Come back this afternoon, and my colleague who'll be on the desk then will give you a document all about it," said the sergeant, winking at the other two.

"All right, I will. I'm not giving up."

"No, don't do that, sir. Yes, miss? How can I help you?"

He was looking at Lyra, and the other two policemen were watching.

She stood up and said, "I don't know if I've come to the right place, but my bicycle was stolen."

"Yes, this is the right place, miss. Fill in this form and we'll see what we can do."

She took the paper he handed her and said, "I'm in a bit of a hurry. Can I bring it back later?"

"Anytime, miss."

Her inquiry not being very interesting, he turned away and joined the conversation about overtime. A moment later, Lyra and Pan were out in the street again.

"Well, what do we do now?" said Pan.

"Go to the left-luggage place, of course."

* * *

But Lyra wanted to see the riverbank first. As they walked across Carfax and down towards the castle, she went over the story with Pan again, each of them being so scrupulously polite and attentive to the other that it was almost painful. Everyone else Lyra could see in the streets or the shops, everyone she'd spoken to in the market, was perfectly at ease with their dæmon. The café owner George's dæmon, a flamboyant rat, sat in the breast pocket of his apron, passing sardonic comments on everything around her, just as she'd done when Lyra was a small child, completely content with George as he was with her. Only Lyra and Pan were unhappy with each other.

So they tried very hard. They went to the allotment gardens and looked at the gate in the high fence around the Royal Mail depot, where the second attacker had climbed over, and at the path from the railway station that the victim had come along.

It was a market day, and as well as the sound of railway cars being shunted in the sidings, and the noise of someone using a drill or a grinder to repair a machine in the Royal Mail building, Lyra heard the mooing of cattle from the pens in the distance. There were people everywhere.

"Someone might be watching us," she said.

"I suppose they might."

"So we'll just wander along as if we're daydreaming."

She looked around slowly. They were standing in the area between the river and the allotments, a roughly tended open meadow where people strolled or picnicked in the summer, or bathed from the riverbank, or played football. This part of Oxford wasn't home territory for Lyra, whose allegiance had lain mostly with the urchins of Jericho, half a mile north. She had fought many battles with the gangs from around here, from St. Ebbe's, in the days before she went to the Arctic and left her world altogether. Even now, a young woman of twenty, educated, a student of St. Sophia's, she felt an atavistic fear of being in enemy territory.

She set off slowly, crossing the grass to the riverbank, trying to look as if she were doing anything other than looking for a murder site.

They stopped to look at a train loaded with coal coming slowly down from their right towards the wooden bridge over the river. Trains never crossed it fast. They heard the trundle of the coal trucks over the bridge, and watched the train swing away to the left on the branch line that made for the gasworks, and into the siding next to the main building where the furnaces roared day and night.

Lyra said, "Pan, if they hadn't attacked him, where was he going? Where does the path lead to?"

They were standing at the southern edge of the allotments, where Pan had been when he first saw the men hide under the willow. The two trees were exactly ahead of them as they looked towards the river, about a hundred yards away. If the man hadn't been attacked, the path would have taken him further along the bank, where the river curved around to the left. Without discussing it, Lyra and Pan moved slowly that way to see where he would have gone.

The path made directly along the bank towards a footbridge over the stream, which in turn led to the narrow streets of back-to-back houses around the gasworks, and the parish of St. Ebbe's proper.

"So that's where he was going," said Pan.

"Even if he didn't know it. Even if he was only following the path."

"And that's where the other man must have come from—the one who didn't come from the mail depot."

"You could get to anywhere from there," Lyra said. "All those tangled old streets in St. Ebbe's, and then St. Aldate's and Carfax . . . Anywhere."

"But we'll never find it. Not by guessing."

They both knew why they were talking like this, at the end of the footbridge over the stream. Neither of them wanted to go and look at the place where the man had been killed.

"We ought to, though," she said, and he said, "Yes. Come on."

They turned back and wandered along the bank of the river, making for the willow and the oak, where rushes grew thickly and the path was muddy. Lyra looked casually all around, but there was no one sinister or threatening: just some children playing by the stream further back, a few men working their allotments, and an elderly couple on the path ahead, walking arm in arm and carrying shopping bags.

They passed the old couple, who smiled and nodded when Lyra said, "Good morning," and then they were under the oak tree. Pan leapt up from Lyra's shoulder and showed her where he'd lain along the branch, and then sprang down again and flowed along the grass towards the willow.

She followed him, looking for signs of a struggle on the ground, but seeing only grass and trampled mud that was no different from the rest of the path.

"Anyone coming?" she said to Pan.

He jumped up to her shoulder and looked around. "A woman with a small child and a shopping bag coming over the footbridge. No one else."

"Let's look in the rushes. About here, was it?"

"Yes. Right here."

"And he pulled the dead man down to the water?"

"In among the rushes, but not all the way down. Not when I was watching, anyway. He probably came back later and did that."

Lyra stepped off the path and down the slope where the rushes grew. They were tall, and the slope was steep, and only six feet or so from the path she was invisible from anywhere in the meadow. It was hard to keep her footing and her shoes would be ruined, but she found her balance and crouched down low and looked around carefully. Some of the rushes had been bent over, their stems broken, and something had been pulled down over the mud, something that might easily have been the size of a man.

But there was no sign of a body.

"We can't lurk about here too long," she said, clambering out. "We really will look suspicious."

"Station, then."

As they walked along the path next to the mail depot, they heard the great bell of Cardinal's College tolling eleven, and Lyra thought of the lecture that she should be attending just then, the last of the term. Annie and Helen would be there, though, and she could borrow their notes; and perhaps that good-looking shy boy from Magdalen would be sitting at the back, as before, and perhaps this time she could have gone to sit right next to him and see what happened; and everything would go back to normal. Except that as long as that locker key was in her pocket, nothing would be normal.

"It used to be you who was impulsive," said Pan, "and me who kept holding you back. We're different now."

She nodded. "Well, you know, things change. . . . We could wait, Pan, and go back to St. Aldate's when that policeman goes off duty. Like this evening, about six, maybe. They can't all be in a conspiracy with him. There must be someone honest there. This isn't . . . this isn't just shoplifting. This is murder."

"I know. I saw it."

"And maybe by doing this we'd be helping the murderer get away with it. By interfering with the investigation. That can't be right."

"That's another thing," he said.

"What?"

"You used to be optimistic. You used to think that whatever we did would turn out well. Even after we came back from the north, you used to think that. Now you're cautious, you're anxious . . . you're pessimistic."

She knew he was right, but it wasn't right that he should speak to her accusingly, as if it was something to blame her for.

"I used to be young" was all she could find to say.

He made no response.

They didn't speak again till they reached the railway station. Then she said, "Pan, come here," and he leapt up at once into her hands. She put him on her shoulder and said quietly, "You're going to have to look out behind. Someone might be watching."

He turned around and settled as she climbed the steps to the entrance. "Don't go straight to the lockers," he murmured. "Go and look at the magazines first. I'll see if there's anyone just hanging about watching."

She nodded and turned left inside the station doors and wandered over to the bookstall. While she flicked through one magazine after another, Pan looked at all the men and women queuing for tickets, or sitting at tables drinking coffee, or checking the timetables, or asking something at the inquiry desk.

"Everyone seems to be doing something," he said quietly. "I can't see anyone who's just hanging about."

Lyra had the locker key ready in her pocket. "Shall I go?" she said.

"Yes, go on. But don't hurry. Just walk naturally. Look at the time or the departures and arrivals board or something. . . ."

She replaced the magazine and turned away from the bookstall. It seemed to her that a hundred pairs of eyes could have been watching, but she tried to look nonchalant as she sauntered across the floor to the other end of the booking hall, where the left-luggage lockers stood.

"All right so far," said Pan. "No one's watching. Just do it now."

Locker number 36 was at waist height. She turned the key and opened the door, and found a battered canvas rucksack inside.

"Hope it's not too heavy," she murmured, and lifted it out, leaving the key in the door.

It was heavy, but she swung it over her right shoulder with no difficulty.

"I wish we could do what Will did," she said.

He knew what she meant. Will Parry had a power of becoming invisible that had astonished the witches of the north, who used to vanish from sight in the same way: by reducing what was interesting about themselves until they were almost unnoticeable. He had practiced it all his life, in order to avoid being spotted by people such as police officers and social workers who might have asked what this boy was doing out of school, and started to make inquiries that would have ended by separating him from his beloved mother, who was troubled by all kinds of unreal fears and obsessions.

When Will had told Lyra about the way he'd had to live, and how difficult it had been to remain unobserved, firstly she'd been astonished that anyone could live in such a solitary way, and secondly she had been moved by his courage, and thirdly she wasn't surprised at all that the witches esteemed his skill so highly.

She wondered, as she did so often, what he was doing now, and whether his mother was safe, and what he looked like these days . . . and Pan murmured, "Good so far. But go a little bit faster. There's a man on the station steps looking at us."

They were on the station forecourt already, where taxis and buses set down passengers and picked them up. Thinking about Will, Lyra had hardly noticed how far they'd come.

"What's he look like?" she said quietly.

"Big. Black woolly hat. Dæmon looks like a mastiff."

She moved a little faster, making for Hythe Bridge Street and the center of the city.

"What's he doing?"

"Still watching . . ."

The quickest way back to Jordan would have been the straightest, of course, but that was also the most dangerous, because she'd be visible all the way along Hythe Bridge Street and then George Street.

"Can he still see us?" she said.

"No—the hotel's in the way."

"Then hold on tight."

"What are you—"

She suddenly darted across the road and ducked under the railings around the coal wharves, where the canal boats came to unload. Ignoring the men who stopped to watch, she ran around the steam crane, behind the Canal Board building, and out across the narrow street into George Street Mews.

"Can't see him," said Pan, craning his neck to look.

Lyra ran on into Bulwarks Lane, a pathway between two high walls no further apart than her own outstretched hands. She was out of sight entirely here: no one to help if she ran into trouble . . . But she came to the end of the lane and turned sharp left along another mews that ran behind St. Peter's Oratory, and then out into New Inn Hall Street, which was busy with shoppers.

"So far, so good," said Pan.

Across the street, and into Sewy's Lane next: a dank little alley next to the Clarendon Hotel. A man was filling a large dustbin and taking his time over it, with his lumpish sow dæmon sprawled on the ground beside him, gnawing a turnip. Lyra leapt over her, causing the man to start backwards and drop the cigarette out of his mouth.

"Oy!" he cried, but she was already out into the Cornmarket, the main shopping street of the city, crowded with pedestrians and delivery vehicles.

"Keep looking," Lyra said, nearly out of breath.

She darted across the road and down an alley next to the Golden Cross Inn, which led to the Covered Market.

"I'm going to have to slow down," she said. "This is bloody heavy."

She walked at a normal pace through the market, watching everyone ahead as Pan was watching behind, and trying to slow her breathing down. Only a short way now: out into Market Street, then left into Turl Street, only fifty yards away, and there was Jordan College. Less than a minute to go. Controlling every muscle, she strolled calmly along to the lodge.

Just as they entered, a figure stepped out of the door into the porter's room.

"Lyra! Hello. Have you had a good term?"

It was the burly, red-haired, affable Dr. Polstead, the historian, who was not someone she wanted to talk to. He'd left Jordan some years before and moved to Durham College, across Broad Street, but no doubt he had business that occasionally brought him back here.

"Yes, thank you," she said blandly.

A group of undergraduates came through at the same moment, on their way to a class or a lecture. Lyra ignored them, but they all looked at her, as she well knew they would. They even fell silent as they went past, as if they were shy. By the time they'd gone through, Dr. Polstead had given up waiting for any fuller response from Lyra and turned to the porter, so she left. Two minutes later, she and Pan were in her little sitting room at the top of Staircase One, where she puffed out her cheeks with relief, dropped the rucksack on the floor, and locked the door.

"Well, we're committed now," said Pan.

FOUR

THE COLLEGE SILVER

"What went wrong?" demanded Marcel Delamare.

The Secretary General was standing in his office at *La Maison Juste*, and the person he was addressing was a casually dressed young man, dark-haired, slim, tense, and sulky, who was leaning back on a sofa with his legs stretched out and his hands in his pockets. His hawk dæmon glared at Delamare.

"If you employ bunglers . . . ," said the visitor.

"Answer the question."

The young man shrugged. "They messed it up. They were incompetent."

"Is he dead?"

"Seems like it."

"But they didn't find anything. Was he carrying a bag, a case of some sort?"

"Can't see that sort of detail. But I don't think so."

"Then look again. Look harder."

The young man waved a hand languidly as if shooing the idea away. He was frowning, his eyes half closed, and there was a faint sheen of sweat on his white forehead.

"Are you unwell?" said Delamare.

"You know how the new method affects me. It puts a severe strain on the nerves."

"You are paid very well to put up with that sort of thing. In any case, I've told you not to use this new method. I don't trust it."

"I'll look, yes, all right, I'll look, but not now. I need to recover first. But I can tell you one thing: there was someone watching."

"Watching the operation? Who was that?"

"No idea. Couldn't tell. But there was someone else there who saw it all."

"Did the mechanics realize?"

"No."

"That's all you can tell me about it?"

"That's all I know. All it's possible to know. Except . . ."

He said no more. The Secretary General was used to this mannerism and kept his patience. Eventually the young man went on:

"Except I think maybe it could have been her. That girl. I didn't see her, mind. But it could have been."

He was looking closely at Delamare as he said that. His employer sat at the desk and wrote a sentence or two on a piece of headed paper before folding it and capping his fountain pen.

"Here you are, Olivier. Take this to the bank. Then have some rest. Eat properly. Keep up your strength."

The young man opened the paper and read it before putting it in his pocket and leaving without a word. But he'd noticed something he'd seen before: at the mention of the girl, Marcel Delamare's mouth trembled.

Lyra put the rucksack down on the floor and sank into the old armchair.

"Why did you hide when Dr. Polstead came through?" she said.

"I didn't," said Pantalaimon.

"You did. You shot under my coat as soon as you heard his voice."

"I just wanted to be out of the way," he said. "Let's open this and have a look." He was peering closely at the rucksack and lifting the buckles with his nose. "It's certainly his. Same smell. Not the sort of cologne that Miriam's father makes."

"Well, we can't do it now," she said. "We've got twenty minutes to get back to St. Sophia's and see Dr. Lieberson."

It was a meeting that each undergraduate had with her tutor near the end of term: an appraisal, a warning to work harder, a commendation for good work done, suggestions for vacation reading. Lyra had never missed such a meeting yet, but if she didn't hurry . . .

She got up, but Pan didn't move.

"We'd better hide this," he said.

"What? No one comes in here! It's perfectly safe."

"Seriously. Think of the man last night. Someone wanted this enough to kill him for it."

Lyra saw the point, and pulled back the worn carpet. Under the floorboards there was a space where they'd hidden things before. It was a tight squeeze, but they got the rucksack in and pulled the carpet back. As Lyra ran downstairs, she heard the Jordan clock chime for eleven-forty-five.

They made it with a minute to spare, and had to sit hot and red-faced through Dr. Lieberson's appraisal. Apparently Lyra had worked well and was beginning to understand the complexities of Mediterranean and Byzantine politics, though there was always the danger of thinking that a superficial mastery of the events was as good as a fundamental understanding of the principles at work underneath. Lyra agreed, nodding hard. She could have written it

41

herself. Her tutor, a young woman with severely cut blond hair and a goldfinch dæmon, looked at her skeptically.

"Make sure to do some reading," she said. "Frankopan's good. Hughes-Williams has a very good chapter on Levantine trade. Don't forget—"

"Oh, trade, yes. Dr. Lieberson, the Levantine trade—sorry to interrupt—did it always involve roses and perfumes and things like that?"

"And smokeleaf, since it was discovered. The great source of rose oil, attar of roses, in medieval times was Bulgaria. But the trade from there suffered from the Balkan wars and the duties the Ottoman Empire imposed on traffic through the Bosphorus, and besides, the climate was changing a little and the Bulgarian rose growers found it harder to cultivate the best sort of plants, so gradually the trade moved further east."

"Do you know why it might be suffering now?"

"Is it?"

Lyra told her briefly about Miriam's father and his problem with obtaining the supplies for his factory.

"That's interesting," said Dr. Lieberson. "History's not over, you see. It's happening all the time. The problem today would mainly be regional politics, I imagine. I'll look into it. Have a good vacation."

The end of the Michaelmas term was marked by a number of ritual occasions, which varied from college to college. St. Sophia's took a narrow-eyed view of ritual in general, and with an air of "If we really must" produced a slightly better dinner than usual when celebration was unavoidable. Jordan, on the other hand, held a Founder's Feast of great splendor and culinary excess. Lyra had always looked forward to the Founder's Feast when she was younger, not because she was invited (she wasn't) but because of the chance it gave her to earn a few guineas polishing the silver. This task had become a tradition of its own, and after a quick lunch with some friends at St. Sophia's (during which Miriam seemed to have cheered up a great deal), Lyra hurried to the pantry at Jordan, where Mr. Cawson, the Steward, was getting out the dishes, the bowls, the plates, the goblets, and the large tin of Redvers' powder.

The Steward was the senior servant in charge of all the college ceremonies, the great dinners, the silver, the Retiring Room and all its luxuries. Lyra had once been more terrified of Mr. Cawson than of anyone else in Oxford, but recently he'd begun to show signs of quite unsuspected humanity. She sat at the long table with its green baize cloth and dabbed a damp cloth into the tin of powder and polished bowls and dishes and goblets until their very surfaces seemed to swim and dissolve in the naphtha lamplight.

"Good going," said Mr. Cawson, turning a bowl over between his palms and scrutinizing the flawless gleam.

"What's it all worth, Mr. Cawson?" she said, taking up the very biggest dish, a shallow platter fully two feet across with a bowl-shaped depression in the center.

"Priceless," he said. "Irreplaceable. You couldn't buy anything like this now, because they don't make 'em anymore. They've lost the skill. That one," he said, looking at the great dish Lyra was polishing, "that's three hundred and forty years old and as thick as two guineas. There's no money value that would make any sense in connection with that. And," he said, sighing, "this Feast is probably the last time we shall use it."

"Really? What's it for?"

"You've never attended a full Feast, have you, Lyra?" the old man said. "Dined in Hall any number of times—High Table often enough—but never a full Feast, am I right?"

"Well, I wouldn't be invited," said Lyra piously. "It wouldn't be right. I'd never be allowed in the Retiring Room afterwards, never mind anything else."

"Hmm," said Mr. Cawson, without any expression at all.

"So I've never seen what this big plate's for. Is it for truffles, at dessert?"

"Try and put it down."

Lyra laid it on the baize, and because of its rounded bottom, the dish tipped over and lay awkwardly to one side.

"It looks uncomfortable," she said.

"Because it's not for putting down, it's for carrying. It's a rose-water dish."

"Rosewater?" Lyra looked up at the old man, suddenly more curious.

"That's it. After the meat, and before they change places for dessert, we take around the rosewater dishes. Four of 'em, and this is the finest. It's for gentlemen and their guests to dab their napkins in, rinse their fingers, whatever takes their fancy. But we can't get the rosewater anymore. We've got enough for this Feast, and that's it."

"Whyever can't you get it? They grow roses everywhere. The Master's garden is full of roses! Surely you could make some rosewater? I bet I could. I bet it's not hard to do."

"Oh, there's no shortage of English rosewater," said the Steward, lifting down a heavy flask from a shelf above the door, "but it's thin stuff. No body to it. The best comes from the Levant, or beyond. Here—sniff this."

He took the stopper out of the flask. Lyra bent over the open vessel and found the concentrated fragrance of every rose that had ever bloomed: a sweetness and power so profound that it moved beyond sweetness altogether and out of the other side of its own complexity into a realm of clear and simple purity and beauty. It was like the smell of sunlight itself.

"Oh!" she said. "I see what you mean. And this is the very last of it?"

"The very last I could get hold of. I think Mr. Ellis, the Chamberlain at Cardinal's, has a few bottles left. But he guards himself close, Mr. Ellis. I shall try to wheedle my way into his affections."

Mr. Cawson's tone was so dry that Lyra was never sure to what extent he was joking. But this rosewater business was too interesting to leave alone.

"Where did you say it came from, the good stuff?" she said.

"The Levant. Syria and Turkey in particular, so I understand; there's some way they can detect the difference between them, but I never could. Not like wine, not like Tokay or Porto—there's a wealth of tastes in every glass, and once you know your way round 'em, there's no mistaking one vintage for another, far less one kind of wine for a different one. But you've got your tongue and your taste buds involved with wine, haven't you? Your whole mouth's involved. With rosewater, you're just dealing with a fragrance. Still, I'm sure there's some that could tell the difference."

"Why is it getting scarce?"

"Greenfly, I expect. Now, Lyra, have you done 'em all?"

"Just this candlestick to go. Mr. Cawson, who's the supplier for the rosewater? I mean, where do you buy it from?"

"A firm called Sidgwick's. Why are you suddenly interested in rosewater?"

"I'm interested in everything."

"So you are. I forgot. Well, you better have this. . . ." He opened a drawer and took out a tiny glass bottle no bigger than Lyra's little finger, and gave it to her to hold. "Pull the cork out," he said, "and hold it steady."

She did, and Mr. Cawson, with the utmost care and the steadiest hand, filled the tiny bottle from the flask of rosewater.

"There you are," he said. "We can spare that much, and since you're not invited to the Feast and you're not allowed in the Retiring Room, you might as well have it."

"Thank you!" she said.

"Now hop it, go on. Oh—if you want to know about the Levant and the east and all that, you better ask Dr. Polstead over at Durham."

"Oh yes. I could. Thank you, Mr. Cawson."

She left the Steward's pantry and wandered out into the winter afternoon. Unenthusiastically she looked across Broad Street at the buildings of Durham College; no doubt Dr. Polstead was in his rooms, no doubt she could cross the road and knock on the door, and no doubt he'd welcome her, full of bonhomie, and sit her down and explain all about Levantine history at interminable length, and within five minutes she'd wish she hadn't bothered.

"Well?" she said to Pan.

"No. We can see him anytime. But we couldn't tell him about the rucksack. He'd just say take it to the police, and we'd have to say we couldn't, and . . ."

"Pan, what is it?"

"What?"

"There's something you're not telling me."

"No, there isn't. Let's go and look in the rucksack."

"Not now. That'll keep. We've got proper work to do, don't forget," Lyra reminded him. "If we make a start on it today, there'll be that much less to do later on."

"Well, let's take the rucksack with us, at least."

"No! Leave it where it is. It's perfectly safe. We'll be back here for the vacation soon, and if it's with us at St. Sophia's, you'll be nagging me to look at it all the time."

"I don't nag."

"You should hear yourself."

When they got back to St. Sophia's, Pan pretended to go to sleep while Lyra checked the references in her final essay and thought again about the rucksack; and then she put on her last clean dress and went down to dinner.

Over the boiled mutton, some friends tried to persuade her to come with them to a concert in the town hall, where a young pianist of striking good looks was going to play Mozart. This would normally have been tempting enough, but Lyra had something else in mind, and after the rice pudding she slipped away, put on her coat, and went down to Broad Street and into a pub called the White Horse.

It wasn't usual for a young lady to go into a pub on her own, but Lyra in her present mood was far from being a lady. In any case, she was looking for someone, and pretty soon she found him. The bar in the White Horse was small and narrow, and in order to be sure the person she was looking for was there, Lyra had to shove her way through the evening crowd of office workers as far as the little snug at the back. In term time it would have been packed with undergraduates, because unlike some other pubs, the White Horse was used by both the town and the gown, but the year was winding down, and the students wouldn't be seen again till mid-January. But Lyra wasn't gown now: this evening she was town, exclusively.

And there in the snug was Dick Orchard, with Billy Warner and two girls whom Lyra didn't know.

"Hello, Dick," she said.

His face brightened, and it was a good-looking face. His hair was black and curly and glossy; his eyes were large, with brilliant dark irises and clear whites; his features were well defined, his skin healthy and golden; it was the sort of face that would look good in a photogram, nothing blurred or smudged about it; and besides, there was a hint of laughter, or at any rate amusement, behind every expression that flitted over it. He wore a blue-and-white-spotted handkerchief around his throat, in the gyptian style. His dæmon was a trim little vixen, who stood with pleasure to greet Pan; they had always liked each other. When Lyra was nine, Dick had been the leader of a gang of boys who hung around the market, and she had admired him greatly for his ability to spit further than anyone else. Much more recently she and he had had a brief but passionate relationship and, what was more, parted friends. She was genuinely pleased to find him there, but of course would never show it, with other girls watching.

"Where you been, then?" Dick said. "En't seen you for weeks."

"Things to do," she said. "People to see. Books to read."

"Hello, Lyra," said Billy, an amiable boy who had been following Dick around since they were in elementary school. "How you doing?"

"Hello, Billy. Is there room for me there?"

"Who's this?" said one of the girls.

They all ignored her. Billy moved up along the bench, and Lyra sat down.

"Hey," said the other girl. "What you doing butting in?"

Lyra ignored her too. "You're not still working in the market, Dick?" she said.

"No, sod that for a lark. Heaving spuds around, piling cabbages up. I'm working at the mail depot now. What you drinking, Lyra?"

"Badger," she said, inwardly delighted. She'd been right about his job.

Dick got up and squeezed out past one of the girls, who protested, "What you doing, Dick? Who's she?"

"She's my girlfriend."

He looked at Lyra with a lazy sort of smile in his eyes, and she looked back, bold and calm and complicit. Then he was gone, and the girl picked up her handbag and went after him, complaining. Lyra hadn't looked at her once. The other girl said, "What'd he call you? Laura?"

"Lyra."

Billy said, "This is Ellen. She works in the telephone exchange."

"Oh, right," said Lyra. "What you doing now, Billy?"

"I'm with Acott's in the High Street."

"Selling pianos? I didn't know you could play the piano."

"I can't. I just move 'em. Like tonight, there's a concert at the town hall, and they got a lousy piano there, so they hired one from us, a good 'un. Took three of us to move it, but you get what you pay for. What you up to? You done your exams yet?"

"Not yet."

"What exams? You a student?" said the girl.

Lyra nodded. Dick came back with a half pint of Badger ale. The other girl had gone.

"Oh, a half. Thank you for my half pint, Dick," said Lyra. "If I'd known you were short of money, I'd have asked for a glass of water."

"Where's Rachel?" said the girl.

Dick sat down. "I didn't get you a pint because there was this article in the paper," he said. "It says women shouldn't drink all that much at once, it's too strong for 'em, it sends 'em mad with strange lusts and desires."

"Too much for you to cope with, then," Lyra said.

"Well, I could manage, but I was just thinking of the innocent bystanders."

"Has Rachel gone?" said the girl, trying to peer through the crowd.

"You're looking very gyptian tonight," Lyra said to Dick.

"You got to show off your best features, en't you," he said.

49

"Is that what you call 'em?"

"You remember my grandad's gyptian. Giorgio Brabandt. He's good-looking too. He'll be in Oxford later this week—I'll introduce you."

"I'm fed up with this," the girl said to Billy.

"Ah, come on, Ellen . . ."

"I'm going with Rachel. You can come or not, as you like," she said, and her starling dæmon flapped his wings on her shoulder as she got up.

Billy looked at Dick, who shrugged; so Billy got up as well.

"See you, Dick. Cheers, Lyra," he said, and followed the girl out through the crowded bar.

"Well, fancy that," said Dick. "We're all alone."

"Tell me about the mail place. What is it you do?"

"It's the main sorting office for the south of England. Stuff comes in on the mail trains in sealed sacks and we open them and sort the post into regions. Then we take it back out in boxes, different colors for different regions, and load 'em onto other trains, or on the zeppelin for London."

"And that goes on all day?"

"All day and night. Round the clock. What you want to know for?"

"I got a reason. Maybe I'll tell you, maybe I won't. What shift are you on?"

"Nights this week. I'll be starting at ten tonight."

"Is there a man who works there—a big hefty man—who was working on Monday night, yesterday night, and who hurt his leg?"

"That's a peculiar question. There's hundreds of people working there, specially this time of year."

"I suppose so. . . ."

"But as it happens, I think I know who you mean. There's a big ugly bugger by the name of Benny Morris. I heard off someone earlier today that he'd hurt his leg falling off a ladder. Pity it wasn't his neck. Funny thing is, he was working last night, first part of the shift anyway, then he cleared off partway through. At least, no one saw him after about midnight. Then this afternoon I hear he's broken his leg, or summing like that."

"Is it easy to get out of the depot without anyone knowing?"

"Well, you couldn't get out the main gate without someone seeing you. But it's not hard to jump over the fence—or to get through. What's going on, Lyra?"

Dick's dæmon, Bindi, had jumped lightly up on the bench beside him and was watching Lyra with bright black eyes. Pan was on the table near Lyra's elbow. They were both following the conversation closely.

Lyra leant in and spoke more quietly. "Last night, after midnight, someone climbed out the depot over the gate by the allotments, and walked along by the river and joined another man, who was hiding among the trees. Then a third man came along the path from the station, and they attacked him. They killed him and hid his body down among the rushes. It wasn't there this morning, because we went to look."

"How d'you know that?"

"'Cause we saw it."

"Why en't you told the police?"

Lyra took a long sip of her beer while keeping her eyes on his face. Then she put it down. "We can't," she said. "There's a good reason."

"What were you doing down there anyway, after midnight?"

"Stealing parsnips. It doesn't matter what we were there for. We were there, and we saw it."

Bindi looked at Pan, and Pan looked back, as bland and innocent as Lyra herself could be.

"And these two men—they didn't see you?"

"If they had, they'd have chased us and tried to kill us too. But this is the point—they weren't expecting him to fight back, but he had a knife and he cut one of them on the leg."

Dick blinked in surprise and drew back a little. "And you saw them shove his body in the river, you said?"

"Down into the rushes, anyway. Then they went off towards the footbridge over to the gasworks, the one helping the other whose leg had been hurt."

"If the body was just in the rushes, they'd've had to go back later and get rid of it properly. Anyone could find it there. Kids play along the bank, there's people going to and fro along the path all the time. During the day, anyway."

"We didn't want to stay and find out," Lyra said.

"No."

She finished her beer.

"Want another?" he said. "Get you a pint this time."

"No. Thanks, but I'm going soon."

"That other man, not the one that was attacked, the one that was waiting. Did you see what he was like?"

"No, not clearly. But we heard him. And that's"—she looked around, and saw that they were still unobserved—"that's why we can't go to the police. 'Cause we heard a policeman talking to someone, and it was the same voice. The exact same voice. The policeman was the man who killed him."

Dick shaped his lips to whistle but didn't blow. Then he took a long drink. "Right," he said. "That is awkward."

"I don't know what to do, Dick."

"Better do nothing, then. Just forget about it."

"I can't."

"That's 'cause you keep thinking about it. Think of something else."

She nodded. That was as good as his advice was going to get. Then she suddenly did think of something else.

"Dick, they take on extra workers at Christmas, don't they, the Royal Mail?"

"Yeah. You fancy a job?"

"Well, I might."

"Just go along the office and ask 'em. It's a good laugh. Hard work, mind. You won't have time to go round being a detective."

"No. I just want to get a feel for what the place is like. It wouldn't be for long, anyway."

"You sure you won't have another drink?"

"Quite sure."

"What you doing for the rest of the evening?"

"Things to do, books to read . . ."

"Stay with me. We could have a good time. You chased them other girls away. You going to leave me all on me own?"

"I didn't chase them away!"

"You scared 'em stiff."

She felt a jolt of shame. She began to blush; she was mortified to remember how unpleasantly she'd behaved to the two girls, when it would have been so easy to be friendly to them.

"Another time, Dick," she said. It wasn't easy to speak.

"You're all promises," he said, but quite good-naturedly. He knew it wouldn't take him long to find another girl to spend the evening with, a girl who had nothing to be ashamed of and who was happy with her dæmon. And they would have a good time, as he'd said. For a moment, Lyra envied this unknown other girl, because Dick was good company and considerate as well as more than good-looking; but then she remembered that after only a few weeks with him, she'd begun to feel confined. There were areas of her life about which she cared passionately, and which he was indifferent to or simply unaware of. She'd never be able to talk to him about Pan and separation, for example.

She stood up, and then bent down and kissed him, which took him by surprise. "You won't be waiting long," she said.

He smiled. Bindi and Pan touched noses, and then Pan leapt to Lyra's shoulder and they moved away through the bar and into the chilly street.

She began to turn left, but stopped, and thought for a second, and then crossed the street instead and went into Jordan.

"What now?" said Pan, as she waved to the porter in the lodge window.

"The rucksack."

They climbed the stairs to their old room in silence. Once she'd locked the door behind them and switched on the gas fire, she rolled back the rug and prized up the floorboard. Everything was as they'd left it.

She retrieved the rucksack and took it to the armchair, under the lamplight. Pan crouched on the little table while Lyra unfastened the buckles. She would very much have liked to tell Pan how uneasy she felt, part guilty, part sad, part overwhelmingly curious. But talking was so difficult.

"Who are we going to tell about this?" he said.

"Depends what we find."

"Why?"

"I don't know. Maybe it doesn't depend on that. Let's just . . ."

She didn't bother to finish the sentence. She folded back the top of the rucksack and found a neatly folded shirt that had once been white and a sweater of coarse dark blue wool, both much darned, and under them a pair of rope-soled sandals, badly worn down, and a tin box about the size of a large Bible, held shut with a couple of thick rubber bands. It was heavy, and the contents didn't move or make a noise when she turned the box around in her hands. It had once contained Turkish smokeleaf, but the painted design was almost worn away. She opened it and found several small bottles and sealed cardboard boxes tightly packed in with cotton fibers.

"Botanical stuff, maybe," she said.

"Is that all?" said Pan.

"No. Here's his toiletry bag or something."

It was made of faded canvas and contained a razor and shaving brush and a nearly empty tube of toothpaste.

"There's something else," Pan said, peering inside the rucksack.

Her hand found a book—two books—and brought them out. Disappointingly, they were both in languages she couldn't read, though one looked from the illustrations like a textbook of botany, and the other, from the way it was laid out on the page, a long poem.

"Still more," said Pan.

At the bottom of the rucksack she found a bundle of papers and brought them all out. They consisted of three or four offprints from learned journals, all concerning botany; a small battered notebook that at a quick look contained names and addresses from all over Europe and beyond; and a small number of handwritten pages. These were creased and stained, and the handwritten words were in a pale pencil. But whereas the journal offprints were in Latin or German, she saw at a quick glance that the written pages were in English.

"Well?" he said. "Are we going to read them?"

"Of course. But not here. The light in here's dreadful. I don't know how we managed to do any work at all."

She folded the pages and put them in an inside pocket, and then replaced everything else before unlocking the door and getting ready to leave.

"And am I going to be allowed to read them too?" he said.

"Oh, for God's sake."

They said not a word on the way back to St. Sophia's.

FIVE

DR. STRAUSS'S JOURNAL

Lyra made herself some hot chocolatl and sat at her little table by the fire, with the lamp close by, to read the document from the rucksack. It consisted of several pages of lined paper torn from an exercise book, by the look of it, covered with writing in pencil. Pan sat, holding himself ostentatiously away from her arm, close enough to read it with her.

From Dr. Strauss's Journal

Tashbulak, 12 September

Chen the camel herder says he has been into Karamakan. Once inside he managed to penetrate to the heart of the desert. I asked what was there. He said it was guarded by priests. That was the word he used, but I know he was searching for another that better expressed what they were. Like soldiers, he said. But priests.

But what were they guarding? It was a building. He

could not say what was inside it. They refused to let him enter.

What sort of building? How big was it? What did it look like? Big like a great sand dune, he said, the greatest in the world, made of red stone, very ancient. Not like a building that people made. Like a hill, then, or a mountain? No, regular like a building. And red. But not like a house or a dwelling. Like a temple? He shrugged.

What language did they speak, the guards? Every language, he said. (I daresay he means every language he knows, which is not a few: like many of his fellow camel men, he is at home in a dozen languages, from Mandarin to Persian.)

Tashbulak, 15 September

Saw Chen again. Asked him why he had wanted to enter Karamakan. He said he had always known stories about the limitless wealth to be found there. Many people had tried, but most had given up before they reached more than a little way, because of the pain of the journey *akterrakeh,* as they pronounce it.

I asked how he overcame the pain. By thinking of gold, he said.

And did you find any? I said.

Look at me, he said. Look at us.

He is a ragged, skeleton-thin figure. His cheeks are hollow, his eyes sunk among a hundred wrinkles. His hands are ingrained with dirt. His clothes would disgrace a scarecrow. His dæmon, a desert rat, is nearly hairless, and her bare skin is covered in weeping lesions. He is avoided by the other camel men, who seem to be afraid of him. The solitary nature of his way of living obviously suits him. The others have begun to avoid me, probably because of my contact with him. They know of his power to separate, and fear and shun him because of it.

Was he not afraid for his dæmon? If she got lost, what would he have done?

He'd have searched for her in al-Khan al-Azraq. My Arabic is patchy, but Hassall told me that meant the Blue Hotel. I queried that, but Chen insisted: al-Khan al-Azraq, the Blue Hotel. And where was this Blue Hotel? He didn't know where it was. Just a place where dæmons go. Anyway, he said, she probably wouldn't go there, because she wanted gold as much as he did. That seemed to be a joke, because he laughed as he said it.

Lyra looked at Pan and saw that he was gazing at the page with fierce intensity. She read on:

Tashbulak, 17 September

The more we examine it, the more it seems that *Rosa lopnoriae* is the parent and the others, *R. tajikiae* and so on, the descendants. The optical phenomena are by some way most marked with *ol. R. lopnoriae*. And the further from Karamakan, the harder it is to grow. Even when conditions have been arranged to duplicate the soil, the temperature, the humidity, etc., of K., so closely as to be more or less identical, specimens of *R. lopnoriae* fail to prosper and soon die. There's something we're missing. The other variants must have been hybridized in order to produce a plant with at least some of the virtues of R. *lop* while being viable in other places.

There is a question about how to write this all up. Of course, the scientific papers will come first. But none of us can overlook the wider implications. As soon as the facts about the roses are known in the world, there will be a frenzy for exploration, for exploitation, and we—this little station—will be elbowed aside, if not actually wiped out. So will all the rose growers nearby. Nor is that all: given the nature of what the optical process discloses, there will be religious and political anger, panic, persecution, as surely as the night follows the day.

Tashbulak, 23 September

I have asked Chen to guide me into Karamakan. There will be gold for him. Rod Hassall will come too. I dread it, but there is no avoiding it. I expected it would be hard to persuade Cartwright to let us make the attempt, but he was all in favor. He can see the importance of it as well as we can. In any case, things here are desperate.

Tashbulak, 25 September

Rumors of violence from Khulanshan and Akdzhar, just 150 kilometers or so to the west. Rose gardens there have been burned and dug up by men from the mountains—at least so it's said. We thought that particular trouble was limited to Asia Minor. Bad news if it's come this far.

Tomorrow we go into Karamakan, if it's possible. Cariad begs me not to. Hassall's dæmon likewise. They are afraid, of course, and my God, so am I.

This pain is agonizing, almost indescribable, completely imperious and commanding. But it isn't quite pain either anymore. A sort of heart-deep anguish and sorrow, a sickness, a fear, a despair almost unto death. All those things, which vary in their intensity. The physical pain grew less after half an hour or so. I don't think I could have borne it for longer. As for Cariad . . . It is too painful to speak of. What have I done? What have I done to her, my soul? Her eyes so wide, so shocked, as I looked back.

I can't write of it.

The worst thing I have ever done, and the most necessary. I pray there will be some future in which we can come together, and that she will forgive me.

The page ended there. As she read it, Lyra felt a movement at her elbow and sensed Pan drawing away. He lay down at the edge of the table with his back to her. Her throat tightened; she couldn't have spoken, even if she knew what to say to him.

She closed her eyes for a moment and then read on:

We have come 4 kilometers into the region and are resting to recover a little strength. It is a hellish place. Hassall was very badly affected at first, but recovered more quickly than I am doing. Chen, by contrast, is quite cheerful. Of course, he has experienced it before.

The landscape is utterly barren. Vast dunes of sand from whose summit you can see nothing except more dunes, and yet more beyond them. The heat is appalling. Mirages flicker at the edge of one's vision and every sound is magnified, somehow; the passage of the wind over the loose sand creates an intolerable scraping, squeaking, as if a million insects lived just under the top layer of sand, and under one's skin too, so that just out of sight these hideous creatures were living a gnawing, chewing, tearing, biting life that eats at one's own inside as well as at the substance of the world itself. But there is no life, vegetable or animal. Only our camels seem unperturbed.

The mirages, if that is what they are, disappear as you look directly at them, but recombine at once when you look away. They seem to be like images of furious gods or devils making threatening gestures. It is almost too hard to bear. Hassall is suffering too. Chen says we should keep asking these deities for forgiveness, reciting a formula of contrition and apology that he tried to teach us. He says the mirages are aspects of the Simurgh, some kind of monstrous bird. It's very hard to make sense of what he says.

It is time to move on.

Karamakan, later

Slow progress. We are camping for the night, despite Chen's advice to keep moving. We simply have no strength left. We must rest and recover. Chen will wake us before dawn so we can travel in the coolest part of the day. Oh, Cariad, Cariad.

Karamakan, 27 September

An appalling night. Hardly slept for nightmares of torture, dismemberment, disemboweling—atrocious suffering that I had to watch, unable to flee or close my eyes or help. Kept being woken by my own cries, dreading to sleep again, unable to prevent it. Oh God, I hope Cariad is not disturbed in this way. Hassall in a similar state. Chen grumbled and went to lie apart, so as not to be disturbed.

He woke us when the dawn was the very faintest lightening of the eastern horizon. Breakfasted on dried figs and slivers of dried camel meat. We rode before the great heat began.

At midday Chen said, There it is.

He was pointing east, towards where I guess the very center of the Karamakan desert to be. Hassall and I screwed up our eyes, shaded them from the sun, peered into the dazzle, and saw nothing.

It is the afternoon now, the hottest part of the day, and we are resting. Hassall rigged up a rough shelter using a couple of blankets to throw a morsel of shade where we all lay, Chen too, and slept a little. No dreams. The camels fold their legs, close their eyes, and doze impassively.

The pain has diminished, as Chen said it would, but there is still a heart-deep wound—a perpetual drag of anguish. Will it ever end?

Karamakan, 27 September, evening

Traveling again. Writing this on camelback. Chen no longer sure of direction. Asked where, he replies, Further. More way to go, but is vague about which way that is. He hasn't seen it since yesterday. When asked, he can't say what exactly he saw. I assume the red building, but

H and I have seen no sign of it, or of any color except the interminable and almost unbearable monotony of sand.

Impossible to estimate the distance we've traveled. Not many kilometers; another day should surely find us at the center of this desolate place.

Karamakan, 28 September

A better night, thank God. Dreams complex and confused but less bloody. Slept deeply till Chen woke us before dawn.

Now we can see it. At first it was like a mirage, flickering, wavering, floating above the horizon. Then it seemed to grow a base and to be attached firmly to the earth. Now it is solidly and unmistakably there—a building like a fortress or a hangar for a vast airship. No details visible at this distance, no doors, windows, fortifications, nothing. Just a large rectangular block, dark red in color. Writing this just after midday, before we crawl under H's shelter and rest during the godawful heat. When we awake, the last lap.

Karamakan, 28 September, evening

We have come to the building and met the priests/soldiers/guards. They seem like all of those things. Unarmed, but powerfully built and threatening of aspect. To the eye they look neither Western European nor Chinese, nor Tartar nor Muscovite; pale skin, black hair, round eyes; perhaps more Persian than anything else. They don't speak English—at least they ignored us when Hassall and I tried to speak to them—but Chen communicates immediately in what I think is Tajik. They are dressed in simple smocks and loose trousers of dark red cotton, the same color as the building, and leather sandals. They seem to have no dæmons, but Hassall and I are beyond being frightened by that now.

We asked through Chen if we could enter the building. An immediate and absolute no. We asked what goes on in there. They conferred, then answered with a refusal to tell us. After more questions, all unhelpfully answered, we got a hint when one of them, more voluble than the rest, spoke rapidly to Chen for a full minute. In the torrent of his speech, Hassall and I both made out, several times, the word *gül*, which means *rose* in many languages of Central Asia. Chen looked at us several times during the man's speech, but when it was over, he would only say, No good. Not stay here. No good.

What did he say about roses? we asked. Chen just shook his head.

Did he mention roses?

No. No good. Must go now.

The guards were watching us closely, looking from us to Chen, from him back to us.

Then I thought to try something else. Knowing that parts of Central Asia had been traveled by the Romans, I wondered whether anything of their language had remained. I said in Latin: We intend no harm to you or your people. May we know what you are guarding in this place?

Immediate recognition and understanding. The voluble one replied at once in the same language: What have you brought as payment?

I said, We did not know payment was necessary. We are anxious because our friends have disappeared. We think they might have come here. Have you seen any travelers like us?

We have seen many travelers. If they come *akterrakeh*, and they have payment, they can enter. One way only, not so. But if they enter, they may not leave.

Then can you tell us whether our friends are inside that red building?

In answer to which he said, If they are here, they are not there, and if they are there, they are not here.

It sounded like a formula, a standard form of words that had been repeated so often its meaning had worn away. At least that told me that others had asked similar questions. I tried another.

I said, You spoke of payment. Did you mean in exchange for roses?

What else?

Knowledge, perhaps.

Our knowledge is not for you.

What payment would be satisfactory?

A life, was the disconcerting answer.

One of us must die?

We will all die.

That was little help, of course. I tried another question. Why can we not grow your roses outside this desert?

The only answer that received was a look of scorn. Then he walked away.

I said to Chen, Do you know of anyone who has gone inside?

He said, One man. He did not return. No one returns.

Frustrated, Hassall and I retreated to our little shelter and discussed what to do. It was a fruitless, painful, repetitious discussion. We were hedged in by imperatives: it's absolutely necessary to investigate these roses; it's absolutely impossible to do so without going in and never returning.

So we examined it again more deeply. Why is it necessary to investigate the roses? Because of what they show us about the nature of Dust. And if the Magisterium hears about what is here in Karamakan, they will stop at nothing to prevent that knowledge from spreading, and to do that, they will come here and destroy the red building and everything in it; and they have armies and armaments in plenty to do that. The recent trouble in Khulanshan and Akdzhar is their work—no doubt about that. They are coming closer.

So we must investigate, and the inevitable consequence of that is that one of us must go in and the other must return with the knowledge we have gained so far. There's no alternative, none. And we cannot do it.

There is still no sign of our dæmons, and our store of food and water is diminishing. We can't stay here much longer.

A note at the end, in a different hand, said:

Later that night Strauss's Cariad arrived. She was exhausted, fearful, damaged. Next day she and Strauss went inside the red building, and I returned with Chen. Trouble coming closer. Ted Cartwright and I agreed that I should set off at once with what little knowledge we have. Pray God I find Strella, and that she will forgive me. R.H.

Lyra put the pages on the table. She felt light-headed. She felt as if she'd caught a glimpse of a long-lost memory, something intensely important that was buried under thousands of days of ordinary life. What was it that had affected her so much? The red building—the desert around it—the guards who spoke in Latin—something buried so deeply that she couldn't be sure if it was true, or a dream, or a memory of a dream, or even of a story she'd loved so much when she was a little child that she'd insisted on it again and again at bedtime, and then put away and forgotten entirely. *She knew something about that red building in the desert.* And she had no idea what it was.

Pan was curled up on the table, asleep, or pretending. She knew why. Dr. Strauss's description of separating from his dæmon, Cariad, had brought back immediately that abominable betrayal of her own on the shores of the world of the dead, when she had abandoned Pan to go in search of the ghost of her friend Roger. The guilt and the shame would still be as fresh in her heart on the day she died, no matter how far away that was.

Perhaps that wound was one reason they were estranged now. It had never healed. There was no one else alive to whom she could talk about it, except for Serafina Pekkala, the witch queen; but witches were different, and anyway she hadn't seen Serafina since that journey to the Arctic so many years before.

Oh, but . . .

"Pan?" she whispered.

He gave no sign that he'd heard. He seemed to be fast asleep, except that she knew he wasn't.

"Pan," she went on, still whispering, "what you said about the man who was killed . . . The man this diary's about, Hassall . . . He and his dæmon could separate, isn't that what you said?"

Silence.

"He must have found her again when he came out of that desert,

67

Karamakan. . . . That must be a place like the one the witches go to when they're young, where their dæmons can't go. So maybe there are other people . . ."

He didn't move; he didn't speak.

She looked away wearily. But her eye was caught by something on the floor by the bookcase: it was the book she'd used to prop the window open, the one Pan had thrown down in distaste. Hadn't she put it back on the shelf? He must have thrown it down again.

She got up to replace it, and Pan saw her and said, "Why don't you get rid of that rubbish?"

"Because it's not rubbish. I wish you wouldn't throw it about like a spoilt child just because you don't like it."

"It's poison, and it's destroying you."

"Oh, grow up."

She laid it on the desk, and he sprang down to the floor, his fur bristling. His tail swept back and forth across the carpet as he sat and stared at her. He was radiating contempt, and she flinched a little but kept her hands on the book.

They said not another word as she went to bed. He slept in the armchair.

SIX

MRS. LONSDALE

She couldn't sleep for thinking of the journal, and the meaning of the word *akterrakeh*. It meant something to do with the journey to the red building, and possibly something to do with separating, but she was so tired that none of it made sense. The man who'd been murdered was able to separate, and it seemed from what Dr. Strauss had written that no one could make the journey if they were intact. Was *akterrakeh* a word in one of the local languages for separation?

The best way to think about it would have been by talking with Pan. But he was unreachable. Reading about the separation of the two men from Tashbulak upset him, angered him, frightened him—perhaps all of those things—just as it did her, but then there'd come the distraction of the novel that he hated so much. There were so many things they had to disagree about, and that book was one of the most toxic.

The Hyperchorasmians, by a German philosopher called Gottfried Brande, was a novel that was having an extraordinary vogue among clever young people all over Europe and beyond. It was a publishing phenomenon: nine hundred pages long, with an unpronounceable title (at least until Lyra had learnt to pronounce the *ch* as a *k*), an uncompromising sternness of style, and nothing that could remotely pass for a love interest, it had sold in the millions and influenced the thinking of an entire generation. It told the story of a young man who set out to kill God, and succeeded. But the unusual thing about it, the quality that had set it apart from anything else Lyra had ever read, was that in the world Brande described, human beings had no dæmons. They were totally alone.

Like many others, Lyra had been spellbound, hypnotized by the force of the story, and found her head ringing with the hammer blows of the protagonist's denunciation of anything and everything that stood in the way of pure reason. Even his quest to find God and kill him was expressed in terms of the fiercest rationality: it was irrational that such a being should exist, and rational to do away with him. Of figurative language, of metaphor or simile, there was not a trace. At the end of the novel, as the hero looked out from the mountains at a sunrise, which in the hands of another writer might have represented the dawn of a new age of enlightenment, free of superstition and darkness, the narrator turned away from commonplace symbolism of that kind with scorn. The final sentence read, "It was nothing more than what it was."

That phrase was a sort of touchstone of progressive thinking among Lyra's peers. It had become fashionable to disparage any sort of excessive emotional reaction, or any attempt to read other meanings into something that happened, or any argument that couldn't be justified with logic: "It's nothing more than what it is." Lyra herself had used the phrase more than once in conversation, and felt Pan turn away in disdain as she did so.

When they woke up the morning after reading Dr. Strauss's journal, their disagreement about *The Hyperchorasmians* was still alive and bitter. As Lyra dressed, she said, "Pan, what's got into you this past year? You never used to be like this. We never used to be like this. We used to disagree about things without this monumental everlasting sulk—"

"Can't you see what it's doing to you, this *attitude* you're affecting?" he burst in. He was standing on top of the bookcase.

"What *attitude*? What are you talking about?"

"That man's influence is baleful. Haven't you seen what's happening to Camilla? Or that boy from Balliol—what's his name, Guy something? Since they started reading *The Hypercolonics* or whatever it's called, they've become arrogant and unpleasant in all kinds of ways. Ignoring their dæmons, as if they didn't exist. And I can see it in you too. A sort of absolutism—"

"*What*? You're not making sense at all. You refuse to know anything about it, but you think you have the right to criticize—"

"Not the *right*, the *responsibility*! Lyra, you're closing your mind. Of course I know about the bloody book. I know exactly what you know. Actually, I probably know more, because I didn't shut down my common sense, or my sense of what's right, or something, while you were reading it."

"You're still fretting because his story does away with dæmons?"

He glared at her and then leapt down to the desk again. She moved back. Sometimes she was very conscious of how sharp his teeth were.

"What are you going to do?" she said. "Bite me till I agree?"

"Can't you *see*?" he said again.

"I can *see* a book I think is extremely powerful and intellectually compelling. I can *understand* the appeal of reason, rationality, logic. No—not the appeal—I'm *persuaded* by them. It's not an emotional spasm. It's entirely a matter of rational—"

"Anything emotional has to be a spasm, has it?"

"The way you're behaving—"

"No, you're not listening to me, Lyra. I don't think we've got anything in common anymore. I just can't stand watching you turn into this rancorous, reductive monster of cold logic. You're *changing,* that's the point. I don't like it. Damn it, we used to warn each other about this sort of—"

"And you think it's all the fault of one novel?"

"No. It's the fault of that Talbot man too. He's just as bad, in a cowardly sort of way."

"Talbot? Simon Talbot? Make your bloody mind up, Pan. There couldn't be two more different thinkers. Complete opposites. According to Talbot, there's no truth at all. Brande—"

"You didn't see that chapter in *The Constant Deceiver?*"

"What chapter?"

"The one I had to suffer you reading through last week. Evidently you didn't take it in, though I had to. The one where he pretends that dæmons are merely—what is it?—psychological projections with no independent reality. That one. All argued very prettily, charming, elegant prose, witty, full of brilliant paradoxes. You know the one I mean."

"But you haven't got any independent reality. You know that. If I died—"

"Neither have you, you stupid cow. If I died, so would you. *Touché.*"

She turned away, too angry to speak.

Simon Talbot was an Oxford philosopher whose latest book was much discussed in the university. Whereas *The Hyperchorasmians* was a popular success that was dismissed as tosh by critics and read mainly by the young, *The Constant Deceiver* was a favorite among literary experts, who praised its elegance of style and playful wit. Talbot was a radical skeptic, to whom truth and even reality were rainbow-like epiphenomena with no ultimate meaning. In the silvery charm of his prose, everything solid flowed and ran and broke apart like mercury spilled from a barometer.

"No," said Pan. "They're not different. Two sides of the same coin."

"Just because of what they say about dæmons—or don't say—they don't pay you enough tribute—"

"Lyra, I wish you could hear yourself. Something's happened to you. You're under a spell or something. These men are *dangerous*—"

"Superstition," she said, and she truly felt contempt for Pan just then, and hated herself for it, and couldn't stop. "You can't look at anything calmly and dispassionately. You have to throw insults at it. It's childish, Pan. Attributing some kind of evil or magic to an argument you can't counter—you used to believe in seeing things clearly, and now you're all bound up in fog and superstition and magic. Afraid of something because you can't understand it."

"I understand it perfectly. The trouble is that you don't. You think those two charlatans are profound philosophers. You're hypnotized by them. You read the absolute drivel they write, both of them, and you think it's the latest thing in intellectual achievement. They're lying, Lyra, both lying. Talbot thinks he can make truth disappear by waving his paradoxes around. Brande thinks he can do it just by bullheaded denial. You know what I think's at the bottom of this infatuation of yours?"

"There you go again, describing something that doesn't exist. But go on, say what you want to."

"It's not just a *position* you're taking up. You half believe those people, that German philosopher and the other man. That's what it is. You're clever enough on top, but underneath you're so bloody naive that you half believe their lies are true."

She shook her head, spread her hands, baffled. "I don't know what I can say," she said. "But what I believe, or half believe, or don't believe, isn't really anyone else's business. Making windows into people's souls—"

"But I'm not anyone else! I *am* you!" He twisted around and sprang up onto the bookcase again, from which he looked down at her with blazing eyes. "You're making yourself *forget*," he said with bitter anger.

"Well, now, I don't know what you mean," she said, genuinely lost.

"You're forgetting everything important. And you're trying to believe things that'll kill us."

"No," she said, trying to keep her voice steady. "You've got it wrong, Pan. I'm simply interested in other ways of thinking. It's what you do when you study. One of the things you do. You see ideas, try to see ideas, with someone else's eyes. You see what it feels like to believe the things they do."

"It's contemptible."

"What is? Philosophy?"

"If philosophy says I don't exist, then yes, philosophy is contemptible. I *do* exist. All of us, we dæmons, and other things too—other *entities*, your philosophers would say—we *exist*. Trying to believe nonsense will kill us."

"You see, if you call it nonsense, you're not even *beginning* to engage with it intellectually. You've already surrendered. You've given up trying to argue rationally. You might as well throw stones."

Pan turned away. They said nothing more as they went to breakfast. This was going to be another silent day. There had been something he'd wanted to tell her about that little notebook from the rucksack, the one with the names and addresses, but now he'd keep that to himself.

* * *

74

After breakfast, Lyra surveyed the pile of clothes that needed washing, and sighed heavily, and began to do something about it. St. Sophia's had a laundry room full of machines where the young ladies could wash their own clothes, an activity felt to be better for their characters than having them washed by servants, which was the way of things for the young gentlemen of Jordan.

She was alone in the laundry room because most of her friends were going home for Christmas, and so would be taking their clothes back with them for washing. Lyra's status as an orphan whose only home was a men's college had aroused the sympathy of several friends in the past, and she'd spent various Christmases in the houses of different girls, interested to see what a family home was like, being made welcome and giving and receiving presents and being included in all the family games and outings. Sometimes there was a brother to flirt with; sometimes she had felt alienated from the close and overemphatic jollity; sometimes she had to put up with a lot of intrusive questioning about her unusual background; and always she came back to the calm and quiet of Jordan College, where only a few Scholars and the servants remained, with pleasure. That was her home.

The Scholars were friendly enough, but remote and preoccupied with their studies. The servants paid attention to important and immediate things, like food, or manners, or little jobs by which she could earn a bit of pocket money, such as polishing the silver. One of the Jordan College servants whose relationship with Lyra had changed over the years was Mrs. Lonsdale. She was called Housekeeper, which wasn't a position that existed in most colleges; but part of her duties had included making sure that the child Lyra was clean and neatly dressed, that she knew how to say please and thank you, and so on, and no other college had a Lyra.

Now that her charge could dress herself and had learnt enough manners to get by, Mrs. Lonsdale had mellowed a good deal. She was a widow—she had been widowed very young and had no children—and she had become so much a part of the college that it was impossible to imagine the place without her. No one had ever tried to define her role exactly or list all her responsibilities, and it would have been impossible to try that now: even the energetic new Bursar, after one or two attempts, had had to retreat graciously and acknowledge her power and importance. But she never acquired power for its own sake. The Bursar knew, as did all the servants, as did all the Scholars and the Master, that Mrs. Lonsdale's considerable influence was always used to strengthen the college and to look after Lyra. And by the time she was entering her twentieth year, Lyra herself had begun to realize that too.

So she had fallen into the habit of visiting Mrs. Lonsdale in her parlor from time to time and gossiping, or asking for advice, or taking her little presents. The woman's tongue was no less caustic than it had been in Lyra's childhood, and of course there were things that Lyra could never have told her, but as far as it was possible, the two of them had become friends. And Lyra noticed with Mrs. Lonsdale, as she'd done with other people who had seemed grand and all-powerful and ageless when she was young, that the housekeeper wasn't that old at all, really. She could easily have children of her own still. But that, of course, was a conversation they would never have.

After she'd lugged her clean clothes back to Jordan and made a second trip to carry all the books she'd need for the vacation, she went to the market and spent some of her silver-polishing money on a box of chocolates, and called on Mrs. Lonsdale at a time when she knew the housekeeper would be taking tea in her parlor.

"Hello, Mrs. Lonsdale," she said, kissing the housekeeper's cheek.

"What's the matter with you, then?" said Mrs. Lonsdale.

"Nothing."

"Don't try fooling me. Something's up. That Dick Orchard giving you the runaround?"

"No, I've finished with Dick," Lyra said, sitting down.

"Good-looking boy, though."

"Yes," said Lyra. "I can't deny that. But we just ran out of things to say."

"Yes, that does happen. Put the kettle on, dear."

Lyra moved the old black kettle from the hearthstone to the little iron stand over the fire while Mrs. Lonsdale opened her box of chocolates.

"Ooh, lovely," she said. "Maidment's truffles. I'm surprised they had any left after supplying the Founder's Feast. Now, what have you been up to? Tell me all about your rich and glamorous friends."

"Not so rich now, some of them," Lyra said, and told her about Miriam's father's trouble, and how she'd had another view of the same matter from Mr. Cawson the day before.

"Rosewater," said Mrs. Lonsdale. "My granny used to make that. She had a big copper pan and she'd fill it with rose petals and spring water and boil it, and distill the steam. Whatever the word is. Run it through a lot of glass pipes and let it turn into water again, and there you are. She made lavender water as well. Seemed a lot of bother to me when you could buy eau de cologne at Boswell's cheap enough."

"Mr. Cawson gave me a little bottle of his special rosewater, and it was—I don't know, so rich and concentrated."

"Attar of roses, that's what they call it. Or maybe that's something different."

"Mr. Cawson didn't know why it was so hard to get hold of now. He said Dr. Polstead would know."

"Why don't you ask him, then?"

"Well . . ." Lyra made a face.

77

"Well what?"

"I don't think Dr. Polstead finds me very easy."

"Why not?"

"'Cause when he tried to teach me a few years ago, I was rude to him, probably."

"What d'you mean, 'probably'?"

"I mean we just didn't get on. You've got to like your teachers, I think. Or if not like them, then feel something in common with them. I've got nothing in common with him at all. I just feel awkward near him, and I think he feels the same."

Mrs. Lonsdale poured the tea. They gossiped for a while longer, about intrigues in the college kitchen involving a feud between the head chef and the pastry chef; about Mrs. Lonsdale's recent purchase of a winter coat, and Lyra's own need for a new one; about Lyra's other friends at St. Sophia's, and their adoration of the handsome pianist who'd just played in the city.

Once or twice Lyra thought of telling her about the murder, the wallet, the rucksack, but held back. There was no one who could help her with it but Pan, and it felt as if they wouldn't be speaking much about anything for some time to come.

Every so often Mrs. Lonsdale glanced at Pantalaimon, who was lying on the floor pretending to sleep. Lyra could tell what she was thinking: What's this coldness about? Why aren't you two speaking? But that wasn't something they could easily talk about in Pan's hearing, and that was a pity, because Lyra knew that the housekeeper would bring some sharp good sense to bear on the subject.

They chatted for an hour or so, and Lyra was about to say goodbye and leave when there was a knock on the parlor door. It opened without waiting for an invitation to come in, which surprised Lyra, and then she was even more surprised, because the visitor was Dr. Polstead.

Several things happened at once.

Pan sat up as if he'd been shocked, and leapt onto Lyra's lap, and she automatically put her arms around him. Dr. Polstead realized that there was a visitor and said, "Oh—Lyra—I do beg your pardon—" which suggested to Lyra that he was in the habit of entering this room, that the housekeeper was a close friend, that he expected to find her alone.

Then he said to Mrs. Lonsdale, "Alice, I'm sorry. I'll come back later," and she said to him, "Don't be silly, Mal. Sit down." Their dæmons—hers a dog, his a cat—were touching noses with great familiarity and friendliness. Pan was watching them fiercely, and Lyra felt an almost anbaric charge in the fur under her hands.

"No," said Dr. Polstead. "It can wait. I'll see you later."

Lyra's presence embarrassed him, that was clear, and his dæmon was now gazing at Pan with a strange intensity. Pan was trembling on Lyra's lap. Dr. Polstead turned and left, his big frame almost too large for the doorway. His dæmon followed. When the door closed, Lyra felt the anbaric charge leave Pan's fur, like water draining out of a basin.

"Pan, what is going on?" she said. "What's the matter with you?"

"Tell you later," he muttered.

"And *Alice? Mal?*" Lyra said, turning to Mrs. Lonsdale. "What's all that, then?"

"Never you mind."

Lyra had never seen Mrs. Lonsdale embarrassed before. She'd have sworn it wasn't possible. The housekeeper was even blushing as she turned away and attended to the fire.

"I didn't even know your name was Alice," Lyra went on.

"I'd have told you if you'd asked."

"And Mal . . . I didn't see him as a Mal. I knew his initial was M, but I thought it was Methuselah."

Mrs. Lonsdale had regained her composure. She sat back in her chair and folded her hands in her lap. "Malcolm Polstead," she said, "is the bravest and the best man you'll ever know, girl. If it wasn't for him, you wouldn't be here now."

"What d'you mean?" Lyra was baffled.

"I told him often enough we ought to tell you about it. But the time was never right."

"About what? What are you talking about?"

"Something that happened when you were very young."

"Well, *what?*"

"Let me talk to him first."

Lyra scowled. "If it's something about me, I ought to be told," she said.

"I know. I agree."

"So why—"

"Leave it to me and I'll talk to him."

"And how long will that take? Another twenty years?"

The old Mrs. Lonsdale would have said, "Don't take that tone with me, child," and accompanied her words with a slap. The new one, this Alice person, just shook her head gently. "No," she said. "I could tell you the whole story, but I shan't till he agrees."

"It's obviously something he feels awkward about. Not as awkward as I do, though. People shouldn't keep secrets about other people from them."

"It's nothing to anyone's discredit. Get off your high horse."

Lyra stayed a little longer, but the friendly mood had passed. She kissed the housekeeper goodbye and left. As she crossed the dark quadrangle of Jordan, Lyra thought of going across the road to Durham College and confronting Dr. Polstead directly, but the thought had no more than entered her mind when she felt Pan tremble on her shoulder.

"Right," she said. "You're going to bloody well tell me what's the matter, and you've got no choice about it."

"Let's get inside first."

"Why?"

"You don't know who might be listening."

The college bell tolled six as she shut the door of her old sitting room behind them. She dropped Pan on the carpet and sat down in the sagging armchair, switching on the table lamp to make the room spring warmly into life around them.

"Well?" she said.

"The other night when I was out . . . didn't you feel anything? Didn't you wake up?"

She thought back. "Yes, I did. Just for a moment. I thought it was when you saw the murder."

"No. I know it wasn't then because I would have felt you waking. It was after that, when I was coming back to St. Sophia's with the man's wallet. It was . . . I . . . Well, someone saw me."

Lyra felt her heart become heavy all at once. She'd known this would happen. He quailed at the look on her face.

"But the thing is, it wasn't a person," he said.

"What the hell d'you mean? Who was it, then?"

"It was a dæmon. Another dæmon, separated, like us."

Lyra shook her head. This made no sense at all. "There isn't anyone like us except the witches," she said. "And that dead man. Was it a witch's dæmon?"

"No."

"And where was this?"

"In the Parks. She was . . . ."

"She?"

"She was Dr. Polstead's dæmon. The cat. I forget her name. That's why just now—"

Lyra felt breathless. She couldn't speak for a moment.

"I don't believe it," she said finally. "I just don't believe it. *They* can separate?"

"Well, she was on her own. And she saw me. But I wasn't sure it was her till he came into the room back there. You saw the way she looked at me. Maybe she wasn't sure it was me till then either."

"But how can *they* . . ."

"People *know* about separation. Other people. The man who was attacked, when his dæmon got me to come to him, she told him I was separated. And he knew what it meant and he told me to take the wallet to my . . . to you."

Another blow to Lyra's heart, as she realized what Dr. Polstead's dæmon must have seen.

"She saw you running back to St. Sophia's, carrying the wallet. She must have thought you'd stolen it. They think we're thieves." She sank back into the chair and put her hands up to cover her eyes.

"We can't help that," he said. "We know we're not, and they'll have to believe us."

"Oh, just like that? When are we going to tell them?"

"We'll tell Mrs. Lonsdale, then. Alice. She'll believe us."

Lyra felt too tired to speak.

"I know it's not a good time . . . ," Pan said, but didn't finish.

"You're not kidding. Oh, Pan."

Lyra had never felt so disappointed, and Pan saw it.

"Lyra, I—"

"Were you *ever* going to tell me?"

"Yes, of course, but—"

"Don't bother now. Just don't say anything. I've got to get changed. I could really, really, really do without this."

She moved listlessly into the bedroom and picked out a dress. They had a dinner with the Master to get through before they'd speak again.

* * *

82

During the vacation, or on evenings like this, dinner at Jordan College was a less formal affair than during term. Sometimes, depending on how many Scholars were present, it wasn't even served in Hall but in a small dining room above the Buttery.

Lyra generally preferred to eat with the servants anyway. It was one of the privileges of her unique position that she could move in any of the circles that made up the complex ecology of the place. A full Scholar would have felt, or been made to feel, she thought, a little ill at ease in the company of the kitchen staff or the porters, but Lyra was just as much at home with them or the gardeners or the handymen as with the higher servants like Mr. Cawson or Mrs. Lonsdale, or with the Master and his guests. Sometimes these guests—politicians or businesspeople or senior civil servants or courtiers—brought with them a breadth of knowledge and a world of experience quite different from the academic specialisms of the Scholars, which were deep indeed, but narrow.

And not a few of these outside visitors were surprised by the presence of this young girl, so apparently confident, so eager to hear what they had to say about the world. Lyra had discovered how to listen, how to respond and encourage these people to say a little more than they meant to, to be indiscreet. She was surprised to find how many of these shrewd and worldly men—and women too— seemed to enjoy the sensation of giving away little secrets, little glimpses into the background of this political maneuver or that business merger. She did nothing with the knowledge she gained in this way, but she was aware that sometimes a Scholar of the college, listening nearby, perhaps an economist or a philosopher or an historian, was grateful to her for unlocking a small revelation or two that they would never have managed to open themselves.

The only person who seemed uneasy about her diplomatic skill, and sometimes even about her presence, was the Master of the college: the new Master, as some still thought of him (and perhaps always would). The old Master, who had taken a particular interest in her and had always been firm about her right to live this strange life in the college but not of it—or of it, but not always in it—had died a year before, very old, greatly esteemed, and even loved.

The new Master was Dr. Werner Hammond: not a Jordan man, or even an Oxford man, but a businessman from the world of pharmaceuticals who had had a distinguished career as a scholar of chemistry before becoming chairman of one of the great medical corporations and enlarging its powers and revenues considerably. Now he had returned to the academic sphere, and no one could say he didn't belong there; his scholarship was impeccable, his command of five languages complete, his tact flawless, his conscientious immersion in the history and traditions of Jordan beyond reproach; but there were some older Scholars who found him a little too good to be true, and wondered whether his Mastership of the college was the real culmination of his career or a stepping-stone on the way to something even grander.

The one thing he had not completely understood about Jordan College was Lyra. Dr. Hammond had never known anything like this strange young self-possessed figure who inhabited the college as if she were a wild bird that had chosen to make her nest in a corner of the oratory roof, among the gargoyles, and was now regarded with protective affection by everyone in the place. He was interested in how this had happened; he made inquiries; he consulted senior members; and the week before the end of term, he sent a note to Lyra inviting her to dine with him in the Master's lodging on the evening after the Founder's Feast.

She was a little puzzled, but not much concerned. Of course he would want to talk to her, or listen, more likely. No doubt there were all kinds of things she could tell him that it would be useful for him to know. She was a little surprised to learn from Mr. Cawson that she was to be the only guest, but he could tell her nothing about the Master's intentions.

Dr. Hammond received her with great friendliness. He was silver-haired and slim, with rimless spectacles and a beautifully cut gray suit. His dæmon was a small and elegant lynx, who sat on the hearthrug with Pantalaimon and made easy and charming conversation. The Master offered Lyra sherry and asked her about her studies, about her schooling, about her life at St. Sophia's College; he was interested to hear about her private study of the alethiometer with Dame Hannah Relf, and told Lyra of how he'd met Dame Hannah in Munich on some corporate business, and of how highly he'd esteemed her, and how she'd been instrumental in some complex negotiations that had eased the passage of an international trade deal with a dusty corner of the Near East. That didn't sound much like Hannah, thought Lyra; she must ask her.

Over the meal, which was served by one of the Master's private staff whom Lyra hadn't seen before, she tried to ask the Master about his previous career, his background, and so on. She was really only making conversation for the sake of politeness; she'd already decided that the man was clever and courteous, but dull. She was slightly interested in whether he was single or widowed; there was no Mrs. Hammond in evidence. The old Master had been a bachelor, but it wasn't a requirement that the Master should be unmarried. A pleasant wife, a young family, would have added a lot to the liveliness of the place, and Dr. Hammond was presentable enough, still young enough to have those desirable additions to his household; but he avoided answering Lyra's questions with great skill and gave not the slightest hint that he thought them intrusive.

Then came dessert, and the purpose of the evening became clear.

"Lyra, I've been meaning to ask you about your position here at Jordan College," the Master began.

And she felt the faintest little sensation, like a tremor in the ground.

"It's a very unusual one," he went on gently.

"Yes," she said, "I'm very lucky. My father sort of put me here, and they just . . . well, put up with me."

"You're how old now? Twenty-one?"

"Twenty."

"Your father, Lord Asriel," he said.

"That's right. He was a Scholar of the college. Dr. Carne, the old Master, was sort of my guardian, I suppose."

"In a way," he said, "though it doesn't seem to have ever been made into a legally valid arrangement."

That surprised her. Why would he have wanted to find that out? "Does that matter," she said cautiously, "now that he's dead?"

"No. But it might have a bearing on the way things move in the future."

"I'm not sure I understand."

"Do you know the origin of the money you're living on?"

Another little earth tremor.

"I knew there was some money that my father left," she said. "I don't know how much, or where it's been looked after. Those were things I never questioned. I suppose I must have thought that things were . . . all right. I mean, that . . . I suppose I thought that . . . Dr. Hammond, may I ask why we're talking about this?"

"Because the college, and I as the Master, are, as it were, *in loco parentis* towards you. In an informal way, because you've never actually been *in statu pupillari*. It's my duty to keep an eye on your affairs until you come of age. There was a sum of money put by for your benefit, to pay for your living expenses and accommodation and so on. But it wasn't put there by your father. It was Dr. Carne's money."

"Was it?" Lyra was feeling almost stupid, as if this was something she should have known about all her life, and it was negligent of her not to.

"So he never told you?" the Master said.

"Not a word. He told me I would be looked after, and there was no need to worry. So I didn't. In a way, I thought the whole college was . . . sort of looking after me. I felt I belonged here. I was very young. You don't question things. . . . And it was his money all the time? Not my father's?"

"I'm sure you'll correct me if I'm wrong, but I believe your father was living as an independent scholar, in a rather hand-to-mouth way. He vanished when you were—what, thirteen years old?"

"Twelve," said Lyra. Her throat had tightened.

"Twelve. That would have been the point when Dr. Carne decided to put a sum of money aside for your benefit. He wasn't a rich man, but there was enough. It was looked after by the college's solicitors, who invested it prudently, paid over a regular sum to the college for your rent and living expenses, and so on. But, Lyra, I have to tell you that the interest on the capital sum was never quite adequate. It appears that Dr. Carne continued to subsidize it from his income, and the money he originally placed with the solicitor for your benefit is now exhausted."

She put down her spoon. The crème caramel suddenly seemed inedible. "What . . . I'm sorry, but this is a shock," she said.

"Of course. I understand."

Pan had come up onto her lap. She moved her fingers through his fur. "So this means . . . I have to leave?" she said.

"You're in your second year of study?"

"Yes."

"One more year to go after this one. It's a pity that none of this was made clear to you before, Lyra, so that you would be prepared."

"I suppose I should have asked."

"You were young. Children take things for granted. Not your fault at all, and it would be very unjust to expose you to consequences you could never have foreseen. This is what I propose. Jordan College will fund the remainder of your education at St. Sophia's. As far as your accommodation outside term is concerned, you may, of course, continue to live here in Jordan, which is, after all, your only home, until you graduate. I understand you have the use of a second room as well as a bedroom?"

"Yes," she said, finding her voice quieter than she had expected.

"Well, this presents us with a little problem. You see, the rooms on that staircase are really needed for undergraduates, for our young men. That is what they were built for, were always intended for. The rooms you occupy could accommodate two first-year undergraduates who currently have to live outside college, which is not ideal. We could at a pinch go back to asking you to use one room only, which would free the second room for one man, but there are matters of propriety, of modesty, one might say, which make it unsuitable. . . ."

"There are undergraduates living on the same staircase," Lyra said. "There always have been. It's never been unsuitable before."

"But not on the same landing. It would not work, Lyra."

"And I'm only here in the vacation," she said, beginning to sound desperate. "During term I live at St. Sophia's."

"Of course. But the presence of your belongings in that room would make it impossible for a young man to make the place properly his own. Lyra, this is what the college can offer. There is a room—a small one, I admit—above the kitchen, currently used as a storeroom. The Bursar will arrange for that room to be furnished and made available to you for the duration of your studies. You may live here as you have done all your life until you graduate. Rent, meals during the vacation, we shall cover all that. But you must understand, this is how things will be in the future."

"I see," she said.

"May I ask—do you have any other family?"

"None."

"Your mother—"

"She vanished at the same time as my father."

"And there are no relations on her side?"

"I never heard of any. Except—I think she might have had a brother. Someone told me that once. But I don't know anything about him, and he's never been in touch with me."

"Ah. I'm sorry."

Lyra tried to pick up a spoonful of her dessert, but her hand was shaking. She put the spoon down.

"Would you care for some coffee?" he said.

"No, thank you. I think perhaps I'd better go. Thank you for dinner."

He stood up, formal, elegant, sympathetic, in his beautiful gray suit and silver hair. His dæmon came to stand beside him; Lyra gathered Pan up in her arms as she stood up too.

"Would you like me to move out at once?" she said.

"By the end of the vacation, if you could manage that."

"Yes. All right."

"And, Lyra, one more thing. You've been used to dining in Hall, to accepting the hospitality of the Scholars, to coming and going freely as if you were a Scholar yourself. It's been put to me by several voices, and I'm bound to say I agree, that that behavior is no longer appropriate. You will be living among servants, and living, so to speak, *as* a servant. It would not be right anymore for you to live on terms of social equality with the academic body."

"Of course not," she said. Surely she was dreaming this.

"I'm glad you understand. You will have things to think about. If it would help at all to talk to me, to ask any questions, please don't hesitate to do so."

"No, I won't. Thank you, Dr. Hammond. I'm in no doubt now about where I belong and how soon I shall have to leave. I'm only sorry to have troubled the college for so long. If Dr. Carne had been able to explain things as clearly as you can, I might have realized much sooner what a burden I was being, and that would have spared you the embarrassment of telling me. Good night."

It was her bland voice, her wide-eyed, innocent look, and she was secretly glad to see they still worked, because he had not the faintest idea how to respond.

He gave a little stiff bow, and she left without another word.

She walked slowly back around the main quad and stopped to look up at the little window of her bedroom, close against the square bulk of the lodge tower.

"Well," she said.

"That was cruel."

"I don't know. If there's no money left . . . I don't know."

"I didn't mean that. You know what I meant. The servant thing."

"Nothing wrong with being a servant."

"All right, those *several voices*, then. I don't believe any Scholar in the college would want us treated like that. He was just deflecting the blame."

"Well, you know what won't help, Pan? Complaining. That won't help."

"I wasn't complaining. I was just—"

"Whatever you were doing, don't do it. There are things to be sad about. Like the rooms . . . We know that little room over the kitchen. There isn't even a window in it. But we should have woken up before now, Pan. We haven't even thought once about money, except the pocket money for polishing the silver and that sort of thing. There were bound to be *costs* . . . for meals and rooms, they cost money. . . . Someone was paying all the time, and we just didn't think about it."

"They let the money run out and they didn't tell us. They should have told us."

"Yes, I suppose they should. But we should have thought to ask . . . ask who was paying. But I'm sure the old Master said that Lord Asriel had left plenty. I'm sure of it."

As if her limbs had been weakened, she stumbled two or three times as she climbed the staircase to her bedroom. She felt bruised and shaken. When she was in bed, with Pan curled up on the pillow, she put the light out at once and lay still for a long time before she fell asleep.

SEVEN

HANNAH RELF

Next morning, Lyra felt shy and nervous about going down for breakfast. She slipped into the servants' dining room and helped herself to porridge, not looking around, just smiling and nodding when someone said hello. She felt as if she'd woken up in chains and couldn't free herself, so had to carry them with her wherever she went, like a badge of shame.

After breakfast she drifted through the lodge, not wanting to go back up to the little rooms that had been her home, feeling too heartsick to do what she'd spoken about to Dick and go in search of a vacation job at the mail depot, feeling almost devoid of energy and life. The porter called her, and she turned.

"Letter for you, Lyra," he said. "D'you want to take it now or pick it up later?"

"I might as well take it now. Thanks."

It was a plain envelope, with her name in a clear, swift hand that she recognized as Dame Hannah Relf's. A little spring of gratefulness gushed in her breast, for she thought that the lady was a true friend, but then it froze almost at once: Suppose she was going to say that Lyra would have to start paying for her alethiometer lessons? How would she manage that?

"Open it, stupid," said Pan.

"Yes," she said.

The card inside said: *Dear Lyra, could you possibly come to see me this afternoon? It's important. Hannah Relf.*

Lyra looked at it numbly. This afternoon? Which afternoon did she mean? Wouldn't she have had to post the letter yesterday? But the date on the card was today's.

She looked again at the envelope. She hadn't noticed that there was no stamp, or that the words *By hand* were written in the top left corner.

She turned to the porter, who was putting other letters into a rack of pigeonholes. "Bill, when did this arrive?" she said.

"About half an hour ago. By hand."

"Thanks . . ."

She put the letter in her pocket and wandered back through the quad and into the Scholars' Garden. Most of the trees were bare, the flower beds seemed empty and dead, and only the great cedar looked alive, though it also looked asleep. It was another of those still, gray days when silence itself seemed to be a meteorological phenomenon, not just the result of nothing happening but a positive presence larger than gardens, and colleges, and life.

Lyra climbed the stone steps that led up the bank at the end of the garden to a spot overlooking Radcliffe Square, and sat on the bench that had been placed there a long time before.

"You know one thing," said Pan.

"What?"

"We can't trust the lock on our door."

"I don't see why not."

"Because we can't trust *him*."

"Oh, really."

"Yes, really. We had no clue that he was going to say that last night. He was all smooth and agreeable. He's a hypocrite."

"What did his dæmon say?"

"Glib, friendly, patronizing stuff. Nothing important at all."

"Well, we haven't got much choice," she said, finding words hard to come by. "He needs our rooms. We're not really part of the college. There's no money left. He's got to . . . got to try and . . . Oh, I don't know, Pan. It's all just so miserable. And now I'm worried about what Hannah's going to say."

"Well, that's just silly."

"I know it is. It doesn't help, though, knowing it."

He stalked to the end of the bench and then leapt across onto the low wall, beyond which was a thirty-foot drop to the cobbles of the square below. She felt a lurch of fear, but nothing would have made her admit it to him. He pretended to stagger and trip and totter on the stone capping, and then, getting no response from Lyra, sank down on his belly into a sphinx posture, paws extended in front, head held high, gazing forward.

"Once we're out, we're out," he said. "We won't be able to set foot in the place again. We'll be strangers."

"Yes, I know. I've thought it all through, Pan."

"So what shall we do?"

"When?"

"When it's all over. When we leave."

"Find a job. Find somewhere to live."

"Very easy, then."

"I know it won't be easy. Actually, I don't know that. It might be very easy. But everyone has to do that. Move away from home, I mean. Go out and make their own life."

"With most people, their home would always let them come

back, and welcome them, and be glad to hear about what they'd been doing."

"Well, good for them. We're different. Always have been. You *know* that. But what we're *not* going to do, not for a single second, you hear me, is make a fuss. Or complain. Or whine that we're not being treated fairly. It *is* fair. He's going to let us stay for another year and a bit, even though the money's run out. He's going to pay for St. Sophia's. That's more than fair. The rest is—well, it's up to us. As it would have been, anyway. We weren't going to live here forever, were we?"

"I don't see why not. We're an ornament to the college. They should be proud to have us."

That made her smile, anyway, for a moment.

"But maybe you're right about the room, Pan. I mean, locking it."

"Ah."

"The alethiometer . . ."

"That's one of the things I meant. We're not *at home* anymore; we've got to remember that."

"One of the things? What are the others?"

"The rucksack," Pan said firmly.

"Yes. Of course!"

"Suppose someone went in there looking around, and found it. . . ."

"They'd think we'd stolen it."

"Or worse. If they knew about the murder . . ."

"We need somewhere better than that. A proper safe."

"Hannah's got one. A safe, I mean."

"Yes. But are we going to tell her?"

He said nothing for a few moments. Then he said, "Mrs. Lonsdale."

"Alice. That's another odd thing. All these things that are changing . . . like ice breaking under your feet."

"We must have known her name was Alice."

"Yes, but to hear *him* calling her Alice . . ."

"Perhaps they're lovers."

That was too silly to deserve a response.

They sat there for a few more minutes, and then Lyra stood up.

"Let's go and make things a bit safer, then," she said, and they set off back to their rooms.

When Lyra visited Hannah Relf, as she did every week during term and quite often during the vacation, she normally took the alethiometer with her, since that was the subject of their study. When she thought of the carefree way she'd carried it with her to the Arctic and out into other worlds, of how she'd thoughtlessly let it be stolen and how she and Will had stolen it back with such care and at such risk, she was amazed at her own confidence, her own luck. Her stock of those qualities felt low at the moment.

So, having made a few changes to the rucksack's hiding place, and having pulled the table over the rug to discourage any search, she made sure the alethiometer was stowed away safely in her bag along with Hassall's wallet before she set off to walk to Dame Hannah's little house in Jericho.

"She can't be wanting to give us another lesson," Lyra said.

"And we can't be in trouble. At least, I hope not."

Although it was still early in the afternoon, Dr. Relf had lit the lamps in her little sitting room, giving it an air of welcoming cheer against the darkening gray outside. Lyra couldn't even guess how many times she'd sat in this room, with Pan and Hannah's dæmon, Jesper, talking quietly on the hearth while she and Dr. Relf pored over a dozen or more ancient books, and tried the alethiometer again, or simply sat and chatted. . . . She loved this mild and learned lady, she realized, loved everything about her and her way of life.

"Sit down, dear. Stop fretting," Hannah said. "There's no reason to fret. But we do have something to talk about."

"It's been worrying me," Lyra said.

"I can see. But now tell me about the Master—Werner Hammond. I know you had dinner with him last night. What did he say to you?"

Lyra shouldn't have been surprised; the lady's perceptions were so quick and accurate as to seem uncanny, or they would have done if Lyra hadn't known of Hannah's skill with the alethiometer. Nevertheless, this did shake her a little.

She gave an account, as full as she could make it, of her dinner with the Master. Hannah listened closely, saying nothing till Lyra had finished.

"But he said one thing I forgot till just now," Lyra concluded. "He said he knew you. He'd met you in some diplomatic context. He wasn't specific about it—he just said how clever you were. Do you know him?"

"Oh, yes, we've met. I saw enough of him to be very careful."

"Why? Is he dishonest? Or dangerous, or something? I'm lost, really," Lyra confessed. "I feel as if the floor has given way. I couldn't argue with what he said; it was just such a shock. . . . Anyway, what do you know about him?"

"I'm going to tell you some things I really ought to keep secret. But because I know you so well, and because I trust you to keep things secret if I ask you to, and because you're in some danger . . . Ah—here's someone I was expecting."

She got up as the doorbell rang. Lyra sat back, feeling light-headed and shaky. Voices came from the little hall, and then Dame Hannah came back with—

"Dr. Polstead," said Lyra. "And . . . Mrs. Lonsdale? You too?"

"Alice, you goose," said that lady. "Things are changing, Lyra."

"Hello, Lyra," said Dr. Polstead. "Don't move. I'll perch here."

Pan crept behind Lyra's legs as Dr. Polstead sat on the sofa next to Alice, looking too large for the little room; his broad ruddy face, a farmer's face, she thought, smiling warmly; his red-gold hair, the exact color of his cat dæmon; his big hands, fingers interlaced, as he leant forward with his elbows on his knees—she felt as if she were catching clumsiness from him, although he had never done anything clumsy. And she recalled the brief period a few years before when he'd been given the task of tutoring her in geography and economic history, and how it had been an embarrassing failure, with each of them clearly resenting this unsuccessful enterprise but neither wanting to say it. He should have acted sooner to bring it to an end, because he was the adult, after all, but she knew she'd been difficult and sometimes insolent, and that much of the blame was hers; they'd just rubbed each other the wrong way, and there was nothing to be done but call an end to it. Since then, they'd both been scrupulously polite and outwardly friendly, while being relieved to see each other for not a moment more than was necessary.

But what Alice had said about him the day before—and now, to see them both on terms of warm friendship with Dame Hannah, when none of them had ever seemed even to know about the others' existence . . . Well, these last few days had exposed a lot of strange links and connections.

"I didn't know you three knew one another," she said.

"We've been friends for—oh, nineteen years," he said.

"It was the alethiometer that told me how to find Malcolm," said Hannah, coming into the room with a tray of tea and biscuits. "He must have been about eleven years old."

"To find him? Were you looking for him, then?"

"I was looking for something that was lost, and it pointed me to Malcolm, who'd found it. We just fell into a sort of friendship."

"I see," said Lyra.

"It was very lucky for me," he said. "Now, what have you said so far?"

"Lyra told me what the Master said to her last night. He told her that she'd been living not on her father's money, as she'd thought, but on Dr. Carne's. Lyra, that is true. The old Master didn't want you to know, but he'd paid for everything. Your father didn't leave a penny."

"And did you know that?" said Lyra. "Have you always known that?"

"Yes, I have," said Hannah. "I didn't tell you because he didn't want me to. Besides—"

"You see, I rather kind of *hate* this," Lyra burst out. "All my life people have hidden things from me. They didn't tell me that Asriel was my father and Mrs. Coulter was my mother. Imagine finding that out, and feeling that everyone in the world knew it and I was the only fool who didn't. Hannah, whatever Dr. Carne said to you, whatever promise you made, it wasn't a good thing to keep it from me. It *wasn't*. I should have known. It would have woken me up. It would have made me think about the money and ask questions about it and find out that there was only a little left. Then I wouldn't have been so shocked yesterday evening."

She'd never spoken like that to her old friend before, but she knew she was right, and so did Hannah, who bowed her head and nodded.

Dr. Polstead said, "In Hannah's defense, Lyra, we didn't know what the new Master was going to do."

"He shouldn't've done that, though," said Alice. "I never trusted him from the moment he arrived."

"No, he shouldn't," said Hannah. "And in fact, Lyra, Alice was keen to tell you about all this while the old Master was still alive. She's not to blame."

"After your twenty-first birthday," said Dr. Polstead, "when you'll be legally able to manage your own affairs, it would have had to come out, and I know that Hannah was planning to speak to you in time for that. He forestalled us."

"Us?" said Lyra. "And *all this*—what is *all this?* I'm sorry, Dr. Polstead, but I don't understand. Are you involved in this somehow? And the other day—what Mrs. Lonsdale, Alice, what she said about you—that took me by surprise too, and for the same reason. You know something about me that I don't, and that's not right. So how are *you* involved?"

"That's one of the things we're going to tell you this afternoon," he said. "It's why Hannah asked me to come. Shall I start?" he asked, turning to the lady, who nodded. "If I leave out anything important, I know Hannah will remind me."

Lyra leant back, feeling tense. Pan climbed onto her lap. Alice was watching them both seriously.

"It began around the time Hannah mentioned just now," Dr. Polstead began, "when I found something that was meant for her, and she found me. I was about eleven, and I was living with my parents at the Trout in Godstow. . . ."

The story that unfolded was stranger than Lyra could have guessed, and listening to it felt like standing on a mountaintop as a wind blew away clouds of fog and mist and disclosed a panorama completely unsuspected only a few minutes before. There were parts of it that were utterly new and unknown, but also there were other parts that had been visible through the fog in a phantasmagoria, and now stood clearly in the sunlight. There was a memory of a night when someone was walking up and down in a moonlit garden, whispering as he held her close, with a great quiet leopard walking alongside. And another memory of a different nighttime garden, with lights in all the trees, and of laughing and laughing for pure happiness, and a little boat. And of a storm and a thunderous knocking at a door in the darkness, but in Dr. Polstead's account there was no horse. . . .

"I thought there was a horse," Lyra said.

"No horse," said Alice.

"Asriel flew us here in a gyropter and landed in Radcliffe Square," Malcolm went on. "And then he put you in the Master's arms and invoked the law of scholastic sanctuary. That law had never been repealed."

"What's scholastic sanctuary? Is it what it sounds like?"

"It was a law that protected Scholars from persecution."

"But I wasn't a Scholar!"

"Oddly enough, that was just what the Master said. So your father said, 'You'll have to make her into one, then, won't you?' And then he left."

Lyra sat back, her heart full, her mind whirling. So much to understand! She hardly knew what to ask about first.

Hannah, who had been listening quietly, leant forward to put another log on the fire. Then she got up to draw the curtains against the darkness outside.

"Well," said Lyra, "I suppose . . . Thank you. I don't mean to sound ungracious or anything. Thank you for saving me from the flood, and everything. This is all so strange. And the alethiometer—this one—"

She reached into her bag and tugged it out, unfolding the black velvet to let it rest on her knee. It glowed in the lamplight.

"The man Bonneville, the one with the hyena dæmon who was chasing you, had it?" she said. "It's so much to take in. Where did he get it from?"

"We found out much later," said Hannah. "He stole it from a monastery in Bohemia."

"Then—shouldn't it go back there?" Lyra said, but her heart sank at the thought of losing this most precious thing, this instrument that had helped her find her way into and out of the world of the dead, that had told her the truth about Will ("He is a murderer") in the only way that would have let her trust him, that had saved their lives and restored the bear king's armor and done a hundred other extraordinary things. Her hands involuntarily tightened around it, and she returned it to the safety of her bag.

"No," said Hannah. "The monks had stolen it themselves from a traveler who made the mistake of taking shelter with them. I took a month once to investigate the provenance of your alethiometer, and it seems to have passed from one set of thieves to another for centuries. When Malcolm pushed it in among your blankets, it was the first time it had changed hands honestly for hundreds of years. And I think that broke the pattern."

"It was stolen from me, once," said Lyra. "And we had to steal it back."

"It's yours, and unless you choose to give it away, it'll be yours for life," said Dr. Polstead.

"And all those other things you told me . . . that fairy: Did you really mean a *fairy*? Or was it that you imagined . . . It can't have been *true*?"

"It was," said Alice. "She was called Diania. She put you to the breast and suckled you. You've drunk fairy milk, and you'd be with her still if Malcolm hadn't fooled her and got us away."

"The flood brought a lot of strange things to light," said Malcolm.

"But why didn't you tell me before?"

He looked a little abashed. How mobile his face was, Lyra thought. He looked like a stranger; it was as if she'd never seen him before.

"We—Alice and I—always said to each other that we would,"

he said, "but the time never seemed to be right. Besides, Dr. Carne made us both promise never to talk to you about Bonneville or anything connected with him. It was part of the sanctuary business. We didn't understand then, but we did later. It was to protect you. But things are changing fast. Now I'll hand over to Hannah."

"When I first met Malcolm," the lady said, "I did something rather reckless. It turned out that he was very well placed to pick up the kind of information I was interested in, and I encouraged him to do that. He sometimes overheard things in his parents' pub, or elsewhere, that were worth noting. He took messages for me, or collected them from other places. He was able to tell me about an abominable organization called the League of St. Alexander, which recruited schoolchildren to inform on their parents to the Magisterium."

"It sounds like . . . ," Lyra said. "I don't know. A spy story or something. It's not very easy to believe."

"I suppose it does. The point was that a lot of the political arguments and struggles that were going on then had to be carried out surreptitiously, anonymously. It was a dangerous time."

"Was that what you were doing? Political things?"

"That sort of thing. It didn't stop. It hasn't stopped. And in some ways things are even more difficult now. For example, there's a bill before Parliament at the moment called the Rectification of Historical Anomalies Bill. It's portrayed as a simple tidying-up measure, to do away with a lot of old statutes that don't make sense anymore or are irrelevant to modern life, such as benefit of clergy, or the right of certain livery companies to catch and eat herons and swans, or the gathering of tithes by monastic bodies that are long gone—ancient privileges that no one's used for years. But tucked away among the obsolete provisions to be abolished is the right of scholastic sanctuary, which is what still protects you."

"Protects me from what?" Lyra found that her voice was shaky.

"From the Magisterium."

"But why would they want to hurt me?"

"We don't know."

"But why hasn't anyone in Parliament noticed this? Isn't anyone arguing against it?"

"It's a very complicated and long-winded piece of legislation—my sources tell me that it was introduced on the urging of an organization gaining power in Geneva: *La Maison Juste*. More to them than you'd think at first, but they're connected to the CCD, I believe. Anyway, it was cleverly done, and you need the eyes of an eagle and the patience of a snail to fight something like that. There was an MP called Bernard Crombie leading the fight against it, but he was killed recently, supposedly in a road accident."

"I read about it," said Lyra. "It was here in Oxford. He was knocked down, and the driver didn't stop. You don't mean he was murdered?"

"I'm afraid so," said Dr. Polstead. "We know what happened, but we can't prove it in court. The point is that the protection that's been around you since Lord Asriel put you in the Master's arms is now, slowly and deliberately, being dismantled."

"And what the new Master said to you last night," said Hannah, "just confirms it."

"So he—Dr. Hammond—he's on the other side? Whatever that is?"

"He's no Scholar," said Alice decisively. "He's only a businessman."

"Yes," said Dr. Polstead. "His background is relevant. We're not sure yet how it all connects, but if that law's passed, it'll give business corporations the chance to help themselves to a good deal of property, for example, whose ownership was never clearly established. If there's any dispute, it'll be resolved in favor of money and power. Even the ruins of Godstow Priory will be up for sale."

"There were men there just the other day measuring things," said Alice.

"The changes Dr. Hammond told you about last night are part of a bigger pattern," said Hannah. "It makes you even more vulnerable."

Lyra couldn't speak. She held Pantalaimon close and looked into the fire. "But he did say . . . ," she began very quietly, and then spoke up: "He did say the college would pay for the rest of my education . . . my time at St. Sophia's. . . . So what does he *want?* Does he want me to finish and get my degree, or—or what? I just don't understand—I can't take this in."

"I'm afraid there's more," said Hannah. "The money that was left you by Dr. Carne—the money Hammond said was all used up—Malcolm can tell you about that."

"In his old age, Dr. Carne was easily confused," said Dr. Polstead, "and money and figures weren't his strong point, in any case. What seems to have happened is that he did put a considerable sum aside—we don't know how much, but there would have been plenty left still—only he was persuaded to invest it in a fund that crashed. It simply failed—very badly managed or deliberately ruined. The money wasn't in the hands of the college solicitor, no matter what Dr. Hammond told you; in fact, the solicitor tried hard to prevent the old Master from investing in that fund, but of course, he had to do what his client wanted. You might know the college solicitor: a very tall man, quite old now. His dæmon is a kestrel."

"Oh yes!" Lyra remembered him: she had never known exactly who he was, but he had always been kind and courteous to her and genuinely interested in her progress.

"They timed it well," Alice put in. "It wasn't long before the old Master began to lose his way, poor old boy. Forgetting things . . ."

"I remember," Lyra said. "It was so sad . . . I loved him."

"Many people did," said Hannah. "But once he'd become unable to manage his affairs, the solicitor had to take power of attorney. If Dr. Carne had wanted to invest the money in the bad fund at that stage, it could have been prevented."

"Just a minute," Lyra said. "Alice said, 'They timed it well.' You don't mean it was intentional—you don't mean *they*, the other side—they lost his money on purpose?"

"It looks very like it," said Dr. Polstead.

"But why?"

"To damage you. You wouldn't even have been aware of it till— well, till now."

"They were—while the old Master was still alive—they were deliberately trying to hurt . . ."

"Yes. We've only just found that out, and it was the thing that prompted us to call you here and tell you about this."

Now she really couldn't speak. It was Pantalaimon who spoke for her.

"But *why*?" he said.

"We have no idea," said Hannah. "For some reason the other side needs you vulnerable, and for the sake of everything good and valuable, we need you safe. But you're not the only one. There are other Scholars protected by scholastic sanctuary. It's been a guarantee of intellectual freedom, and it looks as if it's being torn down."

Lyra ran her hands through her hair. She kept thinking about the man she'd never heard of till then, the man with the three-legged hyena dæmon who had been so determined to get her into his power when she was less than a year old.

"That Bonneville man," she said. "Was he part of the other side too? Is that why he wanted me?"

An expression of contempt and disgust passed over Alice's face, just for a moment.

"He was a complicated man, in a complicated situation," said

Hannah. "He seems to have been a spy, but an independent one, like an independent scholar. He was originally an experimental theologian, a physicist, and entirely on his own, he'd penetrated to the heart of the Magisterium's Geneva headquarters and discovered all kinds of things—an extraordinary amount of material. It was in the rucksack that Malcolm rescued—"

"Stole," he said.

"All right, stole. And Malcolm brought it all back to Oxford. But Bonneville had become a sort of renegade; he was psychotic, or obsessed, or something. . . . He was obsessed with you, with you as a baby, for some reason."

"I think he wanted to use you as a bargaining chip," said Dr. Polstead. "But then—well, at the end he just seemed mad. Deranged. He . . ."

Lyra was astonished at the depth of pain in his face. He was looking directly at Alice, who was returning his gaze with a similar expression. Dr. Polstead seemed unable to speak for a moment. He looked down at the carpet.

Alice said huskily, "This is another reason it's been hard to tell you, dear. You see, Bonneville raped me. He might have done more, but Malcolm . . . Malcolm came to my rescue and . . . well, he did the only thing he could do. We was at the end of our strength, we thought we was at the end of our lives, everything was so horrible and . . ."

She couldn't say any more. Her dæmon, Ben, put his head on her lap and she stroked his ears with a trembling hand. Lyra wanted to put her arms around her, but she couldn't move. Pan was stock-still by her feet.

"The only thing he could do?" she whispered.

Malcolm's dæmon, Asta, said, "Malcolm killed him."

Lyra couldn't speak. Dr. Polstead was still looking down at the floor. He rubbed the heel of his hand across his eyes.

Alice said, "You was bundled up in the boat and he didn't want to leave you there alone, so Asta stayed with you and Malcolm came up to the place where Bonneville was . . . attacking me, and Asta stayed to look after you."

"You separated?" Lyra said. "And you *killed* him?"

"I hated every second of it."

"*How* old were you?"

"Eleven."

Just a little younger than Will, she thought, when the alethiometer had told her that he was a murderer. She looked at Dr. Polstead now with eyes that seemed never to have seen him before. She imagined a stocky ginger-haired boy killing an experienced secret agent, and then she saw another pattern too: the man Will had killed had been a member of the secret service of his country. Were there other correspondences and echoes waiting to be discovered? The alethiometer could tell her, but oh, how long it would take! How quickly she would have done it once, her fingers racing her mind as she flicked the hands around the dial and stepped unhesitatingly down the rungs of linked meanings into the darkness where the truth lay!

Hannah said, "And we must think about keeping that safe too."

Lyra blinked. "The alethiometer? How did you know I was thinking about that?"

"Your fingers were moving."

"Oh," she said. "I'll have to hide everything. I'll have to suppress every movement, every word . . . I had no idea. Not the slightest flicker of an idea about all this. I don't know what to say. . . ."

"Pantalaimon will help you."

But Hannah didn't know about the strain that existed between them these days. Lyra had told no one about that; who would understand it, after all?

"It's getting late," said Dr. Polstead. "If we want any dinner, we'd better be getting back into town."

Lyra felt as if a week had passed. She stood up slowly and embraced Alice, who held her tightly and kissed her. Hannah stood up and did the same, and Lyra kissed her in return.

"This is an alliance now," said Hannah. "Don't ever forget that."

"I won't," said Lyra. "Thank you. I'm still reeling, frankly. There's so much I just didn't know."

"And that's our fault," said Dr. Polstead, "and we'll have to make it up to you. But we will. Are you dining in Hall tonight?"

"No, I must eat with the servants. The Master made that very clear."

Alice muttered, "Bastard," which made Lyra smile a bit. But then she said, "I'm going to the Trout. I'll see you both later."

She set off towards Godstow, and then Lyra and Dr. Polstead began to head back towards the city center, through the streets of Jericho, still busy with shoppers, where the well-lit shop fronts shone warm and safe.

"Lyra," he said, "I hope you won't forget that my name is Malcolm. And Mrs. Lonsdale is Alice."

"That'll take some getting used to."

"I expect many things will. This servant business—it's deliberately designed to humiliate you. There isn't a single Scholar who doesn't value your presence among them. Even though I'm part of Durham now, I know that full well."

"He said that several voices had told him that my dining in Hall, and so on, was no longer appropriate."

"He's lying. If anybody did say that to him, it wasn't one of the Scholars."

"Anyway, if what he wants to do is humiliate me," she said, "it'll fail. It's no humiliation at all to eat with my friends. They're as much family as anything else. If that's what he thinks of my family, so much the worse for him."

"Good."

They said nothing for a minute or so. Lyra thought she would never feel easy in the presence of this Malcolm, no matter what he'd done nineteen years before.

Then he said something that made her feel even more awkward.

"Er—Lyra, I think you and I have something else to discuss, haven't we?"

EIGHT

LITTLE CLARENDON STREET

"Dæmons," she said quietly. He could hardly hear her.

"Yes," he said. "Did you have as big a shock as I did the other night?"

"I think I must have done."

"Does anyone know you and Pantalaimon can separate?"

"No one in this world," she said. Then she swallowed hard and said, "The witches of the north. They can separate from their dæmons. There was a witch called Serafina Pekkala, who was the first I knew about. I saw her dæmon and spoke to him a long time before I saw her."

"I met a witch once, with her dæmon, during the flood."

"And there's a city with an Arabic name . . . a ruined city. Inhabited by dæmons without people."

"I think I've heard of that too. I wasn't sure whether to believe it."

They walked on a little further.

"But there's something else," Lyra began to say, and at the same moment he said, "I think there's—"

"Sorry," she said.

"You go first."

"Your dæmon saw Pantalaimon, and he saw her, only he wasn't sure who she was till yesterday."

"In Alice's room."

"Yes. Only . . . Oh, this is so difficult."

"Look behind," he said.

She turned and saw what he'd already felt: both dæmons walking along together, heads close, talking intensely.

"Well . . . ," she said.

They were at the corner of Little Clarendon Street, which led after a couple of hundred yards to the broad avenue of St. Giles. Jordan College was no more than ten minutes away.

Malcolm said, "Have you got time for a drink? I think we need to talk a bit more easily than we can in the street."

"Yes," she said, "all right."

Little Clarendon Street had been adopted by Oxford's jeunesse dorée as a fashionable destination. Expensive clothes shops, chic coffeehouses, cocktail bars, and colored anbaric lights strung overhead made it seem like a corner of another city altogether— Malcolm couldn't have known what made tears come to Lyra's eyes at that point, though he did notice the tears: it was her memory of the deserted Cittàgazze, all the lights blazing, empty, silent, magical, where she had first met Will. She brushed them away and said nothing.

He led the way to a mock-Italian café with candles in straw-wrapped wine bottles and red-checked tablecloths and travel posters in splashy colors. Lyra looked around warily.

"It's safe here," Malcolm said quietly. "There are other places where it's risky to talk, but there's no danger in La Luna Caprese."

He ordered a bottle of Chianti, asking Lyra first if that was what she'd like, and she nodded.

When the wine was tried and poured, she said, "I've got to tell you something. I'll try and keep it clear in my head. And now I know about you and your dæmon, it's something I can tell you, but no one else. Only I've heard so many things in the last couple of days and my mind's in a whirl, so please, if I don't make sense, just stop me and I'll go over it again."

"Of course."

She began with Pan's experience on the Monday night, the attack, the murder, the man giving him the wallet to take to Lyra. Malcolm listened in astonishment, though he felt no skepticism: such things happened, as he knew well. But one thing seemed odd.

"The victim and his dæmon knew about separating?" he said.

"Yes," said Pan at Lyra's elbow. "They weren't shocked, like most people would be. In fact, they could separate too. She must have seen me up the tree when he was being attacked, and thought it would be all right to trust me, I suppose."

"So Pan brought the wallet back to me at St. Sophia's . . . ," Lyra went on.

"And that was when Asta saw me," Pan put in.

". . . but other things got in the way, and we didn't have a chance to look at it till the next morning."

She pulled her bag up to her lap and took out the wallet, passing it to him unobtrusively. He noticed Pan's tooth marks, and noticed the smell too, which Pan had called cheap cologne, though it seemed to Malcolm something other than that, something wilder. He opened the wallet and took out the contents one by one as she spoke. The Bodleian card, the university staff card, the diplomatic papers, all so familiar; his own wallet had held very similar papers in its time.

"He was coming back to Oxford, I think," Lyra said, "because if you look at the laissez-passers, you can trace his journey from Sin Kiang to here. He'd probably have gone on to the Botanic Garden, if they hadn't attacked him."

Malcolm caught another faint trace of the scent on the wallet. He raised it to his nose, and something distant rang like a bell, or gleamed like the sun on a snowy mountaintop, just for the fraction of a second, and then it was gone.

"Did he say anything else, the man who was killed?"

He addressed the question to Pan, and Pan thought hard before saying, "No. He couldn't. He was nearly dead. He made me take the wallet out of his pocket and told me to take it to Lyra—I mean, he didn't know her name, but he said to take it to your . . . I think he thought we could be trusted because he knew about separating."

"Have you taken this to the police?"

"Of course. That was almost the first thing we did next morning," Lyra said. "But when we were waiting in the police station, Pan heard one of the policemen speak."

"He was the first killer, the one who wasn't wounded," said Pan. "I recognized his voice. It was very distinctive."

"So we asked about something quite different and then left," Lyra went on. "We just thought we shouldn't give the wallet to the very man who'd killed him."

"Sensible," said Malcolm.

"Oh, and there's another thing. The man who was cut on the leg. He's called Benny Morris."

"How d'you know that?"

"I know someone who works at the mail depot, and I asked him if there was anyone there who'd hurt his leg. He said yes, there was a big ugly man called Benny Morris, who sounds just like the man we saw."

"And what then?"

"In the wallet," Lyra said carefully, "there was a left-luggage key—you know, the sort you get with those lockers at the station."

"What did you do with that?"

"I thought we ought to go and get whatever was in it. So—"

"Don't tell me you *did?*"

"Yes. Because he'd sort of entrusted it to us, the wallet, and what was in it. So we thought we ought to go and look after it before the men who killed him realized and went to look for it themselves."

"The killers knew he had some sort of luggage," said Pan, "because they kept asking each other if he'd had a bag, if he'd dropped it, were they sure they hadn't seen it, and so on. As if they'd been told to expect one."

"And what was in the locker?" said Malcolm.

"A rucksack," Lyra said. "Which is under the floorboards in my room in Jordan."

"It's there now?"

She nodded.

He picked up his glass and drained it in one, and then stood up. "Let's go and get it. While it's there, you're in great danger, Lyra, and that's no exaggeration. Come on."

Five minutes later, Lyra and Malcolm turned out of the Broad into Turl Street, the narrow thoroughfare where the main entrance to Jordan College stood under the lodge tower. They were halfway to the lodge when two men, dressed in anonymous workers' clothing, stepped out of the gate and moved away towards the High Street. One of them had a rucksack slung over his shoulder.

"That's it," said Lyra quietly.

Malcolm started to run after them, but Lyra instantly caught his arm. Her grip was strong.

"Wait," she said, "keep quiet. Don't make them turn round. Just let's go inside."

"I could catch them!"

"No need."

The men were walking quickly away. Malcolm wanted to say several things but held his tongue. Lyra was quite calm and in fact seemed quietly satisfied about something. He looked again at the men and followed her into the lodge, where she was talking to the porter.

"Yes, they said they were going to move your furniture, Lyra, but I just saw 'em go out. One of 'em was carrying something."

"Thanks, Bill," she said. "Did they say where they were from?"

"They gave me a card—here it is."

She showed Malcolm the card. It said *J. Cross Removals*, with an address in Kidlington, a few miles north of Oxford.

"Do you know anything about J. Cross?" Malcolm said to the porter.

"Never heard of them, sir."

They climbed the two flights of stairs to her room. Malcolm hadn't set foot on this staircase since he was an undergraduate, but it didn't seem to have changed much. There were two rooms on the top floor on either side of a little landing, and Lyra unlocked the one on the right and switched the light on.

"Good God," said Malcolm. "We should have got here five minutes ago."

The room was in utter confusion. Chairs were overturned, books pulled out of shelves and thrown on the floor, papers in a scattered mass on the desk. The rug was pulled back and thrown in a corner, and a floorboard had been taken out.

"Well, they found it," said Lyra, looking at the floor.

"It was under there?"

"My favorite hiding place. Don't look so bitter. They were bound to search for a loose floorboard. I'd like to see their faces when they open the rucksack, though."

And now she was smiling. For the first time for days, her eyes were free of shadows.

"What will they find?" Malcolm said.

"Two books from the history faculty library, all my last year's notes on economic history, a jersey that was too small for me, and two bottles of shampoo."

Malcolm laughed. She looked through the books on the floor before handing two of them up to him.

"These were in the rucksack. I couldn't read them."

"This one looks like Anatolian," said Malcolm, "some kind of botanical text. . . . And this one's in Tajik. Well, well. What else?"

From among the mass of papers spread all over the desktop and half across the floor, Lyra picked out a cardboard folder very similar to several others. Malcolm sat down to open it.

"And I'll just look in the bedroom," Lyra said, and went across the landing.

The folder was labeled in Lyra's hand. Malcolm supposed that she'd taken her own papers out and put the dead man's in, and so it proved: they seemed to be a sort of diary, written in pencil. But he'd got no further than that when Lyra came back with a battered old smokeleaf tin containing a dozen or so miniature cork-stoppered bottles and some little cardboard boxes.

"This was in the rucksack too," she said, "but I've no idea what's in them. Specimens?"

"Lyra, that was clever. But this is real danger you're in. They already know who you are, somehow, and they know you know about the murder, at least, and they'll soon know that you've got the contents of the rucksack. I'm not sure you should stay here."

"I've got nowhere else to go," she said. "Except St. Sophia's, and they probably know about that too."

She wasn't looking for sympathy: it was said matter-of-factly. The look he remembered so well from when he taught her, that expression of blank insolent obstructiveness, was lurking somewhere at the back of her eyes.

"Well, let's think about that," he said. "You could stay with Hannah."

"That would be dangerous for her, wouldn't it? They must know we're connected. In any case, I think her sister is coming to spend Christmas with her, and there wouldn't be room."

"Have you got any friends you could stay with?"

"There are people I've spent Christmas with before, but that was because they invited me. I've never asked. It would look wrong if I did it now. And . . . I don't know. I just wouldn't want to put anyone . . ."

"Well, it's clear that you can't stay here."

"And this is where I used to feel safest of all."

She looked lost. She picked up a cushion and held it close with both arms around it, and Malcolm thought: Why isn't she holding her dæmon like that? And that brought into focus something he'd noticed without seeing it clearly: Lyra and Pantalaimon didn't like each other. He felt a sudden lurch, as of surprise, and pitied them both.

"Look," he said, "there's my parents' pub in Godstow. The Trout. I'm certain you could stay there, at least over the vacation."

"Could I work there?"

"You mean—" Malcolm was a little nonplussed. "You mean, is it quiet enough to study?"

"No," she said, more scornfully than her eyes suggested she meant. "Work in the bar or the kitchen or something. To pay for my keep."

He saw how proud she was, and how shaken she'd been by the Master's revelation about the money that was not there.

"If you'd like to do that, I'm sure they'd love it," he said.

"Good, then," she said.

How stubborn she was he had more cause to know than most,

but he wondered how many others had seen the loneliness in her expression when she wasn't guarding it.

"And let's not waste time," he said. "We'll go there this evening. As soon as you're ready."

"I've got to tidy . . ." She waved at everything in the room. "I can't leave it like this."

"Just put the books on the shelves and the furniture back—is the bedroom turned over as well?"

"Yes. All my clothes all over the floor, bed upside down . . ."

There was a catch in her voice and a glitter in her eyes. This was an invasion, after all.

"Tell you what," he said. "I'll put the books back and the papers on your desk and I can deal with the furniture in here. You go and put some clothes in a bag. Leave the bed. We'll tell Bill that the removal men were a couple of opportunistic thieves and he should have had more sense than to let them in." He took a cotton shopping bag from the coat hook behind the door. "Can I use this for the rucksack stuff?"

"Yes, of course. I'll go and get some clothes."

He picked up a book that lay on the floor. "Are you reading this?" he said.

It was Simon Talbot's *The Constant Deceiver*.

"Yes," she said. "I'm not sure about it."

"That should please him."

He put the three folders, the two books, and the handful of small bottles and boxes in the bag. Later that night they'd be in Hannah's safe. He'd have to contact Oakley Street, the obscure division of the secret service to which he and Hannah both belonged, and then go to the Botanic Garden, where they must have been expecting the unfortunate Dr. Hassall to have returned by now, with these specimens, whatever they were.

He stood up and began putting the books on the shelves, and presently Lyra came through.

"Ready?" he said. "I've just put the books anywhere. You'll have to sort them out later, I'm afraid."

"Thanks. I'm glad you were with me when we came back. Fooling them with the rucksack trick is all very well, but I hadn't understood how disgusting it would feel to—I don't know. Their *hands* all over my clothes . . ."

Pan had been talking quietly with Asta. No doubt she could tell him all about their conversation later, and no doubt Pan realized it; and no doubt Lyra did too.

"Actually," Malcolm said, "we won't say a word to Bill. He'd want to call the police, and we'd have to explain why he mustn't. So he'd remember it and wonder about it. Much better to say nothing. If he asks, they were removal men, but they had the wrong date."

"And if the police did get involved with this, they'd put two and two together. They'd know I know about the murder. . . . But how did they trace the rucksack anyway? Nobody was following us. . . ."

"The other side's got an alethiometer."

"They must have a good reader, then. This is a very specific address. It's hard to get that sort of detail. I'll have to assume I'm being watched all the time. How loathsome."

"Yes. It is. But now let's get you up to Godstow."

She picked up *The Constant Deceiver*, made sure her bookmark was still in place, and put it in the rucksack to take with her.

Mr. and Mrs. Polstead were not in the least put out when their son appeared with Lyra. They agreed at once to let her stay at the Trout, gave her a comfortable room, agreed that she could work in the bar or the kitchen, wherever she would be most useful, and altogether seemed the most agreeable parents in the world.

"After all, he took you away," said Mrs. Polstead, putting a dish of beef casserole in front of Lyra at the kitchen table. "Only right he should bring you back. Nearly twenty years!"

She was a large woman with something of Malcolm's warm coloring and eyes that were bright blue.

"And I've only just heard about it," said Lyra. "Being taken away, I mean. I was too young to remember anything. Where is the priory? Is it very close?"

"Just across the river, but it's a ruin now. The flood destroyed so much, and it was simply too expensive to repair. Besides, a number of the sisters died that night; there wouldn't have been enough of them left to get it going again. You won't remember Sister Fenella, or Sister Benedicta? No, you were far too young."

Lyra, mouth full, shook her head.

"Sister Benedicta was in charge," Mrs. Polstead went on. "Sister Fenella looked after you most of the time. She was the sweetest old lady you could ever meet. Malcolm loved her dearly—he was devastated when he came back and found she was gone. Oh, I thought I'd never forgive him for making me worry so much. Just vanishing like that . . . Of course, we thought he must be drowned, you too, and Alice. The one good thing was that his canoe was gone. He might have had time to get in that, we thought, and we clung to that hope till he came back, all knocked about and shot and bruised and exhausted. . . ."

"Shot?" said Lyra. The casserole was very good, and she was hungry, but she was even hungrier to hear everything Malcolm's mother could tell her.

"Shot in the arm. He's still got the scar. And so worn out—completely drained. He slept for, ooh, three days. He was ill for a while, actually. All that filthy floodwater, I suppose. How's that casserole? Like another potato?"

"Thank you. It's delicious. What I don't understand is why I never knew about this. I mean, I wouldn't remember anyway, but why didn't anyone tell me?"

"Good question. I suppose at first the problem was just looking after you—problem for the college, I mean. Moldy old place full of Scholars, never had a child running around, and none of them knew what had happened, and Alice wasn't going to tell them. What did Mal tell you about when they took you to Jordan with Lord Asriel?"

"I've only just heard for the first time this afternoon. And I'm trying to adjust. . . . You see, I only ever knew Alice as Mrs. Lonsdale. She was always there when I was little, always keeping me clean and tidy and teaching me manners. I thought . . . Well, I don't know what I thought. I suppose I thought she'd always been there."

"Lord, no. I'll tell you how I know about it—the old Master of Jordan, old Dr. Carne, asked me and Reg to come in and see him: that would have been maybe six months after the flood. We didn't know what it could be about, but we put on our best clothes and went there one afternoon. It was in the summer. He gave us tea in the garden and explained all about it. It seems that Mal and Alice had done what they set out to do, and taken you to Lord Asriel, where they thought you'd be safe. I never heard of anything so blooming reckless in all my life, and I let Mal know how senseless I thought he'd been, but I was proud of him, really, and I still am. Don't you dare tell him, mind.

"Anyway, it seems that Lord Asriel claimed that protection thing—sanctuary—"

"Scholastic sanctuary."

"That's it—on your behalf. And he told the Master he'd have to make you into a Scholar so you'd be properly entitled to it. Then Dr. Carne looked at Mal and Alice, half drowned, worn out, filthy, dirty, bleeding, and said, 'What about these two?' And Lord Asriel said, 'Treasure them.' And then he left.

"So then Dr. Carne set about doing that. He arranged for Mal to go to Radcliffe School and paid for it, and then later on admitted him to Jordan as an undergraduate. Alice wasn't a great one for education, but sharp as a tack, very bright, very quick. The Master offered her a place among the staff, and she soon took over looking after you. She married young—Roger Lonsdale, carpenter, lovely boy, decent, steady. He died in a building accident. She was widowed before she was twenty. I don't know all that happened on that ruddy voyage to London in Malcolm's old canoe—he's never told me half of it, says I'd be too frightened—but one thing was, him and Alice came back fast friends. Inseparable, they were, as far as it could happen, him being at school and all."

"Weren't they before?"

"Deadly enemies. She sneered at him, and he ignored her. Hated each other. She could be a bully—she's four years older, remember, and that's a lot at that age. She used to tease him, pick on him—I had to tell her off once, but he never complained, though he used to set his lips—like this—when he took the dirty dishes in to her to be washed. Then that winter they gave her a bit of work at the priory, helping out with you, letting poor old Sister Fenella take it a little bit easier. Well, you made short work of that casserole. Like some more?"

"No, thanks. It was just what I wanted."

"Baked plums? I put a bit of liqueur in with them."

"Sounds lovely. Yes, please."

Mrs. Polstead dished them up and poured double cream over them. Lyra looked to see if Pan had seen that—before their coldness, he used to tease her about her appetite—but he was sitting on the floor talking to Mrs. Polstead's dæmon, a grizzled old badger.

Mrs. Polstead sat down again. "Malcolm's told me a bit about this new Master of Jordan," she said. "He's treated you badly."

"Well, you see, I really can't tell if he has or not. I'm so confused. Things have been happening so quickly. . . . I mean, if the money I was living on has run out, as he said, I can't challenge that, because I don't know anything apart from what he told me. Did, um, Malcolm tell you about the Master making me leave my rooms?"

It was the first time she'd referred to him as Malcolm, and it felt awkward for a moment.

"Yes. That was a wretched, shabby thing to do. That college is as rich as Ali Baba. They didn't need your rooms for a ruddy student. Throwing you out of a place you'd lived in all your life!"

"All the same, he is in charge, and I . . . I don't know. There are so many complications. I'm sort of losing my grip. I thought I was more sure of things. . . ."

"You stay here as long as you like, Lyra. There's plenty of room, and it'll be useful to have an extra pair of hands. The girl I was expecting to work over Christmas has decided to work in Boswell's instead, and good luck to her."

"I worked there two winters ago. It was nonstop."

"They think it's glamorous at first, perfumes and lotions and whatnot, but it's sheer hard work."

Lyra realized that she must have sold some of Miriam's father's products during her time at Boswell's, but since she didn't know Miriam then, she wouldn't have noticed. Suddenly the world of undergraduate friendships, the calm and frugal life of St. Sophia's, seemed a long way away.

"Now, let me help you with these dishes," she said, and soon she was up to her elbows in soapy water, and feeling very much at home.

* * *

That night, Lyra had a dream about a cat on a moonlit lawn. At first, it didn't interest her, but then, with a start that nearly woke her up (and certainly woke Pantalaimon), she recognized Will's dæmon, Kirjava, who came directly across the grass and rubbed her head on the hand Lyra held out. Will had never known he had a dæmon until she was torn away from his heart on the shores of the world of the dead, just as Pan was torn away from Lyra. And now Lyra seemed to her dreaming self to be recalling things she knew from another time, or perhaps from the future, whose significance was as overpowering as the joy she and Will had felt together. The red building in the journal came into it too: She knew what it contained! She saw why she had to go there! That knowledge was part of everything she knew, immovably. It seemed in her dream memory only yesterday when all four of them had wandered together in the world of the *mulefa*, and that time was surrounded, suffused, with such love that she found herself weeping in her dream, and woke with her pillow soaked with tears.

Pan watched from close by and didn't say a word.

Lyra tried to recall every image from the dream, but it was vanishing by the second. All that was left was that intense, intoxicating, saturating love.

Malcolm rang Hannah's doorbell. Two minutes later they were sitting by her fireside, and he was telling her about the murder, the wallet, the rucksack, and Lyra at the Trout. She listened without interrupting: he was good at recounting events, giving each its due weight, putting them in the most effective order.

"And what's in the bag?" she said.

"Aha," he said, and set it between his feet. "These papers, to begin with. I haven't had time to look, but I'll photogram them tonight. These two books—an Anatolian book on botany, and this."

She took the other book. It was poorly bound and clumsily repaired, and the paper was coarse and fragile, and the typesetting amateurish. It bore the signs of much reading; the boards that covered it were greasy with handling, several pages were dog-eared, and many bore penciled annotations in the same language as the text.

"It looks like poetry," she said, "but I don't know the language."

"It's Tajik," he told her, "and it's an epic poem called *Jahan and Rukhsana*. I can't read all of it, but I recognize that much."

"And what's that other group of papers?"

It was Dr. Strauss's diary, the account of his journey into the desert of Karamakan.

"I think this is the key to the whole thing," said Malcolm. "I stopped at the Lamb and Flag on the way here and read this, and you should read it too. It won't take long."

She took the bundle of paper, intensely curious. "And the poor man was a botanist, you say?"

"I'll go to the Botanic Garden tomorrow and see what they can tell me. There were some little bottles in the rucksack—here they are—and some boxes of what look like seeds too."

She took one of the bottles, held it up to the light, sniffed it, and read the label. "*Ol. R. tajikiae* . . . *Ol. R. chashmiae* . . . Not easy to read. *Ol.* could be *oil*, I suppose—*oleum.* . . . *R.* is *Rosa.*"

"That's my guess too."

"And these are seeds, you think?" She rattled one of the little specimen boxes.

"I imagine so. I haven't had time to open them."

"Let's have a look. . . ."

The lid of the box was tight and took a lot of persuading to open. Hannah tipped the contents carefully into her hand: a few dozen small seeds, irregular in shape and grayish brown in color.

Malcolm read the label on the lid: "*R. lopnoriae* . . . That's interesting. Do you recognize them?"

"They look like rose seeds, but I might be thinking that because of the other things. They *do* look like rose seeds, though. What's interesting?"

"The name of the variety. I suppose it's not surprising to find a botanist carrying seeds. But something's been nagging at my memory. I really think this is Oakley Street business."

"So do I. I'll see Glenys on Saturday—Tom Nugent's memorial service. I'll speak to her then."

"Good," said Malcolm. "It's important enough to lie behind murder and theft, anyway. Hannah, what do you know about Lop Nor?"

"A lake, is it? Or is it a desert? Somewhere in China, anyway. Well, I've never been there. But I heard it mentioned a few months ago in connection with . . . What was it?"

"There's a scientific research station near there. Meteorology, mainly, but they cover a number of other disciplines as well. Anyway, they've lost a number of scientists, inexplicably. They just vanished. I did hear rumors about Dust," Malcolm said.

"I remember now. Charlie Capes told me about it."

Charles Capes was a priest in the hierarchy of the English Church, and secretly a friend of Oakley Street. His position was a risky one; there were severe penalties for apostasy, and there was no appeal from the verdicts of the ecclesiastical courts, which allowed only one defense: overpowering diabolical temptation. In passing information on to Oakley Street, Capes was risking his career, his freedom, and possibly his life.

"So the Magisterium is interested in Lop Nor," said Malcolm. "And possibly roses too."

"You're going to take this material to the Botanic Garden?"

"Yes, but I'll photo all the papers first. And, Hannah . . ."

"What?"

"We're going to have to tell Lyra all about Oakley Street. She's too vulnerable. It's time she knew where to find help and protection. Oakley Street could give her that."

"I nearly told her this afternoon," she said. "But of course I didn't. I think you're right, though, and we must. You know, this reminds me of that other rucksack all that time ago, the one you brought me from Gerard Bonneville. So much material! I'd never seen such a treasure trove. *And* her alethiometer."

"Thinking about alethiometers," he said, "I'm concerned that the other side managed to pinpoint Lyra and the rucksack so quickly. That's not usual, is it?"

She looked troubled. "It sort of confirms what we'd guessed," she said. "People have been talking for months now about a new way of reading the alethiometer. Very unorthodox. Experimental, partly. The new way depends on abandoning the sort of single-viewpoint perspective you have with the classical method. I can't explain exactly how it works, because the only time I tried it I was violently sick. But apparently if you can do it, the answers come much more quickly, and you hardly need the books at all."

"Are there many people using this new method?"

"None in Oxford, to my knowledge. The general feeling is against it. It's Geneva where most of the discoveries have been made. They've got a young man there who's brilliantly gifted. And you'll never g—"

"Lyra? Does she use the new method?"

"I think she's tried once or twice, but without much success."

"And sorry. I interrupted you. What was it that I'd never guess?"

"The name of the young man in Geneva. It's Olivier Bonneville."

NINE

THE ALCHEMIST

As soon as she'd read Strauss's journal, Hannah agreed with Malcolm that Oakley Street needed to see it as soon as possible. Accordingly he spent much of the night photogramming every one of the papers from Hassall's rucksack, together with the title page of each of the books. He put the rolls of film in his refrigerator and went to bed nearer five o'clock than four.

Before they fell asleep, Asta said, "Has she still got her gun?"

Every Oakley Street agent of Hannah's rank had to take an unarmed combat course and pass a test on their marksmanship with a pistol once a year. Hannah looked like a mild gray-haired academic, which is what she was; but she was armed, and she could defend herself.

"She keeps it in that safe of hers," said Malcolm. "I'm sure she'd prefer not to take it out."

"It should be closer at hand than that."

"Well, you tell her. I've tried."

"And what are we going to do about Olivier Bonneville?"

"Can't do anything but speculate at the moment. A son?

Bonneville might have had a son. One more thing to find out. We'll see what Oakley Street knows."

After breakfast, Malcolm delivered the rolls of film to a trusty technician for developing and walked along the High Street to the Botanic Garden. It was a somber gray day with the taste of rain in the air, and the lighted windows of the administrative building glowed brightly against the bulk of a large yew behind it.

A secretary told him at first that the Director was busy, and that he'd need an appointment, but as soon as he said that his visit concerned Dr. Roderick Hassall, her attitude changed. In fact, she looked shocked.

"D'you know where he is?" she said, and her dæmon, a little Boston terrier, stood with hackles raised, uttering a hardly audible whine.

"That's what I've come to discuss with the Director."

"Of course. Sorry. Excuse me."

She left her desk and entered an inner room, the dæmon scampering at her heels. A few moments later, she came out and said, "Professor Arnold will see you now."

"Thanks," said Malcolm, and went in. The secretary closed the door behind him.

The Director was a woman of forty or so, blond, slender, and fierce-looking. She was standing. Her hummingbird dæmon hovered in the air over her shoulder before settling there.

"What do you know about Roderick Hassall?" she said at once.

"I was hoping you could tell me something about him. All I know is what's in here," said Malcolm, and laid the shopping bag on the neatly ordered desk. "I found it at a bus stop, as if someone had forgotten it. There was no one nearby, and I waited for a few minutes to see if anyone would come back and claim it, but no one did. So I thought I'd better see who it belonged to. There's a wallet in there."

Professor Arnold found the wallet and looked at it briefly.

"And seeing that he's a member of your staff," Malcolm went on, "I thought I'd bring it here."

"A bus stop, you said? Where?"

"On the Abingdon Road, the side heading into town."

"When?"

"Yesterday morning."

She put the wallet down and took out one of the folders. After a quick glance at the contents, she did the same with the other two. Malcolm stood waiting for her to speak. Finally she looked at him. She seemed to be weighing him up.

"I'm sorry, my secretary didn't tell me your name," she said.

"She didn't ask me for it. My name's Malcolm Polstead. I'm a Scholar of Durham College. When I mentioned Dr. Hassall's name, though, she looked shocked, and now I have to say that you look the same. It is genuine, I take it, all this? The university cards are real? There is a Dr. Hassall, and he is on your staff?"

"I'm sorry, Dr.—Dr.?" He nodded. "Dr. Polstead, but this has taken me aback. Please—sit down."

He sat in the chair facing the desk. She sat too and lifted the telephone. "I need some coffee," she said, and raised her eyebrows at Malcolm, who nodded. "Could you bring us coffee for two, Joan, please."

She picked up the wallet again and took out cards, papers, money, and laid them all neatly on her blotter.

"Why didn't you . . . ," she began, and stopped, and began again: "Did you think of taking this to the police?"

"The first thing I did was look in the wallet, to find a name, and when I saw the card saying he worked here, I thought it would save time all round if I brought it here directly. Besides, I couldn't help being curious, because when I was looking through the wallet, I caught sight of the name of a place where I spent a little time myself, and I wondered what Dr. Hassall was researching."

"Which place?"

"Lop Nor."

Now she was more than interested. In fact, she was suspicious, even alarmed.

"What were you doing there?" she said. "I'm sorry, that sounded like an accusation."

"I was looking for a tomb. I'm an historian, and the Silk Road has been one of my interests for a long time. I didn't find the tomb, but I did find some other things that made the journey worthwhile. May I ask what Dr. Hassall was doing in Central Asia?"

"Well, he's a botanist, of course, so . . . There's a research institute—we support it together with the universities of Edinburgh and Leiden. He was working there."

"Why there? I don't remember much in the way of plant life around Lop Nor—a few poplars, some grass—tamarisks, I think. . . ."

"For one thing, the climatic conditions—thank you, Joan, just leave it there—aren't easy to replicate further north and west, especially here on the edge of a large ocean. Then there's the soil—there are some unusual minerals in it—and then there's local knowledge. They grow flowers that just . . . can't be grown anywhere else."

"And Dr. Hassall? Is he back in Oxford now? I'm just wondering—and it's none of my business, I know—why you're so alarmed."

"I'm alarmed for him," she said. "The fact is that he's missing. We thought he was dead."

"Really? When did you begin to think that?"

"Some weeks ago. He vanished from the station."

"The station?"

"We call it the station. The research institute at Tashbulak."

"The place near Lop Nor? And he vanished?"

She was looking more and more uncomfortable. She tapped her fingers on the desk: short nails, he noticed, and even a touch of dirt in them, as if she'd been botanizing when he arrived.

"Look, Dr. Polstead," she said, "I'm sorry to seem evasive. The thing is, communications with the station aren't quick or reliable. Obviously, our information about Dr. Hassall was wrong. It's good to have this—these things—very good—because it might mean that he's alive after all, but I'd have expected—if it was him that brought them to Oxford, of course—it would have been wonderful if he'd come here in person. . . . I just can't imagine what anyone was doing leaving them at a bus stop. I'm sure he wouldn't do that. Someone else must have. . . . I'm utterly perplexed. I hope he wasn't . . . Thank you very much, Dr. Polstead, for, for bringing this in."

"What will you do now?"

"You mean, about this? These things?"

She was frightened of something, and frightened separately of betraying the fact to him, a stranger. Her dæmon had not moved from her shoulder, or closed his eyes, which gazed at Malcolm solemnly. Malcolm looked back, trying to seem bland and harmless and helpful.

"It's about roses, isn't it?" he said.

She blinked. Her dæmon turned away and buried his face in her hair.

"Why do you ask that?"

"Two things. One is the specimens—the seeds and the rose oil. The other is that battered book in the red cover. It's an epic poem in the Tajik language called *Jahan and Rukhsana*. It's about two lovers who search for a rose garden. Was Dr. Hassall investigating something to do with roses?"

133

"Yes, he was," she said. "I can't tell you any more because, well, I have to supervise dozens of projects—postgraduate theses, the work done here as well as what they do at Tashbulak, and my own research as well. . . ."

She was one of the worst liars he'd ever met. He felt sorry for her; she was having to improvise a defense when she was in a state of shock.

"I won't bother you anymore," he said. "Thanks for explaining what you could. If for any reason you need to get in touch with me . . ." He laid one of his cards on the desk.

"Thank you, Dr. Polstead," she said, and shook his hand.

"Do let me know if you have any news. I feel as if I've got shares in Dr. Hassall now."

He left the building and went to sit in the garden, where a little weak sunshine was gilding the bare stems of the shrubs, and where two young men were doing something horticultural near the glasshouses.

"Should have told her," said Asta.

"I know. But that would drag Lyra into it. And involve the police, and it was one of them who killed him."

"But the policeman wasn't acting officially, Mal, come on. The one Pan saw is corrupt. The police need to know what happened, and know about him."

"You're absolutely right, and I feel very bad about it."

"But?"

"We'll tell her soon. Tell them soon."

"When?"

"When we've learnt a little more."

"And how are we going to do that?"

"Not sure yet."

Asta closed her eyes. Malcolm wished that Lyra hadn't taken the risk of getting the rucksack from the station alone, but who'd have been able to help her? Not him, clearly. Not then. Once you've witnessed a murder and decided against telling the police, you're really on your own.

And that set him thinking about her again. While Asta lay sphinx-like on the wooden seat beside him, eyes half closed, Malcolm wondered how Lyra was getting on at the Trout, and how safe she'd be there, and a dozen other questions gathered around one central one that he didn't want to look at yet. Had she completely changed from the sullen, contemptuous girl whose manner and tone had been so difficult to deal with when he was teaching her a few years before? She seemed to be much more hesitant, reticent, uncertain of herself. She looked lonely and unhappy, not to make too much of it. And there was her strange, cold relationship with her dæmon. . . . But when they'd spoken in the little restaurant, she'd been almost confiding, almost friendly; and her pleasure in having concealed the things from the rucksack was like a little ripple of laughter, something almost carefree; delightful, anyway.

That central question wouldn't go away. He came back to it helplessly.

He was conscious of his own ox-like clumsiness. He was conscious of all kinds of contrasts—his maturity and her youth, his bulk and her slenderness, his stolidity and her quickness. . . . He could watch her for hours. Her eyes, large and long-lashed and a gloriously vivid blue, more expressive than anyone's he'd known; she was so young, but already he could see where the laughter lines, the lines of sympathy, the lines of concentration would gather in the years to come and make her face even richer and more full of life. Already, on each side of her mouth, there was a tiny crease made by the smile that seemed to hover just under the surface, ready to flower into being. Her hair, dark straw-colored, shortish and untidyish but always soft and shining: once or twice when he was teaching her, bending to look over her shoulder at a piece of written work, he'd caught a faint scent from that hair, not of shampoo but of young warm girl, and drawn away at once. At that time, when they were teacher and pupil, anything like that was so wrong, his mind shut it out before it had even fully formed.

But four years later, was it still wrong to think about it? About Lyra now? Wrong to yearn to put his hands on either side of her face, on those warm cheeks, and bring it gently towards his?

He'd been in love before; he knew what was happening to him. But the girls and women he'd loved in the past had been roughly his own age. Mostly. In the one exception, the difference went the other way. Nothing he knew was any help in this situation, and she was in such danger and difficulty at the moment that bothering her with his own feelings would be unforgivable. But there it was. He, Malcolm Polstead, aged thirty-one, was in love with her. It was impossible to think that she could ever love him.

The quiet of the large garden, the distant conversation of the two young botanists, the regular scraping of their hoes, the purring of his dæmon, all combined with his lack of sleep and his troubled heart to make it tempting to close his eyes and hope to dream of Lyra; so he stood up and said to Asta, "Come on. Let's go and do some work."

At eleven that night, Mr. and Mrs. Polstead were talking quietly in bed. It was the second evening of Lyra's stay at the Trout. She was in her bedroom; the girl who helped in the kitchen, the potboy, the assistant barman had all gone home; there were no guests.

"I can't make her out," said Reg Polstead.

"Lyra? What d'you mean?"

"She seems perfectly cheerful on the surface. Full of, you know, chatter, friendliness. Then sometimes she'll fall quiet and her whole face changes. It's as if she's just had some bad news."

"No," said his wife, "it's not like that. She doesn't look shocked. She looks lonely. She looks as if she's used to it and doesn't expect anything else, but that's what she is. Melancholy."

"She doesn't hardly ever speak to that dæmon either," he said. "It's as if they're two separate people."

"She was such a happy baby. Laughing, singing, full of fun . . . Mind you, that was before, you know."

"Before Malcolm's voyage. Well, *he* was different after that. So was Alice."

"But you'd expect them to be more affected, seeing as they were older. She was just a baby. They don't remember things. And she *is* being badly treated by that college. It's her home—you'd think they'd take better care. Not surprising she's a bit subdued."

"I wonder if she's got any relatives. Malcolm says her father and mother are both long dead."

"If she's got any uncles or aunts or cousins, I don't think much of them," said Mrs. Polstead.

"Why?"

"They should have got in touch. A long time ago. It's an unnatural life for a young girl, cooped up with a lot of old Scholars."

"Maybe she has got relatives, and they don't care about her. She'd be better off without 'em in that case."

"Possibly. Tell you one thing, though—she's a hard worker. I'll have to find something particular for her to do. She does Pauline's couple of jobs quicker and better than Pauline, and Pauline's going to feel shoved aside unless I give Lyra something different."

"We don't need her to work. She could stay as a guest, welcome, far as I'm concerned."

"Me too, love, but it's not for us, it's for her. She's got her college work, but she needs to feel useful. I'm trying to think of something extra, something that wouldn't get done at all if she didn't do it."

"Yeah, maybe you're right. I'll have a think. Night, sweetheart."

He turned over. She read a detective story for five minutes, found her eyelids drooping, and put the light out.

Hannah Relf didn't know it, but Lyra had been experimenting with the new method of reading the alethiometer. This new method wasn't a matter of public knowledge, because there was little public discussion of the alethiometer, but among the small groups of experts, it was a topic of excited speculation.

The instrument in her possession was the one Malcolm had found in Gerard Bonneville's rucksack, and then thrust in among the baby Lyra's blankets when Lord Asriel had handed her to the Master of Jordan. The Master had given it to Lyra when she was eleven, and she'd taken it with her on the great adventure in the Arctic and beyond. At first, she learnt to read it intuitively, as if it was the most natural thing in the world; but before very long she lost the power to do that, and she was left unable to see all the connections and similarities that had once been so clear beneath the symbols on the dial.

The loss of that power was painful. It was a consolation, though a poor, thin one, to know that by diligent study she'd be able to regain some of the ability to read it; but she'd always need the books in which generations of scholars had set down their discoveries about the symbols and the links between them. The contrast, though! It was like losing the power to fly through the air like a swift, and being compensated with a crutch to help her limp along the ground.

And that contributed to her melancholy. Mrs. Polstead was right: melancholy was Lyra's state of mind these days, and since her rift with Pan, she'd had no one to talk to about it. How absurd it was, that the two of them were one person, and yet they found it so hard to talk together or even endure each other's company in silence. More and more she found herself whispering to a phantom, to her idea of what Will was like now in that unreachable world of his.

So the new style of alethiometric technique had come as a welcome distraction. It had spread by rumor, no one knew from whom or from where; but there were stories about dramatic advances in understanding, of a revolution in theory, of sensational feats of readership where the books were simply redundant, superfluous. And Lyra privately began to experiment.

On their second night at the Trout, she was sitting in bed, knees drawn up, blankets around her against the cold, the alethiometer in her loosely cupped hands. The low, sloping ceiling of the bedroom, the wallpaper with its pattern of little flowers, the old worn rug beside the bed—they felt comfortably familiar already, and the gentle yellow light from the naphtha lamp beside her made the room feel warmer than a thermometer would have shown. Pan was sitting beneath the lamp; in the old days, he would have been curled up warmly between her breasts.

"What are you doing?" he said. His tone was hostile.

"I'm going to try the new method again."

"Why? Last time it made you sick."

"I'm exploring. Trying things out."

"I don't like the new method, Lyra."

"But why?"

"Because when you do it, you look as if you're lost. I can't tell where you are. And I don't think you know where you are. You need more imagination."

"*What?*"

"If you had more imagination, it would be better. But—"

"What are you saying? You're saying I haven't got any imagination?"

"You're trying to live without it, that's what I'm saying. It's those books again. One of them saying it doesn't exist, the other saying it doesn't matter anyway."

"No, no . . ."

"Well, if you don't want my opinion, don't ask me about it."

"But I didn't . . ." She didn't know what to say. She felt powerfully upset. He was just looking at her expressionlessly. "What should I do?" she said.

She meant *about us*. But in response he said, "Well, you have to be able to imagine. But in your case, that's not easy, is it?"

"I don't . . . I really have no . . . Pan, I just don't know what you're talking about. It's as if we're speaking different languages. It doesn't connect with . . ."

"What were you going to look up anyway?"

"I'm not sure anymore. You've confused me. But something's wrong with things. I suppose I was going to see if I could find out what it is."

He looked away, and slowly moved his tail from side to side, and then he turned away altogether and sprang onto the old chintz-covered armchair and curled up to sleep.

No imagination? Trying to live without imagination? She had never in her life thought about what her imagination might be. If she had, she might have supposed that that aspect of her self resided more in Pan, because she was practical, matter-of-fact, down-to-earth. . . . But how did she know that? Other people seemed to regard her as being those things, or at least they treated her as if they did. She had friends she would have called imaginative: they were witty, or they said surprising things, or they daydreamed a lot. Wasn't she like that? Evidently not. She had no idea it would hurt so much to be told she had no imagination.

140

But Pan had said it was because of those books. It was true, the narrative of *The Hyperchorasmians* treated with contempt the characters who were artistic, or who wrote poetry, or who spoke about "the spiritual." Did Gottfried Brande mean that imagination itself was worthless? Lyra couldn't remember if he ever mentioned it directly: she'd have to look through the book and see. As for Simon Talbot, in *The Constant Deceiver* his own imagination was on display throughout, in a kind of charming but heartless play with the truth. The effect was dazzling, dizzying, as if there were no responsibilities, no consequences, no facts.

She sighed. She was holding the alethiometer loosely in both hands, letting her thumbs move across the knurled wheels, sensing the familiar weight, half watching the reflection of the lamplight move as she turned it this way and that.

"Well, Pan, I tried," she said, but very quietly. "And so did you, for a bit. You just couldn't keep going. You're not really interested. What are we going to do? We can't go on like this. Why do you hate me so much? Why do I hate you? Why can't we stand being with each other?"

She was no longer sleepy, just wide awake and unhappy.

"Well," she whispered, "it won't make any difference now."

She sat up a little, held the alethiometer more purposefully. There were two points of difference between the new method and the classical one. The first had to do with the placing of the hands on the dial. The classical method required the reader to frame a question by pointing each of the hands at a different symbol, and thus define precisely what it was they wanted to know. But with the new method, all three hands were pointed at one symbol, chosen by the reader. This was felt by classically trained readers to be grossly unorthodox and disrespectful of tradition, besides being unstable; instead of the steady and methodical inquiry made possible by the firmly based triangle of the three hands, the single anchor-hold of the new method allowed a wild and unpredictable chaos of meanings to emerge as the needle darted rapidly from place to place.

The second point of difference had to do with the attitude of the reader. The classical method required a careful, watchful, but relaxed state of mind, which took a good deal of practice to manage. After all, part of the reader's attention had to be available for consulting the books that laid out the multiple meanings of each symbol. The new method, on the other hand, didn't need the books at all. The reader had to abandon control and enter a state of passive vision where nothing was fixed and everything was equally possible. This was the reason why both Hannah and Lyra had had to stop soon after beginning their experiments with it: they'd felt horribly seasick.

Now, sitting in bed and thinking about it, Lyra felt apprehensive.

"Could it go wrong?" she whispered, and, "I could get lost and never come back. . . ."

Yes, that was a risk. Without a fixed perspective or a solid place to stand, it might be like drowning in a wild sea.

In a spirit of mingled desperation and reluctance, she turned the wheels until all three hands pointed to the horse. She didn't know why. Then she held the alethiometer and closed her eyes, letting her mind fall forward like a diver off a high cliff.

"Don't look for a firm place—go into the flow—be with it—let it surge through me—in and out again—there's nothing firm—no perspective . . . ," she muttered to herself.

Images from the dial swung at her and past her, and swung away again. Now she was upside down, now she was soaring, now plummeting into a terrible depth. Images she had known well for almost half her life lowered at her with an alien glare or hid themselves in mist. She let herself drift, float, tumble, holding on to nothing. It was dark and then it was dazzling. She was on an endless plain studded with fossilized emblems under a vast moon. She was in a forest resounding with animal cries and human screams and the whisper of terrified ghosts. Ivy climbed up to envelop the sun and pull it down into a meadow where an angry black bull snorted and stamped.

Through it all she drifted, intentionless, free from any human feeling. Scene after scene unfolded, banal, tender, horrible, and she watched them all, interested but detached. She wondered if she was dreaming, and whether it mattered, and how she could tell what was significant from what was trivial and accidental.

"I don't know!" she whispered.

She had begun to feel that horrible sickness which seemed to be the inevitable consequence of using the new method. She put the instrument down at once and breathed deeply till the nausea passed.

There must be a better way, she thought. Clearly *something* was happening, though it was hard to tell what it was. She wondered what she'd ask if she had some of the books with her and could consult the old authorities about framing a question and interpreting the answer, and at once she knew: she'd ask about the cat in the dream. Was she Will's dæmon, and if so, what did that mean?

She felt uncomfortable to think that, though. The universal skepticism that she'd learnt from Brande and Talbot, in their different ways, made her sternly reject the world of dreams and occult significances. They were childish things, worthless rubbish.

But what was the alethiometer itself, if not a way into that very world? She was horribly divided.

Nevertheless, that shadow-colored cat on the moonlit lawn . . .

She took it up again and turned all three hands to point to the bird, which stood for dæmons in general. She closed her eyes again and cradled the instrument in her lap, holding it without any tension. She tried to summon the mood of the dream, which wasn't hard; in fact, it clung to her mind like a delicate perfume. How the dæmon had come towards her, confident and happy, offering her head for Lyra's knuckles to rub; how her fur had felt almost charged with adoration; how she knew the dæmon was Kirjava, and she was allowed to touch her because she loved Will, and how Will must be nearby . . .

At once the scene changed. Still entranced, she found herself in an elegant building, in a corridor, with windows opening onto a narrow courtyard below, where a large limousine gleamed in the winter sunshine. The walls of the corridor were painted or distempered a pale chalky green in the pale sunshine of a winter afternoon.

And there was the cat dæmon again!

Or . . . just a cat, sitting calmly this time, watching her. Not Kirjava. As Lyra in a fire of hope and disappointment moved towards her, the cat turned and stalked away towards an open door. Lyra followed. Through the doorway she saw a book-lined room where a young man was holding an alethiometer, and it was—

"Will!" she said aloud.

She couldn't help it. His black hair, his strong jaw, the tense way he held his shoulders—and then he looked up at her, and it wasn't Will but someone else, about her age, slim, fierce, arrogant. And he had a dæmon who wasn't a cat: she was a sparrowhawk, perching on the back of his chair, staring at her with yellow eyes. Where was Kirjava now? Lyra looked around: the cat had vanished. A flicker of suspicious recognition passed between Lyra and the young man, but they were recognizing different things: he knew her to be the girl his employer Marcel Delamare wanted so badly for some reason, the girl who had his own father's alethiometer, and she knew him to be the inventor of the new method.

Before he could move, she reached in and pulled the door shut between them.

Then she blinked and shook her head, and found herself in the warm bed at the Trout. She was weak from wonder, and giddy with shock. He had been so like Will—that first moment, what a burst of joy in her breast! And then what a sickening disappointment, followed at once by an uneasy lurch of surprise, that she knew where that place was, and what he was doing, and who he was. And where had the cat gone? Why had she been there, anyway? Was she leading Lyra to the young man?

She didn't notice Pan sitting up tensely, watching her, in the chair beside the bed.

She put the alethiometer on the bedside table and reached for paper and pencil. Working quickly, while the vision was already fading from her mind, she wrote down everything she could.

Pan watched her for a minute or two and then quietly curled up again in the armchair. He hadn't shared her pillow for several nights.

He didn't move till Lyra finished writing and turned out the light, and then he waited a little longer till her steady breathing told him she was asleep. Then he recovered a tattered little notebook from the larger book in which he'd hidden it, and held it firmly in his teeth as he jumped up to the windowsill.

He had already inspected the window, which was not a sash but a casement with a simple iron catch, so he didn't need Lyra's help to open it. A moment later he was outside on the old stone tiles, and then a leap into an apple tree, a dart across a lawn, a scamper across the bridge, and soon he was running freely in the wide expanse of Port Meadow towards the distant campanile of St. Barnabas's Oratory, pale against the night sky. He darted through a group of sleeping ponies, making them shift uneasily: perhaps one of them was the animal whose back he'd leapt on the year before, digging his claws in till the poor creature galloped in a frenzy and finally threw him off, and he'd landed on the grass laughing with delight. That was something Lyra knew nothing about.

Just as she knew nothing about the little notebook he was carrying in his teeth. It was the one from Dr. Hassall's rucksack, the one filled with names and addresses, and he'd hidden it away because he'd seen something in it that she hadn't noticed; and having hidden it, he found that the best time to tell her about it hadn't yet arrived.

He ran on, light and tireless and silent, until he reached the canal that ran along the eastern edge of the meadow. Rather than swim across and risk the notebook, he slipped through the grass until he came to the little bridge across to Walton Well Road and the streets of Jericho. He'd have to be very careful from now on; it wasn't yet midnight, there were several pubs still open, and the yellow streetlights at each corner would have made it impossible to hide if he'd gone that way.

Instead, he kept to the towpath, moving swiftly and stopping frequently to look and listen, until he came to an iron-barred gate on the left. He was through it in a moment, into the grounds of the Eagle Ironworks, whose great buildings loomed high above him. A narrow path led to a similar gate that opened next to the end of Juxon Street, which consisted of a terrace of small brick houses built for the workers at the ironworks or the Fell Press nearby. Pan stayed inside the gate, in the shadow of the buildings, because two men were talking in the street.

Finally one of them opened a door, and they said good night, and the other's footsteps moved away unsteadily towards Walton Street. Pan waited for another minute, and then slipped through the gate and over the low wall in front of the last house.

He crouched beside the little window of the basement, which was dimly lit, and so smoke-covered and dusty that it was impossible to see through. He was listening for the sound of a man's voice, and presently he heard it, a sentence or two in a hoarse conversational tone, answered by a lighter and more musical one.

They were there, and they were working: that was all he needed to know. He tapped on the window, and the voices stopped at once. A dark shape leapt up onto the narrow windowsill, peered out, and a moment later moved out of the way to let the man unlatch the window.

Pan slipped inside and jumped down onto the stone floor of the basement to greet the cat dæmon, whose black fur actually seemed to absorb light. A great furnace was blazing in the center of the room, and the heat was fierce. The place seemed like a combination of blacksmith's forge and chemical laboratory, dark with soot and thick with cobwebs.

"Pantalaimon," said the man. "Welcome. We haven't seen you for a while."

"Mr. Makepeace," said Pan, dropping the notebook in order to speak. "How are you?"

"Active, at least," said Makepeace. "You're alone?"

He was aged about seventy, and deeply wrinkled. His skin was mottled either by age or by the smoke that filled the air. Pan and Lyra had first encountered Sebastian Makepeace a few years before, in a strange little episode involving a witch and her dæmon. They had visited him a number of times since then, becoming familiar with his ironic manner, the indescribable clutter of his laboratory, his knowledge of curious things, and the kindly patience of his dæmon, Mary. She and Makepeace knew that Lyra and Pan could separate: the witch whose deceit had brought them together had once been his lover, and he knew about the power the witches had.

"Yes," said Pan. "Lyra is . . . well, she's asleep. I wanted to ask you about something. I don't want to interrupt you."

Makepeace put on a battered gauntlet and adjusted the position of an iron vessel at the edge of the furnace. "That can go on heating for a while," he said. "Sit down, my boy. I'll smoke while we talk." He took a small cheroot from a drawer and lit it. Pan liked the scent of smokeleaf, but wondered if he'd smell it at all in this atmosphere. The alchemist sat on a stool and looked at him directly. "Very well, what's in that notebook?"

Pan picked it up and held it for him to take, and then told him about the murder and the events that had followed. Makepeace listened closely, and Mary sat at his feet, eyes on Pan as he spoke.

"And the reason I hid it," Pan finished, "and the reason I brought it here, is that your name's in it. It's a sort of address book. Lyra didn't notice that, but I did."

"Let me have a look," said Makepeace. He put on his spectacles. His dæmon sprang up to his lap, and they both looked closely at the list of names of people and their dæmons, and their addresses, in the little book. Each name and address was written in a different hand. They weren't in alphabetical order; in fact, they seemed to Pan to be ordered geographically, east to west, starting from somewhere called Khwarezm and ending in Edinburgh, taking in cities and towns in most European countries. Pan had studied it secretly three or four times, and could find nothing to hint at the connection between them.

The alchemist seemed to be searching for some names in particular.

"Your name's the only one in Oxford," Pan said. "I just wondered if you knew about this list. And why he might have been carrying it."

"You said he could separate from his dæmon?"

148

"Just before he died. Yes. She flew up to the tree and asked me to help."

"And why haven't you told Lyra about this?"

"I . . . It just never seemed to be the right time."

"That's unfortunate," said Makepeace. "Well, you should give it to her. It's very valuable. There's a name for this kind of list: it's known as a *clavicula adiumenti*."

He pointed to a small pair of embossed letters inside the back cover, at the foot next to the spine: C.A. The little book was so rubbed and battered that they were hardly visible. Then he flicked through the pages to about halfway through, took a short pencil out of his waistcoat pocket, and turned the notebook sideways before writing something in it.

"What does that mean?" said Pan. "*Clavicula* . . . And who are these people? Do you know them all? I couldn't see any connection between the names."

"No, you wouldn't."

"What did you write?"

"A name that was missing."

"Why did you turn it sideways?"

"To fit it on the page, of course. I say this again: give it to Lyra, and come back here with her. Then I'll tell you what it means. Not until you're both here together."

"That won't be easy," said Pan. "We hardly talk nowadays. We keep quarreling. It's horrible, and we just can't stop it."

"What do you quarrel about?"

"Last time—earlier this evening—it was imagination. I said she had no imagination, and she was upset."

"Are you surprised?"

"No. I suppose not."

"Why were you arguing about imagination?"

"I don't even know anymore. We probably didn't mean the same thing by it."

"You won't understand anything about the imagination until you realize that it's not about making things up, it's about perception. What else have you been quarreling about?"

"All kinds of things. She's changed. She's been reading books that . . . Have you heard of Gottfried Brande?"

"No. But don't tell me what you think about him. Tell me what Lyra would say."

"Hmm. All right, I'll try. . . . Brande is a philosopher. They call him the Sage of Wittenberg. Or some people do. He wrote an enormous novel called *The Hyperchorasmians*. I don't even know what that means: he doesn't refer to it in the text."

"It would mean those who live beyond Chorasmia, which is to say, the region to the east of the Caspian Sea. It's now known as Khwarezm. And—"

"Khwa—what? I think that name's on the list."

Makepeace opened the notebook again and nodded. "Yes, here it is. And what does Lyra think of this novel?"

"She's been sort of hypnotized by it. Ever since she—"

"You're telling me what *you* think. Tell me what she would say if I asked her about it."

"Well. She'd say it was a work of enormous—um—scope and power . . . A completely convincing world . . . Unlike anything else she'd ever read . . . A—a—a new view of human nature that shattered all her previous convictions and . . . showed her life in a completely new perspective. . . . Something like that, probably."

"You're being satirical."

"I can't help it. I hate it. The characters are monstrously selfish and blind to every human feeling—they're either arrogant and dominating or cringing and deceitful, or else foppish and artistic and useless. . . . There's only one value in his world, which is reason. The author's so rational, he's insane. Nothing else has any importance at all. To him, the imagination is just meaningless and contemptible. The whole universe he describes, it's just *arid*."

"If he's a philosopher, why did he write a novel? Does he think the novel is a good form for philosophy?"

"He's written various other books, but this is the only one he's famous for. We haven't—Lyra hasn't read any of the others."

The alchemist flicked the ash from his cheroot into the furnace and gazed at the fire. His dæmon, Mary, sat beside his feet, eyes half closed, purring steadily.

"Have you ever known anyone and their dæmon who hated each other?" Pan said after a minute had gone by.

"It's more common than you might think."

"Even among people who can't separate?"

"It might be worse for them."

Pan thought: Yes, it would be. Steam was rising from the iron vessel on the fire.

"Mr. Makepeace," he said, "what are you working at now?"

"I'm making some soup," said the alchemist.

"Oh," said Pan, and then realized the old man was joking. "No, what really?"

"You know what I mean by a field?"

"Like a magnetic field?"

"Yes. But this one is very hard to detect."

"What does it do?"

"I'm trying to imagine."

"But if you— Oh, I see. You mean you're trying to perceive it."

"That's right."

"Do you need special equipment?"

"You could probably do it with immensely expensive instruments that used colossal amounts of power and took up acres of space. I'm limited to what's here in my laboratory. Some gold leaf, several mirrors, a bright light, various bits and pieces I've had to invent."

"Does it work?"

"Of course it works."

"I remember the first time we met you, you told Lyra that if people think you're trying to make gold out of lead, they think you're wasting time and they don't bother to find out what you're really doing."

"Yes, I did."

"Were you trying to find this field then?"

"Yes. Now I've found it, I'm trying to discover whether it's the same everywhere, or whether it varies."

"Do you use all the things you've got down here?"

"They all have a use."

"And what are you making in the iron pot?"

"Soup, as I told you."

He got up to stir it. Pan suddenly felt tired. He'd learnt some things, but they weren't necessarily helpful; and now he had to go all the way back across Port Meadow and hide the notebook again, and—sometime—tell Lyra about it.

"*Clavicula* . . . ," he said, trying to remember, and Makepeace added, "*Adiumenti.*"

"*Adiumenti.* I'm going to go now. Thank you for explaining this. Enjoy your soup."

"Tell Lyra, and tell her soon, and come here with her."

The black cat dæmon stood to touch noses with him, and Pan left.

TEN

THE LINNAEUS ROOM

Next morning, a letter arrived by hand at Durham College for Malcolm. He opened it in the porter's lodge and saw that the paper was headed *Director's Office, Botanic Garden, Oxford*, and read:

> *Dear Dr. Polstead,*
>
> *I feel I should have been more frank with you yesterday about Dr. Hassall and his research. The fact is that circumstances are changing rapidly, and the matter is more urgent than it might seem. We have been organizing a small meeting between various parties who have an interest in the case, and I wondered if you could possibly attend. Your knowledge of the area and of the items you found means that you might be able to contribute to our discussion. I wouldn't ask, but it's both serious and urgent.*
>
> *We are meeting this evening at six, here at the Garden. If you can come (and I very much hope you will), please ask at the gate for the Linnaeus Room.*
>
> > *Yours sincerely,*
> > *Lucy Arnold*

He looked at the date on the letter: it had been written that same morning. Asta, on reading it with him from the counter of the porter's window, said, "We should tell Hannah."

"Is there time?"

He had a college meeting at midmorning. He peered into the lodge and read the time from the porter's clock: five past nine.

"Yes, we can do it," he said.

"I meant for her," Asta said. "She's going to London this morning."

"So she is. Better hurry, then," Malcolm said, and Asta leapt down and padded after him.

Ten minutes later he was ringing Hannah Relf's doorbell, and thirty seconds after that she was letting him in and saying, "So you've seen the *Oxford Times*?"

"No. What's that about?"

She held out the newspaper. It was the evening edition from the day before, and she'd turned it to page five, where a headline read, "Body Found at Iffley Lock. Not Drowned, Say Police."

He scanned the story quickly. Iffley Lock was about a mile down the river from where Pan had seen the attack, and the lockkeeper had found the body of a man of about forty, who had been brutally beaten and who appeared to have died before his body entered the water. The police had opened a murder inquiry.

"Must be him," said Malcolm. "Poor man. Well, Lucy Arnold might know by now. Perhaps that's what she's referring to."

"What are you talking about?"

"I came to show you this," he said, and handed her the letter.

"*Circumstances are changing rapidly,*" Hannah read. "Yes. Could well be. She's very cautious."

"Doesn't mention the police. If there was nothing on the body to identify him, they wouldn't know who he was, and she still might not know about it. Do you know anything about her? Ever met her?"

"I know her slightly. Intense, passionate woman—almost tragic, I've sometimes thought. Or felt, rather. I've got no reason for thinking it."

"That doesn't matter. It's part of the picture. Anyway, I'm going to go to this meeting of hers. Will you see Glenys in London, d'you think?"

"Yes. She'll certainly be there. I'll make sure she knows."

She took her overcoat from the hat stand. "How's Lyra getting on?" she said as he held the coat for her.

"Subdued. Not surprising, really."

"Tell her to come and see me when she has an hour or so. Oh, Malcolm—Dr. Strauss's journey through the desert, and the red building . . ."

"What about it?"

"That word *akterrakeh*—any idea what it could mean?"

"None, I'm afraid. It's not a Tajik word, as far as I can tell."

"Oh well. I wonder if the alethiometer could clarify it. See you later."

"Give my regards to Glenys."

Glenys Godwin was the current Director of Oakley Street. Thomas Nugent, who had been Director when Hannah joined the organization, had died earlier in the year, and Hannah was going to his memorial service. Mrs. Godwin had had to retire as a field officer some years before when she contracted a tropical fever which had had the effect of paralyzing her dæmon, but her judgment was both sound and daring, and her dæmon's memory was fine-grained and extensive. Malcolm admired her greatly. She was a widow whose only child had died of the same fever that had infected her, and she was the first woman to head Oakley Street; her political enemies had been waiting in vain for her to make a mistake.

After the memorial service, Hannah managed to speak to her for ten minutes. They were sitting in a quiet corner of the hotel lounge where several other Oakley Street people were having drinks. She briskly summarized everything she knew about the murder, the rucksack, Strauss's journal, and Malcolm's invitation to this hastily summoned meeting.

Glenys Godwin was in her fifties, small and stocky, her dark gray hair neatly and plainly styled. Her face was quick with feeling and movement—too expressive, Hannah had often thought, to be helpful to someone in her position, where a steely inscrutability might have been preferable. Her left hand moved gently over her dæmon, a small civet cat, who lay in her lap, listening closely. When Hannah had finished, she said, "The young woman, Lyra Silvertongue, was it? Unusual name. Where is she now?"

"Staying with Malcolm's parents. They have a pub on the river."

"Does she need protection?"

"Yes, I think she does. She's . . . Do you know about her background?"

"No. Tell me sometime, but not now. Clearly Malcolm must go to this meeting—it's very much Oakley Street business. There's an experimental theology connection; we know that much. A man called . . ."

"Brewster Napier," said the ghostlike voice of her dæmon.

"That's the one. He published a paper a couple of years ago, which first drew our attention to it. What was it called?"

"'Some effects of rose oil in polarized light microscopy,'" said Godwin's dæmon. "In *Proceedings of the Microscopical Institute of Leiden*. Napier and Stevenson, two years ago."

His words were quiet and strained, but perfectly clear. Not for the first time, Hannah marveled at his memory.

"Have you been in contact with this Napier?" Hannah asked.

"Not directly. We checked his background very carefully and quietly, and he's perfectly sound. As far as we know, the implications of his paper haven't been noticed by the Magisterium, and we don't want to prompt them by taking an overt interest ourselves. This business that Malcolm's come across is just another indication that something's stirring. I'm glad you told me about it. You say he's copied all the papers from the rucksack?"

"Everything. I imagine he'll get them to you by Monday."

"I look forward to it."

At about the same time, Lyra was talking to the kitchen helper at the Trout. Pauline was seventeen years old, pretty and shy, inclined to blush easily. While Pan was talking under the kitchen table with her mouse dæmon, Pauline chopped up some onions and Lyra peeled potatoes.

"Well, he used to teach me a bit," Lyra said in answer to a question about how she knew Malcolm. "But I was being horrible to everyone in those days. I never thought of him having a life at all apart from college. I used to think they put him away in a cupboard at night. How long have you been working here?"

"I started last year, just part-time, like. Then Brenda asked me to do a few more hours, and . . . I work at Boswell's too, Mondays and Thursdays."

"Do you? I worked at Boswell's for a bit. Kitchenware. It was hard work."

"I'm in Haberdashery."

She finished the onions and put them in a large casserole on the range.

"What are you making?" said Lyra.

"Just starting a venison casserole. Brenda'll do most of it. She's got some special spices she puts in, I don't know what they are. I'm just learning, really."

"Does she cook one big dish every day?"

"She used to. Mainly roasts and that, joints on the spit. Then Malcolm suggested varying it a bit. He had some really good ideas." She was blushing again. She turned away to stir the onions, which were spitting in the fat.

"Have you known Malcolm for a long time?" Lyra said.

"Yeah. I s'pose. When I was little, he . . . I thought he was . . . I dunno, really. He was always nice to me. I used to think he'd take over the pub when Reg retired, but somehow I can't see that anymore, really. He's more of a professor now. I don't see him so much."

"Would you like to run a pub?"

"Oh, I couldn't."

"It'd be fun, though."

Pauline's dæmon scampered up to her shoulder and whispered in her ear, and the girl bowed her head and shook it slightly to let her dark curls swing down and hide her flaming cheeks. She gave the onions a final stir and put the lid on the casserole before moving it a little away from the heat. Lyra watched without seeming to; she found herself fascinated by the girl's embarrassment, and was sorry to have caused it, without knowing why.

A little later, when they were sitting on the terrace, watching the river flow past, Pan told her.

"She's in love with him," he said.

"What? With *Malcolm*?" Lyra was incredulous.

"And if you hadn't been so wrapped up in yourself, you'd have seen that straightaway."

"I'm not," she said, but she sounded unconvinced, even to herself. "But . . . Surely he's too old?"

"She doesn't think so, obviously. Anyway, I don't suppose he's in love with her."

"Did her dæmon tell you that?"

"He didn't have to."

Lyra was shocked, and she had no idea why. It wasn't shocking: it was just . . . Well, it was *Dr. Polstead*. But then, he was different now. He was even dressing differently. At home in the Trout, Malcolm wore a checked shirt with the sleeves rolled up, showing the golden hair on his forearms, a moleskin waistcoat, and corduroy trousers. He looked like a farmer, she thought, and very little like a scholar. He appeared to be perfectly at home in this world of watermen and farm laborers, of poachers and traveling salesmen; calm and burly and good-natured, he seemed to have been part of this place all his life.

Which of course he had. It was no wonder that he served drinks so expertly, talked so easily with strangers as well as regulars, dealt with problems so efficiently. The evening before, two customers had nearly come to blows over a game of cards, and Malcolm had them outside almost before Lyra had noticed. She wasn't sure that she felt at ease with this new Malcolm any more than with the old Dr. Polstead, but she could see that he was someone to be respected. To fall in love with, though . . . She resolved to avoid talking about him again. She liked Pauline and didn't want to think she'd embarrassed her.

When Malcolm arrived at the Botanic Garden just before six, he saw a light in one window of the administrative building; apart from that, the place was dark. The porter's shutter was closed, and he tapped on it gently.

He heard a movement inside and saw a glow forming at the edge of the shutter, as if someone had arrived with a lamp.

"Garden's closed," said a voice from inside.

"Yes. But I've come for a meeting with Professor Arnold. She told me to ask for the Linnaeus Room."

"Name, sir?"

"Polstead. Malcolm Polstead."

"Right . . . Got it. Main door's open, and the Linnaeus Room is one floor up, second on the right."

The main door of the administrative building faced into the garden. It was faintly lit by a light at the top of the stairs, and Malcolm found the Linnaeus Room just along the corridor from the Director's office, where he'd seen Professor Arnold the day before. He knocked on the door and heard a murmur of conversation come to a stop.

The door opened, and Lucy Arnold stood there. Malcolm remembered Hannah's word: *tragic*. That was her expression, and he knew at once that she'd heard of the discovery of Hassall's body.

"I hope I'm not late," he said.

"No. Please, do come in. We haven't started yet, but there's no one else to come. . . ."

Apart from her, there were five people sitting at the conference table in the light of two low-hanging anbaric lamps that left the corners of the room in semi-darkness. He knew two of them slightly: one was an expert on Asian politics from St. Edmund Hall, and the other was a clergyman called Charles Capes. Malcolm knew him to be a theologian, but Hannah had told him that Capes was in fact a secret friend of Oakley Street.

Malcolm took his place at the table as Lucy Arnold sat down.

"We're all here," she said. "Let's begin. For those who haven't already heard, the police found a body in the river yesterday, and it's been identified as that of Roderick Hassall."

She was speaking with a stern self-control, but Malcolm thought he could hear a tremor in her voice. One or two of the others around the table uttered a murmur of shock, or of sympathy. She went on:

"I've asked you all here because I think we need to share our knowledge about this matter and decide what to do next. I don't think you all know one another, so I'll ask you to introduce yourselves briefly. Charles, could you start?"

Charles Capes was a small, tidy man of sixty or so who wore a clerical collar. His dæmon was a lemur. "Charles Capes, Thackeray Professor of Divinity," he said. "But I'm here because I knew Roderick Hassall, and I've spent some time in the region where he was working."

The woman next to him, about Malcolm's age and very pale and anxious-looking, said, "Annabel Milner, Plant Sciences. I—I'd been working with Dr. Hassall on the rose question before he went to, umm, to Lop Nor."

Malcolm was next. "Malcolm Polstead, historian. I found some papers in a bag at a bus stop. Dr. Hassall's name and university card happened to be among them, so I brought them here. Like Professor Capes, I've worked in the same part of the world, so I was curious."

The person sitting next to him was a slim, dark-featured man in his fifties whose dæmon was a hawk. He nodded to Malcolm and said, "Timur Ghazarian. My area of interest is the history and politics of Central Asia. I had several conversations with Dr. Hassall about the region before he went there."

The next to speak was a sandy-haired man with a Scottish accent. "My name is Brewster Napier. Together with my colleague Margery Stevenson, I wrote the first paper about the rose oil effect in microscopy. In view of what's happened since, I was alarmed and profoundly interested to hear from Lucy this morning. Like Professor Ghazarian, I spoke with Dr. Hassall last time he was in Oxford. I'm shocked to hear about his death."

The final person was a man a little older than Malcolm, with thin fair hair and a long jaw. His expression was somber. "Lars

Johnsson," he said. "I was the director of the research station at Tashbulak before Ted Cartwright took over. The place where Roderick had been working."

Lucy Arnold said, "Thank you. I'll start. The police came to me this morning to ask if I could identify the body that had been found in the river. There was a name tag inside his—inside the dead man's shirt, and they connected his name with the Garden. Staff lists are easy enough to come by. I went with them, and yes, it was him, it was Roderick. I never want to have to do that again. He'd clearly been murdered. The strange thing is that the motive doesn't seem to have been robbery. Yesterday morning, Dr. Polstead"—she looked at him—"found a shopping bag in the Abingdon Road which contained Roderick's wallet and a number of other things, and he brought it to me. Frankly, the police didn't seem very interested in that. I gather they think it was just a meaningless attack. But I've asked you all here because you each have a part of the knowledge we'll need in order to, to move forward with understanding what, what's happened. And what's continuing to happen. This is . . . the thing is . . . I think we're treading on dangerous ground. I'll ask you each to speak in turn, and then we'll open it up to a more general . . . Brewster, could you tell us how it began for you?"

"By all means," he said. "A couple of years ago, a technician in my laboratory noticed that she was having trouble with a particular microscope and asked me to look at it. There was one lens which was misbehaving in an unusual way. You know when you have a smear of dirt or oil on your spectacles, one part of the visual field is blurred—but this wasn't like that. Instead, there was a colored fringe around the specimen she was looking at, quite definite in character. No blurring, no lack of clarity; everything we could see was unusually well defined, and in addition there was that colored fringe, which—well, it moved, and sparkled. We investigated, and discovered that the previous user of the microscope had been examining a specimen of a particular kind of rose from a region of Central Asia and had accidentally touched the lens, transferring a very small quantity of oil from the specimen to the glass. Not very good microscopy, to be honest, but it was interesting that it had that effect. I took the lens and put it aside, because I wanted to see exactly what was happening. On a hunch, I asked my friend Margery Stevenson to have a look at it. Margery's a particle physicist, and something she'd told me a month or two before made me think she'd be interested in this. She was investigating the Rusakov field."

Malcolm sensed a slight shiver of tension around the table, perhaps because he felt it himself. Nobody spoke or moved.

Napier continued: "For those who haven't come across it before, the Rusakov field and the particles associated with it are aspects of the phenomenon known as Dust. Which, of course, is not to be spoken about without the specific authority of the Magisterium. I'm assured by Lucy that you are all aware of the constraints this places on our activities. And our conversations."

He looked directly at Malcolm as he said this.

Malcolm nodded blandly, and Napier went on: "Briefly, Margery Stevenson and I discovered that the oil on the lens made it possible to see various effects of the Rusakov field which had previously only been described theoretically. There have been rumors for a decade or so that something like it had been seen before, but any records had been systematically destroyed by—well, we know who. The question now was whether to keep this discovery secret or make it public. It was too important to say nothing about, but perhaps too dangerous to make much of a noise. Where should we place it? The Microscopical Society of Leiden is not, frankly, a very influential body, and its *Proceedings* are seldom noticed. So we sent a paper there, and it was published a couple of years ago. At first, we heard nothing in response. But more recently both my laboratory and Margery's have been broken into, very skillfully, and we've both been questioned by people we assumed had some connection with Security or Intelligence or something. They were discreet, but quite probing, very persistent, rather alarming, in fact. We told them nothing but the truth in return. That's all I need say for the moment, I think. Except to add that Margery now works in Cambridge, and that I haven't heard from her for the past fortnight. Her colleagues can't tell me where she is, and neither can her husband. I'm extremely anxious about her."

"Thank you, Brewster," said Lucy Arnold. "That's very helpful. Clear and alarming. Dr. Polstead, could you tell us what you know?"

She looked somberly at Malcolm. He nodded.

"As Professor Arnold has told you," he began—but then there came a soft, hurried knock on the door.

Everyone looked round. Lucy Arnold stood up instinctively. Her face was pale. "Yes?" she said.

The door opened. The porter came in quickly and said, "Professor, there's some men wanting to see you. I think maybe CCD. I told 'em you was having a meeting in the Humboldt Room, but they'll be up here soon enough. They en't got a warrant—said they didn't need one."

Malcolm said at once, "Where's the Humboldt Room?"

"In the other wing," said Lucy Arnold, almost too quietly to be heard. She was trembling. No one else had moved.

Malcolm said to the porter, "Well done. Now I'd like you to guide everyone here except me, Charles, and the Director out into the garden and away through the side gate before these men realize what's happened. Can you do that?"

"Yes, sir—"

"Then everyone else please follow. Make as little noise as you can, but go quickly."

Charles Capes was watching Malcolm. The other four got up and left with the porter. Lucy Arnold, gripping the door frame, watched as they hurried away down the corridor.

"Better come back and sit down," said Malcolm, who was replacing the chairs to look as if they hadn't been moved out from the table.

"Nicely done," said Capes. "Now, what shall we be talking about when they arrive?"

"But who are they?" said the Director, sounding distressed. "Are they from the Consistorial Court of Discipline, d'you think? What can they want?"

Malcolm said, "Stay calm. Nothing you've done or we're doing is wrong or illegal or in any way the business of the CCD. We'll say that I'm here because, having brought the bag to you, I wondered if you'd had any news of Hassall. I didn't connect him with the body in the river till you told me about it, as you just have done. Charles is here because I'd been going to see him anyway about the Lop Nor region, and I told him about Hassall's bag, and he mentioned that he knew him, so we decided to come here together."

"What did you ask me about Lop Nor?" said Capes. He was perfectly calm and composed.

"Oddly enough, I asked about the sort of thing you would have told this meeting if we hadn't been interrupted. What were you going to say?"

"It was local folklore, really. The shamans know about those roses."

"Do they? What do they know?"

"They come from—the roses, I mean—from the heart of the

desert of Karamakan. So the story goes. They won't grow anywhere else. If you put a drop of the oil in your eye, you'll see visions, but you have to be determined, because it stings like hell. So I'm told."

"You haven't tried it yourself?"

"Certainly not. The thing about that desert is that you can't enter it without separating from your dæmon. It's one of those odd places—there's another in Siberia, I believe, and I think in the Atlas Mountains as well—where dæmons find it too uncomfortable, or too painful, to go. So the roses come at a considerable cost, you see. A personal cost as well as a financial one."

"I thought people died if they did that," said Lucy Arnold.

"Not always, apparently. But it's horribly painful."

"Was that what Hassall had been going to investigate?" said Malcolm, who knew full well what the answer would be, but who was interested to see whether she did. Or whether she'd admit it.

But before she could answer, there was a knock on the door. It was much louder than the porter's, and the door opened before anyone could respond.

"Professor Arnold?"

The speaker was a man in a dark overcoat and a trilby hat. Two other men stood behind him, similarly dressed.

"Yes," she said. "Who are you, and what do you want?" Her voice was perfectly steady.

"I was told you were in the Humboldt Room."

"Well, we came here instead. What do you want?"

"We want to ask you a few questions," he said, stepping further into the room. The other two men followed him.

"Wait a minute," said Malcolm. "You haven't answered Professor Arnold's question. Who are you?"

The man took out a wallet and flipped it open to show a card. It bore the letters *CCD* in bold uppercase, navy blue on ocher.

"My name's Hartland," he said. "Captain Hartland."

"Well, how can I help you?" said Lucy Arnold.

"What are you discussing in here?"

"Folklore," said Charles Capes.

"Who asked you?" said Hartland.

"I thought you did."

"I'm asking her."

"We were discussing folklore," she said flatly.

"Why?"

"Because we're scholars. I'm interested in the folklore of plants and flowers, Professor Capes is an expert on folklore, among other things, and Dr. Polstead is a historian with an interest in the same field."

"What do you know about a man called Roderick Hassall?"

She closed her eyes for a moment, then said, "He was a colleague of mine. And a friend. I had to identify his body this morning."

"Did you know him?" Hartland asked Capes.

"Yes, I did."

"You?" to Malcolm.

"No."

"Why'd you bring his stuff here, then, yesterday?"

"Because I could see that he worked here."

"Well, why not to the police?"

"Because I didn't know he was dead. How could I? I thought he'd left it there by mistake, and the simplest thing would be to bring it straight to his place of work."

"Where are those things now?"

"In London," Malcolm said.

Lucy Arnold blinked. *Keep still*, Malcolm thought. He saw one of the other two men leaning forward at the far end of the table, his hands on the edge.

"Where in London? Who's got them?" Hartland said.

"After Professor Arnold had looked at them with me, and I'd

heard for the first time that he was missing, we decided that it would be a good idea to ask an expert at the Royal Institute of Ethnology about them. There was a lot of material that had a bearing on folklore, which I know very little about, so I gave it to a friend to take it there yesterday."

"What's your friend's name? Could he confirm this?"

"He could if he was here. But he's going on to Paris."

"And this expert at the—what was it?"

"Royal Institute of Ethnology."

"What's his name?"

"Richards—Richardson—something like that. I don't know him personally."

"You're being a bit bloody careless with this stuff, aren't you? Considering there's a murder involved?"

"As I've just pointed out, we didn't know there was at that stage. Naturally we'd have taken it straight to the police if we had known. But Professor Arnold said the police weren't interested when she mentioned it to them."

"Why are *you* interested?" asked Charles Capes.

"It's my job to be interested in all sorts of things," said Hartland. "What was Hassall doing in Central Asia?"

"Botanical research," said Lucy Arnold.

There was a hesitant knock at the door, and the porter looked in. "Sorry, Professor," he said. "I thought you was in the Humboldt Room. I've been looking all over. These gentlemen found you, then."

"Yes, thank you, John," she said. "They've just finished. Could you show them out?"

With a speculative look at Malcolm, Hartland nodded slowly and turned to go. The other two followed him out, leaving the door open.

Malcolm put his finger to his lips: *Hush*. Then he waited for a count of ten, closed the door, and moved silently to the end of the table, where the man had been leaning. He beckoned the other two to come and look. Crouching down, he looked under the edge and pointed to a dull black object about the size of the top joint of his thumb, which seemed to be stuck to the underside.

Lucy Arnold caught her breath, and again Malcolm put his finger to his lips. He touched the black thing with the point of a pencil, and it scuttled away to the corner by the leg of the table. Malcolm shook his handkerchief open and held it underneath before flicking the creature off with the pencil. He caught it and wrapped up the handkerchief tightly, with the thing buzzing inside it.

"What's that?" whispered Lucy.

Malcolm held it on the table, eased off his shoe, and hit the creature hard with the heel. "It's a spy fly," he said quietly. "They've bred them smaller and smaller, with better memories. It would have listened to what we said next, and flown back to them and repeated it exactly."

"Smallest I've seen," said Charles Capes.

Malcolm checked that it was dead and dropped it out of the window. "I thought it might be an idea to leave it there and let them waste time listening to it," he said. "But then you'd always have to be careful what people said in here, and that would be a nuisance. Besides, it could move about, so you'd never be sure where it was. Better to let them think it just failed."

"It's the first I've heard of a Royal Institute of Ethnology," said Capes. "And what about those papers? Where are they really?"

"In my office," Lucy Arnold said. "There are some samples too—seeds, that sort of thing. . . ."

"Well, they can't stay there," said Malcolm. "When those men come back, they'll have a search warrant. Shall I take the papers away?"

"Why not let me?" said Capes. "I'm curious to read them, apart from anything else. And there are plenty of places to hide things in our cellars at Wykeham."

"All right," she said. "Yes. Thank you. I don't know what to do."

"If you don't mind," said Malcolm, "I'd like to take the book of Tajik poetry. There's something I want to check. You know *Jahan and Rukhsana?*" he added to Capes.

"He was carrying a copy of that, was he? How odd."

"Yes, and I want to find out why. As for the CCD, when they discover there's no Ethnology Institute, they'll come straight back to me," said Malcolm. "But I'll have thought of something else by then. Let's go and get those things right now."

Lyra walked along the river during the afternoon, with Pan in sullen attendance. From time to time he seemed to want to say something, but she was deep in a mood of wintry isolation, so in the end he slouched as far behind her as he could get without arousing suspicion and said nothing.

As the late-afternoon light thickened into gloom under the trees, and a mist that was almost a drizzle began to fill the air, she found herself hoping that Malcolm would be there when she got back to the Trout. She wanted to ask him about—oh, she couldn't remember; it would come to her. And she wanted to watch Pauline with him, to see whether Pan's crazy idea could be true.

But Malcolm didn't come, and she didn't want to ask where he was, in case—in case, she didn't know what; so it was in a state of frustrated melancholy that she went to bed, and there wasn't even anything she wanted to read. She took up *The Hyperchorasmians* and opened it at random, but the heroic intensity that had once intoxicated her now seemed out of reach.

And Pan wouldn't settle. He prowled about the little room, leaping up to the windowsill, listening at the door, exploring the wardrobe, until finally she said, "Oh for God's sake, just go to bloody sleep."

"Not sleepy," he said. "Neither are you."

"Can't you stop fidgeting?"

"Lyra, why are you so difficult to talk to?"

"*Me?*"

"I need to tell you something, but you make it difficult."

"I'm listening."

"No, you're not. Not properly."

"I don't know what I've got to do to listen *properly*. Am I supposed to use the imagination that I haven't got?"

"I didn't mean that. Anyway—"

"Of course you meant it. You said it clearly enough."

"Well, I've thought more since then. When I went out last night—"

"I don't want to hear about it. I knew you were out, and I know you were talking to someone, and I'm just not interested."

"Lyra, it's important. Please listen."

He sprang onto the bedside table. She said nothing, but subsided onto the pillow and looked up at the ceiling.

Finally she said, "Well?"

"I can't talk to you if you're in this mood."

"Oh, this is impossible."

"I'm trying to work out the best way to—"

"Just *say* it."

Silence.

He sighed, and then he said, "You know in the rucksack, all those things we found in there . . ."

"Well?"

"One of them was a notebook with names and addresses in it."

"What about it?"

"You didn't see the name I saw in it."

"Whose name?"

"Sebastian Makepeace."

She sat up. "Where was it?"

"In the notebook, like I said. The only name and address in Oxford."

"When did you see that?"

"When you were flicking through it."

"Why didn't you tell me?"

"I thought you were bound to see it yourself. Anyway, you're not easy to tell anything these days."

"Oh, don't be so stupid. You could have told me that. Where is it now? Has Malcolm got it?"

"No. I hid it."

"Why? Where is it now?"

"Because I wanted to find out why he was in it. Mr. Makepeace. And last night I went out and took it to him."

Lyra almost choked with rage. For a moment she couldn't breathe. She found her entire body trembling. Pan saw it clearly and leapt off the bedside table and onto the armchair.

"Lyra, if you don't listen, I can't tell you what he said—"

"You filthy little rat," she said. She was almost sobbing, and she couldn't recognize her own voice or stop herself saying detestable things, or even know why she was saying them. "You cheat, you thief, you let me down the other night when you let her—his dæmon, the cat—you let her see you with the wallet, and now you do this, you go behind my back—"

"Because you wouldn't listen! You're not listening now!"

"No. Because I can't trust you anymore. You're a fucking stranger to me, Pan. I can't tell you how much I *detest* it when you do this sort of thing—"

"If I hadn't asked him, I'd never—"

"And I used to—oh, how much I used to trust you—you were everything, you were like a rock, I could have . . . *betraying* me like that—"

"*Betray!* Listen to yourself! You think I'll ever forget you betraying *me* in the world of the dead?"

Lyra felt as if someone had kicked her in the heart. She fell back on the bed. "Don't," she whispered.

"It was the worst thing you ever did."

She knew exactly what he meant, and her mind had flown back at once to the bank of the river in the world of the dead, and that terrible moment when she left him behind in order to go and find the ghost of her friend Roger.

"I know," she said. She could hardly hear her own voice through the hammering of her heart. "I know it was. And you know why I did it."

"You *knew* you were going to do it, and you didn't tell me."

"I didn't know! How could I have known? We only heard you couldn't come with us at the last minute. We were together, we'd always be together, that's what I thought, what I wanted, always together forever. But then the old man told us that you couldn't go any further—and Will didn't even know he had a dæmon, he had to do the same thing, leave part of himself behind—oh, Pan, you can't think I *planned* it like that? You can't think I'm that cruel?"

"Then why haven't you ever asked me about it? About what it felt like for me?"

"But we *have* talked about it."

"Only because I brought it up. You never wanted to know."

"Pan, that isn't fair—"

"You just didn't want to face it."

"I was ashamed. I *had* to do it and I was bitterly ashamed to do it and I'd have been ashamed *not* to do it and I've felt guilty ever since, and if you haven't been aware of that—"

"When the old man rowed you out into the dark, I felt torn open," he said. His voice was shaking. "It nearly killed me. But the worst thing, worse than the pain, was the *abandonment*. That you should just leave me there alone. D'you realize how I gazed and stared and called out to you and tried so hard to keep you in sight as you moved off into the dark? The last thing I could see was your hair, the very last thing I could see till the dark swallowed it up. I'd have been willing just to have that, just a little gleam of your hair, just the faintest patch of light that was you, as long as it stayed there so I could see it. I'd have been waiting there still. Just to know you were there, and I could see you. I'd never have moved away as long as I could see that. . . ."

He stopped. She was sobbing. "You think I . . . ," she tried to say, but her voice wouldn't let her. "Roger," she managed, but that was all. The sobbing overtook her completely.

Pan sat on the table and watched her for a few moments, and then with a convulsive movement he twisted away, as if he were weeping too; but neither of them said a word, or made any attempt to reach for the other.

She lay curled in a ball, her head in her arms, weeping till the passion subsided.

When she could sit up, she wiped the tears from her cheeks and saw him lying tense and trembling with his back to her. "Pan," she said, her voice thick with weeping, "Pan, I do realize, and I hated myself then and I'll always hate myself for as long as I live. I hate every part of me that isn't you, and I'll have to live with that. Sometimes I think if I could kill myself without killing you, I might do it, I'm so unhappy. I don't deserve to be happy, I know that. I know the—the world of the dead—I know what I did was horrible, and to leave Roger there would have been wrong too, and I . . . It was the worst thing ever. You're completely right, and I'm sorry, I really am, with all my heart."

He didn't move. In the silence of the night, she could hear him weeping too.

Then he said, "It's not just what you did then. It's what you're doing now. I told you this the other day: you're killing yourself, and me, with the way you're thinking. You're in a world full of color and you want to see it in black and white. As if Gottfried Brande was some kind of enchanter who made you forget everything you used to love, everything mysterious, all the places where the shadows are. Can't you see the *emptiness* of the worlds they describe, him and Talbot? You don't really think the universe is as arid as that. You *can't*. You're under a spell—you must be."

"Pan, there aren't any spells," she said, but so quietly that she hoped he wouldn't hear it.

"And no world of the dead, I suppose," he said. "It was all just a childish dream. The other worlds. The subtle knife. The witches. There's no room for them in the universe you want to believe in. How do you think the alethiometer works? I suppose the symbols have got so many meanings, you can read anything you want into them, so they don't mean anything at all, really. As for me, I'm just a trick of the mind. The wind whistling through an empty skull. Lyra, I really think I've had enough."

"What do you mean?"

"And stop breathing on me. You stink of garlic."

She turned away in humiliation and misery. Each of them lay weeping in the darkness.

When she woke up in the morning, he wasn't there.

ELEVEN

THE KNOT

Fog and cobwebs. Her mind was full of them, and so was the room, so was the dream she'd woken from.

"Pan," she said, and hardly recognized her own voice. "Pan!"

No reply. No scuttle of claws on the floorboards, no featherlight leap onto the bed.

"Pan! What are you doing? Where are you?"

She ran to the window, flung back the curtain, saw the ruins of the priory in the pearly glimmer of dawn. The wide world was out there still, no fog, no cobwebs, and no Pan.

In here? Was he under the bed, in a cupboard, on top of the wardrobe? Of course not. This wasn't a game.

Then she saw her rucksack on the floor beside the bed. She hadn't left it there; and on top of it there was the little black notebook of Hassall's that Pan had spoken about.

She picked it up. It was worn and stained and many of the pages had corners that had been folded back. She flicked through it, seeing now, as he had, how the addresses seemed to trace the course of a journey from a mysterious Khwarezm to a house in the Lawnmarket, Edinburgh. And there was Sebastian Makepeace, in Juxon Street, Oxford, just as he'd said. Why hadn't the name caught her eye? Why hadn't she noticed what Pan was doing when he hid it? How many thousands of other things had she failed to see?

And then a note fell out. She snatched up the scrap of paper with shaking hands.

Pan's claws weren't formed to hold a pencil, but he could write in a fashion by holding one in his mouth.

It said:

GONE TO LOOK FOR YOUR IMAGINATION

That was all. She sat down, feeling weightless, transparent, disembodied.

"How could you be so . . . ," she whispered, not knowing how to finish the question. "How can I live like . . ."

Her alarm clock showed the time to be half past six. The pub was quiet: Mr. and Mrs. Polstead would be getting up soon to make breakfast, to light fires, to do whatever else had to be done every morning. How could she tell them this? And Malcolm wasn't there. She could have told him. When would he come? Surely he'd come soon. There was work to be done. He must come.

But then she thought: How *can* I tell them? How can I show myself to them like this? It would be shameful. It would be worse than mortifying. These people whom she hardly knew, who'd taken her in, whom she was growing to like so much—how could she inflict a monstrosity like herself now, a half person, on them? On Pauline? On Alice? On Malcolm? Only Malcolm would understand, and even he might find her loathsome now. And she stank of garlic.

She would have wept if she hadn't been paralyzed with fear.

Hide, she thought. *Run and hide.* Her mind flew here and there, into the past, into the future and back quickly, into the past again, and found a face she remembered and loved, and trusted: Farder Coram.

He was old now, and he never moved from the Fens, but he was still alive and alert. They wrote to each other from time to time. And above all, he'd understand her predicament now. But how could she get to him? Her memory, rushing from image to image like a bird trapped inside a room, fluttered against something from the White Horse a night or two before. Dick Orchard, and the gyptian knotted handkerchief around his neck. He'd said something about his grandfather—Giorgio something—he was in Oxford now, wasn't that it? And Dick was working the night shift at the mail depot, so he'd be at home during the day. . . .

Yes.

She dressed quickly in her warmest clothes, flung some others into the rucksack, together with the black notebook and a few other things, looked around the little room she'd come to feel so much at home in, and went downstairs in silence.

In the kitchen she found some paper and a pencil and left a note: *Sorry—so sorry—and thank you so much—but I've got to go. Can't explain. Lyra.*

Two minutes later she was walking along the riverbank again, and looking only at the path ahead of her, with the hood of her parka pulled up over her head. If she saw anyone, she'd have to take no notice. People often carried their dæmons, if they were small enough, in a pocket or buttoned inside their coats. She might be doing that. There was no need for anyone to suspect her if she walked on quickly, and it was still early.

But the journey to Botley, where Dick lived with his family, still took most of an hour, even walking fast, and she heard the bells of the city across the expanse of Port Meadow, striking unhelpfully—what? Half past seven? Half past eight? Surely not yet. She wondered what time his night shift finished. If he started work at ten, then he should be coming out sometime soon.

She slowed down as she came to Binsey Lane. It was going to be a rare clear day; the sun was bright now and the air was fresh. Binsey Lane led down from the meadow into the Botley Road, the main route into Oxford from the west. And people would be getting up now, and going to work. She hoped they'd be too busy to look at her, and had their own worries and preoccupations; she hoped that she looked uninteresting, as Will made himself look, as the witches did when they made themselves invisible, so that no one would give them more than a glance, and then forget them at once. She might be a witch herself, with her dæmon hundreds of miles away on the tundra.

That thought sustained her until she reached the Botley Road, where she had to look up to check the traffic before she could cross, and to look for the right little street going off the other side. She'd been to the Orchards' house three or four times: she remembered the front door, even if she'd forgotten the number.

She knocked. Dick should be home by now . . . surely? But what if he wasn't, and she had to explain herself to his mother or his father, who were nice enough, but . . . She almost turned and walked away, but then the door opened, and it was Dick.

"Lyra! What you doing here? You all right?" He looked tired, as if he'd just come home from work.

"Dick, are you on your own? Is there anyone else in?"

"What's the matter? What's happened? There's only me and my gran. Come in. Hang on. . . ." His vixen dæmon was backing away behind his legs and uttering a little cry. He picked her up, and then he saw what the matter was. "Where's Pan? Lyra, what's going on?"

"I'm in trouble," she said, and she couldn't hold her voice steady. "Please, can I come in?"

"Yeah, sure, course you can. . . ."

He moved back to make room in the little hall, and she stepped inside quickly and shut the door behind her. She could see all kinds of consternation and anxiety in his eyes, but he hadn't flinched for a moment.

"He's gone, Dick. He's just left me," she said.

He put a finger to his lips and looked upstairs. "Come in the kitchen," he said quietly. "Gran's awake, and she's easily frightened. She can't make sense of things."

He looked at her again, as if he were unsure who she was, and then led the way along the narrow corridor to the kitchen, which was warm and rich with the smell of fried bacon.

She said, "I'm sorry, Dick. I need some help, and I thought—"

"Sit down. You want some coffee?"

"Yes. Thanks."

He filled a kettle and set it on the range. Lyra sat in the wooden armchair on one side of the fire, holding her rucksack tight against her chest. Dick sat in the other. His dæmon, Bindi, leapt up to his lap and sat close, trembling.

"I'm sorry, Bindi," Lyra said. "I'm sorry. I don't know why he went. Or, I mean, I do, but it's hard to explain. We—"

"We always wondered if you could do this," said Dick.

"What do you mean?"

"Separate. We never seen you do it, but it just felt like if anyone could do it, you could. When did he go?"

"In the night."

"No message or nothing?"

"Not exactly . . . We'd been arguing. . . . It was difficult."

"You didn't want to wait in case he came back?"

"He won't come back for a long time. Maybe never."

"You don't know."

"I think I've got to go and look for him, Dick."

A thin cry came from upstairs. Dick looked at the door. "Better go and see what she wants," he said. "Won't be a minute."

Bindi was out of the door before he was. Lyra sat still and closed her eyes, trying to breathe calmly. When he came back, the kettle was boiling. A spoonful of coffee essence in each mug, a splash of milk, the offer of sugar, and he poured some water into two mugs and handed one to Lyra.

"Thanks. Is your gran all right?" she said.

"Just old and confused. She can't sleep easy, so there's got to be someone here with her in case she gets up and does herself some damage."

"You know the grandfather you mentioned the other night at the White Horse . . . is she his wife?"

"No. This one's Dad's mother. The gyptians are on Mum's side of the family."

"And you said he was in Oxford now?"

"Yeah, he is. He had a delivery to the Castle Mill boatyard, but he's off soon. Why?"

"Could he . . . D'you think I could meet him?"

"Yeah, if you want to. I'll go there with you when Mum gets back."

His mother worked as a cleaner in Worcester College, Lyra remembered. "When would that be?" she said.

"About eleven. But she might be a bit later. Do a bit of shopping or something. Why d'you want to meet my grandad?"

"I need to go to the Fens. There's someone I have to see there. I need to ask the best way of getting there without being seen or caught or . . . I just want to ask his advice."

He nodded. He didn't look very gyptian himself at the moment; his hair was disheveled, his eyes red-rimmed with tiredness. He sipped his coffee.

"I don't want to get you into trouble either," she added.

"Is this something to do with what you told me the other night? Someone being killed near the river?"

"Probably. But I can't see the connection yet."

"Benny Morris is still away from work, by the way."

"Oh, the man with the wounded leg. You haven't told anyone about what I said?"

"Yeah, I put a great big notice up on the bloody canteen wall. What d'you take me for? I wouldn't give you away, gal."

"No. I know that."

"But this is serious stuff, right?"

"Yes. It is."

"Anyone else know about it?"

"Yeah. A man called Dr. Polstead. Malcolm Polstead. He's a Scholar at Durham College, and he used to teach me a long time ago. But he knows about it all because . . . Oh, it's complicated, Dick. But I trust him. He knows things that no one else . . . I can't tell him about Pan leaving, though. I just can't. Pan and me, we'd been quarreling. It was horrible. We just couldn't agree about important things. It was like being split in half. . . . And then this murder happened, and suddenly I was in danger. I think someone knows I saw it. I stayed at Dr. Polstead's parents' pub for a couple of nights, but—"

"Which pub's that?"

"The Trout at Godstow."

"Do they know Pan's . . . disappeared?"

"No. I left before anyone got up this morning. I really need to get to the Fens, Dick. Can I see your grandad? Please?"

There was another cry from upstairs, and a thump, as if something heavy had fallen on the floor. Dick shook his head and hurried out.

Lyra was too restless to sit still. She got up and looked out of the kitchen window at the neat little yard with its cobblestones and bed of herbs, and at the calendar on the kitchen wall with a picture of Buckingham Palace and the changing of the guard, and at the frying pan on the draining board with the bacon fat already beginning to congeal. She felt like crying, but took three deep breaths and blinked hard.

The door opened, and Dick came back. "She's woken up proper now, dammit," he said. "I'll have to take her some porridge. Sure you can't stay here for a while? They'll never know."

"No. I've really got to keep moving."

"Well, take this, then." He held out his blue-and-white-spotted neckerchief, or one very similar, tied in a complicated knot.

"Thanks. But why?"

"The knot. It's a gyptian thing. It means you're asking for help. Show it to my grandad. His boat's called the *Maid of Portugal*. He's a big tough man, good-looking, like me. You won't miss him. He's called Giorgio Brabandt."

"All right. And thanks, Dick. I hope your gran gets better."

"There's only one way that'll end. Poor old girl."

Lyra kissed him. She felt very fond of him. "See you . . . when I get back," she said.

"How long you going to stay in the Fens?"

"As long as I need to, I hope."

"And what was that name again? Doctor something."

"Malcolm Polstead."

"Oh, yeah." He came to the door with her. "If you go up Binsey Lane, past the last house, there's a path through some trees on the right that takes you to the river. Cross the old wooden bridge and keep going a little way and you come to the canal. Go left up the towpath and that'll get you to Castle Mill. Good luck. Just keep bundled up, then maybe they'll think he's . . . you know."

He gave her a kiss and embraced her briefly before seeing her out of the door. Lyra saw the compassion in Bindi's eyes and wished that she could stroke the pretty little vixen, just for the sake of touching a dæmon again, but that was impossible.

Lyra could hear the old woman calling in a quavering voice from upstairs. Dick shut the door, and Lyra was out in the open again.

Back up to the Botley Road, still busy with traffic, and then Lyra went across and set off for the river. She kept her hood up and her head down, and before long she came to the path through the trees and the old wooden bridge that Dick had mentioned. To left and right the slow river extended, upstream through Port Meadow and downstream towards the Oxpens and the murder spot. There was no one in sight. Lyra crossed the bridge and continued on the muddy path between water meadows, and came to the canal, where a line of boats was moored, some with smoke coming out of their tin chimneys, one with a dog that barked furiously until she came closer, when it must have sensed something wrong: it turned and skulked down to the other end of the boat, whining.

A little further along, Lyra saw a woman pegging out some washing on a line strung the length of her boat, and she said, "Good morning, lady. I'm looking for Giorgio Brabandt, of the *Maid of Portugal*. D'you know where he might have moored?"

The woman turned to her, half-suspicious of any stranger and half-mollified by Lyra's correct use of the term of respect for a gyptian stranger.

"He's further up," she said. "At the boatyard. But he's moving on today. You might have missed him."

"Thanks," said Lyra, and walked on fast before the woman noticed anything wrong.

The boatyard extended along an open space on the other side of the canal, under the campanile of the Oratory of St. Barnabas. It was a busy place; there was a chandlery, where Malcolm had gone twenty years before to look for some red paint; there were workshops of different kinds, a dry dock, a forge, and various pieces of heavy machinery. Gyptians and landlopers were working side by side, repairing a hull or repainting a roof or fitting a tiller, and the longest of the boats tied up, and by some way the most richly decorated, was the *Maid of Portugal*.

Lyra crossed the little iron bridge and walked along the quay till she came to the boat. A large man with sleeves rolled up over his tattooed arms was kneeling in his cockpit, reaching down into the engine with a spanner. He didn't look up when Lyra stopped beside the boat, but his black-and-silver keeshond dæmon, ruffed like a lion, stood up and growled.

Lyra approached the boat, steady, quiet, watchful.

"Good morning, Master Brabandt," she said.

The man looked up, and Lyra saw Dick's features—larger, older, coarser, and stronger, but unmistakably Dick. He said nothing, but scowled and narrowed his eyes.

Lyra took the neckerchief out of her pocket and held it carefully in both hands, opening them to display the knot.

He looked at it, and his expression changed from suspicious to angry. A dull red suffused his face. "Where'd you get that?" he said.

"Your grandson Dick gave it to me about half an hour ago. I went to see him because I'm in trouble and I need help."

"Put it away and come aboard. Don't look around. Just step over the side and go below."

He wiped his hands on an oily rag. When she was inside the saloon, he came through to join her and shut the door behind him.

"How'd you know Dick?" he said.

"We're just friends."

"And did *he* put this trouble in your belly?"

For a moment Lyra didn't know what he meant. Then she

blushed. "No! It's not that kind of trouble. I take better care of myself than that. It's that . . . my dæmon . . ."

She couldn't finish the sentence. She felt horribly vulnerable, as if her affliction had suddenly become gross and visible. She shrugged and opened her parka and spread out her hands. Brabandt looked at her from head to foot, and his face lost all its color. He took a step backwards and clutched the door frame.

"You en't a witch?" he said.

"No. Just human, that's all."

"Dear God, then what's happened to you?" he said.

"My dæmon's lost. I think he's left me."

"And what d'you think I can do about it?"

"I don't know, Master Brabandt. But what I want to do is get to the Fens without being caught and see an old friend of mine. He's called Coram van Texel."

"Farder Coram! And he's a friend o' yourn?"

"I went to the Arctic with him and Lord Faa about ten years ago. Farder Coram was with me when we met Iorek Byrnison, the king of the bears."

"And what's your name?"

"Lyra Silvertongue. That's the name the bear gave me. I was called Lyra Belacqua till then."

"Well, why didn't you say so?"

"I just did."

For a moment she thought he was going to slap her for being insolent, but then his expression cleared as the blood came back to his cheeks. Brabandt was a good-looking man, just as his grandson had said, but he was perturbed now, and even a little frightened.

"This trouble o' yours," he said. "When did it come on you?"

"Just this morning. He was with me last night. But we had a terrible quarrel, and when I woke up, he was gone. I didn't know what to do. Then I remembered the gyptians, and the Fens, and Farder Coram, and I thought he wouldn't judge me badly, he'd understand, and he might be able to help me."

"We still talk about that voyage to the north," he said. "Lord Faa's dead and gone now, but that was a great campaign, no doubt about it. Farder Coram dun't move much from his boat these days, but he's bright and cheerful enough."

"I'm glad of that. I might be bringing him trouble, though."

"He won't worry about that. But you weren't going to travel like this, were you? How d'you expect to go anywhere without a dæmon?"

"I know. It'll be difficult. I can't stay where I am, where I was staying, because . . . I'll bring trouble on them. There's too many people coming and going there all the time. I couldn't hide for long, and it wouldn't be fair to them, because I think I'm in danger from the CCD as well. It was just luck I heard from Dick that you were in Oxford, and I thought maybe . . . I don't know. I just don't know where else to go."

"No, I can see that. Well . . ."

He looked out through the window at the busy waterfront, and then down at his big keeshond dæmon, who returned his gaze calmly.

"Well," Brabandt said, "John Faa come back from that voyage with some gyptian children what we'd never've seen again else. We owe you that. And our people made some good friends among the witches, and that was something new. And I got no work on for a couple of weeks. Trade en't good at the moment. You bin on a gyptian boat before? You must've bin."

"I sailed to the Fens with Ma Costa and her family."

"Ma Costa, eh? Well, she wouldn't stand no nonsense. Can you cook and keep a place clean?"

"Yes."

"Then welcome aboard, Lyra. I'm on me own at the moment, since me last girlfriend took a run ashore and never come back. Don't worry—I en't looking for a replacement, and in any case, you're too young for me. I like my women with a bit o' mileage on 'em. But if you cook and clean and do my washing, and keep out o' sight of any landlopers, I'll help you in your trouble and take you to the Fens. How's that?"

He held out his oily hand, and she shook it without hesitation.

"It's a bargain," she said.

At the very moment when Lyra was shaking the hand of Giorgio Brabandt, Marcel Delamare was in his office at *La Maison Juste*, touching a little bottle with the point of a pencil, pushing it sideways, turning it around. The weather was clear, and the sunlight fell across his mahogany desk and sparkled on the little bottle, which was no longer than his little finger, capped with a cork, and sealed with a reddish wax that had dripped halfway down the side.

He picked it up and held it to the light. His visitor waited quietly: a man of Tartar appearance but in shabby European clothes, his face gaunt and sunburned.

"And this is it, the famous oil?" said Delamare.

"So I was told, sir. All I can do is tell you what the merchant said to me."

"Did he approach you? How did he know you were interested?"

"I had gone to Akchi to look for it. I asked among the merchants, the camel dealers, the traders. Finally a man came to my table and—"

"Your table?"

"Trade is done in the teahouses. One takes a table and makes it known that one is ready to trade silk, opium, tea, whatever one

188

has. I had assumed the character of a medical man. Several dealers came to me with this herb, that extract, oil of this, fruit of that, seeds of the other. Some I bought, to maintain my character. I have all the receipts."

"How do you know this is what you wanted? It could be anything."

"With respect, Monsieur Delamare, it is the rose oil from Karamakan. I am happy to wait for my payment until you have tested it."

"Oh, we shall, we shall certainly test it. But what was it that convinced you?"

The visitor sat back in his chair with an air of weary but well-guarded patience. His dæmon, a serpent of a sandy-gray color with a pattern of red diamonds along her sides, flowed over his hands, in and out, through and through his fingers. Delamare caught an air of agitation, strongly subdued.

"I tested it myself," said the visitor. "As the dealer instructed, I put the smallest possible drop on the end of my little finger and touched it to my eyeball. The pain was instant and shocking, which was the reason the dealer had insisted we leave the teahouse and go to the hotel where I was staying. I had to cry out with the shock and the pain. I wanted to wash my eye clear at once, but the dealer advised me to remain still and leave it alone. Washing would only spread the pain further. This is what the shamans do, those who use the oil, apparently. After I suppose ten or fifteen minutes, the worst of it began to subside. And then I began to see the effects described in the poem of *Jahan and Rukhsana*."

Delamare had been writing down the visitor's words as he spoke. Now he stopped and held up his hand. "What poem is this?"

"The poem called *Jahan and Rukhsana*. It relates the adventure of two lovers who seek a garden where roses grow. When the two lovers enter the rose garden after all their trials, guided by the king of the birds, they are blessed with a number of visions that unfold like the petals of a rose and reveal truth after truth. For nearly a thousand years, this poem has been revered in those regions of Central Asia."

"Is there a translation into any of the European languages?"

"I believe there is one in French, but it is not thought to be very accurate."

Delamare made a note. "And what did you see under the influence of this oil?" he said.

"I saw the appearance of a nimbus or halo around the dealer, consisting of sparkling granules of light, each smaller than a grain of flour. And between him and his dæmon, who was a sparrow, there was a constant stream of such grains of light, back and forth, in both directions. As I watched, I became convinced that I was seeing something profound and true, which I would never afterwards be able to deny. Little by little that vision faded, and I was sure the rose oil was genuine, so I paid the dealer and made my way here. I have his bill of sale—"

"Leave it on the desk. Have you spoken to anyone else about this?"

"No, monsieur."

"Just as well for you. The town where you bought the oil—show it to me on this map."

Delamare stood to fetch a folded map from the table and spread it open in front of the traveler. It showed a region about four hundred kilometers square, with mountains to the south and north.

The visitor put on a pair of ancient wire-rimmed spectacles before staring at the map. He touched it at a point near the western edge. Delamare looked, and then turned his attention to the eastern side, scanning up and down.

"The desert of Karamakan is just a little further to the southeast than this map shows," said the traveler.

"How far from the town you mentioned, from Akchi?"

"Five hundred kilometers, more or less."

"So the rose oil is traded that far west."

"I had made it known what I wanted, and I was prepared to wait," said the traveler, taking off his glasses. "The dealer had come to find me especially. He could have sold it at once to the medical company, but he was an honest man."

"Medical company? Which one?"

"There are three or four of them. Western companies. They are prepared to pay a great deal, but I managed to acquire this sample. The bill of sale—"

"You shall have your money. A few more questions first. Who sealed this bottle with wax?"

"I did."

"And it has been in your possession all the way?"

"Every step."

"And does it have a lifetime, so to speak, this oil? Does its virtue fade?"

"I don't know."

"Who buys it? Who are the customers of this dealer?"

"He doesn't only sell oil, monsieur. Other products also. But ordinary ones, you understand, herbs for healing, spices for cooking, that sort of thing. Anyone would buy those. The special oil is used mainly by shamans, I believe, but there is a scientific establishment at Tashbulak, which is"—glasses on, he peered at the map again—"like the desert, just off this map. He has sold oil to the scientists there a small number of times. They were very keen to obtain it, and they paid promptly, though they did not pay as much as the medical companies. I should say there *was* such a place, until recently."

Delamare sat up but not sharply. "There was?" he said. "Go on."

"It was the dealer who alerted me to this. He told me that when he last traveled to the research station, he found the people there in a state of great fear because they had been threatened with destruction if they did not stop their researches. They were packing up, making preparations to leave. But between leaving Akchi and arriving here, I have heard that the establishment has been destroyed. All those who were still there, whether scientific staff or local workers, have either fled or been put to death."

"When did you hear this?"

"Not long ago. But news travels quickly along the road."

"And who was it who destroyed the place?"

"Men from the mountains. That is all I know."

"Which mountains?"

"There are mountains to the north, to the west, and to the south. To the east, only desert, the worst in the world. The mountain passes are safe, or used to be, because the roads are well trod. Maybe not so anymore. All mountains are dangerous. Who knows what sort of men live there? The mountains are the dwelling place of spirits, of monsters. Any human beings who live among them will be fierce and cruel. Then there are the birds, the *oghâb-gorgs*. There are stories told about these birds that would terrify any traveler."

"I am interested in the men. What do people say about them? Are they organized? Have they a leader? Do we know why they destroyed the station at Tashbulak?"

"I understand it was because they believed the work there was blasphemous."

"Then what is their religion? What counts as blasphemy for them?"

The merchant shook his head and spread his hands.

192

Delamare slowly nodded and tapped his pencil on a small pile of folded and stained papers. "These are the expenses you incurred?" he said.

"They are. And of course the invoice for the oil. I would be grateful—"

"You shall be paid tomorrow. Are you staying at the Hotel Rembrandt, as I recommended?"

"I am."

"Stay there. A messenger will bring you your money before very long. I would remind you of the contract we signed so many months ago."

"Ah," said the traveler.

"Yes, ah, indeed. If I learn that you've been talking about this business, I shall invoke the confidentiality clause and pursue you through every court till I have recovered all the money you're being paid and a great deal more besides."

"I remember that clause."

"Then we need say no more. Good morning to you."

The visitor bowed and left. Delamare put the bottle of oil into a desk drawer and locked it, then turned over in his mind the news the merchant had told him. But there was something about the way the man had looked at him while talking about it, something surprised, maybe skeptical, maybe doubtful. It had been hard to read. In fact, Delamare knew quite a lot already about these men from the mountains, and his purpose in asking about them was to find out how much was known by others.

No matter. He wrote a swift note to the Rector of the College of Theophysical Research, and then brought his attention back to the project that was occupying most of his time: a forthcoming congress of the entire Magisterium, of a kind that had never happened before. The oil, and what had happened at Tashbulak, would be at the center of their deliberations, though very few delegates would know that.

Malcolm was detained most of that day by college business, but as the afternoon clouded over, he locked his door and set off for Godstow. He was keen to tell Lyra about the meeting at the Botanic Garden and everything he'd learnt from it, and not just to warn her: he wanted to see her expression as she absorbed all the implications of what had happened. Her emotions came and went so vividly that it seemed to him that she was more in tune with the world than anyone else he'd known. He didn't know quite what he meant by that, and he wouldn't have said it to anyone, least of all her; but it was enchanting to see.

The temperature was falling, and there even seemed like a hint of snow in the air. When he opened the kitchen door at the Trout and went in, the familiar warmth and steam enveloped him like a welcome. But his mother's face, as she looked up from the pastry she was rolling, was tense and anxious.

"You seen her?" she said at once.

"Seen Lyra? What d'you mean?"

She nodded towards the note Lyra had left, which was still in the middle of the table. He snatched it up and read it quickly, then again slowly.

"Nothing else?" he said.

"She left some of her things upstairs. Looks like she took what she could carry. She must've gone out early, before anyone else got up."

"Did she say anything yesterday?"

"She just looked preoccupied. Unhappy, your dad thinks. But she was trying to be cheerful, you could see that. She didn't say anything much, though, and she went to bed early."

"When did she go?"

"She left before we got up. That note was on the table. I thought she might have come to you at Durham, or Alice, maybe. . . ."

Malcolm ran upstairs and into the bedroom Lyra had been using. Her books, or some of them, were still on the little table; the bed was made; there were a few items of clothing in one of the drawers. Nothing else.

"*Fuck,*" he said.

"I wonder . . . ," said Asta from the windowsill.

"What?"

"I just wonder if she and Pantalaimon both went. Or if she thought he'd gone and went after him. We know they weren't . . . they didn't . . . they weren't very happy together."

"But where would he have gone?"

"Just to go out on his own. We know he used to do that. That's when I saw him first."

"But . . ." He was baffled and angry, and far more upset than he could remember being for a long time.

"Though she'd always know that he'd come back," Asta said. "Perhaps this time he just didn't."

"Alice," he said at once. "We'll go there now."

Alice was drinking a glass of wine in the Steward's parlor after dinner.

"Good evening, Dr. Polstead," said the Steward, rising to his feet. "Will you take a glass of port with us?"

"Another time with pleasure, Mr. Cawson," Malcolm said, "but this is rather urgent. May I have a quick word with Mrs. Lonsdale?"

Alice, seeing his expression, stood up at once. They went out into the quad and spoke quietly under the light by the Hall steps.

"What's the matter?" she said.

He explained briefly and showed her the note.

"What'd she take with her?"

"A rucksack, some clothes . . . Not a clue otherwise. Had she come to see you in the last day or so?"

"No. I wish she had. I'd have made her tell me the truth about her and that dæmon."

"Yes . . . I saw there was something wrong, but it wasn't something I could bring up in conversation, with urgent things to talk about. You knew they weren't happy, then?"

"Not happy? They couldn't stand each other, and it was awful to see. How'd she get on at the Trout?"

"They saw the state of mind she was in, but she didn't say anything about it. Alice, you did know she and Pantalaimon could separate?"

Alice's dæmon, Ben, growled and pressed himself against her legs.

"She never spoke about it," said Alice. "But I thought there was something different about them after they come back from the north. She was like someone haunted, I used to think. Shadowed, kind of thing. Why?"

"Just a feeling that Pan might have left, and she went off to try and find him."

"She must've thought he'd gone a long way. If he was just out for a scamper in the woods, he'd have been back before morning."

"That's what I thought. But if you hear from her, or hear anything about her . . ."

"Course."

"Is there anyone else in the college she might have spoken to?"

"No," she said decisively. "Not after the new Master as good as chucked her out, the bastard."

"Thanks, Alice. Don't stand about in the cold."

"I'll tell old Ronnie Cawson that she's missing. He's fond of her.

All the servants are. Well, the original servants. Hammond's got some new buggers that don't talk to anyone. This place en't the same as it used to be, Mal."

A quick embrace, and he left.

Ten minutes later he was knocking on Hannah Relf's door.

"Malcolm! Come in. What's—"

"Lyra's vanished," he said, shutting the door behind him. "She was gone before Mum and Dad were up this morning. Must've been pretty early. She left this note, and no one's got a clue where she's gone. I've just been to ask Alice, but—"

"Pour us some sherry and sit down. Did she take the alethiometer with her?"

"It wasn't in her bedroom, so I suppose she must have done."

"She might have left it there if she was intending to come back. If she thought it would be safe."

"I think she felt safe there. I was going to talk to her this evening, tell her about the business at the Botanic Garden . . . I haven't even told you yet, have I?"

"Does that concern Lyra?"

"Yes, it does."

He told her about the meeting, and what he'd learnt from it, and the men from the CCD.

"Right," she said. "Definitely Oakley Street business. Are you seeing her again?"

"Lucy Arnold—yes. And the others. But, Hannah, I was going to ask—would you be able to look for Lyra with your alethiometer?"

"Yes, of course I could, but not quickly. She might be anywhere by now. What is it, twelve hours or so ago when she left? I'll gladly start looking, but it'll only give me a general idea at first. It might be easier to ask why she's gone, rather than where."

"Do that, then. Anything that'll help."

"The police? What about telling them she's missing?"

"No," he said. "The less attention they pay to her, the better."

"I think you're probably right. Malcolm, are you in love with her?"

The question took him utterly by surprise. "What on earth—where did that come from?" he said.

"The way you talk about her."

He felt his cheeks flaring. "Is it that obvious?" he said.

"Only to me."

"There's nothing I can do about it. Nothing at all. Completely forbidden, by every kind of moral and—"

"Once, yes, but not anymore. You're both adults. All I was going to say was don't let it affect your judgment."

He could see that already she regretted having asked about it. He'd known Hannah for most of his life, and he trusted her completely; but as for her final piece of advice, he thought it was the least wise thing he'd ever heard her say.

"I'll try not to," he said.

TWELVE

THE DEAD MOON

Lyra soon fell into a comfortable enough way of life with Giorgio Brabandt. He wasn't overscrupulous as far as cleaning was concerned; she gathered that his last girlfriend had been a zealot for scrubbing and polishing, and that he was glad to live a little more casually. Lyra swept the floors and kept the galley sparkling, and that satisfied him. Where cooking was concerned, she had learnt a few things in the Jordan kitchens, and she could make the sort of hefty pies and stews that Brabandt liked best: he had no taste for delicate sauces or fancy desserts.

"What we'll do if anyone asks who you are," he said, "is we'll say you're my son Alberto's gal. He married a landloper woman and they live down Cornwall way. He en't been on the water for years. You can be called Annie. That'll do. Annie Brabandt. Good gyptian name. As for the dæmon . . . Well, we'll cross that bridge when we come to it."

He gave Lyra the forward cabin, a cold little place until he put a rock oil stove in there. Wrapped up in bed at night, with a naphtha lamp beside her, she pored over the alethiometer.

She didn't try the new method; she felt uneasy about it. Instead, she gazed at the dial and let her mind hover, not setting off onto a wild sea so much as drifting over a calm one. She kept herself as free from conscious intention as she could manage, asking nothing and puzzling over nothing, and floated in her mind over the Sun or the Moon or the Bull, looking down on each one, taking in all their details with equal attention, gazing into the great depth of the symbol ranges, from the highest levels that were so familiar now to the lower ones fading into darkness further down. She hovered over the Walled Garden for a long time, letting all the associations and connotations of nature and order and innocence and protection and fertility and many, many other meanings float past like exquisite jellyfish, their myriad tendrils of gold or coral or silver drifting in a pellucid ocean.

From time to time she felt a little snag at the drift of her awareness and knew that the young man she'd mistaken for Will was looking for her. She made herself relax, not fight it, not even ignore it, just float, and presently the snag disappeared, like a little thorn that catches for a moment on a traveler's sleeve, only to pull out when the traveler walks on.

She thought constantly about Pantalaimon: Was he safe? Where could he be going? What did he mean by that brief and contemptuous note? Surely he couldn't have meant it literally. It was cruel, he was cruel, and she was cruel too, and it was all a mess, all a dreadful mess.

She hardly thought of Oxford at all. She wondered about writing a note and posting it to Hannah, but that wouldn't be easy: Brabandt seldom stopped during the day, and tended to moor at night on a lonely stretch of water far from any village where there might be a post office.

He was curious about why the CCD was interested in her, but

when she kept saying she had no idea, he realized he wasn't going to get an answer and stopped asking. He had things to tell her about the gyptians and the Fens, though, and on the third night of their journey, when the frost was hardening the grass on the riverbank and the old stove was glowing in the galley, he sat down and talked with Lyra as she made their supper.

"The CCD, they got a down on the gyptians," he told her, "but they daresn't do much to make us angry. Whenever they tried to enter the Fens, we made damn sure they got lured into swamps and dead waterways where they'd never get out. There was one time when they tried to invade the Fens in force, hundreds of 'em, guns and cannons and all. Seems the will o' the wykeses, the jacky lanterns—you heard of them? They shine lights out on the bogs, to lure innocent people off the safe paths—anyways, they heard the CCD was coming, and all the will o' the wykeses come shining their lanterns and flickering this side and that, and the CCD men were so bewithered and bewildered that half of 'em drowned and the other half went mad with fear. That was nigh on fifty year ago."

Lyra wasn't sure that the CCD had existed fifty years before, but she didn't quibble. "So the ghosts and the spirits are on your side, then?" she said.

"Against the CCD, they're on the gyptians' side, aye. Mind you, they chose the wrong time o' the month, them CCD men. They come in the dark of the moon. It's well-known that when the moon's dark, all the bogles and boggarts come out, all the ghouls and the bloody-boneses, and they do powerful harm to honest men and women, gyptian and landloper alike. They caught her once, you know. Caught her and killed her."

"Caught who?"

"The moon."

"Who did?"

"The bogles did. Some say they climbed up and pulled her down, only there en't nothing in the Fens high enough for that; and others say she fell in love with a gyptian man and come down to sleep with him; and still others say she come down of her own accord 'cause she'd heard terrible tales of the things the bogles got up to when she was dark. Anyway, she come down one night, and walked about among the swamps and the bogs, and a whole host of wicked creatures, ghasts, hobgoblins, boggarts, hell-wains, yeth-hounds, trolls, nixies, ghouls, fire-drakes, they come a tippy-toeing after her right into the darkest and doulest part of the Fens, what's known as Murk-Mire. And there she turned her foot on a stone, and a bramble snagged her cloak, and the creeping horrors attacked her, the lady moon, they bore her down in the cold water and the filthy grim old bog, where there's crawling creatures so dark and horrible they en't even got names. There she lay, cold and stark, with her poor little old light just going out, bit by bit.

"Well, by soon after there come along a gyptian man and he'd wandered off his path by reason of the dark, and he was beginning to be fearful on account of the slimy hands he could feel a-gripping his ankles, and the cold claws that scratched at his legs. And he couldn't see a bloody thing.

"Then all of a sudden he did see something. A little dim light a-shining under the water it was, a-gleaming just like the mild silver of the moon. And he must have called out, because that was the dying moon herself, and she heard him and she sat up, just for a moment like, and she shined all around, and all the ghouls and boggarts and goblins they fled away, and the gyptian man could see the path clear as day, and he found his way out of Murk-Mire and back home safe.

"But by that time the moon's light was all gone. And the creatures of the night placed a big stone over where she lay. And things got worse and worse for the gyptians. The creeping horrors come out the murk and snatched away babies and children; the jacky lanterns and the will o' the wykeses shone their glimmers over all the bogs and the marshes and the quicksands; and things too horrible to mention, dead men and ghouls and rawheads and bonelesses, they come creeping round houses at night and swarmed over boats, fingering at the windows, snarling the rudders with weed, pressing their eyes against the slightest little bit of light shining between the curtains.

"So the people went to a wisewoman and asked what they should do. And she said, find the moon, and there'll be an end of the trouble. And then the man who'd been lost, he suddenly remembered what had happened to him, and he said, 'I know where the moon is! She's buried in Murk-Mire!'

"So off they set with lanterns and torches and burning brands, a whole pack of men, carrying spades and pickaxes and mattocks to dig up the moon. They asked that wisewoman how to find her if her light had all gone out, and she said, look for a big coffin made of stone with a candle on top of it. And she made 'em put a stone in their mouths, each one of 'em, to remind 'em not to say a word.

"Well, they traipsed on deep into Murk-Mire, and they felt slimy hands trying to grasp their feet, and scary whispers and sighings in their ears, but then they come to where that old stone was a-lying, with a candle glimmering made of dead man's fat.

"And they heaved up the stone lid, and there was the dead moon lying there, with her strange, beautiful lady's face cold and her eyes closed. And then she opened her eyes, and out there shone a clear silver light, and she lay there for a minute just looking at this circle of gyptian men with their spades and mattocks, all silent because of the stones in their mouths, and then she says, 'Well, boys, it's time I woke up, and I thank'ee all for finding me.' And all around there come a thousand little sucky sounds as the horrors fled back down under the bog. Next thing, the moon was shining down from the sky, and the path was as clear as day.

"So that's the kind of place that's ours, and that's why you better have gyptian friends if you come in the Fens. You come in without permission, the bogles and ghouls'll have you. You don't look like you believe a word of this."

"I do," Lyra protested. "It's only too likely."

She didn't believe it at all, of course. But if it comforted people to believe that sort of nonsense, she thought it was polite to let them do so, even if the author of *The Hyperchorasmians* would have snarled with scorn.

"Young people don't believe in the secret commonwealth," Brabandt said. "It's all chemistry and measuring things, as far as they're concerned. They got an explanation for everything, and they're all wrong."

"What's the secret commonwealth?"

"The world of the fairies, and the ghosts, and the jacky lanterns."

"Well, I've never seen a jacky lantern, but I've seen three ghosts, and I was suckled by a fairy."

"You was what?"

"I was suckled by a fairy. It happened in the great flood twenty years ago."

"You en't old enough to remember that."

"No. I don't remember it at all. But that's what I was told by someone who was there. She was a fairy out of the river Thames. She wanted to keep me, only they tricked her and she had to let me go."

"The river Thames, eh? What was her name, then?"

Lyra tried to remember what Malcolm had told her. "Diania," she said.

"That's right! Damn me, that's right. That's her name. That en't common knowledge. You'd only know that if it was true, and it is."

"I'll tell you something else," she said. "Ma Costa told me this. She said I had witch oil in my soul. When I was a little kid, I wanted to be a gyptian, so I tried to talk in a gyptian way, and Ma Costa laughed at me and said I'd never be gyptian, because I was a fire person and I had witch oil in my soul."

"Well, if she said that, it must be right. I wouldn't argue with Ma Costa. What you cooking there?"

"Stewed eels. They're probably ready now."

"Dish up, then," he said, and poured some beer for them both.

As they ate, she said, "Master Brabandt? D'you know the word *akterrakeh*?"

He shook his head. "It en't a gyptian word, and that's a fact," he said. "Might be French. Sounds a bit French."

"And did you ever hear of a place somewhere called the Blue Hotel? Something to do with dæmons?"

"Yeah, I did hear about that," he said. "That's in the Levant somewhere, that is. It en't a hotel of any kind, really. A thousand years ago, maybe more, it was a great city: temples, palaces, bazaars, parks, fountains, all sorts of beautiful things. Then one day the Huns swept down out the steppes—that's the endless grasslands they have further north, what seem to go on forever—and they slaughtered all the people in that city, every man, woman, and child. It was empty for centuries because people said it was haunted, and I en't surprised. No one would go there for love nor money. Then one day there was a traveler—he might have been a gyptian man—who went there exploring, and he come back with a strange tale, how the place was haunted all right, but not by ghosts: by dæmons. Maybe the dæmons of dead people go there, maybe that's it. I dunno why they call it the Blue Hotel. Must be a reason, though."

"Would that be a secret commonwealth thing?"

"Bound to be."

And so they passed the time as the *Maid of Portugal* sailed nearer and nearer to the Fens.

In Geneva, Olivier Bonneville was becoming frustrated. The new method of reading the alethiometer was refusing to disclose anything at all about Lyra. It hadn't at first; he'd spied on her more than once; but now it was as if some connection was broken, a wire come loose.

He was beginning to discover more about the new method, though. For example, it only worked in the present tense, so to speak. It could reveal events, but not their causes or consequences. The classical method gave a fuller perspective, but at the cost of time and laborious research, and it required a kind of interpretation that Bonneville had little patience for.

However, his employer, Marcel Delamare, was directing all his attention to the forthcoming congress of all the constituent bodies that made up the Magisterium. Since it was Delamare himself whose idea this was, and since he had no intention of making its true purpose clear, but every intention of arranging for it to deliver the resolutions he wanted, and since that involved a great deal of complex politics, Bonneville found himself comparatively unsupervised for a while.

So he decided to try another approach to the new method. He had a photogram of Lyra, which Delamare had given him: it showed her among a group of other young women in academic dress, obviously on some university occasion. They stood formally facing the camera in bright sunlight. Bonneville had cut out the face and figure of Lyra and thrown the rest of the picture away; there was no reason to keep it, because the girls in it were too English to be attractive. He thought that if he looked at Lyra's face in the picture, alethiometer in hand, it might help him focus more clearly on the question of where she was.

So, having swallowed some pills to protect against travel sickness, in case the nausea struck again, he sat in his little apartment as the evening lights came on in the city, turned all three wheels to the image of the owl, and focused his attention on the scrap of photo paper with the picture of Lyra. But that didn't work either, or not as he'd hoped it would. In fact, it generated a blizzard of other images, each of them pin-sharp for a moment and then succumbing to vagueness and blur, but each of them resembling Lyra for the second or so he could see them clearly.

Bonneville narrowed his eyes and tried to keep the pictures in focus for a little longer against the inevitable vertigo. They seemed to have the quality of photograms: all monochrome, some faded or creased, some on photographic paper, some on newsprint, some well lit and professionally taken, others informal, as if taken by someone who wasn't used to a camera, with Lyra screwing up her eyes in the glare of the sun. Several of them seemed to have been taken surreptitiously when she was unaware, showing her lost in thought in a café or laughing as she walked hand in hand with a boy or looking around to cross the road. They showed Lyra at various periods in her childhood as well as more recently, her dæmon always in view. In the later pictures his form was clearly that of some large rodent: that was all Bonneville could tell.

Then with a lurch he seemed to fall into an understanding of what he was looking at. They *were* photograms. They were pinned to a board: he could see a cloth folded back at the top of it, so they were probably kept under cover. Gradually some details of the background emerged: the board was leaning against a wall papered in a faint floral pattern; it stood next to a window across which a curtain of lustrous green silk had been drawn; it was lit by a single anbaric lamp on a desktop below; but whose eyes was he looking through? He had the impression of a consciousness, but—

Something was moving—a hand moved and made Bonneville lurch again and almost vomit, as the viewpoint swung around instantaneously and showed him a white form sweeping across in a blur of wings that set some of the pictures stirring on the board— just a swift dash—a bird—a white owl, just for a moment, and it was gone again. . . .

Delamare!

The owl was Delamare's dæmon. The hand was Delamare's. The floral wallpaper, the green silk curtain, the board of pictures was in Delamare's apartment.

And although Bonneville couldn't see Lyra herself for some reason, he could see pictures of her because it wasn't her he was focusing his mind on but a *picture* of her. . . . All this came to him in a second, as he sank back into his armchair, closed his eyes, and breathed deeply to settle the nausea.

So Marcel Delamare had collected dozens, scores of pictures of Lyra. He'd never mentioned them.

And no one knew. He'd thought that his employer's interest in the girl was professional, so to speak, or political, or something. But this was personal. This was bizarre. It was obsessive.

Well, that was worth knowing.

Next question: why?

Bonneville knew very little about his employer, mainly because he wasn't interested. Perhaps it was time to find things out. The new method would be little use for that, and besides, Bonneville's nauseous headache made him reluctant to think of using the alethiometer again for a while. He'd have to go and ask people: be a detective.

With no clue about where Lyra might have gone, Malcolm and Asta went over and over his conversation with her at La Luna Caprese in Little Clarendon Street.

"Benny Morris . . . ," said Asta. "That name came up at some point."

"Yes. So it did. Something to do with . . ."

"Someone who worked at the mail depot—"

"That's it! The man who was injured."

"We could try the compensation stunt," she said.

So after some work with Oxford city directories and voting registers, they found an address in Pike Street in the district of St. Ebbe's, in the shadow of the gasworks. In the character of a personnel manager from the Royal Mail, Malcolm knocked on the door of a terraced house the next afternoon.

He waited, and no one answered. He listened, but heard only the clanking of railway trucks being shunted into a siding on the other side of the gasworks.

He knocked again. Still there was no response from inside. The trucks had begun to empty their coal, one by one, into the chute below the railway line.

Malcolm waited till the whole train had gone through and the series of distant thunders was replaced by the hollow clank of shunting again.

He knocked a third time, and then heard a heavy limping step inside, and the door opened.

The man standing there was thickset and bleary-eyed, and a strong smell of drink hung around him. His dæmon, a mongrel with mastiff in her, stood behind his legs and barked twice.

"Mr. Morris?" said Malcolm, smiling.

"Who wants me?"

"Your name is Morris? Benny Morris?"

"What if it is?"

"Well, I've come from the personnel department of the Royal Mail—"

"I can't work. I got a certificate from the doctor. Look at the state of me."

"We're not disputing your injury, Mr. Morris, not at all. It's a matter of sorting out the compensation you're due."

There was a pause.

"Compensation?"

"That's right. All our employees are entitled to injury insurance. Part of your wages goes towards it. All we have to do is fill in a form. May I come in?"

Morris stood aside, and Malcolm stepped into the narrow hall and shut the door behind him. Boiled cabbage, sweat, and pungent smokeleaf joined the smell of drink.

"May we sit down?" said Malcolm. "I need to get out some papers."

Morris opened a door into a cold and dusty parlor. He struck a match and lit the gas mantle on a wall bracket. A yellowish light seeped out of it but didn't have the energy to go far. He pulled out a chair from under a flimsy table and sat down, taking care to demonstrate the pain and difficulty the process caused him.

Malcolm sat on the chair opposite, took some papers from his briefcase, and uncapped a fountain pen. "Now, if we could just be precise about the nature of your injury," he said cheerfully. "How did it happen?"

"Oh. Yeah. I was doing some work outside in the yard. Clearing a gutter. And the ladder slipped."

"You hadn't braced it?"

"Oh, yeah, I always brace a ladder. Common sense, innit?"

"But it still slipped?"

"Yeah. It was a wet day. That's why I was clearing the gutter, like, 'cause there was all moss and dirt in it and the water couldn't flow proper. It was all gushing down outside the kitchen window."

Malcolm wrote something down. "Did you have anyone helping you?"

"No. Just me."

"Ah. You see," said Malcolm in a concerned tone, "for full compensation to be paid, we need to be sure that the client—that's you—took every sensible precaution against accident. And when working with ladders, that normally involves having another person to hold the ladder."

"Oh, yeah, well, there was Jimmy. My mate Jimmy Turner. He was with me. He must've gone inside for a second."

"I see," said Malcolm, writing. "Could you let me know Mr. Turner's address?"

"Er—yeah, sure. He lives in Norfolk Street. Number—I can't remember his number."

"Norfolk Street. That'll do. We'll find him. Was it Mr. Turner who went for help when you fell?"

"Yeah . . . This, er, this compensation . . . how much is it likely to be?"

"It partly depends on the nature of the injury, which we'll go into in a minute. And on how long you're likely to be away from work."

"Right, yeah."

Morris's dæmon was sitting as close as she could get to his chair. Asta was watching her, and already the dog was beginning to twitch and look away. The faint beginning of a growl came from

211

her throat, and Morris's hand reached down automatically to grasp her ears.

"How long has the doctor recommended you to stay off work?" Malcolm said.

"Oh, two weeks, about. Depends. It might heal quicker, it might not."

"Of course. And now the injury itself. What damage did you actually do?"

"Damage?"

"To yourself."

"Oh, right. Well, I thought at first I'd broke me leg, but the doctor said it was a sprain."

"Which part of your leg?"

"Er—the knee. Me left knee."

"A sprained knee?"

"I sort of twisted it as I fell."

"I see. Did the doctor examine you properly?"

"Yeah. My mate Jimmy helped me inside, right, and then he went to fetch the doctor."

"And the doctor examined the injury?"

"That's what he did, yeah."

"And said it was a sprain?"

"Yeah."

"Well, you see, this is a little confusing for me, because the information I have is that you were rather badly cut."

Asta saw the man's hand tighten on the ears of his dæmon. "Cut," said Morris, "yeah, I was, yeah."

"It was a cut as well as a sprain?"

"There was glass around. I repaired a window the week before and there must have been some broken glass. . . . Where'd you get this information from anyway?"

"A friend of yours. He said you were rather badly cut behind the knee. I can't quite picture how you came to be cut there, you see."

"Who was this friend? What's his name?"

Malcolm had an acquaintance in the City of Oxford police, a friend from his boyhood—a docile and affectionate child then, and a man of honest decency now. Malcolm had asked him, without saying why, if he knew of a constable at the police station in St. Aldate's who had a heavy, thick voice and a Liverpool accent. Malcolm's friend knew the man at once, and his expression told Malcolm what he thought of him. He gave Malcolm the name.

"George Paston," said Malcolm.

Morris's dæmon uttered a sudden yelp and stood up. Asta was already on her feet, tail slowly swinging from side to side. Malcolm himself sat quite still, but he knew where everything was, and how heavy the table was likely to be, and which leg of Morris's was injured, and he was balanced partly on the chair but partly on his feet, ready to spring. Very quietly, as if from an immense distance, and only for a moment or two, both Malcolm and Asta heard the sound of a pack of dogs barking.

Morris's face, until then heavily flushed, went white.

"No," he said, "wait a minute, wait a minute. George Pas—I don't know anyone called George Paston. Who is he?"

Morris might already have lashed out, except that Malcolm's calm and concerned expression had him utterly confused.

"He says he knows you well," Malcolm said. "As a matter of fact, he says he was with you when you got that injury."

"He wasn't—I told you, it was Jimmy Turner who was with me. George Paston? I've never heard of him. I don't know what you're talking about."

"Well, he came to us, you see," Malcolm said, watching carefully without seeming to, "and he was anxious to let us know that your injury was genuine so that you wouldn't suffer any loss of earnings. He said it was quite a bad cut—a knife was involved—but oddly enough he didn't mention anything about a ladder. Or about a sprain."

"Who are you?" Morris demanded.

"Let me give you my card," said Malcolm, and took from his breast pocket a card that named him as Arthur Donaldson, Insurance Assessor, Royal Mail.

Morris peered at it, frowning, and put it on the table. "What'd he say then, this George Paston?"

"He said you'd suffered an injury, and your absence from work had a good reason for it. Your situation was genuine. And as he was a police officer, naturally we believed him."

"A *police*— No, I don't know him at all. He must've got me confused."

"His account was very detailed. He said he helped you away from the place where the injury happened and brought you home."

"But it was here! I fell off a bloody ladder!"

"What were you wearing at the time?"

"What's that got to do with it? What I normally wear."

"The trousers you're wearing now, for instance?"

"No! I had to throw them away."

"Because they were covered in blood?"

"No, no, you're getting me confused now. It wasn't like that. There was me here and Jimmy Turner, and no one else."

"What about the third man?"

"There wasn't anyone else!"

"But Mr. Paston is very clear about it. There was no ladder in his account. He said you and he had stopped for a chat, and you were attacked by a third man, who cut your leg badly."

Morris wiped his face with both hands. "Look," he said, "I didn't ask for no compensation. I can do without it. This is all mixed up.

This Paston, he's got me confused with someone else. I don't know nothing about what he's saying. It's all lies."

"Well, I expect the court will sort it out."

"What court?"

"The Criminal Injuries Board. All we need now is your signature on this form, and we can go ahead."

"It's all right. Forget it. I don't want no compensation, not if it comes with all these stupid questions. I never asked for this."

"No, you didn't, I agree," said Malcolm, in his most bland and soothing way. "But I'm afraid that once the process has started, we can't go back and undo it. Let's just get this business of the third man out of the way, the man with the knife. Did you know him?"

"I never—there wasn't no third man—"

"Sergeant Paston says you were both surprised when he fought back."

"He en't a sergeant! He's a const—" Morris fell silent.

"I've got you," said Malcolm.

A slow dark red flush moved up from Morris's neck to his cheeks. His fists were clenched, pressing down so hard on the table that his arms were trembling.

His dæmon was growling more loudly than ever, but Asta could see that she'd never attack: she was mortally afraid.

"You en't—" Morris croaked. "You en't nothing to do with the Royal Mail."

"You've only got one chance," said Malcolm. "Tell me everything, and I'll put in a word for you. If you don't do that, you'll face a murder charge."

"You en't the police," said Morris.

"No. I'm something else. But don't get distracted by that. I know enough already to put you in the dock for murder. Tell me about George Paston."

Something of the defiance went out of Morris, and his dæmon

215

backed away as far as she could get from Asta, who simply stood and watched.

"He's . . . he's bent. He's a copper, all right, but he's as twisted as hell. He'll do anything, get you anything, steal anything, hurt anyone. I knew he was a killer, but I never seen him do it, not till . . ."

"It was Paston who killed the other man?"

"Yeah! It couldn't've been me. He'd done my fucking leg by then. I was on the ground, I couldn't move nowhere."

"Who was the victim?"

"I dunno. No need to know. I didn't care who the hell he was."

"Why did Paston want to attack him?"

"Orders, I suppose."

"Orders from whom? From where?"

"Paston . . . He's got someone over him who tells him what jobs he wants done, right—I dunno who that is."

"Paston's never given you any clue?"

"No, I only know what he tells me, and he keeps a lot of it close to his chest. That's all right with me. I don't want to know anything that'll get me into trouble."

"You're in trouble already."

"But I never killed him! Never! That wasn't part of the plan. We was just supposed to smack him a bit and take his bag, his rucksack, whatever he was carrying."

"And did you take it?"

"No, 'cause he wasn't carrying nothing. I says to George he must've had something, he must've left it in the station or passed it to someone else."

"When did you say that? Before or after he was killed?"

"I can't remember. It was an accident. We never meant to kill him."

Malcolm wrote for a minute, two minutes, three. Morris sat slumped without moving, as if all the strength had gone out of him,

216

and his dæmon was whimpering at his feet. Asta, still on guard in case the dæmon made a sudden move, sat down carefully but kept watching.

Then Malcolm said, "This man who tells Paston what to do."

"What about him?"

"Does Paston ever talk about him? Mention a name, for instance?"

"He's a Scholar. That's all I know."

"No, it isn't. You know more than that."

Morris said nothing. His dæmon was lying flat on the floor, her eyes closed tight, but as soon as Asta took a step towards her, she sprang up in alarm and backed away behind the man's chair.

"No!" said Morris, flinching too.

"What's his name?" said Malcolm.

"Talbot."

"Just Talbot?"

"Simon Talbot."

"College?"

"Cardinal's."

"How do you know?"

"Paston told me. He says he's got something on him."

"Paston knows something about him?"

"Yeah."

"Did he tell you what that was?"

"No. He was prob'ly just boasting."

"Tell me as much as you know."

"I *can't*. He'd kill me. Paston—you don't know what he's like. There's no one else that knows this, only me, and if he finds out you know, he'll know it's come from me, and—I've said too much already. I was lying. I never told you nothing."

"In that case, I'll have to ask Paston myself. I'll make sure he knows how helpful you've been."

"No, no, no, please, don't do that. He's a terrible man. You can't imagine what he'd do. Killing's nothing to him. That man by the river—he killed him like killing a fly. That's all it was to him."

"You haven't told me enough about this Talbot man at Cardinal's. Have you met him?"

"No. How would I have done that?"

"Well, how did Paston know him?"

"He's the liaison officer for that group of colleges. If they need any police contact, for any reason, he's the one they speak to."

That made sense to Malcolm. There were arrangements like that in place for all the colleges. The Proctors, the university police, dealt with most matters of discipline, but it was thought to be good for town-gown relations to have regular informal contact with the police.

He stood up. Such was Morris's fear that he shrank back on his chair. Malcolm saw it, and Morris saw that he saw.

"If you say one word to Paston about this, I'll know," said Malcolm. "And you'll be finished."

Morris feebly caught at Malcolm's sleeve. "Please," he said, "don't give me to him. He's—"

"Let go."

Morris's hand dropped away.

"If you don't want to end up on the wrong side of Paston, you'll have to keep your mouth shut, won't you?" Malcolm said.

"Who are you, anyway? That card en't real. You don't come from the Royal Mail."

Malcolm ignored him and walked out. Morris's dæmon whimpered.

"Simon Talbot?" Malcolm said to Asta as they shut the door and walked away. "Well, well."

THIRTEEN

THE ZEPPELIN

Pantalaimon knew he'd have to move at night and hide during the day: that was a given. It was also necessary to follow the river, because that would take him to the heart of London and thence to the docks, and whereas there were plenty of places to hide along the riverbank, there would be far fewer beside the main roads. He'd deal with the city when he got there.

It was harder going than he'd thought it would be. Roaming through Oxford under the moon was one thing, because he knew every corner so well, but he soon realized how much he'd miss Lyra's ability to look things up, to ask questions, to function successfully in a world of human beings. He missed that even more at first than he missed the softness of her flesh, the scent of her warm hair when it needed washing, the touch of her hands, and he missed those terribly: on his first night away he couldn't sleep, no matter how comfortable the mossy fork of an old oak where he curled up.

But it had been impossible. They couldn't live together. She'd become unbearable, with her new hard, dogmatic certainty and the condescending half smile she couldn't conceal when he spoke of things she'd once been eager to hear about, or criticized that loathsome novel which had so warped her understanding.

And *The Hyperchorasmians* was the center of his quest, for the time being. He knew the author's name: Gottfried Brande. He knew Brande was, or had been, a professor of philosophy at Wittenberg. That was all he knew in the way of facts and reason, and it would have to do. But in the realm of dreams and thoughts and memories, he was perfectly at home and perfectly certain: someone had stolen Lyra's imagination, and he was going to find it, wherever it was, and take it home to her.

"What do we know about this Simon Talbot?" said Glenys Godwin.

The Oakley Street Director was sitting in Charles Capes's rooms in Wykeham College together with Capes, and Hannah Relf, and Malcolm. The morning was clear and fresh, and the sun shone through an open window onto the richly spotted fur of Godwin's paralyzed dæmon, where he lay on Capes's desk. Godwin and Capes both had now read all the documents Malcolm had copied, and they had listened with interest to what Malcolm had found out from Benny Morris.

"Talbot's a philosopher," said Capes. "So-called. He doesn't believe in objective reality. It's a fashionable attitude among undergraduates with an essay to write. A flashy writer—witty, if you like that sort of thing—very popular lecturer. He's beginning to acquire a bit of a following among the younger Scholars, mind you."

"More than a bit, I think," said Hannah. "He's rather a star."

"Do we know of any connection between him and Geneva?" asked Malcolm.

"No," said the whisper of Godwin's dæmon. "There could hardly be any common ground, if he means what he says."

"I think the point is that he says nothing means anything very

220

much," said Capes. "It might be quite easy for him to play at supporting the Magisterium. I'm not sure they'd trust *him*, though."

"This police liaison business," said Glenys Godwin. "Talbot's college is Cardinal's, is that right?"

"That's right," said Hannah. "The colleges are organized in groups for that sort of thing. The others in that group are Foxe, Broadgates, and Oriel."

"And presumably there's a Scholar of each college responsible for communicating with the police, if necessary?"

"Yes," said Capes. "Usually a Junior Dean or someone of that sort."

"Find out, please, Charles. See what you can discover about Talbot and this Paston. Malcolm, I want you to concentrate on the rose oil. I want to know everything about it. The research station in Central Asia: What is it? Who runs it? What have they discovered about the oil, if anything? Why can't the roses be grown anywhere else? What's the truth about this extraordinary red building in the middle of the desert, with the Latin-speaking guards, where the roses come from? Is it a delirious fantasy of some sort? I want you to go there yourself as soon as possible. You know the place, you speak the language, I think?"

Malcolm said, "Yes."

That was all he could say. An order like that meant that he'd have no chance to search for Lyra, even if he'd known where to begin.

"And this unrest throughout the Levant and beyond: find out what's behind that. Is it coming from the Lop Nor region and spreading west? Is it connected at all with the rose business?"

"There's something curious about that," said Malcolm. "In Strauss's diary, he mentions that some places not far from the research station had been attacked, rose gardens set on fire, and so

221

on, and he says he was surprised because he thought that sort of thing had been confined to Asia Minor—to Turkey and the Levant, basically. Maybe the unrest didn't originate in Central Asia at all, but further west. Nearer Europe."

Glenys Godwin nodded and made a note. "Find out what you can," she said, and went on, "Hannah, the young woman, Lyra Silvertongue: any idea where she's gone?"

"None, yet. But the alethiometer isn't good at hurrying. I think she's safe, but more than that, I can't tell. I'll keep looking."

"I'd like a brief account of her background and why she's important. I don't know whether she's central or peripheral. Can you put that together quickly?"

"Of course."

"There's a file about her in the mausoleum," said Godwin's dæmon.

He meant the section of Oakley Street's archives in which inactive material was stored. Malcolm and Asta knew that, but couldn't help feeling a little dart of shock at the reminder of that dank and rotting graveyard where he'd killed Gerard Bonneville in order to save Lyra's life.

"Good," said Godwin. "I'll read it when we get back. In the meantime, something's happening in Geneva. D'you know anything about that, Charles?"

"A conference. Or a congress, as they're calling it. All the various bodies of the Magisterium are gathering for the first time in centuries. I don't know what's prompted it, but it doesn't sound good. The best weapon we have against them at the moment is their disunity. If they find a reason for coming together and a way of institutionalizing it, they'll be more formidable than ever."

"Could you find a way of getting there yourself?"

"I daresay I could, but I'm already under suspicion, or so I've been told. They'd make sure I didn't learn very much. I do know one or two people who'd learn more and wouldn't mind telling me about it. There are always journalists, scholars from various places, attending and listening and reporting on events like that."

"All right. Whatever you can do. Let's keep in mind what's at the bottom of this. These roses, this oil they produce, is something the Magisterium is desperate to control. The main instigator in all this seems to be the organization called *La Maison Juste* and its director, Marcel Delamare. Charles, do you know anything about them? Why is it called that, for instance?"

"*La Maison Juste* is the building where their headquarters are. The organization's full title is the League for the Instauration of the Holy Purpose."

"Instauration?" said Glenys Godwin. "I've forgotten what that means, if I ever knew it."

"It means restoration, or renewal."

"And what is this Holy Purpose? Actually, don't bother: I can guess. They want to reinvigorate their sense of righteousness. They'd like a war, and for some reason these roses will give them an advantage. Well, we need to know what that is and cancel it out and, if possible, gain it for ourselves. Let's keep that clearly in mind."

"Oakley Street is hardly in a position to fight a war," said Hannah.

"I was not actually advocating a war," said Godwin. "But if we act intelligently and effectively, we might prevent one. You know why I'm sending you in particular there, Malcolm. I wouldn't ask anyone else to go."

Malcolm did know, and so did Hannah, but Capes didn't and was looking at him curiously.

"It's because my dæmon and I can separate," Malcolm said.

"Ah," said Capes. He looked at Malcolm and nodded.

No one spoke for a few moments.

Something was glinting on the desk: the sunlight was catching the blade of a silver paper knife, and Malcolm felt the familiar presence of the tiny shimmering point, no bigger than an atom, which would slowly become visible and then grow larger into the sparkling loop of light he knew as the spangled ring. Asta looked at him: she felt it too, though it wasn't visible to her. There was no point in his trying to focus on anything for a few minutes, because it would take that long for the ring to grow large enough to see through; so he relaxed his vision and thought about the four human beings in the room, so liberal and tolerant, so civilized, and the organization they embodied.

In that wider perspective, Oakley Street seemed absurd: an organization whose very existence had to be concealed from the nation it had been set up to protect, whose agents were mostly now middle-aged or older and fewer in number than ever, whose resources were so scanty that its Director would have had to travel third-class on a slow train from London and he, Malcolm, would have to subsidize his own travel to Karamakan. What did this decrepit, poverty-stricken, understaffed body think it was doing, taking on the entire Magisterium?

The other three were talking quietly. As the sparkling loop of light drifted towards Malcolm, it encircled each of them in turn when he looked over at them: Charles Capes, slender, bald, faultlessly dark-suited, a red handkerchief in his top pocket, a deep and subtle intelligence in his eyes; Glenys Godwin, warmly dark-eyed, gray hair cut neatly, one hand tirelessly and tenderly caressing her wounded dæmon; Hannah Relf, whom Malcolm loved only a little less than his own mother, slight and gray-haired and frail, whose mind held such knowledge. How valuable these people seemed, in this other perspective, in the light of the spangled ring.

So he sat and listened, and let it drift past him and disappear.

* * *

As Charles Capes had said, it was the first congress the hierarchy of the Magisterium had held for centuries.

There was a hierarchy, in the sense that some of the bodies and individuals were junior and some senior, some more important and some less; but it was not a fixed hierarchy, as it would have been had Pope John Calvin left the Church as he'd found it. Instead, he had repudiated the primacy of his office and divided its power among several agencies. After his death, the office of Pope was never filled again, and the authority that used to go with the title was diverted into many different courses, as a river that had run fast and narrow in the mountains slows down, and spreads out, and cuts many new channels as it finds itself in the flat lands below.

So there was no one clear line of command. Instead, a multitude of different bodies, councils and colleges and committees and courts, grew up and, if they found themselves under an ambitious and talented leader, flourished; or perished and withered, if there was no boldness of vision or depth of courage among their governors. Altogether, the entity known as the Magisterium consisted of a seething mass of rivalrous, jealous, mutually suspicious bodies similar only in their liking for power and their ambition to wield it.

They came, the leaders of these factions, the Director of the Consistorial Court of Discipline, the Dean of the College of Bishops, the Chairman of the Committee for the Propagation of the True Faith, the Secretary General of the Society for the Promotion of Celibate Virtue, the Rector of the Red Chamber, the Master of the School of Dogmatic Logic, the President of the Court of Common Order, the Abbess of the Sisters of Holy Obedience, the Archimandrite of the Priory of Grace, and many, many others— they came because they dared not stay away, in case their absence were interpreted as rebellion. They came from all over Europe and from further south and north and west and east, some eager for conflict, some uneasy at the thought of it; some tempted like hounds by the gamy tang of heresy hunting, others reluctant to leave the peace of their monasteries or colleges for what was bound to be discord and anger and danger.

Altogether, fifty-three men and women assembled in the oak-paneled Council Chamber of the Secretariat of the Holy Presence, which had the advantage of giving the Prefect of that order the right to chair the meeting.

"Brothers and Sisters," the Prefect began, "in the name and the authority of the Most High, we are summoned here today to discuss a matter of burning importance. Our faith has in recent years been challenged and threatened as never before. Heresy is flourishing, blasphemy goes unpunished, the very doctrines that have led us through two thousand years are being openly mocked in every land. This is a time for people of faith to draw together and make our voices heard with unmistakable force.

"And at the same time, there is opening to us in the east an opportunity so rich and promising as to raise the heart of the most despondent. We have a chance to increase our influence and bring our power to bear on all those who have resisted and are still resisting the good influence of the Holy Magisterium.

"In bringing you this news—and you shall hear much more later—I must also urge you all to pray most earnestly for the wisdom we shall need in order to deal with the new situation. And the first question I must put before you is this: Our ancient body, here represented by fifty-three men and women of the utmost faith and probity—is it too large? Are there simply too many of us to make rapid decisions and act with force and effect? Should we not consider the benefits that would flow from delegating matters of great policy to a smaller, a more swift-moving and decisive council, which could provide the leadership that is so necessary in these distracted times?"

Marcel Delamare, representing *La Maison Juste*, listened to the Prefect's words with satisfaction. No one would ever know, but he himself had written the speech for the Prefect to deliver; and he had made sure, by private inquiry, by blackmail, by bribery, by flattery, by threat, that the motion to elect a smaller council would be passed, and he had already decided who should be elected to it, and who should chair it.

He settled comfortably back and folded his arms, and the debate opened.

As darkness was falling at the edge of the Fens, rain started to fall too. It was the time of day when Giorgio Brabandt usually began to look for a likely spot to moor for the night, but as they were so close to his native waters, he was inclined to keep moving. He knew every twist and turn of these mazy waterways, and the lights he sent Lyra to mount at the stem and the stern were a matter of courtesy to any fellow boaters, not a necessity to show the way.

"When do we get into the Fens, Master B?" said Lyra.

"We're there now," he said. "More or less. There en't no frontier nor customs post, nothing like that. One minute you're out, the next minute you're in."

"So how do you know?"

"You got a feeling for it. If you're gyptian, it's like coming home. If you en't gyptian, you feel uncomfortable, nervous, you feel that all them boggarts and horrors is out there in the water, watching you. Don't you feel that?"

"No."

"Oh. Well, we can't be there yet. Or else I en't told you enough stories."

He was standing at the tiller, in oilskins and sou'wester, while Lyra sat just inside the doorway, wrapped in an old coat of his. The stern light threw a yellow outline around his bulky form and lit up the incessant raindrops that filled the air. Lyra was aware of the potatoes cooking on the naphtha stove in the galley behind her; she'd go in soon and cut some slices of bacon to fry.

"When d'you think we'll get to the Zaal?" she said. She was referring to the great meeting hall, the center of the gyptians' communal life.

"Ah, there's a way to tell that."

"What is it?"

"When you're close enough to see it, you're almost there."

"Well, that's helpful. I must—"

He suddenly put up a hand to hush her, and at the same moment his dæmon turned her head to the sky. Brabandt sheltered his eyes with the brim of his sou'wester and peered up too, and Lyra followed their example. She could see nothing, but heard a distant rumble from the clouds.

"Lyra, run forrard and dowse that glim," said Brabandt, easing the throttle back and reaching out with his other hand for the stern light.

The light at the prow was reflected along the length of the cabin roof, so Lyra could see easily enough to run along and jump down into the bow. When she reached up and turned the wick down to extinguish the flame, she could hear the sound more easily, and a moment later she could see the source of it: the pale egglike form of a zeppelin, cruising slowly some way behind them on the starboard side, below the clouds, and showing no lights.

She felt her way back to the cockpit. Brabandt had steered the *Maid* in towards the side and cut the engine to a murmur, and Lyra felt a little jolt as the boat touched the grassy bank.

"You see it?" he said quietly.

"I can see one. Are there more?"

"One's enough. Is it follerin' us?"

"No. I shouldn't think they can have seen the lights yet, not through this rain. And the noise that engine is making, they'd never be able to hear ours."

"I'm going to move along, then," he said.

He pushed the throttle forward, and the engine responded with a gentle rumble. The boat moved on.

"How can you see?" said Lyra.

"Instinct. Keep your trap shut. I need to listen."

She remembered the potatoes, and ran inside to take them off the stove and drain them. The warm, comfortable old cabin, the clean galley, the steam, the smell of the cooked potatoes—they felt like a bulwark against the danger above; but she knew they were nothing of the sort, and that a bomb well aimed would kill her and Brabandt and sink the *Maid of Portugal* in a matter of moments.

She hurried from end to end of the boat, checking all the blinds. There wasn't a single chink. Finally she put out the light in the galley and went back to the cockpit.

The roar of the zeppelin's engine was loud now. It sounded as if it was directly overhead. She squinted up through the lashing rain and could see nothing.

"Psst," said Brabandt quietly. "Look out starboard."

Lyra stood and stared out as hard as she could, ignoring the rain in her eyes, and this time saw a little flickering greenish light. It was inconstant, but it always came back after vanishing for a second or two, and it was moving.

"Is that another boat?" she said.

"It's a will o' the wykes. A jacky lantern."

"There's another!"

A second light, reddish in color, appeared and disappeared not far from the first. Lyra watched them approach each other, touching, disappearing, and then flickering up again a little way apart.

The *Maid of Portugal* continued to move ahead, steady and slow, as Brabandt kept checking left and right, listening, peering, even lifting his face to sniff at the air. The rain was beating down harder than ever. The marsh lights seemed to be keeping pace with the boat, and then Lyra realized that the zeppelin overhead had moved a little in their direction, as if to see what they were. The engine sounded very loud, very close, and she wondered how the pilot could see anything at all in the murk. The *Maid of Portugal* was leaving no wake, and every light on board was out.

"There's another one," Lyra said.

A third light had joined the first two, and now they set up a weird halting, pausing, swerving dance. The cold, inconstant glimmer made Lyra feel uneasy. Only the solid deck beneath her feet and the bulky presence of Giorgio Brabandt saved her from a sickly fear of things that were outside, just beyond the reach of reason, inhabiting the dark.

"It's going that way," said Brabandt.

He was right. As if it was being pulled, the zeppelin was moving to starboard, towards the marsh lights.

Brabandt pushed the throttle further forward, and the narrowboat picked up speed. In the faint glimmer of the marsh lights, Lyra could see him straining every sense, and Anneke, his dæmon, jumped up onto the cabin roof, head moving this way and that to catch a fragment of scent that would help avoid a mudbank or steer round a bend.

Lyra almost said, "Can I help?" but realized as she opened her mouth that if he had a task for her, he'd tell her. So she sat down in the doorway again and kept still, and looked out to starboard, where the marsh lights were flickering more brightly than ever.

Suddenly a line of fire streaked down towards the marsh lights from the teeming sky above. It hit the water and exploded in a blossom of orange and yellow flame, and a moment later Lyra heard the brief whistle of the flight and the solid crump of the explosion.

The marsh lights went out all at once.

"There," said Brabandt. "They broke the law now. They're allowed to fly over, but not to do that."

Anneke was growling as she stood foursquare and gazed at the rapidly fading glow from the rocket.

A moment later a dozen marsh lights flickered again, moving swiftly, darting here and there, even rising and falling. Little jets of fire spurted up from the ground, to flare and go out in a moment.

"That's made 'em angry," said Brabandt. "Trouble is, they're showing us up."

The boat was still purring forward into the dark, but he was right: the marsh lights were so fierce and brilliant now that, small as they were, they illuminated the whole length of the *Maid of Portugal*, streaming with rain and catching every flicker of light.

"They don't like us, the will o' the wykeses, but they like them zeppelins even less," Brabandt said. "But they still don't like us. Wouldn't bother 'em a bit if we got sunk and drowned, or smashed into a thousand splinters."

Anneke suddenly barked, a short yap of alarm. She was looking up, and Lyra, following her gaze, saw a little shape falling from the zeppelin and briskly unfolding into a parachute. Almost at once the wind caught it and tossed it backwards, but a moment later the black shape under the canopy burst into a brilliant flame.

"Flares," said Brabandt as another fell, blossomed, and blazed.

The response from the marsh lights was instant and furious. More and more of them flickered into being and leapt and danced towards the falling flare, and when it reached the water, they swarmed all over it, their cold fire mastering its heat and finally drowning it in a cloud of smoke and a chorus of wet little shrieks and sucking noises.

Suddenly Lyra jumped up and ran inside, feeling her way along the length of the boat to her little cabin in the prow. She felt for her bunk, felt the bedside table, moved her hands over the book and the lamp until they found the velvet bag that held the alethiometer. With that safely in both hands, she moved back through the boat, conscious of the little movements Brabandt was making with the tiller and the throttle, of the roar from the zeppelin's engine somewhere above, of the moaning of the wind. From the galley she saw Brabandt outlined against the flickering marsh lights, and then she was in the doorway again and sat on the bench from where she could see the sky.

"You all right?" said Brabandt.

"Yes. I'm going to see what I can find out."

She was already turning the little wheels of the alethiometer, and peering close in the intermittent glimmer to try to make out the symbols. But it was no good: they were more or less invisible. She held the instrument between her palms and stared fiercely out at the flickering jacky lanterns, aware of a powerful contradiction that almost tore her mind in two. What she wanted to do would involve this secret commonwealth of Brabandt's, and yet she told herself it was nonsense, superstition, nothing but meaningless fancy.

The zeppelin was turning around ahead of them, its searchlight probing the rain and the dark marsh gloom below it. Another minute or two, and it would be facing them, and once it had the *Maid of Portugal* fixed in the glare of the light, nothing would save them.

Pan, Pan, Pan, Lyra thought, *I need you now, you little bastard, you traitor.*

She tried to imagine gathering all the jacky lanterns as if she was herding sheep, but it was so difficult, because, after all, she had no imagination, as Pan had said. What would it be like to do that? She thought harder and harder. She tried to think of herself as a light-herd, and the absent Pan as a light-dog, racing from side to side across the marsh, crouching down still, leaping up again, barking short, sharp commands, running where she thought him to.

And how stupid, she thought, how childish. It's just methane or something. It's just natural, meaningless. Her concentration faltered.

She heard a sob coming from her throat.

Brabandt said, "What you doing, gal?"

She ignored him. She gritted her teeth. Against her will she summoned the absent Pan again, a hellhound now, with glowing eyes and slaver flying from his lips, and she saw the terrified marsh lights fleeing and flocking and circling round as the zeppelin's cold beam of light came closer and closer and she heard the drumming of rain on the great snout-prow of the aircraft, even over the wind and the roar of the engine.

She felt something rising inside her, like a tide, wave upon wave of it, growing and receding and then growing again, a little more each time, and it was anger, it was desire, it was visceral.

"What they doing? Good God—look at that . . . ," Brabandt was saying.

The marsh lights were speeding and climbing, dashing again and again at a spot on the water just ahead of the zeppelin's search-light, and then, with a shriek, something rose out of the marsh that wasn't a jacky lantern or a will o' the wykes but a large bird, a heron or even a stork, heavy and white and terrified by the dart-ing green glimmers that harried it up and up and into the beam of the searchlight, and higher still, snapping at its legs, crowding like hornets at its great hefty body as it lumbered up in fear and hurled itself at the aircraft—

Brabandt said hoarsely, "Hold tight, gal." The searchlight beam was nearly on them.

Then, in an explosion of fire and blood and white feathers, the heron flew straight into the port engine of the zeppelin.

The aircraft lurched and swung to the left at once, and dipped and sagged as the starboard engine screamed and the great slug shape drifted sideways and downwards. The tail heaved itself round, caught by the wind with no port engine to stabilize it, and the craft drifted down and down towards the swamp, and closer and closer to the *Maid of Portugal*, as if it were sinking onto a bed. Little scraps of sound, screams, cries, came whirling through the wind and were snatched away again. By the glow of the dancing marsh lights as well as the fire that was now blazing out of control from the zeppelin, she and Brabandt watched in horror as a figure, two, three, hurled themselves out of the cabin and fell down into the dark. A moment later the great broken shell of the zeppelin collapsed onto the water only fifty yards away from them, surrounded by clouds of steam, and smoke, and flame, and the dance of a thousand marsh lights, capering in triumph. The heat scorched Lyra's face, and Brabandt tilted his sou'wester against it.

It was horrible to watch, but she couldn't look away. The skeleton of the airship showed black against the great blaze of light, and then it crumpled together and fell in with a cascade of sparks and smoke.

"They won't survive that, none of 'em," said Brabandt. "They be all dead now."

"Horrible."

"Aye."

He moved the throttle lever, and the boat moved out into the middle of the watercourse and gathered speed slowly.

"That heron," Lyra said shakily. "The marsh lights were chasing it. They made it fly up into the engine. They knew what they were doing."

And so did I, she thought. *I made it happen.*

"A heron, was it? Might've been. I thought it was a flying boggart. They do fly, some of 'em, making a kind of a whirring noise. Only there was so much else going on, we couldn't a' heard that. That's probably what it was, a flying elf or a spirit out the waters. Summing from the secret commonwealth, what I told you about. Look at the jacky lanterns now."

The marsh lights, dozens of them, had all gathered around the burning wreck, making little darts towards it and out again, flickering and dancing.

"What are they doing?"

"Looking for any survivors. They'll pull 'em down under the water and finish 'em off. Them potaters done yet?"

"Oh—yes."

"Well, don't let 'em get cold. Tell you what, there's a tin of bully beef in the locker. Chop it up with the potatoes and fry the lot. I'm getting peckish."

Lyra felt sick. She couldn't help thinking of the dead men from the zeppelin, burned or drowned or worse, and of that beautiful white bird, driven up without mercy into the blades of the engine. Food was the last thing she wanted just then, but when the hash was cooking she found that, after all, it was a shame to waste it, and it did smell good; so she brought two plates of it to the cockpit, where Brabandt began by scooping up a forkful and dropping it over the side.

"For the will o' the wykeses," he said.

She did the same with hers, and then they ate their supper, sheltering their plates from the rain.

FOURTEEN

THE CAFÉ COSMOPOLITAIN

That same evening, Dick Orchard pushed open the door and went into the public bar of the Trout. He knew many of Oxford's pubs, but like everyone else, he had his favorites, and the Trout was too far out of the way for him to visit often. Still, the beer was good.

He ordered a pint and looked around warily. There was no one among the customers who looked like a scholar: a group of old men playing cards near the fireplace, two men who looked like farmworkers stolidly working their way through a long and winding argument about stock fencing, two younger couples ordering a meal—nothing more than a quiet night in a traditional waterside pub.

When the meal had been ordered and the younger couples were sitting down with their drinks, Dick spoke to the barman, a hefty man of sixty or so with thinning red hair and a genial expression.

"S'cuse me, mate," Dick said. "I'm looking for someone called Malcolm Polstead. D'you know him?"

"He's my son," said the barman. "He's in the kitchen at the moment, having a bite of supper. You want to speak to him?"

"When he's finished. No hurry."

"You've only just caught him, as a matter of fact. He's leaving shortly for somewhere abroad."

"Oh, is he? Lucky I came when I did, then."

"Yes . . . he's got to go and sort out some of his affairs at the university and then he'll be catching a train. I don't think he's got all that long—he'll be off by tomorrow night latest, I'd guess. Why don't you take your drink over to the corner table and I'll let him know you're here, then he can come and say hello before he leaves. What name is it?"

"Dick Orchard. He won't know it, though. It's about . . . It's about Lyra."

The barman's eyes widened. He leant a little closer and said quietly, "You know where she is?"

"No, but she told me the name Malcolm Polstead, so . . ."

"I'll get him now."

Dick took his pint and sat down at the corner table. Something in the barman's manner made him wish he'd come here sooner.

Less than a minute later a tall man, not quite as hefty as his father the landlord, but still someone Dick would have hesitated to tangle with, sat down at the table with him. He held a mug of tea in one hand, and he was wearing a brown corduroy suit. His dæmon, a large ginger cat, touched noses courteously with Dick's vixen, Bindi.

Dick held out his hand, and Polstead shook it firmly.

"You know something about Lyra?" he said.

He spoke quietly, but his voice was very clear. It was deep and resonant, the voice of a singer, perhaps. Dick was puzzled. It wasn't surprising to know the man was a scholar, because of the intelligence in his face, but he had the air of someone who knew his way around the real world.

"Yeah," said Dick. "She's a . . . she's a friend. She came round my house the other morning because she was in trouble, she said, and she asked if I could help her. She wanted to get to the Fens, you see, and my grandad's gyptian, and he happened to be in Oxford just then with his boat, and I gave her a . . . I told her how to introduce herself to him. I think she must've done that and gone off with him. She told me about something that had happened down near the Oxpens, by the river, and—"

"What was that?"

"She saw someone being killed."

Malcolm liked the look of this boy. He was nervous, but he didn't let it get in the way of speaking clearly and frankly.

"How did you know my name?" Malcolm said. "Did Lyra tell you?"

"She said you knew about that business by the river, and she'd been staying here in the Trout, but she had to go, because . . ."

He was finding it hard to say. Malcolm waited. Dick looked around and leant in closer, and finally said almost in a whisper:

"She felt . . . the thing was, her dæmon, Pan . . . he'd gone. He wasn't with her. He'd just disappeared."

And Malcolm thought: *Of course. Of course . . . This changes everything.*

"I'd never seen anyone like that," Dick went on in the same tone. "You know, separated. She was frightened, and she thought everyone'd be looking at her, or worse. There was someone she knew in the Fens, an old gyptian man, she knew she'd be safe with him, and she thought my grandad might be able to take her there."

"What's his name?"

"My grandad? Giorgio Brabandt."

"And the man in the Fens?"

"I dunno. She never said."

"What did she have with her?"

"Just a rucksack."

"What time was this?"

"Quite early. I'd just come home. I work the night shift at the Royal Mail."

"Was it you who told Lyra about Benny Morris?"

"Yeah. I did."

Dick wanted to ask whether Malcolm had found out anything about that man, but he held his tongue. Malcolm was taking out a notebook and pencil. He wrote something down and tore out the page.

"You can trust these two people," he said. "They both know Lyra well. They'll be anxious to know where she's gone. If you could tell them what you've just told me, I'd be very obliged. And if you have the time to come out here, my mother and father would be glad to know if you hear any more from her. But don't tell anyone else."

He passed over the paper, on which he'd written Alice's name and address and Hannah's.

"You going abroad, then?" Dick said.

"Yes. I wish I didn't have to. Listen, there's a possibility that Pan, that her dæmon, might turn up. He'll be just as vulnerable as she is. If he knows you, he might do what she did and ask for help."

"I thought people died when they got separated like that. I couldn't believe it when I saw her."

"Not always. Tell me, do you know anything about a man called Simon Talbot?"

"Never heard of him. Is he summing to do with this?"

"Quite possibly. What's your address, by the way?"

Dick told him, and Malcolm wrote it down.

"You going away for long?" said Dick.

"No way of telling at the moment. Oh—one of the people on that piece of paper, Dr. Relf, would be interested in anything else you can tell her about Benny Morris. He'll be back to work soon."

"You seen him, then?"

"Yes."

"Did he do it?"

"He said he didn't."

"Are you . . . You en't police, are you?"

"No. Just a Scholar. Look, I've got to go—lots to do before I can leave. Thanks for coming here, Dick. When I get back, I'll buy you a drink."

He stood up, and they shook hands.

"Cheers, then," said Dick, and he watched as Malcolm made his way out of the bar. He moves easy for a big man, he thought.

At about the same time, Pantalaimon was crouching in the shadow of a derelict warehouse near a wharf in the Thames estuary, watching three sailors steal a ship's propeller.

There wasn't much light from the sky; a few stars flickered between the ragged clouds, and the moon was somewhere else. There was a feeble glow from the anbaric bulkhead light on the warehouse wall, but very little else to see by except the naphtha lantern in the prow of the rowing boat that had wavered across the creek from a battered old schooner tied up further along the wharf. The schooner was called the *Elsa,* and her captain had spent the day drinking beer after beer and persuading the mate to help him make off with the propeller, which was bolted to the deck of an almost equally squalid-looking coaster that seemed to have no crew at all, and to consist entirely of rust, apart from the four hundredweight of phosphor-bronze on the foredeck. They'd spent hours looking at it through the captain's cracked binoculars and speculating about how much it would fetch in a tolerant shipyard, while two deckhands languidly tossed various splintered planks and bits of rope overboard, the remains of a badly stowed deck cargo that had come apart after a storm in the Channel and was now never going to be paid for.

The tide was coming in, and the jetsam was floating slowly upstream over the rotting skeleton of a barge and the broken bottles and tin cans in the mud as the silent water gradually lifted the coaster upright. Pantalaimon was watching intently. He'd been interested in the *Elsa* since he'd arrived at the filthy little harbor the night before and heard German conversation on the deck. From what he could make out, they were intending to leave with the tide and cross the Channel, heading north for Cuxhaven, near Hamburg. That was when Pan knew he'd have to go with them: Cuxhaven lay at the mouth of the river Elbe, and the city of Wittenberg, where Gottfried Brande lived, lay many miles inland on the same river. It couldn't be better.

The crew of the *Elsa* had been waiting for a cargo, but someone had let them down, or more likely, from what Pan could gather, the skipper had simply got the date wrong. All day long the captain and the mate had bickered on the deck, drinking beer and tossing the bottles over the side, and finally, when the skipper agreed to split the proceeds fifty-fifty, the mate gave in and said he'd help liberate the propeller.

Pan saw his chance to get aboard the *Elsa,* and as soon as the rowing boat began to move across the creek towards the coaster, he crept silently along the wharf and darted up the gangplank. There were four crewmen apart from the skipper and the mate: one of them was rowing the boat, another two were asleep belowdecks, and the fourth was leaning on the rail, watching the expedition. The *Elsa* was older than Pan could guess, patched and mended over and over, her sails worn and shoddy, her deck filthy with grease and rust.

Plenty of places to hide, anyway, thought Pan, and he sat in the shadow of the wheelhouse and watched the thieves clambering up onto the coaster. At least, the mate climbed up, after the skipper tried twice and failed. The mate was a youngish man, lean and long-limbed, whereas the skipper was swag-bellied, bowlegged, and three-quarters drunk, and he'd never see sixty again.

But he was determined. He stood up in the unstable dinghy, hand on the side of the coaster, growling orders at the mate, who was trying to free the nearest davit from enough rust to let it swing out over the water. He kept up a stream of curses and abuse until the mate leant over the side and snarled back at him. The mate's herring gull dæmon added a sardonic squawk. Pan knew no more German than Lyra did, of course, but it wasn't hard to understand the drift of the conversation.

Finally the mate got the davit to move, and then turned his attention to the propeller. The skipper was refreshing himself from a bottle of rum, while his parrot dæmon clung half-insensible to the gunwale. The oily water was slipping into the creek without a murmur, bringing with it ragged clumps of scum and the body of an animal so dead, it was more than half rotted away.

Pan looked at the crewman who was watching from the *Elsa*, and at his dæmon, a scabby-looking rat, who sat at his feet, cleaning her whiskers. He looked back at the little scene across the creek, with the crewman drooping over the oars, more than half asleep, and the mate wielding a spanner on the deck of the coaster above, and the skipper clinging with one hand to a rope hanging from the davit while the other hand lifted the bottle to his lips again. Into Pan's mind came a memory of the night scene from the allotments near the Oxpens, with the Royal Mail depot across the meadow, the wisps of steam rising from the sidings, the bare trees by the river, the distant clank of wire on mooring post, everything silver and calm and beautiful; and, motionless, he felt a thrill of wild exultation at the loveliness of these things and at how the universe was so full of them. He thought how much he loved Lyra and how much he missed her, her warmth, her hands, and how much she would have loved to be here with him, watching, how they would have whispered together and pointed out this detail or that, how her breath would have caressed the delicate fur of his ears.

What was he doing? And what was she doing without him?

That little question wormed into his mind, and he flicked it out. He knew what he was doing. Something had made Lyra immune to the intoxication of night beauty such as this. Something had robbed her of that vision, and he would find it and bring it back to her, and they would never be apart again, and stay together as long as they lived.

The mate had freed the propeller and was looping the rope round and round it, ignoring the growled instructions from the skipper, while the oarsman paddled lethargically to keep the dinghy roughly under the davit. Pantalaimon wanted to see what happened when they lowered the propeller into the boat, and whether the dinghy would sink under it; but he was tired, more than tired, almost delirious with exhaustion, so he prowled the length of the deck until he found a companionway, and then crept down into the bowels of the *Elsa*, found a dark spot, and curled up and fell asleep at once.

Speeches long and short, motions for and motions against, objections, qualifications, amendments, protests, votes of confidence, more speeches and yet further speeches had filled the first day of the Magisterial conference with argument and the Council Chamber of the Secretariat of the Holy Presence with warm, stale air.

Marcel Delamare sat through every word, patient, attentive, and inscrutable. His owl dæmon did close her eyes once or twice, but only to ponder, not to sleep.

They broke at seven for a service of Vespers, followed by dinner. There was no formal seating arrangement; groups of allies seated themselves together, while those with no acquaintance among the other delegates, or those who realized the small influence their own organization could wield, sat wherever they could find space. Delamare watched it all, observing, counting, calculating, but at the same time greeting, exchanging a word here or a joke there, being prompted by a murmur from his dæmon when it would be wise to lay a friendly hand on a shoulder or a forearm, and when a silent twinkle of complicity would be more effective. He paid particular though unobtrusive attention to the representatives of the large corporations who were sponsoring (in the most ethically conscious and, again, unobtrusive way) some aspects of the arrangements: medical insurance, that sort of thing.

When he sat down to eat, it was between two of the least powerful and most timid delegates there, the aged Patriarch of the Sublime Porte in Constantinople and the Abbess of the Order of St. Julian, a tiny body of nuns who by a historical fluke had come to manage a large fortune in stocks and shares and government bonds.

"What did you make of the arguments today, Monsieur Delamare?" said the Abbess.

"All very well put, I thought," he said. "Cogent, honest, from the heart."

"And where does your organization stand on the matter?" said the Patriarch Papadakis: St. Simeon, by courtesy.

"We stand with the majority."

"And which way will the majority vote, do you think?"

"They will vote with me, I hope."

He could assume a pleasant tone when he needed to, and the gentle jocularity of his expression made it clear to his neighbors that this was a jest. They smiled politely.

The candlelight on the long oak tables, the aroma of roast venison, the chink of cutlery on fine porcelain plates, the heady glow of the crimson wine and the golden wine, the unobtrusive swift skill of the servants—it was all very pleasing. Even the Abbess, who lived frugally, found herself approving of these arrangements.

"The Secretariat of the Holy Presence is certainly looking after us very well," she said.

"You can always rely on—"

"Delamare, there you are," said a loud voice, emphasized by a heavy hand on his shoulder. Delamare knew who it was before he turned to look. Only one man interrupted so readily and so rudely.

"Pierre," Delamare said blandly. "Can I help?"

"We haven't been told about the arrangements for the final plenary session," said Pierre Binaud, the Chief Justice of the CCD. "Why's that been left off the schedule?"

"It hasn't. Ask someone from the Office of Ceremonial and they'll explain."

"Hmm," said Binaud, and he left, frowning.

"I do beg your pardon," Delamare said to the Abbess. "Yes, the Secretariat: we can always rely on Monsieur Houdebert, the Prefect. He has a perfect knowledge of how to make events like these move with unruffled serenity."

"But tell me, monsieur," said the Patriarch, "what do you make of the recent troubles we've been having in the Levant?"

"I think you're very wise to use the word *troubles*," said Delamare, filling the old man's water glass. "More than anxieties but less than alarms, hmm?"

"Well, from the viewpoint of Geneva, perhaps . . . ."

"No, I don't mean to downplay their importance, Your Serenity. They are indeed troubling. But it's just this sort of trouble that makes it important for us to speak with one voice, and act with one purpose."

"That's what has been so difficult to achieve," said the Patriarch. "For us in our eastern churches, to feel that we have the authority of the entire Magisterium behind us would certainly be a blessing. Things are getting harder, you know, monsieur. There is more discontent than I have ever known among our people, in their cities and markets and villages. A new doctrine seems to be arising that holds a great attraction for them. We try to confront it, but . . ." He spread his old hands helplessly.

"That is precisely what the new representative council will be perfectly placed to deal with," said Delamare with warm sincerity. "Believe me, the effectiveness of the Magisterium will be greatly magnified. Our truth, of course, is eternal and unchangeable, but our methods have been hampered over the centuries by the need to consult, to advise, to listen, to placate. . . . It is *action* that your situation cries out for. And the new council will deliver that."

The Patriarch looked solemn and nodded. Delamare turned to the Abbess.

"Mother, what is the feeling among your sisters about your place in the hierarchy?" he said. "May I help you to some more wine?"

"How kind. Thank you. Well, we don't have views, really, Monsieur Delamare. It's not our place to have opinions. We are here to serve."

"And very faithfully you do it. But you know, ma'am, I didn't say 'views.' I said 'feeling.' You can argue someone out of their views, but feelings go much deeper and speak more truly."

"Oh, that is certainly true, monsieur. Our place in the hierarchy? Well, I suppose our *feeling* about that would be one of modesty. And—and gratitude. Humility. We don't presume to feel discontented with our lot."

"Quite right. I hoped you'd say that. No—I *knew* you'd say it. A really good woman would say nothing else. Now"—he dropped his voice a little and leant towards her—"suppose a representative council were to emerge from this congress. Would it please your holy sisters if their abbess were to have a seat on that council?"

The good lady was speechless. She opened her mouth twice and closed it again; she blinked; she blushed; she shook her head, and then stopped, and almost nodded.

"You see," Delamare went on, "there's a particular kind of holiness that I think is underrepresented in the Magisterium. It's the kind that serves, as your holy sisters do. But serves with a true modesty and not a false one. A false modesty would be ostentatious, don't you think? It would seek to turn away emphatically from public distinctions and offices while privately lobbying to get them. And then allow itself to be dragged into them, protesting volubly about its unworthiness. I'm sure you've seen that cast of mind. But true modesty would accept that there is a place that one could fill, that one's talents are not illusions, that it would be wrong to turn away from a task if one could do it well. Don't you think?"

The Abbess was looking warm. She sipped her wine and coughed as she swallowed too much at once. Delamare tactfully looked away till she recovered.

"Monsieur, you speak very generously," she said in what was nearly a whisper.

"Not generous, Mother. Merely *juste*."

Her dæmon was a mouse with pretty silver fur. He had been hiding on her shoulder, out of sight of Delamare's owl dæmon, who, sensing their nervousness, had not looked at him once. But now he appeared, just a face and whiskers, and the owl slowly turned and bowed her head to him. The mouse just gazed with bright button eyes but didn't retreat. Presently he crept around onto the Abbess's other shoulder and made a little bow to Delamare's dæmon.

Delamare was talking to the Patriarch again, reassuring, flattering, explaining, sympathizing, and inwardly reckoning: two more votes.

As the first day of the Magisterial conference drew to an end, some of the delegates withdrew to their rooms to read, or to write letters, or to pray, or just to sleep. Others gathered in groups to talk over the day's events; some with old friends, some with new acquaintances who seemed to be agreeable, or of like opinions, or better informed about the politics that lay behind the gathering.

One such group sat with glasses of brantwijn near the great fireplace in the Salon des Étrangers. The chairs were comfortable, the spirits unusually smooth, the room skillfully lit so that chairs were grouped in pools of illumination, with dimmer areas between, isolating each group in a way that reinforced its identity and made it comfortable to be in. As well as money, the Secretariat of the Holy Presence had gifted and experienced designers.

The group by the fire had assembled almost by accident, but they soon found themselves in a state of warm agreement, almost complicity, in fact. They were discussing the personalities who had made the most impact during the day. The Prefect of the Secretariat, naturally, as their host, was one of these.

"A man of calm authority, he seems to me," said the Dean of the Court of Faculties.

"And much experience of the world. Do you know how much property the Secretariat owns?" said the Preceptor of the Temple Hospitalers.

"No. Is it a great deal?"

"I understand they command funds reaching into the tens of billions. Much due to his skill in the world of banking."

Murmurs of admiration went around the little group.

"Someone else who made an impression, I think," said the Chaplain of the Synod of Deacons, "perhaps in a different way, was Saint, Saint . . . the Patriarch of the . . . of the . . . of Constantinople. A very holy man."

"Indeed," said the Dean. "St. Simeon. We are lucky to have him among us."

"He's led his organization for fifty years, no less," said a man none of the others recognized. He was a dapper Englishman, wearing a faultlessly cut tweed suit and a bow tie. "With increasing wisdom, no doubt, but perhaps in recent years a little lessening of strength. Moral authority undiminished, of course."

Nods of assent. The Dean said, "Very true. I'm afraid I don't recognize you, sir. Which body do you represent?"

"Oh, I'm not a delegate," said the Englishman. "I'm reporting on the congress for the *Journal of Moral Philosophy*. My name is Simon Talbot."

"I think I've read something of yours," said the Chaplain. "A very witty piece about, er . . . about, umm . . . about relativism."

"How very kind," said Talbot.

"It's the younger men who hold the future," said a man in a dark suit, who was an executive of Thuringia Potash, one of the corporate sponsors, a powerful pharmaceutical company. "Such as the Secretary General of *La Maison Juste*."

"Marcel Delamare."

"That's it. An extraordinarily able man."

"Yes, Monsieur Delamare is a remarkable man. He seems very keen to promote this idea of a council," said the Preceptor.

"Well, frankly, so are we," said the Thuringia Potash executive. "And I think it would do well to include your Monsieur Delamare in its ranks."

"A clarity of mind, a vigor of perception," murmured Simon Talbot.

All in all, Marcel Delamare could be pleased with his day's work.

The Café Cosmopolitain, opposite the railway station in Geneva, was a long, rectangular, low-ceilinged room, badly lit, not very

clean, the only decoration on the smoke-brown walls being plac-
ards of chipped enamel or faded paper advertising aperitifs or spirits. There was a zinc-topped bar along one side and staff apparently
chosen for their freedom from the constraints of courtesy and com-
petence. If you wanted to get drunk, it would do as well as anywhere else; if you wanted an evening of civility and fine cuisine,
you were in the wrong place.

But it had one great advantage. As a center for the exchange of
information, it was unmatched. The presence within a few hundred meters of a news agency, not to mention several government
bodies as well as the cathedral, and of course the railway, meant
that journalists or spies or members of the detective police could
practice their various trades at the Cosmopolitain with great ease
and convenience. And with the Magisterial Congress now under
way, the place was crowded.

Olivier Bonneville sat at the bar and ordered a dark beer. His
hawk dæmon murmured into his ear, "Who are we looking for?"

"Matthias Sylberberg. Apparently he knew Delamare at school."

"Surely a man like that wouldn't come to a place like this?"

"No, but the people he works with would." Bonneville sipped
his beer and looked around.

"Isn't the man over there a colleague of Sylberberg's?" said his
dæmon. "The fat man with the gray mustache who's just come in."

The man was hanging his hat and coat on a hat stand near the
mirror, and turning to greet the two men at a table beside it.

"Where did we see him before?" said Bonneville.

"At the opening of the Rovelli show at Tennier's gallery."

"So we did!"

Bonneville turned away from the bar and sat with his elbows on
it behind him, watching the bald man sit with the two others. The
newcomer snapped his fingers at one of the surliest waiters, who
nodded briefly at his order and swept away.

"Who are the other two?" Bonneville murmured.

"I don't remember seeing either of them. Unless the one with his back to us is Pochinsky."

"Pochinsky, the art man?"

"The critic, yes."

"I suppose he could be. . . . Yes, you're right."

The man's face became visible briefly in the mirror as he turned to move his chair.

"And the fat man is called Rattin."

"Well remembered!"

"It's a pretty tenuous connection."

"The best we have at the moment."

"So what are we going to do?"

"Introduce ourselves, of course."

Bonneville finished the beer, put his glass on the bar, and set off confidently across the crowded room just as the surly waiter was approaching the men's table. He contrived to trip as someone moved a chair unexpectedly, and lurched against the waiter, who would have dropped the tray had Bonneville not caught it adroitly.

Exclamations of surprise and admiration from the three men—a snarl from the waiter—a flurry of arm waving and shoulder shrugging from the man who had apparently set it all off by moving his chair.

"Your drinks, I think, gentlemen," said Bonneville, putting the tray down on their table and ignoring the waiter, whose lizard dæmon was protesting volubly from the pocket of his apron.

"Very skillfully caught," said Rattin. "You should be a goalkeeper, sir! Or perhaps you are?"

"No," said Bonneville, smiling. He passed the empty tray back to the waiter, and Rattin went on: "You must have a drink with us to thank you for saving ours."

"Indeed, yes," said the third man.

"Well, how generous . . . A dark beer," Bonneville said to the waiter, who scowled and left.

Bonneville was about to pull out a chair when he looked again at the man with the gray mustache, as if recognizing him.

"Isn't it . . . Monsieur Rattin?" he said.

"Yes, it is, but . . ."

"We met a couple of weeks ago at the opening of the Rovelli show at Tennier's gallery. You won't remember, but I found what you said about the artist quite fascinating."

One of the things that Bonneville had noticed in the course of his life was that older men, homosexual or not, could be very susceptible to the flattery of younger ones if it was expressed with frankness and sincerity. The essential thing was to confirm the views of the older ones in such a way as to convey the simple and genuine admiration of a young person who might one day become a disciple. Bonneville's sparrowhawk dæmon, as if eager to continue the flattery, at once hopped onto the back of Rattin's chair to speak with the man's snake dæmon, who lay curled along the top.

Meanwhile, Bonneville turned to Pochinsky. "And you, sir— I don't think I'm mistaken—surely you're Alexander Pochinsky? I've been reading your column in the *Gazette* for years."

"Yes, that's who I am," said the critic. "And are you involved in the world of the visual arts?"

"Only a humble amateur, one who's content to read what the best critics have to say about them."

"You work for Marcel Delamare," said the third man, who hadn't spoken before. "I think I've seen you at *La Maison Juste*. Am I right?"

"Quite right, sir, and very privileged to do so," said Bonneville, holding out his hand to shake. "My name is Olivier Bonneville."

The man gave Bonneville his hand. "Yes," he said, "I've had

occasion to visit *La Maison Juste* on business once or twice. Eric Schlosser."

He was a banker: Bonneville had placed him at last. "Yes," he said, "my employer is a remarkable man. Of course, you're aware of the Magisterial Congress?"

"Did Monsieur Delamare play a part in organizing that?" asked Rattin.

"Yes indeed, a prominent one," said Bonneville. "Your good health, gentlemen!"

He drank, and they reciprocated.

"Yes," Bonneville went on, "working in daily communication with someone whose brilliance is dazzling—well, you know, one can't help but be a little intimidated."

"What is the business of *La Maison Juste*?" said Pochinsky.

"We are continually seeking a way of accommodating the life of the world to the life of the spirit," said Bonneville easily.

"And will this congress help with that?"

"I truly think so. It should bring a clarity, a sharp edge of purpose to the work of the Magisterium."

Rattin said, "And what is *La Maison Juste*? Is it part of the judicial system?"

"It was set up a century ago—the League for the Instauration of the Holy Purpose, that's the official title—and it's been working hard for a long time. But in recent years, under Monsieur Delamare, it's become a potent force for good in the ranks of the Magisterium. Of course, we should always refer to it by that name, really, but the building where we work is so beautiful that I suppose it's a way of paying tribute to it. It was used centuries ago for the examination of heresy and heretics, hence the name."

Bonneville sensed that his dæmon had discovered something important, but he gave no sign of it. Instead, he turned to the critic.

"Tell me, Monsieur Pochinsky," he said, "what do you think about the place of the spirit in the visual arts?"

Pochinsky could talk about that for hours. Bonneville settled back to nurse his drink, to listen with assiduous attention, and to wait for the perfect moment to depart, when he thanked them all for their fascinating conversation and left them with a strong impression of the courtesy, modesty, capability, and charm of the younger generation.

As soon as they were outside, his dæmon flew to his shoulder. Bonneville listened closely as they made their way to the attic apartment where they lived.

"Well?"

"Rattin works with Sylberberg, as you remembered. And Sylberberg knew Delamare at school, and still has an acquaintanceship with him. According to Rattin's dæmon, Delamare had an older sister to whom he was devoted. She was a prominent force in the Magisterium—she set up an organization devoted to some purpose that Rattin couldn't remember, but she was very influential. A beautiful woman, apparently. She married an Englishman called Courtney, Coulson, something like that, but there was a scandal when she had a child by another man. Delamare was devastated when she vanished about ten years ago. He believes that the child was to blame, but as for why he thinks that, Rattin couldn't say."

"A child! Boy or girl?"

"Girl."

"When?"

"About twenty years ago. Lyra Belacqua. She's the one."

FIFTEEN

LETTERS

When Lyra and Giorgio Brabandt arrived at the gyptians' township in the Fens, the great gathering of boats and maze of landing places and paths around the Byanzaal, it was midmorning, and she was nervously aware that other people might not be as tolerant of her dæmonless state as Brabandt had been.

"No need to be anxious," he'd said. "There's witches visit us from time to time these days, after that great fight in the north. We know their ways. You'll just look like one o' them."

"I suppose I could try," she said. "Where's Farder Coram's boat, do you know?"

"Along the Ringland branch, down that way. But you better call on young Orlando Faa first, out of politeness."

"Young" Orlando was in his fifties, at least. He was the son of the great John Faa, who had led the expedition to the north all that time ago. He was smaller than his father, but he had something of the old man's massiveness of nature, and he greeted Lyra solemnly.

"I heard many tales about you, Lyra," said the gyptian leader. "My old dad was full of 'em. That voyage and the battle when you rescued the little kids—I wished I'd been there every time I heard it."

"It was all thanks to the gyptians," Lyra said. "Lord Faa was a great leader. And a great fighter."

His eyes moved around her where she sat at his council table. He couldn't disguise what he was looking for. "You're in trouble, lady," he said gently.

She was moved by his courtesy in using that term, and found her throat too tight to speak for a moment. She nodded and swallowed hard. "That's why I need to see Farder Coram," she managed to say.

"Old Coram's a bit frail now," said Faa. "He dun't go nowhere, but he hears everything and he knows everything."

"I didn't know where else to go."

"No. Well, you stop here with us till you're ready to go on, and welcome. I know Ma Costa'll be glad to see you."

She was. Lyra went to her next, and the boat mother enfolded Lyra in a warm embrace without a moment's hesitation, and hugged her close in the sunshine-flooded galley, rocking them both back and forth.

"What you been doing to yourself?" she said when she finally let go.

"He . . . Pan . . . I don't know. He was unhappy. We both were. And he just left."

"I never heard of such a thing. You poor gal."

"I'll tell you about it, I promise. But I must go and see Farder Coram first."

"You seen young Orlando Faa?"

"He was the first person I called on. I just arrived this morning, with Giorgio Brabandt."

"Old Giorgio? Well, he's a rascal, and no mistake. I want to hear all about it, don't forget. But what's been happening to you? I never seen anyone look so lost, gal. Where are you going to stay?"

That silenced Lyra. For the first time, she realized that she hadn't thought about that for a moment.

Ma Costa saw that and went on, "Well, you're going to stay here with me, goose. Did you think I'd let you sleep on the bank?"

"Will I be in the way?"

"You're not fat enough to be in the way. Get along with you."

"Ma Costa, I don't know if you remember, but you once said— all that time ago—you said I had witch oil in my soul. What did that mean?"

"I haven't the faintest idea, gal. But it looks as though I was right." She looked somber as she said that. Then she opened a cupboard and took out a small biscuit tin. "Here," she said. "When you see Farder Coram, give him these. I made 'em yesterday. He loves a ginger biscuit."

"I will. Thank you."

Lyra kissed her and left to find the Ringland branch. That was a narrower canal than the rest, with several boats moored permanently on the southern bank. The people she passed looked at her curiously, but without hostility, she thought; she carried herself modestly and kept her eyes down, trying to think like Will, trying to be invisible.

It seemed that Farder Coram had a place of high honor among his people, because the path to his mooring was carefully tended and banked with stone, and the verge planted with marigolds and bordered by poplars. The trees were leafless now, but in the summer they'd cast a welcome shade over this stretch of water.

And there was Coram's boat, neat and trim and brightly painted, everything about her looking fresh and lively. Lyra knocked on the cabin roof and stepped down into the cockpit, and peered in through the window in the cabin door. Her old friend was dozing in a rocking chair with a rug over his knees, his dæmon keeping his feet warm, the great autumn-colored cat Sophonax.

Lyra knocked on the glass, and Coram blinked and woke up, and shaded his eyes to look at the door. Then he recognized her and beckoned her inside, with a great smile on his old face.

"Lyra, child! What am I saying? You en't no child, you're a young lady. Welcome, Lyra—but what's happened to you? Where's Pantalaimon?"

"He left me. Just one morning, only a few days ago. I woke up and he was gone."

Her voice trembled, and then her heart overflowed, and she sobbed and wept as never before. She fell to her knees next to his chair, and he leant out to embrace her. He stroked her hair and held her gently as she clung to him and sobbed against his chest. It was like a dam breaking; it was like a flood.

He murmured soft words, and Sophonax jumped up onto his lap to be close to her, purring in sympathy.

Finally the storm subsided. There were no tears left to weep, and Lyra drew away as the old man loosened his embrace. She mopped her eyes and stood up unsteadily.

"Now, you sit down here and tell me all about everything," he said.

Lyra bent down to kiss him. He smelled of honey. "Ma Costa gave me these ginger biscuits for you," she said. "Farder Coram, I wish I'd thought ahead and brought you a proper present—it seems rude to call on you empty-handed. . . . I did find some smokeleaf, though. That's all they had in the post office where we last stopped, me and Master Brabandt. I think I remembered it right, the kind you smoked."

"That's it, Old Ludgate, that's the sort I like. Thank'ee! So you come here on the *Maid of Portugal*, did you?"

"That's right. Oh, Farder Coram, it's been far too long! It seems like a lifetime ago. . . ."

"Seems like yesterday. Seems like the blink of an eye. But before you start, put the kettle on, gal," he said. "I'd do it meself, but I know me limitations."

She made some coffee, and when it was ready, she put his mug on the little table at his right side and sat down on the settle opposite his rocking chair.

She told him much of what had happened since they had last seen each other. She told him about the murder by the river, and about Malcolm, and how she'd learnt about her own past, and how she now felt lost and almost helpless.

Coram listened to Lyra's story without speaking till she'd come to the present moment and her arrival among the gyptians.

"Young Orlando Faa," he said. "He never come to the north with us, because he had to stay in case John never come back. He always regretted that. Well, he's a fine lad. Fine enough. His father, John—well, he was a great man. Simple and true and strong as a beam of oak. A great man. I don't think they make 'em like him anymore, but Orlando's a fine lad, no doubt about it. But times have changed, Lyra. Things as used to be safe en't safe no longer."

"It does feel like that."

"But young Malcolm, now. Did he tell you how he lent Lord Asriel his canoe?"

"He said something about it, but I . . . I was so shaken up by other things that I didn't really take it in."

"Staunch, Malcolm is. When he was a boy, he was just the same. Generous—didn't hesitate to give Lord Asriel his canoe, never knowing if he'd ever see her again. So when Asriel charged me with taking her back, he gave me some money to see her made over—did Malcolm tell you that?"

"No. There's a lot we just haven't had time to talk about."

"Yes, she was a trim little vessel, the *Bell Savage*. She needed to be. I remember that flood well enough, and how it brung things to light that'd been hid for centuries. Maybe longer."

Coram was talking as if he'd known Malcolm more recently than the flood, and Lyra wanted to ask him about that; but she shrank from it, as if it would give too much away. She felt uncertain about so much.

So she said, "D'you know the phrase 'the secret commonwealth'?"

"Where'd you hear that from?"

"From Master Brabandt. He was telling me about the will o' the wykes, things like that."

"Yes, the secret commonwealth . . . You don't hear much talk about that these days. When I was young, there wasn't a single bush, not a single flower nor a stone, that didn't have its own proper spirit. You had to have a mind to your manners around them, to ask for pardon, or for permission, or give thanks. . . . Just to acknowledge that they were there, them spirits, and they had their proper rights to recognition and courtesy."

"Malcolm told me that a fairy caught me and nearly kept me, except that he tricked her into giving me back."

"That's just the sort of thing they do. They en't bad nor wicked, not really, nor partic'ly good neither. They're just there, and they deserve good manners."

"Farder Coram, did you ever hear of a city that's called the Blue Hotel that's empty and ruined except that dæmons live there?"

"What, people's dæmons? Without their folk?"

"Yes."

"No. I never heard of that. Is that where you think Pan's gone to?"

"I don't know what to think, but it could be. Did you ever know anyone who could separate from their dæmon? Except for witches, of course."

"Yes, the witches could do it all right. Like my Serafina."

"But anyone else? Did you know any gyptians who could separate?"

"Well, there was a man—"

Before he could say more, the boat rocked as if someone had come aboard, and then came a knock. Lyra looked up to see a girl of about fourteen balancing a tray on one arm and opening the door with the other, and hastened to help her step down.

"All right, Farder Coram?" the girl said. She was looking at Lyra warily.

"This is my great-niece Rosella," said Coram. "Rosella, this is Lyra Silvertongue. You heard me speak about her many a time."

Rosella put the tray on Farder Coram's lap and shook hands timidly. Her manner was both shy and curious. She was very pretty. Her dæmon was a hare, and he was hiding behind her legs.

"This is Farder Coram's dinner," she said. "But I brung some for you an' all, miss. Ma Costa said you'd be hungry."

On the tray was some fresh bread and butter and pickled herring, and a bottle of beer and two glasses.

"Thank you," said Lyra, and Rosella smiled and left. When she'd gone, Lyra said, "You were going to tell me about a man who could separate. . . ."

"So I was. That was in Muscovy. He'd been to Siberia, to the place the witches go and done what they did. It nearly killed him, he said. He was the lover of a witch, and he thought that if he could separate like them, he'd live as long as they did. Only it didn't work. His witch didn't think no more of him for doing it, and he died soon after, in any case. He was the only man I knew who could do that, or wanted to. Why d'you ask about that, Lyra?"

She told him about the diary in the rucksack of the man who'd been killed by the river. Coram listened without moving, his fork still holding a piece of pickled herring.

"Does Malcolm know about that?" he said when she'd finished.

"Yes."

"Did he say anything to you about Oakley Street?"

"Oakley Street? Where's that?"

"It en't a place, it's a thing. He never mentioned it? Neither him nor Hannah Relf?"

"No. Maybe they would have done if I hadn't left so suddenly . . . I don't know. I know so little, Farder Coram. What is Oakley Street?"

The old man put his fork down and took a sip of beer. "Twenty years ago," he said, "I took a bit of a risk, and I told young Malcolm to say the words *Oakley Street* to Hannah Relf, so as to reassure her that any connection he had with me was safe. I hoped she'd tell him what it was, and she did, and if he never spoke about it, that's because you can trust him. Oakley Street's the name of a department of the secret service, you might say. That's not its real name, it's just a sort of code for it, because the headquarters en't nowhere near Oakley Street itself, which is in Chelsea. It was set up—the department, I mean—in King Richard's time, the king being staunch agin the Magisterium, which was threatening on all sides. It was always an independent body, Oakley Street, under the Cabinet Office, not the War Ministry. It had the full backing of the king and the Private Council, and funds from the Gold Reserves, and it answered to a proper committee of Parliament. But when King Edward come in, the tone of politics, you might say, begun to change a bit, to swing around with the wind. There was ambassadors and, what do they call 'em, high commissioners, legates, exchanged between London and Geneva.

"That's when the CCD got their foothold in this country. It all changed then to what we got now—a government what dun't trust the people, and a people that's afraid of the government, each side spying on the other. The CCD faction can't arrest as many people as hate it, and the people en't got the organization to move agin the CCD. Sort of a stalemate. But it's worse'n that. The other side's got an energy that our side en't got. Comes from their certainty about being right. If you got that certainty, you'll be willing to do anything to bring about the end you want. It's the oldest human problem, Lyra, an' it's the difference between good and evil. Evil can be unscrupulous, and good can't. Evil has nothing to stop it doing what it wants, while good has one hand tied behind its back. To do the things it needs to do to win, it'd have to become evil to do 'em."

"But . . ." Lyra wanted to object to that but didn't know where to start. "But what about when the gyptians and the witches and Mr. Scoresby and Iorek Byrnison destroyed Bolvangar? Wasn't that an example of good beating evil?"

"Yes, it was. A small victory—all right, a big victory, thinking of all them kids we rescued and took back home. That was a big victory. But not a final one. The CCD is stronger than ever, the Magisterium is full of vigor, and little agencies like Oakley Street are starved of funds and run by old people whose best days are long behind 'em."

He sipped the last of his beer.

"But what d'you want to do, Lyra?" he went on. "What've you got in mind?"

"I didn't know until I had a dream. Not long ago I dreamed I was playing with a dæmon, and she wasn't mine, but we loved each other so much. . . . Sorry." She had to swallow hard and brush her eyes. "I knew what I had to do when I woke up. I had to go to the desert of Karamakan and go into a building there because I might find that dæmon again and . . . I don't know why. But I have to find Pan first, because you can't go in without a dæmon and . . ."

She was losing the thread of her own story, not least because she had hardly expressed it to herself before she began to explain it to Farder Coram. And now she could see he was getting tired.

"I'd better go," she said.

"Yes, I can't stay awake all day like I used to. Come back this evening and I'll be refreshed, and I'll have a couple of ideas for you."

She kissed him again and carried the tray back to Ma Costa's boat.

Ma Costa didn't travel much these days; the family had a mooring near the Byanzaal, and as she said to Lyra, it was likely to be her last. She was happy cultivating vegetables and a few flowers on the patch of ground next to the mooring, and happy, she said, to give Lyra a bunk for as long as she needed to stay. She could cook, if she liked.

"Old Giorgio told me you en't a bad cook," Ma had said. "Except for stewed eels, that is."

"What was wrong with my stewed eels?" said Lyra, a little indignant. "He never told me there was anything wrong with them."

"Well, you watch me next time I cook 'em, and learn. Mind you, it takes a lifetime to know how to do 'em proper."

"What's the secret?"

"You gotta cut them on the diagonal. You wun't think it made any difference, but it does."

She went out with her basket. Lyra went to sit on the cabin roof and watched the boat mother make her way along the bank towards the great Byanzaal, with its thatched roof and the marketplace beside it. The canopies of the market stalls were of many colors, the brightest things by far in the gray landscape, where the horizon had to be guessed at in the fading wintry light.

But even if I passed a lifetime here and learnt to stew eels properly, this isn't my home and it never will be, she thought. I found that out long ago.

It was deeply tiring, not knowing how long she'd be here, or how she'd know it was safe to leave, and knowing only that she didn't belong. She stood up wearily, thinking that she might go below and close her eyes; but before she could move, a small boat came along the canal, punted by a boy of about fourteen whose duck dæmon paddled busily beside it. He was moving the boat with skill and power, and as soon as he saw Lyra, he let the punt pole drag in the water to slow down, and swung it left to bring himself in next to the Costas' boat. The duck dæmon flapped her wings and hopped aboard.

"You Miss Silvertongue?" the boy called up.

"Yes," she said.

He fumbled in the breast of his water-green jacket. "Got a letter for you," he said, and handed it up.

"Thanks."

She took it and turned it over to read the address: "Miss L. Silvertongue, c/o Coram van Texel," and Coram or someone had crossed out his name and written in "Mme. Costa, *Persian Queen*." The envelope was made of heavy, expensive paper, and the address was typed.

She realized that the boy was waiting. Then she realized what he was waiting for, and gave him a small coin.

"Toss you for double or quits," he said.

"Too late now," she said. "I've got the letter."

"Worth a try," he said, and dropped it in his pocket before speeding away, moving his punt so fast it actually had a bow wave.

The envelope was too beautiful to tear, so she went below and slit it open with a kitchen knife. She sat at the galley table to read the letter.

The paper was headed *Durham College, Oxford*, but the printed address was crossed out. She didn't know what that could mean, but the letter was signed *Malcolm P.* She was curious to see his handwriting, and glad to find that it was graceful, strong, and legible. He'd written with a fountain pen in blue-black ink.

Dear Lyra,

I heard from Dick Orchard about your predicament, and where you've gone. You couldn't do better than take refuge in the Fens, and Coram van Texel is the best person to advise you about what to do next. Ask him about Oakley Street. Hannah and I were going to tell you about it, but circumstances have overtaken us.

Bill the porter at Jordan tells me that the gossip in the college is that you were arrested by the CCD, and that you've vanished into the prison system. The servants are furious about this, and blame the Master. There's talk of a strike, which would be a Jordan College first, though since that wouldn't bring you back I don't think it will happen; but the Master will find his relations with the staff more than a little strained.

In the meantime, the best thing you can do is learn as much as you can about every aspect of Oakley Street matters that old Coram van Texel can teach you. We've only just begun to talk about important things, you and I, but I sense that you know through the alethiometer, and maybe from other experiences as well, that there are more ways than one, more than two, of seeing things and perceiving their meanings.

What's so important about the Central Asian connection that came with the death of poor Roderick Hassall is that it seems to turn on this very point.

*Give my greetings to Coram, and tell him what you need
to about Hassall, and about Karamakan. That's where I
shall be going next.*

*Finally, please forgive the slightly pompous tone of this
letter. I know I give that impression, and I wish I didn't.*

*Hannah is writing to you too, and she'd love to hear how
you are. A letter in gyptian hands will make its way safely
and quickly to its destination, but I have no idea how.*

> *With warm friendship,*
> *Malcolm P.*

She read it quickly, and then again slowly. She blushed at his
remark about pomposity, because she *had* thought that—in the
time before, that is to say, not since the murder by the river. The
Malcolm she was getting to know now wasn't pompous in the least.

Ma Costa was out at the market, so Lyra had the *Persian Queen*
to herself. She tore a page from her notebook and started to write.

> *Dear Malcolm,*
> *Thank you for your letter. I'm safe here for the moment, but*

She stopped. She had no idea what to say next, or how to talk
to him at all, in fact. She stood up, went out to the stern, looked
around, ran her hands along the tiller, breathed the chilly air deeply
into her lungs, and went in again.

She continued:

> *I know I'll have to move on soon. I must find Pan. I'm
> going to follow every clue, no matter how absurd or
> unlikely. Like Dr. Strauss's diary when he heard about the*

*place called the Blue Hotel. A sort of refuge, I suppose. I've
decided to head for that and see what happens. ~~I must find
him because unless~~*

She stopped, having crossed that out, and rested her head on her
clenched fist. This was like talking into a void. After a minute she
picked up the pen again.

*If I find him there, we'll go on to Karamakan and try and
cross the desert and find that red building. The thing is that
when I first read about it in Dr. Strauss's account, I thought
about it a lot and it affected me like one of those dreams that
stay with you for hours after you wake up. It was familiar,
but I had no idea why. I think I know something about it,
but it's lost and I can't reach it. I probably need to dream
about it again.*

Maybe I'll see you there.

*If I don't come back, I just want to say thank you for
taking care of me in the flood when I was a baby. I wish
memories went further back in our lives than they do so that
I could recall all of it, because the only thing I remember is
little trees with lights in them and being very happy. But of
course that might have been a dream too. ~~I wish~~ I hope one
day we'll be able to talk and I can explain all the things that
led up to me coming here. I don't understand it all myself.
But Pan thought something had stolen my imagination.
That's why he left, to go and look for it. Maybe you could
understand what he meant by that and why it was almost
too hard to bear.*

*Malcolm, please give my love to Hannah and to Alice.
And remember me to Dick Orchard. Oh, and to your*

parents. I've known them for such a little time but I liked
them so much. ~~It would be~~

She crossed out those three words and wrote instead:

~~*I wish*~~

before crossing that out too. Finally she wrote:

I'm very glad we made friends.
                                        Yours,
                                        Lyra

Before she could regret writing it, she sealed it in an envelope she found in a galley drawer and addressed it to Dr. Malcolm Polstead, Durham College, Oxford. She left it propped against the salt pot and went out again.

She was restless. There was nothing to settle to, nothing purposeful to do; she was tired, and yet she couldn't keep still. She wandered along the canal banks, aware of the curious stares of the boat people and the particular way the young men were looking at her. The canals and the Byanplaats were as busy as ever, and soon she became uncomfortable with the sense that so many eyes were on her. Those young men: if Pan had been with her, she'd have been able to stare them back just as boldly, as she'd done a hundred times in the past, or even better, ignore them completely. She knew that they were less self-assured than they looked, and that she could disconcert them in several ways, but knowing that she could do it wasn't the same as being able to do it just then. She was nervous of everything, and it was horrible. She wanted to hide.

Defeated, she turned back to the *Persian Queen* and lay down on her bunk. Quite soon she was asleep.

Pantalaimon, meanwhile, was sleeping too, but intermittently; he would wake up suddenly and remember where he was, and then lie listening to the thudding of the engine, and the groaning and creaking of the old schooner's timbers, and the splash of the waves only inches away through the hull, before sinking again into a shallow slumber.

He woke up out of a dream to hear a scratchy kind of whisper close by, and knew at once that it was the voice of a ghost. He closed his eyes tighter and pulled himself even further into the darkness of the hold, but the whispers went on. It wasn't one, it was several, and they wanted something from him, but they couldn't say it clearly.

"I'm just dreaming," he whispered. "Go away, go away."

The ghosts pressed around him closely, their voices hissing and scratching under the restless dash of the waves.

"Don't come so near," he said. "Get back."

Then he realized that they weren't threatening: they were desperate for the little warmth they could feel from his body. He felt an oceanic pity for these poor chilly phantoms, and tried to peer through his closed eyelids to see their faces clearly; but there was nothing clear about them. The sea had worn them smooth and vague. He still didn't know if he was awake or asleep.

Then he heard the sound of a bolt being slid open. Every pale blank ghost face looked up at once, and then, as a beam of anbaric light stabbed down into the murk, they all vanished, as if they'd never been. Pan crouched deeper into the shadows and held his breath. Now he was awake; there was no doubt about that; he had to open his eyes.

There was a ladder, and a man was clambering down it—two

men. Rain came pelting in with them, splashing and streaming off their oilskins and sou'westers. The first man held a torch, and the second man reached up and swung the hatch cover closed above them. One of the men was the sailor he'd seen the night before, watching from the rail while the captain and the mate stole the propeller.

The first man hung the torch on a nail. The battery was running low, so the light was dim and inconstant, but Pan could see the two of them turning over the boxes and sacks that had been tossed carelessly down into the hold. Most of the boxes seemed to be empty, but then they came across one that clinked with the sound of bottles.

"Ah," said the first man, and tore off the cardboard lid. "Oh, shit, look at this. Typical." He held up a bottle of tomato ketchup.

"Here's some spuds," said the other man, opening a sack. "He can make us some chips, at least. I don't know, though. . . ." The potatoes he was taking out had all grown lengthy pallid shoots, and some of them were rotten.

"They'll do," said the first man. "Fry 'em in diesel and you'll never taste the difference. And here's some sauerkraut, look. And some tinned wurst. A feast, mate."

"Don't go back up yet, though," said the other. "Let 'em wait. Stay out the rain and have a smoke."

"Good idea," said the first man, and they piled a couple of flour sacks against the bulkhead, settled down on them, and dragged out their pipes and smokeleaf. Their dæmons, a rat and a sparrow, came out of the necks of their oilskins and grubbed around by their feet, looking for scraps of anything tasty.

"What's the old man going to do with that bloody propeller?" said one of the men when he'd got his pipe alight. "As soon as the harbormaster spots it, he'll call the cops."

"Who is the harbormaster at Cuxhaven?"

"Old Hessenmüller. Nosy swine."

"Flint'll probably try and offload it on Borkum first. That breaker's yard across from the lighthouse."

"What kind of cargo does he think we'll pick up in Cuxhaven anyway?"

"Not cargo. Passengers."

"Piss off! Who'd pay to sail on this filthy old wreck?"

"I heard him talking, him and Herman. These are a special sort of passengers."

"What's special about them?"

"They en't got no passports, no papers, nothing like that."

"Money? They got any money?"

"No, they en't got that either."

"Then what's in it for the old man?"

"He's got a deal with some big farmer in Essex. There's more and more people coming up the rivers from the south, I don't know, Turkey or somewhere. There's no work for 'em in Germany, but this farmer reckons he likes the idea of a bunch of workers he doesn't have to pay. Well, I suppose he has to feed 'em and give 'em somewhere to sleep, but no wages, sod that for a lark. Slaves, basically. They won't be able to get away because if they en't got papers . . ."

"We're running slaves now?"

"I don't like it either. But whatever happens, he'll do all right, Hans Flint. He always does."

"Mad bowlegged bastard."

They smoked in silence for a few minutes more, and then the first man knocked out his pipe and stamped the ashes deep into the bilgewater slopping to and fro.

"Come on," he said, "get some spuds, and I'll see if I can find some beer. If there's any left."

"Tell you what," said the other. "I'm sick of this. Soon as I get me pay, I'm going to scarper."

"Don't blame yer. Course, Flint'll hold out till he's sold the pro-peller, and then till he's got his fee from the farmer, and he'll go on holding out time and time again. Remember old Gustav? He scarpered in the end without the pay he was owed. Just gave up and buggered off."

He shoved the hatch cover up, and the two of them climbed out into the rain, leaving Pan in the dark and the cold and the solitude. Even the ghosts left him alone; perhaps they were dreams after all.

SIXTEEN

LIGNUM VITAE

Lyra woke up in the early evening, feeling heavy-headed and anxious and not in the least refreshed. After eating a meal of mussels and mashed potato with Ma Costa, and telling her about life at school and college, she did as Farder Coram had suggested and went to see him again. She found him bright-eyed in the lamplight and eager to talk, as if he had a secret to tell her, but he asked her to put another log in the little iron stove and pour them both a glass of jenniver before he'd say anything about it.

She sat in the other armchair and took a sip of the clear, cold spirit.

"Well, now," he said, "it was something you said, or it might have been something I said, or it might have been neither of those, but it set me thinking about this journey of yours. And witches."

"Yes!" she said. "I wonder if we're thinking the same thing. If people think I'm a witch, then they won't—"

"Exactly! If a witch came this far south, like my Serafina did—"

"And she lost her cloud-pine, or it was stolen, or something—"

"Thassit. She'd have to stay earthbound till she found her way

274

back north. We *are* thinking the same thing, gal. But it en't going to be easy. People might accept that you're a witch, and that'd account for Pan being missing, but don't forget they fear witches, and they hate them, sometimes."

"I'll have to be careful, then. But I can be careful."

"You'll have to be lucky too. But you know, Lyra, maybe this *could* work. Except . . . well, that scheme might work with ordinary people. But suppose you met a real witch?"

"Whatever would a witch be doing in Central Asia?"

"Them regions where you're going, in Central Asia, they en't unfamiliar with witches. They travel a long way sometimes, for trade, for learning, for diplomacy. You'll have to work out all you're going to say. And specially what you'll say if you meet a real witch."

"I'll be very young. Only just separated from my dæmon at that place in Siberia . . ."

"Tungusk."

"That's it. And I'm still learning a lot of witch ways. But I don't look like a witch, that's one problem."

"I don't know about that. How many witches did you see when we were in the north?"

"Hundreds."

"Yes, but all from Serafina's clan, or related ones. They look similar, naturally. But they don't all look the same. There's fair-haired witches with Scandinavian-looking eyes and ones with black hair and different-shaped eyes. I think you could *easy* pass for a witch, if it was just a matter of looks."

"And Ma Costa did say once that I had witch oil in my soul."

"There you are, then!" He was becoming enthusiastic about the idea, crazy as it was.

"But then there's language," she said. "I don't speak any of their languages."

"Cross that bridge later. Fetch me that atlas off the bookshelf."

The atlas was old and much used, and the pages were held together by the very last of the stitching. Farder Coram opened it on his lap and turned at once to the pages showing the far north.

"Here," he said, his finger on one of the maps of the Arctic Ocean.

"What's that?" she said, and came around to look over his shoulder.

"Novy Kievsk. This is where you can come from. It's that little island, and there *is* a witch clan there, and it's fiercer and prouder for being so small. You invent a story to explain how something's sent you all the way south on some high purpose. When you were a little gal, you could've spun out a yarn like that for hours on end, and had everyone around listening and half believing every word."

"Yes, I could," she said, and for a moment all the exhilaration of telling a story like that returned to her heart, and the old man saw the light in her eyes as she remembered it. "But I've lost it," she went on. "I can't do that anymore. That was just fancy. I was spinning those tales out of the air, nothing more than that; there was nothing solid in them. Maybe Pan was right, and I haven't got a real imagination. I was bullshitting."

"You were *what?*"

"That's a word Mr. Scoresby taught me. He told me there were truth tellers, and they needed to know what the truth was, so as to tell it. And there were liars, and they needed to know what the truth was, so they could change it or avoid it. And there were bullshitters, who didn't care about the truth at all. They weren't interested. What they spoke wasn't the truth and it wasn't lies; it was bullshit. All they were interested in was their own performance. I remember him telling me that, but I didn't realize it applied to me till much later, after the world of the dead. The story I told there for the ghosts of the kids wasn't bullshit; that was truth. That's why

276

the harpies listened. . . . But with all those other stories I told, I was bullshitting. I can't do it anymore."

"Well, I'm blowed. Bullshitting!" He laughed gently. "But listen, gal, bullshit or not, you're going to need to keep in touch with Hannah Relf and young Malcolm. Are you going to let 'em know before you set off?"

"Yes. When I left here earlier, I got a letter. . . ."

She told him about Malcolm's letter, and what she'd said in reply.

"He says he's off to Central Asia?" he said. "There's only one reason for that. Oakley Street'll have sent him. No doubt there's good cause, but . . . Still, he'll find ways of getting in touch. And I'll tell you something else: there's Oakley Street agents and friends in places you might not suspect, and he'll have let 'em know your predicament, and they'll be keeping an eye out for you."

"How would I know who they are?"

"Leave it to young Malcolm. He'll find ways of doing that."

Lyra fell silent and tried to imagine this journey of several thousand miles, alone, truly alone, and conspicuous too, if her witch disguise was penetrated.

Farder Coram was leaning over the side of his chair and rummaging in the bottom drawer of a little cabinet beside him. With an effort he heaved himself up again.

"Here," he said. "I don't think I ever ordered you to do anything before. I never thought I'd dare. Now you do as I tell you, and don't argue. Take this." He held out a little leather bag closed with a drawstring.

She hesitated.

He snapped, "Take it. Don't argue," and his eyes darkened.

For the first time in her life, she felt afraid of him. She took the little bag, and felt by the weight of it that the coins in there must be gold.

"Is this—"

"Listen to me. I'm telling you what to do. If you won't listen to Farder Coram, you can listen to a senior officer in Oakley Street. I'm giving you this because I got a high regard for you, and for Hannah Relf, and for young Malcolm. Now open it up."

She did, and poured the coins into her hand. They were all kinds of currency, from a dozen or more countries and every kind of shape: mostly round, to be sure, but also square with rounded corners, and octagonal, and seven- or eleven-sided; and some had holes in the middle, and some were worn smooth, and others were clipped or bent; but every single one was heavy and lustrous and gleaming with the purity of gold.

"But I can't—"

"Hush. Hold 'em out."

She did, and he turned them over with a trembling finger and picked out four, which he put in his waistcoat pocket.

"That'll do me. I don't need any more'n that, no matter what happens. The rest is for you. Keep it tight about yourself, but not all in the same pocket. Another thing: if you remember the witches you've seen, you'll recall the little coronet of flowers they wear. Little tiny Arctic flowers. You remember that?"

"Some of them did. Not all. Serafina did."

"The queens always do. Sometimes other witches do as well. It wouldn't do no harm to make yourself a little coronet, something simple, a piece of cotton braid, even. It'd give you an air. Never mind how little it cost. Witches are poor, but they bear theirselves like queens and great ladies. I don't mean conceit and swagger— that's the last thing I mean—but there's a majesty, a kind of pride and awareness, a sense of magnificence. I'm not finding the right words. It can exist in the same place as modesty, strange as it seems. They're modest in their clothing, and they have the bearing of panthers. You could do that. You do it already, only you don't know it."

Lyra asked him to tell her more about Oakley Street, and he told her some things that might be useful, such as a catechism by which she could tell whether or not someone was trustworthy; and she asked about the witches, little details of their life, ways of behaving, habits, as much as she could think of. She felt contented, because she'd made a decision. She was in charge again.

"Farder Coram, I don't know what to say, except thank you."

"We en't finished yet. See that locker up there over the bookshelf? Go and look in there."

She did as he said, and found a mass of notebooks, a roll of something heavy in a soft leather covering, an elaborate leather belt, together with some other bits and pieces she could only examine if she took them out.

"What am I looking for?"

"A short heavy stick. It'd be nearly black by now. It en't round—it's got seven sides."

Her hands found it under the notebooks and brought it out. It was almost black and surprisingly heavy, so heavy it might have been made of brass; but the warmth and the very slight oiliness of the surface showed that it was clearly wood.

"What's this?"

"It's a fighting stick. It's called Pequeno."

"What does that mean?"

"It means Little One, more or less. Little Stick."

It tapered slightly inwards towards the handle, which was bound tightly with some sort of hard cord. At its thickest it was about as thick as three of her fingers together, and the handle was only a little thicker than her thumb. In length it was about the distance between the inside of her elbow and the palm of her hand.

She held it, testing the weight, swinging it lightly to and fro. The balance made it feel almost like part of her.

"What's this wood?" she said.

"It's lignum vitae. The hardest wood in the world."

"Has it got lead or something inside it?"

"No, that's the weight of the wood itself. I got that—where'd I get that?—in High Brazil. A slaver attacked me with it. Trouble is, he wasn't fast enough. His dæmon was an old monkey, and she'd got fat. We took the stick away from him, and I used it ever since."

Lyra imagined the weight of it swung by a strong arm; it would be quite enough to smash a skull.

"Pequeno?" she said. "All right. Pequeno it is." Having a name made it feel more alive to her. She weighed it in her two hands. "Well, thank you, Farder Coram," she said. "I'll take it, though it frightens me. I didn't think I might need to fight. I've never prepared for it."

"No, it didn't look like being necessary, once you come home from that other world."

"I thought all the danger was over. . . . Everything, the good as well as the bad, it was all over. There was nothing left but learning and . . . Well, just that, really."

She looked down. He was watching her tenderly. "That young boy," he said.

"Will."

"I remember Serafina saying to me, last words we ever had, she said that boy has more power of vanishing than a witch, and he don't know it. Imitate him, Lyra, when you can. Be aware all round. Be aware of boys and men. Older men, in particular. There's a time to show your own power, and a time to seem so insignificant, they don't even notice you, and if they do, they forget you in a moment. That's how Will done it, and that's why Serafina was so impressed."

"Yes. I'll remember that. Thank you, Farder Coram."

"You en't never left Will, really, have you?"

"I think about him every day. Probably every hour. He's still the center of my life."

"We could see that, John and me. We could see that then. There was a question come up, as should we let you sleep beside him as you did? You both being, what was it, only twelve, thirteen . . . We talked about that, and it troubled us."

"But you didn't try and separate us."

"No."

"And we never . . . It never seemed to be . . . All we ever did was kiss. Again and again, as if we'd never stop. As if we'd never have to stop. And that was enough. If we'd been older, I don't know, then it wouldn't have been enough. But for us then, it was."

"I think we knew that, so we said nothing."

"That was the best thing you could have done."

"But you got to let him go sometime, Lyra."

"D'you think so?"

"Yes, I do. Serafina taught me that."

They sat in silence for a while. Lyra thought, If I haven't got Pan, and if I must give up Will too . . . But it wasn't really Will, she knew; it was a memory. All the same, she thought, it was the best thing she had. Could she really ever let it go?

She felt the boat rock slightly, and recognized Rosella's step. A moment later the door opened and the girl came in.

"It's time for your hot drink, Farder Coram," she said.

The old man was looking tired. Lyra got up and kissed him good night. "Rosella," she said, "do you know how to stew eels?"

"Yes," said the girl. "It was the first thing my mum showed me when I was little."

"What's the secret of good stewed eels?"

"The secret . . . Well, I dunno if I should tell you."

"Go on, child," said Farder Coram. "You tell her."

"Well, what my mum does, and my gran does it too, is . . . You know the flour you use for thickening the gravy?"

"Yes," said Lyra.

"Well, you toast it a bit first. In a dry pan. Just to give it a bit of color. Not much. My mum says it makes all the difference."

"Best stewed eels you'll ever taste," said the old man.

"Thanks," said Lyra. "That must be it. I'll be off now, Farder Coram. Thank you for everything. I'll come again tomorrow."

Darkness had fallen, and all around her the windows of the gyptian boats were lit, and wood smoke drifted from their chimneys. Lyra passed a group of gyptian boys smoking outside a liquor shop, her age or thereabouts, and they all fell silent as she approached and stared as she passed by. When she'd gone past, one of them spoke, and the others sniggered. She ignored it, but she was very conscious of the stick, and imagined how it would feel in her hand if she ever did wield it in anger.

It was too early for bed, and she still felt restless, so she went to pay a last call on Giorgio Brabandt before he left. There was a slight rain falling as she trod the muddy path to the *Maid of Portugal*'s mooring.

She found Brabandt working by lantern light to clear the weed trap, hauling up strands of dripping weed and cutting them clear of the propeller. Someone was bustling about inside: the lamp was alight in the galley, and she could hear the chink of crockery.

He looked up as she arrived. "How do, gal," he said. "Want to clear some weeds?"

"It looks too difficult for me," she said. "I'd rather watch you and make notes."

"Well, that's not on offer. Get in the galley and say hello to Betty and bring me a cup of tea."

"Who's Betty?" she began to ask, but his head was already down by the trap, his right arm working busily under the water.

Lyra stepped down into the cockpit and opened the door. The steam, the warmth, and the aroma told her that Betty (and Lyra had already guessed that she was Giorgio's latest inamorata-cum-cook) was boiling some potatoes to go with the casserole that stood next to the stove.

"Hello," she said. "I'm Lyra, and you must be Betty."

Betty was plump and fortyish, and at the moment she was pink in the face and her blond hair was a little disheveled. She smiled immediately and held out a warm hand, which Lyra shook with pleasure.

"Giorgio told me all about you," Betty said.

"Then I bet he told you I couldn't stew eels to save my life. What's the secret?"

"Oh, there en't no secret. But did you put an apple in?"

"I never thought of doing that."

"A cooking apple. It cuts the fat a little bit. It boils down so you don't know it's there, but it makes the gravy all silky and just a little bit tart."

"Well, I'll remember that. Thank you."

"Where's my tea?" Giorgio called.

"Oh Lord," said Betty.

"I'll take it out to him," said Lyra.

Betty put three teaspoons of sugar in a big mug of tea, and Lyra carried it out to the cockpit. Giorgio was fitting the cover back on the trap.

"So what you been doing with yourself?" he said.

"Learning things. Betty's just taught me how to stew eels properly."

"High time you knew."

"Ma Costa says only a real gyptian can stew eels. But I think there's more to it than that."

"Course there is. They got to be moon-caught eels, did she tell you that?"

"Moon-caught?"

"Caught at the full moon. What else could it mean? They're the best. Nothing compares to moon-caught eels."

"Well, you never told me that before. That's something else I've learnt. And the secret commonwealth—you taught me about that too."

His expression became serious, and he looked up and down the path. He lowered his voice and said, "Judgment, gal. There's things you can talk about and things you better hold your tongue on. Eels is one of the first, and the secret commonwealth is one of the other."

"I think I realized that."

"Well, take it to heart. Out there on land you'll meet all kinds of different opinions. Some people will hear talk about the secret commonwealth and take it literally, and think you do too, and that you're stupid. Others just scoff, as if they already know it's a lot of moonshine. Both stupid. Keep away from the literal-minded folk, and ignore the scoffers."

"What's the best way of thinking about the secret common-wealth, then, Master Brabandt?"

"You gotta think about it the same way as if you want to see it. You got to look at it sideways. Out the corner of your eye. So you gotta think about it out the corner of your mind. It's there and it en't, both at the same time. If you want to see them jacky lanterns, the absolute worst way is to go out on the marsh with a searchlight. You take a bloody great light, and all the will o' the wykeses and the little sparkers, they'd stay right underwater. And if you want to think about them, it don't do no good making lists and classifying and analyzing. You'll just get a lot o' dead rubbish what means nothing. The way to think about the secret commonwealth is with stories. Only stories'll do."

He blew on his tea to cool it.

"So thassit," he said. "And what you learning all these things for, anyway?"

"Did I tell you about Karamakan?"

"I never heard that name before. What's that?"

"It's a desert in Central Asia. The thing is . . . Well, dæmons can't go into it."

"Why would anyone want to go where their dæmon can't?"

"To find out what's inside. They grow roses there."

"What, in the desert?"

"There must be somewhere hidden where the roses grow. Special roses."

"Ah, well, they would be." He sipped his tea with a loud slurp and pulled out a blackened old smoke pipe.

"Master B, is the secret commonwealth only in Brytain, or all over the world?"

"Oh, it's all over the world, naturally. But I 'spect there's other names for it in other places. Like in Holland, they got a different name for the jacky lanterns. They call 'em *dwaallichts*. And in France they call 'em *feu follets*."

Lyra thought about it. "When I was young," she said, "when I went to the north with the gyptian families, I remember Tony Costa telling me about the phantoms they had in the northern forests, the Breathless Ones, and the Windsuckers. . . . I suppose they must be part of the secret commonwealth of the north."

"Stands to reason."

"And later in another place I saw Specters. . . . They were different again. And that was even in a different world altogether. So maybe there's a secret commonwealth everywhere."

"Wouldn't surprise me a bit," he said.

They sat there quietly for a minute or two, the gyptian packing his pipe with smokeleaf, Lyra helping herself to a sip of his tea.

"Where you going next, Master B?" she said.

"Up north. Nice peaceful work, hauling stone and bricks and cement for that railroad bridge as is going to put us all out of business."

"What'll you do then?"

"Come back here and catch eels. Time I settled down. I'm past me first youth, ye see."

"Oh. I hadn't realized."

"No, I know it dun't show."

She laughed.

"What you laughing for?" he said.

"You take after your grandson."

"Yes, I learnt a lot from young Dick. Or was it the other way round? I can't remember. Did he treat you proper?"

"He treated me very proper."

"Thass all right, then. Cheerio, Lyra. Good luck."

They shook hands, and she looked in and said good night to Betty, and then she left.

Ma Costa was already asleep in the forward cabin of the *Persian Queen*, so Lyra moved carefully as she boarded the boat, treading lightly and making no noise as she prepared for bed.

And once she was tucked up warmly in her bunk, with the little naphtha lamp glowing on the bedside shelf, she found herself wide awake. She thought about writing to Malcolm again; she thought about writing to Hannah; and she thought about something that had never occurred to her before—why she so enjoyed the company of old men like Giorgio Brabandt and Farder Coram.

That caught her attention. She began to think it through.

She liked them a lot, and she'd liked the old Master of Jordan, Dr. Carne, and she liked Mr. Cawson the Steward. And Sebastian Makepeace the alchemist. She liked them much more than most young men. It wasn't because they were too old to be interested in her sexually, and didn't make her feel threatened: Mr. Cawson was known to be a ladies' man, and Giorgio Brabandt had been frank about his own girlfriends, though he'd said she didn't have enough mileage on her to qualify as one herself.

It was something in that region of feelings. Then she had it: she liked being in their company not because they might be attracted to her, but because there was no danger of her being attracted to them. She didn't want to be unfaithful to the memory of Will.

What about Dick Orchard, though? Why didn't her brief romantic liaison with him count as being unfaithful? Probably because neither of them had once used the word *love*. He was frank about what he wanted, and he knew enough to make sure she enjoyed it as much as he did. And he liked her, and made that clear. And she liked the touch of his lips on her skin. There'd been nothing of the all-consuming, all-pervading intensity and ardent passion she and Will had felt together, each for the first time; she and Dick were simply two healthy young people under the spell of a golden summer, and that was quite enough to be.

That dream, though: the one in which she was playing with Will's dæmon on the moonlit grass, stroking her, whispering together, in thrall to each other. The memory of it was still enough to make her body throb and melt and yearn for something impossible, unnameable, unreachable. Something like Will, or like the red building in the desert. Deliberately she let herself drift on a slow current of longing, but it didn't last; she couldn't bring it back; she lay awake with all the longing frustrated, the memory of that love dream fading, no nearer sleep than ever.

Finally, tired and exasperated, she took out her copy of Simon Talbot's *The Constant Deceiver*.

The chapter she was reading began:

ON THE NON-EXISTENCE OF DÆMONS

Dæmons don't exist.

We might think they do; we might talk to them and hold them close and whisper our secrets to them; we might make judgments about other people whose dæmons we think we see, based on the form they seem to have and the attractiveness or repulsiveness they embody; but they don't exist.

In few other areas of life does the human race display so great a capacity for self-deception. From our earliest childhoods we are encouraged to pretend that there exists an entity outside our bodies which is nevertheless part of ourselves. These wispy playmates are the finest device our minds have yet developed to instantiate the insubstantial. Every social pressure confirms us in our belief in them: habits and customs grow like stalagmites to fix the soft fur, the big brown eyes, the merry tricks in a behavioral cavern of stone.

And all the multitudinous forms this delusion takes are nothing more than random mutations of cells in the brain. . . .

Lyra found herself reading on, though she wanted to deny every word. Talbot had an explanation for everything. The fact that children's dæmons appeared to change form, for example, was no more than a representation of the greater malleability of the infant and juvenile mind. That they were usually, but not always, opposite in sex to their person was merely an unconscious projection of the sense of incompleteness felt by the human subject: yearning for its opposite, the mind embodied the complementary gender role in a sexually non-threatening creature, which could fulfill the part without evoking sexual desire or jealousy. The dæmon's inability to move far from the person was simply a psychological expression of a sense of unity and wholeness. And so on.

Lyra yearned to tell Pan about this, and discuss the extraordinary sight of a clever mind attempting almost successfully to deny an obvious reality; but it was too late for that. She put the book down and tried to think like Talbot. His method consisted mainly of saying "X is [no more than, nothing but, only, merely, just, simply, etc.] Y"; and it was easy therefore to construct sentences such as "What we call reality is nothing but a gathering of flimsy similarities held together by habit."

And that didn't help at all, though no doubt Talbot's explanation would have come with a multitude of examples and citations and arguments, each one perfectly reasonable and seemingly impossible to deny, by the end of which the reader would be a step nearer accepting his main argument, the preposterous idea that dæmons did not exist.

She felt unbalanced by his words, in a way that felt like reading the alethiometer with the new method. Things that had been steady were now unfixed; the very ground was shaky; she trembled on the edge of vertigo.

She put *The Constant Deceiver* down and thought about the other book that had made Pan angry, Gottfried Brande's novel *The Hyperchorasmians*. For the first time she realized that the two writers had more in common than she'd thought. The famous sentence that ended *The Hyperchorasmians*—"It was nothing more than what it was"—was constructed exactly like a sentence of Talbot's. Why hadn't she seen that before? And then she remembered that Pan had tried to tell her.

She wanted to talk about it. She took a sheet of paper and started to write to Malcolm. But she must have been tired; her summary of Talbot's arguments seemed both heavy-handed and thin, her description of *The Hyperchorasmians* confused and confusing; she couldn't summon any confidence or ease, and her sentences lay inert on the page. She felt defeated even before she'd finished a single paragraph.

She thought, If there were such things as Specters, this is what it would feel like to be in a Specter's power. The Specters she was thinking of were those dreadful parasites that fed on the inhabitants of Cittàgazze. Now that she was an adult, and Pan's form was fixed, she would be as vulnerable to the Specters as the adults of that world had been. Simon Talbot could never have been to Cittàgazze, so Specters made no appearance in *The Constant Deceiver*. No doubt he'd have a fluent and persuasive argument for denying their existence as well.

She put her pen away and tore up the page. The question was, she thought, was the universe alive or dead?

From somewhere far off on the marshes came the cry of an owl.

Lyra found herself thinking, What does that mean? and simultaneously thought of Talbot's inevitable reply: "It doesn't mean anything." Some years before, in Oxford, she'd had an encounter with the dæmon of a witch, in a little adventure that had culminated in her thinking that everything meant something, if only she could read it. The universe had seemed alive then. There were messages to be read everywhere you looked. Something like the cry of an owl out on the marshes would have been blazing with significance.

Had she just been *wrong* then to feel that? Or immature, naive, sentimental? Simon Talbot would have said both, but charmingly, delicately, wittily. Devastatingly.

She had no answer. A tiny spark of consciousness in the oceanic night, and with her dæmon merely a projection of her unconscious mind, having no real existence at all, wherever he might be now, Lyra felt as unhappy and alone as she had ever done in her life.

"But where is she?"

Marcel Delamare asked the question with enormous and un-concealed patience. The lamplight, glaring from over his shoulder full in the face of Olivier Bonneville, disclosed a hint of clammi-ness, of pallor, of physical unease in the young man. Delamare was glad to see it: he meant to make Bonneville even more uneasy be-fore the interview was over.

"I can't pinpoint her," Bonneville snapped. "The alethiometer doesn't work like that. I know she's traveling, and I know she's go-ing east. More than that, no one could tell."

"Why not?" Very patiently indeed.

"Because the old method, which is the one you want me to use, Monsieur Delamare, is static. It's based on a set of relation-ships which may be very complex but are fixed." He stopped and stood up.

"Where are you going?" said Delamare.

"I'm damned if I'm going to be interrogated with that light in my eyes. I'll sit over here." He slouched to the sofa next to the fireplace. "If you'd let me use the new method, I could find her in no time," he went on, putting his feet up on the tapestry-covered stool. "That's dynamic. It allows for movement. It makes all the difference."

"Take your feet off that stool. Turn to face me so I can see whether you're lying."

In response, Bonneville lay back along the sofa, his head on one arm, his feet on the other. He stared at Delamare briefly, and then put his head back and gazed at the ceiling, nibbling at a fingernail.

"You don't look well," said the Secretary General. "You look as if you've got a hangover. Have you been drinking to excess?"

"Kind of you to ask," said Bonneville.

"Well?"

"Well what?"

Delamare took a deep breath and sighed. "The point is this," he said. "You are doing very little work. The last report you filed was nearly empty of useful content. Our arrangement will come to an end this Friday, unless by then you've made a real and relevant discovery."

"What d'you mean, our arrangement? What arrangement?"

"The arrangement by which you are using the alethiometer. The privilege can easily be—"

"You want to take it away? A lot of good that'll do you. There's no one half as quick as me, even with the old method. If you—"

"It's no longer simply a question of speed. I don't trust you, Bonneville. For a while you seemed to promise an advantage. Now, because of your self-indulgent posturing, that advantage has disappeared. The Belacqua girl has eluded us, and you seem to have no—"

"All right, then," Bonneville said, and stood up. He looked paler than ever. "Have it your own way. Take the alethiometer. Send someone round in the morning to collect it. You'll regret it. You'll say sorry, you'll beg and plead, but I won't lift a finger. I've had enough."

He picked up a cushion from the sofa and seemed about to throw it, probably into the fire; but he just dropped it on the floor and sauntered out.

Delamare tapped his fingers on the desk. It hadn't gone the way he'd planned, and he blamed himself. Once again Bonneville had outwitted, or to be more accurate, out-insolenced him. Unfortunately, the boy was quite right: none of the other alethiometrists was a patch on him for speed or accuracy, and none had mastered the new method. Even though Delamare mistrusted it, he had to admit that the new method had produced some startling results. He suspected that Bonneville was using it despite his prohibition.

Perhaps, the Secretary General thought, it had been a mistake to rely so closely on the alethiometer. The older methods of spying still worked, as they had done for centuries, and the Magisterium's intelligence network was powerful and had a long reach, with agents throughout Europe and across Asia Minor, as well as further east. Perhaps it was time to awaken them. Events were soon going to move fast in the Levant; it would be a wise precaution to put every agent on the alert.

He called in his secretary and dictated several notes. Then he put on his overcoat and hat and went out.

Marcel Delamare's private life was intensely discreet. It was known that he was not married and assumed that he was not homosexual, but that was all. He had few friends and no hobbies, didn't collect ceramics or play bridge or attend the opera. A man of his age and state of health might normally be expected to have a mistress, or to visit a brothel occasionally, but no whispers of that sort ever attended his name. The fact was that journalists didn't find him a very promising subject. He was a dull functionary working in an obscure department of the Magisterium, and that was all. The papers had long given up hope of gaining readers by writing about Monsieur Delamare.

So no one followed when he went out for an evening walk, or

saw him ring the bell of a large house in a quiet suburb, or watched as he was admitted by a woman in the habit of a nun. The light that came on over the door just before she opened it was exceptionally dim.

The nun said, "Good evening, Monsieur Delamare. Madame is expecting you."

"How is she?"

"Adjusting to the new medication, we hope, monsieur. The pain is a little better."

"Good," said Delamare, handing her his coat and hat. "I'll go straight up."

He climbed the carpeted staircase and knocked at a door in a softly lit passageway. A voice from inside told him to enter.

"Maman," he said, and bent over the old woman in the bed.

She turned her cheek to receive the kiss. Her wrinkled lizard dæmon drew back on the pillow, as if there were the slightest danger that Delamare might kiss him too. The room was close and hot, and smelled oppressively of lily of the valley, pungently of embrocation, and faintly of physical decay. Madame Delamare was extremely thin, for reasons of fashion, and had once been handsome. Her sparse yellow hair was stiffly coiffed and she was immaculately made up, though a tiny amount of the scarlet lipstick had seeped into the tight lines that led away from her mouth, and no amount of cosmetics could conceal the savagery in her eyes.

Delamare sat on the chair next to the bed.

"Well?" his mother said.

"Not yet."

"Well, where was she last seen? And when?"

"In Oxford some days ago."

"You'll have to do a great deal better than *that*, Marcel. You are too busy with this congress. When is it going to finish?"

"When I've had my way," he said calmly. He was beyond being irritated by his mother, and a long way beyond being frightened of her. He knew it was safe to discuss the progress of his various projects with her, because no one trusted her enough to believe her if she spoke about them. Besides, her opinions were usefully merciless.

"What were you discussing today?" she said, flicking an imaginary speck of dust from the dove-gray silk of her nightgown.

"The doctrine of embodiment. Where is the boundary between matter and spirit? What is the difference?"

She was too well bred to sneer, exactly; her lips remained pursed; but her eyes blazed with contempt.

"I should have thought that was *perfectly* clear," she said. "If you and your colleagues need to indulge in that sort of adolescent speculation, you've wasted your time, Marcel."

"No doubt. If it's clear to you, Maman, what *is* the difference?"

"Matter is dead, of course. Only the *spirit* gives life. Without spirit, or soul, the universe would be a wasteland of emptiness and silence. But you know this as well as I do. Why are you asking about this? Are you tempted by what these *roses* seem to reveal?"

"Tempted? No, I don't think I'm tempted. But I do think we need to reckon with it."

"*Reckon* with it? What does *that* mean?"

She was most alive when she was animated by venom. Now she was sick and old, he enjoyed provoking her, as one might tease a scorpion that was safely behind glass.

"It means we have to consider what to do about it," he went on. "There are several things we could do. First, we could suppress all knowledge of it, by rigorous investigation, by ruthless force. That would work for a while, but knowledge is like water: it always finds gaps to leak through. There are too many people, too many journals, too many places of learning, who already know something about it."

"You should have suppressed it already."

"No doubt you're right. The second possibility is to go to the root of the problem and wipe it out. There is something unexplained in that desert in Central Asia. The roses will not grow anywhere else, and we don't know why. Well, we could send a force to go there and destroy the place, whatever it is. The amount of rose oil that's ever come this far is very small; supplies of it would dry up and cease altogether, and the problem would wither away. That solution would take longer and cost more than the first, but we could do it, and it would be final."

"I think that is the *least* you should do. Your sister would not hesitate."

"Many things would be much better if Marisa had lived. But there we are. There is a third option."

"And what is that?"

"We could embrace the facts."

"What on *earth* does that mean? What *facts*?"

"The roses exist; they show us something we've always denied, something that contradicts the deepest truths we know about the Authority and his creation; there is no doubt about that. So we could admit it boldly, contradict the teachings of millennia, proclaim a new truth."

The old woman shuddered with revulsion. Her lizard dæmon began to weep, uttering little croaks of terror and despair.

"Marcel, you will withdraw those words *at once*," his mother snapped. "I do not want to have heard them. Take them back. I *refuse* to listen to this heresy."

He watched and said nothing, enjoying her distress. She began to breathe in hoarse, shallow gasps. She gestured with a fluttering

hand, and the sleeve of her nightgown fell back to show her forearm punctured with needle marks, the skin like tissue paper, loose
around the bone. Her eyes were glittering with malice.

"Nurse," she whispered. "Call the nurse."

"The nurse can do nothing about heresy. Calm down. You're not
in your second childhood yet. In any case, I haven't told you the
fourth option."

"Well?"

"Revealing the truth in the way I've described it would not work.
There are too many habits, ways of thought, institutions, that are
committed to the way things are and always have been. The truth
would be swept away at once. Instead, we should delicately and
subtly undermine the idea that truth and facts are possible in the
first place. Once the people have become doubtful about the truth
of anything, all kinds of things will be open to us."

"'*Delicately* and *subtly*,'" she mocked. "Marisa would know how
to show some force. Some *character*. She was all the man you'll
never be."

"My sister is dead. Meanwhile, I am alive, and in a position to
command the course of events. I'm telling you about what I'm going to do because you won't live to see it."

His mother began to snivel. "Why are you talking to me like
this?" she whined. "So cruel."

"I've wanted to be able to treat you like this all my life."

"*Wallowing* in childish resentment," she said shakily, mopping
her eyes and nose with a lace handkerchief. "I have powerful
friends, Marcel. Pierre Binaud came to see me only last week. Be
careful how you behave."

"When I hear you now, I hear Binaud's voice. You were sleeping
with that old goat when I was a boy. The pair of you must make a
fine spectacle these days."

She whimpered and struggled to sit up a little higher. He didn't offer to help. Her lizard dæmon lay panting on the pillow.

"I want a nurse," the old woman said. "I'm *suffering*. You're making me so unhappy, I can't tell you. You only come here to *torment* me."

"I shan't stay long. I'll tell the nurse to give you a sleeping draft."

"Oh no—no—such fearful dreams!"

Her dæmon gave a little shriek and tried to nuzzle her breast, but she pushed him away. Delamare stood up and looked around.

"You should really let some fresh air in here," he said.

"Don't be unpleasant."

"What are you going to do with the girl once I've got her for you?"

"Wring the truth out of her. Punish her. Make her truly sorry. Then, when I've broken her will, I shall *educate* her properly. Give her a true sense of who she is and what her priorities should be. Mold her into the woman her *mother* should have lived to be."

"And Binaud? What part will he play in this educational enterprise?"

"I'm getting tired, Marcel. You don't realize how much I'm suffering."

"I want to know what Binaud plans to do with the girl."

"It's got nothing to do with him."

"Of course it has. The man is corrupt. He reeks of furtive copulation."

"Pierre Binaud is a *man*. You wouldn't know what that means. And he loves me."

Delamare laughed. He didn't do that very often. His mother hit the bed with both bony fists, making her dæmon escape to the bedside table.

"So we're going to see a deathbed wedding, are we?" he said.

"Then he can have your money as well as the girl. I'm afraid I shall be too busy to attend."

He opened one of the windows wide, and the bitter night fell in.

"No, Marcel! Please! Oh, don't be *vile* to me! I shall die of cold!"

He bent over to kiss her goodbye. She turned her face away.

"Goodbye, Maman," said Delamare. "Binaud had better not leave it too long."

Olivier Bonneville hadn't been telling the full truth, but that was nothing unusual. In fact, he hadn't found Lyra because for some reason the new method wouldn't let him. Somehow she'd managed to block his attempts to find her. One more reason for him to feel angry with her, and his anger was growing with his curiosity.

Suspicious by habit as well as inclination, he didn't keep the alethiometer at his apartment; it would be the easiest thing in the world for a practiced thief, especially one commissioned by *La Maison Juste*, to break into his little two and a half rooms and steal anything he had. So he had taken to keeping the alethiometer in a private deposit box at the Banque Savoyarde, a place so discreet that it was almost invisible. The brass plate outside the door in the Rue de Berne said merely *B. Sav.* and was intentionally never polished.

Early the next morning, Bonneville made his way to the bank and gave his name (false) and a password to the official, who opened the door to the private deposit boxes and left. Bonneville took out the alethiometer and slipped it into a pocket, and then put the fat roll of banknotes into another. The only item he left in the box was an unlabeled key, which would open another deposit box in another bank.

Twenty minutes later he was buying a ticket at the Gare Nationale. Of course he took no notice of Delamare's prohibition of the new method; of course he used it anyway. It was from his last session in the classic style, with the books, that he'd learnt that Lyra was moving east and was, as far as he could tell, alone. The new method was showing him nothing about her, and besides, like Lyra, he had found the disconcerting dizziness and nausea almost too much to bear; he thought it might be easier if he questioned the alethiometer for shorter times at longer intervals.

But there still remained the old method, after all, which involved no physical cost. As soon as his train reached Munich, he would take a room at a cheap hotel and begin a thorough search for Lyra. If he had all the books, it would be quicker, no doubt, though by no means as quick as the new method; but he did have two of them—a holograph manuscript of Andreas Rentzinger's *Clavis Symbolorum*, and the single remaining copy of Spiridion Trepka's *Alethiometrica Explicata*, which had been until recently in the keeping of the Library of the Priory of St. Jerome in Geneva. The latter book was without its handsome leather binding. That binding remained on the library shelf, now encasing the unreadable but identically sized memoirs of one of Napoleon's generals, which Bonneville had bought at a secondhand bookstall. Eventually, perhaps quite soon, the theft of the books would be discovered, but by then, Bonneville trusted, he would have returned to Geneva in triumph.

Someone was shaking her.

"Lyra! Lyra!"

It was Ma Costa's voice, and she was leaning over the bunk in the light from the galley through the open door, and there was someone else beside her, and it was Farder Coram, and she heard him too: "Hurry, gal! Wake up!"

"What is it? What's happening?"

"CCD," said Ma Costa. "They've broken the treaty; they're coming into the Fens with a dozen boats or more, and—"

"We got to get you away, Lyra," said Farder Coram. "Hurry up and get dressed. Quick as you can."

She scrambled out of the bunk, and Ma Costa stepped aside as Farder Coram went back into the galley.

"What—how do they know—"

"Here, gal, put this on quickly, over your nightclothes, doesn't matter," the old woman was saying as she thrust a dress into Lyra's hands. Lyra pulled it over her head and, still half asleep, gathered everything loose and stuffed it into her rucksack.

Ma Costa said, "Coram's got a man with a fast boat to take you away. He's called Terry Besnik. You can trust him."

Lyra cast around her dazedly to see if there was anything she'd forgotten. No: there wasn't much, and she had it all. Pan? Where was Pan? Her heart faltered as she remembered, and she blinked and shook her head and said, "All my life I've done nothing but bring the gyptians trouble." Her voice was thick with sleep. "I'm so sorry. . . ."

"That's enough," said Ma Costa, and hugged her so tight, it was hard to breathe. "Now get on outside and don't wait another moment."

Farder Coram in the galley was leaning on two walking sticks and he too looked as if he'd just been woken from sleep. Lyra could hear the quiet rumble of an engine-boat on the water.

"Terry Besnik's a good man," said Coram. "He understands the sittyation. He'll take you to King's Lynn—he knows all the drains and the by-channels—you can get a ferry from there—but quick as you can, Lyra, quick as you can. You got them things I gave you?"

"Yes—yes—oh, Farder Coram . . ."

She embraced him tightly, and felt his bones frail under her hands.

"Go *on*," said Ma Costa. "I can hear gunshots back there."

"Thank you, thank you," Lyra said, and scrambled out and over the side of the narrowboat, to where a hand reached up to help her into the cockpit of another kind of vessel, a launch of dark wood that showed no lights.

"Master Besnik?" she said.

"Hold tight" was all he said.

She could see little of his face. He was stocky, and he wore a dark woolen cap and a heavy jacket. He moved the throttle, and the engine growled like a tiger as the boat surged forward.

SEVENTEEN

THE MINERS

Pantalaimon left the *Elsa* at Cuxhaven at a time when the crew were distracted. Captain Flint had sold the propeller to a boatyard on the island of Borkum, just as the deckhand had predicted, and then refused to share the money equally with the mate, because, he said, as skipper he was far more at risk. In response, the mate stole the captain's whisky and took to his hammock to sulk. An hour out of Borkum, a bush around the *Elsa*'s propeller shaft fell apart, letting the sea into the engine room, and they limped into Cuxhaven with two men pumping resentfully while the mate grumbled nearby. Pan watched it all with fascination. It was easy to keep out of sight on a vessel like the *Elsa*.

They tied up in the evening at a wharf with a crumbling stone warehouse behind it. The "passengers" currently keeping out of sight in the warehouse wouldn't be able to come aboard till the prop shaft bush was replaced, because the whole "passenger" transaction depended on discretion and silence. It wasn't easy to say how long the repair would take either; Flint knew a man who had the necessary spare part, but he was temporarily out of town, or in prison, and his assistant had a long-standing grudge against Flint and was bound to charge a high price. As soon as night fell, Pan darted down the gangway and into the shadows of the main harbor.

Now it was just a matter of finding the river, and setting off upstream till he came to Wittenberg.

At the same time, Lyra was sitting in the forward saloon of a crowded ferry heading for Flushing, on the Dutch coast. She would rather have sat outside, so as to be alone, but it was bitterly cold; so she put up with the oppressive heat and the smells of engine oil, stale food, smokeleaf, beer, dirty clothes, and a persistent hint of vomit. The anbaric strip lights flickered unpleasantly and threw an intrusive pallid glare into every corner. She had to struggle through a crowded doorway and push hard to get to the corner and find a seat.

Her dæmonless state caused less alarm at first than she'd feared. Most of the passengers and staff were preoccupied with their tasks, or busy trying to deal with a crying child, or simply tired and indifferent. The few who did see something strange about her contented themselves with a furtive glance, a muttered word or two, or a gesture for turning away bad luck. She pretended to take no notice, and tried to become inconspicuous.

Among the passengers in the forward saloon were half a dozen men who were obviously traveling together. They were similarly dressed in casual but good-quality cold-weather clothes, they spoke Welsh among themselves, and they had a confident, easy air. Lyra was watching them carefully, because one or two of them had looked at her appraisingly when she pushed her way through the jostling crowd in the doorway and entered the saloon, and said something to each other before looking back at her again. Their companions were ordering drinks, expensive drinks too, and laughing loudly. If Pan had been there, he and Lyra could have played detective, and tried to work out these men's occupation; but they'd have had to go back to their old relationship first, and that was probably gone forever.

Well, she could still do that, she thought, even if she was on her own. She watched the men while trying to seem half asleep.

They were all friends or colleagues: they were together. They were in their thirties or early forties, at a guess, and they looked like manual workers and not like people who sat in offices all day long, because they were fit and they moved with easy balance in the rocking ship, as if they were athletes or even gymnasts. Were they soldiers? That was possible, but then she thought that their hair was too long, and they were too pale: they didn't work outside. They were well paid: the clothes and the drinks testified to that. They were all on the small side too, whereas soldiers were usually bigger, she thought. . . .

That was as far as she got before a bulky middle-aged man sat down next to her. She tried to move to give him more room, but there was a large woman sleeping on the bench to her left who didn't move at all when Lyra gave her a nudge.

"Don't you worry," said the man. "Bit of a squash, no one minds that. Traveling a long way?"

"No," she said indifferently. She didn't look at him.

His dæmon, a small, lively brown-and-white dog, was sniffing curiously around Lyra's rucksack on the floor. She picked it up and held it tightly on her lap.

"Where's your dæmon?" said the man.

Lyra turned and gave him a look of contempt.

"No need to be unfriendly," he said.

Nine years before, when she traveled to the Arctic with Pan always close at hand, Lyra would have effortlessly come up with a story that would explain why the man should leave her alone: she was carrying an infectious disease, or she was on her way to her mother's funeral, or her father was a murderer and was coming back any moment to find her—that story had worked very well on one occasion.

But now she just lacked inventiveness, or energy, or chutzpah. She was tired and lonely and frightened, even by this self-satisfied man and his silly little dæmon, who was now yapping and jumping up at his knees.

"What is it, Bessy?" he said, and lifted her up to make a fuss of her, and let her whisper in his ear. Lyra turned away, but she could still see what he was doing: he was looking at her while whispering with his dæmon.

A little half-stifled whimper came from the dæmon, who tried to scrabble away from Lyra and bury herself in the man's coat. This display of craven attention seeking disgusted Lyra, who closed her eyes and pretended to be asleep. Someone was arguing near the bar—a Welsh voice was raised, there seemed to be a scuffle—but as quickly as it arose, it subsided again.

"There's something wrong here," the bulky man said loudly, not addressing Lyra. "There's something badly wrong."

Lyra opened her eyes and saw one or two heads turning. All the benches were crammed with travelers sitting and sleeping, or eating and drinking, and the noise of the ferry's engines was a perpetual rumble underneath, and the sound of the waves and the wind outside formed another layer of sound, while the conversations nearby and the laughter of the drinkers at the bar a little further away were also clear: but over it all the man's voice insisted again, "I say there's something wrong here. This young woman—something's not right."

His dæmon howled properly, a high quaking shiver of a sound

that touched Lyra's spine with cold. More people were looking now, and the sleeping woman on her left was stirring and working her mouth as she came awake.

Lyra said, "My dæmon is inside my coat. He's not well. It's none of your business."

"No, no, that won't do. I don't think you've got a dæmon at all. My Bess never makes a mistake over that sort of thing."

"You're wrong. My dæmon is not well. I'm not going to disturb him just because you're superstitious."

"Don't speak to me in that tone of voice, young lady. I won't put up with that. You shouldn't be in a public place in the state you are. There's something the matter with you. Something not right."

"What's wrong?" said a man on the bench opposite. "What are you shouting about?"

"She hasn't got a dæmon! I keep telling her, it's not right to come out in public like that. There's something badly wrong—"

"Is that true?" asked the other man, whose rook dæmon was shaking her wings on his shoulder and cawing loudly. Lyra realized he was speaking to her.

"Of course it's not true," she said as calmly as she could manage. "How could I go anywhere without a dæmon?"

"Well, where is he, then?" the first man demanded.

"It's got nothing to do with you," said Lyra, now becoming alarmed by the attention this ridiculous incident was attracting.

"People with that degree of disfigurement ought to keep out of public view," he said, and his dæmon howled again. "Look at the way you're frightening people. Not fit to be seen in public. There are places for people like you to stay. . . ."

A child was beginning to cry, and his mother picked him up ostentatiously, holding his coat clear of Lyra's rucksack, as if it was tainted. The child's dæmon was changing from a mouse to a bird to a puppy and back to a mouse, and kept falling away from him, making them both shriek even louder, until his mother's mastiff dæmon picked her up and shook her.

Lyra held on tight to her rucksack and began to stand up, but found her sleeve held by the bulky man.

"Let me go!" she said.

"Oh, no, you can't just go where you please," he said, looking all around for the support that was beginning to grow in the faces of the people nearby. He clearly thought he was speaking for all of them. "You can't go about in that state," he went on. "You're frightening children. It's a public menace. You're going to come with me, and I'm going to put you in the charge of—"

"It's all right," said another voice, a man's voice with a Welsh accent. Lyra looked up to see two of the men from the group by the bar, easy, confident, a little red-faced, a little drunk, perhaps. "We'll take care of her. You leave her to us, don't you worry."

The man was reluctant to abandon his position at the center of attention, but the two Welshmen were younger and stronger than he was. He let go of Lyra's sleeve.

"You come with us," said the first Welshman. He looked as if he had never in his life been refused or disobeyed. Unsure, she didn't move, and he said "Come on" again.

The other man was looking at her appraisingly. There was no support from anyone nearby. Closed faces, cold and indifferent ones, or faces filled with active hatred were all around; and every dæmon in sight had clambered or flown or crawled to their people's breasts to be safe from the appalling and uncanny figure who had the gall to come among them with no dæmon. Lyra picked her way between their legs and feet and luggage, following the Welshmen.

She thought: Is it all going to end so soon, then? I won't let it. Once we're outside, I'll attack. The stick Pequeno was in her left sleeve, ready to be drawn by her right hand, and she'd already decided where to aim her first blow: on the side of the second man's head, as soon as the door closed behind them.

They reached the door of the saloon, with a growling murmur from the seated passengers and approving, complicit nods from the other Welshmen at the bar. Everybody knew what the two were going to do to her, and not one person objected. Lyra worked the handle of the stick a little way into her palm, and then they were outside in the cold wind with the door banging shut behind them.

The deck was streaming with rain and spray, the boat was pitching hard, and the wind slapped Lyra's face as she pulled out the stick—and then she stopped.

The two men were standing back, hands up, palms forward. Their dæmons, a badger and a canary, stood still and peaceable, one on the deck and the other on a shoulder.

"'S all right, miss," said the taller man. "Just had to get you out of there, that's all."

"Why?" she said, thankful that at least her voice was steady.

The other man held something out. It was the alethiometer's black velvet bag. Lyra lost her balance for a moment, as if she'd been struck.

"What are you doing—how did you—"

"As you come in the saloon, we saw a man put his hand inside your rucksack and take something out. He was very quick. We watched where you went, and we watched him, and before he could clear off, we caught hold of him. He only argued for a second. We got this back off him, and then that fool with the little yapping dæmon started going on at you, so we thought we'll kill two birds with one stone."

She took the velvet bag and opened it: the gleam of gold and the familiar weight of it in her hand told her it was safe.

"Thank you," she said. "Thank you so much."

The taller man's canary dæmon spoke from his shoulder. She said, *"Duw mawr, dydi hi ddim yn ddewines, ydi hi?"*

The man nodded and said to Lyra, "You're a witch, en you? Sorry if that's rude of me, you know, but—"

"How do you know?" said Lyra, and this time she couldn't prevent her voice from shaking.

"We seen your people before," said the other.

The bulkhead light shone yellow on their faces, as naked as hers to the wind and the spray. They stood back further.

"Got all the wind on this side," said the first man. "Bit more shelter round the other way."

They moved away, and she followed them across the open foredeck, struggling to keep her balance, and down the other side of the vessel. The saloon beside them and a lifeboat on its davit above kept the worst of the wind and rain from this side, and there was a bench that was more or less dry a little further along under a feeble light.

The men sat down. Lyra pushed the stick back inside her sleeve and joined them. They sat at one end, leaving plenty of space for her, and pulled the collars of their jackets up against the wind. One had a woolen hat in his pocket and put it on.

Lyra pushed her hood back and turned her face to the light, so she was fully visible.

"I'm Gwyn," said the first man, "and this is Dafydd."

"I'm Tatiana Asrielovna," said Lyra, making a patronymic of her father's name.

"And you *are* a witch, en you?" said Dafydd.

"Yes. I'm traveling like this because I have to. I wouldn't go like this from choice."

"Yes, we could see that," said Gwyn. "You wouldn't choose to go into a pit of fools like that bloody saloon unless you had to."

She suddenly realized something. "Are you miners?" she said.

"How'd you know that?" said Dafydd.

"I worked it out. Where are you going?"

"Back to Sala," said Gwyn. "Sweden, that is. Silver mines."

"That's where we met a witch before," said Dafydd. "She come down that way to buy some silver, and got landlocked. Her, you know, the tree—the pine branch—"

"Cloud-pine."

"Thass it. Someone stole it. We got that back and all."

"She helped us first," said Gwyn. "We owed her one. We helped her, like. Learnt a lot about their life and that."

"Where are you traveling to, Tatiana?" said Dafydd.

"I'm going a long way east. I'm looking for a plant that only grows in Central Asia."

"Is that for, like, a spell or something?"

"It's to make medicine. My queen is ill. Unless I bring back some of that plant, she'll die."

"And why are you going like this, by sea? It's dangerous for you, traveling over the surface of the earth, like."

"Misfortune," she said. "My cloud-pine was lost in a fire."

They nodded.

"Better, if you can, travel by first class," said Gwyn.

"Why?"

"Not so many questions. Not so much curiosity. Rich folk en like us. Them people back in the saloon, that fool of a fat man, there's plenty of arseholes like that—excuse me—wherever you go. And that thief too. If you travel first class and keep yourself kind of apart, you know, what's the word—"

"Aloof," said Dafydd.

"Summing like that. Proud, haughty. People are wary of you then, and they don't dare question you or interfere, you know."

"D'you think?"

"Yes. Take it from me."

"Central Asia," said Gwyn. "That's a long way."

"I'll get there. Tell me, why do Welsh miners work in Sweden?"

"Because we're the best in the world," said Dafydd. "Coleg Mwyngloddiaeth, both of us."

"What does that mean?"

"It's the School of Mining in Blaenau Ffestiniog."

"And you mine for silver?"

"In Sala, yes," said Gwyn. "Precious metals is what we know best."

"That thing we got back for you," said Dafydd. "What is it, if you don't mind me asking? It felt heavy, like gold."

"It is gold," she said. "Would you like to see it?"

"Oh, very much," said Gwyn.

Lyra opened her rucksack. Was she mad? Why in the world should she trust these two strangers? Because they'd helped her, that was why.

They moved closer to look as she opened the black velvet bag and let the alethiometer fall heavily into her palm. It caught every photon that fell on it from the bulkhead light, and gave it back improved.

"*Duw*," said Dafydd. "What's that, then?"

"It's an alethiometer. It was made, I don't know, three hundred years ago, maybe. Can you tell where the gold is from?"

"I'd have to touch it," said Gwyn. "Looking at it now, I can say something straightaway, but I'll have to feel it to be sure."

"What can you see straightaway?"

"It's not twenty-four karat, but then I wouldn't expect it to be. That's too soft for a working instrument. So you have to make an alloy with another metal. I can't see what that is, not in this light. But it's strange. It's almost pure gold, but not quite. I never saw anything like this before."

312

"Sometimes you can taste it," said Dafydd.

"Can I touch it?" asked Gwyn.

Lyra held it out. He took it from her hand and ran his thumb along the gold rim.

"That's not copper nor silver," he said. "That's something else."

He lifted it to his face and held it delicately against the skin over his cheekbone.

"What are you doing?"

"Feeling it. Different nerves in different parts of the skin, see. Sensitive to different stimulations. This is very strange. I can't believe it's . . ."

"Let me try," said Dafydd.

He took it and brought it to his mouth and touched the tip of his tongue to the gold case.

"That's almost all gold. The rest . . . No, I don't believe it."

"It is," said his canary dæmon from his wrist. "I can tell now. It's titanium."

"Aye. I thought so too. But that's impossible," Gwyn said. "They never discovered titanium till about two hundred years ago, and I never heard of a gold alloy of it."

"It's very hard to work," said Dafydd. "But that's what it feels like. . . . What are these hands made of?"

The three hands that Lyra could move with the wheels were made of some black metal. The needle that moved by itself was a lighter color, a sort of stormy gray. She and Will had noticed its resemblance to the color of the blade of the subtle knife, but they had found out nothing about that; even Iorek Byrnison, who reforged the blade when it shattered, had to admit that he had no idea what it was.

Lyra couldn't begin to tell them that without spending a long time explaining it, so she said simply, "I don't think anyone knows."

Dafydd handed the alethiometer back, and she put it away.

"You know," Gwyn told her, "there's a piece of metal in the museum at the Coleg Mwyngloddiaeth that looks like part of a blade, a knife blade, something like that. No one's ever discovered what metal it's made of."

"It's kind of a secret, see," said Dafydd.

"But it looks exactly like that needle. Where does that thing come from, then?"

"Bohemia."

"Well, they had good metalworkers there," said Gwyn. "If the case is an alloy of gold and titanium . . . that's not easy to make. Before modern times I'd say it was impossible. But with that thing, there's no doubt about it. That's what it is. Is that a witch thing, then?"

"No. I'm the only witch who ever touched one of these. There are only six of them in the world that we know about."

"What do you do with it?"

"You ask questions, and read the answers. The trouble is that you need all the old books, with the keys to the symbols, to understand what it says. It takes a long time to learn. All my books are in Novy Kievsk. I can't read it without them."

"Why are you carrying it with you, then? Wouldn't it be safer to leave it at home?"

"It was stolen from me, and I had to go a long way to get it back. It . . ." She hesitated.

"What?" said Dafydd.

"It seems to attract thieves. Like just now. It's been stolen many times. When it was given to me, I thought that was the end of the stealing, but obviously it wasn't. I'll be extra careful. I owe you a great deal."

"Just paying back, like," said Gwyn. "That witch we told you about—she helped us when we fell sick. There was an epidemic. It

314

spread from the mines further north than Sala, sort of a lung disease. We were both a bit poorly. The witch found some herbs that made us better, and then some local idiots stole her cloud-pine. So we got that back for her."

His dæmon, a small badger, was prowling restlessly along the deck, when suddenly she stopped still and gazed towards the stern. Gwyn said something softly in Welsh, and she replied in the same language.

"There's men coming," said Dafydd, translating.

Lyra couldn't see anyone, but it was darker down that way and the wind was whipping her hair across her eyes. She put the rucksack carefully under the bench and felt for her stick. She could see the other two getting ready to jump up and fight, and they looked as if they'd enjoy it; but before it came to that, the two men coming stepped into the pool of light beside a doorway.

They wore uniforms of a kind Lyra didn't recognize: black, smartly tailored, with caps bearing a symbol she couldn't make out. They certainly didn't look maritime: they looked military.

One said, "Show us your travel documents."

Gwyn and Dafydd reached into jacket pockets. The dæmons of the uniformed men were both large wolflike dogs, and they both glared at Lyra with fierce concentration.

The man who seemed to be in charge held out his gauntleted hand for Gwyn's ticket, but Gwyn didn't move.

"First of all," he said, "you're not employees of North Dutch Ferries. I don't know those uniforms. Tell me who you are, and I'll decide if I want to show you my ticket."

The uniformed man's dæmon growled. Gwyn put a hand down to his own badger dæmon's neck.

"Take a good look," said the uniformed man, and took off his cap to show the badge. Lyra saw that it depicted a golden lamp whose flame shot rays of red all around it. "You'll see this more and more, and soon you won't have to ask. This is the badge of the Office of Right Duty. We're constables of that office, and we have the responsibility to check the travel documents of anyone entering continental Europe. Among other things."

Then something entered Lyra's memory, something Malcolm had told her. . . . She said, "The League of St. Alexander. Well done. You can put your cap back on now."

The man opened his mouth to say something, but shut it again, and then opened it only to say, "Beg your pardon, miss?"

"I just want to stop you making a mistake," Lyra went on. "Your organization is new, isn't it?"

"Well, yes," he said. "But the—"

She held up a hand. "It's all right," she said. "I understand. You won't have had time to absorb all the new regulations yet. If I show you this, perhaps you'll know what to do next time."

And she produced the handkerchief that still held the knot Dick Orchard had tied in it. She held it out and let them look for a moment, no more, before putting it away again.

"What's that supp—"

"It's the badge of my agency. It means that my companions and I are on Magisterium business. You should know that. When you see that knot, the best advice I can give you is to look away and forget all about the person who showed it to you. In this case, it means forget my companions as well."

The men looked baffled. One of them spread his hands. "But we weren't told . . . Which agency did you say?" he said.

"I didn't, but I'll tell you, and then we'll say no more about it. *La Maison Juste*."

They'd heard of it, and they knew enough to nod and look serious. Lyra put her finger to her lips. "As if you'd never seen us," she said.

One of them nodded. The other touched his cap in a salute. Their dæmons quiet and subdued, they walked away.

"*Duw annwyl,*" said Gwyn after a moment. "That was good."

"Practice," she said. "But I haven't had to do anything like that for a long time. I'm glad it still works."

"Will they forget about it, then?" said Dafydd. He sounded as impressed as Gwyn.

"Probably not. But they'll be nervous about mentioning it for a while, in case it's something they *should* have known about. We'll be all right till we're ashore, anyway."

"Well, I'm damned."

"What was that you said?" said Gwyn. "The French words?"

"*La Maison Juste.* It's a branch of the Magisterium. That's all I know. I had to distract them before they asked about my dæmon."

"I didn't like to ask before, in case it's impolite, but . . . where is he?"

"Flying home to tell them how far I've got. A thousand miles away or more."

"I can't imagine what it must be like not to have your dæmon nearby," said Dafydd.

"No, it's never easy. But some things are as they have to be." Lyra pulled her coat collar up and tugged the hood of her parka forward.

"God, it's cold," said Gwyn. "You want to try and go inside again? We'd stay with you."

"We could go in the other saloon," said Dafydd. "It's quieter there. Be a bit warmer, like."

"All right," she said. "Thank you."

She rose to follow them, and they made their way along the deck to the aft saloon, which seemed to be occupied mainly by older people who were sleeping. It was darker than the forward saloon, the bar was closed, and only a few people were awake; one small group was playing cards, and the rest were reading.

A clock over the bar showed the time to be one-thirty. The ferry would dock at eight.

"We can sit here," said Gwyn, stopping by a seat against the wall where there was room for three of them. "You can go to sleep," he said to Lyra. "Don't worry. We'll keep an eye on everything."

"It's very kind of you," she said. She sat and clasped the rucksack firmly on her lap. "I'll remember this."

"Aye," said Gwyn. "We'll wake you when it's time to get off."

She closed her eyes, and exhaustion overcame her at once. As she fell asleep, she heard Gwyn and Dafydd on her left talking softly together in Welsh, as their dæmons did the same under their feet.

At the Gasthaus Eisenbahn in Munich, Olivier Bonneville went straight to his ill-lit little room after a dinner of pork and dumplings, and tried to find Lyra. There was something he'd noticed about the new method. . . . It wasn't easy to put into words. . . . He couldn't find any sign of her with it, that was the point, whereas earlier he'd seen her with little difficulty. Something must have happened. Had she found a way of hiding? She'd better not. He was damned if he'd give up.

And there'd been something . . . almost a nudge, as if the alethiometer was giving him a hint. . . . He hadn't thought it dealt in hints. But there was something. . . .

And because the light from the single overhead bulb was so poor, and the print in his stolen books so small, and because he knew the pictures on the dial so well, he didn't try the classical method. He sat in the overstuffed armchair and focused his mind on the girl yet again. He tried to conjure up her face: no success. A blank-faced girl with blond hair, or blondish. Maybe not blond. Light brown? He couldn't see anything. Couldn't even see her dæmon.

What was her dæmon, anyway? Some kind of weasel or ferret?

Something like that. He'd only had a glimpse, but he remembered a broad head, red-brown, a patch of lighter color on the throat—

There was a rustle among twigs and leaves.

Bonneville sat up. He closed his eyes and concentrated. It was dark, of course it was, because it was night, but there was a sort of luminescence from somewhere—undergrowth, leafless brambles, water. . . . Bonneville rubbed his eyes, which made no difference. He made himself relax and tried to subdue the nausea, which was not helped at all by those dumplings. Next time eat less, he thought.

There it was again, that rustling, and a visible movement— immediate nausea. He made it to the washbasin before he threw up. But he nearly had it! So nearly! He rinsed his mouth out with a glass of water and sat down again.

The problem was . . . The question was . . . Whose viewpoint was seeing it? Whose eyes were there to see through? No one's. The point of view was unanchored, and consequently it lurched all over the place. If it kept still, there'd be no nausea. . . . But there were no eyes there. No camera. There was no reason for the viewpoint to be in *this* spot rather than *that*.

All right: try *not* seeing. Try listening instead, or smelling, or both. They didn't depend on a viewpoint in the same way. Bonneville made his mind's eye see nothing but darkness, and focused instead on the other two senses.

That was better at once. He could hear a light wind through bushes, and the occasional brush of an animal's feet against dead leaves, but not dry ones; and he could smell damp, and a larger and more distant river smell, and hear the little murmur of water as the ripples of a wake ran along the bank.

Then more. He could hear the wide night all around. And sounds coming over water from some way off: a large oil engine, the splash of a bow wave, distant voices. The cry of an owl. More rustling in the undergrowth.

He sat perfectly still, eyes closed, looking into a profound blackness. The owl cried again, closer. The vessel was moving away to his right. Then a whiff of something animal, very close.

Startled, he looked, and for a fraction of a second he saw the girl's dæmon outlined against the darkness of a wide river, and no girl. She was nowhere in sight. The dæmon was alone. Quickly he closed his mind's eye again, before the sickness could strike, but he was triumphant. He let it all fade and sat there blinking and smiling, jubilant.

That was why he couldn't see her! She and her dæmon were separated! And the new method: now he knew how that worked. It wasn't the person it was drawn to: it was the dæmon. So many discoveries!

And the fact that he could see photograms of her in Delamare's apartment, as he'd done, was due to the presence of her dæmon in each one.

And now he knew that her dæmon was traveling alone, along a great river. It only remained to discover which one, and that wouldn't take long.

An excellent evening, all told.

EIGHTEEN

MALCOLM IN GENEVA

Malcolm's eyes were giving him trouble. The spangled ring, which he thought of as his personal aurora, had been trembling just out of sight for days; not continuously, but for longer than usual, and never quite appearing. It was as if the world was being projected by a magic lantern on a screen that wasn't quite securely fastened. Asta too, although she couldn't see the ring as he could, was aware of something uneasy in their vision.

They reached Geneva late on a windy afternoon, when the skies were dark with both the approaching evening and a threatening storm. The city was busy, because the Magisterial Congress was just coming to an end. In truth, Malcolm had no need to go through Geneva, and doing so could even have been called reckless; but it would be useful to learn what had been discussed. Besides, he knew that Simon Talbot was attending the congress, and he wanted to find him if he could.

He planned to leave the city by train, but he arrived by bus, because bus stops were less often watched by the authorities than railway stations. He and Asta got off in a dreary suburb, an area of small factories, market gardens, timber yards, and the like. The road ran along the lakeshore for a short way, and in the rapidly gathering dark they could see the lights across the water on the fashionable side of the city, and the great snow-covered mountains beyond, ghostly under the moonless sky. There was a yacht club or something of the sort over there, and in the blustery air they could hear the tapping of the rigging wires against the masts, like a thousand Swiss clocks.

They walked on a little way. Malcolm stopped and rubbed his eyes.

"I can feel it too," said Asta.

"It's as if the damn thing snapped and all the spangles got blown everywhere. If it doesn't make its mind up, we'll have to lie down, but I'd much rather not."

"Talbot."

"That's right. I want to . . . Wait a minute." He was peering at the rusty padlocked gate of a large house behind a stone wall.

"What is it?" she said, and jumped up to his shoulder.

"Something there . . ."

It was nearly dark. Something was moving or fluttering on the gate. He thought at first it was a leaf caught in a spider's web, and next that it might have been some kind of glowworm, but then it resolved into something familiar: the spangled ring itself. It was flickering in the semi-darkness, over the heavy padlock, and it drew him towards itself as if it were reeling in a fish. He went willingly. Asta couldn't see it herself, but she felt the old excitement that came to him.

He reached out towards the twisting, shimmering vision. He wanted to pick it up and hold it in the palm of his hand, knowing that of course he couldn't; but as he touched the padlock, the shackle slipped out of the body with a smooth click, as if it had been recently oiled. The lock hung loose on the hasp.

"Well," said Asta. "Got to go in there now."

They looked in both directions and saw no one. Malcolm removed the padlock and opened the gate, with the spangled ring still flickering in the center of his vision. The gate creaked, but moved easily enough through the weeds that clogged the gravel. The house itself was tall and entirely dark, the windows boarded up, ivy climbing the walls. Its main entrance faced the lake. Malcolm closed the gate, and they made their way towards the building.

"Very un-Swiss, all this neglect," Malcolm said. "Can you see that?"

He was pointing past the house towards the trees at the bottom of the garden, right on the shore.

"Boathouse?" said Malcolm.

"I think so. Yes."

It was just a dark rectangle to his human eyes, but the spangled ring encircled it with brilliance and certainty. They followed the path down towards it, where the gravel was thick with grass and weeds. At least they made no noise as they walked along it.

The door of the boathouse was padlocked, but the wood in which the hasp was set was soft and rotten. Malcolm pulled it away easily, and they stepped inside, Asta first for safety, because Malcolm's vision was now almost totally occupied by the shimmering dazzle of the scotoma.

"Don't move," said Asta. "Just stay there by the door. I'll see for you. There's a boat here, some kind of dinghy or small yacht . . . it's got a mast . . . and there are oars. There's a name . . . *Mignonne*."

Malcolm felt his way down the wall until he was kneeling on the wooden planking, and then reached out into the dark until his hand met the little boat's gunwale. He felt it sway slightly as a ripple passed under the gates, and then he felt another little movement as Asta jumped aboard.

"What are you doing?" he said.

"Just exploring. It's bone-dry inside. No leaks. How are you seeing now?"

"It's clearing a bit. What about the mast and the rigging?"

"Can't tell what's here and what isn't. . . . It all seems in good shape, though."

The spangled ring was getting larger now, and drifting towards him in the way it had. The rest of his vision was returning to normal. He could see the boat dimly against the light from the water outside.

"Well," he said. "Nice to know you, *Mignonne*."

He ran his hand along the gunwale and stood up to let Asta lead the way out. Since the wood holding the hasp was perished, he put a stone on the ground against the door to keep it shut. Asta jumped up to his shoulder again and looked all around.

"It led us here," she said as they went back up the path towards the road.

"Of course it did."

"I mean, it was blatant."

"Rude to ignore it," he said.

Rucksack on his back, small suitcase in hand, he set off towards the city, with Asta padding tirelessly ahead.

The Magisterial Congress was holding its final plenary session. The discussions had been rigorous and exhaustive, but a spirit of unity and concord prevailed, and the election of members to the new representative council had proceeded smoothly and effectively. It was almost a miracle, as more than one delegate remarked to another, how everything had gone so well, without a whisper of rancor or jealousy or suspicion. It was as if the Holy Spirit had possessed the entire gathering. The Prefect of the Secretariat of the Holy Presence, whose efficient staff had organized everything, was widely praised.

The name of the first President of the High Council, as it was going to be called, had taken everyone by surprise. A series of votes had been carried out under conditions of the strictest security, and the winner was announced with great solemnity to be St. Simeon Papadakis, the Patriarch of the Sublime Porte.

It was a surprise, because the Patriarch was so . . . old. But immensely holy, as everyone agreed; a very spiritual man, he seemed to be illumined by a divine light; photograms, once carefully printed, confirmed the fact. There could be no better representative of the sanctity of the entire Magisterium than this modest and kindly man, so wise, so learned, so . . . spiritual.

The news of his election was announced at a press conference, and subsequently much discussed at, among other places, the Café Cosmopolitain. Malcolm knew from earlier visits that it was the first place to go for political and diplomatic gossip. When he arrived, he found the place crowded with visitors, clerics, foreign correspondents, embassy officials, academics, and delegates to the congress, with their entourages. Some were waiting for a train; some were continuing agreeable expense-account conversations that had begun over lunch with representatives of the press, or news agencies, or possibly even spies. The congress would have profound and lasting effects on international relations, certainly including the balance of power in Europe. Naturally the world wanted to know all about it.

Malcolm had been a journalist several times, on previous missions, and he played the part well. As he looked around the Cosmopolitain, there was nothing to distinguish him from a dozen others, and before long he saw the person he was looking for, in conversation with a man and a woman whose faces he recognized: they were literary journalists from Paris.

Malcolm made for their table and stopped, pretending to be surprised. "It's Professor Talbot, isn't it?" he said.

Simon Talbot looked up. There was a slight risk that he'd

recognize Malcolm, who was, after all, a Scholar of his own university; but Malcolm was ready to take that chance, and in any case, he knew that he had done, said, or published nothing that was likely to catch Talbot's attention.

"Yes, that's right," said Talbot, agreeably. "I'm afraid I don't know you, sir."

"Matthew Peterson, *Baltimore Observer*," Malcolm said. "I don't want to interrupt you, but . . ."

"I think we had finished," said the Frenchman. His colleague nodded and closed her notebook. Talbot leant across to shake hands with them both, smiling warmly, and gave them each one of his cards.

"May I?" said Malcolm, indicating a vacant chair.

"By all means," said Talbot. "I don't know your journal, Mr. Peterson. The *Baltimore* . . . ?"

"*Observer*. It's a monthly specializing in literary and cultural matters. We have a circulation of eighty thousand or so, mostly across the Atlantic. I'm the European correspondent. I was wondering how you regarded the outcome of the congress, Professor."

"Intriguing," said Talbot, with another ready smile. He was a slim, dapper man of forty or so, with eyes that could seemingly twinkle at will. His voice was light and musical, and Malcolm could see how he would shine in a lecture room. His dæmon was a blue macaw. He went on: "I daresay many people will be surprised to hear about the elevation of the Patriarch to this new position, to this, ah, ultimate authority, but having spoken to him, I can testify to the simple goodness he embodies. It was a wise decision, I think, to entrust the leadership of the Magisterium to a saint rather than to a functionary."

"A saint? I've seen him referred to as St. Simeon. Is that a courtesy title?"

"The Patriarch of the Sublime Porte holds the title of saint ex officio."

"And the President of the new council will really be the first leader of the entire Church since Calvin renounced the papacy?"

"Undoubtedly. That's why the council was created."

Malcolm was making "shorthand notes" as Talbot spoke. In fact, he was writing random words in the Tajik alphabet.

Talbot lifted his empty glass and put it down again.

"Oh, I'm sorry," Malcolm said. "May I buy you a drink?"

"Kirsch, thank you."

Malcolm waved at a waiter and said, "Do you think a single leader is the best form of government for the Magisterium to adopt?"

"In the flux of history, every kind of leadership emerges and then vanishes again. I wouldn't presume to say that one was better than another. Those terms are the currency of journalism, shall we say, rather than scholarship." His smile became especially charming. A scowling waiter took Malcolm's order, and Talbot lit a cheroot.

"I've been reading *The Constant Deceiver*," said Malcolm. "It's had a big success. Were you expecting a response like that?"

"Oh, no. Not at all. Far from it. But I think perhaps it struck a note that resounded, among younger people especially."

"Your exposition of universal skepticism is very powerful. Is that the reason for its success, d'you think?"

"Oh, I wouldn't like to say."

"I'm intrigued, you see, to find someone so closely associated with that position praising someone for his simple goodness."

"But the Patriarch *is* good. You have only to meet him."

"Shouldn't there be some sort of caveat?"

The waiter brought their drinks. Talbot leant back comfortably and puffed at his cheroot. "Caveat?" he said.

"For example, you might say that he's a transparently good man, but goodness itself is a problematic idea."

A loudspeaker crackled into life and announced in three languages that the Paris train would be leaving in fifteen minutes. A number of people finished their drinks, stood up, put on their coats, and looked around for their luggage. Talbot sipped his kirsch and looked at Malcolm as if he were a promising pupil.

"I think my readers are capable of detecting irony," he said. "Besides, the article I shall write for the *Journal of Moral Philosophy* will be couched in rather more nuanced terms than I might use if I were writing for the *Baltimore Observer*, shall we say."

The twinkle that accompanied that shaft of would-be scholarly wit suddenly reduced it to mere vulgarity. Malcolm was interested to see that Talbot didn't realize it.

"What did you think of the quality of debate at the congress?" he said.

"Very much what one might expect. Most of the delegates were men of the cloth, and their preoccupations were naturally clerical—matters of ecclesiastical law, liturgy, that sort of thing. Though there were one or two speakers who impressed me with their breadth of vision. Dr. Alberto Tiramani, for example, who, I think, is the head of one of the bodies represented at the congress. Certainly a subtle intellect. Something not often combined, as I'm sure you'll have noticed, with a striking clarity of utterance."

Malcolm wrote busily for a moment or two. "I read an article recently," he said when he'd finished, "which made an interesting comparison between your remarks about veracity and the arbitrary nature of language, on the one hand, and the swearing of oaths to tell the truth in courts of law, on the other."

"Really?" said Talbot. "How fascinating." His tone made the words sound like an example of irony, performed for the benefit of the stupid. "Who was the writer of the article?"

"George Paston."

"I don't think I've ever heard of him," Talbot said.

Malcolm was watching closely. Talbot's response was perfect.

He sat back comfortably, calm, slightly amused, enjoying his cheroot. Only his macaw dæmon reacted, shifting from foot to foot on Talbot's shoulder, turning her head for a moment to look at Malcolm, then turning away.

Malcolm made another note and said, "Do you think it's possible to tell the truth?"

Talbot let his eyes brighten. "Ah, well. Where should I begin? There are so many—"

"Imagine you're talking to the readers of the *Baltimore Observer*. Straightforward people, who like a straightforward answer."

"Are they? How depressing. What was the question again?"

"Is it possible to tell the truth?"

"No." Talbot smiled and went on: "You'd better explain the paradox in that answer. I'm sure your readers would enjoy it if it were set out in simple words."

"In a court of law, then, you wouldn't consider yourself bound by an oath to tell the truth?"

"Oh, I should do my best to obey the law, naturally."

"I was intrigued by your chapter in *The Constant Deceiver* about dæmons," Malcolm went on.

"I'm so glad."

"Do you know Gottfried Brande's *The Hyperchorasmians*?"

"I know of it. Isn't it some sort of bestseller? I don't think I could face it."

The macaw dæmon was definitely uncomfortable. Asta, sitting on Malcolm's lap, made no move: her eyes were fixed on the macaw. Malcolm could feel her tension.

Talbot finished his drink and looked at his watch. "Well, fascinating as this has been, I must go. I don't want to miss my train. Good evening, Mr. Peterson."

He held out his hand. Malcolm stood up to shake it and looked directly at the blue macaw, who looked back at him for a moment but then turned her head away.

"Thank you, Professor," Malcolm said. "Bon voyage."

Talbot swung a rusty-brown tweed cloak around his shoulders and picked up a large briefcase. A sharp nod, and he left.

"That was a draw," said Asta.

"I'm not so sure. I think he won. Let's see where he's really going."

A moment in the cloakroom to put on a pair of heavy glasses and a black beret, and Malcolm, with Asta on his shoulder, slipped out into the rain-washed street. There was a heavy drizzle, and most people were walking fast, heads down under their hats or hoods. The black mushrooms of a dozen or more umbrellas filled Malcolm's eyeline, but the blue macaw was impossible to hide.

"There she is," said Asta.

"Going away from the station. As we thought."

The lights from shop windows picked out the dæmon vividly, but Talbot was walking fast, and Malcolm had to hurry to keep him in sight. The man was doing what Malcolm himself would have done if he knew he was being followed, checking in shop windows for a reflection of what was behind him, slowing down unpredictably and then speeding up again, and crossing the road just before the traffic lights changed.

"Let me go after him," said Asta.

It was much easier to follow someone if two of you were doing it, but Malcolm shook his head. The street was too busy; it would be too conspicuous.

"There he goes," he said.

Talbot was turning into the narrow street where Malcolm knew *La Maison Juste* was situated. After a few moments he disappeared from sight. Malcolm didn't follow.

"You really think he won?" said Asta.

"He's a lot cleverer than Benny Morris. I shouldn't have tried to catch him out."

"*She* gave him away, though."

"Well, maybe a draw. But I still think he shaded it. We'd better go and find a train. I don't think it'll be safe here for very long."

"His name is Matthew Polstead," Talbot said. "He's a Scholar of Durham College. Historian. I recognized him at once. Almost certainly an agent of theirs. He knew about my connection with that lout of a policeman who bungled the, the, ah, incident by the river, which means that by now the other side will have got hold of Hassall's notes and other things."

Marcel Delamare listened impassively and watched him across the gleaming desk.

"Did you give anything away?" he said.

"I don't think so. He's fairly sharp, but fundamentally a bumpkin."

"I don't know that word."

"A rustic oaf."

Delamare knew that Talbot's philosophy maintained that nothing was anything, fundamentally, but he didn't question what the Oxford man said. If the phrase "useful idiot" had existed in their world, it would have expressed his opinion of Talbot precisely. The macaw dæmon was looking at Delamare's white owl, preening her feathers, bobbing her head, moving from claw to claw. The owl kept her eyes closed and paid no attention.

Delamare pulled a notepad towards himself and took up his silver pencil. "Can you describe him?" he said.

Talbot could and did, in considerable detail, much of it correct. Delamare wrote swiftly and meticulously.

"How did he know about your connection with the incompetent policeman?" he said when he'd finished.

"That remains to be discovered."

331

"If he's a bumpkin, your arrangement can't have been well hidden. If it was well hidden, he's not a bumpkin. Which is it?"

"Perhaps I'm overemphasizing his—"

"Never mind. Thank you for coming in, Professor. I shall be busy now."

He stood to shake hands, and Talbot gathered his cloak and his briefcase and left, obscurely humiliated, though he wasn't sure how; but his philosophy soon made that feeling disappear.

At the station, Malcolm found a confused crowd of travelers waiting in frustration, and an official of the railway company trying to explain why they couldn't board the train for Venice and Constantinople, as they were expecting to, and as he was too. It was already crowded, and apparently one entire carriage had been requisitioned at the last minute for the exclusive use of the new President of the High Council. Passengers who had booked seats in that carriage would have to wait for the train on the following day. The railway company had tried to find an extra carriage, but none were available, so they were now trying to find hotel rooms so the disappointed passengers could stay overnight.

People around Malcolm were complaining loudly.

"A whole carriage!"

"He's supposed to be a humble, modest man. Give him a title and all of a sudden he becomes a monster of arrogance."

"No, you can't blame him. It's his entourage, insisting on new privileges."

"Apparently the order came from the Prefect of the Secretariat."

"Surprising, given how well everything else was organized . . ."

"Absurd! Exceptionally inconsiderate."

"I have an extremely important meeting in Venice tomorrow! Do you know who I am?"

"They should have thought of this a long time ago."

"Why does he need a whole carriage, in God's name?"

And so on. Malcolm scanned the notice boards, but there were no more departures that evening except local trains to small towns nearby, and one more train for Paris just before midnight, and he wasn't going to Paris.

Asta looked around. "Can't see anyone who looks dangerous," she said. "Talbot wasn't getting this train, was he?"

"I should think he'd be going in the opposite direction. He'll be getting that late one for Paris."

"Are we going to wait for them to find us a hotel room?"

"Certainly not," said Malcolm, who was watching three more officials hurrying towards the crowd with leaflets and clipboards and sheets of paper. "They'll make a list of who everyone is and where they've put them. I think we'd better be anonymous."

Suitcase in hand, rucksack on his back, Asta padding beside him, he left the station quietly and set off to find a room for the night.

The President of the High Council of the Magisterium, the Patriarch of the Sublime Porte, St. Simeon Papadakis, was humbly conscious of being the cause of all this trouble, and settled into his seat in the reserved carriage with deep unease.

"I don't like this at all, you know, Michael," he said to his chaplain. "It's unjust. I did try to protest, but they simply wouldn't listen."

"I know, Your Serenity. But it's for your own protection and convenience."

"That shouldn't matter. I do so dislike being the cause of inconvenience to those other passengers. They are all worthy people, all on holy business, all with appointments to keep and travel connections to make. . . . I don't think it's right at all."

"As the new president, though . . ."

"Well, I don't know. I should have insisted harder, Michael. I should have started in the way I'd like to go on. Simplicity, not ostentation. Would our blessed Savior agree to sitting apart from his fellow passengers? They should have asked me first, you know, before causing all this trouble. I should have put my foot down."

Inadvertently, the chaplain looked down at the Patriarch's feet and then away again. The old man was wearing galoshes over the much-repaired black shoes he wore every day, and something was troubling him: he couldn't seem to find a comfortable position for his legs.

"Are you uncomfortable, Your Holiness?"

"These galoshes are troubling me. . . . I don't suppose . . ."

But it wasn't the galoshes. Like all his other attendants, the chaplain knew that the Patriarch was troubled by pain in one of his legs. The old man tried not to limp, and never mentioned it, but when he was tired, he couldn't conceal it. The chaplain wondered if he should raise the matter with the physician.

"Of course. Let me help you take them off," he said. "You won't need them till we get out."

"That would be very kind. Thank you so much."

As he gently removed the rubber overshoes, the chaplain said, "But you know, Your Holiness, a train carriage especially set aside for the President of the High Council is a very similar kind of thing to the ceremonial and ritual of the Holy Church itself. It marks the natural distance between—"

"Oh, no, no, it isn't the same at all. The ceremonies of the Church, the liturgy, the music, the vestments, the icons—those are holy things intrinsically. They embody holiness. They have sustained the faith of generations past. Sacred things, Michael. Not at all the same as commandeering a whole railway carriage and leaving those poor people in the rain. It's very bad, you know. It shouldn't have happened."

A young, dark-suited, smooth-haired attendant was hovering respectfully nearby. When the Patriarch's galoshes were safely off, he stepped forward and bowed.

"Jean Vautel, Your Serenity. I am blessed enough to have been appointed your new secretary for council business. If you are comfortable, I should like to discuss arrangements for the celebration to mark your election as President. Then there is the matter of—"

"A celebration? What is this?"

"A natural expression of the joy of the people, Your Serenity. It would be a fitting—"

"Oh, dear. I hadn't expected anything like that."

Behind the new secretary, St. Simeon could see other men, strangers, but all busy stowing boxes, files, and suitcases on the luggage racks, and all with the same air of competent zeal that Monsieur Vautel exhibited in every pore.

"Who are all these people?" he said.

"Your staff, Your Holiness. Once we are on our way, I'll bring them forward and present them to you. We have done our best to assemble a team of many talents."

"But I have a staff already . . . ," the old man said, looking helplessly at the chaplain, who spread his hands and said nothing as the train began to move out of the station. The platform was still thronged with passengers.

Malcolm found a cheap place called the Hotel Rembrandt not far from the lakeshore. He registered under one of his false names, found his third-floor room and left his suitcase there, then went out to find something to eat. There was nothing incriminating in the suitcase, but he plucked out one of his hairs and placed it between the door and the jamb so he could see if anyone had entered while he was out.

He found a small brasserie next door to the hotel and ordered pot-au-feu.

"I wish . . . ," he said.

"So do I," said Asta. "But she did."

"'Gone to look for your imagination.' What a thing to have to read. What d'you think he meant?"

"Precisely what he said. He felt them both to be . . . I don't know, diminished perhaps, because of the way she was thinking, as if part of her had vanished. Perhaps she'd stopped believing in her imagination, because of Talbot, partly. So he set out to find it."

"She couldn't have been taken in by that mountebank. Surely?"

"Plenty have been taken in. It's a corrosive thing, his way of thinking. Even corrupting. A sort of universal irresponsibility. Does he say anything specifically about the imagination?"

"No. From time to time he uses the word *imaginative* as a term of disparagement, as if in quotation marks. So that the readers of the *Baltimore Observer* can tell he's being ironic. What did you feel when you spoke to him in Oxford? To Pantalaimon, I mean."

"*Le soleil noir de la Mélancolie*. He said nothing directly about it, but it was there."

"Exactly what I felt about her when we saw her again," said Malcolm. "When she was younger, she was fierce, defiant, insolent even, but there was something melancholy about her even then, don't you think?"

He sat back as the waiter brought his meal. He noticed a man sitting alone at a small table in the corner of the room, a thin and frail-looking middle-aged man who might have been Central Asian, shabbily dressed, wearing much-repaired wire-frame glasses. He saw Malcolm looking at him and turned away.

Asta murmured, "Interesting. He's talking to his dæmon in Tajik."

"A delegate to the congress?"

"Maybe. He doesn't look very pleased with the outcome, if he is. But thinking of Talbot . . . I suppose another reason he's popular is that he'd be easy to imitate in an undergraduate essay."

"Good on a platform too. And I think he *had* read *The Hyperchorasmians*. He didn't want to admit it."

"Harder to see why that's popular."

"I don't think so," said Malcolm. "It's a gripping story that encourages people not to feel bad about being selfish. Plenty of customers for that point of view."

"Surely that's not what Lyra feels?"

"I can't imagine her ever believing that. But between them, they've done something damaging to her, to her and Pantalaimon."

"It must be due to other things as well."

Asta was crouching sphinx-like on the table, her eyes half closed. She and Malcolm were communicating with half murmur, half thought, and it would have been hard for either of them to say whether a remark originated from him or from her. The pot-au-feu was good; the wine Malcolm was drinking was passable; the room was warm and comfortable. It was tempting to relax, but he and Asta kept each other awake.

"He's watching us again," she murmured.

"Was he watching us before? We were watching him."

"Yes, he's curious. But nervous too. Shall we speak to him?"

"No. I'm a respectable Swiss businessman, away from home to show samples of my products to local retailers. It's not likely that I'd be interested in him. Keep watching, but don't let him see."

The Tajik man was eating a frugal meal as slowly as he could, or that was what it looked like to Asta.

"Perhaps he's staying in here for the warmth," Malcolm said.

He was still there when Malcolm finished and paid the bill, and he watched them leave. Malcolm gave him another glance as he closed the door; the man's expression was somber as their eyes met.

Malcolm was cold and tired. No one had disturbed the door. They went to bed, and Asta dozed on the pillow beside him as he read some of *Jahan and Rukhsana* before going to sleep.

At two in the morning there came a knock on his door. He and Asta woke at once, though the knock was very soft.

Malcolm was out of bed in a second. He whispered through the door, "Who's that?"

"Monsieur, I need to speak to you."

The voice was that of the Tajik man: there was no doubt about it. He spoke French, like Malcolm, but his accent was familiar, even in a whisper, even through a door.

"A moment," said Malcolm, and pulled on shirt and trousers.

He unlocked the door as quietly as he could. It was the Tajik man, and he was frightened. The serpent dæmon around his neck was gazing back along the dimly lit corridor. Malcolm offered him the only chair and sat on the bed himself.

"Who are you?" he said.

"My name is Mehrzad Karimov. Monsieur, is your name Polstead?"

"Yes. Why do you want to know?"

"So I can warn you about Marcel Delamare."

"How do you know Marcel Delamare?"

"I have had dealings with him. He has not paid me, and I cannot leave until he does."

"You said you wanted to warn me. What about?"

"He has learnt of your presence in the city and has ordered a watch kept on every road, on the railway station, and on the ferry terminals. He wants to capture you. I heard this from a man I befriended at *La Maison Juste*, who took pity on my situation. And now, monsieur, I think you had better leave quickly, because I saw from my window that the police are actively searching the houses nearby. I do not know what to do."

Malcolm went to the window, stood to one side, and pulled the threadbare curtain away from the wall just enough to see out. There was some kind of movement at the end of the street, and three men in uniform talking under a streetlight.

He let the curtain fall and turned back.

"Well, Monsieur Karimov," he said, "I think that—what is it now?—two-thirty in the morning would be a very good time to leave Geneva. I'm going to steal a boat. Will you come with me?"

NINETEEN

THE PROFESSOR OF CERTAINTY

Pantalaimon had never felt so exposed, except for the terrible first hours of separation from Lyra on the shores of the world of the dead. But even there he hadn't been lonely, because with him then was Will's dæmon, who knew nothing about herself and hadn't even known she existed till she was torn out of his heart. As the little boat had borne Will and Lyra away into the darkness, the two dæmons had shivered on the misty shore, embracing each other for warmth, and Pan had tried to explain everything to the terrified creature, who didn't know her name, or what shape she was, or even that she could change.

And on his journey up the river Elbe, through cities and forests and well-tended fields, he often thought back to that desolate time made warm by their companionship, and wished above everything for a companion now. He even wished for Lyra. If only they were making this journey together! It would be an adventure; it would be filled with love and excitement. . . . What had he done to her? How must she be feeling now? Was she still at the Trout in Godstow? Or was she looking for him? Was she safe?

It nearly made him stop and go back. But he was doing this for her. She was incomplete; something had been stolen from her, and he was going to get it back. That was why he crept along riverbanks and past power stations, and slipped aboard barges laden with rice, or sugar, or slates, or guano, and scampered through boatyards and along wharves and embankments, keeping to the shadows, staying in the undergrowth, avoiding the daylight, alert to every threat from every direction. Cats wouldn't take him on, but several times he had to flee from dogs, and once from wolves; and always and everywhere hide from human beings and their dæmons.

But finally he reached Wittenberg, and then came the even harder problem of finding the house of Gottfried Brande.

What would Lyra do? Well, he thought, to start with, she'd probably go to a library and look in local reference books or town directories of one sort or another, and if those things failed, she'd start asking directly. Well-known people could never really keep their addresses secret; the postal authorities would know them; doubtless local newspapers would know too. Even passersby in the street or the marketplace might have an idea where the city's most famous resident lived, and Lyra was very good at asking people things.

But those ways were impossible for a dæmon on his own.

The barge he arrived on was tied up to a buoy in the river, because the nearest quay was fully occupied. Pan waited until it was fully dark, and then slipped over the side and swam through the icy water to a patch of bare ground under some trees. The earth was frost-hard, the air still and heavy with the smells of coal, and timber, and something sweet that might have been molasses. Further back downstream, just outside the city walls, the barge had passed an area of tents and rough shanties, where people had been cooking over fires or sleeping huddled under blankets of canvas or roofs of cardboard. Pan could see the glow of the fires still, and smell the wood smoke, and for a minute he was tempted to go back and investigate; but then he shook himself dry and ran away from the river and into the city, keeping close to the walls, looking at everything.

The narrow streets were lit by gaslamps, whose soft light cast soft shadows. Pan moved with obsessive care, only leaving the darkness of an alley or an oratory porch when he was sure there was no one looking, and skirting the edges of the open squares and marketplaces. There were few people about: it was clearly a well-behaved city that went to bed early and took a dim view of pleasure. Everything was clean; even the refuse outside kitchen doors was separated into precisely labeled municipal bins.

Pan thought it was going to be impossible. How could he ever find out where Brande lived without asking someone? But how could he, a dæmon on his own, speak to anyone without making himself horribly conspicuous? The doubts increased, and then he found himself thinking of something else: what was he actually going to do when he came face to face with the author of *The Hyperchorasmians*, assuming he ever did? Why had he never thought about that?

He crouched under a boxbush in a little expanse of grass and trees in a triangle of space where three roads met. It was a residential area: tall neat houses, an oratory with a spire, some other kind of building in a large garden. The trees were bare; it would be some time before spring woke them up. Pan was cold, and tired, and discouraged, and he longed more than ever for Lyra's arms, for her breast, for her lap. He had been utterly reckless, utterly foolish, petulant, selfish, and proud. He hated what he'd done. He hated himself.

There was a signboard above the wall around the garden across the street. It stood under a large conifer, and there was no streetlamp nearby; but just then a tram came past, and in its headlights and the glow from the lighted interior, he read the words:

ST. LUCIA SCHULE FÜR BLINDE

A school for the blind!

As soon as the tram had turned the corner, he darted across the road and leapt up to the top of the wall, and from there into the pine tree, and a minute later he was curled up in a comfortable fork in the branches, where he fell asleep at once.

In the dawn, Pan scouted the school grounds and the outbuildings. It wasn't a large place, but it was carefully tended and as clean and tidy as the rest of the city. The main school building was built with brick and plain almost to the point of severity, so much like St. Sophia's College, in fact, that the sight of it in the early light brought a pang of homesickness. On the other side of the main building was a neat garden, bare at this time of year, but with a little fountain playing in a pool, and a gravel drive leading to the main gates.

Pan wasn't sure what he'd do, but not being seen would be just like being invisible, and he'd improvise when the time came. He found a dense little shrubbery on one side of a close-cut lawn, from which he could see the whole of the main building, and settled down to watch.

It was a boarding school for girls. He was familiar with the sort of routine that governed the day in such a place, and he listened to the bell that signaled time to get up and time to go to breakfast, the sounds of female voices, the clatter of knives and forks on china plates, and he smelled the fragrance of toast and coffee; and he saw shutters over dormitory windows being opened wide, lights coming on, adult figures moving to and fro; and then breakfast was over, and from another part of the building came the sound of young voices raised in a hymn. He knew it all so well.

At some point in the morning the pupils would come out for air and exercise, and then he'd take whatever chance he could find. In the meantime, he explored the school grounds. Behind the shrubbery was a continuation of the stone wall he'd scaled to get in, and he could hear a busy street on the other side of it. He'd be able to escape that way if he really needed to, but he didn't want to leap down among pedestrians and traffic. It would be better to find a quieter corner where he wouldn't be so conspicuous, and he found one behind a wooden shed that contained gardening tools.

Right now, however, the shrubbery was the best place to hide, so he went back there and made a discovery. Someone had created a little shelter from branches and leaves against a big pine trunk on the side that faced away from the school. The way to it was thickly overgrown and would have been hard for an adult to get through, but a young person, if they were slim, would be able to do it easily. Inside the shelter, Pan found a tin box under a heap of dry leaves. It was locked, and it was heavy with the sort of weight a thick book would give it. Someone's secret diary? But how could she write if she couldn't see?

He heard the bell ring and put everything back. Then he climbed the tree trunk a little way and waited.

It wasn't long before she came. She was about fourteen years old, and slender, and dark-haired. She wore a skirt and blouse of blue cotton and a paint-stained white apron, and her bare knees were badly scratched, no doubt from the bushes she'd had to push her way through in order to hide the box. Her dæmon was a chinchilla.

Pan watched as she felt for the leaves, pulled out the tin, and unlocked it with a little key on a chain around her wrist. She took out a battered book, as thick and heavy as Pan had guessed, and settled down with her back against the tree trunk to read it. What he hadn't realized was that the book was thick because, of course, it was printed in the raised-dot alphabet that blind people could read with their fingers. As she moved her hand across the page, she whispered to the little dæmon on her shoulder, reading it aloud to him. Within a minute they were both completely engrossed in the story.

Pan felt bad to be spying on them, so he climbed down the trunk, taking care to scratch his claws on the rough bark so they could hear him coming. They both heard and turned their faces up in alarm.

"I'm sorry to interrupt you," Pan said in the German he and Lyra had both struggled with for years until they began to memorize poetry in it.

"Who are you?" the girl whispered.

"Only a dæmon," he said. "My girl is nearby, watching to see if anyone comes."

"So you're not blind? What are you doing here?"

"Just exploring. My name is Pantalaimon. What's yours?"

"Anna Weber. And Gustavo."

"May I sit with you for a little?"

"Yes, if you tell me what shape you have."

"I'm a . . ." He didn't know the German word.

The chinchilla dæmon had no more sight than she did, but his other senses were briskly alert. He touched noses with Pan, and sniffed, and twitched his ears, and then whispered to Anna. She nodded.

"*Marder,*" she said.

"Oh. In my language it's *marten*. What are you reading?"

She blushed. Pan wondered whether she knew he could notice. "It's a love story," she said, "but one we're not supposed to know about because . . . it's kind of grown-up. . . . That's why I hide it out here. My friend lent it to me."

"We read a lot, me and Lyra."

"That's a strange name."

"Have you read *The Hyperchorasmians?*"

"No! Oh, but we'd love to. We're longing to read that. But the school won't allow it. One older girl got into terrible trouble for bringing it in. You know the author lives here in this city?"

Pan felt a shiver of luck. "Does he? Do you know where?"

"Yes. It's famous. People come from all over the world to visit him."

"Where is his house?"

"In the street behind the Stadtkirche. They say he never leaves it—his house, I mean—because he's so famous and people stop him to talk all the time."

"Why won't the school let you read it?"

"Because it's dangerous," she said. "Lots of people think so. But it sounds so exciting. Did you read it with . . . Lyra?"

"Yes. We didn't agree about it."

"I'd love to hear what she thought about it. Was it as exciting as people say?"

"Yes, it was, but—"

The bell rang. Anna closed her book at once and felt for the tin box. "Got to go in," she said. "They don't give us long. Will you come and talk to us again?"

"If I can. I'd like to. Do you know what Brande's house looks like? Sorry. That was a silly question."

"Well, no, but it's called the *Kaufmannshaus*. It's famous." She swiftly and deftly locked the box and thrust it back among the leaves. "Bye!" she said, and scrambled away through the undergrowth.

Pan felt bad about deceiving her. If he and Lyra were ever reconciled, he'd make sure they came back here to visit Anna and bring her some books. But the luck! He felt as they'd done in the Arctic town of Trollesund, meeting the aeronaut Lee Scoresby and Iorek Byrnison the armored bear, the very best allies they could possibly have found. That felt as if he and Lyra had been blessed, or as if some power was looking after them, and so did this.

He moved quietly around the grounds until he came to the caretaker's hut, and then jumped up on the roof and across onto the wall. The narrow side street below was deserted, but he could hear the sound of traffic from the main road beyond the school. To be safe, he should wait till dark, and he knew it, but it was so tempting to jump down and run hard. . . .

In which direction, though? She'd mentioned the Stadtkirche, the town church. Pan looked around, but the tall houses blocked the view ahead. Keeping low, he scampered along till he came to the spot where he'd entered the grounds the night before. Through the branches of the bare trees on the little triangle of grass, he could see two square towers of pale stone, each capped with a black dome and lantern. That might be it.

Before he could stop himself, he leapt down from the wall and raced into the street just after two trams had crossed in the middle. One or two pedestrians saw him and blinked or shook their heads, but he was across too soon for anyone to see him clearly, and then he scrambled up the trunk of an old cedar and vanished from view. He looked down carefully and saw that the passersby were moving on as if nothing had happened. Perhaps they thought their eyes were tricking them.

He climbed round the trunk a little way and looked for the towers of the Stadtkirche, and soon found them again.

Maybe he could get there by moving from roof to roof. The

houses were tall and narrow, with no gaps between them, opening directly onto the pavement without the little basement area that was common in English town houses. He darted across the road and into a small alley, climbed a drainpipe, slipped into the gutter it drained, and then onto the tiles and up to the ridge of a roof. Now he could see the church towers in the pale sunlight, and many other tall buildings besides, and no one could see him. It was almost like being on the roof of Jordan College long ago. He settled down to sleep by a warm chimney and dreamed of Lyra.

"Wittenberg!" said Olivier Bonneville aloud, and jubilantly. He couldn't stop himself, and it didn't matter, because he was alone in his cabin on the old river steamer, which was right over the engine room. The clanking and wheezing and thudding were more than enough to cover his voice, had anyone been listening outside.

He'd been watching Pantalaimon with the alethiometer ever since he'd first seen him on the riverbank, in brief snatches so as not to let the nausea build up. It wasn't long before he realized that Lyra's dæmon was traveling up the Elbe. Bonneville traveled at once by train to Dresden, further up the river from wherever Pantalaimon was, where he booked a cabin on this surely soon-to-be-retired steamboat, which traveled strenuously up and down the river between Prague and Hamburg. They were in Meissen when he saw Pan climb up the side of a building and look across the rooftops towards a church with two towers. It was a familiar sight: there was an engraving showing the famous Wittenberg Stadtkirche on the wall of Marcel Delamare's office.

Bonneville swiftly shuffled through the scatter of papers on his bunk and found the boat company's timetable. Meissen was six hours' journey from Wittenberg. Not long now, in fact.

* * *

Rooftop to rooftop . . . Pan should have thought of that before. The old houses were built joining one another, or with only a very narrow alley between them, and people seldom looked up, because their attention was focused at ground level, on traffic and cafés and shop windows. Pan's nature was suited to high things, and his footing was secure, so rooftops it was.

He scouted the whole district, unseen and unsuspected by those below. In the early afternoon he found a house that looked promising, just behind the Stadtkirche, as the girl had said; and by creeping down a drainpipe and looking across the street, he could even make out the words *Das Kaufmannshaus* in Gothic letters on a brass plate by the front door. There was little traffic; it was a very quiet street. He took a risk and ran across, making for an alley three or four houses further along, and then there was another climb, and then he was on the roof of Gottfried Brande's house.

It was steeper than its neighbors, but the tiles gave Pan quite enough grip. He made his way over the ridge, past a cluster of tall brick chimneys, and down towards the rear of the house.

There was someone playing in the garden.

That there was a garden at all was surprising, because none of the other houses he could see had more than a small paved courtyard. But the *Kaufmannshaus* had a square of grass, two or three small trees, and a summerhouse where a girl was throwing a ball against the wooden wall and spinning round before trying to catch it. He could hear the regular thud of the ball, the little gasps of satisfaction when she caught it, the hisses of disappointment when she didn't. Her dæmon was something so small, he couldn't make it out: just a little scamper on the lawn. He might have been a mouse.

Was there any point in waiting? Of course not. Pan looked down from the gutter and saw to his satisfaction that the rear wall of the house was covered in ivy. A moment later he was moving down through the leaves silently, watching the girl as he did. She didn't notice. As he reached the gravel path at the foot of the wall, she threw the ball again, spun round, and this time stopped halfway round because she saw him.

The ball hit her on the shoulder and fell to the grass. She snapped a cross word and picked it up, and then turned back to throw it again, ignoring Pan.

He was still at the foot of the wall, under a tall window. He watched her throw the ball again and again, taking no notice of him, and then he stalked across the path, making no noise at all, and walked across the grass towards her and sat down in the shadow of the house, only a few feet away from the girl. She could see him without even turning her head, but she went on playing as if he wasn't there.

She was about fifteen years old, blond and slender, with an expression of discontent that looked as though it had settled on her face for life. Two little frown lines had already marked her forehead. She wore a formal white dress with puffed sleeves, and her hair was tied up elaborately: the dress was too young for her, and the hairstyle too old; she looked as if nothing about her was right, and she knew it.

Throw, thud, spin, catch.

Her mouse dæmon had seen Pan and made a movement as if to approach him, but she saw and hissed. The dæmon stopped and crept back.

Throw, thud, spin, drop.

Pan said, "Is this the house of Gottfried Brande?"

"What if it is?" she said, snatching up the ball from the ground.

"I've come a long way to see him."

"He won't talk to you."

"How do you know?"

She shrugged and threw the ball again, and caught it.

"Why are you playing a little children's game?" Pan said.

"Because he pays me to."

"What? Why?"

"It gives him pleasure, I suppose. He watches me from the window. He's working now, but he still likes to hear the sound."

Pan looked at the house. There was no sign of movement, but the ground-floor window facing the garden was slightly open.

"Can he hear us talking?"

Another shrug, another catch.

He said, "Why won't he talk to me?"

"He won't even look at you. What are you doing on your own, anyway? It's not natural. Where's your person?"

"I'm looking for her imagination."

"You think he's got it?"

"I think he stole it."

"What would he want with that?"

"I don't know. But I've come to ask him about it."

She looked at him then, disdainfully. The last of the watery sunshine was just touching the top of the two trees; the shadow of the house across the garden was already chilling the air.

"What's your name?" Pan said.

"Nothing to do with you. Oh, this is too strange for me." She threw the ball to the ground and turned away, shoulders slumped. Then she sat down on the step of the summerhouse, and her dæmon ran up her arm and buried his face in her hair.

"Does he pay you to play all day long?" Pan asked.

"He's given up everything else."

He tried to think what that could mean; she wasn't likely to give him a clear answer. "Is he in the house now?"

"Where else? He never goes out."

"Which room would he be in?"

She sat up impatiently. "Oh, for God's sake. The study, of course. That open window."

"Is there anyone else there apart from him?"

"There are servants, naturally. It won't do you any good, you know."

"Why are you so sure?"

She gave a heavy sigh, as if his question was too stupid to deserve an answer. Then she turned away, leant over, and laid her head on her folded arms. Two glittering little black eyes stared at him from the fortress of her hair.

"Go away," she said, her voice muffled. "Too many ghosts. You think you're the first? They keep coming back, and he won't say a word."

Pan wasn't sure what he'd heard. He wanted to know much more about this discontented girl. So would Lyra, he thought, but she'd know how to talk to her, and he didn't.

"Thanks," he said quietly.

He left her and ran across the lawn. There was a light in the study window now, or perhaps he only noticed it because the late-afternoon light was fading fast. He saw an open window on the floor above and scampered up in the ivy and darted through.

He found himself in a bedroom: it was austere like a monk's cell, bare floorboards, no pictures or bookshelves, one narrow bed with thin bedclothes very tightly tucked in, a bedside table with nothing but a glass of water on it.

The door was slightly open. He went through and made his way down the steep stairs into a dark hall, with a door nearby that led (to judge from the smell of cabbage) to the kitchen, and another door from which came a powerful smell of smokeleaf. He crept along the wall, trying to make no noise with his claws on the polished wooden floor, and paused outside that door.

Brande's voice (it could only have been his: clear and forceful and precise) sounded as if he were giving a lecture.

". . . and it is clear that no further examples are necessary. Here the reign of stupidity comes to its final phase, characterized at first by a bloom of decadence, and then by the flowering of every kind of extravagant, timorous, and crepuscular piety. At this point—"

"Sorry, Professor," came a woman's voice. "What sort of piety?"

"Extravagant, timorous, and crepuscular."

"Thank you. Sorry."

"You have not worked for me before, I think?"

"No, Professor. The agency explained—"

"Continue. At this point everything is in place for the coming of the strong leader, which will form the subject of the next chapter."

He stopped. There was silence for a few seconds.

"That is all," he said. "Kindly tell the agency that I would be obliged if they would send a different stenographer tomorrow."

"I'm sorry, Professor. I was the only person available—"

"Are you sorry? If it is your fault, you should be sorry. If it is not, there is no blame to be sorry for. A mistake is your fault. An incapacity is not."

"I know I'm not used to— I trained for business and commerce, and the terms you use are unfamiliar—I know you want to get it right. . . ."

"It is right."

"Of course. Sorry."

"Goodbye," he said, and Pan heard the sound of a chair being moved, some papers being stacked, a match being struck.

A few moments later a young woman came out of the room, shrugging herself into a shabby overcoat and trying to hold back a bundle of papers and a pen case from falling on the floor. It was no use: they tumbled out from under her arm, and the parrot dæmon, who'd flown to the newel post of the stairs, said something disparaging.

She ignored him and bent to pick them up, and at the same moment she caught sight of Pan, who had nowhere to hide. He tried to stand as still as possible against the wall.

Her eyes widened. She took a sharp breath, and her dæmon uttered a quiet squawk of alarm.

Pan's eyes met hers. He shook his head.

"It's not possible," she whispered.

"No," he whispered back. "Not possible."

The parrot was actually whimpering. From the doorway came a strong smell of smokeleaf. The young woman scooped up her papers and hastened to open the front door and leave even before she had her coat fully over her shoulders. The parrot flew ahead of her, and the door slammed shut.

There was nothing to be gained by waiting. Pan walked through the doorway into the cigar-burdened, book-lined study, where Gottfried Brande was sitting at a large desk, watching him.

He was a large-boned man, gaunt and stiff, with short gray hair and very light blue eyes. He was dressed formally, as if he were about to give an academic lecture, and his expression was one of stark terror.

Pan looked for his dæmon. She was a very large German shepherd, and she lay on the carpet at his feet, apparently asleep, or pretending to be. She looked as if she were trying to make her great size as small as possible.

Brande hadn't moved, but he looked away from Pan and stared into the corner of the room. Unless that was the natural expression his face fell into, the terror still possessed him. Pan was disconcerted: of all the reactions he'd expected, this was not one.

He stalked across the room and leapt up onto the desk.

Brande closed his eyes and turned his body away.

"You've stolen Lyra's imagination," said Pan.

No movement from Brande, not a word.

"You've stolen it," Pan said. "Or corrupted it. Or poisoned it. You've made it small and unkind. I've come here to make you undo the damage you've done."

Brande felt for the ashtray with a trembling hand and put his cigar down. His eyes were still closed.

"What were you dictating just now?"

No response.

"It didn't sound much like a novel. Have you given up writing fiction?"

Brande's eyelids flickered open, just a tiny fraction of an inch, and Pan saw him trying to look sideways. Then they closed again.

"Who's the girl outside? Why do you pay her to play silly games?" As Pan said that, he realized that he hadn't heard the thud of the ball against the summerhouse since he left her there. "What's her name? How much do you pay her?"

Brande sighed, but furtively, as if he were trying not to show it. Pan heard his dæmon moving quietly on the floor—turning over, perhaps—and then came a muffled whimper.

Pan stalked to the edge of the desk and looked down at her. She had her face tucked down, with one paw over her eyes. There was something odd about her, and it wasn't just that a big, powerful creature should be showing so much fear. It was uncanny, and it made him think of something the girl had said.

He turned back to the man and said, "She told me there are ghosts here. Too many ghosts. They keep coming back, she said. D'you think I'm a ghost? D'you think that's what I am?"

Brande's eyes were tight shut. He looked as if he thought keeping absolutely still would make him invisible.

"Because I wouldn't have thought you believed in ghosts," Pan went on. "I'd have thought you'd scoff at the very idea. You'd feel nothing but contempt for anyone who did believe in them. There's a page on that very subject in *The Hyperchorasmians*. Have you forgotten your own words?"

Still no response.

"Your dæmon. Is she a ghost? There's something strange about her. Oh, but of course, I forgot: you don't believe in dæmons. She's trying to pretend she's not there, like you are. Too many ghosts, the girl said. Did she mean dæmons? Like me? Do they come at night or in the day? If you opened your eyes, could you see any now? What do they do? Do they talk to you? Do they feel your eyes and try and pull them open? Or maybe come right inside your eyelids and press themselves against your eyes? Can you fall asleep with them watching you all night?"

Finally Brande moved. He opened his eyes and swung around in his chair to look down at his dæmon. His expression was ferocious, and for the first time Pan felt a little afraid of him.

But he said nothing except to summon the dæmon: "Cosima! Cosima! Come with me."

The dæmon stood up unwillingly, and keeping her head low and her tail tucked under her, she moved all around the edge of the room towards the door. Brande stood up to go with her, but then the door flew open with a crash.

It was the girl from the garden. The German shepherd dæmon flinched back and cowered, Brande glared at the girl without moving, and Pan sat down on the desk to watch.

"Ach!" said the girl, making a face, shaking her head. "This room is full of them! You should make them go away. You shouldn't let them—"

"Silence!" growled Brande. "We shall not talk about such things. You have a disease of the brain—"

"No! No! I'm so *tired* of this!"

"Sabine, you are incapable of making rational judgments. Go to your room."

"No! I won't do that, I won't! I came here because I thought you'd love me and be interested in me, and I can do nothing that pleases you except playing that stupid game with the ball. I hate it. I hate it."

So she was called Sabine, and she thought he'd love her. Why would she think that? Could she be his daughter? Pan remembered so well the passionate exchange between Lyra and Lord Asriel in the luxurious prison the bears had built, and his head rang with echoes of what she'd said then.

The girl was trembling violently. Tears dashed from her eyes as she tugged the pins out of her hair and shook her head wildly so that the elaborate coiffure dissolved into a chaos of stormy blond.

"Sabine, control yourself. I will not have a display like this. Do as I tell you and—"

"Look at him!" she cried, pointing at Pantalaimon. "Another ghost out of the dark. And I suppose you pretended not to see him too, like all the others. I hate this life here. I won't live like this. I can't!"

Her dæmon became a wren and flew around her head, calling piteously. Pan looked at Brande's dæmon again and saw her lying with her back to the girl, head under a paw. Brande himself looked tormented with misery.

"Sabine," he said, "calm yourself. These are delusions. Put them out of your mind. I cannot reason with you if you behave like this."

"I don't want your reason! I don't want that! I want love. I want affection. I want a little kindness! Are you completely incapable of—"

"I have had enough," said Brande. "Cosima! Cosima! Come with me."

The dog dæmon got to her feet, and immediately the wren flew at her like a dart. The dog howled and fled from the room, and Sabine cried out loud. Pan knew very well why: it was the heart-deep pain of feeling her wren dæmon leaving her as he tried to pursue the dog. Brande stood helplessly watching her clutch her breast and sink fainting onto the carpet, as Pan found himself standing in amazement: Brande and his dæmon could separate! The man showed no sign of the pain that had made Sabine cry aloud and reach out towards the little bird, trying to snatch him out of the air.

Finally the dæmon returned to her and fell into her hands. Meanwhile, Brande stepped past her and followed his dæmon out of the study and towards the stairs, and Pan left Sabine sobbing on the floor.

Brande can separate! Pan thought again with confusion as he scampered up the stairs after him. Were the professor and the German shepherd like him and Lyra, then? Did they hate each other? But it didn't seem like that either. Something else was happening. Brande went into the bare little bedroom, and before he could shut the door, Pan darted through after him. The dæmon was cowering on the bare floorboards in front of the empty fireplace. Brande stood beside her and turned to face Pan. Now he looked haunted, and even tragic.

"I want to know about Dust," said Pan.

That startled Brande. He opened his mouth as if to speak, and then seemed to recollect that he was trying to ignore Pan and looked away again.

"Tell me what you know about it," said Pan. "I know you can hear me."

"There is no such thing," Brande muttered, looking at the floor.

"No such thing as Dust?"

"No—such—thing."

"Well, at least you can talk now," Pan said.

Brande looked at his bed, and then at the window, and then at the bedroom door, which was still open. "Cosima," he said.

The dog dæmon took no notice.

"Cosima, please," he said. His voice almost broke.

She buried her face even more deeply into her paws. Brande groaned; it sounded like genuine anguish. He looked at Pan again, almost as if begging a torturer for mercy.

Pan said, "You could pretend you could see me, and pretend you could hear me, and pretend to talk to me. That might work."

Brande closed his eyes and sighed deeply. Then he moved towards the door and left the room. The dæmon stayed where she was, and Pan followed Brande as he crossed the landing and climbed another staircase, darker and steeper than the main one, and unfastened the latch on a door that led into a bare attic. Pan was close on his heels.

He went in, and once more Pan followed him before he could shut the door.

"Are you afraid of me?" Pan said.

Brande turned and said, "I am afraid of nothing. I do not acknowledge fear. It is not a valuable emotion. It is parasitic on human energy."

There were three small windows in the attic, letting in the last of the daylight. Bare floorboards, bare rafters, heavy swags of cobweb, and dust—ordinary, everyday dust everywhere.

Pan said, "Tell me about Dust, now you can talk."

"This is dust," said Brande, sweeping his hand along a rafter and blowing on his fingers to disperse it. The grains whirled meaninglessly through the air and sifted down to the floor.

"You know what I mean," said Pan. "You just refuse to believe in it."

"It does not exist. Belief and disbelief are both irrelevant."

"And the scientists who discovered it? Rusakov? And the Rusakov field, what about that?"

"A fraud. Those who claim such things are either deluded or corrupt."

The man's contempt was like a blowtorch that turned things to ice. Pan was afraid of the force of it, but he didn't move. He was fighting for Lyra.

"What about imagination?"

"What about it?"

"Do you believe in that?"

"What does it matter what anyone believes? The facts are indifferent to belief."

"You imagined the story of *The Hyperchorasmians*."

"I constructed it from first principles. I built a narrative to show the logical outcome of superstition and stupidity. Every passage in the book was composed impersonally and rationally, and in a state of full awareness, not in some morbid dreamland."

"Is that why the characters are so unlike real people?"

"I know more about people than you do. Most people are weak and stupid and easily led. Only a few are capable of doing anything original."

"They don't seem like real people at all. Everything that makes people interesting is just . . . it's just not there."

"You're expecting the sun to describe shadows. The sun has never seen a shadow."

"But the world is full of shadows."

"That is not interesting."

"Is Sabine your daughter?"

Brande didn't answer. Throughout their conversation he had looked at Pan no more than three times, and now he turned completely to face the gloom at the other end of the attic, which was deepening steadily.

"She is, then," Pan said. "And how did you learn to separate from your dæmon—what's she called?—Cosima?"

The philosopher's head dropped slowly onto his chest. Again he said nothing.

"I came here," Pan said, "because reading your novel persuaded my Lyra that the things she believed in were false. It made her bitterly unhappy. It was as if you'd stolen her imagination and taken away her hope with it. I wanted to find them and take them back to her, and that's why I came to speak to you. Have you got anything for me to tell her when I go back to her?"

"Everything is what it is and nothing else," said Brande.

"That's it? That's all you have to say?"

Brande remained completely still. In the gloom he looked like an abandoned sculpture after a museum had been ransacked.

"Do you love your daughter?" said Pan.

Silence and stillness.

"She said she came here," Pan went on. "Where did she live before that?"

No reply.

"When did she come? How long has she been here?"

Perhaps there was the slightest movement of the man's shoulders, but it wasn't enough to call a shrug.

"Was she living with her mother? In another city, maybe?"

Brande breathed deeply, with a very slight shudder.

"Who chooses her clothes? Who does her hair? Do you want her to look as she does?"

Silence.

"Does she have any opinion about that sort of thing? Have you ever asked her? Does she go to school? What's happening about her education? Has she got any friends? Do you allow her outside the house and garden?"

Brande began to move as if he were carrying a great burden. He shuffled towards the far corner of the attic, where it was now almost completely dark, and sat down on the floor and drew his knees up, and then put his face in his hands. He was like a child who thinks that if he hides his eyes, he won't be seen by anyone else. Pan felt a wave of compassion begin to build up in himself and tried to resist it, because of what this man's ideas had done to Lyra; but then he realized that she'd have felt the same compassion, and that Brande's ideas had failed.

The door into the attic was still open. Pan went silently out and down the stairs. At the foot of the main staircase, in the hall, the girl was sitting, tearing up a sheet of paper into little pieces and dropping them like snowflakes.

She looked up when Pan came past and said, "Have you killed him?"

"No, of course not. Why is his dæmon like that?"

"No idea. They're both stupid. Everyone's stupid. This is hateful."

"Why don't you leave?"

"Nowhere to go."

"Where's your mother?"

"Dead, of course."

"Haven't you got any other relatives?"

"None of your bloody business. I don't know why I'm bothering with you. Why don't you just piss off?"

"If you open the door, I will."

With a snort of contempt, she did. He went down the steps into the street, where the gaslamps glowed through a gathering mist. If there had been anyone passing by, their footsteps would have been muffled, their outlines vague, their shadows full of possibility, threat, and promise, but of course the sun would have seen nothing of that.

He didn't know where to go next.

At the same time, only a few streets away, Olivier Bonneville was disembarking from the ferry.

TWENTY

THE FURNACE MAN

At the same time, Lyra was in a railway carriage on the outskirts of the city of Prague. She had found it quite easy to buy a ticket in Paris without arousing too much suspicion, and it seemed that her imitation-of-Will method was working. Either that or the citizens of the European towns she passed through were unusually incurious, or unusually polite. Or preoccupied: there was a tension in the streets, and she'd seen more uniforms like those she'd encountered on the ferry—groups of black-dressed men guarding a building, or standing in discussion on corners, or speeding out of underground garages in patrol cars with harsh air-cooled engines.

Or perhaps it was that a person with no visible dæmon wasn't unimaginable. She had seen a woman in Amsterdam without one, beautiful, dressed in the height of fashion, confident, even arrogant, and indifferent to the curiosity of passersby; and a man in Bruges had no dæmon, and made it worse for himself by the shameful, unhappy, self-conscious way he moved along a busy street, hugging the shadows. She learnt from both those examples, and bore herself with modesty and calm confidence. It was far from easy to do, and from time to time, when she was alone, she gave way to tears; but no one would know that.

She'd been brought to Prague by the flicker of a memory that darted into her mind as she saw the name of the city on a railway timetable. She and Pan had once, some years before, spent an evening poring over an old street map of the place, mentally constructing an image of it, building by building. This was where the alethiometer had been invented, after all; and when she saw the name again, she recognized the little spark of memory as the secret commonwealth at work. She was becoming sensitive to these half-whispered promptings, getting better at recognizing when they were not guesswork.

In Prague, though, she would have to make a decision. At the city was a junction of the Central European Railway Company, where lines of one gauge went north and east towards Kiev and Muscovy, and lines of a different and broader gauge went south through Austria-Hungary and Bulgaria towards Constantinople. The northern route would be the obvious one to take if she were going straight on to Central Asia and Karamakan; but that would do her no good, because she needed to find Pan before she tried to reach the place where the roses grew.

And he was—where? The Blue Hotel was the only clue she had, and its Arabic name suggested it lay a good deal further south than Muscovy. If she took the northern route and changed trains at Kiev, she could take a different route south to Odessa and cross the Black Sea by ferry to Trebizond and make her way south from there to Arabic-speaking lands; but without a stronger clue she might as well stick a pin in the atlas. The southern route through Constantinople was less complicated but might take longer—or it might be quicker; and she didn't know what her destination was in any case, except for the Arabic name of al-Khan al-Azraq.

What was more, the alethiometer was little help. The new method had such unpleasant physical consequences that after her first success she'd only tried it once again, and learnt nothing. She could make a little progress with her existing knowledge of the symbols, but without the books it was like trying to thread a needle while wearing boxing gloves.

The only idea she had about what to do next if she did manage to find Pan was bound up with the phrase *the Silk Road*, the route of the ancient camel trains that led directly into Central Asia. But the Silk Road wasn't a railway. It wasn't even a single road: it was a multitude of different routes. It wouldn't be swift and easy; she would have to go at the walking pace of whatever animals they used for transport—camels, no doubt. It would be a long journey, and unless she and Pan were somehow reconciled, it would be a hard one.

She'd been thinking about it for some time. She hadn't spoken to anyone since she'd said goodbye to the Welsh miners in Bruges—anyone, that is, except for waiters and railway officials. She longed for her dæmon; even the unfriendly Pan of recent months was at least another voice, another point of view. How hard it was to think when half of your self was missing!

It was already dark when the train drew into the station in the heart of Prague. She was glad of that, and she thought it might not be too unusual to see a young woman traveling alone, because Prague was a sophisticated city, and students of music and other arts came from all parts of Central Europe, and beyond, to study there.

She handed in her ticket at the barrier and moved away from the rush-hour crowd of passengers to look for an information office where she might find timetables and, if she was lucky, a map. The main concourse was built and decorated in a flamboyant baroque style, with sculptures of naked gods and goddesses holding up every window frame or gaslamp, and stone vegetation twining around every column. Every wall was set with pilasters and niches. There was hardly a surface that was plain and clear, and Lyra was glad of that, because she felt safer in all the visual confusion.

She made herself look firmly at a point ahead of her and walk towards it with confident determination. It didn't matter if it was a coffee stall or the steps to the administrative offices: anything would do; she just had to look as if she made this journey every day.

And she was successful. No one stopped and stared; no one shouted out in angry fear to denounce this freakish young woman with no dæmon; no one seemed to notice her at all. When she reached the end of the concourse, she looked around for the ticket office, where she hoped to find someone who spoke English.

Before she saw it, however, she felt a hand on her arm.

She jumped with alarm and instantly thought: Wrong! I mustn't look fearful. The man whose hand it was stood back, himself alarmed at causing such a reaction. He was middle-aged, spectacled, dressed in a dark suit and a discreet tie, carrying a briefcase: every inch a law-abiding and respectable citizen.

He said something in Czech.

She shrugged, trying to look rueful, and shook her head.

"English?" he said.

She nodded reluctantly. And then, with an even greater shock than she'd felt a moment ago, she realized that, like her, he had no dæmon. Her eyes widened, her mouth opened to speak, she glanced over his shoulder, to left and right, and then she shut her mouth again, uncertain what to say.

"Yes," he said quietly. "We have no dæmons. Walk calmly with me, and we will not be noticed. Pretend you know me. Pretend to talk."

She nodded and fell into step beside him as he walked through the rush-hour throng, making for the main exit.

"What is your name?" she said quietly.

"Vaclav Kubiček."

Something about that was familiar, but the impression came and went in a second.

"And yours?"

"Lyra Silvertongue. How did you know I . . . Did you just see me and decide to speak to me on impulse?"

"I was expecting you. I didn't know your name or anything about you except that you were one of us."

"One of . . . one of who? And how were you expecting me?"

"There is a man who needs your help. He told me you were coming."

"I . . . Before we do anything else, I need a railway timetable."

"Do you speak any Czech?"

"Not a word."

"Then let me ask for you. Where do you want to go?"

"I need to know the times of the trains to Muscovy, and those of the other railway to Constantinople."

"Please come with me. I shall get those for you. There is an information bureau through that door," he said, pointing to the corner of the great concourse.

She went with him. Inside the bureau he spoke rapidly to the official behind the desk, who asked him something in return. Kubiček turned to Lyra and said, "Do you desire to travel all the way to Constantinople, if you go that way?"

"Yes, all the way."

"And similarly, all the way to Moscow?"

"Beyond Moscow. How far does the line go? Does it go on through Siberia?"

He turned to translate. The official listened, and then swiveled round in his chair to take two leaflets from the rack beside him.

Kubiček said, "He was not very helpful. But I do know that the Muscovy line goes as far as Irkutsk on Lake Baikal."

"I see," said Lyra.

The official slid the leaflets across the desk, his eyes tired and unseeing, and then went on with the work he'd been doing. Lyra put the leaflets in her rucksack and then turned away with Kubiček, thinking that this man was clearly practiced at Will's art; perhaps she could learn from him.

She said, "Where are we going, Mr. Kubiček?"

"To my house in the old city. I shall explain as we walk."

They left the station and stood facing a busy square where traffic was flowing swiftly. The shopfronts were brightly lit; there were cafés and restaurants thronged with people; trams went past with a smooth humming from the anbaric wires above them.

"Before you say anything else," said Lyra, "what did you mean when you said that I was one of us? Who is *us*?"

"Those whose dæmons have deserted them."

"I had no idea—" Lyra began, but then the traffic lights changed, and Kubiček set off quickly across the road, so she had to say no more until they reached the other side. She began again: "Until recently I didn't realize that this could happen to anyone. Anyone other than me, I mean."

"You felt alone?"

"Desperately. We could separate, but of course, we kept that secret as far as we could. Then in recent months . . . I don't know how to describe it to you. I don't know you at all."

"There are some of us in Prague. A small number. We met by chance, or by hearing about one another from those who are not afraid of us—we do have a few friends—and we have discovered other networks of acquaintanceship in other places. It is a secret society, if you like. If you tell me where you are going next, I can give you names and addresses of some people like us in that place. They will understand and help, if you need it. If I might suggest . . . we should move away from this light."

She nodded and walked on beside him, marveling at what he'd said.

"I had no idea," she said again. "I knew nothing about this way of being. I was sure people would see it at once and hate me for it. Some did, in fact."

"We have all experienced that."

"When did your dæmon leave? Is that a question it's polite to ask? You see, I know so little."

"Oh, we can talk of this very openly among ourselves. One thing I should say is that before she left, we knew that we could separate."

He glanced at Lyra, who saw and nodded.

"I think that is common among us," he went on. "There is a sudden danger, or an emergency, some absolutely compelling reason, and you separate for the first time. It is agonizing, of course. But you survive, no? And then it is easier. In our case, we came to disagree about many things, and to find that we were unhappy together."

"Yes . . ."

"Then one day she must have decided that we would be less unhappy if we were apart," he went on. "She may have been right in her case. Anyway, she left. Maybe there is a secret society of dæmons too, as there is of us. Maybe they help one another, as we do. Maybe they watch us. Maybe they have forgotten all about us. We manage to live, all the same. We are quiet; we attract very little attention. We do no harm."

"Have you tried to find her?"

"Every time I open my eyes, I hope she will be there. I have walked down every street, every alley; I have looked in every park, every garden, every church, even in every café; but we all do this, we all begin by doing this. It is my dread that I will see her with a man who is me, who is my double. But so far . . . nothing.

"But I did not find you in order to tell you about myself. Earlier this week, something else happened. A man arrived in our city and came to my house, who . . . I would describe him to you, but I cannot find the words, in Czech or English or Latin. He is the strangest person I have ever known, and his predicament is appalling. He knows about you, and he says that you will be able to help. I agreed to invite you to meet him and listen to what he has to say."

"He said I— But how did he know about me?"

And she'd been thinking that she could move across Europe and on into Asia unnoticed, unsuspected.

"I don't know. There is much about him that is mysterious. He too has lost his dæmon, but in a different manner. . . . It is very hard to describe, but you will understand at once when you see him. You will understand, but perhaps you will not believe what you see. Possibly this is something that we in Prague would find easier to believe than those who live elsewhere. The hidden world exists, with its own passions and preoccupations, and from time to time its affairs leak through into the visible world. In Prague, maybe the veil between the worlds is thinner than in other places—I don't know."

"The secret commonwealth," said Lyra.

"Indeed? I did not know that expression."

"Well, if I can help, I will. Of course. But my most important task is to go east."

They went on towards the river, the Vltava. Kubiček explained that the river was the route by which most travelers entered and left the city, though the railway was beginning to rival it in popularity. His own house, Kubiček said, lay on the other side of the river, in the Malá Strana.

"Have you heard of Zlatá ulička?" he asked.

"No. What is that?"

"It is the street where people think the alchemists used to make their gold. It is very close to my apartment."

"Do people still believe in alchemy?"

"No. Educated people do not. So they think alchemists are fools for pursuing a goal that does not exist, and they take no notice of them, and fail to see what they are really doing."

A bell rang in her memory: Sebastian Makepeace, the Oxford alchemist! He'd told her almost the same thing four years before.

They came to the river. Kubiček looked carefully all around before stepping forward towards the bridge, a wide, ancient structure with statues of kings and saints set along the parapet. The houses on the other side were old, crowded together, with narrow streets and crooked alleys between them, and high above behind them stood a castle that was lit by floodlights. Despite the cold, the bridge was busy and the streets crowded; lights glowed from every shop window and tavern, and gaslamps flared between the statues on the bridge.

At the foot of the bridge on the Malá Strana side of the river, there was a landing stage where a paddle steamer was carefully drawing up. As Lyra and Kubiček went further across, they could see a number of passengers on the deck waiting for the gangway to be lowered so they could come ashore. They hadn't been on a pleasure cruise; they were carrying suitcases, or rucksacks, or boxes tied with string, or loaded baskets and carrier bags. They looked as if they were fleeing some disaster.

"Did your strange man arrive on a boat like this?" said Lyra.

"Yes."

"Where are those people traveling from?"

"From the south; ultimately, from the Black Sea or further. The boats travel on from here to the north, where this river joins the Elbe, and from there to Hamburg and the German Ocean."

"Does every boat that lands here carry passengers like those? They look like refugees."

"More and more of them arrive every day. The Magisterium has begun to encourage each province of the Church to regulate its territory with a firmer hand. In Bohemia things are not yet as savage as elsewhere; refugees are still given sanctuary. But that can't go on indefinitely. We shall have to begin turning them away before too long."

In their short walk through the city, Lyra had already noticed a few people huddled in doorways or sleeping on benches. She'd supposed they were beggars, and she was sorry to see that such a fine city cared so little for the poor. Now she watched as a family came down the gangway onto the landing stage: an old woman leaning on a stick, a mother with a baby in her arms, and four other children, all under ten, by the look of them. Each child carried a box or a bag or a suitcase, and they were all struggling. Behind them came an old man and a boy in his early teens carrying a rolled-up mattress between them.

"Where will they go?" said Lyra.

"At first, to the Bureau of Asylum. After that, onto the streets if they have no money. Come. This way."

Lyra walked a little faster, as he did. Once across the river, they made for the twisting maze of little alleys under the castle. Kubiček took so many turns that she soon lost track of where they might be.

"You will help me find the way back to the station?" she said.

"Of course. We are quite close now."

"Can you tell me anything about this man you want me to see?"

"His name is Cornelis van Dongen. Dutch, as you may guess. I would rather let him tell you the rest."

"Suppose I can't help him? What will he do then?"

"Then it would be much the worse for me, and for all the citizens of the Malá Strana, and beyond the Malá Strana too."

"That's giving me a large responsibility, Mr. Kubiček."

"I know you will bear it."

She said nothing, but she felt for the first time how stupid she'd been to walk into this warren of ancient houses and alleyways with a man she knew nothing about.

Here and there a gaslight flaring on a bracket shone on the wet street, on the cobbles, on the shutters over the windows. The noise of the traffic, the clatter of iron wheels on stone, the drone of the anbaric trams, grew less and less noticeable as they went further in. There were fewer people to be seen, though sometimes they would pass a doorway with a man lounging against the wall, or a woman standing under a lamp. They would look at Kubiček and Lyra and mutter a comment, or cough consumptively, or simply sigh.

"Not far now," said Kubiček.

"I'm completely lost," said Lyra.

"I'll show you the way out, don't worry."

Around one more corner, and then Kubiček took a key from his pocket and unlocked the heavy oak door of a tall house. He went in ahead of Lyra and struck a match, lighting a naphtha lamp and holding it up so she could see to pick her way through the columns of books that stood on both sides of the narrow hall. There were bookshelves too, rising to the ceiling, but clearly Kubiček had long ago filled them, and had to resort to the floor. The steps of a staircase that led up into the gloom were themselves laden with books on each side. The air of the place was cold and damp, with the smell of leather bindings and old paper overlying that of cabbage and bacon.

"Please come this way," said Kubiček. "My guest is not actually inside the building. I am a book dealer, and . . . You will understand in little more than a minute."

Carrying the lamp, he led Lyra into a little kitchen, which was clean and tidy and clear of books except for three small piles on the table. Kubiček put the lamp down and unlocked the back door.

"Please, will you come this way?" he said.

Apprehensive, Lyra followed. Kubiček had left the lamp inside, and the little yard behind the house was almost dark but for the glow of the city that pervaded the air above. But for that, and for—

Lyra caught her breath.

In the little courtyard stood a man in rough clothes who gave off such heat that she couldn't go close. He was like a furnace. She could see his gaunt face, alive with anguish, and she had to gasp as two little flames broke out from under his eyelids, to be dashed away like tears by his angry hand. His eyes were glowing like coals: black over a flaring, breathing red. He had no dæmon that Lyra could see.

He spoke to Kubiček, and flame spilled out of his mouth. His voice had the quiet roaring, bubbling sound of an overfed fire in a small fireplace, the kind of fire that threatens to set the chimney ablaze.

Kubiček said in English, "This is Lyra Silvertongue. Miss Silvertongue, may I introduce Cornelis van Dongen?"

Van Dongen said, "I cannot shake your hand. I salute you. Please, I beg you, help me."

"If I can, I will, but—how? What can I do for you?"

"Find my dæmon. She is nearby. She is in Prague. Find her for me."

She supposed he meant with the alethiometer. And she'd have

to use the new method, and that would leave her prostrate with sickness.

"I need to know—" she began, but shook her head, helpless.

The dark man who burned like a furnace stood with hands out-stretched, palms upward, pleading. A row of little flames broke out from under the fingernails of his left hand, and he crushed them out in his right palm.

"What do you need to know?" he said, his voice sounding like that of a gas flame.

"Oh, everything—I don't know! Is she—like you?"

"No. I am all fire, and she is all water. I long for her. She is long-ing for me. . . ."

Tears of flame gushed from his eyes, and he stooped to pick up a handful of earth and rubbed it into them until the flames went out. Lyra was filled with pity and horror. She could make him out a little more clearly now her eyes were accustomed to the dark, and his face seemed like that of a wounded animal, aware of its suffer-ing but of nothing that could explain it, so the whole universe was complicit in its pain and terror. The man's clothing, she realized in passing, was made of asbestos cloth.

Her expression must have been visible to him, and it made him shrink away, ashamed, which added to the shame she felt herself. What could she do? What in the world could she do?

But she had to do something.

"I need to know more about her," she said. "Her name, for ex-ample. Why you're separated. Where you come from."

"Her name is Dinessa. We come from the Dutch Republic. My father is a natural philosopher, and my mother died when we were young. My dæmon and I loved to help my father in his workshop, his laboratory, where he worked on his magnum opus, which was the isolation of the essential principles of matter. . . ."

As he spoke, the heat coming from his body seemed to increase, and Lyra found herself stepping back a little. Kubiček was standing in the doorway, respectfully attending to everything they said. The yard they were in seemed to be shared by the other buildings behind, whose windows overlooked it; and as Lyra turned her face away for a second's relief from the heat, she saw lights glowing and one or two people moving around, but no one was looking out.

"Please go on," she said.

"I said that Dinessa and I loved to help him in his work. It felt grand and important to us. All we knew was that he was having conversations, interchanges, with immortal spirits, and what they had to say was far above our understandings. One day he spoke to us about the elements of fire and water. . . ." He broke off for a few moments to sob helplessly in great gouts of flame.

Kubiček said, "Van Dongen, please—not so much . . ." He was looking anxiously up at the windows of the buildings overlooking the little courtyard.

"I am a human being!" the furnace man cried. "Even now I am *human!*"

He pressed his hands over his eyes and rocked back and forth. There was nothing he needed so much as an embrace, and such a human contact would never be offered.

"What happened?" urged Lyra, helpless with pity.

"My father was interested in change," Van Dongen said after another moment. "In one thing becoming another, while other things do not change. Naturally we trusted him and thought no harm could come of what he did. We were proud to be helping with such a great task. So when he wanted to work with us, with the connection between the two of us, while Dinessa could still change, we agreed at once.

"It was a long process that wearied and troubled us, me and

my dæmon, but we persevered and did all that he asked of us. My father was anxious about our safety, anxious about everything, because he truly loved us as much as he loved knowledge. And in the course of one experiment, he assimilated our essential self to the elements: me to the nature of elemental fire, her to that of elemental water. Then he found he could not undo this operation—that it was permanent. I am like this, and my dæmon cannot live in the air but has to breathe water and live her life in it." A flame broke out on his brow, and he swiped a hand across to smother it.

"Why were you separated?" Lyra said.

"Once we were transformed in that way, we were each other's only comfort and consolation, but now we could never touch, never embrace. It was a torment. We had to remain hidden in the house and grounds, my dæmon in a pool of water and myself in a hut constructed of iron sheets. The servants were bribed to keep quiet about us. My father did everything he could to keep us concealed, but it was costing him money; he was selling everything he could to meet the expense. We didn't know. How would we know? We knew nothing. Finally he came to us and said, 'I am so sorry, my child, but I can afford to keep you concealed no longer. The Magisterium has heard rumors, and if they find out about you, they will arrest me and kill you. I have had to ask the advice of a great magician. He is coming tomorrow to see you. Maybe he will be able to help.'

"False words! Oh, false hopes and false words!"

Cascades of flame ran down his cheeks, and the blaze lit up the backs of all the other buildings, and made flaring shadows on the walls. Lyra stood helplessly watching. Van Dongen wiped his asbestos sleeve over his face and brushed off little sparks that fell to the ground and squirmed and flared and died quickly.

Kubiček stepped forward a little way and said, "Please, Van Dongen, please try to avoid exciting yourself. This is the only place we can talk without danger to the building, but anyone could look out at any time, and—"

"I know. I know. Please forgive me."

He sighed, and a cloud of smoke and flame gushed from his mouth, and vanished in the air.

Van Dongen sank to his knees, and then twisted himself down to sit on the ground cross-legged. His head was bowed, his hands in his lap.

"The magician arrived. He was called Johannes Agrippa, and he looked at us, at me and Dinessa, and went to my father's study to talk in private. There he made my father an offer: he would pay a considerable sum to take my dæmon away, but he would not take me. My father accepted the offer. As if she was an animal, as if she was a block of marble, he gave that man my dæmon, my only companion, the one being who could understand the full misery of our existence. She begged and pleaded, I sobbed and implored, but he was stronger, he had always been stronger, and he went through with his transaction. My dear dæmon was sold to the magician, and arrangements were made to transport her to the city of Prague, where he lived. The agony of parting was indescribable. I was kept from them by force until they were far away, and as soon as I was free I set off to find her. But here she still is, somewhere, and I would tear down every wall and set every house ablaze, I would bring about a conflagration that would dwarf every great fire that ever burned, but she would perish in the process and I would be destroyed before I saw her again.

"I must know where she is, Miss Silvertongue. I believe you could tell me. Please tell me where to find my dæmon."

Lyra said, "How do you know about me?"

"In the world of the spirits your name is famous."

"What is this world of the spirits? It is nothing I know about. I don't know what spirit is."

"Spirit is what matter does."

That disconcerted her. She didn't know how to respond, and then Kubiček said, "It is your secret commonwealth, perhaps."

Lyra turned back to Van Dongen and said, "Do you know how the alethiometer works? How I use it?"

He looked bewildered. He spread his hands, and at once a flame broke out in the center of each palm. He beat them on the ground to put them out.

"Alethi—" He shook his head. "I don't know that word. What is that?"

"I thought that's what you wanted me to use. The alethiometer. It tells the truth, but it's very hard to read. Isn't that what you meant?"

He shook his head. Little tears ran down his cheeks like lava. "I don't know! I don't know!" he cried. "But you will know! You will know!"

"But that's all I've got. . . . No, wait. There's this too."

It was the battered notebook that Pan had left with his cruel note, the one carried all the way from Central Asia by the murdered man, Hassall. She realized that that was where she'd seen Kubiček's name before, and why she'd felt that flicker in her memory. She tugged the notebook out of her rucksack and flicked through it urgently to find the entry for Prague.

It was too dark to read, so she had to kneel beside the furnace man and use the fierce light from his eyes to see it by. And yes, there was Kubiček, with his address in the Malá Strana. There were five names with Prague addresses, including Kubiček's, each written in a different hand with a different pen. But there was also one more, written sideways to fit on the page, and in pencil, and there it was: Dr. Johannes Agrippa.

"Got it!" said Lyra, and tried to look more closely, but the light from Van Dongen's eyes was too hot to bear. She scrambled up and said, "Mr. Kubiček, can you read it? I can't quite make out the address."

Van Dongen got to his feet too, eager to see. He was beating his hands together, striking sparks out of himself that whirled in the air like tiny Catherine wheels. One of them flew all the way to Lyra's hand and stung like a needle thrust. She gasped and slapped it out, and stepped away hastily.

"Oh—sorry—sorry . . . ," the Dutchman said. "Just read it. Read it."

"Please, not so loud!" said Kubiček. "I beg you, Van Dongen, keep your voice down! The address is . . . Ah. I see."

"What is it? Where does he live?" came in a subdued roar of flame from Van Dongen's throat.

"Starý železniční most forty-three. That is not far away. It's a place where . . . I suppose a sort of area of workshops. Under an old railway bridge. I would not have expected—"

"Take me there!" said Van Dongen. "We'll go now."

"If I told you where it was—if I gave you a map—"

"No! Impossible. You must help. You, miss, you will come too. He will respect you, at least."

Lyra doubted that, but she would have to go with them if she wanted Kubiček to guide her to the railway station afterwards. She nodded. In any case, she was curious, and relieved to have been spared a session with the new method.

Kubiček said, "Please, Van Dongen, walk quietly and say little. We are just three people walking home, nothing more than that."

"Yes, yes. Come on."

Kubiček led the way through the house and outside, the Dutchman walking with the greatest care between the piles of books, and Lyra keeping her distance from him as she followed.

The dark lanes and crooked streets of the Malá Strana were mostly empty, with only a cat or two prowling or a rat scuttling into an alley. They saw no human beings until they came out to a rough patch of ground beside a high factory wall. There was a group of men gathered around a brazier, sitting on boxes or piles of sacks, smoking and staring at them as they passed. Kubiček murmured a polite greeting, which the men ignored, and Lyra felt the force of their interest as their heads turned to follow her as she stumbled over the uneven ground, trying to avoid the potholes and the oil-tinted puddles. Van Dongen didn't even appear to see the men, and they didn't seem interested in him; he was intent only on the stone arches of the old railway bridge towards which they were moving.

"Is that the place? Is that it?" he said, and a jet of flame gushed out and ballooned above him before fading. Lyra heard a grunt of alarm from the men around the brazier.

In front of them the old bridge reared high above the waste ground. Under each of the arches was a door, some of wood, some of rusted steel, some of little more than cardboard. Most were padlocked. Two of them were open, with naphtha lamps throwing a yellow pool of light on the ground outside. In one, a mechanic was assembling an engine, his monkey dæmon handing him the parts, and in the other, an elderly woman was selling a small packet of herbs to a ravaged-looking younger woman, who might have been pregnant.

Van Dongen was striding up and down the row of doors, looking for number 43.

"It's not here!" he said. "There's no forty-three!"

Gouts of flame coughed out with his words. The mechanic stopped with a carburetor in his hand and looked out at them.

"Van Dongen," pleaded Kubiček, and the Dutchman shut his mouth. He was breathing heavily. His eyes glowed like searchlights.

"The numbers aren't in order," Lyra said.

"In Prague, houses are numbered in the order in which they were built," Kubiček whispered. "It is the same with these workshops. You have to check every one."

He kept looking back at the men around the brazier. Lyra glanced as well, and saw that two of them were now standing up and watching. Van Dongen was hurrying from door to door along the whole length of the waste ground, looking quickly at each one, leaving a trail of cinders and burnt grass. Lyra went along behind him, checking more closely, and found some of the numbers easy to read, painted roughly in white or scrawled in chalk, but others faded and peeling and nearly impossible to make out.

But then she saw a door more solidly built than most, of dark oak with heavy iron hinges. A bronze lion mask was fastened beside it to the bricks of the arch itself. The number 43 was scratched, as if with a nail, in the center of the door.

She stepped back and called softly, "Mr. Kubiček! Mr. Van Dongen! This is the one!"

They both came at once, Kubiček treading delicately through the puddles, Van Dongen at a rush. Lyra was somehow in charge now, though she didn't know why. She knocked firmly on the door.

A voice spoke instantly from the bronze lion. "Who are you?" it said.

"Travelers," Lyra answered. "We have heard of the wisdom of the great master Dr. Johannes Agrippa, and we want to ask for his guidance."

Only then did she realize that the voice had spoken in English, and that she had automatically responded in the same language.

"The master is busy," said the lion mask. "Come back next week."

"No, because we shall be long gone by then. We need to see him now. And . . . I have a message from the Dutch Republic."

Kubiček was clutching Lyra's arm, and Van Dongen was wiping away the little flames breaking out all around his mouth. They waited for a short while, and then the mask spoke again: "Master Agrippa will grant you five minutes. Enter and wait."

The door opened by itself, and a gust of smoky air, laden with dusty odors of herbs and spices and minerals, wafted out to surround them. Van Dongen immediately tried to push past Lyra, but she put out her hand and held him back—at once regretting it: her palm and fingers felt as if she'd tried to pick up a piece of red-hot iron.

She clutched the hand to her breast, trying not to cry out, and went into the workshop ahead of the other two. The door closed behind them at once. The brick walls and the concrete floor were lit very dimly by a single pearl hanging by a thread from the ceiling, its glow brightening and fading with a rhythm like breathing. In its light they saw—nothing. The place was empty.

"Where should we go?" Lyra said.

"Down," came in a whisper from the air.

Van Dongen pointed to the corner. "There!" A great billow of flame came out of his mouth and spread across the ceiling before vanishing.

In the light from his voice they saw a trapdoor. Van Dongen hastened to pull up the iron ring at one end, but Lyra said, "No! Don't you touch anything. In fact, don't you come down at all. You stay up here till I tell you. Mr. Kubiček, make sure he does."

"Soon, soon," said Kubiček to the Dutchman, and they both retreated to the far corner as Lyra lifted up the trapdoor.

A flight of wooden steps led down almost immediately inside the entrance towards a cellar lit by a lurid flare. Lyra made her way down and halted at the foot to look in at the room. It had a vaulted ceiling, black with the smoke of centuries. A large furnace stood in the very center, under a copper hood that went up through the ceiling as a chimney. Around the walls, hanging from the ceiling, or standing on the floor were a thousand different objects: retorts and crucibles; earthenware jars; open-topped boxes containing salt, or pigment, or dried herbs; books of every size and age, some lying open, some crammed into shelves; philosophical instruments, compasses, a photo-mill, a camera lucida, a rack of Leyden jars, a Van de Graaff generator; a jumble of bones, some of which might have been human; various plants under dusty glass domes; and an immensity of other objects. Lyra thought: Makepeace! It reminded her powerfully of the Oxford alchemist's laboratory.

And standing by the furnace, in the red glare from the burning coals, was a man in rough workman's clothing, stirring a cauldron in which something pungent was boiling. He was reciting what might have been a spell in what might have been Hebrew. What she could see of his face showed him to be of middle years, proud, impatient, and strong, the master of considerable intellectual force. He didn't seem to have seen her.

For a moment she was reminded of her own father, but she moved away from that thought at once, and looked at the other large object in the cellar, which was a tank of stone some ten feet long and six wide, with sides as high as her waist.

And the tank was full of water, and in the water, twisting, speeding from end to end and back again, twining herself like honeysuckle growing up a branch, never still, never less than perfectly graceful and lovely, was the mermaid-formed dæmon of Cornelis van Dongen: Dinessa, the water sprite.

She was beautiful, and naked, and her black hair streamed out behind her like fronds of the most delicate seaweed. As she turned at the far end of the tank, she caught sight of Lyra and, like the quickest fish, darted towards her.

Before she could break the surface, Lyra put her finger to her lips and pointed to the magician deep in his spell. The water sprite understood and fell still, looking up through the surface at Lyra with eyes that implored. Lyra nodded and tried to smile, and then noticed what stood over the tank: a vast complexity of iron pistons, valves, connecting rods, wheels, crankshafts, and other parts whose names she didn't know and whose function was unguessable.

Lyra heard a cry from behind her, and a gust of flame singed her hair. She turned to see Van Dongen halfway down the steps, with Kubiček trying to hold him back but flinching from the pain. Lyra's scorched palm throbbed in sympathy.

And then they were at the bottom, on the cellar floor—

At once a tumult broke out. The stuffed crocodile hanging from the ceiling twisted in its chains, and writhed and lashed its tail and roared; a row of dusty glass bottles, gallon-sized or larger, containing strange specimens, fetuses, homunculi, cephalopods, glowed with light as the dead creatures inside beat their fists on the glass or sobbed with fury or hurled themselves from side to side; a metal bird in a dusty cage sang raucously; the water in Dinessa's tank shrank away from Van Dongen and rose up in a great wave to stand suspended and trembling in the air, with the water dæmon inside, like an insect trapped in amber, though she saw her man and reached both arms out of the water and into the air, calling, "Cornelis! Cornelis!"

It was all happening too quickly for anyone to stop. Van Dongen, crying "Dinessa!" hurled himself at the standing wave, and Dinessa burst out of it and into his arms.

They came together in an explosion of steam and flame. For a second Lyra could see their faces, lurid, enraptured, pressing themselves together in a final embrace. Then they were gone, and something was happening among the machinery above the tank. Jets of superheated steam were forcing their way into the cylinders and slamming the pistons to and fro, making the connecting rods swing backwards and forwards as they turned a gigantic wheel, everything moving with the smooth ticking of lubricated machinery.

Lyra and Kubiček could only stand back in shock. Then she turned to the sorcerer, who was shutting his book with the air of having completed a long and arduous task.

"What have you done?" she found herself saying.

"Started my engine," he said.

"But how? Where are they, the man and his dæmon?"

"They are both fulfilling the destiny they were created for."

"They weren't created for this!"

"You know nothing about it. I arranged for their birth, I brought the dæmon here for this work, but her boy escaped. No matter. I arranged for you to find him and bring him here. Now your part is over, and you can leave."

"Their father betrayed them, and you did this to them!"

"I *am* their father."

Lyra was dazed. The machinery was working faster now. She could feel the whole cellar trembling with the force of it. The crocodile had fallen still, apart from the slow swing of its tail; the homunculi in their bottle had stopped screaming and banging on the glass and were floating contentedly in the fluid that contained them, which was now glowing a faint and steady red; the metal bird in its cage, its golden feathers now gleaming with rich enamels and precious stones, was singing as sweetly as a nightingale.

Agrippa stood calmly, book in hand, as if waiting for Lyra to ask a question.

"Why?" she said. "Why do it like this? Why sacrifice two lives? Couldn't you build a fire in the normal way?"

"This is not a normal fire."

"Tell me *why*," Lyra said again.

"This is not a normal engine. Not a normal fire. Not normal steam."

"That's all they were? Just a different kind of *steam*? Steam is steam."

"Nothing is only itself."

"That's not true. Nothing is any more than what it is," Lyra said, quoting Gottfried Brande, feeling uneasy as she did.

"You've fallen for that lie, have you?"

"You think it's a lie?"

"One of the biggest lies ever told. I thought you would have more imagination than to believe it."

That took her aback. "What do you know about me?" she said.

"As much as I need to."

"Will I ever find my dæmon?"

"Yes, but not in the way you think."

"What does that mean?"

"Everything is connected."

Lyra thought about that. "What is *my* connection with this?" she said.

"It has brought you to the one man who can tell you whether to go east or south on the next stage of your journey."

Then she felt dizzy. This was all impossible, and it was all happening. "Well?" she said. "Which way should I go?"

"Look in your *clavicula*." He gestured towards her notebook.

She turned to the page with the added lines in pencil, and found under his name and address something she'd missed before: the words *Tell her to go south.*

"Who wrote this?" she said.

"The same man who wrote my name and address: Master Sebastian Makepeace."

Lyra had to grasp the side of the stone tank. "But how did he—"

"You'll find that out in due course. There's no point in my telling you now. You would not understand."

She felt a light touch on her arm and looked around to see Kubiček, looking pale and nervous.

"In a minute," said Lyra, and to Agrippa she said, "Tell me about Dust. You know what I mean by Dust?"

"I have heard of Dust, of the Rusakov field, of course I have. You think I still live in the seventeenth century? I read all the scientific journals. Some of them are very funny. Let me tell you something else. You have an alethiometer, do you not?"

"Yes."

"The alethiometer is not the only way to read Dust, not even the best way."

"What other ways are there?"

"I will tell you one, that is all. A pack of cards."

"You mean the tarot?"

"No, I do not. That is an egregious modern fraud designed to extract money from gullible romantics. I mean a pack of cards with pictures on them. Simple pictures. You will know it when you see one."

"What can you tell me about something called the secret commonwealth?"

"That is a name for the world I deal with, the world of hidden things and hidden relationships. It is the reason that nothing is only itself."

"Two more questions. I want to find a place called the Blue Hotel, al-Khan al-Azraq, to look for my dæmon. Have you heard of that?"

"Yes. It has another name: it's sometimes called Madinat al-Qamar, the City of the Moon."

"And where is it?"

"Between Seleukeia and Aleppo. You can reach it from either of those cities. But you will not find your dæmon without great pain and difficulty, and he will not be able to leave with you unless you make a great sacrifice. Are you ready for that?"

"Yes. And my second question: what does the word *akterrakeh* mean?

"Where have you heard that expression?"

"In connection with a place called Karamakan. It's a way of traveling, or something like that. When you have to go *akterrakeh*."

"It's Latin."

"What? Really?"

"*Aqua terraque.*"

"Water and land . . ."

"By water and by land."

"Oh. So that means—what?"

"There are some special places where you can only go if you and your dæmon travel separately. One must go by water, the other by land."

"But this place is in the middle of a desert! There isn't any water."

"Not so. The place you mean is between the desert and the wandering lake. The salt marshes and shallow streams of Lop Nor, where the watercourses shift and move about unpredictably."

"Ah! I see," she said.

What Strauss wrote on those tattered pages she'd found in Hassall's rucksack had suddenly become clear. So much became clear! The men had had to separate from their dæmons to travel to the red building, and Strauss's dæmon had arrived successfully, so he and she could enter; but Hassall's dæmon hadn't made it, though they must have found each other later. So that was how it worked; and she'd only be able to go there herself if Pan agreed to go through Lop Nor while she went through the desert; and then she'd be able to go into the red building. And as the clarification spread through her mind, blowing away all the mist and doubt, she remembered the feeling she'd had when she first read Strauss's journal: she was certain that she knew what was in the building. The knowledge flickered with promise like a mirage, but it still trembled just out of her reach.

She stood in the smoky cellar, with the steady, confident beat of the pistons and the connecting rods and the valves above her testifying to the unity at last of Cornelis and Dinessa, and tried to bring her attention back to Agrippa.

"How do you know about that?" she said. "Have you made the journey yourself?"

"No more questions. Be on your way."

Kubiček pulled at her sleeve, and she went with him to the staircase. She looked back at the cellar, where everything was alive, and where great hidden purposes were at work. Agrippa was already reaching for a box of herbs, clearing a space on a workbench, taking down a set of scales. The steam engine had settled down into a quiet, powerful rhythm, and then Lyra saw the magician reach out a hand and take a small box that had seemingly floated to him by itself. Little lights glowed over a number of different jars, bottles, boxes around the shelves, and beside two drawers in a great mahogany cabinet. The sorcerer took something from every container lit in this way, and as he did so, the spirit (Lyra could find no other word) responsible for the light flew across the cellar and joined its fellow on the bench. Everything in his cellar seemed alive and full of purpose, and Agrippa was perfectly busy, perfectly calm and in charge of what he was doing, completely fulfilled, and eager for the next stage in his work.

She followed Kubiček up the stairs and out into the empty waste ground. The men had gone, and the brazier was burning low. The cold air flooded into her grateful lungs and connected her with the night sky, as if it was a wind from the millions of stars.

"Well, it's clear that I need the train for the south," she said. "Will I make it to the station on time?"

A bell in the nearby cathedral struck two.

"If we go there at once," said Kubiček.

She went with him through the old city to the river and across the bridge. Lights glowed in some of the boats on the water; a cargo barge went past, moving on the current with a load of great pine logs towards the Elbe, and Hamburg, and the German Ocean; a tram trundled along the rails at the far end of the bridge, with three late travelers in its lighted interior.

Neither of them spoke till they reached the station. Then Kubiček said, "I'll help you buy your ticket. But first, let me see your *clavicula*."

He flicked through the little notebook.

"Ah," he said with satisfaction.

"What are you looking for?"

"To see if it had the name and address of someone in Smyrna. There is no one like us in Constantinople, but if you go on to Smyrna, you will find this lady helpful."

She put the little notebook away and shook his hand, forgetting till it was too late that her own had been painfully scorched.

"You had a strange evening in Prague," said Kubiček as they went towards the one lighted window in the booking office.

"But valuable. Thank you for your help."

Five minutes later she was inside a sleeper cabin, alone, exhausted, in some pain from her burned hand, but alive and exultant, with a destination and a clear purpose at last. And five minutes after that the train began to move, and she was fast asleep.

TWENTY-ONE

CAPTURE AND FLIGHT

Marcel Delamare was seldom angry. His disapproval took the form of a quiet, cold, precisely measured punishment administered to those who had annoyed him. It was done so subtly that those who suffered it were at first flattered to think they had attracted his attention, until they realized its unpleasant consequences.

But what Olivier Bonneville had done was more than annoying. It was direct and flagrant disobedience, and the punishment it deserved was exemplary. The Consistorial Court of Discipline was the body best able to deal with offenses of that kind, and Delamare made sure they had every detail necessary to find Bonneville, arrest and interrogate him, including some facts about his background that Bonneville himself didn't know.

The young man was not as cunning as he thought he was, and his trail wasn't hard to follow. The ticket he'd bought in Dresden would allow him to travel all the way downriver to Hamburg, so the CCD agents at various cities along the Elbe kept watch at all the stopping points; and as soon as Bonneville disembarked at the quay in Wittenberg, he was seen and followed by the single agent there, who promptly sent a message to Magdeburg, only a few hours downstream, asking for help.

Their quarry himself wasn't aware that he was being followed. He was an amateur, and his tracker was a professional, after all, who watched Bonneville check into a shabby little guesthouse, and then sat in the café opposite waiting for his colleagues to arrive from Magdeburg. They had hired a fast engine-boat; they wouldn't be long.

Bonneville had spent much of the day with the alethiometer, hunched over his lap in the airless cabin, watching Pantalaimon's movements through the city, from his conversation with the girl at the school for the blind to the rooftop journey and his second conversation with a young girl, who was rather prettier than the first one. But the nausea was too much for Bonneville at that point, and he had to sit out on deck to clear his head of it, and by the time he'd recovered, Lyra's dæmon was talking to some old man about philosophy. It was so difficult: looking made him sick, but hearing told him nothing about where the dæmon was. He had to look occasionally, or know nothing.

His room at the guesthouse was no less stuffy than his cabin on the boat, the only difference being the smell of cabbage rather than the smell of oil; so, rather than bring on another bout of nausea, he decided to go for a walk in the evening streets and clear his head. If he kept his eyes open, he might see the creature anyway.

The CCD man watched from the café as Bonneville sauntered out, with his dæmon, some kind of hawk, on his shoulder. He was carrying a small bag, but he'd left his suitcase in the guesthouse, so presumably he'd be returning. The agent left a few coins on the table and followed.

As for Pantalaimon, he was in the garden at St. Lucia's School for the Blind, curled up in the tree where he'd hidden that morning.

He wasn't asleep; he was watching all the evening activity through the lighted windows, and hoping that the girl Anna would come out to visit her book again. But, of course, she wouldn't: it was cold and damp, and she'd be eating supper with her friends in the warmth. Pan could hear their voices across the dark lawn.

He thought about Gottfried Brande and Sabine. Perhaps they were still there, still quarreling, in that tall house with the barren attic. Pan reproached himself: he should have questioned Brande differently. He should have tried to speak to that mysterious dæmon Cosima. He should have been more patient with the girl, above all. She was so like Lyra in some ways—and the thought brought an almost physical pang of longing. He supposed that Lyra was at the Trout still, and he imagined her talking to Malcolm, and Asta, the beautiful gold-red cat, joining in. He imagined Lyra tentatively reaching out to touch her, knowing everything about what that gesture would mean. But no: impossible. He banished that thought at once.

But he couldn't go back to her without what he'd come to seek. He was restless. For the first time he wondered what he'd meant when he spoke of Lyra's imagination. He didn't know, but he knew he wouldn't go back without it.

It was no good: he'd never go to sleep. He was too irritated with himself. He stood up and stretched, and leapt onto the wall and left the garden for the darkness of the streets.

Bonneville strolled towards the Stadtkirche, looking into every doorway, every alley, and up to every roof. In order not to attract attention, he tried to seem like a tourist, or a student of architecture. He wondered whether it would help to have a sketch pad and pencil, but mist was gathering, and no one would be out sketching in conditions like this.

In the bag he carried, as well as the alethiometer, was a coal-silk net, extremely strong and light, in which he intended to catch the girl's dæmon before taking him somewhere private and interrogating him. He could see that happening in his mind's eye, because he'd practiced it many times; and he was so quick with the net, so skillful, that he thought it was a great pity that no one would see him in action with it.

He stopped at a café in the main square and drank a glass of beer, looking all around, listening to the conversations nearby, talking quietly with his dæmon.

"That old man," he said. "The old man in the attic."

"We've heard those kinds of arguments before. The things he said. He's probably famous."

"I'm just trying to place him."

"You think the dæmon'll still be with him?"

"No. They weren't being friendly. The dæmon was accusing him of something."

"Something to do with *her*."

"Yes . . ."

"You think he'll go back there?"

"Maybe. If we knew where the house was, perhaps."

"We could talk to him."

"I don't know, though," he said. "If the dæmon's gone, the old man won't necessarily know where. They weren't on those kind of terms."

"The other girl might know something," said his dæmon. "She might be his daughter."

Bonneville found that suggestion more appealing. He was good with girls too. But he shook his head, and said, "It's all too speculative. We need to focus on *him*. I'm going to try something. . . ."

He reached into his bag. The hawk dæmon, who suffered from the nausea just as he did, said hurriedly, "No, no, not now."

"I won't look. Just listen."

She shook her head and turned away. There were half a dozen customers in the café, mostly middle-aged men who seemed to be settled for the evening, talking and smoking or playing cards. None of them were interested in the young man at the corner table.

He held the alethiometer on his lap, with both hands around it. His dæmon fluttered from the back of his chair to the table. He closed his eyes and thought about Pantalaimon, and at first he could only summon up images of what he looked like, and the hawk dæmon murmured, "No. No."

Bonneville breathed deeply and tried again. He kept his eyes open this time, looking at his half-empty glass, and listened for the scratch of claws on cobbles, the noise of traffic, busy city streets; but all he heard was the mournful blast of a foghorn.

Then he realized that he was hearing it in real life, because he saw two of the men at the other tables turn their heads in the direction of the river and speak to each other, nodding. There was the sound again, but coming into Bonneville's mind from another place altogether was that scratch of claws, men's voices, the splash of water, a deep thud as something large and heavy bumped into something large and immobile, the creak of rope on damp wood. A steamer tying up at the quay?

So Lyra's dæmon was on the move again.

"That's it," Bonneville said, standing up and packing the alethiometer into his bag. "If we go there right now, we might see him get aboard, and then we'll have him."

He paid the bill quickly, and they left.

Pantalaimon was watching from the shadows at the side of the ticket office. According to the notice on the wall, this boat was going all the way upstream to Prague. That would do.

The quay was well lit, though, and the numbers of people coming down the gangway or going up made it quite impossible for him to get on board that way, even in the fog that was blurring the edges of everything visible.

But there was always the water. Without stopping to think, he raced out from beside the ticket office and made for the edge of the quay. But he hadn't got halfway across when something fell over him—a net—

He was snatched to a halt and tumbled over and dragged along the flagstones, struggling, twisting, snapping, tearing, biting; but the net was too strong, and the young man holding it was merciless. Pan felt himself swung into the air, caught a glimpse of his captor's face, dark-eyed, vicious, of astonished passengers watching, unable to move, and then several other things happened at once. He heard the roar of a smaller engine-boat thrown into reverse gear as it pulled up to the quay, exclamations from the passengers, a violent curse from the young man swinging the net, and then the sound of running feet over the stones, and a deep man's voice saying, "Olivier Bonneville, you're under arrest."

The net fell to the ground, with Pan struggling harder than ever, and only getting more entangled.

He didn't stop tearing at it to watch, but he was aware of the men running from the engine-boat, of the young man (Bonneville! *Bonneville!*) loudly protesting, of the word *dæmon* coming from different voices in tones of shock and fear, and then of the hideous touch of an unknown human hand around his neck. It lifted him up and held him close to a man's face, to a smell of beer and smokeleaf and cheap cologne, and to bloodshot eyes that bulged horribly.

The net was still tangled around him. He tried to bite through it, but that hand around his neck was tightening like an iron band. Dimly he heard the young man's voice saying angrily, "I have to say my employer, Marcel Delamare of *La Maison Juste*, will not be at all pleased by this. Take me somewhere quiet, and I shall explain—"

That was the last Pan heard before he fainted.

Mignonne promised to be as light and graceful as Malcolm's boyhood canoe, *La Belle Sauvage*, had been, but the sail that he found and tried to hoist was frail and rotting. That was clear even in the darkness: it came apart in his hands.

"Oars it is, then," said Malcolm, who knew that a boat that sailed well might be a brute to row. But there was no choice, and in any case, the sail was white, or had been, and would show up far too well on a dark night.

In the light of a match he saw that the boathouse gates were fastened with another padlock, and found it harder to shift than the one on the door had been. He finally wrenched it free, and there was the lake in front of them.

"Ready, monsieur?" he said, holding the little boat steady against the landing stage as the other man got in.

"Ready, yes. If God wills."

Malcolm pushed off and let the boat drift away from the shore until there was room to set the oars and start rowing. The boathouse stood in a small bay under the shelter of a rocky headland, and he expected the water to be more or less calm just there, and choppy outside the bay; but to his surprise, once they were out on the open water, with the whole length of the great lake curving away in front of them, the surface was as flat as glass.

The air felt heavy to move through, and clammy; everything was uncannily still. Malcolm enjoyed the sensation of using his muscles again, after days of traveling, but it was almost like being indoors. When he spoke to Karimov, he found himself lowering his voice.

"You said that you had some dealings with Marcel Delamare," he said. "What was his business with you?"

"He commissioned me to bring him some rose oil from the desert of Karamakan, but he has not yet paid me, and I feared he was holding back the money in order to keep me in Geneva because he wants to do me harm. I would have left before now, but I am penniless."

"Tell me about this oil."

Karimov told him everything he'd told Delamare, and then added, "But there was something curious. When I told him of the destruction of the research station at Tashbulak, he seemed not to be surprised, though he pretended to be. Then he asked me questions about the men from the mountains who attacked the station, and I answered truthfully, but again I felt that he knew what he expected to hear. So I held back one thing."

"What was the thing you didn't tell him?"

"The men from the mountains did not destroy the place entirely. They were forced to flee by— And this is where it becomes hard to believe, monsieur, because they were forced to flee by a monstrous bird."

"The Simurgh?"

"How do you know that? I was not going to say that name, but—"

"I read about it in a poem."

That was true: it was a great bird that guided Jahan and Rukhsana to the rose garden in the Tajik poem. But it wasn't the whole truth: Malcolm also remembered it from the diary of Dr. Strauss, which the murdered Hassall had brought back from Tashbulak. The camel herder Chen had told them that the mirages they saw in the desert were aspects of the Simurgh.

"You know *Jahan and Rukhsana*?" said Karimov, clearly surprised.

"I have read it, yes. Naturally I took it to be a fable. Are you saying that such a thing as the Simurgh exists?"

"There are many forms of existence, monsieur. I would not say that it was this one or that one, or any other. Possibly one we know nothing about."

"I see. And you said nothing about this to Delamare?"

"That is correct. It is my belief, based on what I observed during my interview with him, that he knows a great deal about the men from the mountains, and he did not wish me to know that he did. It makes me afraid that he will have me arrested and imprisoned, or worse, and that is why he was keeping me trapped in this city. When I learnt about your situation, monsieur, I felt it was my duty to tell you what I knew."

"I'm very glad you did."

"May I ask in turn what Monsieur Delamare wants with you?"

"He believes I am his enemy."

"And is he correct?"

"Yes. In the matter of Tashbulak and the rose oil, especially. I think he wants to use it for some evil purpose, and if I can stop him, I will. But first I need to know more about it. You found someone who was trading in it, for example. Is there much trade in this oil?"

"Not very much. It is extremely expensive. It was used some-what in the old days, when people believed in shamans who could enter the spirit world. But now not so many believe that."

"Is it used for anything else? Do people take it for pleasure, for example?"

"There is not much pleasure to be had, Monsieur Polstead. The pain is extreme, and the visual effects are more easily obtained with other drugs. I think there are some doctors who use it to relieve various chronic conditions, both physical and mental, but it is so expensive that only the very rich can afford it. It was only the learned investigators at Tashbulak who had any interest in it, and much of their work was secret."

"Have you ever visited the station at Tashbulak?"

"No, monsieur."

Malcolm rowed on. The silence over the lake was profound, the air stifling, almost as if all the oxygen had been withdrawn.

After some time Karimov said, "Where are we going?"

"You see that castle?" Malcolm said, pointing to a crag on the shore not far ahead of them. At the summit stood a building whose massive towers bulked against the skyline only dimly, because there was no light from moon or stars.

"I think so," said Karimov.

"That marks the border with France. Once we're past that, we should be safe, because Geneva has no jurisdiction there. But—"

Between the *b* and the *t* of that word, the entire sky came alight, and then fell dark again. Then came another flash, even brighter, and this time Malcolm and Karimov saw the forked and many-branched lightning stab its way to the ground at the same moment as they felt the first drops of rain, heavy gouts that slammed hard into their faces. Only after both men had turned their collars up and pulled their hats on more tightly did the thunder arrive, with a deafening crack that seemed to split their heads open. It rolled around the lake, rebounding from the mountains and making Malcolm's head ring with its force.

Already a wind was rising. It stirred the water up into waves, and then flung them into spray that lashed Malcolm's face even more fiercely than the rain. He'd done some lake sailing in the past, and he knew how suddenly storms could arrive, but this was exceptional. There was no point in trying to get past the castle on the headland: he hauled the boat to starboard and rowed as hard as he could for the nearest shore, seeing his way by flashes of lightning as the huge whips of incandescence lashed the ground and threw a garish light over the mountains. The thunder followed close behind it now, loud enough to shake the little boat, or so they felt. Asta had crawled inside Malcolm's greatcoat and was lying there, warm and relaxed, with a perfect confidence that transmitted itself to him, which he knew was her intention, and he blessed her for it.

The little *Mignonne* was bobbing this way and that in the chaos, and shipping water fast. Karimov was using his fur hat to scoop out as much as he could. Malcolm hurled all the strength of his arms and his back into the labor, digging the oars deep into the water and straining every muscle to keep the boat from being tossed or blown further back on the lake.

When he looked over his shoulder, he could see little but darkness and deeper darkness, but the deeper darkness was looming high above them now. It was forest, growing right down to the shore. He could hear the wind in the pines, even behind the deafening drumming of the rain and the monstrous crashing explosions of thunder.

"Not far!" Karimov shouted.

"I'll go straight in. See if you can grab a branch."

Malcolm felt a shock and a grinding sensation as the *Mignonne*'s wooden hull met a rock. There was no avoiding it: he could hardly see anything, and there was no sandy beach for the boat to land on gently. Rocks, and more rocks, and after one final lurch and scrape, she was immobile. Karimov was trying to stand up and find a branch to seize, but he kept losing his balance.

Malcolm held on to the gunwale and stepped over the side, thigh-deep before his feet found anything solid. The rocks were tumbled and irregular, but at least they were large and they wouldn't roll under his weight and break an ankle.

"Where are you?" Karimov called.

"Nearly ashore. Keep still. I'll tie us up as soon as I can."

He felt his way towards the bow, and then found the painter. When he'd untied it in the boathouse, he'd noticed how old and worn it was, but it had been good manila cord when it was made, and it might have a little strength still. Asta climbed up onto his shoulder and said, "Up and to your right."

He reached in that direction and found a low-hanging bough, which felt solid enough to trust, but it was too far for the painter.

"Karimov," he called. "I'll hold the boat steady while you get out. We'll just have to feel our way to the bank, but we're wet enough already. Get everything you need and go carefully."

A lightning flash, very close, threw a sudden searchlight on them. The bank was only a yard or two beyond the bow, thick with bushes, and rising steeply out of the water. Karimov gingerly put his left leg overboard and felt around for something solid.

"I can't reach. . . . I can't find any rock—"

"Hold on to the boat and put both legs down."

Another lightning flash. Malcolm thought, What's the drill for surviving a storm if you're in a forest? Avoid tall trees, to begin with; but if you couldn't see anything . . . The lightning had set off another of his spangled-ring episodes. The little thing twisted and scintillated in front of the lashing darkness all around, just at the moment when his hand found a branch low enough for the rope to reach.

"Here!" he shouted. "This way. Here's the bank."

Karimov was floundering towards him. Malcolm found his hand and gripped it tight, and pulled the older man along towards the bushes and then out of the water.

"Got everything you need?"

"I think so. What do we do?"

"Keep together and climb up away from the water. If we're lucky, we'll find somewhere to shelter."

Malcolm hauled his rucksack and suitcase out of the boat and lugged them over the rocks and up into the undergrowth. It felt as if they were at the base of a steep slope, maybe even at the foot of a cliff. . . . There might be an overhanging rock, if they were lucky.

They had only been climbing for a minute when they found something even better.

"I think—here's a . . . just over this big rock . . ."

Malcolm shoved his suitcase ahead of him and reached down to pull Karimov up.

"What is it?" said the Tajik.

"A cave," said Malcolm. "A dry cave! What did I tell you?"

The officers took Olivier Bonneville to the nearest police station and requisitioned the interview room. Strictly speaking, the CCD had no formal relations with the police force in Wittenberg, or anywhere else in greater Germany; but a CCD badge worked like a magic key.

"How dare you treat me like this?" Bonneville demanded, of course.

The two agents took their time settling onto the chairs on the other side of the table. Their dæmons (vixen and owl) were watching his with unpleasant vigilance.

"And what have you done with that dæmon?" Bonneville went on. "I've been pursuing him, on the express orders of *La Maison Juste*, all the way from England. You'd better not have lost him. If I find that—"

"State your full name," said the agent who'd first seen him. The other man was taking notes.

"Olivier de Lusignan Bonneville. What have you done with—"

"Where are you staying in Wittenberg?"

"None of your—"

The interrogator had long arms. One of them reached out before Bonneville could move, and slapped his face hard. The hawk dæmon screamed. Bonneville hadn't been hit since his elementary school days, having learnt very young that there were better ways than violence to make life miserable for his enemies, and he wasn't used to shock and pain. He sat back and gasped.

"Answer the question," said the agent.

Bonneville blinked hard. His eyes were watering. One side of his face was bright red and the other was dull white. "What question?" he managed to say.

"Where are you staying?"

"A guesthouse."

"Address?"

Bonneville had to think hard to remember. "Friedrichstrasse seventeen," he said. "But let me advise you—"

That long arm shot out again and seized him by the hair. Before Bonneville could resist, his head was slammed facedown on the table. His dæmon screamed again and flew up flapping wildly before tumbling down.

The agent let go. Bonneville sat up trembling, with blood streaming from a broken nose. One of the agents must have rung a bell, because the door opened and a policeman came in. The note-taking man stood up and spoke to him quietly. The policeman nodded and went out.

"You don't advise me," said the interrogator. "I hope that alethiometer's not been damaged."

"I'm not likely to damage it," said Bonneville thickly. "I read it better than anyone else; I know everything about it; I treat it with the utmost care. If it's damaged, it wasn't damaged by me. It's the property of La Maison Juste, and I read it on the specific instructions of the Secretary General, Monsieur Marcel Delamare."

To his annoyance, he couldn't keep his voice steady or stop his hands from shaking. He dragged a handkerchief from his pocket and held it to his face. His nose hurt abominably, and his shirtfront was drenched with blood.

"That's curious," said the interrogator. "Seeing as it was Monsieur Delamare himself who reported it missing and gave us your description."

"Prove it," said Bonneville. His disordered mind was beginning to pull itself together, and in the mist of pain and shock he could just make out the shape of a plan.

"I still don't think you've got this the right way round," the interrogator said, smiling. "I ask, and you answer. Any minute now I'm going to hit you again, just to remind you. You won't see where that one's coming from either. Where's Matthew Polstead?"

Bonneville was baffled. "What? Who the hell is Matthew Polstead?"

"Don't tempt me. The man who killed your father. Where is he?"

Bonneville felt as if his mind was coming loose from his body. His dæmon, now on his shoulder again, gripped tightly with her claws, and he knew what she meant at once.

"I didn't know him by that name," he said. "You're right. I've been looking for him. What have you done with that dæmon I caught? He was going to lead me to that Polstead man."

"The polecat or whatever he is is nicely tied up next door. I take it he's not Polstead's dæmon. Whose is he?"

"The girl who's got my father's alethiometer—he's hers. If the Geneva reader's found out that much, then I have to say I'm surprised. He's not usually that quick."

"Reader? What d'you mean, reader?"

"Alethiometer reader. Look, I can't concentrate with this bleeding. I need to see a doctor. Get me fixed up, and I'll talk to you."

"Trying to make conditions now? I wouldn't if I was you. What's that girl's dæmon got to do with Polstead? And how come the dæmon's running around without her? Creepy, that's what that is. Unnatural."

"Come on, there are aspects of this that are confidential. What security clearance have you got?"

"You're asking me questions again. I did warn you about that. You know you've got another clout coming any second now, I'd say."

"That won't help," said Bonneville, who had managed to control the shaking of his voice by this time. "I don't mind telling you what I'm doing, since we're on the same side, but as I say, I need to know the level of your security clearance. If you tell me that, I might even be able to help you."

"Help us with what? What d'you think we're doing? We been looking for you, boy. We got you now. And why the fuck should we help you?"

"There's a bigger picture. D'you know *why* you've been looking for me?"

"Yeah. 'Cause the boss told us to. That's why, you bit of jelly."

Bonneville's eyes were beginning to close. The blow must have bruised his cheekbones or his eye sockets or something, he thought, but don't show pain, don't be distracted. Stay calm.

He said steadily, "There's a connection between my father, what my father was doing, and his death, and this man Polstead, and the girl Lyra Belacqua. Right? Monsieur Delamare has given me the job of finding out more about it because I can read the alethiometer and because I've already discovered a good deal. To start with, the connection involves Dust. Got it? You understand that? You know what that means? My father was a scientist, as they call them now. An experimental theologian. He was investigating Dust, where it comes from, what it means, the threat it holds. He was killed and all his notes were stolen, and so was his alethiometer. The girl Belacqua knows something about it, and so does that Polstead man. That's why I'm here. That's what I'm doing. That's why you'd be much better advised helping me than wasting our time with this sort of thing."

"Then why did Monsieur Delamare tell the CCD that he wanted you arrested?"

"You sure that's what he said?"

The interrogator blinked. For the first time he looked a little unsure. "I know the orders we received, and they've never been wrong before."

"What's just been happening in Geneva?" Bonneville demanded.

"What d'you mean?"

"I mean, what's been going on? Why is the city full of priests and bishops and monks and so on? This congress, that's what I mean. Obviously, since it's the most important development in the Magisterium for centuries, it's important to keep security tight."

"So?"

"So messages get enciphered. Instructions are relayed by different routes. Code words are used. Sometimes information's deliberately scrambled. This Polstead, for example. Did they give you a description of him?"

The interrogator looked at his colleague, the man who was taking notes.

"Yes," said the notetaker. "Big man. Red hair."

"Just what I mean," Bonneville said. "That information's not meant for the public. I know what his real name is, and I know he doesn't look like that. The red hair and the size—those details tell me something *else* about him."

"What?"

"I can't tell you, obviously, unless I know your security clearance. Maybe not then, depending on what it is."

"Level three," said the notetaker.

"Both of you?"

The interrogator nodded.

"Well, I can't, then," said Bonneville. "Look, I tell you what. Let me talk to that dæmon. You can sit in; you can hear what he tells me."

There was a knock, and the door opened. The policeman who'd been sent to investigate the guesthouse came in, carrying Bonneville's rucksack.

"Is it in there?" said the interrogator.

"No," said the policeman. "I searched the room, but there was nothing else."

"If you were looking for the alethiometer," said Bonneville, "you only had to ask. I've got it with me, of course."

He took it out of his pocket and placed it in front of him on the table. The interrogator reached out for it, but Bonneville moved it back.

"You can look, but don't touch," he said. "There's a connection that builds up between the instrument and the reader. It's easily disturbed."

The interrogator peered closely at it, and so did the other man. Bonneville thought: A knife in his eye now—that would teach him a lesson.

"How d'you read it, then?"

"It works by symbols. You have to know all the meanings of each of those pictures. Some of them have over a hundred, so it's not something you can just pick up and do at once. This one belongs to the Magisterium, and it's going back there as soon as I've finished the mission they sent me on. So I'll tell you again: let me talk to that dæmon before he thinks of a good story."

The interrogator looked at his colleague. They both stood up and moved to a corner of the room, where they spoke too quietly for Bonneville to hear. In the pause, the tension that was helping Bonneville stay calm and stop his hands trembling began to seep away. His dæmon felt it, and gripped his shoulder so fiercely that she drew blood. It was just what he needed. When the men turned back to him, he was calm and composed, despite the bloody mess in the middle of his face.

"All right, then," said the interrogator, as the other man opened the door.

Bonneville put the alethiometer away and picked up his rucksack to follow them. They were speaking to the policeman, who turned and took a ring of keys from his pocket and looked through them for the right one.

"We're going to watch," said the interrogator. "And we're going to make a note of everything you ask, and everything he says in reply."

"Of course," said Bonneville.

The policeman opened the door, and then stopped suddenly.

"What's the matter?" said the interrogator.

Bonneville pushed him aside and went in past the policeman. It was a room just like the one next door, with a table and three chairs. The coal-silk net was lying on the table, bitten to shreds, and the window was open. Pantalaimon had escaped.

Bonneville turned to the CCD men in a fury that wasn't in the least assumed. Blood flowing thickly over his mouth and chin, nearly blind with pain, he denounced them and the police for their boneheaded stupidity and criminal carelessness, and threatened them with the wrath of the entire Magisterium in this life, and the certainty of hell in the next.

It was a fine performance. He certainly thought so himself a few minutes later, as he sat in a comfortable chair under the hands of the police doctor, and shortly afterwards stalked away towards the railway station, with his possessions intact and his pride in full flower. The bandage covering his nose was the badge of an honorable wound; the loss of Pantalaimon irrelevant. He had a new target now, one so interesting and so unexpected that it was like a revelation, an epiphany.

It rang in his head like the tolling of a bell: the man who had killed his father, this large man with red hair, this man called Matthew Polstead.

TWENTY-TWO

THE ASSASSINATION OF THE PATRIARCH

Lyra arrived in Constantinople tired and anxious, completely unable to put out of her mind what had happened in Prague, or to understand what it meant. Her feeling of certainty and purpose had been brief and evanescent. She felt as if she had been used by some hidden power, as if all the events on her journey, and for long before, had been arranged with meticulous care with only one purpose: and it was a purpose that had nothing to do with her, and one that she'd never understand, even if she knew what it was. Or was it the beginning of madness to think like that?

The only thing she could find any satisfaction in was the matter of being inconspicuous. She had a mental checklist: Where am I looking? How am I moving? Am I showing any feeling? She went through everything that might draw attention to her and suppressed it. As a result, she could now walk along a crowded street and hardly be noticed. It gave her a rueful kind of amusement to recall how, only a few months ago, she'd sometimes attracted looks of admiration or desire, and had played at ignoring them haughtily while enjoying the power they gave her. Now what she had to feel pleased with was being ignored.

The much harder thing was being without Pantalaimon.

She was aware of a few things concerning her dæmon. He was not in danger; he was traveling; he was intent on something; but that was all. And although she picked up the alethiometer several times, in the solitude of her hotel room or railway sleeping compartment, she soon put it away again. The sickness brought on by the new method was unbearable. She did try the classic method, brooding over the images, trying to recall a dozen or so meanings for each one and composing a question; but the answers she got were enigmatic or contradictory or simply opaque. Occasionally she felt a spasm of passionate fear, or of pity, or of anger, and knew he was feeling those things too; but she had no idea why. All she could do was hope, and she kept trying to do that, in spite of the fear and the loneliness.

She spent some time writing to Malcolm. She told him about everything she saw and heard. She related the events involving the burning Dutchman and the alchemist, and told him the advice Agrippa had given her about her journey, and posted the letters to Malcolm care of the Trout in Godstow; but whether he'd ever get them, and whether she'd ever receive an answer, she had no idea.

She felt so alone. She felt as if her life had gone into a kind of hibernation, as if part of her was asleep and maybe dreaming the rest. She let herself be passive; she accepted whatever happened. When she found that the ferry to Smyrna had just left and that she'd have to wait two days for another, she heard the news calmly, found a cheap hotel, and wandered about the ancient city of Constantinople modestly and unobtrusively, looking at oratories and museums and the great merchants' houses along the waterfront, sitting in one of the many parks under trees that were still bare. She bought an English-language newspaper and read every word of every article, lingering over coffee in a warm and smoky café near the vast Oratory of the Holy Wisdom, which rose like a giant bubble of stone above the buildings around it.

The newspaper told her of attacks on property in the country-side, of rose gardens set aflame or dug up, of workers and their families slaughtered when they tried to defend their workplaces. There had been a spate of such attacks as far south as Antalya and as far east as Yerevan. No one knew what had set off this frenzy of destruction. The attackers were known simply as "the men from the mountains," and according to some reports these men demanded that their victims spurn their religion and take up a new one, but no one had any details about that. Other reports said nothing about religion, and only mentioned the looting and the destruction, and the inexplicable hatred expressed by the attackers towards roses and their scent.

Other news in the paper concerned the forthcoming celebrations in honor of the Patriarch, St. Simeon Papadakis, on his election as President of the new High Council of the Magisterium. There was going to be a lengthy service in the Oratory of the Holy Wisdom, in the presence of over a hundred senior clergy from all over the province, followed by a procession through the city. The celebrations would include the consecration of a new icon of the Virgin Mary, which had appeared miraculously at the tomb of a fourth-century martyr, accompanied by various signs attesting to its supernatural origin, such as blossom on a honeysuckle growing over the grave, various sweet odors, the sound of heavenly flutes, and so on. Sweet odors, thought Lyra. . . . To the men from the mountains, such things were anathema. To the established hierarchy of the Church, they were the mark of heavenly favor. If the religious world was going to split, it might well be over a small thing like the scent of a rose.

Malcolm would know why it was all happening. She'd write to him about it in her next letter. Oh, but it was so lonely.

She made herself read more about this new High Council. The celebrations in honor of the Patriarch were happening that very morning—her second day in Constantinople—and she decided to go along and watch. It would be something to do.

As a matter of fact, while Lyra was thinking about him, St. Simeon was stirring uneasily in his marble bath and thinking about the mystery of the Incarnation. His dæmon, the sweet-voiced Philomela, nodded beside him on her golden perch. The currents that the saint's body set up in the scummy water were uncomfortably cold now, and he called out, "Boy! Boy!"

He could never remember the name of any of the boys, but it didn't matter. All boys were very similar. However, the feet he heard coming in answer to his call were not a boy's feet, being heavy and slow: a shuffle instead of a light, darting step.

"Who is that? Who is that?" said the saint, and his dæmon answered, "It is Kaloumdjian."

The Patriarch extended a quivering hand and peered up at the bulky form of the eunuch. "Help me up, Kaloumdjian," he said. "Where is the boy?"

"His master the devil came last night and took him away. How should I know where the boy is? There is no boy to be found."

In the dim lantern light, it was hard to see Kaloumdjian except as a gigantic shadow, but his delicate, creamy voice was unmistakable. The saint felt himself lifted and placed dripping on the wooden duck board, and a moment later swathed roughly in clean heavy cotton.

"Not so rough," he said. "I'll fall over if you shake me like that. The boy would be gentle. Where has he gone?"

"No one knows, Your Blessedness," said the eunuch, toweling less vigorously. "There will be another very soon."

"Yes, no doubt. And the water, you know, it gets cold more

quickly than it used to. I am sure there is something wrong. The oil—do you think the oil could make it lose heat? A new kind of oil, perhaps? It doesn't smell the same. It has a harsher quality. If the chemical composition is slightly different, you see, that might allow the molecules of heat to pass through the film of oil more easily. I am sure there is something like that going on. I must ask St. Mehmet to look into it."

Behind him, Kaloumdjian's goose dæmon dipped her head towards the bath and smelled the water. The eunuch said, "The oil is not the same, because the merchant who used to supply it has been summoned to the Court of the Three Windows."

"You don't say? The scoundrel! What has he done?"

"Fallen into debt, Your Blessedness. As a result, he could obtain no more credit from the suppliers, and furthermore they too are in trouble, and likely to go out of business."

"But what about my rose oil?"

"This is an inferior product from Morocco. It is all we could get."

St. Simeon made a small noise expressive of disappointment. Kaloumdjian knelt heavily to towel the holy shanks while the Patriarch's frail hand rested on his shoulder.

"No boys, no oil . . . What is the world coming to, Kaloumdjian? I hope the boy is safe, at any rate. I was fond of the little wretch. Do they just run away, do you think?"

"Who can tell, Your Blessedness? Perhaps he thought they were going to make a eunuch of him."

"I suppose he might have thought that. Poor little fellow. I hope he is safe. Now, Kaloumdjian, you will make sure that the water is sold cheaply. It would be wrong to let people think they were getting the same quality as before. I am quite firm about this."

The saint's bathwater, being sanctified by contact with his person, was bottled and sold at the palace gates. St. Simeon was about the only man in the palace who did not know that the officials took a homeopathic attitude to its quality, and diluted it several-fold. But saints were not expected to be worldly about such matters; a previous Patriarch, expressing surprise when he discovered the gallons and gallons on sale, had to be assured that the holiness of the water caused it to expand in size, and that a number of bottles routinely burst from sacramental exuberance.

"My drawers, Kaloumdjian, if you please," said the Patriarch, and still holding on to the soft bulk of the eunuch's shoulder, he stepped shakily into the silk garment before letting the eunuch fasten the ribbon around his little potbelly. In the process, Kaloumdjian took a close look at the suppurating ulcer on the saint's right shin, which must have been causing him abominable pain, but about which he said not a word. It will kill him in six months, Kaloumdjian thought, as he eased the old man's arms tenderly into the sleeves of his undervest and helped his damp and bony feet into the slippers.

St. Simeon, for his part, was grateful after all that it was Kaloum-djian and not the boy who was dressing him, because the boy had no idea which way round to hold the cope, for example, and had once done up thirty-five of the buttons on the undervest before discovering that the last one lacked a hole to go into, and had to undo them all and start again; so the saint had to pay attention and direct the operation, which was trying. Kaloumdjian required no guidance, and the Patriarch was able to withdraw his attention and attempt once again to think about the mystery of the Incarnation, which was trying in a different way.

So he stopped thinking about that and said, "Kaloumdjian—tell me: these men from the mountains of whom we hear so much talk—do you know anything about them?"

"I have a distant cousin in Yerevan, Your Blessedness, whose family were put to the sword by a band of men who wanted them to abjure the Holy Church and the doctrine of the Incarnation in particular."

"But that is appalling," the old man said. "And have they been found and punished, these heretics?"

"Alas, no."

"His whole family?"

"Almost all, except for my cousin Sarkisian, who was at the market when it happened, and for a young girl, a servant, who saved herself by promising to believe what the men told her to."

"The poor child!" The saint's dim eyes filled with tears for the little girl, who would now go to hell. "Do you suppose, Kaloumdjian, that these men from the mountains have made away with the boy?"

"Perfectly possible, Your Blessedness. Take my hand now."

The saint obediently took the great soft hand he saw in front of him, and with Kaloumdjian's help, he braced himself against the weight of the little nightingale dæmon who struggled to his shoulder, though in truth she weighed barely more than a handful of petals. With Kaloumdjian's goose waddling ahead, they made their way out of the bath chamber and into the vestry, where the Patriarch's outer robes were being prepared. The process was not so much a putting-on as a climbing-in, and indeed the outermost garment was constructed not unlike a tepee or yurt, with a frame of sticks and laths that allowed the saint to rest against it during the rigors of the long liturgy. There was even a vessel skillfully placed to collect the saint's urine, so that nothing need interrupt the service or trouble the Patriarch, who like many elderly men felt his bladder behaving more and more capriciously.

Kaloumdjian delivered the Patriarch into the care of the three subdeacons. St. Simeon let go of his hand with some reluctance and said, "Thank you, dear Kaloumdjian. Please see if you can find out more about, you know, the matters we discussed. I would be so grateful."

The eunuch saw what the Patriarch didn't, the little Brother Mercurius's bright, inquisitive, sympathetic glance flicker at once from under his charmingly tousled hair, flick to the Patriarch's face, and then to the eunuch's, and then back to the Patriarch. Kaloum-djian's heavy eyes rested on the subdeacon for a second longer than Brother Mercurius found comfortable, but the young man understood their message and folded his hands as he turned his modest attention to the saint.

The old man said the first prayer, and on went the cassock. Brother Mercurius was swift to kneel, his hands fluttering at the buttons and stroking the heavy silk over the Patriarch's legs, as if to adjust the hang, but he watched for the helpless flinch as his hand brushed the right shin. Worse than last time! That was worth knowing.

Another prayer as the skullcap went on, another for the hood, another for the surplice, another for the stole, another for the girdle, one each for the sleeves, left and right, that covered the plain arms of the surplice. Each of these vestments was embroidered so thickly with gold and jewels that the Patriarch was becoming more like a piece of ancient mosaic than a human being, and their combined weight was making the old man tremble.

"Soon, Holy One, soon," murmured Brother Mercurius, and knelt again to adjust the front of the lower garments as the great enfolding cope, with its substructure of tough struts and crosspieces, was maneuvered into place around the saint's shoulders.

"Brother," said the senior subdeacon warningly, and Brother Mercurius modestly ducked aside, managing to imply both a humble desire to serve and a rueful self-deprecation: how silly to forget that this was Brother Ignatius's job! His little jerboa dæmon skipped out of the way helpfully.

"Brother . . . Brother . . . young Brother," said the old man, "please be good enough to trim the lamps in the corridor to the council room. Twice now I have nearly missed my step along there."

"Of course, Your Blessedness," said Brother Mercurius, bowing to conceal his disappointment. Now it would be the other two who supported the saint on his entrance.

The subdeacon slipped out of the vestry and found the eunuch waiting in the corridor—waiting for something, or just standing, but in either case disconcerting. That face, a great moon of raw pastry! Brother Mercurius offered him a quick, modest smile and set about adjusting the lamps, which needed no adjusting, as he well knew. Those at the further end, close to the council chamber, were mounted a little higher than the rest, which allowed Brother Mercurius to make much of the awkwardness of dealing with them while listening for any scraps of conversation he might hear through the door.

But they were cunning, these bishops and archbishops and archimandrites. Two thousand years of subtle statesmanship are not easily outfoxed by a pretty young subdeacon with a winning manner. Behind the door outside which Brother Mercurius was disingenuously lingering, three prelates from Syria were discussing raisins. Their fellow synod members, all one hundred and forty-seven of them, were disposed around the council chamber, engaging in similarly meaningless small talk. They would not start their business until the emptying bell rang to signify that everyone but themselves had been escorted from the palace.

Hearing the doors from the vestry open, Brother Mercurius turned away from the lamp he'd been fiddling with and smoothed his hands down over his slim flanks before standing modestly to one side, ready to dart forward and open the door to the great chamber.

"Back, fool, back," came a whisper in a well-known voice. The Archdeacon Phalarion, who had appeared from the vestry, was the supervisor of ritual, and the office of opening the door was very firmly his. Brother Mercurius bowed and tiptoed back along the corridor, keeping so close to the wall that he was moving sideways rather than forward. It was because he was doing that, and because he was about halfway along, that he had the best view of all of them of what happened next.

The first thing was that the eunuch's goose dæmon, from the door of the vestry, honked suddenly and loudly: a great goose cry of fear and danger.

Kaloumdjian turned to see what had frightened her, and the next instant a scimitar sliced his head from his shoulders. The head tumbled with a hefty thud, and a very long second or two later, down came his body to follow it, spouting blood. His dæmon had already vanished.

Archdeacon Phalarion hurled himself at the jostling figures that were coming out of the vestry, and was borne to the ground in a moment. The Patriarch, supported by the two subdeacons, was too stiff to turn and look and too bewildered to speak, and the subdeacons themselves, caught between horrible fear and the desire to protect the old man, did not move either, but were both killed as they gazed back over their shoulders. They fell aside like the mold of a sculpture that has just been cast in bronze: stiff, dead things that only serve to contain the work of art within, which is now born and visible for the first time.

That work of art, the Patriarch himself, stood radiant in his robes and supported still by the armature inside the cope. His expression, which Brother Mercurius could see very clearly in the radiance of the lamps, was like that of someone who has just understood the solution to a profound and complex problem—as it might be, the mystery of the Incarnation. But unlike the eunuch and the subdeacons, the saint was not lucky enough to die from the first blow that struck him. His assailants—three of them—hacked and stabbed and sawed at the stiff, half-wooden figure while his frightened dæmon fluttered high and fell back and careered into the wall and spun around on the floor, and drops of liquid music flew around.

St. Simeon, meanwhile, was waving his arms slowly like a beetle on its back, despite the fact that one of them had lost its hand; and presently the nightingale's song fell silent and the old man lolled in his sustaining robes, quite unable to fall over.

Brother Mercurius saw the three white-robed swordsmen, now much more vividly colored than a few seconds previously, push the old man over to make sure he was dead. He saw them look around and behind, from where shouts and cries of anger and pursuit could now be heard, running feet, the clatter of pikes; he saw them turn their hawk faces towards him, he felt the appalling beauty of their gaze, he nearly swooned as he saw them rush towards him, and he thought of the door behind him, the door—

It opened *this* way, and if he planted his back against it and waited to be slaughtered, it might hold the men up long enough for the palace guards to arrive. Brother Mercurius knew that, within the smallest fraction of a second. He also knew that it was not in his nature to do that sort of thing, and that it was in his nature to be agreeable, to make things easy and convenient, and that this was the way God had made him, and there was no changing now.

So in that same moment and before the assassins had come halfway down the corridor, Brother Mercurius had turned and grasped the handle and pulled the great door open. The terrified prelates inside, hearing the cries and the sounds of struggle from the corridor, had gathered like sheep in the center of the chamber, and the assassins were able to charge full at them through the open doorway and slaughter a dozen or so before the pursuing guards caught up and fell on them from behind.

Brother Mercurius did not want to look at the body of the Patriarch, but he knew that it would be a good thing to be discovered praying beside it, so while the killing, the cries, the splashing, the thudding, the scraping and wailing and clashing from the council chamber filled his ears, he made his way delicately back to the tumbled structure containing what was left of the saint and fell to his knees, taking care to daub himself with as much blood as he could bear, and to let the tears flow freely down his cheeks.

It would be wrong to say that Mercurius was already envisaging the icons that would in time depict the martyrdom of St. Simeon Papadakis, and ensuring that an essential component of the scene, perhaps even its defining element, was the presence of the young and devoted subdeacon splashed with the martyr's blood and with his large eyes cast upwards in prayer.

That is to say, that picture was indeed in his mind, but not at the forefront. He was mainly preoccupied with the enthralling questions of the succession, of the weeks of politics that would now unfold, of the possibility of promotion now that the two other subdeacons of the bathhouse had been killed. He was also intoxicated by the look in the beautiful eyes of the assassins as they rushed towards him in the corridor. He had never in all his life seen anything quite so thrilling.

Meanwhile, in the main body of the great cathedral, out of earshot of the assassination of St. Simeon, the congregation—including Lyra—stood in their hundreds under the vast dome, waiting for the service proper to begin, while a choir of deep male voices sang a hymn whose length and slowness conveyed a strong impression of eternity.

Part of Lyra's unobtrusiveness policy consisted of not asking any questions or starting any conversations, so she had to make do with whatever she could gather from everything that was going on around her. She absorbed the congregation's patience and trance-like stillness, intensified by the music, until a moment came when one of the singers faltered.

It sounded as if he had been struck in the heart during a long-held high note. A sort of cough or gasp interrupted the line of music, succeeded by a sighing uncertainty in the other voices. After a minute or so they seemed to gather themselves and continue, only to come to a halt after another phrase or so, although that was clearly not the end of the hymn.

The choir was hidden, so no one could see what had caused the interruption. The rapt mood of the service had vanished in a second; from a single congregation they had fractured into several hundred anxious individuals. People looked all around, they tried to peer over the heads of those in front, and after a moment came other sounds from the choir: cries, shouts, the clash of steel on steel, and even at one point a gunshot, which made everyone in the congregation start at once, so they looked like a field of wheat under a sudden gust of wind.

People had moved at first away from the walls to gather more closely in the center of the vast building. Lyra went with them, unable to see very much but listening hard to the hubbub and the violent struggle that was taking place beyond the iconostasis. To add to the noise, several people had begun to pray aloud in tones of desperation.

Lyra turned to whisper to Pan, and of course he wasn't there, and again she felt a stab of abandonment. She gathered herself and went through her checklist, dealing one by one with the things that might make her conspicuous, so that once she was in control, she seemed only like the meekest, most passive, least determined bystander, no one worth taking an interest in.

In this mask of modesty she made her way towards the edge of the vast floor and along the wall to the doors. Several other people were already hurrying out, and Lyra could see there would be a problem if the exit got blocked. Rather than wait and be trapped inside, she slipped through the melee and shoved hard until she was outside on the marble steps, blinking in the sunlight, being forced downwards as more and more people poured through the door and spread out in front of the building.

There was confusion in the public square as rumors of assassination, massacre, bloodshed spread with the speed of fire. Lyra could only guess what was being said, but then she heard some words in English and turned to the speaker.

He was a gaunt and tonsured man in a form of clerical dress, something severe and monastic, and he was speaking rapidly to a party of English men and women, mostly middle-aged or elderly, who looked fearful and sorrow-struck.

A woman at the edge of the group had a kind face that was vivid with concern, and her greenfinch dæmon was looking at Lyra sympathetically.

"What's happening? Does anyone know?" Lyra said, breaking her rule.

Hearing an English voice, the woman turned to her and said, "They think he's been killed—the Patriarch—no one knows for certain—"

Another member of the group called out to the monk, "What did you actually see?"

The monk laid his hand across his forehead in a gesture of

desperate helplessness and raised his voice: "I saw men with swords—dressed in white—they were killing all the clergy—His Holiness the Patriarch was the first to fall—"

"Are they still in there?"

"I couldn't say—I fled—I'm ashamed to admit it—I fled instead of staying to die like the others. . . ."

Tears were falling down his cheeks, his voice was high and broken, and his mouth was trembling.

"It's important to bear witness," someone said.

"No!" cried the monk. "I should have stayed! I was called to be a martyr, and I fled like a coward!"

The woman who'd spoken to Lyra shook her head and murmured in dismay, "No, no."

The monk's dæmon was a small monkey-like creature, who ran up and down his arm and rubbed her fists into her eyes, wailing in self-pity. The woman turned away, frowning, but then her dæmon whispered in her ear, and she looked back at Lyra again.

"You—excuse me—I can't believe that you—am I making a mistake? Your dæmon . . ."

"No, you're right," Lyra said. "My dæmon's not . . . He's gone."

"You poor girl," said the woman with genuine sympathy.

This was so far from the reaction Lyra expected that she didn't know how to respond. "Are you, umm . . . are you part of this group?"

"No, no. I just heard them speaking in English, so . . . Were you inside the cathedral? Do you know what's happening?"

"No . . . The choir stopped singing, and then—but look, someone's coming out."

In the throng at the top of the steps, outside the entrance, there was a disturbance as people seemed to be pushed aside, and then came four or five soldiers in the ceremonial uniform of the Patriarchal Guard. They were forming a protective square around a young man in clerical dress whose bloodstained face and large, lustrous eyes seemed, even on that sunny morning, to be lit by a spotlight, so clear was every change of expression, from sorrow and pity to patient courage and on to a rapturous acceptance of the late saint's martyrdom. He was speaking, and half chanting words that were obviously familiar prayers, because the crowd seemed to find themselves transformed into an impromptu congregation, and murmured responses whenever he paused.

The woman whispered, "I don't think I've ever seen such a shameless opportunist. He'll do well out of this terrible business."

Lyra thought so too. The little coxcomb was now appearing to feel faint, and gripping the arm of the most handsome of the guards, who blushingly held him up. The priest's dæmon said something that drew a sigh of warm sympathy from those nearby. Lyra turned away, and so did the woman.

"Don't go," the woman said, and Lyra looked at her properly for the first time. She saw a woman in a well-preserved middle age, with a plain, good-humored face whose red cheeks were not entirely due to the sun.

"I can't stay here," said Lyra, though there was no reason why she couldn't, and since this was (from an Oakley Street point of view) where the most important events were happening, no doubt she should stay and make notes.

"Spare five minutes," said the woman. "Come and have some coffee with me."

"Well," Lyra said, "all right, I will. Thank you."

The sirens of an ambulance howled through the square, which was getting fuller every minute, as more people poured out of the cathedral and still more came hurrying in from the four roads that met in front of it. Another ambulance arrived to join the first one in trying to thrust a way through the crowd.

The young priest on the steps, still clinging to the guard, was now talking to three or four people who were busy scribbling into notebooks.

"Reporters already," said the woman. "He's having the time of his life."

She turned her back and strode vigorously through the crowd. Lyra went with her. As they left the square, they could hear a different kind of siren, coming from the first police cars that were arriving.

Five minutes later they were sitting outside a little café in a side street. Lyra was glad of the woman's presence at the table with her.

The woman was called Alison Wetherfield, she told Lyra, and she worked as a teacher in the English school in Aleppo. She had come to Constantinople on vacation.

"But I'm not sure how much longer the school will be able to survive," she said. "The city's holding out, but in the countryside people are getting very nervous."

"I feel I should know what's going on," said Lyra. "Why do people feel nervous now?"

"There's a lot of unrest. The awful business this morning is part of it. People are feeling brutalized by the laws, exploited by their bosses, discriminated against by social structures they've got no means of changing. It's been like that for years: there's nothing new about it. But it's a fertile soil for the rose panic to flourish in. . . ."

"The rose panic?"

"It's a new sort of fanaticism. Rose growers are being persecuted, their gardens set ablaze or plowed over by these men from the mountains, as they're called, who say that the rose is an abomination to the Authority. I hadn't realized it had spread this far."

"They're feeling the effects already in Oxford," said Lyra, and told her about the rosewater problem at Jordan College. She might have regretted revealing where she came from, as it went against every principle she was trying to obey, but the sheer relief and pleasure of talking to someone sympathetic was too much to resist.

"But what are you doing, traveling in this part of the world?" asked Alison Wetherfield. "Have you come here to work?"

"I'm just passing through. I'm on my way to Central Asia. Just waiting for a ferry."

"A long way to go yet, then. And what are you going to do there?"

"Research for the thesis I have to write."

"What's your subject?"

"History, basically, but I wanted to see things you can't find in libraries."

"And . . . you . . . the thing I noticed about you . . ."

"No dæmon."

"Yes. Is your journey about him too?"

Lyra nodded.

"Mainly about him?"

Lyra sighed and looked away.

"You're going to Madinat al-Qamar," Alison said.

"Well . . ."

"No need to try and hide it. I'm not shocked or surprised. I know someone else who set out to go there, but I don't know what happened to him. I'd tell you to be careful, but you look sensible enough to realize that yourself. Do you know how to find it?"

"No."

"There are so many dead towns, dead villages, in that part of the desert. You could spend years looking for the right place. You'll need to find a guide."

"It does exist, then?"

"As far as I know. I thought it was just a legend or a ghost story when I first heard about it. To be honest, I find all that sort of thing—well, I don't know—unconvincing. Irrelevant, really. There's enough trouble and difficulty in this world, enough sick people to look after, enough children to teach, enough poverty and oppression to fight without worrying about the supernatural. But then I'm lucky. I'm perfectly at home in the world and perfectly happy with my dæmon and the work I do. I realize that other people aren't so lucky. Why did your dæmon leave you?"

"We quarreled. I had no idea it would lead to this. I didn't think it was possible. But we didn't speak for a long time, and one day he just vanished."

"How painful for you!"

"Oh, the pain . . . Yes, but the hardest thing was just having no one to talk to. And sometimes give good advice."

"What d'you think he'd say to you now?"

"About my journey, or about today?"

"Today."

"Well, he'd have mistrusted that young priest."

"Quite right."

"And he'd make me take notes about everything."

"He'd be a good journalist."

"And he'd have made friends with your dæmon at once. That's one of the things I miss most."

Alison's greenfinch dæmon was listening intently, and now he sang a few notes of sympathy. Lyra thought she should change the subject before she revealed too much.

"What about this new High Council?" she said. "What d'you think that'll mean?"

"I don't think anyone knows yet. It's come rather out of the blue. I hope it won't mean that there's a much more ferocious orthodoxy. The system we've had for hundreds of years was flawed, no one claimed it was perfect, but one merit it did have was room for disagreement of a limited kind. If there's one voice imposing one will on us all . . . I can't see it leading anywhere very good, I'm afraid."

In the background, the noise of sirens had been continuous. Now another sound joined it: the clangor of a loud bell in a campanile nearby. A few seconds later another bell joined in. For a moment Lyra thought of the bells of Oxford and felt intensely homesick, but it was only a moment. From other buildings in the area more bells began to ring, and presently yet another sound thrust its way over them: the harsh thud-thud-thud of a gyropter.

Lyra and Alison looked up and saw first one and then two more of the aircraft circling the dome of the Holy Wisdom.

"What that's likely to be," said Alison, "is the first sign of official panic. Quite soon—in fact, any minute, I'd guess—there'll be police patrols demanding to see everyone's documents, and arresting anyone they don't like the look of. Such as you, my dear. If you take my advice, you'll go straight back to your hotel and stay there till your ferry goes."

Lyra felt a great weariness descend on her. Oh, Pan, she thought. She forced herself to stand up and shook the woman's hand. "Thank you for talking to me," she said. "I'll remember you."

She left and went back to her hotel. On the way she saw a police patrol in the process of arresting a young man who was fighting back fiercely, and in another street she saw a different patrol retreating from a crowd of angry men who were tearing up the roadway and throwing cobblestones at them. She walked carefully and stayed invisible as far as she could; even the hotel receptionist at her dingy little desk didn't notice as she walked past.

Once inside her room, she locked the door.

* * *

News of the assassination spread wide and quickly. Several news agencies picked up the fact that the martyred Patriarch, so aged, so holy, was also the President of the new High Council of the Magisterium.

In Geneva it registered at once. The council—or those members who lived and worked in the city, and whose numbers, by the blessed workings of Providence, constituted a quorum—met at once, and opened with shocked prayers for the dead St. Simeon, whose presidency had been so short.

Then they turned immediately to the matter of the succession. It was clear, in these anxious times, that the question should be resolved quickly, and it was also clear that the only possible candidate was Marcel Delamare. More than one council member saw the hand of Providence there too.

So he was elected unanimously. With sorrow and reluctance he accepted the great responsibility, proclaiming his unworthiness in phrases so perfectly turned they might almost have been composed in advance of the terrible and utterly unpredictable events in Constantinople.

But even in his evident modesty and hesitation he had the calmness of mind and clarity of vision to suggest a few slight amendments to the constitution, all in the interests of firmness, resolution, and efficiency in, as the phrase had it, these anxious times. In order not to distract the holy work of the council with needless elections, the President's term of office was increased from five to seven years, and there were to be no restrictions to the number of times an individual could serve. Furthermore, the President was to be granted executive powers, which would be needed in order to allow swift action in these anxious, etc.

Thus, for the first time in six centuries, the Magisterium had one sole leader, invested with all the authority and power that had previously run through many channels. Shorn and parceled no longer, the might of the Church now flowed through the office and the person of Marcel Delamare.

And the first to feel how swiftly the new dispensation could act, and how disagreeable its actions could be, was Pierre Binaud, the Chief Justice of the Consistorial Court of Discipline. He was removed from that office within an hour, and he would never interrupt anyone again.

As he signed the order, Marcel Delamare thought of the sister he had admired so much. He thought of his mother too, and looked forward to seeing her again.

TWENTY-THREE

THE SMYRNA FERRY

After a night in her hotel room listening to the sirens, the shouting, the breaking windows, the gyropters thudding overhead, and occasionally the gunshots, Lyra felt tired and oppressed. But the Smyrna ferry left that day, and she couldn't hide in the hotel forever.

She went down for breakfast and then stayed in her room till it was time to check out. According to the receptionist, who had read it in the morning paper, the assassins had all been killed when the guard stormed the cathedral. The rioting since had been the work of some men from the mountains, he didn't know more, exploiting the general panic. It was all over now, he told her. The civil police were in command.

The hotel staff were glad to see her leave, because they were all afraid of her. She felt their alarm and dread, and since there was no point in trying to be invisible to them, she tried to dispel it by being friendly, but there was nothing she could do to acquire a dæmon. She felt glad to put the place behind her and make for the port.

The ferry left in the late afternoon and would arrive in Smyrna on the second morning afterwards. Lyra could have paid for a cabin, but after her temporary imprisonment in the hotel, she wanted to spend as much time as possible in the open. On the first evening, she ate by herself in the dingy restaurant and then sat on deck, wrapped in a blanket in a comfortable wicker reclining chair, watching the lights on the shore as they went past, and the night-fishing boats, and the starry sky.

She was thinking about Alison Wetherfield. A teacher, a woman of clear decency and certainty, someone she would like to emulate . . . She reminded Lyra of Hannah Relf. The fears Alison expressed about the new High Council were like her own, though Lyra hadn't managed to think them through. Since Pan left, her focus had been entirely on her own predicament, and . . . No, it had begun before that. When they'd first become estranged? Probably. Self-preoccupation was not something Lyra admired in others, but here she was, thinking of nothing else. Good women like Hannah and Alison found other things to fret about, or better still, didn't fret at all. Good women . . .

It was so complicated. She remembered Malcolm describing the sisters in Godstow Priory, who had been so kind to him when he was a boy, and who'd taken in the baby Lyra and looked after her before the flood came. Clearly what they did was good, and equally clearly much of what the Magisterium did was not; but were they part of the Magisterium because of their beliefs, or something else altogether because of their activities? She thought she'd been certain about things when she came back from the north, but the things she'd learnt during her adventures there seemed so far away now; all that remained was a scatter of vivid impressions, of personalities such as Lee Scoresby and Mary Malone, and of events like the fight between the bears, and above all of the moment when she and Will kissed in the little wood in the world of the *mulefa*. She'd hugged to herself the phrase "the Republic of Heaven," but never analyzed what it might mean. When she'd thought about it at all, she'd thought that rationality was the very foundation stone of the Republic of Heaven.

That was the Lyra who wrote essays and passed examinations. That Lyra had enjoyed disputing with Scholars and searching out the weaknesses in someone else's arguments, and cracking them open with a flourish to disclose the assumptions, the inconsistencies, the dishonesties concealed within them. That was the Lyra who had found the writing of Gottfried Brande so intoxicating, and that of Simon Talbot so disturbing.

She hadn't been prepared for the revolution in her mind caused by Giorgio Brabandt and his stories of the secret commonwealth. She would once have dismissed things like that with scorn. But now, under her blanket on the deck, watching all the little points of light in the dark sky or on the dark shore, feeling the little tremor of the engines and the constant gentle rocking as the ferry moved south over the calm sea, she wondered if she'd got everything wrong.

A thought that followed naturally: Was that why Pan had left her?

Time seemed to be suspended during that quiet night on the sea. She thought calmly and systematically back to the time of her first estrangement from Pan. The memories came obediently out of the dark, links on a long chain. His anger when she had been unkind to a younger girl at school, against her natural inclination and in spite of every prompting from him, mocking her inability to distinguish between the author and the narrator in a novel set for examination. An impatient word to a servant at St. Sophia's. A scoffing refusal to go to an exhibition of paintings on religious themes by the parent of a friend. Her delight in seeing so much philosophy taken apart and trampled on by Gottfried Brande. Her behavior—and now it all came back to her, bright with shame—her behavior towards Malcolm, when he'd been just Dr. Polstead. Small things, perhaps, but a hundred of them, and they kept coming. Her dæmon had seen all that, and disliked it, and then he'd had enough.

She tried to defend herself against this self-summoned tribunal. But her defense was feeble, and she soon stopped pretending. She was profoundly ashamed. She *had* done wrong, and her wrongdoing was bound up, somehow, with a vision of the world from which the secret commonwealth was excluded.

The stars wheeled slowly around the pole. The ferry moved steadily along the coast. From time to time the lights of a village glimmered on the shore, their reflections shaken into a thousand silver or gold flakes by the myriad movements of the water. Once or twice she saw a different kind of light, a glow from the fishing boats, each with a lantern in the prow, setting out their nets to catch bluefish or squid. They gave her another image: she was enticing monsters out of the darkness of herself. And she remembered what the dead child Roger, once her closest friend, had told her about the harpies in the world of the dead: they know every bad thing you've ever done, and they whisper about them to you all the time. She was getting a foretaste of that now.

She wondered: Did the harpies belong to the secret commonwealth? Was the world of the dead, the world they dwelt in, part of that? Or had she imagined it, and was her imagination just a spindrift of falsity?

Well, she thought, what was the secret commonwealth, anyway? It was a state of being that had no place in the world of Simon Talbot, or the different world of Gottfried Brande. It was quite invisible to everyday vision. If it existed at all, it was seen by the imagination, whatever that was, and not by logic. It included ghosts, fairies, gods and goddesses, nymphs, night-ghasts, devils, jacky lanterns, and other such entities. They were neither well-nor ill-disposed to human beings by nature, but sometimes their purposes intersected or coincided with human ones. They had a certain power over human lives, but they could be defeated too, as the fairy of the Thames had been tricked by Malcolm when she had wanted to keep Lyra with her and not let her go. . . .

A steward came along the deck to tell those passengers still out-side (there were only a handful of them) that the bar was shortly going to close. Two men got up from their deck chairs and went inside. Lyra said, "Thank you," her only phrase of Anatolian. The steward nodded and passed on.

She returned to her thoughts. Did the night-ghasts and fairies and jacky lanterns and other citizens of the secret commonwealth exist only in her imagination? Was there a logical, rational, sci-entific explanation for such things? Or were they inaccessible to science and baffling to reason? Did they exist at all?

"Such things" included dæmons, surely. They certainly did if Brande and Talbot were right about them. Neither of those schol-ars would see anything wrong with a young woman who had no dæmon. Alison Wetherfield, on the other hand, had seen what was different about Lyra straightaway, as most people did, but un-like most people was warm in her sympathy. The loud man on the Channel ferry had seen it and was warm in his hatred and fear. Dæmons certainly existed for most people.

She couldn't get any further at that point. The sky full of stars seemed dead and cold, everything in it the result of the mechani-cal, indifferent interactions of molecules and particles that would continue for the rest of time, whether Lyra lived or died, whether human beings were conscious or unconscious: a vast, silent, empty indifference, all quite meaningless.

Reason had brought her to this state. She had exalted reason over every other faculty. The result had been—was now—the deepest unhappiness she had ever felt.

But we shouldn't believe things because it makes us happy to, she thought. We should believe things because they're true, and if that makes us unhappy, that's very unfortunate, but it's not the fault of reason. How do we see that things are true? They make sense. True things are more economical than false ones: Occam's razor; things are more likely to be simple than complicated; if there is an explanation that leaves out things like imagination and emotion, then it's more likely to be true than one that includes them.

But then she remembered what the gyptians had said: Include things, don't leave them out. Look at things in their context. Include everything.

She felt a little spring of hope when she remembered that. She thought on: When I believed in the jacky lanterns, I saw more of them. Was that delusional? Was I making them up or seeing them? Was it rational to lift the little red fruit to Will's lips, in that little sunlit wood, and relive the act they'd heard Mary Malone describe, the one that had made her fall in love? Had reason ever created a poem, or a symphony, or a painting? If rationality can't see things like the secret commonwealth, it's because rationality's vision is limited. The secret commonwealth is *there*. We can't see it with rationality any more than we can weigh something with a microscope: it's the wrong sort of instrument. We need to imagine as well as measure. . . .

But then she remembered what Pan had said about her imagination, and that cruel little note in the bedroom at the Trout. Pan had left in order to look for a quality she didn't have.

And Dust? Where did that come in? Was it a metaphor? Was it part of the secret commonwealth? And the burning Dutchman!

What would reason say about him? He couldn't exist. He was a delusion. She had dreamed it all. It hadn't happened—

Before she could examine that question, the ferry hit something. Lyra felt the shock almost before she heard the bang and the rending sound of metal being torn, and then came a roar from the engines as the helmsman immediately signaled FULL ASTERN. The ferry shuddered, lurching awkwardly like a horse refusing a jump, and as the propeller thrashed the water, Lyra heard something else: human voices crying out in pain or panic.

She threw off the blanket and ran to the rail. She could see very little from where she was—amidships—so she hurried forward, having to grab the rail as the boat plunged and shook.

More people were coming out to see what was happening, from the bar, from their cabins, or, like her, from sleeping places on the deck. Voices rose all around, their meaning clear whatever the language:

"What's the matter?"

"Have we run aground?"

"I can hear a baby—"

"Someone put a spotlight on!"

"Look—in the water—"

The momentum of the vessel was still greater than the power of the screw, and it hadn't yet come to a halt. And Lyra, looking down where the last speaker was pointing, saw planks, broken wood, a lifebelt, other unidentifiable detritus from a shattered boat. And people—bodies in the water—heads, faces, arms, screaming, waving, sinking, and struggling up again. They seemed to be floating past, but it was only the ferry still moving forward.

Finally the bite of the propeller in the water overcame the forward momentum and pulled the vessel to a halt. The sound of the engines fell at once.

More voices now, shouting from the deck, from the bridge—men's voices, in Anatolian—and deckhands came running to throw ropes over the side, and lifebelts, and to lower a boat that swung from its davit over the deck.

The scene in the water was lit by a spotlight that was being hastily rigged on the foredeck, and by the light from every window or porthole on the port side. It became clear that the ferry had run down this smaller boat, which must have been showing no lights, and that the boat was carrying a large number of passengers, far more than its size would suggest it could; because the whole side of the boat had now drifted into view, lying dead in the water, with a dozen or more men and women clinging to it.

A woman kept trying to push a baby up onto it, herself sinking below the water every time she tried, and the baby was screaming and struggling, and no one helped.

Lyra couldn't stop herself crying out, "Help her! Help her!"

Each of the men clinging to the overturned boat was in fear for his own life, and had no strength left to help the woman; and after several attempts to get the baby safe, the woman herself sank under the surface, leaving the baby still struggling, its little voice choked with water. Lyra, like the other passengers watching, could only call out in horror and point, and finally one of the men let go, grabbed the baby by an arm, and flung it up onto the rocking planks before sinking himself and drifting away into the dark.

By that time the deckhands had got the lifeboat down, and while two men plied the oars, another leant over the stern and pulled the swimmers on board. Meanwhile, others had rigged a gangplank from an opening in the side of the ferry, where light spilled out over the water, showing the wrecked boat, the swimmers still struggling, and some people who were drowned already and who floated limp on the rocking water, facedown.

Lyra thought that if the ferry had cut the boat in two, there must be some people on the starboard side as well as on the port. She ran across the deck, which was now thronged with passengers trying to see what was happening, and found she was right: there were people in the water on that side too, not so many but just as desperate, and no one had seen them. They had nothing but scraps of planking to hold on to, and they were calling for help, but no one could hear them.

Lyra saw an officer running down the companionway from the bridge, and seized his sleeve. "Look! More people this side! They need a lifeboat here too!"

He shook his head, unable to understand, but she pulled his arm and pointed down.

He said something short and sharp and wrenched her hand off his sleeve. His dæmon, a lemur of some kind, was chittering fearfully in his ear, staring and pointing at Lyra. The man looked at Lyra with revulsion, seeing no dæmon, and said something angry.

"The boat!" she shouted. "Lower the boat on this side! They're drowning!"

A deckhand heard her, looked over and saw where she was pointing, and spoke quickly to the officer, who gave a curt nod and moved away. The deckhand ran to the lifeboat and began to make the davit ready to lower it. Another man joined him.

Lyra ran inside and darted down the steps two at a time, making for the gangway. She found a number of the rescued people already on board, huddling and shivering, and passengers and crew handing out blankets and helping those who were injured. She pushed through the crowd of those who had just come to stare, and went out onto the swaying gangway to help pull the remaining victims out. They were mostly young men, but there were women and children too, people of every age. They looked as if they had come from

North Africa or the Levantine countries. Their clothes were poor and thin, and although one or two clung to rucksacks or shopping bags, they had no other possessions at all. Perhaps their few things had gone down with the boat.

The starboard lifeboat was on the water now, and more and more of the victims were being pulled to safety. Lyra helped to haul two young men and five children up onto the platform, and the last person to make it there was a very old woman, stiff with fear, being pulled along by a boy of twelve or so, who might have been her grandson. Lyra tugged him up first, and then, between them, they hauled the old woman aboard.

She was shaking with cold—they were all cold—and Lyra, despite the exertion and her warm jacket, was soon shivering too. She peered out at the lapping water, scattered with wreckage and bits of clothing and unidentifiable objects that were once so important that people thought it worth carrying them away when they fled. Had they been fleeing from something? It looked like it.

"Lyra?"

She turned in alarm. It was Alison Wetherfield, warm and anxious. Lyra hadn't realized she was on the ferry.

"I think they've got everyone out on this side," Lyra said.

"Come and help. These sailors don't know what to do once they've got them aboard."

Lyra followed her. "Where do you think these people are from?" she said. "They look like refugees."

"That's exactly what they are. They're probably farmers or rose gardeners, fleeing from the mountain men."

Lyra thought of the people she'd seen disembarking from the river steamer in Prague: Had they too come from this part of the world? Was this happening all over Europe?

But there was no time to think about that. In the saloon they found sixty, maybe seventy people, all soaking wet, all freezing cold, the children crying, old people lying helpless, their dæmons feebly clinging to their sodden clothes; and more people limped or tottered in every minute as the last survivors were pulled out of the sea. And not only survivors: the sailors had picked up a number of bodies from the water too, and the cries of their relatives as they recognized this child, that woman, made Lyra's heart turn over with sorrow.

But Alison was everywhere, calling instructions to the crew, comforting a frightened mother, enfolding a baby in a blanket snatched from a passenger, calling for the ship's cook and demanding hot drinks, hot soup, bread and cheese for the survivors, some of whom seemed to be near to starvation. Lyra followed and helped carry out her instructions, giving out blankets, picking up a baby who seemed to belong to no one and was too frightened or too shocked even to cry, and rocking it on her breast.

Little by little the chaos crystallized into a sort of rough order. Alison was the source of that. She was abrupt, she was rude, she was impatient, but everything she said was clear, and every instruction made sense, and, as well as giving the ferry passengers things to do that were obviously helpful, she radiated an air of certainty and experience.

"You looking for dry clothes for that child?" she said, seeing Lyra nonplussed by her burden.

"Well, yes."

"The woman over there in the green coat's got some. You'll have to change the child's nappy. Ever done that?"

"No."

"Well, it's common sense. Work it out. Get the child dry and clean and warm before you do anything else."

Lyra was glad to obey, and made a creditable job of it, she

thought. Once the child (who turned out to be a boy) was washed and wrapped up warmly, she supposed he would need feeding, and began to look for something he could eat, only to be stopped by a woman with wild eyes, still wearing the sodden clothes she'd been pulled out of the sea in, who pointed at the baby and herself, sobbing with relief. Lyra handed him over, and at once the woman put him to her breast, chilly and damp though that was; and a moment later the child was sucking passionately.

Then Alison called her over to help with a different problem. A girl of five or six years old, all alone, warm and dry at least by now and in the clothes of another and slightly bigger child, was seemingly mesmerized or frozen with horror. She could hardly move; her mouse dæmon clutched at her neck, shivering; her eyes were focused on the middle distance, no matter what was in front of her.

"Her family's all drowned," said Alison. "Her name's Aisha. She only speaks Arabic. She's in your charge now."

And she turned away to deal with a sobbing little boy. Lyra nearly quailed, but the girl's frozen gaze and the terror in the eyes of her tiny dæmon decided her. She crouched down beside her and took her limp and frozen hand.

"Aisha," she whispered.

The dæmon crept down into the neck of the big sweater the girl was wearing, and Lyra thought: Pan, you should be here. This dæmon needs you. You shouldn't have left me.

"Aisha, ta'aali," she said, trying to recall the Arabic vocabulary the Scholars at Jordan had drilled into her so many years before. "Ta'aali," she said again, hoping it meant "Come."

She stood, holding on to the child's all but lifeless hand, and tugged gently. The girl didn't resist, didn't obey, just seemed to float with her, as if she had no bodily presence at all. Lyra was desperate to take her away from the crying, the noise of voices raised in sorrow or desperation, the sight of the rows of dead partly covered by blankets or sheets, away from all the confusion and distress.

On the way out of the saloon she picked up a round Turkish flatbread and a small carton of milk from the buffet. She led the child to the wicker chair she'd been half sleeping in when the ferry had run into the other boat; it was wide enough for them both, and the blanket was still there. She laid the bread and milk on the deck beside her and wrapped herself and the child in the blanket. She scrupulously avoided touching the little dæmon, who trembled and whispered at the girl's neck, more alive, it seemed, than Aisha was herself.

Lyra picked up the bread. "Aisha, *khubz*," she said. "*Inti ja'aana?*"

She broke off a piece and offered it. Aisha didn't seem to hear or see. Lyra nibbled it herself, hoping the child would see that it was harmless, but again there was no response.

"Well, I'll just hold you, and the bread's here when you need it," she whispered. "I'd tell you in Arabic, but I didn't pay enough attention to my lessons when I was little. I know you're not understanding this, but you've had enough to deal with tonight and I won't be giving you a test on it. I just hope I can make you warm."

The girl lay at Lyra's side, in her left arm, and a great coldness seemed to emanate from her frail body. Lyra tucked the blanket around her again, making sure she was covered.

"Well, you're really cold, Aisha, but it's a big blanket and you'll warm up soon. We'll warm each other up. You can go to sleep if you feel like it. Don't worry if you can't understand me. Of course, if you spoke to me, I wouldn't understand you either. We'd just have to wave our hands and pull faces. And point. We'll probably understand in the end."

She nibbled another piece of the bread.

"Look, if you don't take some soon, I'll have eaten it all and that'll look very fine, won't it, me scoffing the food they brought for you and the other people from your boat. It'd be a scandal. I'd be in all the papers, exposed as a thief and an exploiter of the dispossessed, and there'd be a picture of me looking guilty and you looking reproachful. . . . I'm sure this isn't helping. I just thought if I kept on whispering . . . I know! I'll sing you a song."

From somewhere very deep and very far back there came the words of one nursery rhyme after another, little bits of nonsense with rhymes and tunes and rhythms that the baby Lyra had loved without understanding them at all. She'd been somewhere warm on a lap or in someone's arms, and the lulling words and the simple tunes were part of the warmth and the safety, and she sang them very softly to the child, pretending that Aisha was Lyra and Lyra was . . . Who could it have been? It must have been Alice, sharp-tongued, caustic Alice with the soft breast and the warm arms.

After a few minutes she found a little, chilly presence at her neck. The child's dæmon was cuddling up against her, knowing no better, and it was all Lyra could do to keep her voice steady as she sang, because she herself had missed that feeling so much, so much. And presently they all fell asleep together.

And she dreamed of the cat again, the dæmon cat. She was entwining herself between Lyra's legs as they stood on that moonlit lawn, and the atmosphere of love and bliss was still there, but shot through now with anxiety. She had to do something. She had to go somewhere. The cat was urging her to follow, taking a few steps away, turning to look back at her, coming back and then going away again, and now she wasn't sure she was Will's dæmon after all. The moonlight bleached out all the colors: this was a black-and-white world.

She tried to follow the cat, but her legs wouldn't move. At the edge of the trees the dæmon looked back once more and then moved away into the darkness. Lyra was overwhelmed with love and loss and sorrow, and tears ran down her sleeping cheeks.

They woke to a bright morning. The sun hadn't yet appeared over the mountains, but the air was clear and clean, and the sea was as still as glass. The steady, quiet beat of the engines was the only sound, until Lyra heard the calls of seabirds too, and human voices nearby.

"Aisha," she whispered. "Are you awake? *Sihiiti?*"

She felt a frightened little scamper. The girl's dæmon had been sleeping between the two of them, and woke to find the presence of this stranger alarming. He darted back to Aisha's breast, and the girl sensed his fear and felt it too, and she drew away with a little whimper of anxiety.

Lyra sat up gently and tucked the blanket around the child. It was sharply cold without it. Aisha watched her every movement, as if Lyra would murder her unless she kept guard.

"Aisha, don't be scared of me," Lyra said quietly. "We've been asleep and it's morning. Here—look—eat a bit of this bread. It's pretty stale, but it's all right."

She gave the child the rest of the flatbread. Aisha took it and nibbled the edge, not daring to take her eyes off Lyra, who smiled at her. There was no smile in response, but Lyra was glad to see her unfrozen from that mesmerized horror of the night.

"There's some milk too," she said.

She twisted the top of the carton and tore off the tab. Aisha took it and drank, handing it back to Lyra when she'd had enough. That little reaction itself was encouraging. Lyra held it for her while Aisha ate a little more bread.

She thought, Sometime soon she's going to remember what

happened, and realize that she's lost everyone. And then what? Her mind moved over different possibilities: Aisha in the company of others like her, moving laboriously westwards in the hope of refuge, hungry, cold, robbed of the little she had. Or being taken in by a family who didn't speak her language, who treated her as a slave, who beat her and starved her, who sold her to men who would use her little body in any way they liked. Or being turned away from house after house, begging for shelter on a winter night. But people were better than that, surely? Wasn't the human race better than that?

She wrapped the blanket more carefully around the little girl and held her close, turning her head away so her tears wouldn't run down onto Aisha's face.

Slowly around them the ship was coming awake. Other people had been sleeping on the deck, wrapped up in blankets or huddling close together, and now they were beginning to stir, talking in quiet tones or sitting up stiffly.

Aisha said something. Lyra could hardly hear her, and couldn't understand anyway, but something in the way the child was moving made it clear what she meant, and Lyra stood up and helped her up too, draping the blanket around her to keep in the warmth, and led her to a lavatory. She waited outside, still half-asleep, and listened to the voices around in the hope of hearing a word or two that she understood. Little shreds and snatches, splinters of meaning, like flying fishes appearing for a moment above the water and then disappearing again: that was all.

Then the note of the engines slowed, and the slight movement changed as the boat seemed to be turning tightly. Not again, thought Lyra, but a few moments later it began to pitch a little and lean into the turn. In the confined and overheated passageway, with no sight of the sea, Lyra began to feel a little queasy, and when

Aisha came out, she took the child's hand and led her out on deck again, where the air was fresh. Aisha held her hand readily enough, and her dæmon seemed more active and less fearful than he'd been in the night. He was whispering in the girl's ear and watching Lyra all the time. Aisha murmured a word or two in response.

Lyra saw a queue of people forming on the deck outside the main saloon and led Aisha to join it, hoping it was for breakfast. And so it turned out to be: fresh flatbreads and a little cheese. Lyra took some and went back to the chair, where Aisha sat huddled under the blanket, bread in one hand and cheese in the other, and nibbled steadily.

Then Lyra noticed that the ferry had indeed changed direction and was now slowing down and moving towards a harbor under the rocky hills of an island.

"I wonder where this is," she said to Aisha.

The child simply stared at her and then at the hills, the little town of white-painted houses, the fishing boats in the harbor.

"Well, how's she doing?" said Alison Wetherfield, appearing suddenly beside them.

"She's eating, at least," said Lyra.

"What about you? Have you eaten something?"

"I thought the food was for the refugees."

"Well, go and buy something from the cafeteria. I'll wait here. You won't be any use if you're hungry."

Lyra did, and came back with bread and cheese for herself and a spice cake for the child. The only drink available was a sweet mint tea, which was hot, at least. Every part of the vessel was crowded and noisy and alive with voices expressing fear, curiosity, anger, and sorrow; and Lyra was grateful for it, because she was definitely less interesting than the situation they were all in, and she could pass among people without being noticed at all.

When she got back to the child, she found her talking freely to

Alison. Freely, but quietly and with eyes lowered, and in a monotone. Lyra tried to follow her words, but could make out very little; perhaps Aisha spoke a dialect of Arabic different from the classical kind they taught at Jordan College. Or perhaps Lyra simply hadn't paid attention to her lessons.

She offered the spice cake, and the child looked up just once as she accepted it, and then cast her eyes down again; and Lyra knew in a moment that the trust of the night was gone, and Aisha now felt the fear every human being felt for someone so mutilated as to be without a dæmon.

"I'm going to wash," she said to Alison, not noticing that the woman had seen Aisha's fear and the immediate sadness it had caused Lyra.

When she came back, hoping she looked refreshed, she said, "Where are we? What's this place?"

"One of the Greek islands. I don't know which one. The refugees will go ashore here, no doubt. I don't expect the Greeks will refuse to let them land. They'll take them to the mainland eventually and they'll settle somewhere."

"What'll happen to her?"

"I've spoken to a woman who'll look after her. We can only do so much, Lyra. There comes a point when we have to accept that other people can do more."

Aisha was now finishing the spice cake, her eyes still firmly cast down. Lyra wanted to stroke her hair but held back, not wanting to frighten her.

The ferry had come to rest against a quay, and deckhands were making it fast to bollards at the bow and the stern. There was a loud clatter of chains as a gangway was lowered, and a little crowd was already gathering on the waterfront to see what had brought the ferry to their harbor.

Lyra stood at the rail and watched the activity unfold, and

gradually fell into a kind of trance. Perhaps she hadn't slept well, or perhaps her energy was depleted, but she found herself withdrawing little by little into a labyrinth of daydream and speculation, all involving dæmons.

The moment in the night when the little mouse dæmon had cuddled against her: had that really happened? She was as sure of it as she could be of anything, but (as so often now) it was the meaning that was a mystery.

Perhaps there was no meaning. That's what Simon Talbot would say. She felt a lurch of revulsion, and then she thought something else: she'd felt at the time that the poor little dæmon was attracted by her warmth, the greater certainty of her adulthood, by the simple fact of her being in charge and offering comfort. Now it occurred to her that there was another interpretation. Perhaps it was the little dæmon himself who sensed a loneliness and desolation in Lyra, and came to give her comfort—not the other way round at all. And it had worked. That thought was a shock, but it convinced her. She wanted to express her gratitude, but when she turned to look at the child again, she found that it would be impossible; there was no point where they could meet and understand each other. The moment in the night was an end point, not a starting point.

"Can I do anything to help?" she said to Alison when the woman got up and lifted the child to her feet.

"I've decided I should go ashore to see that they're looked after properly. I've got no authority; all I can do is boss people, but it seems to work. I'll wait for a later boat—I doubt the captain will want to lose more time than he needs to. You stay on board and gather yourself, and go on and find your dæmon. That's what you need to do. If you go through Aleppo, don't leave without seeing Father Joseph at the English school. He's not hard to find, and he's a very good man. Goodbye, my dear."

A brisk kiss, and she led Aisha away. The child didn't look back. Her dæmon was a little bird now, of a kind that Lyra didn't recognize, and he'd probably already forgotten what he'd done in the night, though Lyra knew that she never would.

She sat down in the wicker chair. In the warmth of the Aegean morning, she soon fell asleep.

TWENTY-FOUR

THE BAZAAR

Malcolm and Mehrzad Karimov spent the night in their dry cave, and woke to a warm, sunny morning. By staying in the forest, they managed to cross the border without being discovered. They could see, from their path among the trees higher up the mountain, the long queues of traffic that had built up on either side of the frontier post, and exchanged a silent glance of relief. From that point on, the journey was untroubled. Malcolm paid for Karimov's ticket as far as Constantinople, and they arrived two days after the assassination of the Patriarch.

They found the city in a state of feverish anxiety. Their travel documents were examined three times before they could manage to leave the railway station, and Malcolm's cover identity as a scholar traveling to study various documents in the libraries of that city was thoroughly ransacked. It stood up because it was genuine, and the details of his contacts and sponsors and hosts had all been rigorously checked before he left London; but the manner of the soldiers who examined it was hostile and suspicious.

He said goodbye to Karimov, whom he'd come to like a great

deal. He had told Malcolm everything he knew about Tashbulak and the work of the scientists there, and about the desert of Karamakan, and about the poem *Jahan and Rukhsana*, long passages of which Karimov knew by heart. He was going to pick up some business in Constantinople, he said, and join a caravan further along on the Silk Road.

"Malcolm, thank you for your companionship on this journey," he said as they shook hands outside the railway station. "May God keep you safe."

"I hope he'll do the same for you, my friend," said Malcolm. "Go well."

After finding a cheap hotel, he set out to call on an old acquaintance of his, an inspector in the Turkish police who was an unofficial friend of Oakley Street. But on his way to the police headquarters, he realized that he was being followed.

It wasn't hard to see, in shop windows and the glass doors of banks and office buildings, the young man who was on his trail. The only way of following someone with real success, without being detected, was to have a team of three people doing it, all trained and experienced; but this young man was on his own and had to stay close. Without looking at him directly, Malcolm had plenty of time to examine him: his dark good looks, his slender build, and his nervous, sudden movements and pauses were clearly visible in the wealth of reflections Malcolm saw around him. He didn't look Turkish; he might have been Italian; in fact, he might have been English. He was wearing a green shirt, dark trousers, and a pale linen jacket. His dæmon was a small hawk. His face was badly bruised, and there was a plaster across the bridge of his nose.

Malcolm moved gradually towards the more crowded streets, where his follower would need to come nearer. He wondered whether the young man was familiar with the city: at a guess, he thought not. They were in the neighborhood of the Grand Bazaar, and Malcolm meant to lead him into the crowded alleys of the bazaar itself, where he'd have to come even closer.

He came to the great stone archway that led into the bazaar and paused to look up at it, giving his follower time to see where he was going, and strolled inside.

Immediately, before the young man could see, he stepped into a little shop selling rugs and textiles. There were over sixty different lanes in the bazaar, and hundreds of shops. It wouldn't be hard to escape from his follower, but Malcolm wanted to do something different: to turn the tables and follow *him*.

A few seconds later, the young man hurried in at the great gate and looked around, craning to peer along the crowded alley, looking quickly to left and right—too quickly to see anything clearly. He was agitated. Malcolm, among the hanging rugs, was facing away from the alley, but was watching in the back of his wristwatch, which consisted of a mirror. The rug seller was busy attending to a customer and gave Malcolm no more than a quick glance.

The young man began to hurry along the alley, and Malcolm stepped out to follow him. He had a linen cap in his pocket, and he put it on now to hide his red hair. The lane they were in was one of the wider ones, but shops and stalls crowded close on both sides, and the whole alley was hung thickly with clothes, shoes, carpets, brushes, brooms, suitcases, lamps, copper cooking vessels, and a thousand other things.

Malcolm moved unobtrusively through it all, following the young man without ever looking at him directly, in case he suddenly looked around. His nervousness surrounded him like a vapor. His hawk dæmon sat on his shoulder, her head twitching this way and that, occasionally seeming to face backwards like an owl, and Malcolm saw every movement and moved closer and closer.

Then the boy—he was hardly a man—said something to his dæmon, and Malcolm saw his face more clearly. And that raised an apparition in his mind, no more than the ghost of a memory of another face, and he was back in his parents' inn on a winter evening as Gerard Bonneville sat by the fire with his hyena dæmon and gave Malcolm such a warm smile of complicity that—

Bonneville!

This was his son. This was the Magisterium's celebrated alethiometrist.

"Asta," Malcolm whispered, and his dæmon leapt up into his arms and climbed to his shoulder. "It is, isn't it?" he murmured.

"Yes. No doubt about it."

The alleys were crowded, and Bonneville uncertain; he seemed so young, so inexperienced. Malcolm followed the boy into the heart of the bazaar, closer, closer, little by little, moving through the crowds like a ghost, unseen, unsuspected, unfelt, subduing his own personality, watching without looking and seeing without staring. Bonneville was becoming despondent, to judge by his bearing; he'd lost his quarry; he wasn't sure of anything.

They came to a sort of crossroads, where an ornate fountain stood under the high arched roof. Malcolm guessed that Bonneville would stop there and look all around, and he did, Malcolm seeing it in the back of his watch, with his head turned away.

"He's drinking," said Asta.

Malcolm moved quickly, and while the boy's head was still bent down to the water, he came to stand right behind him. The hawk dæmon was looking to left and right, and then, as Malcolm knew she would, she turned and saw him only an arm's length away.

It gave Bonneville a great shock. He jerked back and up from the water, whirled around—and there was a knife in his right hand.

At once Asta sprang at the boy's dæmon and bore her down into the stone trough where the water ran. Malcolm reacted in the same moment, just as the razor-sharp blade sliced through the left arm of his jacket and the skin beneath. Bonneville had swung his hand so hard that he was off balance for a fraction of a second, and in that moment Malcolm slammed his right fist with all his strength into the boy's solar plexus, the kind of blow that would have ended a boxing match at once; and Bonneville, all breath and power gone, slumped back over the trough and dropped the knife.

Malcolm kicked it away and picked the boy up with one hand gripping his shirtfront.

"My knife," Bonneville gasped in French.

"It's gone. You're going to come with me and talk," said Malcolm in the same language.

"Like hell."

Asta's claws were firmly fixed in the hawk dæmon's throat. She gripped harder, and the hawk screamed. Both dæmons were soaking wet, and Bonneville was wet through himself, and both frightened and defiant.

"You've got no choice," said Malcolm. "You're going to come and sit down and drink some coffee with me and talk. There's a café just around the corner. If I'd wanted to kill you, I could have done it anytime during the last fifteen minutes. I'm in charge. You do as I say."

Bonneville was winded and trembling, and hunched over as if his ribs were broken, which they might very well have been. He was in no condition to argue. He did try to shake off Malcolm's grip on his arm, without the slightest success. It had all happened so quickly that hardly anyone had noticed. Malcolm took him to the café and made him sit in the corner, his back to a wall hung with photograms of wrestlers and film stars.

Malcolm ordered coffee for them both. Bonneville sat hunched forward, caressing his dæmon with trembling fingers, stroking the water off her feathers.

"Fuck you, man," he muttered. "You've broken something. A rib or, I don't know, something in my chest. Bastard."

"You've been in the wars, haven't you? How did you get that broken nose?"

"Piss off."

"What do you know about the murder of the Patriarch?" said Malcolm. "Did Monsieur Delamare send you here to see it done successfully?"

Bonneville tried to conceal his surprise. "How do you know—" he began, but stopped.

"I ask the questions. Where's your alethiometer now? You haven't got it on you, or I'd know."

"You'll never have it."

"No, because Delamare will. You took it without permission, didn't you?"

"Fuck you."

"I thought so."

"You're not as clever as you think."

"I daresay you're right, but I'm cleverer than you think. For example, I know the names and addresses of Delamare's agents in Constantinople, and now that you realize I can follow you, you'll know that I'll very soon find out where you're staying. Ten minutes after that, they'll know."

"What are their names, then?"

"Aurelio Menotti. Jacques Pascal. Hamid Saltan."

Bonneville gnawed his lower lip and looked at Malcolm with hatred. The waiter came with their coffee, and couldn't help looking at the boy's wet shirt and bandaged nose and at the blood now seeping through the cut in Malcolm's sleeve.

"What do you want?" said Bonneville when the waiter had gone.

Malcolm ignored the question and sipped the scalding coffee. "I'll say nothing to Menotti and the others," he said, "if you tell me the truth now."

Bonneville shrugged. "You wouldn't know if it was the truth or not," he said.

"Why did you come to Constantinople?"

"Nothing to do with you."

"Why were you following me?"

"My business."

"Not after you pulled a knife on me. It's mine too."

Another shrug.

"Where's Lyra now?" Malcolm said.

Bonneville blinked. He opened his mouth to speak, changed his mind, tried to sip his coffee, burned his mouth, put the cup down.

"So you don't know?" the boy said eventually.

"Oh, I know exactly where she is. I know why you're following her. I know what you want from her. I know the way you use the alethiometer. Know how I know that? It leaves a trail, did you realize?"

Bonneville looked at him, narrow-eyed.

"She discovered that straightaway," Malcolm went on. "You've been leaving a trail all through Europe, and they're following you, and eventually they'll pick you up."

The boy's eyes flickered for a moment in what would have been a smile if he'd let it. *He knows something,* thought Asta to Malcolm.

"Shows how much you know," Bonneville said. "Anyway, what's this trail? What do you mean by that?"

"I'm not going to tell you. What does Delamare want?"

"He wants the girl."

"Apart from that. What does he want to do with this new High Council?"

Why did Delamare want Lyra? was the one question Malcolm wanted to ask, but he knew he'd never get the answer by asking it.

"He's always wanted power," said Bonneville. "That's all. Now he's got it."

"Tell me about the business with the roses."

"I don't know anything about it."

"Yes, you do. Tell me what you know."

"I'm not interested in it, so I took no notice."

"You're interested in anything that gives you any power, so I know you'll have heard about the rose business. Tell me what Delamare knows."

"It's no advantage to me to tell you anything."

"That's just what I mean. You're shortsighted. Raise your eyes to the horizon. It would be a great advantage to you not to have me against you. Tell me what Delamare knows about the rose business."

"What will I get in return?"

"I won't break your neck."

"I want to know about this trail."

"You can work that out for yourself. Come on—roses."

Bonneville sipped his coffee again. His hand was steadier now. "A man came to see him a few weeks ago," he said. "A Greek, or a Syrian, I don't know. Maybe from further east. He had a sample of rose oil from a place way out in Kazakhstan or somewhere. Lop Nor. They mentioned Lop Nor. Delamare had the sample analyzed."

"Well?"

"That's all I know."

"That's not good enough."

"It's all I know!"

"What about the business in Oxford that went wrong?"

"That was nothing to do with me."

"So you know about it. That's useful. Delamare was behind that as well, obviously."

Bonneville shrugged. He was beginning to regain his confidence. It was time to shake it again.

"Did your mother know how your father died?" Malcolm said.

The boy blinked and opened his mouth to speak, closed it again, shook his head, picked up his coffee cup, but put it down again almost at once, seeing his own hand tremble.

"What do you know about my father?"

"More than you, obviously."

The hawk dæmon shook herself away from Bonneville's hand and sprang to the tabletop, her claws gripping the tablecloth and pulling it into ridges. Her fierce eyes were fixed on Malcolm's, and Asta stood up on the chair next to his, watching her.

"I know you killed him," Bonneville said. "You killed my father."

"Don't be stupid. I was only ten, eleven, something like that."

"I know your name. I know you killed him."

"What is my name, then?"

"Matthew Polstead," said Bonneville with contempt.

Malcolm took out his passport, his genuine one, and showed the boy his name. "Malcolm, see? Not Matthew. And look at my date of birth. It was only eleven years before your father died. There was a great flood, and he drowned. As for Matthew, he's my older brother. He found your father's body in the Thames, near Oxford. He had nothing to do with killing him."

He took back his passport. The boy looked both rebellious and disconcerted.

"If he discovered the body, he must have stolen my father's alethiometer," he said sullenly. "I want it back."

"I heard about an alethiometer. I heard about what your father did to his dæmon too. Did you know about that? I thought it might run in the family."

Bonneville's hand moved to his dæmon's neck, to stroke it or hold her steady, but she shook her wings impatiently and moved away, further onto the table. Asta put her front paws on the table and stood up, watching intently.

"What?" said Bonneville. "Tell me."

"You tell me what I want to know first. Roses. Oxford. The alethiometer. The girl. The death of the Patriarch. Everything. Then I'll tell you about your father."

The boy's eyes were glaring like his dæmon's. He sat tensely on the edge of his chair, both hands on the table, and Malcolm stared implacably back. After several seconds Bonneville's eyes dropped, and he sat back and began to chew at a fingernail.

Malcolm waited.

"What d'you want first?" said Bonneville.

"The alethiometer."

"What about it?"

"How you came to read it."

"When I was a kid, my mother told me about how my father had been given his by these monks in Bohemia or somewhere. They had it for centuries, but they recognized that he was a genius at reading it and they saw he had to have it. When I heard that, I knew it would be mine one day, so I started reading all about the symbols and how to interpret them. And when I first touched the one the Magisterium has, I found I could read it easily. So they began to rely on me. I could read it more quickly and better, more accurately, than anyone they'd ever seen. So I became their chief reader. I used it to ask what had happened to my father, how he died, where his alethiometer was now, a lot of questions like that.

They led me to that girl. That bitch has got it. They murdered him, and she stole it."

"Who murdered him?"

"The Oxford people. Maybe your brother."

"He drowned."

"The fuck you know about it, if you were only ten years old."

"Tell me about this new method."

"I just found it out."

"How?"

Bonneville was vain enough to respond. "You wouldn't understand. No one would unless they had a thorough classical training. Then you have to rebel against it and find something new, like I did. At first, it made me throw up and I saw nothing and felt nauseated. But I stuck to it. I tried again and again. I wasn't going to let it beat me. And in spite of being nauseated, I could make connections much more quickly. It became famous, my new method. The other readers tried it. But they could only do it weakly, uncertainly; they couldn't handle it. It was talked about all over Europe. But no one can do it properly except me."

"What about the girl? I thought she could do it."

"She's better than most. I admit that. But she hasn't got the strength. You need a kind of power, stamina, force, and I guess girls haven't got it."

"Why do you think she has the alethiometer that your father had?"

"I don't have to think it. I just know it. It's a stupid question. It's like asking how I worked out that this tablecloth's white. You don't have to work it out."

"All right. Now tell me why the Patriarch Papadakis was killed."

"It was bound to happen. As soon as Delamare arranged for him to head this new High Council, the poor old bastard was doomed.

See, Delamare had it all worked out from the start. The only way he could be the single unchallenged leader was to set up a structure where there *was* a leader. The Magisterium hasn't had that since, I don't know, hundreds of years ago, but as soon as there was a single leader, all Delamare had to do was have him killed in circumstances that led to panic, then step in and calm that panic with some emergency regulations, and modestly offer himself. He's in charge now for life. Unlimited powers. You got to admire that sort of resolution. I could handle him, but no one else can."

"In that case, why are you on the run?"

"What the fuck d'you mean? I'm not on the run," Bonneville blustered. "I got a secret mission from Delamare himself."

"They're looking for you. There's a reward, didn't you know?"

"How much?"

"More than you're worth. Someone will betray you in the end. Now tell me about the roses. What did they do with the sample of oil?"

"They analyzed it. The oil from that place has got various properties that they haven't got to the bottom of yet. They need a larger sample. I got hold of a tiny amount—I know a girl in the Geneva laboratory, and in exchange . . . Well, she gave me a piece of blotting paper with a few drops on it. I found out one thing straightaway. It protects against the nausea in the new method. With enough of it, you could use the new method and never suffer the ill effects. But I only had that little bit."

"Go on. What else?"

"You know what they mean by Dust?"

"Of course."

"With the oil, they can see that. And lines of power. Or fields. Maybe fields. The girl in the lab said it was a field. And they could see not just chemicals and kinds of light but human interactions.

If Professor Zitski had touched this specimen but not that one, he showed up somehow, because they could check it against the other things he'd touched. And Professor Zotski would have his mark on it too, if he had. If Zotski had been thinking about the thing, or he'd ordered how the experiment was to be set up, he'd show up in the field."

"And what was Delamare's reaction to this?"

"You've got to understand, he's not a simple man. He's got layer on layer of complexity, he's subtle, he seems to contradict himself and then you see he's thought several moves ahead. . . . The new High Council, that'll let him do things he wasn't able to before. He's going to send an expedition to this rose place, Lop Nor, wherever. Not for trade, though. I mean armed. They're going to capture it. He's going to control it all. He's not going to let anyone else have the oil."

"What do you know about this armed expedition? Who's commanding it?"

"Fuck, I don't know," said Bonneville. He was sounding impatient, bored, and Malcolm could see that he needed the constant attention of a listener to stop him losing concentration and becoming irritated.

"Want some more coffee?"

"All right."

Malcolm signaled to the waiter. Bonneville's dæmon had shut her eyes and let him return her to his shoulder.

"This girl in the laboratory," Malcolm said. "In Geneva."

"Nice body. Too emotional, though."

"Are you still in contact with her?"

Bonneville thrust his right forefinger into and out of his closed left fist several times. Malcolm knew what the boy wanted then: the sexual admiration of an older man. He let a slight smile into his expression.

"She'll find things out for you?"

"She'll do anything. But there's no oil left, I told you."

"Have they tried to synthesize it?"

Bonneville's eyes narrowed. "You sound like you're trying to recruit me as a spy," he said. "Why should I tell you anything?"

The waiter came back with their coffee. Malcolm waited till he'd gone, and then said, "The circumstances haven't changed."

He wasn't smiling anymore. Bonneville gave an elaborate shrug.

"I've told you plenty. Now you tell me something. How did that girl Belacqua get hold of my father's alethiometer?"

"As far as I know, it was given to her by the head of her father's college in Oxford. Jordan College."

"Well, how did *he* get hold of it?"

"I've no idea."

"So why did he give it to her?"

"I know nothing about it at all."

"How do you know her anyway?"

"I used to teach her."

"When? How old was she? Did she have the alethiometer then?"

"She was about fourteen, fifteen. I taught her history. She never mentioned the alethiometer. I certainly never saw it. I had no idea she had it until recently. Is that why Delamare wants to find her?"

"He'd like the alethiometer, certainly. He'd be glad to have a second one. Then he could play me off against the other readers. But that isn't why he wants to find her."

"Well, why does he?"

Malcolm could see the temptation playing over Bonneville's expression. He knew something that Malcolm didn't, and the pleasure of telling it was too strong to ignore.

"You mean you don't know?" he said.

"There are a lot of things I don't know. What is it in this case?"

"I don't know how you failed to know this. Obviously your sources aren't up to much."

Malcolm sipped his coffee and watched Bonneville's knowing smirk broaden. "Obviously," he said. "Well?"

"Delamare is her uncle. He thinks she killed his sister, her mother. He must have been in love with his sister, if you ask me. Obsessed with her, anyway. He wants to punish her, Silvertongue, Belacqua, whatever her name is. Wants to make her pay."

Malcolm was profoundly surprised. He'd had no idea that the Mrs. Coulter he'd once met, in Hannah Relf's little house on a winter afternoon just before the great flood, had any siblings at all. But why should she not? People did. And did Lyra know about this brother, this uncle? He wanted to talk to her urgently, now, this minute. And he had to show no reaction. He had to feel no reaction. He had to feel no more than mildly interested.

"Does he know where she is?" he said. "Have you told him?"

"Your turn," said Bonneville. "Tell me about my father. Who killed him?"

"I told you. No one killed him. He drowned."

"I don't believe you. Someone killed him. When I find out who that was, I'll kill him."

"Have you got the nerve to do that?"

"No question. Tell me about his dæmon. You said something about his dæmon."

"She was a hyena. She'd lost a leg because he mistreated her. He beat her savagely. I heard it from a man who saw him doing it. He said it made him sick to see it."

"You think I'll believe that?"

"It's of no interest to me whether you believe it or not."

"Did you ever see him?"

"Only once. I saw his dæmon, and she frightened me. She came

470

out of the bushes in the dark and looked at me and pissed on the path I was walking on. Then he came out and saw what she was doing, and laughed. They went ahead further into the wood, and I waited for a long time before I dared go on. But I never saw him again."

"How did you know his name?"

"I heard people talking about him."

"Where was this?"

"In Oxford during the flood."

"You're lying."

"And you're boasting, and you've got far less control over the alethiometer than you think you have. You read it in a state of confusion and seasickness, and guesswork. I don't trust you an inch, because you're a slippery, vicious little brat. But I've given my word. I won't tell Menotti or the others where you are. Unless you try something against me, in which case I won't bother with them; I'll find you and kill you myself."

"Easy to say."

"Easy to do."

"Who are you, anyway?"

"An archaeologist. The best advice I can give you is to crawl back to Delamare and apologize fulsomely. Then stay put."

Bonneville sneered.

"Is your mother still alive?" Malcolm said.

A flush came into the boy's cheeks. "Never you fucking mind," he said. "She's got nothing to do with you."

Malcolm watched him and said nothing. After a minute Bonneville stood up.

"I've had enough," he said.

He picked up his dæmon and squeezed out past the next table. Malcolm smelled the cologne he was wearing and recognized the scent as one that a number of young men seemed to be affecting: a citrus-based product called Galleon. So Bonneville was conscious of fashion, and wanted to be attractive, and perhaps was; it was another fact that might be useful. The young man was holding himself gingerly, as if his ribs still hurt. Malcolm watched him out of the café and away past the fountain to be lost in the crowd.

"D'you think he knows about Lyra and Pan not being together?" said Asta.

"Hard to say. It's the sort of thing he'd boast about, if he did."

"He'll kill her if he finds her."

"Then we must find her first."

TWENTY-FIVE

THE PRINCESS CANTACUZINO

The ferry didn't reach Smyrna till late in the following afternoon. During the day Lyra hardly moved, staying in her wicker chair and stirring only to fetch some coffee and bread, thinking about what she should do next, and looking through the little notebook, the *clavicula*. The name Kubiček had pointed to was that of a Princess Rosamond Cantacuzino, and it was the rose in her name that decided it. Lyra set off for her house as soon as she left the boat.

The princess lived in one of the great houses further along the waterfront. The city was a famous center of trade; in earlier times, merchants had made enormous fortunes from buying and selling carpets, dried fruit, grain, spices, and precious minerals. For the sake of the cool breezes in summer, and the views of the mountains, the richest families had long settled in splendid mansions along the palm-shaded corniche. The Cantacuzino house stood back from the road, behind a garden whose neatness and complexity of planting spoke of great wealth. Lyra thought that great wealth would help a lot if you'd lost your dæmon; you could pay for well-guarded privacy.

And thinking that, she wondered if she'd ever get inside the house to meet the princess. She almost quailed. Why did she want to meet her, anyway? Well, to ask for advice about the rest of her journey, obviously. And if Kubiček had her on his list, there must have been at least one occasion when she'd agreed to be helpful to those like herself. *Courage!* Lyra thought.

She walked through the gate and along a gravel path between symmetrical beds of tightly pruned roses whose buds were just beginning to show. A gardener at work in a far corner looked up and saw her, and straightened his back to watch as she made, with all the confidence she could assume, for the marble steps up to the entrance.

An elderly manservant answered the bell. His crow dæmon gave one hoarse croak as soon as she saw Lyra, and the old man's hooded eyes flickered with a moment's understanding.

"I hope you can speak English," Lyra said, "because I have little Greek and no Anatolian. I have come to present my compliments to Princess Cantacuzino."

The servant looked her up and down. She knew her clothes were shabby, but she also remembered Farder Coram's advice, and tried to imitate the way the witches bore themselves: supremely at ease in their ragged scraps of black silk, as if they wore the most elegant couture.

The butler inclined his head and said, "May I tell the princess who is calling?"

"My name is Lyra Silvertongue."

He stood aside and invited her to wait in the hall. She looked around: heavy dark wood, an elaborate staircase, a chandelier, tall palms in terra-cotta pots, the smell of beeswax polish. And cool, and quiet. The sound of traffic on the corniche, the stir of the air in the outside world, were all hushed behind the layers of wealth and custom that hung like heavy curtains all around.

The butler returned and said, "The princess will see you now, Miss Silvertongue. Please follow me."

He'd come from a door on the ground floor, but now he began to climb the stairs. He moved slowly, wheezing a little, but his posture was soldierly and upright. On the first floor he opened a door and announced her, and Lyra walked past into a room flooded with light, overlooking the bay and the harbor and the distant mountains. It was very large, and it seemed full of life: an ivory-colored grand piano covered in a dozen or more silver-framed photograms, many modern paintings, crowded white-painted bookshelves, and elegant light-colored furniture, all made Lyra like it at once. A very old lady sat in a brocaded armchair near the great windows, dressed all in black.

Lyra approached her. She wondered for a moment if she ought to curtsy, but decided immediately that it would look ridiculous, and simply said, "Good afternoon, Princess. It's very good of you to see me."

"Is that how you were brought up to address a princess?" The old woman's voice was dry, astringent, amused.

"No. That didn't form part of my lessons at all. I can do several other things quite well, though."

"I'm glad to hear it. Bring that chair forward and sit down. Let me look at you."

Lyra did as she was told and looked back calmly as the old woman scrutinized her. The old woman was both fierce and vulnerable, and Lyra wondered what her dæmon had been, and whether it would be polite to ask.

"Who were your people?" said the princess.

"My father's name was Asriel, Lord Asriel, and my mother was not his wife. She was called Mrs. Coulter. How did you know . . . I mean, why did you say *were*? How could you tell they weren't alive?"

"I can tell an orphan when I see one. I met your father once."

"Did you?"

"It was at a reception in the Egyptian embassy in Berlin. It must have been thirty years ago. He was a very handsome young man, and very rich."

"He lost his wealth when I was born."

"Why was that?"

"He wasn't married to my mother, and there was a court case—"

"Oh! Lawyers! Have *you* any money, child?"

"None at all."

"Then you will be of no interest to lawyers, and all the better for it. Who gave you my name?"

"A man in Prague. He was called Vaclav Kubiček."

"Ah. A very interesting man. A scholar of some repute. Modest, unassuming. Did you know of him before you went to Prague?"

"No, not at all. I had no idea there could be anyone else who . . . I mean, without . . . He was very helpful to me."

"Why are you traveling? And where are you going?"

"I'm going to Central Asia. To a place called Tashbulak, where there's a botanical research station. I'm going there to find out the answer to a puzzle. A mystery, really."

"Tell me about your dæmon."

"Pantalaimon . . ."

"A good Greek name."

"He settled in the form of a pine marten. He and I discovered we could separate when I was about twelve. We had to. At least, I had to keep a promise, which meant leaving him behind and going into a place where he couldn't come. Nothing . . . Almost nothing has ever felt worse. But after a while we found each other again, and I think he forgave me. And we were together after that, though we had to keep our separating very secret. We didn't think anyone could do it except witches. But for the last year or so we've been quarreling. We couldn't stand each other. That was horrible. And one day I woke up and he'd just gone. So I'm searching for him, really. I'm following clues . . . little things that don't make rational sense. . . . In Prague I met a magician who gave me a clue. And I'm relying on chance. It was by chance that I met Mr. Kubiček."

"There's a great deal you're not telling me."

"I don't know how long you'll be interested for."

"You don't suppose my life is so full of fascinating events that I can pass up the chance to listen to a stranger in the same depleted condition as I am myself?"

"Well, it might be. Full of fascinating events, I mean. I'm sure there's no shortage of people who'd like to meet you, or friends who could come and talk. Perhaps you have a family."

"I have no offspring, if that's what you mean. No husband. But in another sense I am smothered by family; this city, this country are full of Cantacuzinos. What I have instead of a family is— yes, I have a handful of friends, but they are embarrassed by me, they make allowances, they avoid painful subjects, they're full of kindly understanding, and as a result conversation with them is a kind of purgatory. When Mr. Kubiček came to see me, I was nearly dead with boredom and despair. Now the people who come here through him and through two or three other people of our sort in other places are the most welcome of guests. Will you take some tea with me?"

"I would love to."

The princess rang a little silver bell on the table beside her. "When did you arrive in Smyrna?" she said.

"This afternoon. I came straight from the port. Princess, why did your dæmon leave you?"

The old lady held up a hand. She heard the door open. When

the butler came in, she said, "Tea, Hamid," and he nodded deeply and went out again.

The princess listened. When she was satisfied that the servant had gone, she turned back to Lyra.

"He was a particularly beautiful black cat. He left me because he fell in love with someone else. He became utterly fascinated by a dancer, a nightclub dancer."

Her tone made it clear that she meant "someone little better than a prostitute." Lyra was silent, intrigued.

"You will be wondering," the princess went on, "how he could possibly have come to know such a woman. My social circle and hers would normally never touch. But I had a brother whose physical appetites were insatiable, and whose gift for making unsuitable alliances caused the family a great deal of embarrassment. He introduced the woman one evening into a soirée. He was perfectly open about it—'This young woman is my mistress,' he would say when meeting people—and to do her justice, she was remarkably pretty and graceful. I could feel her attractiveness myself, and my poor dæmon became besotted at once."

"Your *poor* dæmon?"

"Oh, I felt sorry for him. To be so abjectly dependent on a woman of that kind. It was a sort of madness. I felt every little quiver of it, of course, and I tried to speak to him about it, but he refused to listen, refused to control his feelings. Well, I daresay they were beyond control."

"What about her dæmon?"

"He was a marmoset or something of that kind. Lazy, incurious, vain. Quite indifferent to what was going on. My brother persisted in bringing the girl to the opera, to race meetings, to receptions, and whenever I was present too, my dæmon's obsession would force me to seek her company and experience his passion for her. It became unendurable. He would get as close as he could and talk quietly, whispering into her ear, while her own dæmon preened and yawned nearby. In the end—"

The door opened, and she stopped while the butler came in with a tray, which he set on the little table to her right. He bowed and left, and she completed the sentence:

"In the end it became notorious. Everyone knew about it. I have never been so unhappy."

"How old were you?"

"Nineteen, twenty, I can't remember. It would have been the natural thing for me to accept the attentions of any one of a number of young men my parents thought suitable, and to marry, and so on. But this absurdity made that impossible. I became an object of ridicule."

She spoke calmly, as if the young woman who had been her twenty-year-old self were someone else entirely. She turned to the tray and poured tea into two pretty cups.

"How did it end?" said Lyra.

"I begged, I pleaded with him, but he was lost in his madness. I said we would both die if he didn't stop, but nothing would make him stay with me. I even—and this will show you how abject a human being can become—I even left my parents and went to live with her myself."

"The dancer? You went to live with her?"

"It was reckless. I pretended to be in love with her, and she was happy enough with that. I lived with her, I forsook all my family responsibilities, I shared her bed, her table, her wretched occupation, because I could dance too, I was graceful, I was no less pretty than she was. She had a little talent, but no more than that. Together we attracted a bigger audience; we had a great success. We danced in every nightclub from Alexandria to Athens. We were offered a fortune to dance in Morocco, and an even greater one to dance in South America. But my dæmon wanted more, always more. He wanted to be hers and not mine. Her dæmon became a slave of poppy, which didn't affect her; but she turned to my dæmon, and when he felt his own obsession returned, I knew it was time for me to leave.

"I was ready to die. One night—we were in Beirut—one night I tore myself away from them. He was clinging to her, she was holding him tight, crushing him to her breast, all three of us were sobbing with pain and terror; but I wouldn't stop. I wrenched myself apart from him and left him there with her. From that day to this, I have been alone. I came back to my family, who regarded it all as a mildly amusing addition to the family legends. I could not marry, of course, in my solitary state; no one would have had me."

Lyra sipped her tea. It was delicately scented with jasmine.

"When did you meet my father?"

"It was a year before all that."

Lyra thought, But that can't be true. He wouldn't have been old enough.

"What do you remember most about your time with the dancer?" she said.

"Oh, that's easy. The hot nights, our narrow bed, her slender body, the scent of her flesh. That will never leave me."

"And were you in love with her, or were you still pretending?"

"You can pretend and pretend that sort of thing until it comes true, you know." The old woman's face was calm and deeply lined. Her eyes were very small amid the wrinkles, but bright and still.

"And your dæmon . . ."

"Never came back. She died, the dancer, oh, a long time ago. But he never came back to me. I think he might have gone to al-Khan al-Azraq."

"The Blue Hotel—is that . . . is it true, that story? About the ruined city where no one but dæmons can live?"

"I believe so. Some of my visitors—people from Mr. Kubiček, I mean—have been on their way there. No one has come back, as far as I know."

Lyra's mind was racing over deserts and mountains, to a ruined city stark and silent under moonlight.

"Now I have told you my story," said the princess, "you must tell me something remarkable. What have you seen on your journey that might interest an old lady without a dæmon?"

Lyra said, "When I was in Prague . . . It seems a long time ago, but it was really only last week. I got off the train, and before I'd even tried to find out about the timetable, Mr. Kubiček spoke to me. It was as if he'd been waiting for me, and as it turned out, he had. . . ."

She recounted the entire story of the furnace man and was rewarded by utter stillness and concentration. When she finished, the princess sighed with satisfaction.

"And he was the magician's son?" she said.

"Well, so Agrippa claimed. Cornelis and Dinessa . . ."

"It was a cruel game to play with him and his dæmon."

"I thought so too. But he was determined to find Dinessa, and he did."

"Love . . . ," said the princess.

"Tell me more about the Blue Hotel," said Lyra. "Or what's the other name—Madinat al-Qamar—the City of the Moon. Why is it called that?"

"Oh, no one knows. It's a very old idea. My nurse used to tell me ghost stories when I was very young, and it was she who told me about the Blue Hotel. Where are you going next?"

"Aleppo."

"Then I shall give you the names of some people there who are in our condition. One of them might know a little about it. Of course, it is a subject of horror and superstitious dread. Not to be spoken of in front of people who are entire, and easily frightened."

"Of course," said Lyra, and sipped the last of her tea. "This is such a lovely room. Do you play the piano?"

"It plays by itself," said the princess. "Go and pull out the ivory knob on the right of the keyboard."

Lyra did, and at once a mechanism inside the piano began playing the keys, which were depressed as if by an invisible pair of hands. The sounds of a sentimental love song of fifty years before filled the room. Lyra was delighted, and smiled at the princess.

" 'L'Heure Bleue,' " the old lady said. "We used to dance to that."

Lyra looked back at the piano, at the multitude of silver-framed photograms, and suddenly fell still.

"What is it?" said the princess, startled by Lyra's expression.

Lyra pressed in the knob to stop the music, and picked up one of the photograms with a trembling hand. "Who is this?" she said.

"Bring it to me."

The old lady took it and peered through a pair of pince-nez. "It is my nephew, Olivier," she said. "My great-nephew, I suppose I should say. Do you know him? Olivier Bonneville?"

"Yes. That is, I haven't actually met him, but he . . . he thinks I've got something that belongs to him, and he's been trying to get it back."

"And have you?"

"It belongs to me. My father . . . my father gave it to me. Monsieur Bonneville is wrong, but he won't accept it."

"Always a very stubborn boy. His father was a ne'er-do-well who probably died a violent death. Olivier is related to me on his mother's side, and she too is dead. He has expectations of me. If it were not for those, I should certainly never see him."

"Is he in Smyrna now?"

"I hope not. If he comes here, I shall say nothing about you, and if he asks, I shall lie through my teeth. I am a good liar."

"I used to be good at lying when I was young," Lyra said. She was feeling a little calmer. "These days I find it more difficult."

"Come here and kiss me, my dear," said the princess, and held out her hands.

Lyra was glad to do so. The old lady's papery cheeks smelled of lavender.

"If you do go to al-Khan al-Azraq," said the princess, "and if it really is a ruined city inhabited by dæmons, and if you see a black cat, and if his name is Phanourios, tell him that I would be glad to see him again before I die, but that he had better not leave it too long."

"I shall."

"I hope that your quest goes well, and that you solve your mystery. There is a young man involved, I take it."

Lyra blinked. The princess must have meant Malcolm. Of course, he *was* young to her. "Well," she said, "not . . ."

"No, no, not my great-nephew, of course not. Now, if you come this way again, do not fail to come and see me, or I shall haunt you."

She turned to a little ormolu desk beside her, took out a piece of paper and a fountain pen, and wrote for a minute or so. Then she blew on the paper to dry the ink and folded it in half before giving it to Lyra.

"One of these people will be sure to help," she said.

"Goodbye. I'm very grateful indeed. I shan't forget the things you've told me."

Lyra left and closed the door quietly. The butler was waiting in the hall to see her out. When she left the garden, she walked a little further until she was out of sight of the house, and then leant against a wall to recover her composure.

She had been nearly as shocked as if Bonneville had come into the room himself. He had the power to disturb her, even as a picture. This had all the quality of a warning from the secret commonwealth. It said, "Be on your guard! You never know when he'll appear."

Even in Smyrna, she thought, he might find her.

TWENTY-SIX

THE BROTHERHOOD OF
THIS HOLY PURPOSE

By the evening of the day after his encounter with Olivier Bonneville, Malcolm was in a city three hundred miles south of Constantinople. It was the capital of the rose-growing district in the ancient Roman province of Pisidia, and he'd gone there to meet an English journalist called Bryan Parker, a foreign correspondent who specialized in security matters, whom he knew from Oakley Street business. Malcolm told him a little about the journey to Central Asia, and what had sent him on that quest, and Parker instantly said, "Then you must come with me to a public meeting this evening. I think we can show you something interesting."

As they walked to the theater where the meeting was due to take place, Parker explained that the rose growing and processing industry was a valuable part of the region's economy, and that it was now under a great strain.

"What's the source of the problem?" said Malcolm as they went into the old theater.

"A group of men—no one knows where they come from, but

they're always referred to as the men from the mountains. They've been burning rose gardens, attacking the growers, smashing their factories. . . . The authorities can't seem to do anything about it."

The auditorium was crowded already, but they found a couple of seats at the back. There was a large number of middle-aged or older men wearing respectable suits and ties, and Malcolm guessed them to be the owners of the gardens. There were several women too, with sun-browned faces; he'd gathered from Parker that the industry was intensely conservative, with differing roles played by men and women workers, so perhaps these were some of the women who gathered the flowers, while the men were involved in the distilling of the rosewater and the production of the oil. Apart from them, the other members of the audience seemed to be towns-people, some of them possibly journalists or local politicians.

Men were coming and going on the stage, some engaged in erecting a large banner, which Parker said was that of the trade association sponsoring the meeting.

Eventually every seat was taken, with people standing at the back and along the sides. It was too full to satisfy any fire regulation that Malcolm was familiar with, but perhaps they had a more relaxed attitude about such things here. There were armed policemen, though, at every entrance, looking nervous, Malcolm thought. If there was any trouble this evening, a lot of people could easily get hurt.

Finally the organizers decided that they were ready to begin. A group of men in suits, carrying briefcases or bulging files of paper, came out onto the stage, and some of them were recognized and applauded or cheered by the audience. Four of them sat at a table, and a fifth came to a lectern and started to speak. At first, the loud-speakers howled with feedback, and he stood back, alarmed, and tapped the microphone, and a technician hurried out to adjust it.

Malcolm was watching everything, looking around unobtrusively, and as the speaker began again, he noticed something: the armed police had quietly vanished. There'd been a man at each of the six exits. Now there were none.

Parker was whispering a précis of what the speaker was saying. "Welcome to everyone—time of crisis in the industry—soon hear a report from each of the rose-growing regions. Now he's reading out some figures—this man is not the greatest speaker in the world. . . . Basically, production is down, turnover is down—now he's introducing the first speaker—a grower from Baris."

There was a scatter of applause as the next speaker left the table and came to the lectern. Whereas the previous man had a bureaucratic manner and a soporific voice, this older man spoke with force and passion from the start.

Parker said, "He's telling what happened at his factory. Some men from the mountains came early one morning and gathered all his workers together and forced them at gunpoint to burn down the factory, feeding the flames with the precious oil. Then they brought a bulldozer and dug up every corner of his gardens and poured poison—I don't know what sort—on the land so nothing could grow there again. Look—he's weeping with passion—this was a place owned by his great-great-grandfather, cared for by his family for over a hundred years, employing all his children and thirty-eight workers. . . ."

Murmurs of anger, or sympathy, or agreement came from the audience. Clearly many others had had similar experiences.

"He's saying where was the police force? Where was the army? Where was any protection for honest citizens like him and his family? It seems his son was killed in a skirmish with these men, who simply vanished afterwards—no one was caught, no one punished. Where is the justice? That's what he's saying."

The man's voice had risen to a pitch of rage and sorrow, and the audience joined in, clapping, shouting, stamping. Shaking his head, sobbing, the farmer left the lectern and sat down.

"Is there anyone from the government here?" Malcolm said.

"The only politicians here are from the local administration. No national figures."

"What's been the response of the national government so far?"

"Oh, concern, of course—sympathy—stern warnings—but also a curious tone of caution, as if they're too frightened to criticize these vandals."

"Curious, as you say."

"Yes, and it's making people angry. This next speaker is from the wholesalers' trade association. . . ."

He was another dull speaker. Parker whispered the gist of what he said, but Malcolm was more interested in what was going on in the auditorium.

Parker noticed and said, "What? What are you looking at?"

"Two things. Firstly the police have vanished, and secondly they've closed all the exits."

They were sitting at the right-hand end of the last row but one, which was close to the exit on that side. It had been a noise from there that had alerted Malcolm: it sounded like the sliding of a bolt.

"You want me to go on translating this dull man?"

"No. But be ready to smash that door open with me when the time comes."

"They open inwards."

"But they're not heavy or strong. Something's going to happen, Bryan. Thank you for suggesting this."

They didn't have to wait long.

Before the speaker had finished, three men appeared on the platform behind him, carrying guns: two had rifles, one had a pistol.

The audience gasped and fell still, and the speaker turned to see what had happened, and grasped the lectern and went pale. Out of the corner of his eye, Malcolm caught a movement at the other side of the hall. He turned his head a little to look and saw a door on that side open briefly to let in a man with a rifle. Then it shut again. Malcolm turned all around: the same thing had happened at all six exits.

The young man with the revolver had pushed the speaker aside and begun to talk himself. His eyes were pale, but his black hair and beard were long and thick. His voice was clear and light and harsh in quality, and full of calm conviction.

Malcolm leant his head a little sideways, and Parker whispered:

"He's saying that everything you know is going to change. Things that you are familiar with will become strange and alien, and things you have never imagined will become normal. This is beginning now in many parts of the world, not just in Pisidia. . . ."

The men who'd entered with him came to the two sides of the stage and faced out into the audience. No one moved. Malcolm could almost feel everyone holding their breath.

Parker went on as the man continued: "You and your families and your workers have been tending your gardens for far too long. The Authority does not want roses, and you are displeasing him by growing so many. The smell of them is sickening to him. It is like the dung of the devil himself. Those who grow roses and those who deal in oils and perfumes are pleasing the devil and offending God. We have come to tell you this."

He paused for a moment, and then the farmer who had spoken so passionately couldn't contain himself for another moment. He pushed back his chair and stood up. All three gunmen on the stage turned to him at once, guns pointed at his heart. The man spoke, without the microphone, but in a voice so loud and clear that everyone heard.

Parker whispered, "He says this is a new teaching. He has not heard it before. His forefathers, his family, his cousins who grow roses in the next village, they all thought they were doing the will of God by tending the flowers he created and preserving the beauty of their scent. This doctrine is new and strange, and it will be strange to everyone he knows and to everyone in this hall."

The gunman spoke, and Parker translated, "It replaces every other doctrine, because it is the word of God. No other doctrine is necessary."

The farmer came out from behind the table and confronted the gunman directly. His broad and stocky frame, his red face, the passion in his eyes made a vivid contrast with the cool and slender young man holding the revolver.

The farmer spoke again, even more loudly, in what was almost a bellow: "What will become of my family and my workers? What will become of the merchants and craftsmen who depend on the roses we grow? Will it please God to see them all poor and starving?"

The gunman answered, and Malcolm leant close to hear Parker's whisper: "It will please God to see them no longer involved in that evil trade. It will please him to see them turn away from their false gardens and set their eyes on the one true garden, which is paradise."

Without moving his head, Malcolm looked to left and right and saw the men on either side slowly scanning the audience, back to front and back again, their rifles unwaveringly swinging from side to side with their gaze at head-level to the audience.

The farmer said, "What are you going to do, then?"

The gunman replied, "The question is not what we are going to do. There is no question that needs to be asked about us, because we submit to the will of God, which is without question."

"I can't see the will of God! I see my roses, my children, my workers!"

"You need not worry. We shall tell you the will of God. We understand how your life is complicated, how things seem to contradict one another, how everything is full of doubt. We have come to make things clear."

The farmer swung his head and lowered it like a bull, and seemed to be gathering his strength. He spread his feet, as if to find a firmer purchase on the earth, though it was only a wooden stage; and finally he said, "And what is the will of God?"

The young gunman said, and Parker whispered, "That you dig up and burn every one of your rosebushes and smash every piece of your distilling apparatus. That you destroy every vessel that contains the dung of Satan, which you call perfume and oil. That is the will of God. In his infinite mercy, he has sent me and my companions to inform you of this and make sure it is done, so that your women and your workers may live lives that are pleasing to God instead of filling the air with the foul stench from the bowels of hell."

The farmer tried to say something else, but the gunman lifted his hand and held the revolver only a foot away from the old man's head.

"When you light that fire," he said, "the fire that will consume your gardens and your factories, it will light a beacon of truth and purity to shine all over the world. You should rejoice at being given this opportunity. My companions in the brotherhood of this holy purpose are numbered in the thousands of thousands. The word of God has spread so fast that it is like a forest fire, and it will spread further and further until all the world is burning with the love of God and the joy of perfect obedience to his will."

All this time the farmer's dæmon, a heavy-beaked old raven, had been raising her wings and snapping her beak on his shoulder;

and the gunman's, a large and beautiful sand-colored desert cat, had been standing tense and watchful at his side.

Then the farmer shouted, "*I will never burn my roses!* I will never deny the truth of my senses! The flowers are beautiful, and their scent is the very breath of heaven! You are wrong!"

And the raven plunged down towards the cat, and the cat leapt up towards the raven, but even before they met, the gunman pulled the trigger and sent a bullet through the old man's head. The raven vanished in midair and the farmer fell dead, blood pulsing from the hole in his skull.

The audience cried out, but any further noise was stilled at once by the movement of the gunmen, who stepped forward, all of them, and raised their rifles to their shoulders. No one said a word, but there was the sound of sobbing from several parts of the auditorium.

The young man spoke again, and Parker translated: "That was an example of what you must not do from now on, and an illustration of what will happen if you disobey us. . . ."

He went on in the same style. Malcolm put his hand on Parker's sleeve; he'd heard enough. He whispered, "Where does the stage door open?"

"Into an alley on the right of the main building."

"Is there another way out of the alley, or is it a dead end?"

"The only way out goes past the front of the theater."

The gunman finished his speech and had given another instruction.

"Hostages," whispered Parker.

The remaining speakers on the stage were told to lie down on their faces, with their hands behind their heads. One or two of them were old, or hampered by arthritis; the gunmen forced them down anyway. Then at another order the six men by the exits stepped forward and each indicated to the nearest audience member that he or she should stand up and go with him.

The woman sitting in front of Malcolm began to do that, but Malcolm stood up first. He turned to the gunman and pointed to himself. The gunman shrugged, and the woman sat down heavily.

"What are you doing?" said Parker.

"Wait and see."

Malcolm stepped out into the aisle and put his hands up as the gunman indicated. Other hostages, two of them women, were doing the same and being ordered down towards the stage. Malcolm watched and followed their example.

He reached the stage with the rifle prodding his back. There were steps on each side, and he climbed them, as the others were doing. As the first woman had to step past the body of the old farmer, where a pool of blood was still slowly growing larger, her dæmon dog suddenly howled and refused to step in it. She tried to pick him up, but the gunman behind her pushed hard with his rifle and she fell over into the blood herself. She cried out in horror, and another of the hostages helped her up and kept his arms around her as she sobbed and nearly fainted.

Malcolm watched with close interest. The young man in charge had made a bad mistake. He should have let his cat dæmon deal with the raven and avoided shooting altogether. The situation was getting more complicated every second, and the gunmen had no plan to deal with it—a death, hostages, a whole audience imprisoned, but now with no one to hold them at gunpoint, all the intruders being on the stage, guarding their hostages. At any moment someone would run to an exit and try to get out, and then there'd be a panicked scramble to leave, in which anything could happen. Malcolm saw the young man looking at everything, calculating swiftly, working it all out, and then give a few harsh sentences of command.

Three of the men who'd come from the auditorium turned back and covered the audience with their rifles. The other three gestured at the six hostages, including Malcolm, to follow the leader into the wings at stage left. Malcolm was sure that the leader was improvising, and that hostages had never been part of his plan, but he had to admit that the young man was forceful and decisive. If he was going to be stopped, it would have to be soon.

And it was Malcolm who'd have to do it. He hadn't had many fights as a boy, because he was big and strong and most people liked him, and in the playground scuffles he was forced into he'd found himself bound by a sense of chivalry and fairness. Oakley Street had got rid of that. And as soon as he stepped into the wings, there came a piece of outrageous luck. Oakley Street had taught him what to do about that too: use it at once and don't wait.

He found himself in a crowded confusion of long black curtains, which were swaying and releasing a thin shower of dust. And just ahead of him, holding the pistol, was the young man who'd shot the farmer, and he was about to sneeze.

Seeing that, Malcolm shook the nearest curtain hard and the dust fell more thickly. For no more than a couple of seconds the curtains cut them off from everyone else, and as the young man opened his mouth and shook his head and blinked in the shower of dust, trying to hold back the sneeze, Malcolm kicked him very hard in the groin.

The sneeze came at the same moment. Helpless, the man dropped the gun and uttered a stifled grunt. Malcolm stepped forward, seized the young man's hair with both hands, and smashed his head downwards, at the same time bringing his own knee up hard into his face. Then he let go with one hand and, grabbing the man's beard, slammed it sideways while pulling his hair the other way. There was a loud *crack*, and the gunman's dæmon vanished before he hit the floor.

"This way!" said Asta quietly, at the level of Malcolm's head.

He saw she was clinging to a ladder, black-painted iron rungs set into the brickwork, and he swung himself up silently, holding his breath, until he was above head height. His clothes were dark; there was very little to see, even if anyone had looked in the right direction. And all around were the dark hanging curtains, swaying in the confusion as the men and their hostages fumbled their way through.

And Asta was up higher already, on a gantry, looking down through the steel mesh floor at the doubt and confusion below, where some men had halted, some hostages were calling out in fear, and where the leader's body was lying, half hidden by a curtain. A moment later, Malcolm was climbing the ladder again. He moved out onto the gantry and waited.

Asta whispered, "What now?"

"They'll find his body in a minute, and—"

It was less than that. One of the gunmen fell over it and called out first in surprise and annoyance and then, when he realized what it was, in high alarm.

Malcolm watched as the others responded in various ways: at first, none of them could see what had caused the alarm, and some called out to ask, while others, closer by, fumbled their way past the enveloping curtains and almost fell over the body of their leader and the man who still lay sprawled in terror beside it.

Complicating the scene were the hostages, who themselves were terrified and confused. One or two took immediate advantage of the distraction and fled further into the maze of curtains and darkness in the wings. Others clung together, too frightened to move, and that meant more blundering collisions and cries of alarm.

"They didn't plan this very well," said Asta.

"Neither did we."

The gunmen were now engaged in a desperate argument. There

was no point in Malcolm's wishing that all the hostages would vanish into safety: things were as they were. At some point the gunmen would work out that the only person who could have killed their leader was the hostage who had disappeared, and then they'd begin to look for him, and then they'd find the ladder, and then they'd look up, and then they'd shoot him.

But this was a gantry. It spanned the stage. Surely there'd be another ladder at the other end, and Asta darted away to look and came back: there was. A few moments later Malcolm had climbed down, and found himself in a similar black-curtained space at stage right.

And now what held him up was doubt. The one thing he must not do was make it more likely that innocent people would be shot, but how best to manage that? He might be able to find his way out of the building without being seen, but shouldn't he stay and try to find a way to save them?

"Just go," Asta whispered. "Don't be foolhardy. We can't stop them if we can't argue with them, and we can't speak their language. We can be much more use outside. How will it help Lyra for us to be shot dead in here? They'll do that as soon as they see you. Come *on*, Mal."

She was right. He moved towards the back wall: There must be a door in here somewhere. . . . And there was, and it was unlocked. Turning the handle very carefully, he opened the door and stepped through before closing it again. Now he was in almost total darkness, but in the dim glow of an anbaric fire alarm he could make out a narrow flight of stairs. Before going up, though, he looked back at the door, and sure enough, there was a bolt. He could hear the noise of arguing getting louder; someone was shouting, and there were feet running on the stage. More voices joined in from the auditorium.

He slid the bolt home with as little noise as possible.

Asta looked at him from the foot of the stairs, thinking, ??

"No," he said. "There's another door just along there."

He moved past the stairs and along a short corridor, seeing very little, but confident: Asta's eyes caught every photon there was to catch.

The door had a push bar, not a handle, like a fire exit.

"These make a noise," said Malcolm. "I wonder if I can do it without banging. . . ."

Left hand on the vertical bolt, right hand on the bar. Stop and listen. There was a distant hubbub, but it was voices, not shots. He eased the bar inwards, and felt the bolt slide down.

A waft of cold air, laden with the smells of size and paint and turpentine, came out of the dark as he pushed the door open. There also came the sense of a large space with a high ceiling.

"Scenery painting," said Asta.

"That means there'll be a door to the outside for deliveries. Can you see it? A big door."

"There's a bench right in front of you—a workbench—go left a bit—that's it. Now you can walk straight ahead. . . . Five more steps—here's the back wall."

Malcolm felt the wall and moved along to the right. Almost at once, his hands found a large entrance closed with a roller shutter, and next to it a normal-sized door. It was locked.

"Mal," said Asta, "there's a key on a nail beside the door."

The key fitted the lock, and a moment later they were outside the building and in a small yard open to the alley beyond.

Malcolm listened carefully, but heard nothing more than the normal sounds of urban traffic. There was nothing unusual going on: no police cars, no crowds of people rushing out, no gunshots, no screams. They went out and turned right to bring themselves round to the theater entrance.

"So far, so good," said Asta.

The theater foyer was glowing with light. It was empty—
Malcolm supposed that the staff had all fled. He stepped inside
and listened hard while Asta raced to the stairs and made for the
dress circle. Malcolm could hear voices raised from the auditorium, several voices, but not in anger or denunciation or pleading. They sounded like a large committee discussing a point of
order.

A minute went by, and Malcolm was about to move further in
when a small shadow appeared from the staircase, and Asta jumped
up onto the box-office counter to speak quietly.

"I can't make it out," she said. "The men with guns are on the
stage, and they're arguing with some people from the audience—
farmers, maybe, hard to tell, but some women too—and someone's
found a rug and laid it over the body of the man they shot, and they
brought the leader's body out onstage too, and someone was tearing
down a curtain to cover him with."

"What is the audience doing?"

"I couldn't see them clearly, but they're mostly still in their seats
and they seem to be listening. Oh, and Bryan is there! On the
stage, I mean. It looks as if he's taking minutes."

"No threatening, then? No guns?"

"They're holding their guns, but not pointing them at anyone."

"I wonder if I should go back in."

"Whatever for?"

That was a good question, in the circumstances. There didn't
seem to be much for him to do.

"Back to Calvi's, then," he said.

Calvi's was the bar where he'd arranged to meet Bryan Parker
earlier in the evening.

"Might as well," said Asta.

* * *

498

Thirty minutes later, Malcolm was sitting at a table with a glass of wine and a dish of grilled lamb. And as if they'd planned it, in came Parker. He pulled out a chair and beckoned a waiter.

"Well, what happened?" said Malcolm.

"They were horribly baffled. They ushered the hostages back onto the stage. We could see that something had gone wrong with their plans, but of course we had no idea what. I'll have the same as this gentleman," Parker said to the waiter, who nodded and left.

"What then?"

"Then there was a stroke of good luck. It turned out that Enver Demirel was in the audience. Heard of him? No? Conservative politician in the provincial assembly, young, very bright. He stood up and called out—and that took some courage, because the gunmen were very frightened, very jumpy—offering his help to moderate a discussion between all the parties. That was where the rest of us realized for the first time that their leader wasn't there, because, the way he'd been speaking before, he wasn't one for discussions of any sort.

"Anyway, they accepted Demirel's offer, and I must say—I was never an admirer of his—he was superb. Calmed everything down, explained it all to the audience as he went along. And then we heard what had frightened the gunmen: their leader had been killed, and no one had seen it happen, and the killer had vanished."

"Extraordinary."

"Then I decided to join in. All good copy. I offered my services as secretary to the discussion. Demirel recognized me and urged the men to agree, which they did. Little by little, you see, moving the whole thing towards talk and away from violence."

"Clever."

"And cleverer still. The big mystery was who had killed the leader. They found him in the wings with his neck broken. Had he

499

fallen? Had he been attacked? If so, by whom? There was no sign of anyone else around, and all the hostages were just as mystified as the gunmen, and just as frightened. That was the point when Demirel introduced the idea of divine justice. At least—let me get this right—he heard it in a remark from one of the hostages, and skillfully tended it, not putting out any ideas himself, just allowing time for that notion to develop. The dead leader had been the one who killed the farmer. The retribution occurred so quickly that it seemed very likely to have a supernatural cause."

"Quite possibly."

"Then someone asked if all the hostages who'd come up were still there. There was a count, and a lot of complicated yes he did no he didn't yes he was no he wasn't, and in the end they agreed that since every other explanation was impossible, it must have been the case that there had been an angel among the hostages, that he'd struck down the leader as punishment for shooting the farmer, and then vanished, probably flown back to heaven."

"No doubt."

"Or to Calvi's."

"Improbable," said Malcolm blandly.

The waiter brought Parker's food, and Malcolm asked for another bottle of wine.

"Anyway," Parker went on, "Demirel persuaded them to give up their guns into his charge, in exchange for which they could leave the theater and disappear. A discussion about that, and then they agreed. So that's what they did. I must say, I've changed my view of that man. It was brilliantly done. He moved the atmosphere of the whole thing, the whole complicated situation, away from passion and towards rationality, and once they'd got there, it was clear to everyone that even letting them get away without punishment would be better than a massacre. So in the end it was a fair outcome for everyone. Except the poor farmer, obviously."

"Quite. Bryan, there was a phrase that young man used—'the brotherhood of this holy purpose.' Have you heard that before?"

Parker shook his head. "New to me," he said. "Why? It sounds like the sort of slogan any of these fanatics might use."

"It probably is. You kept your promise, anyway."

"What promise?"

"To show me something interesting. Another glass?"

TWENTY-SEVEN

THE CAFÉ ANTALYA

The afternoon was far advanced; the sun had already set behind the mountains, and the air was cooling rapidly. Lyra had to move: she had to find somewhere to stay. She set off towards the center of the city, past apartment buildings and office blocks and government ministries and banks, and soon the daylight was all gone, and the light she saw by came instead from naphtha lamps hung outside shops or the more brilliant gaslights shining out from windows and open doors. The air was fragrant with the smells of grilling meat and spiced chickpeas, and Lyra realized that she was hungry.

The first hotel she tried turned her down at once: the receptionist's look of superstitious horror made it clear why. The second place did the same, with fulsome expressions of regret and apology. They were small places, family-run, in quiet streets, not the large glittering palaces that served statesmen and plutocrats and rich tourists. Perhaps she'd be better off in one of those, she thought, but shuddered at the expense.

The third place she tried was more welcoming, simply by being less interested. The young woman at the desk was perfectly indifferent as Lyra signed the register and took her room key, and turned back to her photo magazine at once. Only her dog dæmon seemed concerned, and whined softly and hid behind her chair as Lyra passed.

The room was small and shabby and overheated, but the light worked and the bed was clean and there was a little balcony overlooking the street. Lyra found that she could sit on a chair half in the room and half on the balcony and see along the street in both directions.

She locked the room and went out briefly, coming back with a greaseproof paper bag containing grilled meat and peppers and some bread, and with a bottle of luridly colored orange drink. She sat on the chair and ate and drank, finding little pleasure in the gristly meat and the sickly liquid, but thought grimly that at least she was keeping her strength up.

The street below was narrow, but clean and well lit. On the side opposite her balcony was a café whose pavement tables were empty but whose interior was crowded and bright. Shops to left and right sold hardware, or shoes, or newspapers and smokeleaf, or cheap clothes, or sweetmeats. It was busy; it looked as if everywhere was going to stay open long into the evening. People were slowly wandering along, or passing the time talking with friends, or sitting and smoking together beside a hookah, or haggling with shopkeepers.

She fetched a blanket from the bed, and put the light out, and settled herself comfortably to watch everything. She wanted to see people and their dæmons: she felt hungry for their completeness. There was a stout man, short, bald, mustached, in a voluminous blue shirt, who had been standing in the doorway of his shop when Lyra began to watch, and who showed no sign of moving except to step out of the way when a customer wanted to go past. His dæmon was a monkey with a bag of peanuts and a loud cheerful voice, who carried on a raucous dialogue with him and with any of the friends who stopped to pass the time. There seemed to be plenty of them. Another fixture was a beggar who sat on the pavement with a kind of lute on his lap, occasionally playing a mournful snatch of melody for a few bars before breaking off to call for alms. Another was a woman in a black headscarf who was involved in a long discussion with two friends while their children squabbled and stole sweets from the stall behind them.

Lyra watched: their dæmons observed the owner without seeming to, and prompted the children, who struck like snakes when he turned away for a second. Their mothers were quite aware of this, and accepted sweets from the children's hands without breaking off their conversation.

Occasionally a couple of policemen, guns at their waists, helmets low over their eyes, strolled along, looking at everything. People avoided returning their stare. Their dæmons, large and powerful dogs, stalked closely at their heels.

Lyra thought about the princess's story. She wondered what the dancer's name had been, and if there was a picture of her anywhere in the archives of a Levantine newspaper. What was happening, anyway, when people fell in love? She'd heard enough about her friends' love affairs to know that dæmons complicated the matter, but deepened it too when it worked. Some girls seemed to be attracted to this boy or that, only for their dæmons to be indifferent or even hostile. Sometimes it was the other way round: the dæmons passionately attracted, their people kept apart by dislike. And the princess's story had shown her yet another human possibility. Was it possible, though, as the old lady had said, for pretending to be in love to turn into actual love?

She looked down at the street again, huddling the blanket up around her shoulders. The stout man in the blue shirt was now smoking a cheroot, passing it up to the monkey dæmon on his shoulder, and talking volubly to two other men whose dæmons were sharing a bag of nuts between them, cracking the shells in their teeth and throwing them into the gutter. The lute player had found another tune, and had even gathered an audience of two children who gazed at him, hand in hand, the little boy nodding with his dæmon approximately in time with the rhythm. The women with the sweet-stealing children had gone, and the sweetmeat seller was busy folding and stretching a hank of red-brown toffee.

Gradually, as Lyra watched, she found her mood lifting. She'd hardly been aware of feeling anxious, but that was because anxiety was everywhere, built into the very molecules of the world, or so it had seemed. But now it was disappearing, like heavy gray clouds thinning and dispersing and finding their great banks of vapor drifting into wisps that wafted away into invisibility, leaving the sky clear and open. She felt her whole self, including the absent Pan, becoming light and free. Something good must have happened to him, she thought.

And she found herself thinking about roses and Dust. The street below her was saturated in Dust. Human lives were generating it, being sustained and enriched by it; it made everything glow as if it was touched with gold. She could almost see it. It brought with it a mood that she hadn't felt for so long that it was unfamiliar, and she welcomed it almost apprehensively: it was a quiet conviction, underlying every circumstance, that all was well and that the world was her true home, as if there were great secret powers that would see her safe.

She sat there for an hour, unconscious of the time, sustained by this new strange mood, and then went to bed and fell instantly asleep.

Pantalaimon was making his way south. And east. That was all he could tell. For as long as he could, he stayed beside water: river, lake, or sea, it didn't matter which, as long as there was somewhere nearby to dive into and swim away. He avoided towns and villages. As he traveled through rougher and stranger country, he felt himself becoming wilder, as if he were really a pine marten and not a human being.

But he was a human being, or part of one, and he felt just as Lyra did: unhappy, and guilty, and wretchedly lonely. If he ever saw Lyra again, he would run towards her, and he imagined her bending to greet him, arms wide, and they'd both swear eternal love and promise never to part again, and it would all go back to the way it used to be. At the same time, he knew it wouldn't, but he had to hold on to something in the dark nights, and imagination was all he had.

When he finally saw her, she was sitting in the shade of an olive tree on a hot afternoon, and she looked as if she was asleep. His heart leapt, and he bounded towards her—

But of course it wasn't Lyra. It was a girl a few years younger, maybe sixteen or so, with a shawl covering her hair and a mixture of clothes that hadn't been hers, because they were a mixture of expensive and shabby, of new and old, of the too-big and the too-small. She looked exhausted. She looked hungry and dirty. She'd been weeping before she fell asleep, or maybe even during the sleep itself, because there were tears still on her cheeks. She looked as if she'd come from somewhere in North Africa, and she had no dæmon.

Pan looked around very carefully and quietly, and looked at her from all sides, but he wasn't wrong: she was alone. Not even a dæmon as small as the smallest mouse was hiding near her, or curled up close by her head as it lay on a bank of dusty moss.

She was in danger, then. He leapt up into the olive tree above her, perfectly silent, and climbed high until he could see all around: the blue gleam of the sea, the near-white stone of the mountain on whose slopes the tree was growing, the dry green of the grass being cropped by a few skinny sheep. . . .

Sheep, so there might be a shepherd nearby. But Pan couldn't see anyone, shepherd or not. He and the girl seemed to be the only humans alive. Well, he could look after her, and pretend to be her dæmon, and guard her from suspicion at least.

He climbed down and settled at her feet to doze.

When she woke up soon afterwards, she sat up slowly and painfully, rubbing her eyes, and then, seeing Pan, jumped to her feet and backed away.

She said something, but he couldn't understand it. She knew he was a dæmon, of course, and she was looking for his person, and she was terrified.

He stood and bowed his head in greeting. "My name is Pantalaimon," he said clearly. "Can you speak English?"

She understood. She looked around again, wide-eyed and sleepy still, as if it might have been a dream.

"Where is your . . . ," she said.

"I don't know. I'm looking for her, and she's probably looking for me. Where's your dæmon?"

"There was a shipwreck. Our boat was sunk. I thought he must be dead, but he can't be, because I'm alive, I think, only I can't find him anywhere. What did you say your name was?"

"Pantalaimon. What's yours?"

"Nur Huda el-Wahabi." She was still dizzy from tiredness. She sat down slowly.

"This is too strange," she said.

"Yes, it is. But I've had a bit longer to get used to it, maybe. We've been separated for . . . Well, I can't remember, but it seems like a long time. When was your ship wrecked?"

"Two nights—three nights—I don't know. My family—my mother, my little sister, my grandmother—we were all in a boat, just a small boat, because of the men from the mountains—a big ship ran us down. We were all in the water, everyone, and the sailors in the big ship tried to save us, but some of us were carried away. I called and called until my throat was sore and my dæmon wasn't with me and I was so frightened and everything was hurting and in the dark I couldn't see anyone, anything, and I was sure I would drown, and Jamal would die, wherever he was—it was the worst thing I ever felt. But when the sun came up, I could see some mountains, so I tried to swim towards them, and finally there was a beach and I swam there and just fell asleep on the sand. I had to hide from people when I woke up, in case . . . You know."

"Yes. Course you did. I suppose Lyra must be doing the same."

"Her name is Lyra? I had to steal things, like these clothes. And food. I'm so hungry."

"How did you come to speak English so well?"

"My father is a diplomat. We lived in London for a while when I was younger. Then he was sent to Baghdad. We were safe until the men from the mountains came. Lots of people had to flee, but my father had to stay. He sent us away."

"Who are these men from the mountains?"

"No one knows. They just come from the mountains and . . ." She shrugged. "People try to escape. They come to Europe, but where . . . I don't know. I would cry, but I've cried so much, I haven't got any tears left. I don't know if Mama is alive, or Papa, or Aisha, or Jida . . ."

"But you know your dæmon is alive."

"Yes. Alive somewhere."

"We might find him. Have you heard of the Blue Hotel? Al-Khan al-Azraq?"

"No. What is that?"

"It's a place where dæmons go. Dæmons without their people. I'm going there myself."

"Why are you going there if your girl is somewhere else?"

"I don't know where else to go. Your dæmon might be there."

"What did you call it? The Blue Khan?"

"Al-Khan al-Azraq. I think people are afraid of it."

"It sounds like Moontown. Moon City, maybe. I don't know what it would be in English."

"Do you know where it is?" he said eagerly.

"No. In the desert somewhere. When I went to school in Baghdad, the other kids used to talk about this place where there were night-ghasts and ghouls and people with their heads chopped off, horrible things. So I was afraid of it. But then I thought it probably wasn't real anyway. Is it real?"

"I don't know. But I'm going to find it."

"Do you really think my dæmon could be there?"

She reminded him of the Lyra of a few years ago, before their estrangement: eager, curious, openhearted, half child still, but with the shadow of suffering on her.

"Yes, I do," he said.

"Could I—"

"Why don't we—"

They both spoke together, and stopped.

Then: "I could pretend to be your dæmon," he said. "We could go there together. No one would know, if we just behaved normally."

"Really?"

"It would help me too. A lot. Honestly."

Some way off down the slope below them, someone was playing a reed pipe. A thin musical knocking of bells followed it as the sheep began to move.

"Let's do that, then," said Nur Huda.

* * *

In the morning Lyra remembered the mood of calmness and certainty like a dream, incomplete but still powerful. She hoped she could retain it for a long time, and revisit it whenever she needed to.

It was going to be a warm day. Spring was coming, and for some reason that made her think of one of the papers she'd found in the wallet of the murdered Dr. Hassall: the brochure for the shipping line, listing the ports of call for a cruise on the SS *Zenobia*, with Smyrna being among the ports; and someone had written the words *Café Antalya, Süleiman Square, 11 a.m.* against the date of the ship's visit. That was several weeks away, but she could still go and look at the Café Antalya, and maybe have breakfast there.

First she went out and bought some new clothes: a flowered skirt, a white shirt, and some underclothes. Remembering the etiquette, she haggled the price down to what she felt was a respectable level. The shopkeeper was the man in the blue shirt, who was indifferent to her lack of a dæmon, though his own monkey dæmon jumped up to a shelf as far away as she could get; but Lyra managed to seem so calm and matter-of-fact that the monkey was merely disconcerted.

Then she went back to the hotel and washed her hair, toweling it roughly dry and shaking her head to let it fall where it would; and then she put on the new clothes and paid her bill, and went out to find Süleiman Square.

The air was fresh and clear. Lyra bought a tourist map of the city center and walked the half mile or so to the square, which was shaded by trees just coming into leaf and overlooked by the statue of a lavishly medaled Turkish general.

The Café Antalya was a quiet and old-fashioned place, with starched white tablecloths and dark wood paneling. It might have been the kind of place where a young woman on her own, let alone one without a dæmon, might have felt unwelcome; it had an air of old-fashioned masculine formality and style; but the elderly waiter showed her to a table with every courteous attention. She ordered coffee and pastries, and looked around at the other customers: businessmen, perhaps, a father and mother with a young family, one or two older men dressed with fastidious elegance, one wearing a fez. There was one man on his own, writing busily in a notebook, and while she waited for her coffee, she played an Oakley Street sort of game and watched him without looking directly. He wore a linen suit with a blue shirt and a green tie, and a panama hat lay on the chair beside him. He was in his forties or early fifties, fair-haired, slim, strong, and active-looking. Perhaps he was a journalist.

The waiter brought her coffee, a plate of elaborate pastries, and a little carafe of water. She thought, Pan would say I'd better eat no more than one of those. Across the café the journalist was closing his notebook. Without looking, Lyra knew that his dæmon—a small white owl, with large black-rimmed yellow eyes—was watching her. She sipped her coffee, which was intensely hot and sweet. The journalist stood up, put on his hat, and came straight towards her, making for the exit; but then he stopped in front of her, raised his hat, and said quietly, "Miss Lyra Belacqua?"

She looked up, genuinely startled. The glare of the owl dæmon on his shoulder was ferocious, but the man's expression was friendly, puzzled, interested, a little concerned, but most of all surprised. His accent was New Danish.

"Who are you?" said Lyra.

"My name is Schlesinger. Bud Schlesinger. If I said the words *Oakley Street* . . ."

Lyra remembered Farder Coram's voice, instructing her in his warm tidy boat, and said, "If you said that, I'd have to say, *Where is Oakley Street?*"

"*Oakley Street is not in Chelsea.*"

"That's true as far as it goes."

"It goes as far as the Embankment."

"So I've heard . . . Mr. Schlesinger, what on earth is going on?"

They had been speaking very quietly.

"May I join you for a moment?" he said.

"Please do."

His manner was free, informal, friendly. He was possibly even more taken aback by this encounter than she was.

"What—"

"How—"

They both spoke at the same time, and were both still too surprised to laugh.

"You first," she said.

"Is it Belacqua, or Silvertongue?"

"It was Belacqua. The other name is what I'm called now. Among friends. But—oh, it's complicated. How did you know about me?"

"You're in danger. I've been looking for you for over a week. There's been a general call for news of your whereabouts—that is, among Oakley Street agents—because the High Council of the Magisterium—you've heard about the new constitution?—has ordered your arrest. Did you know about that?"

She felt dizzy. "No," she said. "First I've heard."

"The last news we had of you was in Buda-Pesth. Someone saw you, but couldn't make contact. Then there was a report that you were in Constantinople, but that wasn't a definite sighting."

"I've tried not to leave a trail. When—why—what does the Magisterium want to arrest me for?"

"Blasphemy, among other things."

"But that's not against the *law. . . .*"

"Not in Brytain. Not yet. This is not a matter of public knowledge—there isn't a price on your head, nothing of that sort.

The council has let it be known discreetly that your arrest will be pleasing to the Authority. The way these things work now, a word of that sort will be sufficient justification to make it happen."

"How did you know who I was?"

He produced a pocketbook, and took out a printed photogram. It showed an enlargement of Lyra's face taken from the matriculation photogram Lyra and her contemporaries had posed for in their first term at St. Sophia's.

"There are hundreds of copies of this in circulation," he said. "With the name Belacqua. I was kind of on the lookout, not because I expected you to come through Smyrna, but because I know Malcolm Polstead."

"You know Malcolm?" she said. "How?"

"I did my doctorate in Oxford, oh, I guess, twenty years ago. It was around the time of the great flood. That's when I first met him, but of course he was just a kid then."

"Do you know where he is?"

"What, right now? No, I don't. But he wrote me a short while ago, enclosing a letter for you, under the name Silvertongue. The letter's in the safe in my apartment. He said to look out for you."

"A letter . . . Is your apartment nearby?"

"Not far. We'll go get it in a minute. Apparently Malcolm's on his way east. There's some big operation going on involving Central Asia—that's all he said—and we've heard something on the same lines from local eyes and ears."

"Yes. I think I know what that's about. It involves a desert in Sin Kiang, near Lop Nor, a place where . . . Well, a place where dæmons can't go."

Schlesinger's dæmon spoke. "Tungusk," she said.

"Like that," said Lyra, "but further south."

"Tungusk, where the witches go?" said Schlesinger.

"Yes. But not that. Like it, but somewhere else."

"I can't help noticing . . . ," he said.

"No. No one can help noticing."

"I'm sorry."

"Don't be sorry. It's relevant. I can do what the witches do and separate from my dæmon. But then he disappeared, my dæmon, and before I do anything else, I have to find him. So I'm going to a place called . . . the Blue Hotel. Or sometimes the City of the Moon, Madinat al-Qamar."

"There's something familiar about that name. . . . What is that place?"

"Oh, a story. Maybe just a travelers' tale . . . They say there's a ruined city there that's inhabited by dæmons. It might be nonsense. But I've got to try."

"Oh, be careful," said the owl dæmon.

"I don't know. Maybe they're ghosts and not dæmons. I don't even know where it is, exactly." She pushed the plate of pastries towards him, and he took one. "Mr. Schlesinger," she went on, "if you wanted to travel on the Silk Road to Sin Kiang, to Lop Nor, how would you go about it?"

"You specifically want to go that way rather than, say, by rail to Muscovy and then through Siberia?"

"Yes. I want to go that way. Because I think on the road I'd be able to hear a lot of news, gossip, stories, information."

"You're right about that. Well, your best bet is Aleppo. That's the western terminus, if I can put it like that, for one of the main routes. Join a caravan there and go as far as they'll take you. I can tell you the man to see."

"Who's that?"

"His name is Mustafa Bey. The Bey is a courtesy title. He's a merchant. He doesn't travel much himself anymore, but he has interests in many ventures, caravans, cities, factories, enterprises the whole length of the Silk Road. It's not one road, but I guess you knew that—it's a whole bundle of trails and roadways and tracks. Some go south round a desert or a mountain range, some go further north. Depends on what the caravan master decides."

"And if I went to see this man Mustafa Bey, would he be suspicious of me? Of the way I am?"

"I don't think so. I don't know him very well, but I think he's interested almost entirely in profit. If you want to travel with one of his caravans, just show him you can pay."

"Where can I find him? Is he well-known there?"

"Very well-known. The best place to find him is in a café called Marletto's. He's there every morning."

"Thank you. I'll remember that. D'you know why I came to this café today?"

"No. Why?"

Lyra told him about the shipping brochure, and the annotation marking the appointment in that very café. "It was found on the body of a man who'd just arrived in Oxford from Tashbulak, the place Oakley Street is interested in. He was a botanist, working with roses. We think that was why he was killed. But we've got no idea who was going to keep this appointment, him or someone else, or both."

Schlesinger wrote a note in his diary. "I'll make sure to be here on that date," he said.

"Mr. Schlesinger, do you work full-time for Oakley Street?"

"No. I'm a diplomat. But I'm bound to Oakley Street by old ties of friendship, besides actually believing in what they stand for. Smyrna is a kind of a crossroads; there are always things to watch, or people to keep an eye on. And once in a while, something to do. Now, tell me what Oakley Street knows about your present situation. Do they know where you are? Do they know about your plan to visit this Blue Hotel, if it exists?"

She thought for a few moments. "I don't know. There's a man called Coram van Texel, a gyptian from the Fens, a retired Oakley Street agent, who knows; he's an old friend, and he can be trusted. But . . . in the light of day, I'm not sure about the Blue Hotel anyway. It all sounds so improbable. Secret commonwealth business."

She used the phrase to see whether he'd heard it before, but he merely looked puzzled. "Now you've told me, I have to pass it on," he said.

"I understand that. What's the best way of getting to Aleppo?"

"There's a good train service twice a week. One leaves tomorrow, I think. Listen, Miss Silvertongue, I really am anxious about your safety. You look too much like this picture. You ever thought of a disguise?"

"No," she said. "I thought not having a dæmon might be a sort of disguise. People don't like looking at me, because they're frightened or disgusted. They look away. I've been getting used to that. Trying to be inconspicuous. Or invisible, like the witches. It works some of the time."

"Can I make a suggestion?"

"Of course. What?"

"My wife used to be on the stage. She's done this before a few times—changing someone's look. Nothing drastic. Just a few details to help people's eyes see someone different from you. Would you come to my apartment with me now and let her help you? We'll pick up Malcolm's letter at the same time."

"Is she at home now?"

"She's a journalist. She's working at home today."

"Well," Lyra said, "I think that might be a good idea."

Why did she trust this Bud Schlesinger? He knew about Oakley Street, and about Malcolm heading this way too, but an enemy might know those things and use them to trap her. It was partly her mood. The morning was sparkling; things were intensely themselves; even the Turkish general on the stone plinth had a roguish light in his eye. She felt she could trust the world.

So twenty minutes later she stepped out of the shuddering, creaking, ancient elevator in Schlesinger's apartment building and waited as he opened the door.

"Excuse the lack of domestic airs and graces," he said.

It was certainly a place of color. On every wall hung rugs and other textiles; there were dozens of paintings and several walls of bookshelves. Schlesinger's wife, Anita, was colorful too: slender and dark-haired and dressed in a scarlet smock and Persian slippers. Her dæmon was a squirrel.

As Schlesinger explained the circumstances, she examined Lyra curiously, but it was a professional curiosity, full of life and understanding. Lyra sat on a large sofa and tried not to feel self-conscious.

"Right," said Anita Schlesinger. She too was New Danish, her accent a little less marked than her husband's. "Now, Lyra, I'm going to suggest three things. One is simple: you wear a pair of spectacles. Plain glass. I've got some. The second thing is to cut your hair much shorter. And the third thing is to dye it. How d'you feel about that?"

"Intrigued," said Lyra carefully. "Would those things make a big difference?"

"You're not trying to fool your friends or anyone who knows you well. It won't do that. What you're trying to do is make someone who's got a picture in his mind of a blondish girl without glasses not look at you twice. They'll be looking for someone who doesn't look like you. It's superficial, but superficial is the level most interactions work at. Do they know you haven't got your dæmon with you?"

"I'm not sure about that."

"Because that's a pretty big giveaway."

"I know. But I've tried to make myself invisible. . . ."

"Hey! I'd love to do that. You must tell me how. But first, can I cut your hair?"

"Yes. And dye it. I can understand the reason—all you said makes sense. Thank you."

Bud brought Lyra the letter from Malcolm, and then he had to leave. He shook Lyra's hand and said, "Seriously, you're in real danger. Don't forget that. It might be safer to stay in Smyrna till Mal gets here. We could keep you out of sight."

"Thank you. I'll think hard about that."

Lyra was burning to read the letter, but she put it away for now and focused on Anita, who was keen to hear about the witches and their way of becoming invisible. Lyra told her everything she knew. And that led to Will, and how he'd worked the same sort of spell without knowing it; and that led somehow to Malcolm, and everything he'd told her about the flood, and how she'd never known about it when she was his pupil, and how differently she saw him now.

It was the sort of conversation she hadn't had for a long time, and she had no idea how much she'd missed that sort of easy, friendly chatter. She thought, This woman would make an irresistible interrogator. No one could help telling her things. She wondered how often Anita had helped her husband with Oakley Street business.

Meanwhile, Anita was cutting Lyra's hair, a little at a time, stepping back and looking critically, checking in the mirror.

"We're aiming to change the shape of your head," she said.

"That sounds alarming."

"Without surgery. Your hair's naturally wavy and thick and takes up a lot of space, even though it isn't very long. We just want to make it a bit self-effacing. The dye will make a bigger difference. But a lot of what you call being invisible depends on the way you hold yourself. I recognize that. I acted with Sylvia Martine once."

"Really? I saw her Lady Macbeth. Terrifying."

"She could put it on at will. I was walking down the street with her one day. We'd just been rehearsing and it was a normal sort of busy city street, people going past, not noticing anything. And she said—you know her name was really Eileen Butler—she said, 'Let's call Sylvia.'

"I didn't know what she meant. But we'd been talking about audiences, and fans, and followers, and she said that, and I didn't know what to expect.

"Well, her dæmon was a cat, as you probably remember if you saw her onstage. A perfectly ordinary cat. But something happened to him then, or he did something, and instantly he became—well, I don't know how to put it. He became more visible. As if a spotlight had come on, focused right on him. And the same was true of her. One second she was Eileen Butler, nice-looking, but just an ordinary passerby. The next second she was Sylvia Martine, and everyone in the street knew it. People saw her, they came up to speak, they crossed the street to ask for her autograph, and within a minute she was pretty well surrounded. It happened outside a hotel—I think she knew exactly what would happen, and did it somewhere where we could escape. The commissionaire let us in and kept everyone else back. Then she was Eileen Butler again. I wasn't a bad actress, but she was a star, and the difference is colossal, magical. Something supernatural about it. I was too shy to ask how she did it, *becoming* Sylvia in that way, but her dæmon had something to do with it. He said very little; he just—I don't know—became more visible. Extraordinary."

"I believe it," said Lyra. "I believe every word of it. I wonder if you can learn to do it. Or whether it's only possible for a few people."

"I don't know. But I've often thought it would be dreadful to have that sort of power and not be able to turn it off. Sylvia could manage it—she was full of good sense—but in the case of someone vain or silly, it would drive them mad in the end. Make them a monster. Well, I can think of a few stars like that."

"I want to do just the reverse. Can I see what it looks like now?"

Anita stood aside, and Lyra looked in the mirror. Her hair had never been so short. She liked it, liked the lightness, liked the air it gave her of being alert and birdlike.

"We've only just started," said Anita. "Wait till you see it dyed."

"What color do you suggest?"

"Well, dark. Not hard black—that wouldn't go with your general coloring. A darkish chestnut brown."

Lyra submitted willingly. In all her life it had never occurred to her to have her hair colored; it was curious to find herself in the hands of someone so good at this whole business, so interested in it, so knowledgeable.

After applying the dye, Anita made some lunch, just bread and cheese and dates and coffee, and told Lyra about her journalistic work. She was currently writing a piece for an English-language paper in Constantinople about the state of the Turkish theater. Journalism sometimes overlapped with her husband's diplomatic work, and she'd seen something of the crisis in the world of rose gardens and precious oils and perfumery. She told Lyra about the numbers of gardens she knew about that had been destroyed, and of the merchants who dealt in those goods and who'd seen their factories and warehouses burned down.

"It's happening much farther east as well," she said, "as far as Kazakhstan, apparently. A kind of mania."

Lyra told her about her friend Miriam, whose father had gone bankrupt. "That was when I first heard about it. Only a few weeks ago—it feels like a lifetime. Am I really going to be a brunette? Miriam wouldn't recognize me. She always wanted me to do more with my hair and so forth."

"Well, let's look," said Anita.

They rinsed out the dye, washed her hair, and then Lyra sat impatiently as Anita dried it.

"I think that's worked very well," she said. "Let me just . . ."

She ran her fingers through Lyra's hair, settled it slightly differently, and stood back.

"A success!" she said.

"Show me! Where's the mirror?"

It was a new face that looked back at her. Lyra's main thought, almost her only thought, was would Pan like this? But at the back of her mind was another: as soon as Olivier Bonneville finds me again with the alethiometer, he'll know I look like this, and then so will the Magisterium.

"Haven't quite finished yet," said Anita. "Put these on."

It was a pair of horn-rimmed spectacles. Now Lyra was a different person altogether.

"You'll have to go on doing all that witch stuff about being invisible," Anita reminded her. "That won't change. Dowdy. You need to be dowdy. Dull. Low-powered. You need dull clothes, not bright colors. And I'll tell you something else," she added, brushing Lyra's new hair, "you'll have to hold yourself differently. You've naturally got a springy, active way of moving. Think yourself heavy. Slow."

Then her dæmon spoke. He'd been watching all this, saying little, occasionally nodding with approval, but now he perched on the back of a chair and said directly, "Make your body heavy and slow, but don't forget what your mind's doing. You need to look like someone who's suffering from a depression of the spirits, because that makes people turn away. They don't like looking at suffering. But it's very easy to become depressed by mimicking it. Don't fall into that trap. Your dæmon would tell you that, if he was here. Your body affects your mind. You need to act, not be."

"That's it," said Anita. "That's your note from Telemachus."

"It's a very good one," said Lyra. "Thank you. I'll do the reverse of what Eileen Butler did to become Sylvia Martine, but not in my mind."

"And what are you going to do now?" said Anita.

"Buy a railway ticket for Aleppo. Get some dowdy clothes."

"The Aleppo train leaves tomorrow. Where are you going to stay tonight?"

"Not in the same hotel. I'll find another one."

"You certainly won't. You'll stay here tonight. Anyway, those glasses need adjusting. They keep sliding down your nose."

"Are you sure? I mean, about me staying?"

"Yes. I know Bud will want to hear more from you."

"Then . . . thank you."

The spectacles adjusted, Lyra went out in her new persona. She bought a dull brown skirt and as dowdy a sweater as she could find; she bought a ticket for the Aleppo train; and then she found a small café and ordered hot chocolatl. When it was on the table in front of her, a mound of whipped cream slowly subsiding into the liquid, she looked at her name on the envelope in his clear hand. It wasn't one of the heavy college envelopes, but a flimsy one of coarse yellowing paper, and it bore a Bulgarian stamp. How absurd to find her hands shaking as she tore it open!

> Dear Lyra,
>   I wish you'd keep still so I could catch up with you. This part of the world is becoming more unstable by the day, and the kinds of thing I can say in a letter are getting fewer

and fewer the more likely it is that the letter will have been opened before it reaches you.

If you come across an Oakley Street friend in Smyrna, you can rely on him with total confidence. Actually, if you're reading this letter, you know that already.

You're now being watched and followed, though you probably haven't noticed yet. And those who are watching now know that you've been warned about it.

I understand your reason for taking the route you've chosen, and why you want to travel through that particular region. I shall search for you there if our paths don't cross beforehand.

There's a lot I'd like to say to you, but nothing I want to share with the other eyes that may read this letter along the way. I've learnt a number of things I want to talk to you about: matters of philosophy not least. I want to hear about everything you've seen and felt.

I hope with every fiber of my being that you're safe. Remember everything Coram told you, and keep watchful.

> With the warmest of wishes,
> Malcolm

Lyra had seldom been so frustrated. All those general warnings! And yet he was right. She looked carefully at the envelope again and saw that the flap had been stuck down twice, the second time not quite over the first. When she wrote back, which she'd do as soon as she had paper and a pen, she'd have to write in exactly the same terms to Malcolm.

She read the letter through again twice, and then drank her cooling chocolatl and walked (carefully, dowdily, aware of everything around) back to the Schlesingers' apartment.

But before she even turned the corner into the quiet street where their building stood, she heard the sound of sirens, and the harsh engines of police cars or fire trucks, and she saw above the rooftops a plume of dirty smoke rising into the air. People were running; the engines and the sirens came closer.

She went to the corner of the street and looked round. It was the Schlesingers' building, and it was ablaze.

TWENTY-EIGHT

THE MYRIORAMA

Lyra turned away from the blazing building at once and walked steadily (dowdily, heavily) towards the center of the city. Her mind carried on half of a dialogue with Pan, urgent and frightened, but none of it showed on her face or in her bearing.

"I should stop—I should find out if they're safe—I know I can't—it would only make it worse for them, apart from anything else—it's because of me that it happened—whoever set the fire is probably watching to see if anyone runs out, or . . . I'll write to them as soon as—I can't stay here in Smyrna now. Got to get out as soon as possible. Who am I? What was my witch-name? Tatiana . . . And a patronymic—Tatiana Asrielovna. Maybe that gives too much away. Giorgio . . . Georgiovna. If only I had a passport in that name—but witches don't need *passports*—I'm a witch. A witch disguising herself as a, what was it, *dowdy* girl—depressed and dowdy—just so people don't look at me. Oh, God, I hope Anita and Bud are all right. Perhaps he's still at his office and doesn't know about it—I could go and tell him—but I don't know where that is. . . . I must be Oakley Street–ish about this.

If it was intended for me, then I'd be dangerous for them. What should I do? Get away. But the train doesn't leave till—oh, get *another* train. Where does the next train stop? No trains for Aleppo. There's one for a place called Seleukeia—Agrippa mentioned that! Go there today and . . . the Blue Hotel. The City of the Moon. Between Seleukeia and Aleppo. That's what I'll do. Maybe first find somewhere quiet and try the new method again . . . People get their sea legs and then they stop feeling seasick. . . . Perhaps I could try that. And get together with Malcolm. Yes! But I don't know where he is—the letter was posted in Bulgaria but he could be anywhere now—he could have been arrested—in prison—he could be dead. . . . Don't think like that. Oh, Pan, if you're not at the Blue Hotel, I don't know if I can go any further. . . . Why do dæmons go there? But I've got the princess's list of names in Aleppo—and that merchant there Bud Schlesinger told me about this morning, what was his name—Mustafa Bey. Oh, this is horrible. Danger all around . . . People who want to kill me—even the Master of Jordan only wanted to put me in a smaller room—not *kill* me—I wonder how Alice is now? Pan, we might not like each other much, but at least we're on the same side—and if they kill me, then you . . . you won't survive, in the Blue Hotel or anywhere else—self-preservation, Pan, if only for that—why did you go there? Why *there*? Did someone kidnap you? Is it a kind of prison camp? Will I have to rescue you? Who's keeping you captive? The secret commonwealth will have to help—if I get there—if I find Pan—if . . ."

The one-sided conversation sustained her for part of the way to the station. It was so hard to make herself move slowly, though, to be dull and depressed; every particle of her body wanted to run, to dart across the squares and open spaces, to look all around every second, and she had to keep a firm hold on the image she wanted to project. Being invisible was hard work, unrewarding, soul-crushing work.

She was passing through a district where a number of temporary camps had been set up for the people displaced from their homes further east. In the next few days, perhaps, these people would be trying to find passage across the sea to Greece, and perhaps some of them would suffer shipwreck and drown. Children were running about on the stony ground, fathers stood in groups talking or sat smoking in the dust, mothers washed clothes in galvanized buckets or cooked over open fires, and there was a barrier that was invisible and intangible between them and the citizens of Smyrna, because they had no homes; they were like people without dæmons, people missing something essential.

Lyra wanted to stop and ask them about their lives and what had brought them to this state of things, but she had to be invisible, or at least forgettable. Some of the young men glanced at her, but not for long; she felt their flickering attention like the touch of a snake's tongue, and then it withdrew. She was successfully uninteresting.

At the railway station she tried one counter after another until she found someone who could speak French, which she thought would be safer than English. The train for Seleukeia was a slow one, stopping at what seemed like every station on the way, but that suited her. She bought a ticket and waited on the platform in the late-afternoon sun, hoping she was transparent.

There was an hour and a half to wait. She found an empty bench near the cafeteria, and she sat there and kept watch all around while trying to seem invisible. She had one shock as she came to the bench and saw her reflection in the café window: who was this dark-haired stranger in glasses?

Thank you, Anita, she thought.

She bought some food and drink for the journey and returned to the bench. She couldn't stop her thoughts circling back to the Schlesingers' apartment building. If Anita hadn't spotted the fire soon enough . . . If she hadn't managed to get out . . . Thoughts that didn't bear thinking kept crowding in and shouldering aside her pretended passivity.

A train came in and disgorged a platform-full of travelers. Among them were several families who looked only a little better off than the people she'd seen in the camp and on the streets: mothers in heavy clothing and headscarves, children carrying toys or torn shopping bags or sometimes younger brothers or sisters, old men harassed and exhausted, carrying suitcases or even cardboard boxes containing clothes. She remembered the riverboat docking in Prague and the refugees getting off. Would any of these people make it that far?

And why was the cause of this great movement of people not reported in Brytain? She had never heard of anything like it. Did the press and the politicians think that it would have no effect on her country? Where were these desperate people hoping to get to, anyway?

She mustn't ask. Mustn't show any interest at all. Her only hope of getting to the city of the dæmons and finding Pan was to hold her tongue and restrain every instinct of curiosity.

So she watched as the newcomers gathered their possessions and slowly dispersed. Perhaps they'd make for the port. Perhaps they'd find a shelter in one of the camps. They might have a little more money than the people she'd seen shipwrecked, which had allowed them to take the train; they might find somewhere affordable to lodge. Before very long they had all left the station, and then Lyra found the platform getting busier with people from Smyrna itself, commuting home after their day's work. When the Seleukeia train came in, it filled up quickly with these commuters. She realized that if she wanted a seat, she'd better move quickly, and hurried to get on board, and found one just in time.

It was a corner seat. She made herself small and insignificant. The first person to sit next to her was a heavy man in a homburg hat who looked at her curiously as he set his bulging briefcase down beside him. It was only when his mongoose dæmon whispered in his ear, curling herself around his neck and peering myopically at Lyra, that he realized something was wrong. He said something sharply in Turkish.

"*Pardon,*" Lyra murmured, sticking to French. "*Excusez-moi.*"

If she had been a child, her dæmon would be a puppy abjectly wagging his tail and trying to appease this big, important, powerful man. That was the mood she tried to project. He wasn't happy about it, but as the only result of moving away from her would be that he'd have to stand, he remained in his seat and turned away in extravagant distaste.

No one else seemed to notice, or they were all too tired to care. The train steamed slowly from one suburban station to the next, and then out of the city and through a series of country towns and villages, the carriage gradually emptying as it went. The heavy man with the bulging briefcase said something as he stood up to leave, half to her, half to the other people nearby, but again no one took any notice.

After an hour or so the towns and villages thinned out, and the train gathered speed a little. The evening was advancing; the sun had vanished behind the mountains, the temperature in the compartment was falling, and when the conductor came through to inspect tickets, he first had to light the gaslamps before he could see.

The carriage consisted of a number of separate compartments linked by a corridor along one side. In Lyra's compartment, once the commuters had all got off, there were three other travelers, and in the new light of the gaslamp she studied them without looking directly. There was a woman in her thirties with a pale-looking child of six or so, and an elderly man with a mustache and heavy-lidded eyes, wearing an immaculate light gray suit and a red fez. His dæmon was a small and elegant ferret.

The man was reading an Anatolian newspaper, but not long after the conductor had lit the lamp, he folded the paper with great care and set it on the seat between himself and Lyra. The little boy was watching him solemnly, thumb in mouth, head leaning against his mother's shoulder. When the old man folded his hands in his lap and closed his eyes, the child turned to stare at Lyra, sleepy, puzzled, troubled. His mouse dæmon kept up a whispering conversation with the mother's pigeon dæmon, the two of them flicking glances at Lyra and looking away again. The woman herself was thin, drawn, poorly dressed, and seemed worn down by anxiety. They had one small suitcase, battered and clumsily repaired, on the rack above them.

Time went past. The daylight vanished, and the world outside the compartment narrowed to the reflection of the little space itself in the window. Lyra began to feel hungry, and opened the bag of honey cakes she'd bought at the station. Seeing the child gazing at them with obvious desire, she held out the bag to him, and then to his mother, who flinched as if in fear; but they were both hungry, and when Lyra smiled and gestured to say, "Please take one," first the little boy and then his mother slowly reached in and took one out.

The woman murmured a phrase of thanks almost too quietly to be heard, and nudged the boy, who whispered the same words.

They ate the honey cakes at once, and it was clear to Lyra that it was the first food they'd had for some time. The elderly man had opened his eyes, and he was watching the little transaction with serious and considered approval. Lyra held out the bag to him, and after a brief interval of surprise, he took a cake, and unfolded a snow-white handkerchief and laid it across his lap.

He said to Lyra a sentence or two in Anatolian, obviously in appreciation, but all she could do in response was say, "*Excusez-moi, monsieur, mais je ne parle pas votre langue.*"

He inclined his head, smiled with dignified courtesy, and ate the cake in several small bites. "That was a most delicious honey cake," he said in French. "Very kind of you."

There were two left in the bag. Lyra was still hungry, but she had some bread and cheese too, so she offered the cakes to the mother and her child. The boy was keen but anxious, and the woman at first tried to refuse; but Lyra said in French, "Please take them. I bought far too many for myself. Please do!"

The man translated her words, and finally the woman nodded and let the boy have one; but she wouldn't take the last for herself.

The man had an attaché case of brown leather, and he opened it and took out a vacuum flask. It was the sort that had two cups as part of the top, and he unscrewed them both and set them on the case next to him, where his ferret dæmon held them steady as he filled them with hot coffee. He offered the first cup to the mother, who refused, though she seemed to want it; and then to the child, who shook his head, doubtful; and then to Lyra, who took it gratefully. It was intensely sweet.

And that reminded her of the bottle of carbonated orange drink that she'd bought at the station. She found it and offered it to the child. He smiled, but looked up to his mother, who smiled too and nodded her thanks; and Lyra unscrewed the top and handed it to him.

"Are you traveling a long way, mademoiselle?" the old man said. His French was flawless.

"A very long way," Lyra said, "but on this train, only to Seleukeia."

"Do you know that city?"

"No. I shan't be there long."

"Perhaps that would be wise. I understand that civil order is somewhat disturbed there. You are not French, I think, mademoiselle?"

"You're right. I come from further north."

"You are traveling a long way from your homeland."

"Yes, I am. But it's a journey I have to make."

"I hesitate to ask, and if I am being impolite, I most sincerely beg your pardon, but it seems to me that you are one of the women of the far north, those known as the witches."

He used the word *sorcières*. Lyra, intensely wary, looked at him directly, but could see only courteous interest.

"That is true, monsieur," she said.

"I admire your courage in coming so readily among the lands of the south. I am emboldened to speak like this because I traveled a great deal myself at one time, and many years ago I was so lucky as to fall in love with a witch from the far north. We were very happy, and I was very young."

"Such encounters do happen," she said, "but in the nature of things, they cannot last."

"Nevertheless, I learnt a good deal. I learnt a certain amount about myself, which was no doubt useful. My witch, if I may call her that, came from Sakhalin, in the far east of Russia. May I know the name of your homeland?"

"In Russian it's called Novy Kievsk. We have our own name, which I'm not allowed to pronounce away from there. It is a small island, and we love it fiercely."

"May I ask what has brought you to travel among us?"

"The queen of my clan has fallen sick, and the only cure for her disease is a plant that grows near the Caspian Sea. Perhaps you are wondering why I am not flying there. The fact is that I was attacked in St. Petersburg, and my cloud-pine was burnt. My dæmon flew home to tell my sisters what had happened, and I am traveling like this, across the earth, slowly."

"I see," he said. "I hope your journey is successful, and that you return with the cure for your queen's malady."

"That is kind of you, monsieur. Are you traveling to the end of this line?"

"Merely as far as Antalya. My home is there. I am retired, but I still retain an interest in some business affairs in Smyrna."

The child had been watching them with the sort of exhaustion that is beyond sleep. Lyra realized that he was ill: how had she not seen that before? His face was pale and gaunt, the skin around his eyes dark and drawn. He needed to sleep more than anything else in the world, but his body wouldn't let him. He still held the half-empty bottle of orange drink, and his mother took it from his limp fingers and screwed the top on.

The old man said, "I am going to tell this little fellow a story." He reached into an inner pocket of his silk jacket and took out a pack of cards. They were narrower than ordinary playing cards, and when he laid one down on the attaché case on his knees, facing the child, Lyra saw that it showed a picture of a landscape.

Something jogged her memory, and she was back in that smoky cellar in Prague, with the magician telling her about cards and pictures. . . .

The card showed a road running from one side to the other, and beyond the road a stretch of open water, a river or a lake, with a sailing boat on it. Beyond the water was part of an island where a castle stood on a wooded hill. On the road, two soldiers in scarlet uniforms were riding splendid horses.

The old man began to speak, describing the scene or naming the soldiers or explaining where they were going. The little boy, leaning in to his mother's side, watched with those exhausted eyes.

The man laid another picture card next to the first. The two landscapes fitted together perfectly: the road moved on, and on this card a path led towards a house standing among trees at the edge of the water. Evidently the soldiers turned off the road and went to knock at the door of the house, where a farmer's wife gave them some water from the well beside the path. As he mentioned each event, each little object, the old man touched a silver pencil to the card, showing precisely where it was. The little boy peered closer, blinking as if he found it hard to see.

Then the old man spread out the rest of the cards in his hands facedown and offered them to the boy, asking him to take one. He did, and the old man laid it next to the last. As before, the picture seamlessly continued the landscape of the previous one, and Lyra saw that the whole pack must be like that, and it must be possible to put them together in an uncountable number of ways. This time the picture showed a ruined tower, with the road running across as ever in front of it, and the lake continuing behind. The soldiers were tired, so they went into the tower and tied up their horses before lying down to sleep. But flying over the tower was a large bird—there it was—a gigantic bird—a bird so huge that it flew down and seized one of the horses in each claw and took them up into the sky.

So Lyra judged to be what was happening, from the way the old man mimed the bird's flight and uttered the terrified neighing of the captured horses. Even the mother was listening closely, wide-eyed like her son. The soldiers woke up. One was about to fire his rifle at the bird, but the other held him back because the horses would certainly die if the bird dropped them. So they set off on foot to follow the bird, and the story went on.

Lyra leant back, attending to the old man's voice without understanding it, but happy to guess and watch the expressions come and go on the faces of the boy and his mother, and gradually enliven them both, bringing a flush of warmth to their sallow cheeks, brightening their eyes.

The old man's voice was melodious and comforting. Lyra found herself slipping backwards into slumber, into the easy sleep of her childhood, with Alice's voice, not so musical but soft and low, telling her a story about this doll or that picture as her eyes fell heavily, softly, closed.

When she woke up, it was some hours later. She was alone in the compartment, and the train was steaming steadily up a gradient among mountains, as she could see through the window: a starlit panorama of bleak rocks and cliffs and ravines.

After a moment's slow confusion, she suddenly thought: The alethiometer! She flung open her rucksack, plunged her hand inside, and found the familiar heavy roundness in its velvet bag. But there was something else on her lap, a little pasteboard box with a bright label saying MYRIORAMA. It was the old man's pack of picture cards. He had left it for her.

The light from the gaslamp was inconstant, flaring briefly before sinking to a faint flicker and then rising again. Lyra stood up and looked at it closely, but there was no means of turning it up or down. There must be a problem with the supply. She sat down again and took out the cards, and in one of the flares of light she noticed something, some words written on the back of one of the cards, in an elegant hand in pencil. They were in French:

> Dear young lady,
>   Please take my advice and be very careful when you
> reach Seleukeia. These are difficult times. It would be best
> if you did not even cast a shadow.
>   With my most earnest wishes for your well-being.

It wasn't signed, but she remembered the silver pencil he'd been using to point out details in the pictures. She sat there troubled and lonely in the inconstant gaslight, unable to sleep anymore. She found her bread and cheese and ate a little, thinking it might strengthen her. Then she took out Malcolm's last letter and reread it, but it brought her little comfort.

She put it back and reached for the alethiometer again. She wasn't intending to read it, or to use the new method: just to hold something familiar and be comforted by it. The light was too poor to see the symbols clearly in any case. She held the instrument on her lap and thought about the new method. All the time she was trying to resist the temptation to try it there and then. She would look for Malcolm, of course, but with no idea where to start, and it would be fruitless, and leave her sickened and weak. So she shouldn't do it. And anyway, what was she thinking of, intending to look for Malcolm? It was Pan she should look for.

She gathered the little cards together with an automatic hand. That was the phrase that came to her, as if her hand were purely mechanical, not alive at all, as if the messages from her skin and her nerves were changes in the anbaric current along a copper wire, not anything conscious. With that vision of her body as something dead and mechanical came a sense of limitless desolation. She felt not only as if she were dead now, but that she'd always been dead, and had only dreamed of being alive, and that there was no life in the dream either: it was only the meaningless and indifferent jostling of particles in her brain, nothing more.

But that little chain of ideas provoked a spasm of reaction, and she thought, No! That's a lie! That's a slander! I don't believe it!

Except that she did believe it, just then, and it was killing her.

She made a helpless movement with her hands—her automatic hands—which disturbed the little cards in her lap and sent some of them falling to the floor of the carriage. She leant down to pick them up. The first one she found showed a woman, alone, crossing a bridge. She was carrying a basket, and was herself wrapped up in a shawl against a cold day. She was looking out of the picture as if directly at Lyra, who saw her with a little jar of self-recognition. She set the card down on the dusty seat beside her, and picked up another at random and set it beside the first.

This one showed a number of travelers walking along beside some packhorses. They were going in the same direction as the woman, from left to right, and the bundles on the animals' backs were large and heavy-looking. Make them camels instead of horses, sweep away the trees and replace them with a sandy desert, and they could be a camel train on the Silk Road.

As faintly as a bell tolling just once a mile away on a summer evening, as tenuous as the fragrance of a single flower borne indoors through an open window, there came to Lyra the notion that the secret commonwealth was involved in this.

She picked up one more card. It was one of those the old man had come to in his story, the one with the farmhouse and the well among the trees. She saw what she hadn't seen before: there were roses growing over an archway outside the door.

She thought: I could *choose* to believe in the secret commonwealth. I don't have to be skeptical about it. If free will exists, and I have it, I can choose that. I'll try one more.

She shuffled the cards and then cut them and turned over the one on the top. She laid it next to the last. It showed a young man, a knapsack on his back, walking towards the packhorses and the woman with the basket. To the uninflected eye, he probably looked no more like Malcolm than the woman with the basket resembled her, but that didn't matter.

The train began to slow down. The whistle blew, and a lonely sound it made, which Lyra seemed to hear echoing among the mountains. There was a French poem she used to know, about a horn blowing in a forest. . . . There were isolated lights on the slopes, and then more lights, lit buildings and streets: they were coming into a station.

Lyra gathered all the cards together and put them with the alethiometer in her rucksack.

The train came to a halt. The name of the station, painted on a board, was not one she recognized; at all events it wasn't Seleukeia; and it didn't seem to be a large place, but the platform was crowded. It was packed with soldiers.

She moved further into the corner and held her rucksack on her lap.

TWENTY-NINE

NEWS FROM TASHBULAK

The message brought to Glenys Godwin by the Cabinet Office messenger was brief and to the point:

> *The Chancellor of the Private Purse would be obliged if*
> *Mrs. Godwin would attend on him this morning at 10:20.*

It was signed with what looked like a contemptuous and indecipherable scribble, in which Godwin recognized the signature of the Chancellor, Eliot Newman. It arrived at her Oakley Street office at nine-thirty, giving her enough time to cross London to the Chancellor's office in White Hall, but not enough to consult her colleagues or do very much more than to say to her secretary, "Jill, the time's come. They're going to close us down. Tell all the Heads of Section that Christabel is now in operation."

"Christabel" was the name for a long-standing plan to withdraw and conceal the most important of all the active papers. Christabel status was constantly reviewed, and only the Section Heads were aware of it. If the word got around as quickly as it could, the papers concerning the bulk of Oakley Street's current projects would be on their way to various locations—these to a locked room behind a laundry in Pimlico, those to the safe of a diamond merchant in Hatton Garden, others to a cupboard in the vestry of a church in Hemel Hempstead—by the time Godwin entered the office in White Hall to which she'd been summoned.

The assistant private secretary who met her at the door was so young, he could hardly have been shaving for more than a year, she thought, and he regarded her with exquisitely polite condescension; but she treated this junior functionary like a favorite nephew, and even managed to extract a little information from him about what she could expect.

"Frankly, Mrs. Godwin, it's all arisen from the forthcoming visit of the new President of the High Council of the Magisterium—but of course, I didn't tell you that," the young man said.

"A wise person knows when to keep things dark. An even wiser person knows when to let the light in," Glenys Godwin said gravely as they climbed the stairs. It was the first she'd heard about Delamare visiting London.

The assistant private secretary was duly impressed by his own wisdom, and showed her into the outer office before softly knocking at the inner door and announcing the visitor in deferential tones.

Eliot Newman, the Chancellor of the Private Purse, was a large man with slick black hair and heavy black-rimmed spectacles, whose dæmon was a black rabbit. He had been in office less than a year; Glenys Godwin had met him only once, and had had to listen to a lengthy and ignorant explanation of why Oakley Street was useless, expensive, and counter-modern—that being the latest way of describing anything His Majesty's Government did not like. Newman didn't stand up to greet his visitor and didn't offer to shake her hand. It was precisely as she had expected.

"This little department of yours, what d'ye call it, the . . ." The Chancellor knew perfectly well, but he picked up a paper and peered down at it as if to remind himself of the name. "The Intelligence Division of the Office of the Private Purse," he read fastidiously.

He sat back as if he'd finished a sentence. Since he hadn't, Godwin said nothing and continued to look at him mildly.

"Well?" said Newman. Every tone of his voice was designed to express barely controlled impatience.

"Yes, that's the full name of the department."

"We're closing it down. It's disrecognized. It's an anomaly. Counter-modern. A useless money pit. Besides which, the political tendency is iniquitous."

"You'll have to explain what you mean by that, Chancellor."

"It expresses a hostility to the new world we're in. There are new ways of doing things, new ideas, new men in charge."

"You mean the new High Council in Geneva, I take it."

"Yes, I do, of course I do. Forward-looking. Not bound by convention and propriety. HMG is of the opinion that that's where the future lies. It's the correct way to go. We must reach out the hand of friendship to the future, Mrs. Godwin. All the old ways, the suspicions, the plotting, the spying, the gathering of endless pages of useless and irrelevant so-called information, must come to an end. And that very much includes the ramshackle outfit you've been battening on to for years past. Now, we're not going to treat you badly. Staff will all be reassigned positions in the domestic civil service. You'll have a decent pension and some sort of bauble, if that's what you fancy. Accept with good grace and no one'll be any the worse. In a year or two, Oakley Street—yes, I know what you call yourselves—Oakley Street will have vanished forever. Not a trace left."

"I see."

"A team from the Cabinet Office will come over this afternoon to begin the transition. You'll be dealing with Robin Prescott. First-class man. You'll hand over everything to him and be out of your office and home pruning the roses by the weekend. Prescott will deal with all the details."

Godwin said, "Very well, Chancellor. The authority for this comes entirely from this office, I take it?"

"What d'you mean?"

"You represented it as a move towards modernity and away from the habits of the past."

"That's right."

"And that turn towards streamlined efficiency is strongly identified with you in the public mind."

"I'm pleased to say it is," said the Chancellor, a little suspicion creeping into his manner. "Why?"

"Because unless you manage the announcement with some caution, it will look like appeasement."

"Appeasing who, for God's sake?"

"Appeasing the High Council. I gather the new President is visiting soon. To do away with the very body that's done more than any other branch of government to curb Geneva's influence on our affairs would look to those who know about these things like an act of extraordinary generosity, if not actually abject self-damage."

Newman's face had darkened to a dull crimson. "Get out and put your affairs in order," he said.

Godwin nodded and turned to go. The assistant private secretary opened the door for her and accompanied her down the marble stairs to the entrance, seeming all the way to be on the point of saying something, and not to be able to find the words.

As they reached the great mahogany doors that opened onto White Hall, the young man finally found something to say. "Can I—er—could I perhaps call a taxi for you, Mrs. Godwin?"

"Kind of you, but I think I'll walk part of the way," she said, and shook the young man's hand. "I wouldn't tie yourself too closely to the Office of the Private Purse if I were you," she added.

"Really?"

"Your chief is cutting off the branch he's sitting on, and he'll take the whole office down with him. That's an educated guess. Cultivate some alternative sources of power. Always a wise precaution. Good day."

She left and walked up White Hall a little way before turning into the War Office and asking a porter to take a message to Mr. Carberry. She wrote a few lines on one of her cards and handed it to the man before leaving and making her way down to the gardens on the Embankment that faced the river. It was a clear bright day, with big dazzling clouds moving busily across the blue sky, and the air felt almost sparkling. Glenys found a bench near the statue of some long-dead statesman and sat down to enjoy the river. The tide was high; a string of barges pulled by a sturdy little tug was moving upstream, carrying a cargo of coal.

"What will we do?" said her dæmon.

"Oh, we'll flourish. It'll be like the old days."

"When we were young and full of energy."

"We're wilier now."

"Slower."

"Cleverer."

"More easily damaged."

"We'll have to put up with that. Here's Martin."

Martin Carberry was a Permanent Secretary at the War Office and an old friend of Oakley Street. Glenys stood up to greet him, and by unspoken agreement and long habit they began to stroll along together to talk.

"Can't stay long," Carberry said. "Meeting with the Muscovite Naval Attaché at twelve. What's up?"

"They're closing us down. I've just been with Newman.

Apparently we're counter-modern. Of course we'll survive, but we'll have to go a little undergroundish. What I want to know now, quite urgently, is what the new High Council in Geneva is up to. I gather the chief man's coming here in a couple of days."

"Apparently so. There's talk of a memorandum of understanding, which will change the way we work with them. What they're up to—well, they're assembling a large strike force in Eastern Europe. That's what the Muscovite chap's coming here to talk about, not surprisingly. There's been a lot of diplomatic activity in the Levant—Persia too—and further east."

"We've been aware of that, but our own resources are stretched, as you can imagine. If you had to put a fiver on it, what would you say this strike force was being set up to do?"

"To invade Central Asia. There's talk of a source of valuable chemicals or minerals or something in a desert in the middle of some howling wilderness, and it's a matter of strategic importance for the Magisterium not to let anyone else get at it before they do. There's a very strong commercial interest as well. Pharmaceuticals, mainly. It's all a bit *blurred*, to tell you the truth. Reports rely too much on rumor, or gossip, or old wives' tales. Our interest at the moment lies in keeping the peace with Geneva. We haven't yet been asked to contribute the Brigade of Guards, or even some secondhand water cannons, but no doubt we'd regard it favorably if we were."

"They can't invade anywhere without an excuse. What'll it be, d'you think?"

"That's what all the diplomacy's about. I heard that there is or was some sort of science place—a research institute or something— at the edge of the desert concerned. There were scientists from various countries working there, including ours, and they've been under pressure from local fanatics, of whom there are not a few, and the casus belli will probably be a confected sense of outrage that innocent scholars have been brutally treated by bandits or terrorists, and the Magisterium's natural desire to rescue them."

"What are the local politics?"

"Confused. The desert and the moving lake—"

"A moving lake?"

"It's called Lop Nor. Really an immense area of salt marshes and shallow lakes where earth movements and changes in the climate play Old Harry with the geography. Anyway, national borders are flexible, or changeable, or negotiable. There is a king who claims to rule there, but he's really a vassal of the empire of Cathay, which is as much as to say that it depends on the current state of the emperor's health whether Peking feels like exercising power or not. What's Oakley Street's interest in this?"

"There's something going on there, and we need to know about it. Now that we've been officially disrecognized—"

"Lovely word."

"A coinage of Newman's, I think. Anyway, now that we've ceased to exist, I want to cover as many angles as I can reach while I still can."

"Of course. But you've got a contingency plan? You must have seen this coming?"

"Oh, yes. This just adds another layer of difficulty. But this government will fall in the end."

"Very sanguine. Glenys, if I need to contact you at any point—"

"A note chez Isabelle will always find me."

"Right. Well, good luck."

They shook hands and parted. Isabelle was an elderly woman who had been an agent herself until arthritis had forced her to retire. She now ran a restaurant in Soho often used as an informal post office by people in the trade of intelligence.

Glenys walked along the Embankment. There was a tourist boat moving slowly past, with a loudspeakered voice pointing out the sights. The sun shone on the river, on the arches of Waterloo Bridge, on the distant dome of St. Paul's Cathedral.

Carberry had confirmed much of what she'd already suspected. The Magisterium under its new President was intent on capturing and possessing the source of this rose oil, and was willing to muster an army and take it several thousand miles to do so. Anyone who was in the way could expect to be crushed without mercy.

"Pharmaceuticals," said Godwin.

"Thuringia Potash," said her dæmon.

"Must be."

"They're enormous."

"Well, Polstead will know what to do," said Godwin, and anyone who didn't know her would have heard nothing in her voice but boundless confidence and certainty.

The doorman at the New Danish consulate in Smyrna said, "Mr. Schlesinger is busy. He cannot see you now."

Malcolm knew the procedure. He took a small-denomination banknote from his pocket and picked up a paper clip from the desk.

"And this is my card," he said.

He clipped the card to the banknote, which vanished at once into the doorman's pocket.

"Two minutes, sir," the man said, and set off up the stairs.

It was a tall building on a narrow street near the ancient bazaar. Malcolm had been here twice before, but this was a new doorman, and something about the district had changed. People were watchful now; an air of casual well-being had vanished. The cafés were largely empty.

He heard footsteps on the stairs and turned to greet the consul, but Bud shook his head, set his finger to his lips, and came down to meet him.

A warm handshake, and Schlesinger nodded towards the door.

"Not safe?" said Malcolm quietly as they walked along the street.

"Listening wires everywhere. How are you, Mal?"

"Fine. But you look a wreck. What's been happening?"

"The apartment was firebombed."

"No! Is Anita all right?"

"Got out just in time. But she lost a lot of work, and—well, there's not much left. You found Lyra yet?"

"Have you seen her?"

Schlesinger told him how he'd first seen Lyra in the café, and recognized her from the photogram.

"Anita helped her change her appearance a little. But . . . she went out before the place was bombed, and we never saw her again. I say *we* never did, but I've asked around, and it seems she went to a nearby café and read a letter, which would have been the one from you that I passed on, and then went to the railroad station and caught a train towards the east, but not the fast Aleppo train. One that stops everywhere and crawls to . . . I think Seleukeia is the final stop, near the border. That's the last I've managed to find out."

"And she still hadn't found her dæmon?"

"No. She had this idea he was in one of the dead towns outside Aleppo. But listen, Malcolm, something else has just come up. This is urgent. I'm going to take you to see a man called Ted Cartwright. Just up here." Malcolm was aware that Bud was checking in all directions, and he did the same, seeing no one. Schlesinger turned into an alley and unlocked a shabby green door. When they were inside, he locked it again, and said, "He's in poor shape, and I don't think he's got long. Up the stairs."

As Malcolm followed, he tried to place the name Ted Cart-wright. He knew he'd heard it before: someone had spoken it, in a Swedish accent, and there'd been a penciled scrawl on tattered paper. . . . Then he had it.

"Tashbulak?" he said. "The director of the research station?"

"Yup. He arrived yesterday, after God knows what sort of journey. This is a safe house, and we've arranged a nurse and a stenographer . . . but you need to hear it from his own lips. Here we are."

Another door, another lock, and they were inside a small, neat studio flat. A young woman in a dark blue uniform was taking the temperature of a man lying on the single bed. He was covered in nothing but a sheet. His eyes were closed, and he was sweating, and emaciated, and his face was blistered with sunburn. His thrush dæmon clung to the padded headboard, dusty and weary. Asta jumped up beside her, and they whispered together.

"Is he any better?" asked Bud quietly.

The nurse shook her head.

"Dr. Cartwright?" said Malcolm.

The man opened his eyes, which were red-rimmed and blood-shot. They flickered constantly without focusing on anything, and Malcolm wasn't sure if Cartwright could see him at all.

The nurse put her thermometer away, made a note on a chart, and stood up to let Malcolm have her chair. She went across to a table where boxes of pills and other medical supplies were neatly stacked. Malcolm sat down and said, "Dr. Cartwright, I'm a friend of your colleague Lucy Arnold, in Oxford. My name is Malcolm Polstead. Can you hear me clearly?"

"Yes," came in a hoarse whisper. "Can't see much, though."

"You're the director of the research station at Tashbulak?"

"Was. Destroyed now. Had to escape."

"Can you tell me about your colleagues Dr. Strauss and Roderick Hassall?"

A deep sigh, ending in a shuddering moan. Then Cartwright took another breath and said, "Did he get back? Hassall?"

"Yes. With his notes. They were immensely helpful. What was this place they were investigating? The red building?"

"No idea. It was where the roses came from. They insisted on going into the desert. I shouldn't have let them. But they were desperate; we were all desperate. The men from the mountains . . . Shortly after I sent Hassall home . . . Simurgh . . ."

His voice faded. From behind him Schlesinger whispered to Malcolm, "What was that last word?"

"Tell you in a minute. . . . Dr. Cartwright? Are you still awake?"

"The men from the mountains . . . they had modern arms."

"What sort of arms?"

"Up-to-date machine guns, pickup trucks, all new and plentiful."

"Who was funding them? Do you know?"

Cartwright tried to cough, but couldn't summon the strength to clear his throat fully. Malcolm could see how it hurt him, and said, "Take your time."

He was aware that behind him Bud had turned to talk to the nurse, but his attention was focused on Cartwright, who was gesturing, asking for help to sit up. Malcolm put his arm around the man's back to lift him up, feeling how hot he was, and how light, and again Cartwright tried to cough, racked with wheezing, hacking efforts that seemed to strain his very skeleton.

Malcolm half turned round to ask Bud or the nurse to bring another pillow or a cushion.

There was no one there.

"Bud?" he said.

Then he realized that Bud was there, on the floor, unconscious, his owl dæmon lying on his chest. The nurse had vanished.

He let Cartwright down gently and darted to Bud, and saw a syringe next to him on the carpet. An empty vial lay on the table.

Malcolm flung open the door and ran to the stairs. The nurse was already at the bottom, and she turned to look up at him, and there was a pistol in her hand. He hadn't noticed how young she was.

"Mal—" began Asta, but she fired.

Malcolm felt a crippling blow, but couldn't tell where he'd been hit, and he fell at once and slid tumbling down the stairs to lie half-stunned at the foot, where the nurse had been standing a moment before. He pushed himself up and then saw what she was doing.

"No! Don't do it!" he cried, and tried to scramble over to her.

She was standing inside the front door, holding the pistol under her chin. Her nightingale dæmon was shrieking with fear and fluttering at her face, but her eyes were clear and wide and blazing with righteousness. Then she pulled the trigger. Blood, bone, and brain exploded against the door, the wall, the ceiling.

Malcolm sank to the floor. A crowd of sensations was gathering around him, among which he could smell yesterday's cooking, and see sunlight glowing on the blood against the faded green paint of the door, and hear a ringing in his ears from the gunshot and the distant howling of wild dogs and a liquid trickle from the nurse's blood as the last pulsing of her heart forced it out of her shattered head, and the soft voice of his dæmon whispering next to him.

And pain. There it was. A throb of it, then another and another, and then one long, deep, focused, and brutal assault on his right hip.

He felt it, and found his hand wet with blood. It was soon going to hurt a lot more, but there was Bud to see to. Could he get back up the stairs?

He didn't try to stand, but hauled himself across the wooden floor and then up, step by step, with his arms and his left leg.

"Mal, don't force it," said Asta faintly. "You're bleeding a lot."

"See if Bud's all right. That's all."

He managed to stand up on the landing and made it into the sickroom. Bud was still lying unconscious, but he was breathing clearly. Malcolm turned to Cartwright, and had to sit down on the edge of the bed. His leg was rapidly stiffening.

"Help me up," Cartwright whispered, and Malcolm tried to pull him upright, with some difficulty, and leant him against the headboard. His dæmon fell clumsily on to his shoulder.

"The nurse—" Malcolm began, but Cartwright shook his head, which set off another bout of coughing.

"Too late," he managed to say. "She's paid by them too. She's been giving me drugs. Making me talk. And just now, poison . . ."

"Being paid—you mean, by the men from the mountains?" Malcolm was baffled.

"No, no. No. Them too. All part of the big medical—" More coughing, and retching too. A dribble of bile left his lips and fell from his chin.

Malcolm mopped it with the sheet and said quietly, urgently, "The big medical . . . ?"

"TP."

It meant nothing to Malcolm. "TP?" he repeated.

"Pharmaceut . . . funding. TP. Company lettering on their trucks . . ."

Cartwright's eyes closed. His chest heaved, the breath rattling in his throat. Then his entire body clenched and relaxed, and he was dead. His dæmon drifted into invisible particles and melted into the air.

Malcolm felt the strength drain out of his body as the pain in his hip grew more insistent. He should look at the wound; he should attend to Schlesinger; he should report to Oakley Street. He had never felt the desire to go to sleep so powerful and urgent.

"Asta, keep me awake," he said.

"Malcolm? Is that you?" came a blurred voice from the floor.

"Bud! You OK?"

"What happened?"

Schlesinger's dæmon was standing groggily and stretching her wings as Bud struggled to sit up.

"The nurse drugged you. Cartwright's dead. She was drugging him."

"What the hell! . . . Malcolm, you're bleeding. Stay there, don't move."

"She injected you with something while I had my back turned. Then she ran downstairs and I ran after her, like a fool, and she shot me before killing herself."

Bud was holding on to the end of the bed. Whatever drug the nurse had injected into him was short-acting, because Malcolm could see the clarity returning to his friend's face second by second. He was looking at Malcolm's blood-soaked trouser leg.

"All right," he said. "First thing we do is get you out of here and call a doctor. We'll go out the back way through the bazaar. Can you walk at all?"

"Stiffly and slowly. You'll have to help me."

Bud stood up and shook his head to clear it. "Come on, then," he said. "Oh, here, put this on. It'll hide the blood."

He opened a wardrobe and took out a long raincoat, and helped Malcolm put it on.

"Ready when you are," Malcolm said.

A couple of hours later, after a doctor Bud trusted had examined and dressed Malcolm's wound, they sat with Anita, drinking tea in the consulate, where they were staying while their apartment was being rebuilt.

"What did the doctor say?" said Anita.

"The bullet clipped the hip bone but didn't break it. Could have been much worse."

"Does it hurt?"

"Yes, a lot. But he gave me some painkillers. Now tell me about Lyra."

"I'm not sure you'd recognize her now. She's got short dark hair and glasses."

Malcolm tried to imagine this dark-haired girl wearing glasses, without success. "Could anyone have followed her to your apartment?" he said.

"You mean, was that why they bombed it?" said Bud. "Because they thought she was there? I doubt it. In the first place, we weren't followed when we left the café. In the second place, they know where I live anyway: there's no secret about that. For the most part the agencies leave each other alone, apart from the usual secret-service attentions. Bombing, arson—they're not the local style. I'm worried about what happened to her after she took the train to Seleukeia."

"What was she going to do there? Did she tell you?"

"Well, she had a strange idea. . . . It's the kind of thing anyone might think was crazy, but somehow as she spoke about it . . . In the desert between Aleppo and Seleukeia there are dozens, maybe hundreds, of empty towns and villages. Dead towns, that's what they call them. Nothing there but stones and lizards and snakes.

"And in one of those dead cities, well: this is what they say. Dæmons live there. Just dæmons. Lyra heard a story about it, oh, way back, in England, from some old guy on a boat. And she met an old woman here in Smyrna called Princess Cantacuzino, who told her about it as well. And Lyra was going to go there and look for her dæmon."

"You don't sound as if you believe it."

Schlesinger drank some of his tea and then said, "Well, I had no idea. But the princess is an interesting woman; there was a huge scandal about her years ago. If she ever writes her memoirs, there's a bestseller in it. Anyway, her dæmon had left her, like Lyra's had. If Lyra gets as far as Seleukeia—"

"What do you mean, *if* she gets that far?"

"I mean, these are bad times, Mal. You've seen the numbers of people fleeing from the trouble further east? The Turks have been mobilizing their army in response. They expect trouble, and so do I. That young woman's moving right into the thick of it. And as I say, if she makes it to Seleukeia, she'll still have to travel on somehow to this Blue Hotel. What'll you do when you find her?"

"Travel together. We're going further east, to where the roses come from."

"On behalf of Oakley Street?"

"Well, yes. Of course."

"Don't try and tell us that's all it is," said Anita. "You're in love with her."

Malcolm felt a great weariness oppress his heart. It must have shown in his expression, because she went on, "Sorry. Ignore that. None of my business."

"One day I'll write *my* memoirs. But listen: before he died, Cartwright said something about the men from the mountains who attacked the research station. He said they were funded by something called TP. Ever heard of that?"

Bud blew out his cheeks. "Thuringia Petroleum," he said. "Bad guys."

"Potash," said Anita. "Not Petroleum."

"Damn, that's right: Potash. Anita wrote a piece about them."

"It wasn't published," Anita continued. "The editor was nervous about it. It's a very old company. They've been digging up potash in Thuringia for centuries. They used to supply companies that made fertilizer, explosives, chemical stuff, generally. But about twenty years ago TP began to diversify into manufacturing as well, because that's where the profit was. Arms and pharmaceuticals, mainly. They're enormous, Malcolm, and they used to loathe publicity, but markets don't work like that, and they're having to adapt to new ways of doing things. They had a big success with a painkiller called treptizam, made a lot of money, and put it all into research. They're privately owned, no shareholders demanding dividends. And they've got good scientists. What are you looking at?"

Malcolm had reached uncomfortably into his pocket to take out a little bottle of pills. "Treptizam," he read.

"There you are," said Bud. "The name of every product they make contains the letters *T* and *P*. And Cartwright thought they were funding the terrorists? The men from the mountains?"

"He saw the initials on the trucks they came in."

"They're after the roses."

"Of course they are. That explains a lot. Anita, could I see that story of yours? I'd like to read about the background."

She shook her head. "Most of my files went up with the apartment," she said. "All that work."

"Could that have been the reason for bombing the place?"

She looked at Bud. He nodded reluctantly. "One of them," he said.

"I'm so sorry. But for now I'd better follow Lyra's trail."

"I told Lyra to seek out a guy in Aleppo called Mustafa Bey. He's a merchant. He knows everyone and everything. It's likely that she'll go to him first if she gets there. I would. Anyway, you'll find him at Marletto's Café."

* * *

Bud bought Malcolm some clothes to replace the blood-soaked ones, and a stick to help him walk, and went with him to the railway station, where he was going to take the express for Aleppo.

"What'll you do with the safe house?" Malcolm asked.

"The police are there already. Someone reported the sound of the shots. We got out just in time, but we won't be able to use it again. It'll all be in my report to Oakley Street."

"Thanks, Bud. I owe you a lot."

"Say hello to Lyra, if . . ."

"I'll do that."

As the train left, Malcolm settled himself painfully in the air-conditioned comfort and took out the battered copy of *Jahan and Rukhsana* from Hassall's rucksack, in an attempt to take his mind off the pain in his hip.

The poem told the story of two lovers and their attempts to defeat Rukhsana's uncle, the sorcerer Kourash, and gain possession of a garden where precious roses grew. It was highly episodic; the story had many turns and byways, and brought in every kind of fabulous creature and outlandish situation. At one point Jahan had to harness a winged horse and fly to the moon to rescue Rukhsana, who had been imprisoned by the Queen of the Night, and at another Rukhsana used a forbidden amulet to overcome the threats of the fire fiend Razvani, and further elaborations followed each adventure, like little vortices of consequence spinning away from the main flow. In Malcolm's view the story was almost insufferable, but the whole thing was redeemed by the poet's rapturous descriptions of the rose garden itself, and the physical world as a whole, and of the pleasures of the senses that were enjoyed by those who reached it in a state of knowledge.

"Either it means something," Malcolm said to Asta, "or it means nothing."

"My bet is on something," she said.

They were alone in the compartment. The train was due to stop in an hour's time.

"Why?" he said.

"Because Hassall wouldn't have burdened himself with it unless it meant something."

"Maybe it only meant something close and personal to him, and there's no other significance."

"But we need to know about him. It's important to know why he valued that poem."

"Maybe it's not the poem so much as this particular book. This edition. Even this copy."

"As a code book . . ."

"Something like that."

If two people each had a copy of the same book, they could send messages to each other by looking for the word they wanted and writing the page number, the line number, and the number of the word in the line, and if the book was unknown to anyone else, the code was practically unbreakable.

Alternatively, the particular copy could itself carry a message if the letters or words wanted were indicated in some way, by a pencil dot or something similar. The trouble with that method was that the message was equally readable by the enemy, if it fell into their hands. It was hardly secret at all. Malcolm had spent some time looking for such marks, and several times had thought he'd found some, only to conclude that they were flaws in the cheap coarse paper rather than anything intended.

"Delamare is Lyra's uncle," said Asta.

"So what?"

Sometimes he could be very slow. "Kourash is Rukhsana's uncle. He's trying to capture a rose garden."

"Oh! I see. But who's Jahan?"

"Oh, really, Mal."

"They're lovers."

"It's the essence of the situation that matters."

"It's a coincidence."

"Well," she said, "if you say so. But you were looking for a reason to find this book important."

"No. I already think it's important. I was looking for a good reason why. An accidental coincidence or two is just not convincing."

"On its own. But when there are lots of them . . ."

"You're playing devil's advocate."

"There's a good reason for the devil's advocate. You have to be skeptical."

"I thought you were being credulous."

They were fencing. They often did, with him arguing X and her arguing Y, and then in a flash they'd change sides and argue the opposite, and eventually something would emerge that made sense to them both.

"That place she's looking for," Asta said, "that dead town: Why d'you think dæmons live there? Is there somewhere like that in the poem?"

"Damn it, actually there is. Rukhsana's shadow is stolen, and she has to get it back from the land of the zarghuls."

"Who are they?"

"Devils who eat shadows."

"Does she get it back?"

"Yes, but not without sacrificing something else . . ."

They sat in silence for a while.

"And I suppose . . . ," he began.

"What?"

"There's a passage in which Rukhsana is captured by the enchantress Shahzada, the Queen of the Night, and Jahan rescues her. . . ."

"Go on."

"The thing is that he tricks her by tying her silk sash in a clever knot that she can't undo, and while she's trying to do that, he and Rukhsana escape."

He waited. Then she said, "Oh! The fairy of the Thames and the box she couldn't open!"

"Diania. Yes, the same kind of thing."

"Mal, this is . . ."

"Very similar. I can't deny that."

"But what does it *mean*, for things like that to turn up? It might be just a matter of temperament whether you find it meaningful."

"That would make it meaningless," he pointed out. "Shouldn't it be true whether you believe in it or not?"

"Maybe refusing to see is the mistake. Maybe we should make a commitment. Decide. What happens at the end of the poem?"

"They find the garden and defeat the sorcerer and get married."

"And live happily ever after . . . Mal, what are we going to do? Believe it, or not? Does it mean what it seems to mean? And what does *mean* mean anyway?"

"Well, that's easier," he said. "The meaning of something is its connection to something else. To us, in particular."

The train was slowing down as it moved through the outskirts of a town on the coast.

"It wasn't going to stop here, was it?" said Asta.

"No. It might just be slowing down because they're working on the next track or something."

But it wasn't that. The train slowed down even further, and entered the station at a crawl. In the fading afternoon light Malcolm and Asta could see a dozen or so men and women gathered around a platform from which someone had been giving a speech, or perhaps saying a ceremonial farewell. A man in a dark suit and a wing-collared shirt was stepping down, hands were being shaken, embraces bestowed. Clearly he was someone important enough for the railway company to change their schedules for. A porter in the background picked up two suitcases and came to put them on the train.

Malcolm tried to move, because his leg was stiffening, but the pain was relentless. He couldn't even stand up.

"Lie down," said Asta.

The train began to move once more, and Malcolm felt a great resignation settle over him like falling snow. The strength was draining out of him minute by minute. Maybe he'd never move again. His body was failing, and the sensation drew him back twenty years to that dreadful mausoleum in the flood where he'd had to go to the very edge of his strength to save Alice from Gerard Bonneville. . . . Alice would know what to do now. He whispered her name, and Asta heard and tried to respond, but she was dazed with pain as well, and when he fainted, so did she. The ticket inspector found her unconscious on his breast. A pool of blood was gathering on the floor.

THIRTY

NORMAN AND BARRY

Alice Lonsdale was sorting some linen, putting aside those sheets and pillowcases that could be mended, and tearing up for dusters and cleaning rags those beyond help, when Mr. Cawson the Steward opened the door and came in.

"Alice," he said, "the Master wants to see you." He looked serious, but then he never looked lighthearted.

"What's he want me for?" said Alice.

"He's seeing all of us. Collections for servants, I expect."

Collections was the term for an annual meeting between student and tutor at which the student's progress was assessed.

"Has he seen you yet?" said Alice, hanging up her apron.

"Not yet. You heard anything from young Lyra?"

"No, and I'm worried sick, I don't mind saying."

"She seems to have vanished off the face of the earth. The Master's in the Bursar's office, because they're redecorating his."

Alice had no particular anxiety about seeing the Master, though she had never cared for him, and since hearing how he'd treated Lyra, she detested him thoroughly. She knew she did her job well, and had enlarged the duties she'd originally been engaged to carry out to such an extent that in the Bursar's view, and in the Steward's, and certainly in that of the old Master too, she was essential to the smooth running of the college. In fact, two or three other colleges had taken the revolutionary step of appointing housekeepers of their own, in imitation, thus breaking a centuries-old Oxford habit of employing only male senior servants.

So she was confident that whatever Dr. Hammond wanted to see her about, it wouldn't be dissatisfaction with her work. In any case, that would have been a matter for the Domestic Bursar, not the Master. Curious.

She knocked on the door of the Bursar's secretary, Janet, and went in. Janet's dæmon, a squirrel, immediately scampered across to greet Ben, Alice's dæmon, and Alice felt a little shiver of apprehension, without knowing why. Janet, a slight, pretty woman in her thirties, was looking anxious, and kept glancing at the Bursar's office door. She put her finger to her lips.

Alice came closer. "What's going on?" she said quietly.

Janet whispered, "He's got a couple of men with him from the CCD. He hasn't said they are, but you can tell."

"Who else has he seen?"

"No one."

"I thought he was seeing all the servants."

"No, that's what he told me to tell Mr. Cawson. Alice, do be—"

The office door opened. The Master stood there himself, with a bland smile of welcome.

"Mrs. Lonsdale," he said. "Thank you so much for coming. Janet, could we have some coffee?"

"Of course, sir," she said, more startled than Alice, more nervous.

"Do come in," said Dr. Hammond. "I hope I'm not disturbing your work, but I thought we might have a chat."

Alice went in as he held the door. There were two men in there with him, as Janet had said, both seated. Neither of them stood up, or smiled, or offered to shake hands. Alice could project a beam (that was how she thought of it) of intense coldness when she wanted to, and she did then. The men didn't move or change their expressions, but she knew the beam had reached its target.

She sat down in the third chair in front of the desk, between the two strangers. Alice was slim, she could move with great elegance, she was not beautiful—she would never be that, nor pretty, nor conventionally attractive—but she could embody an intense sexuality. Malcolm knew that. She let it show now, just to disconcert them. The Master went behind his desk and sat down, making a meaningless remark about the weather. Still Alice hadn't said a word.

"Mrs. Lonsdale," Hammond said, having settled himself, "these two gentlemen are from a government agency concerned with matters of security. They have a few questions to ask, and I thought it would be better all round for the college if it happened quietly here in my presence. I hope everything is well with you?"

"Mr. Cawson told me you were seeing all the servants. He said it was just an internal matter. Domestic. He obviously didn't know about these two policemen."

"Not policemen, Mrs. Lonsdale. Civil servants, perhaps? And as I say, I thought it best to maintain a certain discretion."

"In case I wouldn't come if I heard they were here?"

"Oh, I'm sure you know where your duty lies, Mrs. Lonsdale. Mr. Manton, would you like to begin?"

The older of the two men was sitting on Alice's left. She looked at him just once, and saw a blandly good-looking face, a neat gray suit and a striped tie, and the body of a man too interested in weight lifting. His dæmon was a wolf.

"Mrs. Lonsdale," he said. "My name is Captain Manton. I—"

"No, it isn't," she said. "Captain isn't a name; it's a rank. Captain in what, anyway? You look like a secret policeman. Is that what you are?"

As she spoke to him, she looked directly at the Master. He returned her gaze with no expression at all.

"We don't have secret police in this country, Mrs. Lonsdale," the man replied. "Captain is my rank, as you observe. I'm an officer in the regular army, seconded for security duties. My colleague here is Sergeant Topham. We're interested in a young woman you know. Lyra Belacqua."

"Belacqua's not her name."

"I believe she goes by the nickname Silvertongue. But legally that is not her name. Where is she, Mrs. Lonsdale?"

"Fuck off," said Alice calmly. Her eyes were still on the Master's face, and his expression hadn't changed in the slightest. However, a delicate pink was beginning to show in his cheeks.

"That attitude isn't going to help you," said Manton. "At this moment in time, in this informal setting, it's just bad manners. But I should warn you—"

The door opened, and Janet came in with a tray.

"Thank you, Janet," the Master said. "Just leave it on the desk, if you would."

Janet couldn't help looking at Alice, whose gaze was still fixed on the Master.

Alice said to the agent, "Yes? You were going to warn me about something?"

A tiny frown appeared on Hammond's forehead, and he glanced at Janet. "Just leave the tray," he said.

"I'm still waiting," said Alice. "Someone was going to warn me about something."

Janet put the tray down. Her hands were shaking. She crossed to the door, almost tiptoeing, and went out. Hammond sat forward and began to pour the coffee.

"That really wasn't very wise, Mrs. Lonsdale," said Manton.

"I thought it was quite clever."

"You're putting your friend in danger."

"I don't know how you work that out. Am *I* in danger?"

The Master passed one cup to Manton, another to his colleague. "I think it would really help, Mrs. Lonsdale," he said, "if you simply answered the questions."

"Alice? May I call you Alice?" said Manton.

"No."

"Very well. Mrs. Lonsdale. We're concerned about the well-being of the young woman—young lady—who used to be in your care at Jordan College. Lyra Belacqua."

He said the name firmly. Alice said nothing. Hammond was now watching, narrow-eyed.

"Where is she?" said the other man, Topham. It was the first time he'd spoken.

"I don't know," said Alice.

"Are you in contact with her?"

"No."

"Did you know where she was going when she left?"

"No."

"When did you last see her?"

"A month, maybe. I don't know. You're from the CCD, aren't you?"

"That's neither here nor—"

"I bet you are. I ask that because some of your thugs came here, came to this college, to her room, the last day I saw her. Got themselves let into a place that ought to have been safe. Made a right mess of it. So you'll have a record of that date. That's when I last knew where she was. As far as I know, you might have taken her yourselves since then. She might be locked up in one of your filthy dungeons right now. Have you looked?"

She was still staring at Hammond. The pink had left his cheeks, which were now becoming pale.

"I believe you know more than you're telling us, Mrs. Lonsdale," said Manton.

"Oh, is that what you believe? And is it true because you believe it?"

"I think you know more than—"

"You answer my question, and I might answer yours."

"I'm not playing a game, Mrs. Lonsdale. I have the authority to ask questions, and if you don't answer them, I'll arrest you."

"I thought a place like Jordan College was safe from this sort of bullying interference. Was I wrong, Dr. Hammond?"

"There used to be a concept known as scholastic sanctuary," said the Master, "but that's long out of date. In any case, it only offered protection to Scholars. College servants have to answer questions here, just as they do outside. I really advise you to answer, Mrs. Lonsdale."

"Why?"

"Cooperate with these gentlemen, and the college will make sure you have legal representation. But if you adopt an attitude of truculent hostility, there's little I can do to help."

"Truculent hostility," she said. "I like the sound of that."

"I'll ask you again, Mrs. Lonsdale," said Manton. "Where is Lyra Belacqua?"

"I don't know where she is. She's traveling."

"Where is she going?"

"Dunno. She never told me."

"Well, you see, that's one thing I don't believe. You're very close to that young woman. Known her all her life, so I understand. I don't believe she'd just take off on a whim and never tell you where she was going."

"On a whim? She left because your thugs were chasing her. She was afraid, and I don't blame her. There used to be a time when there was justice in this country. I don't know if you remember it, Dr. Hammond. Maybe you were somewhere else. But in my lifetime it used to be that you had to have cause to arrest someone, and—what did you call it?—*truculent hostility* wasn't cause enough."

"But that's not what the problem is," said Manton. "You can be as truculent as you like; it makes no difference to me. I'm not interested. If I arrest you, it won't be because of your emotional attitude but because you refuse to answer a question. I'll ask you again—"

"I've answered it. I've told you I don't know where she is."

"And I don't believe you. I think you do, and I'm going to make damn sure you tell me."

"And how are you going to make damn sure? You going to lock me up? Torture me? What?"

Manton laughed. Topham said, "I don't know what lurid stories you've been reading, but we don't torture people in this country."

"Is that true?" Alice asked Hammond.

"Of course. Torture is forbidden under English law."

Before any of them could react, Alice stood up and went swiftly to the door. Her dæmon, Ben, usually self-contained and even languid, was quite capable of ferocity, and he snarled and snapped at the dæmons of the two CCD men to keep them back while Alice opened the door and went out into Janet's office.

Janet looked up from her desk in alarm. The Bursar, Mr. Stringer, had arrived and was standing beside her, sorting through some letters. Alice had time to say, "Janet—Mr. Stringer—witnesses—" before Topham caught hold of her left arm.

Janet said, "Alice! What—"

567

The Bursar stared in astonishment, and his dæmon fluttered from one shoulder to the other. A moment later, Alice swung her right hand round and slapped Topham's face hard. Janet gasped. Ben and the other two dæmons were snarling, biting, grappling, and Topham kept a tight grip on Alice's arm, and then spun her round and slammed the arm up behind her back.

"Tell people!" Alice cried. "Tell the whole college. Tell people outside! I'm being arrested for—"

"That's enough," said Manton, who had come to join Topham, and who now took hold of Alice's other arm, in spite of her struggles.

"This is what happens now in this college," Alice said, "under that man. This is what he allows. This is the way he likes to—"

Manton shouted to drown her voice. "Alice Lonsdale, I'm arresting you for obstructing an officer in the performance of his duty—"

"They're trying to find Lyra!" Alice shouted. "That's who they really want! Tell everyone—"

She felt her arms pulled backwards and tried to go with it, but then the click of a lock and a hard metal edge digging into her wrists told her she was pinioned. She fell still. No point in fighting handcuffs.

"Dr. Hammond, I must protest—" the Bursar began, as the Master came out of the inner office.

Topham had slipped a chain around Ben's neck, attached to a long, stout stick wrapped in leather. It was humiliating for the dæmon, and he fought furiously, snarling and tearing and snapping. Topham was good at this, trained, practiced, and ruthless. Ben had to submit. Alice knew, though, that Topham would have a hard time when he tried to take the chain off.

Hammond said to the Bursar, "Raymond, this is a sad and quite unnecessary business. I do beg your pardon. I was quite clearly wrong to think we could deal with it tactfully."

"But why is it necessary to use this degree of force? I'm absolutely appalled, Master. Mrs. Lonsdale is a college servant of long standing."

"These men en't ordinary police, Mr. Stringer," Alice said. "They're—"

"Take her outside," said Manton.

Topham began to pull, and she resisted.

"Tell people!" Alice shouted. "Tell everyone you know! Janet, tell Norman and Barry—"

Topham pulled so hard she lost her footing and fell on the floor. Ben plunged and snarled and fought at the end of the chain, his teeth snapping an inch from Manton's throat.

"Raymond, step inside with me for a moment" were the last words Alice heard from the Master, as she saw him put his arm around the Bursar's shoulders and draw him into the inner office. The last thing she saw was Janet's terrified face, and then she felt the prick of a sharp needle in her shoulder, and she lost consciousness.

Quite early that afternoon, as soon as Janet, the Bursar's secretary, could get away, she cycled hard up the Woodstock Road towards the Wolvercote turn. Her squirrel dæmon, Axel, sat in the basket on the handlebars, cold and fearful.

Janet had often been to the Trout with Alice and other friends. She knew at once what Alice's last words meant: Norman and Barry were the two peacocks at the inn. The original Norman and Barry had drowned in the great flood, but their successors always bore the same names, because Malcolm's mother said it saved time.

She pedaled hard through Wolvercote and along to Godstow, and turned in at the garden of the Trout, hot and breathless.

"Your hair's all over the place," said Axel.

"Oh, for goodness' sake. Stop fussing."

She smoothed it down and went into the parlor. It was a quiet time of day; there were only two drinkers in the bar, gossiping by the fire; Mrs. Polstead was polishing glasses, and smiled a welcome.

"Don't usually see you at this time of day," she said. "Afternoon off?"

"I need to tell you something urgent," Janet said in her quietest voice. The drinkers by the fire took no notice.

Mrs. Polstead said, "Come into the Terrace Room," and led the way along the corridor. The two dæmons, squirrel and badger, followed them close behind.

As soon as the door was closed, Janet said, "Alice Lonsdale. She's been arrested."

"*What?*"

Janet told her what had happened. "And she said, as they took her away, she said to me, 'Tell Norman and Barry,' and of course I knew she didn't mean the peacocks, I knew she meant you and Reg. I don't know what to do. It was awful."

"CCD, you think?"

"Oh, yes. No doubt at all."

"And the Master didn't do anything to stop it?"

"He was on their side! He was helping them! But it's all round college now, obviously, about Alice, and everyone's furious. Like they were when he took Lyra's rooms away, and then when she vanished. But there's nothing you can do, is there? He hasn't broken any laws; it's quite within his power. . . . But poor Alice . . . Good for her, though, she got in a good slap on one of those thugs. . . ."

"I imagine she would. You wouldn't want to get on the wrong side of Alice. But the Bursar, though. What did he say?"

"After he came out of the office with the Master, he was—I don't know how to put it—subdued. Not himself. Ashamed, even. It's a horrible place now, Jordan," Janet finished passionately.

"It wants clearing out," said Brenda. "Why don't you come with me?"

"Where?"

"Jericho. I'll tell you why on the way."

The two women cycled together, urgently, along the towpath through Port Meadow, down to the boatyard, over the footbridge, and along Walton Well Road and into Jericho.

Malcolm's mother had known Hannah Relf almost as long as he had, and knew she'd want to know at once about this. Brenda Polstead had a shrewd idea about the secret hinterland her son shared with Dame Hannah, although she'd never asked either of them about it. She knew Hannah would know the right people to talk to, who'd be able to help, who else to warn.

They turned into Cranham Street, but stopped at once.

"That's her house," said Brenda.

Outside Hannah's house stood an anbaric van, and a man was putting several boxes in the back. They watched as he came out twice, each time with an armful of cardboard boxes or files.

"That's one of the men from this morning," Janet whispered.

They pushed their bicycles along the pavement, towards the van. As Topham came out with a third armful of files, he turned and saw them. He glared at them, but said nothing and shut the van before going back inside.

"Come on," said Brenda.

"What are we going to do?"

"We're just going to call on Hannah. Perfectly normal thing to do."

Janet followed as Brenda pushed her bike forthrightly up to the house and leant it on the little garden wall. Brenda's badger dæmon, broad-snouted, heavy-shouldered, was close at her heels as she rang the doorbell. Janet waited a few feet further back.

There were voices inside, male voices, and Hannah's too. Theirs were raised and hers wasn't. Brenda rang the doorbell again. She looked at Janet, who looked back at this stocky woman in her fifties, in her tweed overcoat that was a little too tight, with her expression of calm determination. Janet saw Malcolm very clearly in his mother at that moment, and she had admired him greatly (and silently) for a long time.

The door opened, and Brenda turned back to face the other man, the one who was in charge.

"Yes?" he said, cold and hard.

"Well, who are you, then?" said Brenda. "We've come to visit my friend Hannah. Are you doing some work for her?"

"She's busy at the moment. You'll have to come back later."

"No, she'll see me now. She's expecting me. Hannah," she called, loud and clear. "It's Brenda. Can I come in?"

"Brenda!" Hannah called, and her voice sounded tight and high-pitched, and then was cut off.

"What's going on?" said Brenda to the captain.

"It's absolutely nothing to do with you. Dame Relf is helping us with some important inquiries. I'm going to ask you to—"

"*Dame Relf,*" said Brenda with powerful scorn. "Get out of the way, you ignorant bully. Hannah! We're coming in."

Before the man's dæmon could do more than snarl, Brenda's badger had the wolf's paw in his crushing jaws and was shouldering her out of the way. The captain put his hands on Brenda's breast and tried to push her back, but she swung her right hand and cracked him so hard on the side of the head that he stumbled and nearly fell.

"Topham!" he called.

Brenda was past him already and at the sitting room door. She saw Hannah inside, sitting upright and uncomfortable as the other man twisted her arm behind her back.

"What do you think you're doing?" Brenda said.

Behind her she could hear a scuffle, and Janet said loudly, "Don't you touch me!"

Hannah said, "Brenda—be careful—" Topham twisted her arm further, and Hannah grimaced.

"Let her go at once," Brenda demanded. "Take your hands off, stand back, move right away. Go on."

Topham's reply was to twist even harder. Hannah couldn't help a little gasp of pain.

Suddenly something cannoned into Brenda's back and she fell forward into the little room, right over the chair Hannah was sitting in. Janet fell with her—Manton had flung her forward to shake her hands off his sleeves—and all three women tumbled onto the hearth, just a forearm's length away from the fire.

Topham had lost his grip on Hannah's arm, and under the impact of the other two he fell back against the glass cabinet that held Hannah's collection of porcelain, crashing with it to the floor.

Brenda was the first to stand up, and in her hand was the poker from the little stand of fire irons. Janet, in imitation, had picked up the shovel. Hannah had fallen badly and didn't seem able to move, but Brenda stepped across her and confronted the two men implacably.

"Now turn around, go outside, and leave," she said. "You're not getting any further with this. I don't know who you think you are or what you think you're doing, but by God you're not going to get away with it."

"Put that down," said Manton to Brenda. "I warn you—"

He tried to seize it. She swiped him hard across the wrist, and he took a step backwards.

Topham was still struggling to get up from the broken frame and shattered glass of the cabinet. Brenda glanced at him and was pleased to see him bleeding from a cut hand.

"And *you*," Brenda said, "how dare you manhandle an elderly woman, you cowardly thug. Go on, get out."

"All those boxes—" said Janet.

"Yes, stealing as well. You can take them out of your van before you go."

"I remember you," said Manton to Janet. "You're the secretary from Jordan College. You can say goodbye to that job."

"And what have you done with Alice Lonsdale?" Brenda said. "Where have you taken her? What's she supposed to have done?"

Janet was trembling with shock, but Brenda seemed to have no fear, confronting the two CCD men as if all the moral power in the situation belonged to her, which it did.

"You seem to be unaware that we have authority to carry out investigations—" Manton began, but Brenda's voice overwhelmed his.

"No, you haven't, you thief, you coward, you thug. No one has the authority to come into anyone's house without a warrant—you know that, and I know that. Everyone knows it. Nor do you have the authority to arrest people without a cause. Why did you arrest Alice Lonsdale?"

"Nothing to do with—"

"It's got everything to do with me. I've known that woman since she was a child. There's not a criminal bone in her body, and she's been a first-rate servant to Jordan College too. What did you do to the Master to make him give her up?"

"That's got nothing—"

"You can't give me a reason because there isn't one, you wretch, you bully, you sneaking villain. What have you done with her? Tell me!"

Janet was helping Hannah get up. The sleeve of the old woman's cardigan was scorched, even burned: she had actually fallen on the fire for a moment, but hadn't uttered a sound. Burning pieces of coal were beginning to scorch the hearthrug, and Janet bent to scoop them up quickly with the shovel. Meanwhile, Topham was picking a piece of glass out of his hand, and Manton was turning away from Brenda's fierce demand.

"Come on," he said to the sergeant.

"You're not giving up?" said Topham.

"Waste of time. Outside now."

"We'll find her," said Brenda. "We'll have her out of your custody, you lawless vermin. The day'll come when the bloody CCD is drummed right out of this country with your tails between your legs."

"We en't—" began Topham, but Manton said, "Enough, Sergeant. That's enough. On our way."

"Captain, we could *take her*."

"Not worth the trouble. We know *you*," he said, looking at Janet, "and we'll have *you* before long," he went on, looking at Hannah, "and we'll find out who *you* are easy enough, and you'll be in real trouble," he finished, looking at Brenda.

Just the coldness in his eyes was enough to frighten Janet, but she felt defiant too, having helped in a small way. It might be worth losing her job to feel like that for a minute or two.

Hannah was brushing the last sparks from her sleeve as the men left.

"Are you burned?" Brenda said. "Let's have a look. Roll your sleeve up."

"Brenda, I don't know how to thank you," Hannah said.

Janet noticed that the old woman wasn't trembling at all, though she could feel that she was herself. She took the little brush from the fire-iron stand and swept up what she could of the ashes and the mess, but it was hard to manage with shaking hands.

"And I'm so grateful to you too," Hannah went on. "I'm sorry, but I don't know who you are. It was very brave of you both."

"Janet is the Bursar's secretary from Jordan," said Brenda. "She was there when they came for Alice this morning, and she came to tell me as soon as she could, and I thought we'd better warn you. Did they take anything valuable?"

"Only my tax returns and household bills and that sort of thing. I'm glad to see the back of them, frankly. The valuable things are all in the safe, but I'm going to have to move them now. D'you know, I'd love a cup of tea. How about you both?"

Next morning Janet went in to work as usual, and thought the porter gave her an odd look as she went in through the lodge. The Bursar was waiting in his office, and he called her in as soon as he heard her arrive.

"Good morning," she said carefully.

He was sitting behind his desk playing with a piece of cardboard: tapping it on the blotter, flexing it this way and that, smoothing down a crease. He didn't look at her.

"Janet, I'm sorry, but I've got some unfortunate news," he said.

He was speaking quickly. He still didn't look at her. She felt her stomach about to sink, and held her tongue.

"I—um—it's been made clear to me that it would be difficult to—ah—continue your employment," he said.

"Why?"

"It seems that you unfortunately made a, umm, well, a bad impression on the two officers who came here yesterday. I must say I saw nothing of that sort myself—always valued your complete professionalism—and it may be that their attitude was a little excessive—nevertheless, these are not easy times, and . . ."

"Did the Master put you up to this?"

"I beg your pardon?"

"Yesterday. When he called you in there after they'd taken Alice. What did he say to you?"

"Well, it was confidential, obviously, but he did stress the extreme difficulty we have in maintaining the independence of an institution like this, which is, after all, part of the national community and not separate from it. The pressures that bear on all of us . . ."

His voice simply trailed away, as if he had no more strength. And to do him justice, she thought, he did look about as miserable as a man could look.

"So the Master tells you to sack me, and you do it?"

"No, no, it wasn't . . . It . . . this came from a different source. A far more, how shall I say, authoritative . . ."

"It used to be the Master who had authority in the college. I don't think the old Master would have put up with being told what to do by someone else."

"Janet, you're not making this very easy. . . ."

"I don't want to make it easy. I want to know why I'm to be dismissed, after doing my job well for twelve years. *You've* never had a complaint about me, have you?"

"Well, not as such, but it seems that yesterday you did interfere with some important men in the execution of their duty."

"Not here, though. Not in college. Did I interfere yesterday when they were here?"

"It doesn't matter where."

"I'd have thought it mattered quite a lot. Did they tell you what they were doing?"

"I didn't speak to them directly."

"Well, I'll tell you. They were stealing the property of an old lady and treating her brutally, and I happened to see it going on, and me and my friend stepped in and helped her. And that's all, Mr. Stringer, that's all that happened. Is this the kind of country we're living in now, that people can be sacked from jobs they do well just because they inconvenience bullies and thugs from the CCD? Is that the kind of place this is?"

The Bursar put his head in his hands. Janet had never in her life spoken to an employer like that, and she stood with fast-beating heart while he sighed heavily and three times tried to say something.

"It's very difficult," he said. He looked up, but not at her. "There are things I can't explain. Pressures and tensions that . . . umm . . . college staff, domestic staff are quite properly protected from. These are times unlike any . . . I have to protect the staff from . . ."

She said nothing as his words faded into silence.

"Well, if you've got to get rid of *me*," she said finally, "why did they arrest Alice? And what have they done with her? Where is she now?"

All he could do was sigh and lower his head.

She began to gather her own few possessions from the desk where she worked. She felt light-headed, as if part of her was somewhere else and dreaming of this, and she'd wake up soon and find everything normal.

Then she went into his office again. He looked utterly diminished.

"If you can't tell me where she is as an employer," she said, "can you tell me as a friend? She is my friend. She's everyone's friend. She's part of the college—she's been here ages, much longer than me. Please, Mr. Stringer, where have they taken her?"

He was pretending he couldn't hear her. His face was turned down; he sat perfectly still; he was pretending she wasn't there, and that no one was asking him questions, and he seemed to think that if he sat still and didn't look at her, what he pretended would come true.

She felt a little sick. She put her things in a shopping bag and left.

Several hours later Alice was sitting, her ankles shackled, in a closed railway carriage with a dozen other figures similarly restrained. Some of them had swollen eyes and lips, bloody noses, bruised cheekbones. The youngest was a boy of eleven or so, chalk-pale and wide-eyed with fear; the oldest, a man of Hannah's age, gaunt and trembling. Two dim anbaric bulbs, one at each end of the carriage, provided the only light. As an ingenious extra way of keeping the prisoners still, cages of some bright metal covered in silvery mesh were attached underneath the hard benches that ran the length of the carriage, and each prisoner's dæmon was locked in one of them.

There was little conversation. Their guards had thrown them roughly inside, manhandled their dæmons into the cages, slapped the shackles on their ankles, and told them nothing. The carriage had been on a siding in the empty countryside when the prisoners had been brought there, and a locomotive had arrived after an hour or so to pull the carriage—somewhere.

The young boy was sitting opposite Alice. After they had been moving for half an hour, he began to fidget, and Alice said, "You all right, love?"

"I need the toilet," he said in a whisper.

Alice looked up and down the carriage. The doors had been locked at each end—they had all heard the sound, and seen the large keys—and there was no lavatory, and she knew full well that no one would come if they called.

"Stand up and turn around and do it behind the bench," she said. "No one'll blame you. It's their fault, not yours."

He tried to do as she said, but it was too hard to turn around with his ankles shackled. He had to urinate on the floor in front. Alice looked away till he'd finished. He was bitterly ashamed.

"What's your name, love?" she said.

"Anthony." She could hardly hear him.

"You stick to me," she said. "We'll help each other. I'm Alice. Don't worry about peeing on the floor. We'll all be doing it in the end. Where d'you live?"

They began to talk, and the train moved on into the night.

THIRTY-ONE

LITTLE STICK

The noises of shouting voices, heavy boots on concrete, the trundle of iron wheels as a large trolley went past the train window laden with what looked like boxes of ammunition, all combined with the violent hiss of steam, filled the air and made Lyra listen hard for a language she recognized or a voice that wasn't harsh and commanding. There was loud male laughter too, and more shouted orders. Men in desert camouflage uniforms were staring in at her, and making remarks about her, and then moving past towards the door of the carriage.

Invisible, she thought. *Dowdy. Undesirable.*

The compartment door slid open with a bang. A soldier looked in and said something in Turkish, in reply to which she could only shake her head and shrug. He said something to the other men behind him and came in, heaving his heavy pack up onto the rack and unslinging the rifle he was carrying. Four others joined him, jostling, laughing, staring at her, treading on one another's feet.

She kept her own feet out of the way and made herself as small as possible. The soldiers' dæmons were all dogs, fierce ones, shoving each other and snarling—and then one of them stopped and stared at her with sudden interest, and threw her head back and howled with fear.

Every other sound stopped. The dæmon's soldier bent to stroke her in reassurance, but the others had all registered what had caused the howling and began to howl too.

A soldier snapped at Lyra, asking a question, fierce and hostile. Then a sergeant appeared at the door, evidently demanding to know what was happening, at which the soldier with the first howling dæmon pointed at Lyra and said something with an air of superstitious hatred.

The sergeant barked a question at her, but he too was frightened.

In answer she said, *"J'aime le son du Cor, le soir, au fond des bois."*

It was the first thing that came to mind: a line of French poetry. The men stood perfectly still, waiting for a cue, waiting for the sergeant to indicate what the proper response should be, and all, by the look of them, full of dread.

Lyra spoke again: *"Dieu! Que le son du Cor est triste, au fond des bois."*

"Française?" said the sergeant hoarsely.

The eyes of every man and dæmon were on her. She nodded, then held up her hands as if to say "I surrender! Don't shoot!"

There must have been something in the contrast between their big male healthy power, the weapons they carried, the snarling teeth of their dæmons, and this dæmonless, dowdy, timid girl with the dull clothes and the glasses, something comic; because first the sergeant smiled, and then began to laugh; and then the others, responding, saw the contrast too and joined in the laughter; and Lyra smiled and shrugged, and moved up a little more to make room. The sergeant said again, *"Française,"* and added, *"Voilà."*

The only soldier apparently willing to sit next to her was a heavily built, dark-skinned, big-eyed man with an air of being able to enjoy things. He said something to her in a friendly enough tone, and she replied with more French poetry:

"*La nature est un temple où de vivants piliers / Laissent parfois sortir de confuses paroles.*"

"Ah," he said, nodding confidently.

Then the sergeant spoke to them all, giving orders, looking at her a couple of times, as if the orders included instructions about how to behave towards her. With a final look at her and a nod, he left and went to push his way through the other soldiers still crowding onto the train.

It took several minutes to get them all on board, and Lyra wondered how many of them there were, and where the officer in charge was. She soon found that out, because, obviously prompted by the sergeant, a tall young man in a smarter uniform than the rest looked in at the compartment door and spoke to her.

"You are French, mademoiselle?" he said in careful and strongly accented French.

"Yes," she said in the same language.

"Where are you traveling to?"

"Seleukeia, monsieur."

"Why you have not . . ." He clearly didn't know the French word, and indicated his own hawk dæmon, who was clutching his epaulette and staring with yellow eyes.

"He disappeared," she said. "I am looking for him."

"It is not possible."

"But it is. It happened. You can see."

"You are going to look in Seleukeia?"

"Everywhere. I will search everywhere."

He gave a baffled nod. He seemed to want to know more, or to forbid something, or require something, but not to know what. He looked around at the soldiers in the compartment, and then withdrew. More men were passing along the corridor; doors were slamming; a voice called on the platform, and a guard blew a whistle.

The train began to move.

Once they were out of the station, and leaving the lights of the town for the darkness of the mountains again, the soldier nearest the door leant out and looked both ways along the corridor.

Evidently satisfied, he nodded to the man opposite, who produced a bottle from his pack and pulled out the cork. Lyra smelled a tang of powerful spirits, and remembered another occasion when she'd had the same sensation: outside Einarsson's bar in the Arctic town of Trollesund, seeing the great bear Iorek Byrnison drinking spirits from an earthenware jug. If only she had his company on this journey! Or the company of Farder Coram, who'd been with her then.

The bottle was being passed around. When it reached the man next to her, he took a deep pull and then breathed out loudly, filling the air with fumes. The man opposite waved them away in mock disgust before taking the bottle himself. Then he hesitated, looked at Lyra with a knowing smile, and offered it to her.

She smiled back briefly and shook her head. The soldier said something and offered it again, more forcefully, as if daring her to refuse.

Another man spoke to him, apparently criticizing. The soldier took a pull at the spirits and said something hard and unfriendly to Lyra before passing the bottle on. She tried to become invisible but made sure her stick was just inside the rucksack.

The bottle went around the compartment again; the talk became louder and looser. They were talking about her, there was no doubt about that: their eyes moved over her body, one man was licking his lips, another clasping the crotch of his trousers.

Lyra gathered the rucksack to herself with her left arm and began to stand up, intending to leave, only for the man opposite to push her back into the seat and say something to the man by the door, who reached up and pulled down the blind over the corridor window. Lyra stood up again, and again the soldier pushed her back, this time squeezing her breast as he did. She felt a flood of dread invading her bloodstream.

Well, she thought, here it comes.

She stood up a third time, her right hand grasping the handle of her stick Pequeno, and when the soldier's hand came forward, she whipped the stick out of the rucksack and smashed it down so hard that she heard the crack of bone a moment before he yelled in pain. His dæmon leapt up at her, and she lashed the stick across her dog face, sending her howling to the floor. The man was cradling his broken hand, white-faced, unable to speak or utter a sound except a high tremulous whimper.

She felt another man's hands on her waist and gripped the stick tight and swung it backwards, luckily hitting him on the temple with the end of the handle. He shouted and tried to grab her arm, so she twisted round and sank her teeth into his hand, feeling a flame of pure ferocity blaze up in her heart. She drew blood: she bit deeper—a length of skin came away in her teeth, and his hand fell off her arm. His face loomed close, insensate with fury: she stabbed the stick up into the soft flesh under his jaw, and as he reared up and away from that, she lashed it harder than she'd hit anything else in her life across his nose and mouth. He grunted and fell back, gushing blood, and then his dæmon too was leaping for Lyra's throat. She brought up her knee as hard as she could, knocking the dæmon aside, and then felt other hands—two men's hands—on her wrist, up inside her skirt, fumbling at her underwear, gripping it, tearing it aside, and thrusting fingers at her, and other hands on the stick, twisting it, tearing it out of her fingers, and then with feet, teeth, forehead, knees, she fought as she had seen Iorek Byrnison fight, reckless, heedless of pain, fearless, but she was outnumbered; even in the crowded little compartment they had more room, more strength, just more hands and feet than she did; and they had dæmons, who were now growling, roaring, barking with fury, teeth bared, spittle flying, and still she fought and struggled—and it was the noise from the dæmons that saved her, because suddenly the door was flung open and there was the sergeant, who took it all in at once and said a word to his dæmon, a massive brute, who tore at the soldiers' dæmons, teeth in their necks, flinging them aside as if they weighed nothing, and the men fell back on the seats, bloodied and broken-boned, and Lyra was still standing, her skirt torn, her fingers blood-soaked and wrenched, her face cut and scratched, blood trickling down her legs, her eyes aflood with tears, trembling in every muscle, sobbing, but standing, still standing, facing them all.

She pointed to the man who had her stick. She had to support her right hand with her left wrist to do it.

"Give it to me," she said. "Give it back to me."

Her voice was thick with tears and shaking so much, she could hardly articulate the words. The man tried to shove the stick down beside him on the seat. With the last of her strength she flung herself at him and tore at his face, his hands, with nails and teeth and fury, but found herself lifted away effortlessly and held up in the air by the sergeant's left arm.

He snapped the fingers of his right hand at the soldier, whose eyes and nose were now bleeding thickly. The man handed up the stick. The sergeant put it in his pocket and then barked an order. Another soldier picked up Lyra's rucksack and handed it to him.

Another harsh sentence or two, and he carried the struggling

Lyra out into the corridor and put her down. He jerked his head, indicating that she should follow him, although she could barely stand; and then he shoved his way forcefully through the men who had come out into the corridor to see what was going on. Lyra had to go with him: he had the rucksack and the stick. Shaking so violently she almost lost her balance, feeling the blood trickling past her mouth and the wetness on her legs, she did her best to follow.

Every soldier's eyes were staring, taking in every detail, greedy to know more. She stumbled through the midst of them, trying to hold herself steady, simply that; once the train lurched over a poor section of track, and she almost fell, but a hand came out to hold her upright; she pulled her arm away and moved on.

The sergeant was waiting outside the last compartment in the next carriage. Standing in the doorway was the officer—major, captain, whatever he was; and as she reached him, the sergeant handed her the rucksack, which had never seemed so heavy.

"Thank you," she managed to say in French. "And my stick."

The officer asked the sergeant something. The sergeant took the stick out of his pocket and gave it to the officer, who looked at it curiously. The sergeant was explaining what had happened.

"My stick," Lyra said, steadying her voice as much as she could. "Are you going to leave me entirely defenseless? Let me have it back."

"You have already put three of my men out of action, I am told."

"Am I supposed to let myself be raped? I'd kill them all first."

She had never felt so ferocious and so weak. She was really on the point of falling to the floor, and at the same time, she was ready to tear out his throat to get her stick back.

The sergeant said something. The officer replied, and nodded, and reluctantly handed Lyra back the stick. She tried to open her rucksack, and failed, and tried again, and failed, and began to cry, to her immense anger. The officer stood aside and indicated the seat behind him. The compartment was empty apart from his valise, a multitude of papers spread out on the opposite seat, and a half-finished meal of bread and cold meat.

Lyra sat down and tried a third time to open her rucksack. This time she managed, though it made her realize how damaged her fingers were: torn nails, swollen joints, a wrenched thumb. She wiped her eyes with the heel of her left hand, took several deep breaths, gritted her teeth—at which point she found one of them broken, and explored it with her tongue. Half of it was missing. Too bad, she thought. She gathered her resolution and worked at the rucksack buckles with her painful fingers. Her left hand was so sore and weak and swollen, she touched the back of it tenderly, and thought she felt a broken bone. Finally she got the rucksack open and found the alethiometer, the pack of cards, and her little purse of money. She slipped the stick down inside and buckled it again, and then leant back and closed her eyes.

Every part of her seemed to hurt. She could still feel those hands tearing at her underclothes, and wanted to wash more than anything else in the world.

Oh, Pan, she thought. Are you satisfied now?

The officer had been speaking quietly to the sergeant. She heard him reply and then move away, and the officer came back into the compartment and slid the door shut.

"Are you in pain?" he said.

She opened her eyes. One of them seemed to prefer to stay closed. She touched the flesh around it with her right hand: it was already swollen.

She looked at the young man. It wasn't really necessary to say anything. She held out her trembling hands to show him the damage.

"If you will permit me," he said.

He sat down opposite and opened a little clothbound case. His hawk dæmon jumped down and looked as he moved the contents around: rolls of bandage, a little pot of salve, bottles of pills, small envelopes probably containing powders of one sort or another. He unfolded a clean cloth and uncapped a brown bottle to sprinkle some liquid on it.

"Rosewater," he said.

He handed it to her and indicated that she might clean her face with it. It was marvelously cool and soothing, and she held it over her eyes until she felt able to look at him again. She lowered the cloth, and he sprinkled it with more rosewater.

"I thought rosewater was difficult to obtain," she said.

"Not for officers."

"I see. Well, thank you."

There was a mirror over the seat opposite, and she stood up shakily and looked at herself, almost recoiling when she saw the mess of blood over her mouth and nose. Her right eye was nearly closed.

Invisible, she thought bitterly, and set to work cleaning herself. More applications of rosewater helped, and so did the salve in the little pot, stinging at first and then diffusing a deep warmth, along with a strong herbal smell.

Finally she sat down and took a deep breath. It was her left hand, she thought, that hurt the most. She touched it tentatively again. The officer was watching.

"I may?" he said, and took the hand with great gentleness. His own hands were soft and silky. He moved it to and fro, just a little this way and that, but it hurt her too much to let him continue. "Possibly a broken bone," he said. "Well, if you will ride on a train with soldiers, you must expect a little discomfort."

"I have a ticket that permits me to ride on this train. It does not say that the journey includes assault and attempted rape. Do you *expect* your soldiers to behave like that?"

"No, and they will be punished. But, I repeat, it is not wise for a young woman to travel alone in the present circumstances. May I offer you a little eau de vie as a restorative?"

She nodded. The movement hurt her head. He poured the spirit into a little metal cup, and she sipped it carefully. It tasted like the best brantwijn.

"When does the train arrive in Seleukeia?" she said.

"In two hours."

She closed her eyes. Hugging the rucksack close to her breast, she let herself sink into a doze.

Only a few seconds later, it seemed, the officer was squeezing her shoulder. Her heavy consciousness was reluctant to leave the slumber behind; she wanted to sleep for a month.

But outside the window she could see the lights of a city, and the train was slowing down. The officer was gathering his papers together, and then he looked up as the door slid open.

The sergeant said something, perhaps reporting that the men were ready to leave the train. He looked at Lyra as if assessing the damage. She looked down: time to be modest again, inconspicuous, dowdy. But inconspicuous, she thought, with a black eye and a broken hand and cuts and scratches all over? And no dæmon?

"Mademoiselle," said the officer. She looked up and saw the sergeant was holding something out to her. It was her spectacles, with one lens broken and one arm missing. She took them without a word.

"Come with me," said the officer, "and I shall help you leave the train first."

She didn't argue. She stood up, with some difficulty and pain, and he helped her lift the rucksack to her shoulders.

The sergeant stood aside to let them out of the compartment. All along the train, as far as she could tell, soldiers were gathering their weapons and possessions and shoving their way into the corridor, but the officer called out, and the nearest ones moved back out of the way as Lyra followed him towards the door.

"A little advice," he said as he helped her stiffly down onto the platform.

"Well?"

"Wear a niqab," he said. "It will help."

"I see. Thank you. It would be better for everyone if you disciplined your soldiers."

"You have done that yourself."

"I should not have had to."

"Nevertheless, you defended yourself. They will think twice before behaving badly again."

"No, they won't. You know that."

"You are probably right. They are trash. Seleukeia is a difficult city. Do not stay here long. There will be more soldiers arriving by other trains. Better move on soon."

Then he turned away and left her alone. His men watched her from the train windows as she limped along the platform towards the ticket hall. She had no idea what she could do next.

THIRTY-TWO

HOSPITALITY

She walked away from the station and tried to look as if she had every right to be there and knew where she was going. Every part of her body hurt, every part felt tainted by the hands that had thrust their way to her flesh. Her rucksack was a hideous burden: how had it become so heavy? She longed for sleep.

It was the dead of night. The streets were empty of people, poorly lit, and hard. There were no trees, no bushes, no grass; no little parks or squares with a patch of greenery; nothing but hard pavements and stone-built warehouses, or banks, or office buildings; nowhere to lay her head. The place felt so quiet, she thought that there must be a curfew, and that if she were found wandering, she would be arrested. She almost longed for that: she could sleep in a cell. There was no sign of a hotel, not even a single café, nowhere that might be intended for the refreshment or repose of travelers. This place made an outcast of every visitor.

Only once did she hear any sign of life, and that was when, nearly crazed with exhaustion and at the limit of pain and unhappiness, she risked knocking at a door. Her intention was to throw herself on the mercy of whoever lived there, in the hope that their culture had a tradition of hospitality to strangers, in the face of all the evidence to the contrary. Her timid knock, with bruised knuckles, awoke only a man, clearly a night watchman or security guard of some kind, on duty just inside. His dæmon woke him with a frenzy of howling, and he snarled a curse at whoever had dared to knock. His voice was full of hate and fear. Lyra hurried away. She could hear him cursing and shouting for a long time.

Finally she could go no further. She simply crumpled at a spot shaded from the glare of the nearest streetlight by the corner of a building, and curled up around the rucksack, and fell asleep. She was too hurt and tired even to sob; the tears flowed from her eyes with no impulsion; she felt them cold on her cheek, her eyelids, her temple, and did nothing to stanch them; and then she was asleep.

Someone was shaking her shoulder. A low voice was whispering anxious, urgent words that she couldn't understand. Everything hurt.

It was still dark. When she opened her eyes, there was no light to dazzle her. The man leaning over her was dark too, a deeper darkness, and he stank terribly. There was another figure nearby; she could see his face, pale against the night, looking this way and that.

The first man stood back as she struggled to sit up on the cold stone and to loosen her limbs a little. It was so cold. They had a cart, and a long-handled shovel.

More words, in that urgent low voice. They were gesturing: get up, stand, get up. The stench was sickening. As she painfully moved her limbs and forced herself up, she understood: these were night-soil men, making their rounds, emptying the city's latrines and cesspits: an occupation for the lowest and most despised class of people.

She tried French: "What do you want? I am lost. Where are we?"

But they could only speak their own language, which sounded neither Anatolian nor Arabic. At any rate, she couldn't understand, except to see that they were anxious, and anxious for her.

But she was so cold, so full of pain. She tried to stop shivering. The first man said something else, which seemed to be: Follow, come with us.

Even burdened with their stinking cart, they moved faster than she could, and she caught some of their anxiety when they had to slow down for her. They kept looking all around. Finally they came to an alley between two imposing stone buildings, and turned into it.

There was just the very faintest hint in the sky that the night was going; nothing as much as light, just a slight dilution of the dark. She understood: they had to finish their rounds by daylight, and they wanted her out of sight before then.

The alley was very narrow, and the buildings crowded close above. She was getting used to the smell—no, she wasn't; she never would; but it was no worse than it had been. One of the men lifted the latch on a low door and opened it quietly. Instantly a female voice inside, heavy with sleep but awake at once, uttered a short fear-filled question.

The man replied, equally briefly, and stood aside to indicate Lyra. A woman's face emerged dimly from the gloom, strained, fearful, prematurely aged.

Lyra stepped forward so as to be more clearly visible. The woman scanned her for a moment and then reached out a hand to take hers. It was the broken hand, and Lyra couldn't help a cry of pain. The woman shrank back into the darkness, and the man spoke urgently again.

"Sorry, sorry," said Lyra quietly, though she felt like howling with agony. She could feel that the hand was swollen and hot.

The woman emerged a second time and beckoned, taking care not to touch. Lyra turned to express her thanks somehow, but the men were already hastening away with their stinking cart.

She stepped forward carefully, ducking under the low lintel. The woman shut the door, and total darkness enveloped them; but Lyra heard a rustling movement, and then the woman struck a match and lit the wick of a little oil lamp. The room smelled of nothing but sleep and cooked food. In the yellow glow Lyra could see that her hostess was very thin, and that she was younger than she'd seemed.

The woman indicated the bed, or rather a mattress heaped with various coverings: it was the only place to sit down apart from the floor. Lyra put her rucksack down and sat on the corner of the mattress, saying, "Thank you—it's very kind—*merci, merci*—"

It was only then that she noticed that she hadn't seen the woman's dæmon. And with a little jolt she realized that the men had no dæmons either.

She said, "Dæmon?" and tried to indicate her own lack of one, but the woman clearly didn't understand, and Lyra just shook her head. There was nothing else she could do. Perhaps these poor people had to do the job they did because, without having dæmons, they were less than human in the eyes of their society. They were the lowest caste there was. And she belonged with them.

The woman was watching her. Lyra pointed to her own breast and said, "Lyra."

"Ah," said the woman, and pointed to herself, saying, "Yozdah."

"Yozdah," repeated Lyra carefully.

The woman said, "Ly-ah."

"Lyra."

"Ly-ra."

"That's it."

They both smiled. Yozdah indicated that Lyra could lie down, and Lyra did, and then she felt a heavy rug being pulled up over her, and at once she fell asleep, for the third time that night.

She woke up to the sound of low voices. Daylight was filtering in through a bead curtain across the doorway, but it was gray, with no direct sunshine in it. Lyra opened her eyes to see the woman Yozdah and a man, presumably one of the two who had brought her there, sitting on the floor and eating from a large bowl between them. She lay and watched them before moving; the man looked younger than the woman, and his clothes were shabby, but she couldn't detect any of the stink from his profession.

She sat up carefully and found her left hand too painful even to open fully. The woman saw her move and said something to the man, who turned to look and then stood up.

Lyra urgently needed a privy, or something of the sort, and when she tried to convey this, the man looked away and the woman understood and led her outside through another door into a little yard. The latrine was in the far corner, and meticulously clean.

Yozdah was waiting in the doorway when she came out, holding a jar of water. She mimed holding out her hands, and Lyra did that, guarding her left from the shock of the cold water as best she could when Yozdah poured it over them. She offered Lyra a thin towel, and beckoned her inside.

The man was still standing, waiting for her to come back, and indicated that she should sit on the carpet with them and eat from the bowl of rice. She did so, using her right hand, as they did.

Yozdah said to the man, "Lyra," and pointed to her.

"Ly-ra," he said, and pointed to himself and said, "Chil-du."

"Chil-du," Lyra said.

The rice was sticky and almost flavorless but for a little salt.

Still, it was all they had, and she tried to take as little as possible, since they hadn't expected a guest. Chil-du and Yozdah spoke quietly to each other, and Lyra wondered what language they were speaking; it was like none that she'd heard before.

But she had to try to communicate with them. She spoke to them both, turning from one to the other and saying as clearly as she could, "I want to find the Blue Hotel. Have you heard of the Blue Hotel? Al-Khan al-Azraq?"

They both looked at her. He was politely mystified, and she was anxious.

"Or Madinat al-Qamar?"

They knew that. They drew back, they shook their heads, they put up their hands as if to ban any further mention of that name.

"English? Do you know anyone who speaks English?"

They didn't understand.

"*Français? Quelqu'un qui parle français?*"

Same response. She smiled and shrugged and ate another morsel of rice.

Yozdah stood up and took a pan from the open fire and poured boiling water into two earthenware cups. Into each one she dropped a pinch of some dark, gritty-looking powder, and scooped a lump of what might have been butter or soft cheese in after it. Then she stirred each cup with a stiff brush, making both cups froth up, and gave one to Chil-du and the other to Lyra.

"Thank you," Lyra said, "but . . . ," and pointed to the cup and then to Yozdah. That seemed to breach some point of etiquette, for Yozdah frowned and looked away, and Chil-du gently pushed Lyra's hand away.

"Well," said Lyra, "thank you. I expect you can use the cup when I've finished. It's very generous of you."

The drink was too hot to sip, but Chil-du was drinking it by sucking at the edge with a noisy splashing sound. Lyra did the same. It tasted both bitter and rancid, but inside it there was a taste not unlike tea. She found after several noisy slurpings that it was sharp and refreshing.

"It's good," she said. "Thank you. What is it called?"

She pointed to her cup and looked inquisitive.

"*Choy*," said Yozdah.

"Ah. It *is* tea, then."

Chil-du spoke to his wife for about a minute, making suggestions, perhaps, or maybe giving instructions. She listened critically, making an interjection here, asking a question there, but finally saying something that was plainly in agreement. They both glanced at Lyra throughout. She watched, wary, listening for any words she might understand, trying to interpret their expressions.

When the conversation was over, Yozdah stood up and opened a wooden chest, which looked as if it was made of cedar, and was the only beautiful or costly-seeming object in the room. She took out a folded piece of cloth, black in color, and shook it out of its folds. It was surprisingly long.

Yozdah looked at her and beckoned, so Lyra got up. Yozdah was refolding the cloth a different way and indicating that Lyra should watch, so she did, trying to memorize the sequence of folds. Then Yozdah stepped behind her and began to fasten the cloth around her head, first putting one edge across the bridge of Lyra's nose so that the cloth hung over the lower part of her face, and then winding the rest around her head to conceal every part of it except her eyes. She tucked the ends in on both sides.

Chil-du was watching. He gestured at his own head, and Yozdah understood and tucked away the last strand of Lyra's hair.

He said something that clearly signified approval. Lyra said, "Thank you," hearing her voice muffled.

She hated it, but she could see the sense. She was impatient to be on her way, as if she knew what her way was, or where; and there was nothing to keep her here, especially since they had no language in common.

So she put her palms together in what she hoped would be understood as a gesture of thanks and of farewell, and bowed her head, and picked up her rucksack and left. She bitterly regretted having nothing to give them but money, and thought briefly of offering them a couple of coins, but feared that they'd feel she was insulting their hospitality.

She made her way out of the little alley, where the night-soil cart stood at one side, looking as if it was ashamed of itself. It wasn't locked to anything; who would want to steal such an object? The street outside was dazzling with brilliant sunshine, and Lyra soon began to feel hot under the abominably confining veil and head-scarf.

However, no one looked at her. She had become what she'd been trying to become ever since the beginning of this journey: invisible. Combined with the dowdy-depressed way of moving recommended by Anita Schlesinger, the veil made her actively resistant to other people's interest. Men in particular walked in front of her as if she had no more substance or importance than a shadow, barged ahead at street crossings, took no notice at all. And little by little she began to feel a kind of freedom in this state.

It was hot, though, and getting hotter as the sun rose higher. She made her way towards where she thought the center of the city must be, in the direction of more traffic, more noise, bigger shops, and more crowded streets. At some point, she thought, she might find someone who spoke English.

There were large numbers of armed police, some sitting on the pavement playing dice, some standing scrutinizing every passerby, some inspecting the items a poor hawker was trying to sell from his suitcase, others eating and drinking at a food stall placed illegally in the road. Lyra watched them closely, and felt their eyes when they did deign to notice her, a brief incurious flick at her hidden face, the automatic and inevitable glance at her body, then the look away. Not even her lack of a dæmon provoked a glimmer of attention. Despite the heat, it really was almost like being liberated.

As well as the police, there were soldiers sitting in armored cars or patrolling with guns held across their chests. They looked as if they were waiting for an uprising they knew was coming but didn't know when. At one point Lyra nearly walked into a squad who seemed to be interrogating a group of boys, some so young that their dæmons kept flickering between one abject form and another, trying to appease the men with guns and faces ablaze with anger. One boy dropped to his knees and held his hands out, pleading, only for a rifle butt to slam into the side of his head and drop him on the road.

Lyra very nearly cried out, "No!" and had to hold herself back from running up to protest. The boy's dæmon had changed into a snake and squirmed brokenly in the dust until the soldier's dæmon put a heavy foot on her, and she and the boy fell still.

The soldiers were aware that Lyra was watching. The man who'd hit the boy looked up and shouted something, and she turned and walked away. She hated being helpless, but the thought of this man's violence made her feel every bruise, every cut from the attack on the train, and the memory of those hands thrusting up inside her skirt made her very entrails cold with repugnance. Her first task was to get out of this place alive and active, and that meant remaining inconspicuous, however hard that was.

She moved on further into the busy streets, into an area of shops and small businesses, repairers of furniture, sellers of secondhand bicycles, makers of cheap clothing and the like. Always the presence of the police, always the sight of soldiers. She wondered about relations between the two forces. They seemed to be keeping scrupulously apart, with a formal politeness when they had to pass one another on the street. She wished Bud Schlesinger would suddenly appear to guide her calmly through the maze of difficulties here, or Anita, to keep her cheerful with encouragement and conversation, or Malcolm—

She let that thought linger until it faded.

The closer she came to the center of the city, the more she felt uncomfortable, because the pain in her left hand got a little worse with each throb of blood through the arteries near her broken bone. She looked at every shop sign, every notice board, every brass plate on every building, looking for a sign that might mean English was spoken there.

In the end the sign she found was on an oratory. A little limestone basilica, roofed with red-brown terra-cotta tiles, in a dusty graveyard where three olive trees grew out of the gravel, bore a wooden sign that said *The Holy Chapel of St. Phanourios* in English, French, and Arabic, followed by a list of the times of services and the name of the priest in charge, a Father Jerome Burnaby.

Princess Cantacuzino . . . Hadn't she said that her dæmon was called Phanourios? Lyra stopped to look into the enclosure. Beside the basilica stood a little house in a palm-shaded garden where a man in a faded blue shirt and trousers was watering some flowers. He looked up as she watched, and gave a cheerful wave. Encouraged by this, Lyra moved cautiously towards him.

He put down his watering can and said, *"As-salamu aleikum."*

She went a little closer, into the garden itself, which was rich with many kinds of green leaves, but where the only flowers were deep red.

"*Wa-aleikum as-salaam,*" she said quietly. "Do you speak English?"

"Yes, I do. I'm the priest in charge here, Father Burnaby. I am English. Are you? You sound English."

He sounded as if he came originally from Yorkshire. His dæmon was a robin who watched Lyra from the handle of the watering can with her head cocked. The priest himself was burly and red-faced, older than she'd thought from the road, and his expression radiated a shrewd kind of concern. He reached out a hand to steady her as she stumbled over a stone.

"Thank you . . ."

"Are you all right? You don't look well. Not that it's easy to tell . . ."

"May I sit down?"

"Come with me."

He led her into the house, where it was a little cooler than outside. As soon as the door closed behind her, Lyra unwound the headscarf-veil and took it off with relief.

"What have you been doing to yourself?" he said, taken aback by the cuts and the bruising on her face.

"I was attacked. But I just need to find—"

"You need a doctor."

"No. Please. Let me just sit down for a minute. I'd rather not—"

"You can have a glass of water, anyway. Stay there."

She was in a small hallway, where there stood one flimsy-looking cane chair. She waited till he came back with the water and said, "I didn't mean to—"

"Never mind. Come in here. It's not very tidy, but at least the chairs are comfortable."

He opened a door into a room that seemed to be part study and part junk shop, where books lay everywhere, including on the floor. She was reminded of the house of Kubiček in Prague; how long ago that seemed!

The priest moved a dozen books from an armchair. "You take this chair," he said. "The springs are still intact."

She sat down and watched as he distributed the books into three separate piles, corresponding, she supposed, to three aspects of the subject he was reading about, which seemed to be philosophy. His robin dæmon was perching on the back of the other armchair, watching her with bright eyes.

Burnaby sat down and said, "Obviously you need some medical attention. Let's take that as read. I'll give you the address of a good doctor in a minute. Now tell me what else you need. Apart from a dæmon. We'll take that as read too. How can I help?"

"Where are we? This is Seleukeia, I know that much, but is it far from Aleppo?"

"A few hours by motor. The road isn't very good, though. Why do you want to go there?"

"I want to meet someone there."

"I see," he said. "May I know your name?"

"Tatiana Prokovskaya."

"Have you tried the Muscovite consul?"

"I'm not a Muscovite. Only my name is."

"When did you arrive in Seleukeia?"

"Late last night. It was too late to find a hotel. I was looked after very kindly by some poor people."

"And when were you attacked?"

"On the train from Smyrna. By some soldiers."

"Have you seen a doctor at all?"

"No. I've spoken to no one except the people who helped me, and we had no language in common anyway."

"What were their names?"

"Chil-du and Yozdah."

"A night-soil man and his wife."

"Do you know them?"

603

"No. But their names are not Anatolian—they're Tajik. They mean Forty-Two, the man, and Eleven, the woman."

"Tajik?" she said.

"Yes. They're not allowed to have personal names, so they're given numbers instead, even for the men, odd for the women."

"That's horrible. Are they slaves or something?"

"Something like that. They can take up only a limited number of occupations: grave digging is a common one. And the night-soil business."

"They were very kind. They gave me this veil, headscarf, this . . . niqab, is it?"

"You were wise to wear it."

"Mr. Burnaby—Father—what should I call you?"

"Jerome, if you like."

"Jerome, what is happening here? Why are there soldiers on the street and in the train?"

"People are restless. Frightened. There have been riots, arson, persecutions. . . . Since the martyrdom of St. Simeon, the Patriarch, there's been a sort of martial-ecclesiastical law in force. The rose garden troubles are at the bottom of it all."

Lyra thought about that. Then she said, "The people—last night—they had no dæmons. Like me."

"May I ask how you were deprived of your dæmon?"

"He vanished. That's all I know."

"You were lucky not to be stopped this morning. Those without dæmons, often Tajiks, are not allowed to be seen in the hours of daylight. If they'd thought you were a Tajik, you would have been arrested."

Lyra sat still for a moment, and said, "This is a horrible place."

"I can't deny that."

She sipped the water.

"And you want to get to Aleppo?" he said.

"Would it be hard to do that at the moment?"

"This is a trading city. You can find anything here for money. But it will be more expensive now, such a journey, than it would be in peaceable times."

"Have you heard of a place," she said, "called the Blue Hotel? A place where lost dæmons go?"

His eyes widened. "Oh—please—be careful," he said, and actually got up out of his chair and patrolled the room, looking out of both windows, one facing the street and the other the narrow vegetable garden next to the house. His robin dæmon was twittering her alarm and flew towards Lyra before turning and making for the safety of the priest's shoulder.

"Be careful about what?" Lyra said. She was a little bewildered.

"The place you mentioned. There are powers that are not of this world, spiritual powers, evil powers. I really do advise you not to go there."

"But I'm trying to find my dæmon. You know I am. If the place exists, then he might be there. I must go and try. I'm—I'm incomplete. You must see that."

"You don't know that your dæmon is there. I have seen cases—I could tell you of examples of real spiritual evil arising in places where . . . among people who . . . No, no, I really do counsel you not to go there. Even if it does exist."

"Even if? You mean it might not exist?"

"If such a place did exist, it would be wrong to go there."

Lyra thought, Is this Bolvangar again? But she couldn't waste time telling him about that. "If I were asking," she said, "as a—I don't know—simply as a journalist or something, if I were asking how one might get there if one wanted to, would you tell me?"

"Well, in the first place, I don't know how to get there. It's all rumor, myth, maybe even superstition. But I expect your friend the night-soil man might know, if anyone would. Why don't you ask him?"

"Because we can't speak each other's language. Look, never mind. I haven't got the strength to go anywhere at the moment. Thank you for listening. And for the glass of water."

"I'm sorry. Don't feel you have to go. I'm only concerned for your welfare, spiritual and . . . Sit here and rest. Stay awhile. I really think you should let a doctor have a look at your injuries."

"I'll be all right. But I've got to go now."

"I wish there was something you'd let me do."

"All right," she said. "Just tell me about travel between here and Aleppo. Is there a train?"

"There used to be. Till quite recently, in fact, but they've stopped allowing them. There is a bus, twice a week, I think. But . . ."

"Is there any other way of getting there?"

He drew in his breath, tapped his fingers, shook his head. "There are camels," he said.

"Where would I find a camel? And someone to guide me?"

"You realize that this city is a terminus of many of the Silk Road trails? The great markets and warehouses are in Aleppo, but a substantial number of goods come here to be taken onwards by sea. And there's inward trade as well. Train masters load their camels here for journeys as far as Peking. Aleppo is just a step for them. If you go to the harbor—that's what I'd do—go to the harbor and ask for a train master—they speak every language under the sun. Forget the other idea, I do beg you. It's moonshine, deluding, dangerous. Really. By camel, Aleppo would be two days or so away. Maybe three. Have you got friends there?"

"Yes," she said easily. "Once I get there, I'll be safe."

"Well, I wish you good luck. Sincerely. And remember, the Authority never wishes for his creation to be split apart. You were created with a dæmon, and he is somewhere now longing to be reunited with you. When that happens, nature will be restored a little, and the Authority will be happy."

"Is he happy that those poor Tajik people have to live like that?"

"No, no. The world is not an easy place, Tatiana. There are trials we are sent. . . ."

She stood up, surprised at the effort it took, and had to hold on to the back of her chair.

"You're not well," he said, and his tone was gentle.

"No."

"I . . ."

He stood too, and clasped his hands together. His face was expressing a whole sequence of thoughts and feelings, and he even made a curious writhing movement as if he wanted to burst out of chains or shackles.

"What is it?" Lyra said.

He said, "Sit down again. I haven't told you the full . . . I haven't told you the truth. Please. Sit down. I shall try."

He was plainly moved. He was struggling against something, and at the same time ashamed to reveal it.

Lyra sat down, watching every expression that came and went on the priest's face.

"Your Tajik friends," he said quietly, "their dæmons will have been sold."

She wasn't sure she'd heard him. "What? Did you say *sold*? People *sell* their dæmons?"

"It's poverty," he said. "There's a market for dæmons. Medical knowledge here is quite advanced, unlike other things. Big corporations are behind it. They say the medical companies are experimenting here before expanding into the European market. There's a surgical operation. . . . Many people survive it now. Parents will sell their children's dæmons for money to stay alive. It's technically illegal, but big money brushes the law aside. . . . When the children grow up, they're not full citizens, being incomplete. Hence their names, and the occupations they have to take up.

"There are dealers. . . . I know where—I can even tell you where to find them. This is not knowledge I'm proud of transmitting. In fact, every bone in my body is rebelling. . . . I can't forgive myself for knowing this. There are men who can supply a dæmon for those who are without one. It sounds atrocious. It sounds absurd. When I first heard about it, when I moved to this living, to look after this chapel, I thought it was something fit only for the confessional, and I admit I suffered—I struggled to believe it. But I have heard it from several quarters. People tell priests things like this. It seems that if a person such as yourself, who has suffered in this way, suffered the loss of a dæmon, if such a person has enough money, they can call on the services of a *dealer* who will supply them with . . . will sell them a dæmon who will pass as their own. I have seen a few people in that condition. They have a dæmon; she, he goes everywhere with them, appears to be close and understanding, but—"

"You can tell," said his own robin dæmon. Her voice was sweet and quiet. "They look disconnected, in some deep way. It's very disturbing."

"I struggled with this," the priest went on. "Struggled to understand it and come to terms with it, but . . . my bishop gave me no guidance. The Magisterium denies that this is happening, but I know it is."

"It's not possible," said Lyra, "surely! Why would any dæmon agree to pretend to belong to someone else? They're *us*. They're part of us. They must miss us just as we miss them. Have *you* ever been separate from your dæmon?"

He shook his head. His dæmon said something quietly, and he took her in both hands and brought her close to his face.

"And why do the dæmons stay with strangers? How could they bear it?"

"It might be better than to remain where they are . . . where they've been severed."

"And . . . *dealers?*" Lyra went on. "Is this *allowed?* Are they *licensed* or something?"

"I've heard . . . ," he began, and then, "This is speculation and rumor, you understand. . . . Well, some of the dæmons they sell are those removed from the Tajiks. The majority of them die, apparently, but—and this is very much an underground, you know, illicit sort of transaction—but the authorities turn a blind eye to it because the corporations behind it are more powerful than politics now. Oh, you spoke the truth when you said this was a horrible place, Tatiana."

"Tell me more about the Blue Hotel," said Lyra.

He looked unhappy.

"Please," she added. "I've come a very long way to find my dæmon. If he's anywhere near here, then I must keep him away from those dealers. And if the Blue Hotel is a place where dæmons go, it must be safe for them. Where is it? What is it? What do you know about it?"

He sighed. "People keep away from it," he said, "out of fear . . . I do believe there are evil powers involved. As far as I've heard—I had one parishioner who went to look for it out of curiosity, and he came back marked, changed, diminished. . . . It's not a hotel. That's just a euphemism. It's a dead town. One of hundreds. I have no idea why it's known as the Blue Hotel. But something rules there, something attracts dæmons, maybe dæmons who've been severed and then escaped. . . . It is not a good place, Tatiana. I'm convinced of that. *Please* don't . . ."

"Where can I find one of these dealers?"

He put his head in his hands and cried, "I wish I had said nothing!"

"I'm glad you did. Where can I find them?"

"Everything about this is illegal, immoral. Everything is dangerous. Both legally and spiritually. Do you understand what I mean?"

"Yes, but I still want to know. Where do I go? What do I ask for? Do they have a special name for these people, for this transaction?"

"Are you determined to do this?"

"It's the only clue I've had. Yes, of course I'm determined, and so would you be. These people who buy dæmons—how do they find the dealers? Please, Mr. Burnaby—Jerome—if you don't tell me everything you know, I might fall into even more danger. Is there a special place they go to? A particular marketplace, a café, something like that?"

He murmured something, and Lyra was about to ask him to say it again when she realized that he was talking to his dæmon. And it was the dæmon who answered.

"There is a hotel near the docks," she said. "It's called the Park Hotel, though there's no park nearby. People in your condition do go there and take rooms for a few days. Dealers will hear about it and call on them. The hotel management is discreet, but they charge a high price."

"The Park Hotel," Lyra repeated. "Thank you. I'll go there. What street is it on?"

"A backstreet called Osman Sokak," said Burnaby. "Near the swing bridge."

"Osman . . ."

"Osman Sokak. An alley, really."

Lyra stood up. This time she felt steadier. "I'm most grateful," she said. "Thank you, Mr. Burnaby."

"I can imagine how difficult it must be to find yourself in your position—but I beg you, please simply go home."

"There's nothing simple about going home."

"No," he said. "It was too easy to say."

"And I'm not going to buy a dæmon. That would be a horrible transaction."

"I should never—" He shook his head and went on, "If at any point you need help, please call on me."

"That's kind of you. I'll remember. But I'll go now, Father Burnaby."

She remembered the veil with a sigh. She carefully arranged it across the bridge of her nose and around the back and over the top of her head, tucking the ends inside. She checked herself in the mirror over his hall table: it looked neat enough. And safe. And nullifying.

She shook the priest's hand and left the coolness of his house for the heat of the morning, and began to walk doggedly towards the docks. She could see the tall necks of cranes in the quivering distance, and possibly the masts of ships as well, so that was clearly the way to go. "Osman Sokak," she repeated to herself.

If she hadn't already discovered that this city was a less agreeable place than Smyrna, the walk to the docks would have convinced her. No one seemed to have ever had the thought of planting a tree or cultivating some bushes or even a patch of grass, or of making the neighborhoods places for pleasure or comfort and not just stonyhearted business. The sun blazed down on the dusty streets with nothing to mitigate its glare. There were no benches to rest on, not even at the infrequent bus stops, and no cafés either, it seemed. If you wanted to rest, you would have to sit on the ground, and find what shade you could between the buildings, most of which were blank-faced factories or warehouses or dingy apartment blocks. The only shops were small and functional, their goods laid out with a casual indifference in the full sun, vegetables wilting in the heat or bread gathering the dust of the traffic. The citizens moved about without looking at one another, their heads down, unwilling to acknowledge anyone or anything. And everywhere, patrols: the police cruising slowly in their blue vans, soldiers on foot, sauntering, guns held across their chests.

Through it all, increasingly weary and painful and oppressed, Lyra moved grimly towards the docks. When she found the little backstreet called Osman Sokak, she was nearly ready to weep, but she managed to keep her composure as she entered the shabby building that called itself Par Hotel, the *k* having fallen off and disappeared.

The desk clerk was both torpid and sullen, but a flash of reptilian interest seemed to spark deep in his lizard dæmon's eyes as she noticed that Lyra had no dæmon. No doubt the clerk would earn a commission when he spread the word that a customer had arrived. He gave Lyra the key to a room on the first floor and left her to find the way herself.

Once inside the hot little room, she tore off the veil and flung it into the corner, and lay down carefully on the bed: carefully because her injuries were merging into a single great pain, which felt not as if it were in her but as if she were in it. She felt sick and desolate. After crying a little she fell asleep.

She woke an hour later to find tears still on her cheeks, and to hear someone knocking at the door.

"Wait a moment," she called, and hastily arranged the veil.

She opened the door a little way. A middle-aged man in a suit stood there, with a briefcase in one hand.

"Yes?" she said.

"You are English, mademoiselle?"

"Yes."

"I am in a position to help you."

"Who are you?"

"My name is Selim Veli. In fact, Dr. Selim Veli."

"What are you offering?"

"You do not have something very necessary, and I can supply what you need. May I come into your room and explain?"

His own dæmon was a parrot, who was watching Lyra from his shoulder with her head cocked. Lyra wondered if she was really his own dæmon or one that he himself had bought; and knew that she would normally be able to tell at once, but all her certainties were dissolving now.

"Wait a moment," she said, and shut the door before making sure her stick was near to hand.

She opened the door again and let him in. He was formal and correct in manner, his clothes were clean and recently pressed, and his shoes gleamed.

"Please sit down, Dr. Veli," she said.

He took the only chair, and she sat on the bed.

"I don't know whether this is conventionally approved of," she said, "but I'm not used to wearing a niqab, and I'm going to take this one off."

He nodded gravely. His eyes widened a little when he saw her injured face, but he said nothing.

"Tell me what you came for," she said.

"The loss of a dæmon is a grave event in anyone's life. In many cases it is even fatal. The need exists for a supplier of what is wanted by those who have no dæmon, and I can fulfill that need."

"I want to find *my* dæmon."

"Of course you do, and I hope with all my heart that you are successful. How long has he been gone?"

"A month . . . more."

"And you are still in good health, apart from . . ." He gestured delicately towards her face.

"Yes."

"Then there is every likelihood that your dæmon will be too. What is his name, and what form does he have?"

"Pantalaimon. He's a pine marten. Where do you acquire the dæmons that you sell?"

"They come to me. It is a purely voluntary transaction. There are dealers, I regret to say, who buy and sell dæmons taken by force, or without consent."

"You mean the dæmons that belong to the poor Tajiks?"

"Tajiks, yes, sometimes others. They are regarded with disgust and scorn for selling their dæmons, but if you have seen how poor people are forced to live, you will not withhold your compassion. I have nothing to do with that business. I will not touch it."

"So your dæmons came by themselves."

"I represent only dæmons who have freely decided to sever their previous connection."

"And how much do you charge?"

"It depends on the age, the appearance, the form. . . . Other characteristics come into play as well. Languages spoken, social background . . . We aim for a close match, you see. There is always the risk that the person from whom the dæmon was severed will die, in which case the dæmon also will pass away. I can offer an insurance policy against that, which will cover the cost of a replacement."

Lyra was sickened, but made herself say, "And what is the price?"

"For a dæmon of the highest quality, closely matched, the price would be ten thousand dollars."

"And the very cheapest?"

"I do not deal in poor-quality dæmons. Other dealers would charge you less, no doubt. You would have to engage with them."

"But if I were to bargain with you?"

"Ah, a price is a number on which we must both agree." His manner was that of a high-class merchant discussing the purchase of a fine work of craftsmanship.

"And how do people get on with their new dæmons?" she said.

"Every case is different, of course. Clients take a risk. With goodwill on both sides, a satisfactory arrangement can be reached in time. The aim is a modus vivendi which will pass muster in normal social circumstances. The perfect oneness and sympathy that each party has lost, that they had from birth . . . I would be lying if I said that was always reached. But a sort of satisfactory tolerance and even, in time, affection is certainly possible."

Lyra stood up and walked to the window. The afternoon was a long way advanced; the pain she felt was not in the least abated; the heat was nearly intolerable.

"In the nature of this kind of transaction," the dealer continued, "there can hardly be any possibility of advertising. But it may be of interest to you to know the names of some satisfied clients."

"Well, who have you sold dæmons to?"

"To Signor Amedea Cipriani, the Chairman of the Banco Genovese. To Madame Françoise Guillebaud, Secretary General of the European Forum for Economic Understanding. To Professor Gottfried Brande—"

"What? To *Brande?*"

"As I said, Professor Gottfried Brande, the distinguished German philosopher."

"I've read his books. He's a profound skeptic."

"Even skeptics need to move about in the world, to appear

normal. I found him a fine German shepherd bitch, very like his own original dæmon, he told me."

"But *him* . . . How ever did he come to lose his dæmon?"

"That was a private matter, and no concern of mine."

"But in one of his books he says dæmons don't exist."

"That is a question to be discussed between him and his followers. I daresay he will not make public the fact that he has made this transaction."

"No," she said, feeling slightly dazed. "And how do the dæmons feel about being bought and sold?"

"They are in a condition of loneliness and desolation. They are grateful to be introduced to someone who will care for them."

Lyra tried to imagine Pan coming to this dealer, being sold to some lonely woman, trying to fit into a stranger's life, to feign affection, to receive confidences, all the while putting up with physical contact from someone who would always be a stranger. A lump came to her throat and tears to her eyes, and she turned away for a moment.

"Well, I have another question," she said after a pause. "How can I get to the Blue Hotel?"

She turned back to see him a little surprised. He gathered himself almost at once and said, "I have no idea. I have never been there myself. I am inclined to believe that no such place exists."

"But you have heard of it?"

"Of course. Rumor, superstition, gossip . . ."

"Well, that's all I need to know. Goodbye, Dr. Veli."

"With your permission, I shall leave a small selection of photograms. And my card." He leant forward and spread out some pictures on the bed.

"Thank you and goodbye," she said.

With a bow, the dealer left. Lyra picked up one of the photograms. It showed a cat dæmon, his fur patchy and thin, standing in a silver cage. As far as she could tell, his expression was one of rage and defiance.

Stuck to the bottom of the picture was a label on which some typed words said:

NAME: Argülles
AGE: 24
LANGUAGES SPOKEN: Tajik, Russian, Anatolian
Price on application.

The card bore the dealer's name and an address in the city, and that was all. She tore it and all the pictures up and threw them in the wastepaper basket.

A few minutes later came another knock. She didn't bother with the veil this time; the dealer was an elderly Greek, who made the same response when she asked about the Blue Hotel. He left within five minutes.

The third came half an hour later. Again she said that she didn't want to buy a dæmon; all she wanted was to get to the Blue Hotel. He didn't know, so she said goodbye and shut the door.

She was desperately uncomfortable, hot, hungry, thirsty, and a bad headache added to her other unhappinesses. Her broken hand was swollen and darkened and throbbing with pain. She sat and waited.

An hour went past. She thought, The word's got around that I don't want to buy a dæmon, and they've given up bothering to come.

She felt half inclined to lie down and die. But her body wanted food and drink, and she took that to be a sign that her body at least wanted to go on living. She put on the veil and went out to buy some bread and cheese and some bottled water and, if she could find any, some painkilling medication.

Veiled though she was, the shopkeepers treated her with hostile suspicion. One refused to sell her anything and kept making gestures to ward off some evil influence, but another took her money and sold her what she wanted.

When she returned to the hotel, she found a man waiting outside her room.

The first three had been respectably dressed, and conducted themselves like professional businessmen with valuable goods to sell. This man looked like a beggar; his clothes were little better than rags, his hands were ingrained with dirt, and he had a scar that began on his left cheek, passed across the bridge of his nose, and continued to his right ear, white against his nut-brown sunburned face. He could have been any age between thirty and sixty. A scattering of gray stubble was all the hair he had, but his face was mobile and unlined. His eyes were intelligent and vivid, and he spoke in a light, swift voice whose accent seemed a blend of the entire Levant. His dæmon was a gecko, sitting on his shoulder.

"Miss! I am so glad to see you. I have been waiting here without a pause. I know what you want. The word is out. Does the young lady want to buy a dæmon? No, she does not. Is she interested in visiting the Roman temple sites? Another day, maybe. Is she waiting for a merchant of gold or ivory, or perfume or silk or dried fruit? No. I am going to anticipate your deepest desire, lady. I know what you want. Is it not true?"

Lyra said, "I want to open my door and sit down inside my room. I'm tired and hungry. If you want to sell me something, tell me what it is when I've eaten and rested."

"With the greatest of pleasure. I shall wait here. I shall not go away. Take as long as you need. Make yourself entirely comfortable, and then call on me, and I will serve you with all the honesty at my command."

He bowed, and sank into a cross-legged pose against the wall of the corridor opposite her door. He put his palms together in a gesture that possibly meant respect, though there was a slight gleam of mockery in his eyes. She unlocked her door and went inside, locking it again before taking off the veil, and sat down with her bread and cheese and warm water, and swallowed two of the painkillers.

She ate and drank, and felt a little better for it, and then washed her hands and face and tidied her short hair before opening the door.

He was still there, cross-legged, patient, and he stood up at once with a lithe energy.

"Very well," she said. "Come in and tell me what you have to sell."

"Did you enjoy your meal, madam?" he said when she'd shut the door.

"No. But it was necessary to eat. What is your name?"

"Abdel Ionides, madam."

"Please sit down. Don't call me madam. You can call me Miss Silvertongue."

"Very good. That is a name expressive of personal qualities, and I dare to ask about the interesting people who must have been your parents."

"That name was given me by a king, not by my parents. Now, what have you got to sell?"

"Many things. I can supply almost anything. I add the 'almost' to testify to my honesty. Now, most people who come to this hotel are in a sorry condition, having lost their dæmons but still remained alive. Their suffering is pitiable, and my heart is a warm and easily moved organ, so if they ask me to find them a dæmon, that is what

I shall do. I have performed that task many times. May I say something about the condition of your health, Miss Silver?"

"What do you want to say?"

"You are in some pain. I have a truly marvelous salve, from the most mysterious region of the deepest east, which is guaranteed to relieve pains of every kind and origin. For only ten dollars' equivalent, I can sell you this wonderful medication." He took a small tin from his pocket, like the containers shoe polish came in, but smaller and unlabeled. "Please—try just a small amount—you will be convinced, I assure you," he said, taking off the lid and holding it out.

The salve was pinkish in color and greasy. She took a very small dab on the tip of her right forefinger and applied it to her broken hand. She couldn't feel any difference, but she didn't feel like arguing, and the price wasn't high.

She paid the money, causing him a little surprise, and then she realized that he'd been expecting her to bargain. Well, too bad. She put the tin on the bedside table and said, "Do you know a man called"—she picked up the card left by her earlier visitor—"Dr. Selim Veli?"

"Oh, indeed. A man of substance and renown."

"Is he honest?"

"That is like asking whether the sun is hot. Dr. Veli's honesty is a byword throughout the entire Levant. But do you mistrust him, Miss Silver?"

"He told me he had sold a dæmon to someone whose name I knew, and I was surprised. I didn't know whether to believe him."

"Oh, you can believe him without hesitation or fear."

"I see. Where do— How do those who sell dæmons acquire them?"

"There are many ways. I can see you are a lady of a tender heart, so I shall not tell you some of the ways in which this happens. But from time to time a dæmon will be lost, unhappy, even unwanted, if you can believe that dreadful truth, and we take him or her into our care and try to find a congenial companion for them in the hope of making a liaison that will last, after all, for a lifetime. When we are successful, the happiness we feel is almost equivalent to that of our lucky clients."

His gecko dæmon, orange and green in color, scuttled briskly over his arms and shoulders and the top of his head. Lyra saw her slip out her tongue and lick the surface of her eyes, and then whisper a quick word or two in the man's ear.

"Well," said Lyra, "I don't want a replacement for my dæmon. I want to go to Aleppo."

"I can guide you there with great facility and convenience, Miss Silver."

"And on the way I want to go somewhere else. I have heard of a place called the Blue Hotel."

"Ah, yes. I am familiar with that name too. Sometimes we refer to it by the name of Selenopolis, or Madinat al-Qamar. They are words that mean the city or the town of the moon."

"Do you know how to get there?"

"I have been there twice. I had not thought I would ever go there again, but I perceive the course of your thinking, and I dare to say we could agree on a price for me to take you there. But it is not a pleasant place."

His gecko dæmon spoke from his left shoulder. "It is horrible," she said, her voice high and quiet. "Our price will be high to pay for the suffering that I will undergo. For choice, we would never go there again. But if it is your will, then it will be our duty. I shall not say our pleasure."

"Is it far from here?"

"One, maybe two days' journey by camel," said Ionides.

"I have never ridden a camel."

"Then we shall have to teach you. But there is no other way. No road, no rail. Only the desert."

"Very well, then name your price."

"One hundred dollars."

"That's too high. It sounds like something worth sixty."

"Oh, Miss Silver, you mistake the nature of this journey. This excursion to the world of the night is not just a matter of *tourism*. This is not a Roman temple or a ruined theater, with picturesque columns and fallen masonry, and a little stall that sells lemonade and souvenirs. We shall be treading on the borders of the invisible, trespassing in the realm of the uncanny. Is this not worth a higher price than the sum you named, which would hardly cover the hire of one camel? Make it ninety."

"Still too much. I can summon the uncanny whenever I want to. I have spent weeks of my life in the presence of the invisible and the uncanny. They are not strange to me. What I want is a guide to take me to this city or town or village of the night. I offer you seventy dollars."

"Alas, you want to travel like a beggar, Miss Silver. For a journey of this danger and consequence, it is a sign of respect to the inhabitants, and of respect to your humble guide, and not least of respect to your own dæmon to travel in a manner that expresses the quality of your breeding and the width of your sympathies. Eighty dollars."

She was tired. "All right, eighty dollars," she said. "Twenty-five before we start, twenty-five when we get to the Blue Hotel, and thirty when we get to Aleppo."

He shook his head sadly. His dæmon, perching on it, kept her eyes on Lyra as his head moved. "I am a poor man," he said. "And I shall still be a poor man after this journey. I had hoped to be able to save a little from this fee, against the poverty of old age, but I see that will be impossible. Nevertheless, you have my word. Thirty for each stage of the journey, then."

"No. Twenty-five, twenty-five, and thirty."

He bowed his head. The dæmon jumped off and into his open hands, and licked her eyes again.

"When would you like to start?" Ionides said.

THIRTY-THREE

THE DEAD TOWN

All the next day Lyra rode her camel in a little enclosed tent of pain. Ionides managed everything with good humor and perfect tact; he knew when to be quiet and when she wouldn't mind a friendly remark; he found somewhere shady to rest at noon, and made sure she kept drinking enough water.

After their midday rest, he said, "It is really and quite genuinely not far now, Miss Silver. I estimate that we shall arrive in the neighborhood of Madinat al-Qamar at about sunset."

"Have you ever been into the place?" she asked.

"No. To be immaculately candid, Miss Silver, I was afraid. You mustn't underappreciate the degree of fear that is aroused in persons who are complete by the thought of a company of separated dæmons, or of the process of separation that must have occurred."

"I don't under-whatever the fear. I used to feel it myself. I've been causing it in other people for two and a half thousand miles."

"Yes, of course. I would never assume you didn't deeply and thoroughly know that. But the result of that emotional reaction is that I was too frightened to follow my clients into the purlieus of the Blue Hotel. I told them so with perfect frankness. They went in alone. I brought them there, but I never guaranteed the outcome of their search. All I guaranteed was to take them to the Blue Hotel, which I did. One hundred percent. The rest was up to them."

She nodded; she was almost too tired to say anything. They rode on. The little pot of Ionides's salve was in her pocket, and balancing as best she could, she prized it open and applied a dab to the back of her abominably aching hand, and then, experimenting, to her temples. The headache she'd had for days was still firmly in residence, and the glare from the sand all around was helping not at all. But a marvelous coolness quite soon began to soothe her brow, and the glare even seemed to dim slightly.

"Mr. Ionides," she said, "tell me more about this salve."

"I bought it from a train master who had just arrived from Samarkand. Its virtues are quite well-known, I assure you."

"Where does it originally come from?"

"Oh, who knows, very much further east, beyond the highest mountains in the world. No camel trains make the journey through the mountain passes. It is too high and too arduous even for camels. Anyone who wishes to transport goods from that side to this, or this side to that, has to negotiate with the *bagazhkti*."

"And what's that? Or they?"

"They are beings who are like humans in that they have a language and can speak, but unlike us in that if they have a dæmon, it is internal or invisible. They are like small camels, no hump, long neck. They hire themselves out for purposes of transport. Bad-tempered, very unpleasant, oh, I can't tell you. Arrogant. But they can climb the high passes with loads of unbelievable size."

"So if this salve came from beyond the mountains . . ."

"It will have been carried part of the way by the *bagazhkti*. But the *bagazhkti* have another virtue. The mountains are infested with large birds of a carnivorous rapacity, which are known as *oghâb-gorgs*. Enormously dangerous. Only the *bagazhkti* have found a way of fighting off these birds. The *bagazhkti* can spit their offensive and venomous saliva very accurately for a not-inconsiderable distance. The birds find this not at all enjoyable, and quite commonly retreat. So in paying for the services of the *bagazhkti*, a train master will also ensure his survival and that of the goods he carries. But as you will realize, Miss Silver, it adds to the cost. May I ask how is your pain now?"

"It's slightly better, thank you. Tell me, did you know about this salve? Did you specifically ask for it?"

"Yes, I did know, and that is why I managed to find a merchant likely to have it."

"Has it got a special name?"

"It is called *gülmuron*. But there are many cheap kinds that do not have any beneficial effects. This is the true *gülmuron*."

"I'll remember that. Thank you."

The pain in her hand was just about bearable, but to add to all the other discomforts, she began to feel a familiar deep dragging ache low in her belly. Well, it was due. There was even something reassuring in it: if that part's working, then at least my body's still in good order, she thought.

But it was uncomfortable nonetheless, and she was profoundly glad when the sun touched the horizon and Ionides said it was time to make camp.

"Are we there?" she said. "Is this the Blue Hotel?"

Looking around, she saw a low range of hills—not even hills: not much more than rocky slopes—to the right, and endless flat desert to the left. Directly ahead was a mass of broken stone, with little to show at a first glance that there had ever been a town there, though the last rays of the sun did illuminate the top of a line of columns made of light-colored limestone much eroded by wind, which she might not have noticed otherwise. While Ionides bustled around tethering the camels and making a fire, Lyra climbed the nearest rock and looked steadily into the mass of jumbled boulders, and in the rapidly fading light, she did begin to make out some regular shapes: a rectangular set of tumbled walls, an arch that had tilted slightly without actually falling, a paved open space that might have been a market or forum.

It was all lifeless. If there were any dæmons there, they were hiding well and keeping very quiet.

"Are you sure this is the right place?" she said, joining Ionides at the fire, where he was grilling some kind of meat.

"Miss Silver," he said in a tone of deep reproach, "I did not think of you as a die-hard skeptic."

"Not a die-hard one, but just a little cautious. Is this the place?"

"Guaranteed. There are the remains of the town—all those rocks, they used to be buildings. Even now some of the walls are still standing. You have only to walk among them to know that you are in what used to be a center of commerce and culture."

She stood watching the shadows lengthen as Ionides turned the meat and mixed some flour with a little water and slapped the dough flat before cooking it in a long-blackened frying pan. By the time the food was ready, the sky was nearly dark.

"A good sleep, Miss Silver, and you will be awake bright and early to investigate the ruins in the morning," he said.

"I'm going in tonight."

"Is that altogether one hundred percent wise?"

"I don't know. But it's what I want to do. My dæmon is in there, and I want to find him as soon as possible."

"Of course you do. But there may be other things than dæmons in there."

"What things?"

"Phantoms. Ghasts of this kind or that. Emissaries of the Evil One."

"Do you believe that?"

"Of course. It would be an intellectual failure to do anything else."

"There are philosophers who say that the failure would be to believe, not to disbelieve."

"Then excuse me, Miss Silver, but they have separated their intelligences from their other faculties. And that is not an intelligent thing to do."

She said nothing at first, because she agreed with him—agreed instinctively, if not yet intellectually; part of her was still in thrall to the cast of mind of Talbot and Brande. But it came to her clearly, as she swallowed the last of her tender meat and hot bread, how incongruous it was to bring any of that university skepticism to the Blue Hotel.

"Mr. Ionides, have you ever heard the term 'the secret commonwealth'?"

"No. What does it refer to?"

"To the world of half-seen things and half-heard whispers. To things that are regarded by clever people as superstition. To fairies. Spirits, hauntings, things of the night. The sort of thing you said the Blue Hotel is full of."

"'The secret commonwealth' . . . No, I have never heard the expression."

"Perhaps there are other names for it."

"I am sure there are many."

He wiped the frying pan around with the last of the bread and ate it slowly. Lyra was so tired, she felt on the verge of delirium. She wanted to sleep quite desperately, but she knew that if she gave in and put her head down, she wouldn't wake up till the morning was filling the sky. Ionides pottered about their little camp, covering the fire, gathering his blankets, rolling a smokeleaf cigarette. Finally he settled down to huddle in the dark shade of a camel-sized rock. Only the tiny glow of his cigarette showed he was there at all.

Lyra stood up, feeling every one of the separate pains and injuries. The hand was worst; she took a very little of the rose salve on her right forefinger and rubbed it in as gently as a butterfly landing on a grass blade.

Then she put the salve in her rucksack with the alethiometer, and stepped away from the fire and towards the tumbled ruins. The moon was climbing the sky, and the vast sweep of the Milky Way stretched above, every one of those minute specks a sun in its own system, lighting and warming planets, maybe, and life, maybe, and some kind of wondering being, maybe, looking out at the little star that was her sun, and at this world, and at Lyra.

Ahead of her the dead bones of the town lay almost white in the moonlight. Lives had been spent here—people had loved one another and eaten and drunk and laughed and betrayed and been afraid of death—and not a single fragment of that remained. White stones, black shadows. All around her, things were whispering, or it might only have been night-loving insects conversing together. Shadows and whispers. Here was the tumbled ruin of a little basilica: people had worshipped here. Nearby a single archway topped with a classical pediment stood between nothing and nothing. People had walked through the arch, driven donkey carts through, stood and gossiped in its shade in the heat of a long-dead day. There was a well, or a fountain, or a spring: at any rate, someone had thought it worth cutting stones and forming a cistern, and a representation of a nymph above it, now blurred and smoothed by time, the cistern dry, the only trickle that of the insect sounds.

So she walked on, further and further into the silent moonscape of the City of the Moon, the Blue Hotel.

* * *

And Olivier Bonneville watched. He was lying among some rocks on the slope nearest the little camp; he had been there since shortly after Lyra and Ionides had arrived. He was watching through binoculars as Lyra picked her way among the stones of the dead town, and beside him lay a loaded rifle.

He had made himself as comfortable as he could be without a fire. His camel knelt some way behind, chewing something resistant and appearing to think deeply.

The view Bonneville had of Lyra was the first time he had ever seen her in the flesh. He was taken aback by how different she looked from the photogram, the short black hair, the tense and strained expression, the obvious exhaustion and pain in every movement. Was it the same girl? Had he mistakenly followed someone else? Could she have changed this much already?

He half wanted to follow her right into the ruins, and confront her close to. At the same time, he feared to do that, guessing that it would be much easier to shoot someone from a distance, in the back, than to do it when they were face to face. He considered the man who was with her, the camel man, the guide, to be a slight nuisance, but no more than that. A few dollars would pay him off.

Lyra was still brightly visible in the moonlight, an easy target as she picked her slow way through the stones. Bonneville was a good shot: the Swiss were keen on such things as military service and hunting and marksmanship. But if he wanted to shoot her cleanly, he had better do it before she moved very far into the Blue Hotel.

He put down the binoculars and took the rifle, carefully, silently, knowing everything about its weight and its length and the feeling of the stock against his shoulder. He lowered his head to look along the barrel, and moved his hips a fraction of an inch to settle himself more securely.

Then he had a horrible shock.

There was a man lying next to him, and looking at him, no more than three feet to his left.

He actually gasped aloud, "Ahh . . . ," and twisted away involuntarily, and his dæmon burst up into the air, flapping her wings in panic.

The man didn't move, in spite of the way the rifle barrel was waving wildly in Bonneville's shaking hands. He was monstrously, inhumanly calm. His gecko dæmon sat on a rock just behind him, licking her eyeballs.

"Who—where did you come from?" said Bonneville hoarsely. He spoke in French, by instinct. His dæmon glided down to his shoulder.

The camel man, Lyra's guide, replied in the same language, "You didn't see me because you took your eyes off the whole picture. I've been watching you for two days. Listen, if you kill her, you'll be making a big mistake. Don't do it. Put your gun away."

"Who are you?"

"Abdel Ionides. Put the rifle down, now. Put it down."

Bonneville's heart was hammering so hard that he thought it must be audible. The blood pounded in his head as he made his hands relax and push the rifle away.

"What do you want?" he said.

Ionides said, "I want you to leave her alive for now. There is a great treasure, and she is the only one who can get it. Kill her now and you'll never have it, and more importantly, neither will I."

"What treasure? What are you talking about?"

"You don't know?"

"Again, what are you talking about? Where is this treasure? You don't mean her dæmon?"

"Of course not. The treasure is three thousand miles to the east, and as I said, no one can get it but her."

"And you want her to get it so you can have it?"

631

"What do you think?"

"Why should I care what you want? I don't want treasure from three thousand miles away. What I want is what she has now."

"And if you take that, she will never find the treasure. Listen to me: I speak to you harshly, but I have to admire you. You are resourceful, courageous, hardy, inventive. I like all those qualities, and I want to see them rewarded. But at the moment you are like the wolf in the fable who seizes the nearest lamb and arouses the shepherd. Your attention is in the wrong place. Wait, and watch, and learn, and then kill the shepherd, and you will be able to have the entire flock."

"You're speaking in riddles."

"I am speaking in metaphor. You are intelligent enough to understand that."

Bonneville was silent for a few moments. Then he said, "What is this treasure, then?"

Ionides began to talk, quietly, confidently, confidentially. In the fable that Bonneville knew, it was a fox, but he enjoyed being compared to a wolf, and above all else he enjoyed the praise of older men. As the moon rose higher, as Lyra in the distance slowly made her solitary way into the dead and dæmon-haunted town, Ionides went on talking, and Bonneville listened. When he looked at the dead city again, Lyra had vanished.

She was out of sight because she'd turned to avoid a broken mass of gleaming marble that had once been a temple. There she found herself at one end of a colonnade, which cast black bars of shadow across the snow-white stone of the path.

And there was a girl sitting on a fallen piece of masonry, a girl of sixteen or so, of North African appearance and shabby dress. She wasn't a phantom: she cast a shadow, as Lyra herself did, and like her, she had no dæmon. She stood up as soon as she saw Lyra. In the moonlight she looked tense and full of fear.

"You are Miss Silvertongue," she said.

"Yes," said Lyra, astonished. "Who are you?"

"Nur Huda el-Wahabi. Come on, come quickly. We have been waiting for you."

"We? Who—? You don't mean . . . ?"

But Nur Huda tugged urgently at Lyra's right hand, and they hurried together along the colonnade, towards the heart of the ruins.

Thus she there waited untill eventyde,
　　Yet living creature none she saw appeare:
　　And now sad shadowes gan the world to hyde,
　　From mortall vew, and wrap in darkenesse dreare;
　　Yet nould she d'off her weary armes, for feare
　　Of secret daunger, ne let sleepe oppresse
　　Her heavy eyes with natures burdein deare,
　　But drew her selfe aside in sickernesse,
And her welpointed wepons did about her dresse.

EDMUND SPENSER, *The Faerie Queene*, III XI 55

To be concluded . . .

ACKNOWLEDGMENTS

I owe many people thanks for their help in writing this story, and I'll acknowledge them all in full at the end of the final book. But there are three debts I would like to pay now. One is to the great work of Katharine Briggs, *Folk Tales of Britain*, where I first read the story of the dead moon. The second is to the poet and painter Nick Messenger, from whose account of a voyage in the schooner *Volga* in his poem *Sea-Cow* I have borrowed the story of the phosphor-bronze propeller. The third is to Robert Kirk (1644–1692), whose wonder-filled book *The Secret Commonwealth, or an Essay on the Nature and Actions of the Subterranean (and for the Most Part) Invisible People Heretofore Going Under the Names of Fauns and Fairies, or the Like, Among the Low Country Scots as Described by Those Who Have Second Sight* has been an inspiration in many ways, not least in reminding me of the value of a good title. So I stole it, or some of it.

There are three characters in this novel whose names are those of real people whose friends wanted to remember them in a work of fiction. One is Bud Schlesinger, whom we saw first in *La Belle Sauvage*; the second is Alison Wetherfield, whom we shall see again in the final book; and the third is Nur Huda el-Wahabi, who was one of the victims of the terrible fire at Grenfell Tower. I'm privileged to be able to help commemorate them.

THE EPIC WORLD OF
HIS DARK MATERIALS